BLACK MOON INN

BLACK MOON INN

Burnt Offerings
Blue Moon

Laurell K. Hamilton

FANTASY

Published by arrangement with
The Berkley Publishing Group
a member of Penguin Putnam Inc.
375 Hudson Street
New York, New York 10014

ISBN 0-7394-0046-0

The Penguin Putnam Inc. World Wide Web site address is
   http://www.penguinputnam.com

The Science Fiction Book Club World Wide Web site address is
   http://www.sfbc.com

PRINTED IN THE UNITED STATES OF AMERICA

Contents

BURNT
OFFERINGS

For my grandmother, Laura Gentry,
who at 4' 11" taught me that you could be
small, female, and still be tough.

Acknowledgments

To my brother-in-law, Officer Shawn Holsapple, who should have been mentioned in these pages long ago.

Thanks for firefighter info to Paty Cockrum, who among her many talents is also a volunteer firefighter. To Bonnee Pierson, also a volunteer firefighter. To Florence Bradley, member of the Birmingham Fire and Rescue Service Department. She does this firefighting stuff for a living.

Thanks also to Dave Cockrum, who came up with the color for Asher's eyes.

As always to my writing group, the Alternate Historians: Tom Drennan, N. L. Drew, Deborah Millitello, Rett MacPherson, Marella Sands, Sharon Shinn, and Mark Sumner. I would be lost without you guys.

Here's the address for the newsletter: Laurell K. Hamilton Fan Club, 2200 Old Highway 21, Suite 162, Imperial, MO 63052.

I look at every piece of mail personally, which explains the slow response time. I'll be getting help soon, which should speed things up.

For those on the information super highway, here's my e-mail address: Laurell K aricia.com

I don't read the computer messages. Someone else handles all the techie stuff.

1

Most people don't stare at the scars. They'll look, of course, then do the eye slide. You know, the quick look, then drop the gaze, then just have to have that second look. But they make it quick. The wounds aren't like freak show bad, but they are interesting. Captain Pete McKinnon, firefighter and arson investigator, sat across from me, big hands wrapped around a glass of iced tea that our secretary, Mary, had brought in for him. He was staring at my arms. Not the place most men look. But it wasn't sexual. He was staring at the scars and didn't seem a bit embarrassed about it.

My right arm had been sliced open twice by a knife. One scar was white and old. The second was still pink and new. My left arm was worse. A mound of white scar tissue sat at the bend of my arm. I'd have to lift weights for the rest of my life or the scars would stiffen and I'd lose mobility in the arm, or so my physical therapist had said. There was a cross-shaped burn mark, a little crooked now because of the ragged claw marks that a shapeshifted witch had given me. There were one or two other scars hidden under my blouse, but the arm really is the worst.

Bert, my boss, had requested that I wear my suit jacket or long-sleeved blouses in the office. He said that some clients had expressed reservations about my ah . . . occupationally acquired wounds. I hadn't worn a long-sleeved blouse since he made the request. He'd turned the air conditioner up a little colder every day. It was so cold today I had goose bumps. Everyone else was bringing sweaters to work. I was shopping for midriff tops to show off my back scars.

McKinnon had been recommended to me by Sergeant Rudolph Storr, cop and friend. They'd played football in college together, and been friends ever since. Dolph didn't use the word "friend" lightly, so I knew they were close.

"What happened to your arm?" McKinnon asked finally.

"I'm a legal vampire executioner. Sometimes they get pesky." I took a sip of coffee.

"Pesky," he said and smiled.

He sat his glass on the desk and slipped off his suit jacket. He was nearly as wide through the shoulders as I was tall. He was a few inches short of Dolph's six foot eight, but he didn't miss it by much. He was only in his forties, but his hair was completely grey with a little white starting at the temples. It didn't make him look distinguished. It made him look tired.

He had me beat on scars. Burn scars crawled up his arms from his hands to disappear under the short sleeves of his white dress shirt. The skin was mottled pinkish, white, and a strange shade of tan like the skin of some animal that should shed regularly.

"That must have hurt," I said.

"It did." He sat there meeting my eyes with a long steady look. "You saw the inside of a hospital on some of that."

"Yeah." I pushed the sleeve up on my left arm and showed the shiny place where a bullet had grazed me. His eyes widened just a bit. "Now that we've proven we're big tough he-men, can you just cut to the chase? Why are you here, Captain McKinnon?"

He smiled and draped his jacket over the back of his chair. He took the tea off my desk and sipped it. "Dolph said you wouldn't like being sized up."

"I don't like passing inspections."

"How do you know you passed?"

It was my turn to smile. "Women's intuition. Now, what do you want?"

"Do you know what the term firebug means?"

"An arsonist," I said.

He looked expectantly at me.

"A pyrokinetic, someone who can call fire psychically."

He nodded. "You ever seen a real pyro?"

"I saw films of Ophelia Ryan," I said.

"The old black-and-white ones?" he asked.

"Yeah."

"She's dead now, you know."

"No, I didn't know."

"Burned to death in her bed, spontaneous combustion. A lot of the firebugs go up that way, as if when they're old they lose control of it. You ever see one of them in person?"

"Nope."

"Where'd you see the films?"

"Two semesters of Psychic Studies. We had a lot of psychics come in and talk to us, demonstrate their abilities, but pyrokinetics is such a rare ability, I don't think the prof could find one."

He nodded and drained the rest of his tea in one long swallow. "I met Ophelia Ryan once before she died. Nice lady." He started to turn the ice-filled glass round and round in his large hands. He stared at the glass and not at me while he talked. "I met one other firebug. He was young, in his twenties. He'd started by setting empty houses on fire, like a lot of pyromaniacs. Then he did buildings with people in them, but everybody got out. Then he did a tenement, a real firetrap. He set every exit on fire. Killed over sixty people, mostly women and children."

McKinnon stared up at me. The look in his eyes was haunted. "It's still the largest body count I've ever seen at a fire. He did an office building the same way, but missed a couple of exits. Twenty-three dead.''

"How'd you catch him?''

"He started writing to the papers and the television. He wanted credit for the deaths. He set fire to a couple of cops before we got him. We were wearing those big silver suits that they wear to oil rig fires. He couldn't get them to burn. We took him down to the police station, and that was the mistake. He set it on fire.''

"Where else could you have taken him?'' I asked.

He shrugged massive shoulders. "I don't know, somewhere else. I was still in the suit, and I held onto him. Told him we'd burn up together if he didn't stop it. He laughed and set himself on fire.'' McKinnon sat his glass very carefully on the edge of the desk.

"The flames were this soft blue color almost like a gas fire, but paler. Didn't burn him, but somehow it set my suit on fire. The damn thing is rated for something like 6,000 degrees, and it started to melt. Human skin burns at 120 degrees, but somehow I didn't melt into a puddle, just the suit. I had to strip it off while he laughed. He walked out the door and he didn't think anyone would be stupid enough to grab him.''

I didn't say the obvious. I let him talk.

"I tackled him in the hallway and slammed him into a wall a couple of times. Funny thing, where my skin touched him, it didn't burn. It was like the fire crawled over a space and started on my arms, so my hands are fine.''

I nodded. "There's a theory that a pyro's aura keeps them from burning. When you touched his skin, you were too close to his own aura, his own protection, to burn.''

He stared at me. "Maybe that is what happened, because I threw him hard up against the wall over and over. He was screaming, 'I'll burn you. I'll burn you alive.' Then the fire changed color to yellow, normal, and he started to burn. I let him go and went for the fire extinguisher. We couldn't put the fire on his body out. The extinguishers worked on the walls, everything else, but it wouldn't work on him. It was as if the fire was crawling out of his body from deep inside. We'd dampen some of the flames, but there was just more of it until he was made of fire.''

McKinnon's eyes were distant and horror-filled as if he was still seeing it. "He didn't die, Ms. Blake, not like he should of. He screamed for so long and we couldn't help him. Couldn't help him.'' His voice trailed off. He just sat there staring at nothing.

I waited and finally said, gently, "Why are you here, Captain?''

He blinked and sort of shook himself. "I think we've got another firebug on our hands, Ms. Blake. Dolph said that if anyone could help us cut the loss of life, it was you.''

"Psychic ability isn't technically preternatural. It's just talent like throwing a great curve ball.''

He shook his head. "What I saw die on the floor of the station that day wasn't human. It couldn't have been human. Dolph says you're the monster expert. Help me catch this monster before he kills.''

"He or she hasn't killed yet? It's just property damage?'' I asked.

He nodded. "I could lose my job for coming to you. I should have bucked this up the line and gotten permission from the chain of command, but we've only lost a couple of buildings. I want to keep it that way."

I took in a slow breath and let it out. "I'll be happy to help, Captain, but I honestly don't know what I can do for you."

He pulled out a thick file folder. "Here's everything we've got. Look it over and call me tonight."

I took the folder from him and sat it in the middle of my desk blotter.

"My number's in the file. Call me. Maybe it's not a firebug. Maybe it's something else. But whatever it is, Ms. Blake, it can bathe in flames and not burn. It can walk through a building and shed fire like sprinkling water. No accelerant, Ms. Blake, but the houses have gone up as if they've been soaked in something. When we get the wood in the lab, it's clean. It's like whatever is doing this can force the fire to do things it shouldn't do."

He glanced at his watch. "I'm running late. I'm working on getting you on this officially, but I'm afraid they'll wait until people are dead. I don't want to wait."

"I'll call you tonight, but it may be late. How late is too late to call?"

"Any time, Ms. Blake, any time."

I nodded and stood. I offered my hand. He shook it. His grip was firm, solid, but not too tight. A lot of male clients that wanted to know about the scars squeezed my hand like they wanted me to cry "uncle." But McKinnon was secure. He had his own scars.

I'd barely sat back down when the phone rang. "What is it, Mary?"

"It's me," Larry said. "Mary didn't think you'd mind her putting me straight through." Larry Kirkland, vampire executioner trainee, was supposed to be over at the morgue staking vampires.

"Nope. What's up?"

"I need a ride home." There was just the slightest hesitation to his voice.

"What's wrong?"

He laughed. "I should know better than to be coy with you. I'm all stitched up. The doc says I'll be fine."

"What happened?" I asked.

"Come pick me up and I'll tell all." Then the little son of a gun hung up on me.

There was only one reason for him to not want to talk to me. He'd done something stupid and gotten hurt. Two bodies to stake. Two bodies that wouldn't have risen for at least another night. What could have gone wrong? As the old saying goes, only one way to find out.

Mary rescheduled my appointments. I got my shoulder holster complete with Browning Hi-Power out of the top desk drawer and slipped it on. Since I'd stopped wearing my suit jacket in the office, I'd put the gun in the drawer, but outside the office and always after dark I wore a gun. Most of the creatures that had scarred me up were dead. The majority I'd done personally. Silver-plated bullets are a wonderful thing.

2

Larry sat very carefully in the passenger seat of my Jeep. It's hard to sit in a car when your back has fresh stitches in it. I'd seen the wound. It was one sharp puncture and one long, bloody scrape. Two wounds, really. He was still wearing the blue T-shirt he'd started in, but the back of it was bloody and ragged. I was impressed he'd kept the nurses from cutting it off of him. They had a tendency to cut off clothing that stood in their way.

Larry strained against the seat belt, trying to find a comfortable position. His short red hair had been freshly cut, tight enough to his head that you almost didn't notice the curls. He was five foot four, an inch taller than me. He'd graduated with a degree in preternatural biology this May. But with the freckles and that little pain wrinkle between his clear blue eyes, he looked closer to sixteen than twenty-one.

I'd been so busy watching him squirm that I'd missed the turnoff to I-270. We were stuck on Ballas until we got to Olive. It was just before lunch, and Olive would be packed with people trying to shove food in their mouths and rush back to work.

"Did you take your pain pill?" I asked.

He tried to sit very still, one arm braced on the edge of the seat. "No."

"Why not?"

"Because stuff like that knocks me out. I don't want to sleep."

"A drugged sleep isn't the same thing as regular sleep," I said.

"No, the dreams are worse," he said.

He had me there. "What happened, Larry?"

"I'm amazed you've waited this long to ask."

"So am I, but I didn't want to ask in front of the doctor. If you start asking questions of the patient, the docs tend to wander off and treat somebody else. I wanted to know from the doctor who stitched you up just how serious it was."

"Just a few stitches," he said.

"Twenty," I said.

"Eighteen," he said.

"I was rounding up."

"Trust me," he said. "You don't need to round up." He grimaced as he said it. "Why does this hurt so much?" he asked.

It might have been a rhetorical question, but I answered it anyway. "Every time you move an arm or a leg you use muscles in your back. Moving your head and muscles in your shoulders makes muscles in your back move. You never appreciate your back until it goes out on you."

"Great," he said.

"Enough stalling, Larry. Tell me what happened." We were stopped behind a long line of traffic leading up to the light on Olive. We were stuck between two small strip malls. The one on our left had fountains and V. J.'s Tea and Spice, where I got all my coffee. To our right was Streetside Records and a Chinese buffet. If you came up Ballas at lunch time, you always had plenty of time to study the shops on either side.

He smiled, then grimaced. "I had two bodies to stake. Both vamp victims that didn't want to rise as vampires."

"They had dying wills, I remember. You've been doing most of those lately."

He nodded, then froze in mid-gesture. "Even nodding my head hurts."

"It'll hurt more tomorrow."

"Gee, thanks, boss. I needed to know that."

I shrugged. "Lying to you won't make it hurt less."

"Anybody ever tell you your bedside manner sucks?"

"Lots of people."

He made a small *hmph* sound. "That I believe. Anyway, I'd finished the bodies and was packing up. A woman rolled in another body. Said it was a vamp with no court order attached."

I glanced at him, frowning. "You didn't do a body without paperwork, did you?"

He frowned back. "Of course not. I told them, no court order, no dead vampire. Staking a vamp without a court order is murder, and I'm not going to be up on charges because someone screwed the paperwork. I told them both that in no uncertain terms."

"Them?" I asked. I eased up the line of traffic, a little closer to the light.

"The other morgue attendant had come back in. They went out in search of the misplaced paperwork. I was left with the vampire. It was morning. He wasn't going anywhere." He tried to look away and not meet my eyes, but it hurt. He ended up staring at me, angry.

"I went out for a cigarette."

I looked at him and had to slam on the brakes when the traffic just stopped. Larry was flung into the seat belt. He groaned, and when he was finished writhing on the seat, he said, "You did that on purpose."

"No, I didn't, but maybe I should have. You left a vampire body alone. A vampire that might have had enough kills to deserve a court order of execution, alone in the morgue."

"It wasn't just the cigarette, Anita. The body was just lying there on the gurney. It wasn't chained or strapped. There were no crosses anywhere. I've done executions. They plaster the vamps with silver chains and crosses until it's hard to find the heart. It just didn't look right. I wanted to talk to the medical examiner.

She has to approve all vampires before execution, or somebody does. Besides the ME smokes. I figured we could have one together in her office.''

"And," I said.

"She wasn't in, and I went back to the morgue. When I got there, the woman attendant was trying to pound a stake through the vamp's chest.''

It was lucky we were at a dead stop in traffic. If we'd been moving, I'd have plowed into someone. I stared at him. "You left your vampire kit unattended.''

He managed to look embarrassed and angry at the same time. "My kit doesn't include shotguns like yours does, so I figured, who would bother it.''

"A lot of people will steal things out of the bag for souvenirs, Larry.'' Traffic started to creep forward and I had to watch the road instead of his face.

"Fine, fine, I was wrong. I know I was wrong. I grabbed her around the waist and pulled her off the vampire.'' His eyes slid downward, not looking at me. This was the part that bothered him, or the part he thought would bother me. "I turned my back on her to check the vampire. To make sure she hadn't hurt him.''

"She did your back," I said. We inched forward. We were now trapped between Dairy Queen and Kentucky Fried Chicken on one side, and an Infiniti car dealership and a gas station on the other. The scenery was not improving.

"Yeah, yeah. She must have thought I was down for the count because she left me and went back to the vampire. I disarmed her, but she was still trying to get to the vampire when the other attendant came in. It took both of us to pin her. She was crazy, manic.''

"Why didn't you draw your gun, Larry?'' His gun was sitting in his vampire kit because a shoulder holster and his back wound did not mix. But he went armed. I'd taken him out to the shooting range, and out on vampire hunts until I trusted him not to shoot his foot off.

"If I'd drawn my gun, I might have shot her.''

"That's sort of the point, Larry.''

"It's exactly the point," he said. "I didn't want to shoot her.''

"She could have killed you, Larry.''

"I know.''

I gripped the steering wheel tight enough to mottle my skin, white and pink. I let out a long breath and tried not to yell. "You obviously don't know, or you would have been more careful.''

"I'm alive, and she's not dead. The vampire didn't even get a scratch. It worked out all right.''

I pulled out onto Olive and started creeping towards 270. We needed to head north towards St. Charles. Larry had an apartment over there. It was about a twenty-minute drive, give or take. His apartment looked out over a lake where geese nested in the spring and congregated in the winter. Richard Zeeman, junior high science teacher, alpha werewolf, and at that time, my boyfriend, had helped him move in. Richard had really liked the geese nesting just under the balcony. So had I.

"Larry, you are going to have to get over this squeamishness or you're going to get killed.''

"I'll keep doing what I think is right, Anita. Nothing you can say will change my mind.''

"Dammit, Larry. I don't want to have to bury you.''

"What would you have done? Shot her?"

"I wouldn't have turned my back on her, Larry. I could have probably disarmed her or kept her busy until the other attendant arrived. I wouldn't have had to shoot her."

"I let things get out of control," he said.

"Your priorities were screwed. You should have neutralized the threat before you checked on the victim. Alive, you could help the vamp. Dead, you're just another victim."

"Well, at least I've got a scar you don't have."

I shook my head. "You'll have to try harder if you want a scar I don't have."

"You let a human shove one of your own stakes into your back?"

"Two humans with multiple bites, what I used to call human servants, before I knew what the term really meant. I had one pinned and was stabbing him. The woman came at my back."

"So yours wasn't a mistake," he said.

I shrugged. "I could have shot them when I first saw them, but I didn't kill humans as easily back then. I learned my lesson. Just because it doesn't have fangs doesn't mean it can't kill you."

"You used to be squeamish about shooting human servants?" Larry asked.

I turned onto 270. "No one's perfect. Why did the woman have a hard-on to kill the vampire?"

He grinned. "You're going to love this one. She's a member of Humans First. The vampire was a doctor in the hospital. He'd tucked himself into a linen closet. It was where he always slept the day away if he'd had to stay too late in the hospital to drive home. She just popped him on a gurney and wheeled him down to the morgue."

"I'm surprised she didn't just push him out into the sunlight. The last sunlight of the day works as well as noonday."

"The linen closet he used was on the basement floor just in case someone opened the door at the wrong time of day. No windows. She was afraid someone would see her before she could get him up in the elevator and outside."

"She really thought you would just stake him?"

"I guess so. I don't know, Anita. She was crazy, really crazy. She spit at the vampire and us. Said we'd all rot in hell. That we had to cleanse the world of the monsters. The monsters were going to enslave us all." Larry shivered, then frowned. "I thought Humans Against Vampires was bad enough, but this splinter group, Humans First, is genuinely scary."

"HAV tries to work within the law," I said. "Humans First doesn't even pretend to care. They claimed they staked that vampire mayor in Michigan."

"Claimed? You don't believe them?"

"I think someone near and dear to his household did it."

"Why?"

"The cops sent me a description and some photos of the security precautions he'd taken. Humans First may be radical, but they don't seem very well organized yet. You'd have had to plan and be very lucky to get to that vampire during the day. He was like a lot of the old ones, very serious about his daytime safety. I think whoever did it is happy to let the right-wing radicals take the blame."

"You tell the police what you think?"

"Sure. That's why they asked."

"I'm surprised they didn't have you come down and see it in person."

I shrugged. "I can't go personally to every preternatural crime. Besides, I'm technically a civilian. Cops are sort of leery about involving civilians in their cases, but more importantly, the media would be all over it. The Executioner Solves Vampire Murder."

Larry grinned. "That's a mild headline for you."

"Unfortunately," I said. "Also, I think the killer is a human. I think it's just someone he was close to. It's like any well-planned murder except for the victim being a vampire."

"Only you would make a locked-room vampire murder sound ordinary," Larry said.

I had to smile. "I guess so." My beeper went off, and I jumped. I pulled the damn thing off my skirt and held it where I could see the number. I frowned at it.

"What's wrong? Is it the police?"

"No. I don't recognize the number."

"You don't give out your beeper number to strangers."

"I'm aware of that."

"Hey, don't get grumpy at me."

I sighed. "Sorry." Larry was slowly wearing me down on my aggression threshold. He was, by sheer repetition, teaching me to be nicer. Anybody else and I would have fed them their head in a basket. But Larry managed to push my buttons just right. He could caution me to be nicer and I didn't slug him. The basis of many a successful relationship.

We were only minutes from Larry's apartment. I'd tuck him into bed and answer the call. If it wasn't the police or a zombie-raising, I was going to be pissed. I hated being beeped when it wasn't important. That's what beepers are for, right? If it wasn't important stuff, I was going to rain all over somebody's parade. With Larry asleep, I could be as nasty as I wanted to be. It was almost a relief.

3

When Larry was safely tucked in bed with his Demorol, so deeply asleep that nothing short of an earthquake would have woken him, I made my phone call. I still didn't have the faintest idea who it was, which bothered me. It wasn't just inconvenient, it was unnerving. Who was giving out my private numbers and why?

The phone didn't even finish a ring before it was picked up. The voice on the other end was male, soft, and panicked. "Hello, hello."

All my irritation vanished in a wash of something very close to fear. "Stephen, what's wrong?"

I heard him swallow on his end of the phone. "Thank God."

"What's happened?" I made my voice very clear, very calm, because I wanted to yell at him, to force him to tell me what the hell was going on.

"Can you come down to St. Louis University Hospital?"

That got my attention. "How bad are you hurt?"

"It's not me."

My heart slid up into my throat, and my voice came out squeezed and tight. "Jean-Claude." The moment I said it, I knew it was silly. It was just after noon. If Jean-Claude had needed a doctor, they would have had to come to him. Vampires did not travel well in broad daylight. Why was I so worried about a vampire? I happened to be dating him. My family, devout Catholics, are simply thrilled. Since I'm still a little embarrassed about it, it's hard to defend myself.

"It's not Jean-Claude. It's Nathaniel."

"Who?"

Stephen's breath went out in a long-suffering sigh. "He was one of Gabriel's people."

Which was another way of saying he was a wereleopard. Gabriel had been the leopards' leader, their alpha, until I killed him. Why had I killed him? Most of the wounds he'd given me had healed. It was one of the benefits of the vampire marks. I didn't scar quite so easily anymore. But there was a curl of scars high up on my buttocks and lower back, faint, almost dainty, but I would always have a little reminder of Gabriel. A reminder that his fantasy had been to rape me, to make me cry out his name, then kill me. Though knowing Gabriel, he probably hadn't been so picky on when I died, after, or during—either would have worked for him. As long as I was still warm. Most lycanthropes aren't into carrion.

I sounded casual about it, even in my own head. But my fingers traced along my back as if I could feel the scars through my skirt. Had to be casual about it. Had to be. Or you start screaming, and you don't stop.

"The hospital doesn't know Nathaniel's a shapeshifter, do they?" I said.

He lowered his voice. "They know. He's healing too fast for them not to know."

"So why whisper?"

"Because I'm out in the waiting room on a pay phone." There was a sound on the other end like he'd had to take the receiver away from his mouth. He muttered, "I'll be off in just a minute." He came back on. "I need you to come down, Anita."

"Why?"

"Please."

"You're a werewolf, Stephen. What are you doing babysitting one of the kitty-cats?"

"I'm one of the names in his wallet in case of emergencies. Nathaniel works at Guilty Pleasures."

"He's a stripper?" I made it a question because he could have been a waiter, but it wasn't likely. Jean-Claude owned Guilty Pleasures, and he would never have wasted a shapeshifter off-stage. They were too damned exotic.

"Yes."

"The two of you need a ride?" It was my day for it, I guess.

"Yes, and no."

There was something in his voice that I didn't like. An unease, a tension. It wasn't like Stephen to be cagey. He didn't play games. He just talked. "How did Nathaniel get hurt?" Maybe if I asked better questions, I'd get better answers.

"A customer got too rough."

"At the club?"

"No. Anita, please, there's no time. Come down and make sure he doesn't go home with Zane."

"Who the hell is Zane?"

"Another of Gabriel's people. He's been pimping them out since Gabriel died. But he's not protecting them like Gabriel did. He isn't alpha."

"Pimping them out? What are you talking about?"

Stephen's voice rose high and far too cheerful. "Hello, Zane. Have you seen Nathaniel yet?"

I couldn't really hear the answer, just the buzz of all the people in the waiting room. "I don't think they want him to go just yet. He's hurt," Stephen said.

Zane must have stepped very close to the phone, very close to Stephen. A low, growling voice came through the wire. "He'll go home when I say he goes home."

Stephen's voice held an edge of panic. "I don't think the doctors will like that."

"I don't give a shit. Who are you talking to?"

For his voice to be that clear he had to have Stephen pinned against the wall. Threatening him, without saying anything specific.

The growling voice was suddenly very clear. He'd taken the phone from Stephen. "Who is this?"

"Anita Blake, and you must be Zane."

He laughed, and it sounded too low, as if his throat were sore. "The wolves' human lupa. Oh, I'm so scared."

Lupa was the word the werewolves used for their leader's mate. I was the first human so honored. I wasn't even dating their Ulfric anymore. We'd broken up after I saw him eat somebody. Hey, a girl's got to have some standards.

"Gabriel wasn't scared of me either. Look where it got him," I said.

Zane was quiet for a handful of heartbeats. He breathed over the phone like a dog panted, heavy, but not like he was doing it on purpose, more like he couldn't help it. "Nathaniel is mine. Keep off of him."

"Stephen isn't one of yours," I said.

"Does he belong to you?" I could hear cloth moving. A sense of movement on the other end of the phone that I didn't like. "He is sooo pretty. Have you tasted these soft lips? Has this long yellow hair swept over your pillow?"

I knew without seeing it that he was touching Stephen, caressing him to match the words. "Don't touch him, Zane."

"Too late."

I gripped the phone tight and forced my voice calm, even. "Stephen's under my protection, Zane. Do you understand me?"

"What would you do to keep your pet wolf safe, Anita?"

"You don't want to push that button, Zane. You really don't."

He lowered his voice to an almost painful whisper. "Would you kill me to keep him safe?"

I usually have to meet someone at least once before threatening to kill them, but I was about to make an exception. "Yeah."

He laughed, low and nervous. "I see why Gabriel liked you. So tough, so sure of yourself. Sooo dangerous."

"You sound like a bad imitation of Gabriel."

He made a sound that was somewhere between a hiss and a *bah*. "Stephen shouldn't have interfered."

"Nathaniel's his friend."

"I am all the friend he needs."

"I don't think so."

"I am taking Nathaniel with me, Anita. If Stephen tries to stop me, I'll hurt him."

"You hurt Stephen, I hurt you."

"So be it." He hung up.

Shit. I ran for my Jeep. I was thirty minutes away, twenty if I pushed it a lot. Twenty minutes. Stephen wasn't dominant. He was a victim. But he was also loyal. If he thought Nathaniel shouldn't go with Zane, he'd try and keep him. He wouldn't fight for him, but he might throw his body in front of the car. I had no doubts at all that Zane would drive right over him. Best case scenario. Worst case scenario was Zane would take both Stephen and Nathaniel. If Zane acted as much like Gabriel as he talked, I'd rather have taken my chances with the car.

4

My second emergency room in less than two hours. It was a red-letter day even for me. Good news was that none of the injuries were mine. Bad news was that that might change. Alpha or not, Zane was a shapeshifter. They were able to bench-press medium-size elephants. I was not going to arm-wrestle him. Not only would I lose, but he'd probably pull the arm out of my socket and eat it. Most lycanthropes liked to try and pass for human. I wasn't sure Zane sweated little details like that.

Yet I didn't want to kill Zane if I didn't have to. It wasn't mercy. It was the thought that he might force me to do it in public. I didn't want to go to jail. The fact that the punishment worried me more than the crime said something about my moral state. Some days I thought I was becoming a sociopath. Some days I thought I was already there.

I carried silver-plated bullets in my gun at all times. Silver worked on humans, as well as on most supernatural beings. Why keep switching to normal ammo that only did humans and a very few creatures? But a few months ago I'd met a fairie that had damn near killed me. Silver didn't work on fairies, but normal lead did. So I'd taken to keeping a spare clip of regular bullets in the glove compartment. I peeled off the first two rounds of my silver clip and replaced them with lead. Which meant I had two bullets to discourage Zane with, before I killed him. Because, make no mistake, if he kept coming after I'd pumped him full of two Glazer Safety Rounds, which hurt a hell of a lot even if you could heal the damage, the first silver bullet was not going to be aimed to wound.

It wasn't until I was going through the doors I realized that I didn't know Nathaniel's last name. Stephen's name wasn't going to help me. Damn.

The waiting room was packed. Women with crying babies, children racing through the chairs belonging to no one, a man with a bloody rag around his hand, people with no visible injury staring dully into space. Stephen was nowhere in sight.

Screams, the sound of breaking glass; metal clanked to the floor. A nurse ran out of the far hallway. "Get more security, now!" A nurse behind the admittance desk punched buttons on the phone.

Call it a hunch but I was betting I knew where Stephen and Zane were. I flashed my ID at the nurse. "I'm with the Regional Preternatural Investigation Team. Can I help?"

The nurse clutched my arm. "You're a cop?"

"I'm with the police, yes." Prevarication at its best. As a civilian attached to a police squad you learn how to do that.

"Thank God." She started to pull me towards the noise.

I pulled my arm free and took out my gun. Safety off, pointed at the ceiling, ready to go. With normal ammo I wouldn't have pointed at the ceiling, not with a hospital full of patients above me, but Glazer Safety Rounds aren't called safety rounds for nothing.

The back area was like every emergency area I'd ever been in. Curtains hung from metal tracks so you could make lots and lots of little individual examining rooms. A handful of curtains were closed, but patients were sitting up, staring through the curtains, watching the show. A wall divided the room down the middle to the corridor, so there wasn't much to see.

A man wearing green surgical scrubs went flying through the air from around that wall. He smacked into the opposite wall, slid down it heavily, and lay very still.

The nurse with me ran towards him, and I let her go. What lay beyond, what was tossing doctors around like toys, wasn't a job for a healer. It was a job for me. Two more figures in surgical scrubs lay on the floor, one male, one female. The woman was awake, eyes wide. Her wrist was at a 45 degree angle, broken. She saw my ID clipped to my jacket. "He's a shifter. Be careful."

"I know what he is," I said. I lowered the gun just a touch.

Her eyes flinched, and it wasn't pain. "Don't shoot up my trauma center."

"Try not to," I said and moved past her.

Zane stepped out into the corridor. I'd never seen Zane before, but who else could it be? He was carrying someone in his arms. I thought at first, a woman, because the hair was long and shining brown, but the exposed back and shoulders were too muscular, too male. It had to be Nathaniel. He fit easily into the taller man's arms.

Zane was about six foot, stretched tall and thin. He wore only a black leather vest on his thin, pale upper body. His hair was cotton-white, cut short on the sides with the top long in moussed spikes.

He opened his mouth and snarled at me. He had fangs, upper and lower, like a great cat. Sweet Jesus.

I pointed the gun at him and let out the air in my body until I was still and quiet. I was aiming for a line of shoulder above Nathaniel's still form. At this distance I'd hit it.

"I'll only ask once, Zane. Put him down."

"He's mine, mine!" He took striding steps down the hallway, and I fired.

The bullet spun him halfway around, and staggered him to his knees. The shoulder I'd hit stopped working, and Nathaniel slid out of his arms. Zane got to his feet with the smaller man tucked under his good arm like a doll. The flesh of his shoulder was already reknitting, rebuilding itself like a fast-forward picture of a flower blooming.

Zane could have tried to rush past me, to use his speed, but he didn't. He just came walking towards me as if he didn't believe I'd do it. He should have believed.

The second lead bullet took him square in the chest. Blood exploded out of his pale skin. He fell onto his back, spine bowing, struggling to breathe with a hole the size of a fist in his chest. I went for him, not running, but hurrying.

I walked wide around him, out of arm's reach, and came up a little behind him, and to the side. The shoulder I'd shot was still limp, his other arm trapped under Nathaniel's body. Zane gasped up at me, brown eyes wide.

"Silver, Zane, the rest of the bullets are silver. I'll make it a head shot and blow your freaking brains all over this nice clean floor."

He finally managed to gasp out, "Won't." Blood filled his mouth and spilled down his chin.

I pointed the gun at his face, about eyebrow level. If I pulled the trigger, he was gone. I stared down at this man I'd never met before. He looked young, nowhere close to thirty. A great emptiness filled me. It was like standing in the middle of white noise. I felt nothing. I didn't want to kill him, but I didn't care if I did. It didn't matter to me. It only mattered to him. I let that knowledge fill my eyes. That I didn't give a damn one way or the other. I let him see it, because he was a shapeshifter, and he'd understand what I was showing him. Most people wouldn't. Most sane people anyway.

I said, "You are going to leave Nathaniel alone. When the police arrive, you are going to do everything they tell you to do. No arguments, no fighting, or I will kill you. Do you understand me, Zane?"

"Yes," he said, and more blood flowed in a heavy line from his mouth. He started to cry. Tears welled down his bloodstained face.

Crying? The bad guys aren't supposed to cry.

"I'm so glad you've come," he said. "I tried to take care of them, but I couldn't. I tried to be Gabriel, but I couldn't be him." His shoulder had healed enough that he covered his eyes with his hand so we couldn't see him cry, but his voice was thick with tears, as well as blood.

"I'm so glad you've come to us, Anita. I'm so glad we're not alone anymore."

I didn't know what to say. Denying that I was going to be their leader seemed a bad idea with bodies littering the area. If I refused his offer, he might get nasty again and I'd have to kill him. I realized suddenly with something like a physical jolt that I didn't want to kill him. Was it the tears? Maybe. But it was more than that. It was the fact that I'd killed their alpha, their protector, and never given a thought what that might do to the rest of the wereleopards. It had never occurred to me that there was no second in command, no one to fill Gabriel's place. I certainly couldn't be their alpha. I didn't turn furry once a month. But if it would keep Zane from tearing up any more doctors, I could play along for a while.

By the time the cops arrived, Zane was healed. He'd curled around Nathaniel's unconscious body like it was a teddy bear, still crying. He stroked Nathaniel's hair and muttered over and over, "She'll keep us safe. She'll keep us safe. She'll keep us safe."

I think the "she" was me, and I was in way over my head.

5

Stephen lay in the narrow hospital bed. His curly blond hair was longer than mine, sweeping across the white pillow. Angry red and pink scars crisscrossed his delicate face. He looked like he'd been shoved through a window, which is exactly what had happened. Stephen, who didn't outweigh me by twenty pounds, had stood his ground. Zane had finally shoved him through a wire-mesh safety window. Like shoving someone through a wire cheese grater. If it had been a human being, they'd be dead. Even Stephen was hurt, badly hurt. But he was healing. I couldn't literally see the scars fading. It was like trying to watch a flower bloom. You knew it happened, but you never got to see it. I'd glance back at him, and there'd be one less scar. It was unnerving as hell.

Nathaniel was in the other bed. His hair was longer than Stephen's. Waist length, I was betting. Hard to judge since I'd only seen him prone. It was the darkest of auburns, almost brown but not. It was a rich, deep mahogany. The hair lay on the white sheets like the pelt of an animal, thick and shining.

He was pretty rather than handsome, and couldn't have been more than five foot six. The hair helped the illusion of femininity. But his shoulders were disproportionately broad, part weightlifting, but part genetics. He had great shoulders, but they belonged on someone about half a foot taller. He had to be eighteen to strip at Guilty Pleasures. His face was slender, jaw too smooth. He might have been eighteen, but he wasn't much over. Maybe someday he'd grow into the shoulders.

We were in a semiprivate room on the isolation ward. The floor that most hospitals kept for lycanthropes, vamps, and other preternatural citizens. Anything they thought might be dangerous. Zane would have been dangerous. But the cops had carted him away, wounds nearly healed. His flesh had pushed my bullets out onto the floor like rejected bits of organ. I didn't think we needed the isolation ward for Stephen and Nathaniel. I could be wrong on Nathaniel, but I didn't think so. I trusted Stephen's judgment better than that.

Nathaniel hadn't regained consciousness. I'd asked what his injuries were, and they told me, because they still thought I was a cop, and I'd saved their asses. Gratitude is a wonderful thing.

Someone had pretty much gutted Nathaniel. I don't mean just cut open his gut with a knife. I mean opened him up and let his intestines fall onto the floor; they found bits of debris on his intestines. There were signs of severe trauma to other parts of the body. He'd been sexually abused. And yes, a prostitute can be raped. All it takes is saying no. No one, not even a lycanthrope, would agree to being raped while their insides were spilling onto the floor. The rape could have been first, then they tried to kill him. It was a touch less sick done in that order. A touch.

There were marks on his wrists and ankles like he'd been chained. The marks were rubbed bloody like he'd struggled, and they weren't healing. Which meant that they'd used chains with a high silver content so it would hurt and not just hold. Whoever had done this to him knew ahead of time they'd be getting a lycanthrope. They were prepared. Which raised some very interesting questions.

Stephen said Gabriel had been pimping the wereleopards out. I understood why people would want something as exotic as a wereleopard. I knew that sado-masochism existed. Shapeshifters could take a hell of a lot of damage. So the combination even made a certain sense. But this was beyond sex games. I'd never heard of anything this brutal outside of a serial-killer case.

I couldn't leave them alone, unprotected. Even without the threat of sexual murderers, there was still the wereleopards. Zane might have cried and kissed my feet, but there were others. If they had no pack structure, no alpha, they had no one to tell them to leave Nathaniel alone. Without a leader it might be a matter of having to back down or kill each of them individually. Not a pleasant thought. Real leopards don't sweat who's in charge much. They don't have pack structures, but shapeshifters aren't animals, they're people. Which meant no matter how sol-itary and uncomplicated the animal form, the people half will find a way to screw things up. If Gabriel had hand-picked his people, I couldn't trust that they wouldn't come and try for Nathaniel again. Gabriel had been one sick kitty, and Zane hadn't impressed me much either. Who you gonna call for reinforcements? The local werewolf pack, of course. Stephen was a member of their pack. They owed him protection.

There was a knock on the door. I took the Browning out and held it on my lap underneath the magazine I'd been reading. I'd managed to find a three-month-old copy of *National Wildlife*, with an article on Kodiak bears. The magazine hid the gun nicely.

"Who is it?"

"It's Irving."

"Come in." I left the gun out, just in case somebody would try to push in behind him. Irving Griswold was a werewolf and a reporter. For a reporter he was a good guy, but he wasn't as careful as I was. When I saw he was alone, then I would put the gun up.

Irving pushed the door open, smiling. His frizzy brown hair encircled his head like a brown halo with the bald spot gleaming in the middle. Glasses perched on a small nose. He was short and gave the impression of being round without being fat. He looked like anything but a big bad wolf. He didn't even look much like a reporter, which was one of the things that made him such a great interviewer but would probably always keep him from being on-camera material. He worked for the *St. Louis Post-Dispatch*, and had interviewed me many times.

He closed the door behind him.

I put up the gun.

His eyes widened. He spoke low, but not in a whisper. "How's Stephen?"

"How did you get in here? There's supposed to be a cop on the door."

"Gee, Blake, I'm glad to see you too."

"Don't mess with me, Irving. There's supposed to be a guard out there."

"He's talking to a very pretty nurse at the desk."

"Dammit." I was not a real cop, so I couldn't go around yelling at them, but it was tempting. There was a law floating around Washington that might give vampire hunters federal badges soon. Sometimes I thought it was a bad idea. Sometimes, I didn't.

"Talk to me fast before I get kicked out. How is Stephen?"

I told him. "You don't care about Nathaniel?"

He looked uncomfortable. "You know that Sylvie is *de facto* pack leader while Richard is out of town working on his master's degree, right?"

I sighed. "No, I didn't know."

"I know you're not talking to Richard since you broke up, but I'd think someone else would have mentioned it."

"All the other wolves creep around me like there's been a death. No one talks about Richard to me, Irving. I thought he'd forbidden them to talk to me."

"Not to my knowledge."

"I'm surprised you didn't come in here asking for a story."

"I can't do this story, Anita. It's too close to home."

"Because you know Stephen?"

"Because everyone involved is a shapeshifter and I'm just a mild-mannered reporter."

"You really think you'd lose your job if they found out?"

"Job, hell. What would my mother say?"

I smiled. "So you can't play bodyguard."

He frowned. "You know, I hadn't thought about that. When one of the pack got hurt in public where it couldn't be hidden, Raina always used to ride to the rescue. With her dead, I don't think we have any alphas that aren't hiding what they are. No one I'd trust to guard Stephen, anyway."

Raina had been the wolf pack's old lupa before I took the job. Technically the old lupa doesn't have to die to step down, unlike the Ulfric, or King Wolf. But Raina had been Gabriel's playmate. They'd shared certain hobbies, like making pornographic snuff films starring shapeshifters and humans. She'd been helping film while Gabriel tried to rape me. Oh, yeah, Raina had made it a real pleasure to punch her ticket.

"That's the second time you've ignored Nathaniel," I said. "What gives, Irving?"

"I told you Sylvie is in charge until Richard gets back in town."

"So?"

"She's forbidden any of us to help the wereleopards in any way."

"Why?"

"Raina used the wereleopards in her porno movies a lot, along with the wolves."

"I've seen one of the films. I wasn't impressed. Horrified, but not impressed."

Irving looked very serious. "She also let Gabriel and the cats punish wayward pack members."

"Punish?" I made it a question.

Irving nodded. "Sylvie was one of the ones who got punished, more than once. She hates them all, Anita. If Richard hadn't forbid it, she'd have used the pack to hunt the leopards down and kill them all."

"I've seen what Gabriel and Raina thought was fun and games. I think I'm on Sylvie's side for once."

"You cleaned house for us, you and Richard. Richard killed Marcus and now he's Ulfric, pack leader. You killed Raina for us, and now you're our lupa."

"I shot her, Irving. According to pack law, so I'm told, using a gun negates the challenge. I cheated."

"You're not lupa because you killed Raina. You're lupa because Richard picked you as his mate."

I shook my head. "We aren't dating anymore, Irving."

"But Richard hasn't picked a new lupa, Anita. Until he does, the job's yours."

Richard was tall, dark, handsome, honest, truthful, brave. He was perfect except for being a werewolf. Even that had been forgivable, or so I thought. Until I saw him in action. Saw the whole enchilada. The meat had been raw and squirming, the sauce a little bloody.

Now I was dating just Jean-Claude. I wasn't sure how much of an improvement dating the head vampire of the city was over dating the head werewolf, but I'd made my choice. It was Jean-Claude's pale, pale hands that held my body. His black hair that curled over my pillow. His midnight-blue eyes that I stared into while we made love.

Good girls do not have premarital sex, especially with the undead. I didn't think good girls had regrets about ex-boyfriend A, when they've chosen boyfriend B. Maybe I'd been wrong. Richard and I avoided each other when we could. Which had been for most of the last six weeks. Now he was out of town. Easy to avoid each other now.

"I won't ask what you're thinking about," Irving said. "I think I know."

"Don't be so damn smart," I said.

He spread his hands wide. "Occupational hazard."

That made me laugh. "So Sylvie's forbidden anyone to help the leopards. Where does that leave Stephen?"

"He went against her direct orders, Anita. For someone as low in the pack structure as Stephen, that took guts. But Sylvie won't be impressed. She'll tear him up, and she won't allow anyone to come down and baby-sit them. I know her that well."

"I can't do this twenty-four hours a day, Irving."

"They'll heal in a day or so."

I frowned at him. "I can't sit here for two days."

He looked away from me and went to stand beside Stephen's bed. He stared down at the sleeping man, hands clasped in front of him.

I walked over to them. I touched Irving's arm. "What aren't you telling me?"

He shook his head. "I don't know what you mean."

I turned him around, made him face me. "Talk to me, Irving."

"You aren't a shapeshifter, Anita. You aren't dating Richard anymore. You need to get out of our world, not further into it."

He looked so serious, solemn, that it scared me. "Irving, what's wrong?"

He just shook his head.

I grabbed him by both arms and resisted the urge to shake him. "What are you hiding?"

"There is a way for you to get the pack to guard Stephen and even Nathaniel."

I took a step back. "I'm listening."

"You outrank Sylvie."

"I'm not a shapeshifter, Irving. I was the new pack leader's girlfriend. I'm not even that anymore."

"You're more than that, Anita, and you know it. You've killed some of us. You kill easily and without remorse. The pack respects that."

"Gee, Irving, what a rousing endorsement."

"Do you feel badly about killing Raina? Did you lose sleep over Gabriel?"

"I killed Raina because she was trying to kill me. I killed Gabriel for the same reason, self-preservation. So no, I didn't lose any sleep."

"The pack respects you, Anita. If you could find some pack members that are already outed as shifters and convince them that you're scarier than Sylvie, they'd guard them, both of them."

"I am not scarier than Sylvie, Irving. I can't beat them to a pulp. She can."

"But you can kill them." He said it very quietly, watching my face, searching my expression.

I opened my mouth, closed it. "What are you trying to get me to do, Irving?"

He shook his head. "Nothing. Forget I said it. I shouldn't have said it. Get more cops in here and go home, Anita. Just get out of it while you can."

"What's going on, Irving? Is Sylvie a problem?"

He looked at me. His usually cheerful eyes, solemn, thoughtful. He shook his head. "I've got to go, Anita."

I grabbed his arm. "You go nowhere until you tell me what's happening."

He turned back to me slowly, reluctantly. I let go of his arm and stepped back. "Talk."

"Sylvie has challenged everyone higher in the pack than she is, and won."

I looked at him. "So?"

"Do you understand how unusual it is for a woman to fight her way to second in command. She's about five foot six, small-boned. Ask how she's winning."

"You're being coy, Irving. That's not like you. I'm not going to play Twenty Questions with you. Just tell me."

"She killed the first two people she fought. She didn't have to. She chose to. The next three challenges she made just agreed she was dominant to them. They didn't want to risk being killed."

"Very practical," I said.

He nodded. "Sylvie's always been that. She finally picked one of the inner circle to fight. She's too small to be one of the enforcers; besides I think she was afraid of Jamil, and Shang-Da."

"Jamil? Richard didn't drive him out? But he was one of Marcus's and Raina's flunkies."

Irving shrugged. "Richard thought the transition would go smoother if he kept some of the old guard in power."

I shook my head. "Jamil should have been driven out or killed."

"Maybe, but actually Jamil seems to support Richard. I think it really surprised him when he wasn't killed instantly. Richard has earned his loyalty."

"I didn't know Jamil had any loyalty," I said.

"None of us did. Sylvie fought and won the place of Geri, second in command."

"She kill for it?"

"Surprisingly, no."

"Okay, so Sylvie's tearing up the pack. She's second in command. Great, so what?"

"I think she wants to be Ulfric, Anita. I think she wants Richard's job."

I stared at him. "There's only one way to be Ulfric, Irving."

"To kill the old king," Irving said. "Yeah, I think Sylvie knows that."

"I haven't seen her fight, but I've seen Richard fight. He outweighs her by a hundred pounds, a hundred pounds of muscle, and he's good. She can't beat him in a fair fight, can she?"

"It's like Richard is wounded, Anita. The heart's gone out of him. I think if she challenged and really wanted it, she'd win."

"What are you telling me? That he's depressed?" I asked.

"It's more than that. You know how much he hates being one of the monsters. He'd never killed anyone until Marcus. He can't forgive himself."

"How do you know all this?"

"I listen. Reporters make good listeners."

We stared at each other. "Tell me the rest."

Irving looked down, then up. "He doesn't discuss you with me. The only thing he said was that even you couldn't accept what he was. Even you, the Executioner, were horrified."

It was my turn to look down. "I didn't want to be."

"We can't change how we feel," Irving said.

I met his eyes. "I would if I could."

"I believe you."

"I don't want Richard dead."

"None of us do. I'm afraid of what Sylvie would do without anyone to stop her." He motioned to the other bed. "First order of business would be hunting down all the wereleopards. We'd slaughter them."

I took in a deep breath and let it out. "I can't change how I feel about what I saw, Irving. I saw Richard eat Marcus." I paced the small room, shaking my head. "What can I do to help?"

"Call the pack and demand that they acknowledge you as lupa. Make some of them come here and guard both of them against Sylvie's express orders. But you have to give them your protection. You have to promise them that she won't hurt them, because you'll see to it that she can't.''

"If I do that and Sylvie doesn't like it, I'll have to kill her. It's like I'm setting her up to be killed. That's a little premeditated even for me.''

He shook his head. "I'm asking you to be our lupa. To be Richard's lupa. To show Sylvie that if she keeps pressing, Richard may not kill her, but you will.''

I sighed. "Shit.''

"I'm sorry, Anita. I wouldn't have said anything, but . . .''

"I needed to know,'' I said. I hugged him, and he stiffened in surprise, then hugged me back.

"What was that for?''

"For telling me. I know Richard won't like it.''

The smile faded from his face. "Richard has punished two pack members since he took over. They challenged his authority, big time, and he nearly killed them both.''

"What?'' I asked.

"He sliced them up, Anita. He was like someone else, something else.''

"Richard doesn't do things like that.''

"He does now, not all the time. Most of the time he's fine, but then he snaps and goes into a rage. I don't want to be anywhere near him when he loses it.''

"How bad has he gotten?'' I asked.

"He's got to accept what he is, Anita. He's got to embrace his beast, or he's going to drive himself mad.''

I shook my head. "I can't help him love his beast, Irving. I can't accept it either.''

Irving shrugged. "It's not so bad being furry, Anita. There are worse things . . . like being the walking dead.''

I frowned at him. "Get out, Irving, and thanks for telling me.''

"I hope you're still thankful in a week.''

"Me, too.''

Irving gave me some phone numbers and left. Didn't want anyone to stay too long. People might suspect him of being more than just a reporter. No one seemed to worry about my reputation. I raised zombies, slew vampires, and was dating the Master of the City. If people began to suspect me of being a shapeshifter, what the hell difference would it make?

Three names of submissive pack members who Irving thought were tough enough to play bodyguard and weak enough to be bullied. I didn't want to do this. The pack was based on obedience: punishment and reward, mostly punishment. If the pack members I called refused me, I had to punish them, or I wasn't lupa, wasn't strong enough to back Richard. Of course, he probably wouldn't be grateful. He seemed to hate me now. I didn't blame him. He'd hate me interfering.

But it wasn't just Richard. It was Stephen. He'd saved my life once and I still hadn't returned the favor. He was also one of those people that was everyone's victim, until today. Yeah, Zane had nearly killed him, but that wasn't the point. He'd put friendship above pack loyalty. Which meant that Sylvie could withdraw pack protection from him. He'd be like the wereleopards, anybody's meat. I couldn't let that happen to him, not if I could stop it.

Stephen might end up dead. Richard might end up dead. I might have to kill Sylvie. I might have to maim or kill a few pack members to make my point. Might, might, might. Damn.

I'd never killed before except in self-defense or for revenge. If I put my hat in the ring, it would be premeditated, cold-blooded murder. Maybe not in a technical sense, but I knew what I would be starting in motion. It was like dominoes. They all stayed straight and neat until you hit one of them; then there was no stopping them. I would end up with a pretty pattern on the floor: Richard solidly in power, Stephen and the wereleopards safe, Sylvie backed down, or dead. The first three things were going to happen. It was Sylvie's choice how the last bit turned out. Harsh, but true. Of course, there was one other option. Sylvie could kill me. That would sort of open things up for her again. Sylvie wasn't exactly ruthless, but she didn't let anyone get in her way. We shared that trait. No, I am not ruthless. If I was, I'd have just called Sylvie into a meeting and shot her on the spot. I wasn't quite sociopath enough to do it. Mercy will get you killed, but sometimes it's all that makes us human.

I made the calls. I chose a man's name first, Kevin, no last name. His voice was thick with sleep, gruff, like he smoked.

"Who the hell is this?"

"Gracious," I said, "very gracious."

"Who is this?"

"It's Anita Blake. Do you know who I am?" When trying to be threatening, less is more. Me and Clint Eastwood.

He was quiet for nearly thirty seconds, and I let the silence build. His breath had sped up. I could almost feel his pulse quickening over the phone.

He answered like he was used to strange phone calls and pack business. "You're our lupa."

"Very good, Kevin, very good." Condescending is also good.

He coughed to clear his throat. "What do you want?"

"I want you to come down to St. Louis University Hospital. Stephen and Nathaniel have been hurt. I want you to guard them for me."

"Nathaniel, he's one of the wereleopards."

"That's right."

"Sylvie's forbidden us to help the wereleopards."

"Is Sylvie your lupa?" Questions are great, but only if you know the answers. If you ask questions and the answers surprise you, you look silly. Hard to be threatening when you look ill-informed.

He was quiet for a second. "No."

"Who is?"

I heard him swallow. "You are."

"Do I outrank her?"

"You know you do."

"Then get your butt down here, and do what I ask."

"Sylvie will hurt me, lupa. She really will."

"I'll see that she doesn't."

"You're just Richard's human girlfriend. You can't fight Sylvie, not and live."

"You're right, Kevin. I can't fight Sylvie, but I can kill her."

"What do you mean?"

"If she hurts you for helping me, I'll kill her."

"You can't mean that."

I sighed. "Look, Kevin, I've met Sylvie. Trust me when I say that I could point a gun at her head and pull the trigger. I can and will kill Sylvie if she forces me to. No jokes, no bluffs, no games." I listened to my voice as I said it. I sounded tired, almost bored, and so serious it was almost frightening.

"All right, I'll do it, but if you let me down she may kill me."

"You have my protection, Kevin, and I know what that means in the pack."

"It means I have to acknowledge you as dominant to me," he said.

"It also means that if anyone challenges you, I can help you fight your battles. Seems like a fair trade."

Silence filled the phone lines again. His breathing had slowed, deepened. "Promise me you won't get me killed."

"I can't promise that, Kevin, but I can promise that if Sylvie kills you, I'll kill her for you."

Silence, shorter this time. "I believe you would. I'll be at the hospital in forty minutes or less."

"Thanks, I'll be waiting."

I hung up and made the other two calls. They both agreed to come down. I'd drawn a line in the sand with Sylvie on one side and me on the other. She wasn't going to like it, not one little bit. Couldn't blame her. If our places were reversed, I'd have been pissed. But she should have left Richard alone. Irving had said it was like Richard was wounded, like the heart had gone out of him. I'd helped put that wound there. I'd cut his heart into tiny little pieces and danced on them. Not deliberately. My intentions were good, but you know what they say about good intentions.

I couldn't love Richard, but I could kill for him. Killing was the more practical of the two gifts. And lately I'd become very, very practical.

6

Sergeant Rudolph Storr showed up before the baby-sitting werewolves could arrive. I'd called him myself. He was the man in charge of the Regional Preternatural Investigation Team, RPIT, or RIP. A lot of people call us RIP, for Rest in Peace. Hey, at least they know who we are.

Dolph is six foot eight, built like a pro-wrestler, but it isn't just physical size that makes him impressive. He'd taken a squad that had been meant as a joke to appease the liberals and made it work. RPIT had solved more preternatural crimes in the last three years than any other police unit. Including the FBI. Dolph had even been invited up to lecture at Quantico. Not bad for someone who'd been given his command as a punishment. Dolph wasn't exactly an optimist, few cops are, but give him lemons and he made damn fine lemonade.

He closed the door behind him and stared down at me. "The doctor said my detective was in here. I just see you."

"I never said I was a detective. I said I was with the squad. They assumed the rest."

He shook his head. His black hair actually hid the tops of his ears. He was overdue for a hair cut. "If you were playing cop, why didn't you yell at the uniform that was supposed to be on this door?"

I smiled up at him. "I thought I'd leave that to you. I assume he knows that he was a bad boy."

"I took care of it," Dolph said.

He stayed standing at the door. I stayed sitting in my chair. I'd actually managed not to pull my gun on him. I was happy about that. He was staring at me hard enough to hurt without flashing a gun at him.

"What's going on, Anita?"

"You know everything I know," I said.

"How did you happen to be Johnny-on-the-spot?"

"Stephen called me."

"Tell me," he said.

I told him. I even put in the part about the pimping. I wanted that stopped.

The cops are pretty good at stopping crime, if you tell the truth. I left out a few things, like me having killed the wereleopards' old alpha. It was the only thing I left out. For me, it was almost the same as being honest.

Dolph blinked at me and took it all down in his trusty notebook. "Are you saying that our victim allowed someone to do this to him?"

I shook my head. "I don't think it's that simple. I think he went there knowing they'd chain him up. He knew there'd be sex and pain, but I don't think he knew they'd come this close to killing him. The doctors actually had to give him blood. His body was going into shock faster than it could fix itself."

"I've heard of wereanimals healing from worse wounds than this," Dolph said.

I shrugged. "Some people heal better than others even among the shapeshifters. Nathaniel is pretty low in the power structure, so I'm told. Maybe part of being weak is not healing as well." I spread my hands wide. "I don't know."

Dolph searched back through his notes. "Someone dropped him off at the emergency entrance wrapped in a sheet. No one saw anything. He just appeared."

"No one ever sees anything, Dolph. Isn't that the rule?"

That earned me a small smile. It was nice to see the smile. Dolph wasn't too happy with me lately. He'd only recently found out that I was dating the Master of the City. He didn't like it. He didn't trust anyone that socialized with the monsters. Couldn't blame him.

"Yeah, that's the rule. Are you telling me everything you know about this, Anita?"

I raised a hand in a scout's salute. "Would I lie to you?"

"If it suited your purpose, yes."

We stared at each other. The silence grew thick enough to walk on. I let it sit there. If Dolph thought I was going to break first, he was wrong. The strain between us wasn't this case. It was his disapproval of my choice of dates. His disappointment in me was always there now. Pressing, weighted, waiting for me to apologize or say, shucks, just kidding. The fact that I was dating a vampire made him trust me less. I understood. Two months ago, even less, and I'd have felt the same way. But here I was dating who, and what, I was dating. Dolph and I, both, had to deal with it.

And yet, he was my friend, and I respected him. I even agreed with him, but if I could ever get out of this damn hospital, I had a date with Jean-Claude tonight. Regardless of my doubts about Richard, morals in general, and the walking dead, I wanted the date. The thought of Jean-Claude waiting for me made my body tight and warm. Embarrassing, but true. I don't think anything short of giving up Jean-Claude would have satisfied Dolph. I wasn't sure that was an option anymore for a lot of reasons. So I sat and looked at Dolph. He stared back. The silence grew thicker with each tick of the clock.

A knock on the door saved us. The officer, now attentively on the door, whispered something to Dolph. Dolph nodded and closed the door. The look he gave me was even less friendly, if that was possible.

"Officer Wayne says that there are three relatives of Stephen's out here. He also says that if they're all relatives, he'll eat his gun."

"Tell him to pucker up," I said. "They're fellow pack members. Werewolves consider that closer than family."

"But legally it's not family," Dolph said.

"How many of your men you want to lose when the next shapeshifter comes through that door?"

"We can shoot them just as good as you can, Anita."

"But you still have to give them a warning before you shoot them, don't you? You still have to treat them like people instead of monsters or you end up in front of the review board."

"Witnesses say you gave Zane, no last name, a warning."

"I was feeling generous."

"You were shooting him in front of witnesses. That always makes you generous."

We went back to staring at each other. Maybe it wasn't just dating a vampire. Maybe it was the fact that Dolph was the ultimate cop and he was beginning to suspect that I was killing people, murdering people. People who hurt me or threatened me did have a tendency to vanish. Not many, but enough. And less than two months ago I'd killed two people where the bodies couldn't be hidden. Self-defense both times. Never saw the inside of a courtroom. Both assassins with records longer than I was tall. The woman's fingerprints had been the answer to several political killings that Interpol had lying around. Big-time bad guys that no one really mourned, at least not the cops.

But it fed Dolph's suspicions. Hell, it did everything but confirm them.

"Why'd you recommend me to Pete McKinnon, Dolph?"

He didn't answer for so long, I thought he wasn't going to, but finally he said, "Because you're the best at what you do, Anita. I may not always approve of your methods, but you help save lives, put away the bad guys. You're better on a murder scene than some of the detectives on my squad."

For Dolph, this was a speech. I opened my mouth, closed it, then said, "Thanks, Dolph. Coming from you, that's a big compliment."

"You just spend too much time with the damn monsters, Anita. I don't mean who you date. I mean all of it. You've played by their rules so long, sometimes you forget what it's like to be normal."

I smiled. "I raise the dead for a living, Dolph. I've never been normal."

He shook his head. "Don't purposely misunderstand what I'm saying, Anita. It's not the fur or the fangs that make you a monster, not always. Sometimes, it's just where you draw the line."

"The fact that I play with monsters is what makes me valuable to you, Dolph. If I played it straight, I wouldn't be as good helping you solve preternatural crimes."

"Yeah, sometimes I wonder if I'd left you alone, not gotten you to consult with us, if you'd be . . . softer."

I frowned at him. "Are you saying you blame yourself for what I've become?" I tried to laugh it off, but his face stopped me.

"How often did you go to the monsters on one of my cases? How often did you have to make bargains with them to help put away a bad guy? If I'd left you alone . . ."

I stood up. I reached out to him, then let my hand fall back without touching him. "I'm not your daughter, Dolph. You're not my keeper. I help the police because I like it. I'm good at it. And who else you gonna call?"

He nodded. "Yeah, who else? The shifters outside can come in and . . . visit the patients."

"Thanks, Dolph."

He took in a long breath and let it out in a big rush of air. "I saw the window that your friend Stephen got shoved through. If he'd been human, he'd be dead. It's just luck that no civilians were killed."

I shook my head. "I think Zane was being careful of the humans, at least. With the strength he has, it would have been easier to kill than to maim."

"Why would he have cared?"

"Because he's in jail, and he gets a bail hearing."

"They won't let him out," Dolph said.

"He didn't kill anyone, Dolph. Since when haven't you seen someone *not* get bail for assault and battery?"

"You think like a cop, Anita. It's what makes you good."

"I think like a cop and like a monster. That's what makes me good."

He nodded, closed his notebook and slipped it into an inner pocket of his jacket. "Yeah, that's what makes you good." He left without another word. He sent in the three werewolves and closed the door.

Kevin was tall, dark, scruffy and smelled like cigarettes. Lorraine was neat and prim like a second-grade schoolteacher. She smelled of White Linen perfume and blinked nervously at me. Teddy, his preference not mine, weighed around three hundred pounds, most of it muscle. He'd buzzed his hair down to a fine dark prickle, and his head looked too small for his massive body. The men looked scary, but it was Lorraine's handshake that left power vibrating down my skin. She looked like a scared rabbit and had enough power to be the big bad wolf.

Within twenty minutes I was free to leave. The mismatched trio of werewolves had divided the shifts so that one of them would be with the boys at all times. Did I trust the new wolves to guard them? Yeah. Because if they abandoned their posts and let Stephen get killed, I really would kill them. If they tried their best and were simply not strong enough, fine, but if they just gave up . . . I'd given Stephen, and now, Nathaniel, my protection. I wasn't kidding. I made sure that all of them knew that.

Kevin said it best, "If Sylvie shows up, we'll send her to you."

"You do that."

He shook his head, playing with an unlit cigarette. I'd told him he couldn't smoke it, but even touching it seemed to comfort him. "You've pissed in her pond. I hope you can clean it up."

I smiled. "Eloquent, Kevin, very eloquent."

"Eloquent or not, Sylvie is going to bust your ass if she can."

The smile widened. I couldn't help it. "Let me worry about my own ass. My job is to keep your ass out of the sling, not mine."

The three werewolves looked at me. There was something on all their faces, almost the same expression, but I couldn't read it. "Being lupa is more than just fighting for dominance," said Lorraine in a small voice.

"I know that," I said.

"Do you?" she asked, and there was something childlike in the question.

"I think so."

"You kill us if we fail you," Kevin said, "but will you die for us? Will you risk the same price you ask us to pay?"

I liked Kevin better when he wasn't being eloquent. I stared at these three strangers. People I'd just met. Would I risk my life for them? Could I ask them to risk their lives for me if I wasn't willing to return the favor?

I looked at them, really looked at them. Lorraine's small hands clutching her purse so tightly her hands shook. Teddy, who stared at me with calm, accepting eyes, but there was a challenge in them, an intelligence that you might miss if you just looked at the body. Kevin, who looked like he should be in an alley looking for a fix, or in a bar drinking up his share of whiskey. There was something underneath the cynicism. It was fear. Fear that I'd be like all the rest. A user who didn't give a damn about them. Raina had been that, and now Sylvie. The pack was supposed to be their refuge, their protection, not the thing they feared most.

Their warm, electric power filled the room, flowed out of them, dancing over my body. They were nervous, scared. Strong emotions made most shapeshifters leak power. If you were sensitive to it, you'd feel it. I'd felt it a lot over the years. This time was different somehow. I didn't just sense the power, my body reacted to it. Not merely a shivering of skin, a line of goose bumps, but something deeper. It was almost sexual, but that wasn't it either. It was as if the power had found a part of me, caressed a part of me, that I never knew was there.

Their power filled me, touched something, and I felt it, whatever it was, open up like a switch being thrown. A rush of warm energy welled up inside of my body and spread out through my skin, as if every pore of my body was emitting a warm line of air. It brought a soft gasp to my throat. I knew the taste of the power, and it wasn't Jean-Claude. It was Richard. Somehow, I'd tapped into Richard's power. I wondered if he felt it all the way out of state, studying for his degree.

Six weeks ago to save both their lives, I'd let Jean-Claude bind the three of us to each other. They were dying, and I couldn't let them go. Richard had invaded my dreams by accident, but mostly Jean-Claude had kept us apart because anything else was too painful. This was the first time I'd felt Richard's power since then. The first time I knew for certain that the tie was still there, still strong. Magic is like that. Even hate can't kill it.

I suddenly had the words, words I couldn't have known. "I am lupa, I am the all-mother, I am your guardian, your refuge, your peace. I will stand with you against all harm. Your enemies are my enemies. I share blood and flesh with you. We are lukoi, we are pack."

The warmth cut off abruptly. I staggered. Only Teddy's hand kept me from falling to the floor. "Are you all right?" he asked in a voice as deep and impressive as the rest of him.

I nodded. "I'm fine, I'm fine." As soon as I could, I stepped back. Richard had felt the pull hundreds of miles away, and he'd cut me off. He'd slammed the door shut without knowing what I was doing, or why. A rush of rage danced down inside my head like a silent scream. He was so angry.

We were both bound to Jean-Claude. I was his human servant and Richard was his wolf. It was a painful intimacy.

"You aren't lukoi," Lorraine said. "You aren't a shapeshifter. How did you do that?"

I smiled. "Trade secret." Truth was, I didn't know. I'd have to ask Jean-Claude tonight. I hoped he could explain it. He was only the third master vampire in their long history to have bound both a mortal and a shapeshifter into a single bond. I suspected strongly that there wasn't a manual, and that Jean-Claude winged it more often than I wanted to know.

Teddy went down on his knees. "You are lupa." The other two followed him. They abased themselves like good little submissive wolves, though Kevin didn't like it, and neither did I. But I wasn't sure how much was form and how much was necessary. I wanted them submissive because I didn't want to have to fight anybody, or kill anybody. So I let them crawl on the floor and run their hands along my legs, and sniff my skin like dogs. Which is when the nurse came in.

Everybody got up off the floor. I tried to explain and finally stopped. The nurse just stood there staring at all of us, a strange frozen smile on her face. She finally backed out without doing a damn thing. "I'll send Doctor Wilson in to check on them." She nodded her head too often and too rapidly and shut the door behind her. If she'd been wearing heels, I'd have bet we could have heard her run.

So much for not being one of the monsters.

7

Tucking in the baby-sitting werewolves made me late for my date. Taking time to read McKinnon's file made me later, but if there was a fire tonight, it'd be embarrassing not to be prepared. I learned two things from the file. One, that all the fires had been started after dark, which made me think instantly of vampires. Except that vampires couldn't start fires. It wasn't one of their abilities. In fact fire was one of the things they feared most. Oh, I'd seen a few vamps that could control existing flames to a small extent. Make a candle flame rise or fall, parlor tricks, but fire was the element of purity. Purity and the vamps didn't mix. The second thing I learned from the file was that I didn't know much about fires in general or arson in particular. I was going to need a book or a good lecture.

Jean-Claude had made reservations at Demiche's, a very nice restaurant. I'd had to run home, to my new rented house, to change. It had put me late enough that I'd arranged to meet him at the restaurant. The trouble with fancy dates was where to put my weapons. Women's dress clothes are the ultimate challenge to concealed-weapon carry.

Formals hid more but made grabbing the weapon harder. Anything form-fitting made it difficult. Tonight I was wearing a spaghetti-strap formal with slits so high on either side, I'd had to make sure that the hose were a matching off-black, and the underwear was lacy and black. I knew myself well enough to know that sometime during the evening I'd forget and flash the undies. And if I had to go for the gun, I'd certainly flash. So why wear it? Answer: I had a Firestar 9mm pistol tucked inside a bellyband.

The bellyband was an elastic strap that went over the underwear, but under the outerwear. It was designed to wear under a button-down dress shirt. Pull the shirt up with the free hand, pull the gun out, and violà, start shooting. The bellyband didn't work well under most formals, because you had yards of cloth to raise before you could get to the gun. It was better than nothing, but only if the bad guy was patient. But this dress, all I had to do was put my hand up through one of the slits. I had to pull the gun out, down, and out from under the dress, so it still wasn't speedy, but it wasn't bad. The bellyband also did not work with an especially form-fitting dress. Nobody gains weight in the shape of a gun.

I'd actually found a strapless bra that matched the black panties, so once I took off the gun and dress, I was wearing lingerie. The shoes were higher heels than I'd normally accept, but it was either that or hem the dress. Since I refuse to sew, heels it was.

The one major drawback to the spaghetti straps was that it showed off all my scars. I'd thought about buying a little cover-up jacket, but this wasn't a dress that was meant for a jacket. So screw it. Jean-Claude had seen the scars before, and the few people rude enough to give second glances could have an eyeful.

I was getting pretty good at makeup, eye shadow, blusher, lipstick. The lipstick was red—very, very red. But I had the coloring for it. Pale skin, black curly hair, pure brown eyes. I was all contrasts and strong colors the bright red lipstick matched. I was feeling pretty spiffy until I got a glimpse of Jean-Claude.

He was sitting at the table, waiting for me. I could see him from the entryway, though the maitre d' was two people ahead of me. I didn't mind. I enjoyed the view.

Jean-Claude's hair is black and curly, but he'd done something to it so it was straight and fine, falling past his shoulders, curled under at the ends. His face seemed even more delicate, like fine porcelain. He was beautiful, not handsome. I wasn't sure what saved his face from being feminine—some line of his cheek, bend of his jaw, something. You would never mistake him for anything other than male. He was dressed in royal blue, a color I'd never seen him in. A short jacket of a shining, almost metallic cloth was overlaid with black lace in a pattern of flowers. The shirt was his typical frilled, à la 1600's shirt, but it was a rich, vibrant blue, down to the mound of ruffles that climbed up his neck to frame his face and spill out the sleeves of the jacket to cover the upper half of his slender white hands.

He held an empty wineglass in his hand, spinning the stem of the glass between his fingers, watching the light spill through the crystal. He couldn't drink wine more than a sip at a time and mourned it.

The maitre d' led me through the tables towards him. He looked up, and seeing his face full-on made my chest tight, and it was suddenly hard to breathe. The blue so close to his face made his eyes bluer than I'd ever seen them, not the color of midnight skies, but cobalt blue, the color of a good sapphire. But no jewel ever had that weight of intelligence, of dark knowledge. The look in his eyes as he watched me walk towards him made me shiver. Not cold, not fear. Anticipation.

In the heels, and with the slits on both sides of the dress, there was an art to walking. You had to sort of throw yourself into it, a sling-back, slouching, hip-swinging walk, or the dress wrapped around your legs and the heels twisted at your ankles. You had to walk like you knew you could wear it and look wonderful. If you doubted yourself, hesitated, you'd fall to the floor and turn into a pumpkin. After years of my not being able to wear heels and dress clothes, Jean-Claude had taught me in a month what my stepmother couldn't teach me in twenty years.

He stood, and I didn't mind, though once upon a time I'd pissed off a prom date by standing every time that he did for the other girls at the table. One, I'd mellowed since then; two, I could see the rest of Jean-Claude's outfit.

The pants were black linen, clinging smooth and perfect to his body, so form-fitting that I knew there was nothing under the pants but him. Black boots climbed his legs to the knees. The boots were soft, crepe-like leather, wrinkled and pettable.

He glided towards me, and I stood there watching him come. I was still half afraid of him. Afraid of how much I wanted him. I was like a rabbit caught in headlights, frozen, waiting for death to come. But did the rabbit's heart beat fast and faster? Did its breath come like a choking thing into its throat? Was there an eager rush to the fear, or was there just death?

He wrapped his arms around me, drawing me close. His pale hands were warm as they slid over my bare arms. He'd fed on someone tonight, borrowed their warmth. But they'd been willing, even eager. The Master of the City never went begging for donors. Blood was about the only bodily fluid I wouldn't share with him. I slid my hands over the silk of his shirt, underneath the short jacket. I wanted to mold my body against his stolen warmth. I wanted to run my hands over the roughness of the linen, contrasting it to the smoothness of the silk. Jean-Claude was always a sensual feast, right down to his clothing.

He kissed my lips lightly. We'd learned that the lipstick came off. Then he tilted my head to one side and breathed along my face, down my neck. His breath was like a line of fire along my skin. He spoke with his lips just above the big pulse in my neck. "You are lovely tonight, *ma petite*." He pressed his lips against my skin, softly. I let out a shuddering breath and drew back from him.

It was a greeting among the vampires to plant a light kiss above the big pulse in the throat. It was a gesture reserved for the very closest friends. It showed great trust and affection. To refuse it meant you were angry or distrustful. It still seemed too intimate for public consumption to me, but I'd seen him use it with others and seen fights start with a refusal. It was an old gesture just coming back into vogue. In fact, it was becoming a chic greeting among entertainers and others of the same ilk. Better than kissing the air near someone's face, I guess.

The maitre d' held my chair. I waved him off. It wasn't feminism, but lack of grace. I never managed to be scooted under a table without the chair banging my legs or being so far from the table I had to finish scooting forward on my own. So the heck with it, I'd do it myself.

Jean-Claude watched me struggle into my chair, smiling, but he didn't offer to help. I'd finally broken him of that at least. He sat down in his own chair with a graceful fall. It was an almost foppish movement, but he was like a cat. Even at rest there was the potential of muscle under skin, a physical presence that was utterly masculine. I used to think it was vampire trickery. But it was him, just him.

I shook my head.

"What's wrong, *ma petite*?"

"I felt pretty spiffy until I saw you. Now I feel like one of the ugly stepsisters."

He tut-tutted at me. "You know you are lovely, *ma petite*. Shall I feed your vanity by telling you how much?"

"I wasn't fishing for compliments." I gestured at him and shook my head again. "You look amazing tonight."

He smiled, dipping his head to one side so his hair swept forward. *"Merci, ma petite."*

"Is the hair permed straight?" I asked. "It looks great," I added hastily, and it did, but I hoped it wasn't as permanent as a perm. I loved his curls.

"If it was, what would you say?"

"If it was, you'd have just said so. Now you're teasing me."

"Would you mourn the loss of my curls?" he asked.

"I could return the favor," I said.

He widened his eyes in mock horror. "Not your crowning glory, *ma petite, mon Dieu.*" He was laughing at me, but I was used to it.

"I didn't know you could get linen that tight," I said.

His smile widened. "And I did not know you could hide a gun under such a . . . slender dress."

"As long as I don't hug anybody, they'll never know."

"Very true."

A waiter came and asked if we wanted drinks. I ordered water and Coke. Jean-Claude declined. If he could have ordered anything, it would have been wine.

Jean-Claude brought his chair over to sit almost beside me. When dinner came, he'd move back to his place setting, but picking out the meal was part of the night's entertainment. It had taken me several dinner dates to realize what Jean-Claude wanted—no, almost needed. I was Jean-Claude's human servant. I bore three of his marks. One of the side effects of the second mark was that he could take sustenance through me. So if we'd been on a long sea voyage, he wouldn't have had to feed off of any humans on the boat. He could live through me for a time. He could also taste food through me.

For the first time in nearly four hundred years he could taste food. I had to eat it for him, but he could enjoy a meal. It was trivial compared to some of the other things he'd gained through the bonding, but it was the thing that seemed to please him most. He ordered food with a childlike glee and watched me eat, tasting it as I did. In private he'd roll on his back like a cat, hands pressed to his mouth as if trying to drain every taste. It was the only thing he did that was cute. He was gorgeous, sensual, but rarely cute. I'd gained four pounds in six weeks eating with him.

He slid his arm over the back of my chair, and we read the menu together. He leaned close enough for his hair to brush my cheek. The smell of his perfume, oh, sorry, cologne, caressed my skin. Though if what Jean-Claude wore was cologne, then Brut was bug spray.

I moved my head away from the caress of his hair, mainly because the feel of him this close was all I could think about. Maybe if I'd taken him up on his invitation to live with him at the Circus of the Damned, some of this heat would have dissipated. But I'd rented a house in record time in the middle of nowhere so my neighbors wouldn't get shot up, which is why I moved out of my last apartment. I hated the house. I wasn't a house kinda gal. I was a condo kind of gal. But condos had neighbors, too.

The lace overlay on his jacket was scratchy against my nearly bare shoulders. He put his hand on my shoulder, smoothing his fingertips across my skin. His leg brushed my thigh, and I realized I hadn't heard a damn thing he'd said. It was embarrassing.

He stopped talking and looked at me, gazed at me from inches away with those extraordinary eyes. "I have been explaining my menu choices to you. Have you heard any of it?"

I shook my head. "Sorry."

He laughed, and it hovered over my skin like his breath, warm and sliding over my body. It was a vampire trick but low on the scale, and had become public foreplay for us. In private we did other things.

He whispered against my cheek. "No apologies, *ma petite*. You know it pleases me that you find me . . . intoxicating."

He laughed again, and I pushed him away. "Go sit on your side of the table. You've been here long enough to know what you want."

He moved his chair dutifully back to his place setting. "I have what I want, *ma petite*."

I had to look down and not meet his eyes. Heat crept up my neck into my face, and I couldn't stop it.

"If you mean what do I want for dinner, that is a different question," he said.

"You are a pain in the ass," I said.

"And so many other places," he said.

I didn't think I could blush more. I was wrong. "Stop it."

"I love the fact that I can make you blush. It is charming."

The tone in his voice made me smile in spite of myself. "This is not a dress to be charming in. I was trying for sexy and sophisticated."

"Can you not be charming as well as sexy and sophisticated? Is there some rule about being all three?"

"Slick, very slick," I said.

He widened his eyes, trying for innocent and failing. He was many things, but innocent wasn't one of them.

"Now, let's start negotiating on dinner," I said.

"You make it sound like a chore."

I sighed. "Before you came along, I thought food was something you ate so you wouldn't die. I will never be as enamored of food as you are. It's almost a fetish with you."

"Hardly a fetish, *ma petite*."

"A hobby, then."

He nodded. "Perhaps."

"So just tell me what you like on the menu, and we'll negotiate."

"All that is required is that you taste what is ordered. You do not have to eat it."

"No, no more of this tasting shit. I've gained weight. I never gain weight."

"You have gained four pounds, so I am told. Though I have searched diligently for this phantom four pounds and cannot find them. It brings your weight up to a grand total of one hundred and ten pounds, correct?"

"That's right."

"Oh, *ma petite*, you are growing gargantuan."

I looked at him, and it was not a friendly look. "Never tease a woman about her weight, Jean-Claude. At least not an American twentieth-century one."

He spread his hands wide. "My deepest apologies."

"When you apologize, try not to smile at the same time. It ruins the effect," I said.

His smile widened until a hint of fang peeked out. "I will try to remember that for the future."

The waiter returned with my drinks. "Would you like to order, or do you need a few minutes?"

Jean-Claude looked at me.

"A few minutes."

The negotiation began.

Twenty minutes later I needed a refill on my Coke, and we knew what we wanted. The waiter returned, pen poised, hopeful.

I'd won on the appetizer, so we weren't having one. I'd given up the salad, and let him have the soup. Potato-leek soup, hey, it wasn't a hardship. We both wanted the steak.

"The petite cut," I told the waiter.

"How would you like that prepared?"

"Half well-done, half rare."

The waiter blinked at me. "Excuse me, madam?"

"It's an eight-ounce cut, right?"

He nodded.

"Cut it in half, and cook four ounces of it well-done, and four ounces of it rare."

He frowned at me. "I don't think we can do that."

"At these prices you should bring the cow out and have a ritual sacrifice at the table. Just do it." I handed him the menu. He took it.

Still frowning, he turned to Jean-Claude. "And you, sir?"

Jean-Claude gave a small smile. "I will not be ordering food tonight."

"Would you like wine with dinner, then, sir?"

He never missed a beat. "I do not drink—wine."

I coughed Coke all over the tablecloth. The waiter did everything but give me the Heimlich. Jean-Claude laughed until tears trailed from the corners of his eyes. You couldn't really tell it in this light, but I knew that the tears were tinged red. Knew that there would be pinkish stains on the linen napkin when he was done dabbing his eyes. The waiter fled without having gotten the joke. Staring across the table at the smiling vampire, I wondered if I got the joke or was the butt of the joke. There were nights when I wasn't sure which way the grave dirt crumbled.

But when he put his hand out to me across the table, I took it. Definitely, the butt of the joke.

8

Dessert was raspberry-chocolate cheesecake. A triple threat to any diet plan. Truthfully, I preferred my cheesecake straight. Fruit, except for strawberries, and chocolate just muddied the pure cream cheese taste. But Jean-Claude liked it, and dessert took the place of the wine I'd refused to order with dinner. I hated the taste of alcohol. So Jean-Claude's choice of dessert. Besides, the restaurant did not serve plain cheesecake. Not artistic enough, I guess.

I ate all the cheesecake, chased the last chocolate curl across the plate, and pushed it away. I was full. Jean-Claude had laid his arm across the tablecloth, rested his cheek on his arm, and closed his eyes, swooning, trying to savor every last taste. He blinked at me, as if coming out of a trance. He spoke, head still resting on his arm, "You have left some whipped cream, *ma petite.*"

"I'm full," I said.

"It is real whipped cream. It melts on the tongue and glides across the palate."

I shook my head. "I am done. If I eat any more, I'll be sick."

He gave a long-suffering sigh and sat back up. "There are nights when I despair of you, *ma petite.*"

I smiled. "Funny, I think the same thing about you sometimes."

He nodded his head, making a small bow. "Touché, *ma petite*, touché." He stared off past my shoulder and stiffened. The smile didn't fade from his face. It was wiped clean. His face was its blank unreadable mask. And I knew without turning around that someone was behind me, someone he feared.

I managed to drop my napkin, and picked it up with my left hand. With my right hand I drew the Firestar. When I sat back up, the gun was in my hand in my lap. Though shooting up Demiche's seemed like a bad idea. But hey, it wouldn't be the first bad idea I'd had.

I turned to see a couple walking towards us through the tables and crystal. The woman looked tall until you got a glimpse of the heels she was wearing. Stiletto, four inches. I'd have broken my ankle trying to walk in them. The dress was white, square necked, form-fitting, and more expensive than my entire outfit, even if you threw in the gun. Her hair was a white-blond so pale it matched the dress and the simple white mink stole curled around her shoulders. The hair was piled in a mound atop her head with a sparkle of silver and the crystal fire of diamonds to frame the hair like a crown. She was chalk-white, and despite the expert makeup I knew she hadn't fed yet tonight.

The man was human, though there was a thrumming energy to him that made me want to take back the human part. He was tanned that wonderful rich brown that olive skin can manage. His hair was a luxuriant curling brown, shaved short on the sides, but done so it fell in curls near his eyes. The eyes were pure brown and watched Jean-Claude steadily, joyously, but it was a dark joy. He was dressed in a white linen suit, complete with silk tie.

They stopped at our table like I knew they would. The man's handsome face was all for Jean-Claude. I might as well have not been there. He had very strong features, from high cheekbones to an almost-hooked nose. An inch either direction and his face would have been homely. Instead, it was striking, compelling, handsome in an utterly masculine way.

Jean-Claude stood, hands loose at his side, face beautiful and empty. "Yvette, it has been a long time."

She smiled wonderfully. "A very long time, Jean-Claude. You remember Balthasar?" She touched the man's arm, and he obligingly slid it around her waist. He planted a chaste kiss on her pale cheek. He looked at me then for the first time. It wasn't a look I'd ever gotten from a man. If it had been a woman, I'd have said she was jealous. The vampire's English was perfect. Her accent was pure French.

"Of course, I remember him," Jean-Claude said. "Time spent with Balthasar was always memorable."

The man turned back to Jean-Claude then. "But not memorable enough to keep you with us." He, too, sounded French, but there was an undercurrent of some other language. It was like mixing blue and red and getting purple.

"I am master of my own territory. It is what everyone dreams of, is it not?"

"Some dream of a seat on the council," Yvette said. Her voice was still mildly amused, but there was an undercurrent now, like swimming in dark water when you know there are sharks.

"I do not aspire to such lofty heights," Jean-Claude said.

"Really?" Yvette said.

"Truly," Jean-Claude said.

She smiled, but her eyes stayed distant and empty. "We shall see."

"There is nothing to see, Yvette. I am content where I am."

"If that is so, you have nothing to fear from us."

"We have nothing to fear regardless," I said. I smiled when I said it.

Both of them looked at me as if I was a dog that had done an interesting trick. I was really beginning not to like either of them.

"Yvette and Balthasar are envoys of the council, *ma petite*."

"Bully for them," I said.

"She doesn't seem very impressed with us," Yvette said. She turned full-face to me. Her eyes were greyish-green, with tiny flecks of amber dancing round the pupils. I felt her try to suck me under with those eyes, and it didn't work. Her power raised goose bumps on my skin, but she couldn't capture me with her eyes. She was powerful, but she wasn't a master vampire. I could feel her age like an

ache in my skull. A thousand years, at least. The last vamp I'd met who was that
old had cleaned my clock. But Nikolaos had been Master of the City, and Yvette
would never be that. If a vamp hadn't attained master status in a thousand years,
she, or he, was never going to. A vamp gained power and abilities with age, but
there was a limit. Yvette had reached hers. I stared into her eyes, let her power
tickle across my skin, and wasn't impressed.

She frowned. "Impressive."

"Thanks," I said.

Balthasar stepped around her and went to one knee in front of me. He put one
hand on the back of my chair and leaned into me. If Yvette wasn't a master, then
he wasn't her human servant. Only a master vampire could make a human servant.
Which meant he belonged to someone else. Someone I hadn't met yet. Why did I
get the feeling I'd be meeting that someone soon?

"My master is a council member," Balthasar said. "You have no idea what
kind of power he wields."

"Ask me if I care."

Anger flared across his face, darkening his eyes, making his grip on my chair
tight. He laid his hand on my leg just above my knee and started to squeeze. I'd
played with the monsters long enough to know what supernatural strength feels
like. His fingers dug into my flesh, and I knew he could keep squeezing until
muscle popped and he bared my bones to the air.

I grabbed his silk tie and pulled him close, and shoved the barrel of the Firestar
into his chest. I watched the surprise chase across his face from inches away.

"Bet I can blow a hole in your chest before you can crush my leg."

"You wouldn't dare."

"Why not?" I asked.

A touch of fear flowed through his eyes. "I am the human servant of a council
member."

"Not impressed," I said. "Try door number two."

He frowned at me. "I don't understand."

"Give her a better reason not to kill you," Jean-Claude said.

"If you shoot me here in front of witnesses, you will go to jail."

I sighed. "There is that." I jerked him close enough that our faces almost
touched. "Take your hand off my knee, slowly, and I won't pull this trigger. Keep
hurting me, and I'll take my chances with the police."

He stared at me. "You would do it, you really would do it."

"I don't bluff, Balthasar. Remember that for future reference, and maybe I
won't have to kill you."

His hand eased, then moved slowly away from me. I let him move back, his
tie sliding through my hand like a fishing line. I eased back in my chair. The gun
had never made it out from under the tablecloth. We'd been the soul of discretion.

The waiter came over anyway. "Is there a problem?"

"No problem," I said.

"Please bring our check," Jean-Claude said.

"Right away," the waiter said. He watched a little nervously while Balthasar
got to his feet. Balthasar smoothed down the wrinkles in his linen pants, but there's
only so much you can do with linen. It really isn't meant to be knelt in.

"You have won the first round, Jean-Claude. Be careful that it does not become a Pyrrhic victory." Yvette said. She and Balthasar left without ever taking a table. Guess they weren't hungry.

"What's going on?" I asked.

Jean-Claude sat back down. "Yvette is a council toady. Balthasar is the human servant of one of the most powerful council members."

"Why are they here?"

"I believe it is because of Mr. Oliver."

Mr. Oliver had been the oldest vampire I'd ever met. The oldest one I'd ever heard hinted at. He'd been a million years old, no joke, a million years, give or take. For all those with a head for prehistory, yes, that does mean he wasn't *Homo sapiens. Homo erectus*, and able to walk around during the day, though I never saw him cross direct sunlight. He'd been the only vamp to ever fool me for even a few moments into thinking he was human, which is nicely ironic, since he wasn't human at all. He'd had a plan to take out Jean-Claude, take over the vamps in the area, and force them to slaughter humans. Oliver had thought a slaughter like that would force the authorities to make vamps illegal again. He thought vampires would spread too quickly with legal rights and take over the human race. I'd sort of agreed with him.

His plan might have worked if I hadn't killed him. How I managed to kill him is a long story, but I'd ended up in a coma. A week unconscious, gone, so close to death that the doctors didn't know how I survived. Of course, they hadn't been too clear on why I was in a coma to begin with, and no one felt like explaining vampire marks and *Homo erectus* vampires.

I stared at Jean-Claude. "The crazy son of bitch that tried to take you out last Halloween?"

"*Oui.*"

"What about him?"

"He was a council member."

I almost laughed. "No way. He was old, older than sin, but he wasn't that powerful."

"I told you he agreed to limit his powers, *ma petite*. I did not know who and what he was at first, but he was the council member known as the Earthmover."

"Excuse me?"

"He could cause the earth to shake by his power alone."

"No way," I said.

"Yes way, *ma petite*. He agreed not to cause the earth to swallow the city because it would be blamed on an earthquake. He wanted the bloodletting to be blamed on vampires. You remember his plan was to drive vampires back to being illegal. An earthquake would not do that. A bloodbath would. No one, not even you, believes that a mere vampire can cause an earthquake."

"Damn straight, I don't." I stared at his careful face. "You're serious."

"Deadly serious, *ma petite*."

It was too much to take in all at once. When in doubt ignore and be terribly unimpressed. "So we took out a council member, so what?"

He shook his head. "There is no fear in you, *ma petite*. Do you understand what danger we are all in?"

"No, and what do you mean the 'danger we are all in'? Who else is in danger besides us?"

"All our people," he said.

"Define 'all,' " I said.

"All my vampires, anyone that the council considers ours."

"Larry?" I asked.

He sighed. "Perhaps."

"Should I call him? Warn him? How much danger?"

"I am not sure. No one has ever slain a council member and not taken their place."

"I killed him, not you."

"You are my human servant. The council sees all that you do as an extension of my actions."

I stared at him. "You mean anyone I kill is your kill?"

He nodded.

"I wasn't your servant when I killed Oliver."

"I would keep that bit of knowledge to ourselves."

"Why?"

"They may not kill me, *ma petite*, but a vampire hunter who killed a council member would be executed. There would be no trial, no hesitation."

"Even though I'm your human servant now?"

"That might save you. It is one of our most stringent laws not to destroy another's servant."

"So they can't kill me because I'm your servant."

"But they can harm you, *ma petite*. They can harm you so very much that you may wish for death."

"You mean torture?"

"Not in a traditional sense. But they are masters at finding that which terrifies you most and using it against you. They will use your desires against you and twist everything you are into a shape of their choosing."

"I've met master vampires that could sense your heart's desire and use it against you."

"Everything you have seen of us before, *ma petite*, is like a distant dream. The council is the reality. They are the nightmare on which we are all based. The thing that even we fear."

"Yvette and Balthasar didn't seem that scary to me."

He looked at me. There was no expression on his face. It was a mask, smooth, pleasant, hidden. "If they did not frighten you, *ma petite*, it is only because you do not know them. Yvette is a toady of the council because they are powerful enough to give her a ready supply of victims."

"Victims? You aren't talking about human prey, are you?"

"It can be human. But Yvette is considered perverted even by other vampires."

I wasn't sure I wanted to know, but . . . "Perverted in what way?"

He sighed and looked down at his hands. They lay very still on the tablecloth. It was like he was pulling away from me. I could see the walls clicking back into place. He was rebuilding himself into Jean-Claude, Master of the City. It was a shock to realize that there had been a change. It had been so gradual that I hadn't realized that with me, on our dates, he was different. I don't know if he was more himself or more what he thought I wanted him to be, but he was more "relaxed," less guarded. Watching him put on his public face while I sat across from him was almost depressing.

"Yvette loves the dead."

I frowned at him. "But she's a vampire. That's redundant."

He stared at me, and it wasn't a friendly look. "I will not sit here and debate with you, *ma petite*. You share my bed. If I were a zombie, you would not touch me."

"That's true." It took me a handful of seconds to understand what he'd just said. "Are you telling me that Yvette likes to have sex with zombies, real rotting corpses?"

"Among other things, yes."

I couldn't keep the disgust off my face. "Good Lord, that's . . ." Words failed me. Then I found a word. "She's a necrophiliac."

"She will use a dead body if nothing else is available, but her true joy is the rotted animated corpse. She would find your talent most appealing, *ma petite*. You could raise her an unending stream of partners."

"I wouldn't raise the dead for her amusement."

"Not initially," he said.

"No, not under any circumstances."

"The council has a way of finding circumstances that can force you to do almost anything."

I watched his face and wished I could read it. But I understood. He was hiding from them, already. "How deep is the hole we're in?"

"Deep enough to bury us all, if the council chooses."

"Maybe I shouldn't have put the gun up," I said.

"Perhaps not," he said.

The check came. We paid. We left. I made a stop at the ladies' room on the way out and retrieved the gun. Jean-Claude took my car keys, so I wouldn't have to handle anything but the gun. It was a short walk from bathroom to door. Black gun against a black dress. Either no one noticed, or no one wanted to get involved. What else was new?

9

The parking lot was a dark expanse of shining blackness with pools of light spot-lighting gleaming cars. Jaguars, Volvos, and Mercedes were the dominant species in the lot. I caught a glimpse of my Jeep at the far end of a line. I lost sight of it as we walked between the cars. Jean-Claude held my car keys cupped in his hand so they didn't rattle as he moved. We weren't holding hands, or anything else now. I had the Firestar in a two-handed grip, pointed at the ground, but ready. I was scanning the parking lot. My eyes flicking back and forth. I wasn't coy about it. A cop would have known what I was doing from yards away. I was searching for danger, searching for targets.

I felt both silly and nervous. The skin across my bare shoulders was trying to crawl down my spine. It was silly, but I'd have felt better in jeans and a shirt. More secure.

"I don't think they're out here," I said softly.

"I'm sure you are right, *ma petite*. Yvette and Balthasar have delivered their message and run back to their masters."

I glanced at him before turning my attention back to the parking lot. "Then why am I in combat mode?"

"Because the council travels with an entourage. We have not seen the last of them tonight, *ma petite*. Of that, I can promise you."

"Great."

We came around the last cars between us and my Jeep. There was a man leaning against the Jeep. The Firestar was just suddenly pointing at him. No thinking, just paranoia—oh, sorry, caution.

Jean-Claude froze beside me, utterly motionless. The old vampires can do that—just seem to stop, stop breathing, stop moving, stop everything. As if, if you looked away, they might just disappear.

The man leaned on the back of my Jeep in profile. He was in the middle of lighting a cigarette. You'd have thought he hadn't seen us, but I knew better. I was pointing a gun at him. He knew we were there. The match flared, showing one of the most perfect profiles I'd ever seen. His hair shone golden in the light, shoulder-length, thick waves to frame his face. He tossed the match to the pavement with a practiced flick of his hand. He took the cigarette from his mouth and raised his face skyward. The street light played along his face and golden hair. He blew three perfect smoke rings and laughed.

That laugh trailed down my spine as if he'd touched me. It made me shiver, and I wondered how the hell I'd thought he was human.

"Asher," Jean-Claude said. That one word was spoken without emotion, empty of meaning. But it was all I could do not to look at Jean-Claude's face. I knew who Asher was, but only by reputation. Asher and his human servant, Julianna had traveled with Jean-Claude across Europe for a couple of decades. They'd been a ménage à trois, the closest thing Jean-Claude had had to a family since he became a vampire. Jean-Claude had been called away to his dying mother's bedside. Asher and Julianna had been taken by the Church. Read witch-hunters.

Asher turned and gave us his right profile. The street light that had caressed the perfection of his left side seemed harsh now. The right side of his face looked like melted candle wax. Burn scars, acid scars, holy water. Vampires couldn't heal damage done by holy objects. The priests had had a theory that they could burn the devil out of Asher, one drop of holy water at a time.

I kept the gun on him, solid, no wavering. I'd seen worse, recently. I'd seen a vampire whose face had rotted away on one side. An eye had been rolling in a bare socket. Compared to that, Asher was a *GQ* cover boy. The thing that made the scarring worse somehow was that the rest of him was so perfect. It made it worse somehow, more obscene. They'd left his eyes pure, and the midline of his face, so his nose, the fullness of his mouth, sat in a sea of scars. Jean-Claude had saved him before the zealots killed him, but Julianna had been burned as a witch.

Asher never forgave Jean-Claude for the death of the woman they both loved. In fact, last I'd heard, he was asking for my death. He would kill Jean-Claude's human servant as revenge. The council had refused him up until now.

"Step away from the Jeep, slowly," I said.

"Would you shoot me for leaning against your car?" He sounded amused, pleasant. The tone in his voice, the way he chose his words, reminded me of Jean-Claude when I'd first met him. Asher pushed to his feet using just his body. He blew a smoke ring at me and laughed again.

The sound slithered across my skin like the touch of fur, soft and feeling— oh, so slightly—of death. It was Jean-Claude's laugh, and that was unnerving as hell.

Jean-Claude took a deep, shuddering breath and stepped forward. He didn't block my line of sight though, and he didn't tell me to put the gun down. "Why are you here, Asher?" His voice held something I'd seldom heard, regret.

"Is she going to shoot me?"

"Ask her yourself. I am not the one holding the gun."

"So it is true. You do not control your own servant."

"The best human servants are those that come willingly to your hand. You taught me that, Asher, you and Julianna."

Asher threw the cigarette on the ground. He took two quick steps forward.

"Don't," I said.

His hands were balled into fists at his side. His anger rode the night like close lightning. "Never, never say her name again. You don't deserve to speak her name."

Jean-Claude gave a shallow bow. "As you wish. Now, what do you want, Asher? Anita will grow impatient soon."

Asher stared at me. He looked at me from head to toe, but it wasn't sexual, though that was in there. It was like he was looking me over, like I was a car he was thinking of buying. His eyes were a strange shade of pale blue. "Would you really shoot me?" He turned his head so that I couldn't see the scars. He knew exactly how the shadows would fall. He gave a smile that was supposed to melt me into my socks. It didn't work.

"Cut the charm and give me a reason *not* to kill you."

He turned his head so that a sheet of golden hair spilled over the right side of his face. If my night vision had been worse, it might have hidden the scars.

"The council extends their invitation to Jean-Claude, Master of the City of St. Louis, and his human servant, Anita Blake. They request your presence this night."

"You may put up the gun, *ma petite*. We are safe until we see the council."

"Just like that," I said. "Last I heard, Asher here wanted to kill me."

"The council refused his request," Jean-Claude said. "Our human servants are too precious to us for them to agree."

"Very true," Asher said.

The two vampires stared at each other. I expected them to try vampiric powers on each other, but they didn't. They just stood there, looking at one another. Their faces gave nothing away, but if they'd been people and not monsters, I'd have told them to hug and make up. You could feel their pain on the air. I realized something I hadn't before. They had loved each other once. Only love can turn to such bitter regret. Julianna had been their link, but it hadn't just been her they loved.

It was time to put the gun up, but irritatingly, I'd have to flash the parking lot. I was really going to have to invest in more dressy pants suits. Dresses just sucked for concealed carry.

There was no one else but the three of us in the parking lot. I turned my back on both of them and raised the dress enough to put up the gun.

"Please, don't be modest on my account," Asher said.

I smoothed the dress into place before I turned around. "Don't flatter yourself."

He smiled, and the look on his face was amused, condescending, and something else. That "something else" bothered me. "Modest. Were you also chaste before our dashing Jean-Claude found you?"

"That's enough, Asher," Jean-Claude said.

"She was a virgin before you?" He made it a question and then threw his head back and laughed. He laughed until he had to lean against the Jeep to steady himself. "You, wasted on a virgin. It is simply too perfect."

"I wasn't a virgin, not that it's any of your damn business."

The laughter stopped so abruptly, it was startling. He slid down to the ground, sitting on the dark pavement. He stared up at me through a curtain of golden hair. His eyes looked strange and pale. "Not virginal, but chaste."

"I've had enough games for one night," I said.

"The games are just beginning," he said.

"What's that supposed to mean?" I asked.

"It means, *ma petite*, that the council await us. They will have many games for us to play, none of them pleasant."

Asher rose to his feet like he'd been pulled by strings. He stood, brushing himself off. He settled his black overcoat more solidly into place. It was hot for a long coat. Not that he would necessarily care, but it was odd. Vamps usually tried to blend in better than that. Made me wonder what was underneath the coat. You could hide a pretty big gun under an ankle-length coat. I'd never met a vampire that carried a gun, but there was always a first time.

Jean-Claude had said we were safe until we reached the council, but that didn't mean Asher couldn't pull a weapon then and blow us away. It had been beyond careless to put up my gun without patting Asher down first.

I sighed.

"What is wrong, *ma petite*?"

Asher was a vampire. How much more dangerous could he be with a gun? But I couldn't do it. "Let me test my understanding. Is Asher going to ride in the car with us to the meeting?"

"I must, to give you directions," Asher said.

"Then lean against the Jeep."

He frowned at me in an amused, condescending sort of way. "Excuse me?"

"I don't care if you're the second coming of the Antichrist, you can't sit behind me in my own car until I know you're not carrying a weapon."

"*Ma petite*, he is a vampire. If he is sitting behind you in a car, he is close enough to kill you without a gun."

I shook my head. "You're right. I know you're right, but the point isn't logic, Jean-Claude. The point is that I simply can't let him in the car behind me without knowing what's under the coat. I just can't." It was true. Paranoid, but still true.

Jean-Claude knew me better than to argue. "Very well, *ma petite*. Asher, would you be so kind as to face towards the Jeep."

Asher smiled brilliantly at both of us, flashing fang. "You want to pat me down? I could rip you into pieces with my bare hands, and you're worried I have a gun?" He chuckled, a low, skin-prickling sound. "That is so very cute."

Cute? Me? "Just do it, please."

He turned to face the Jeep, still laughing softly.

"Hands on the hood, feet apart." I got out the gun one more time. Maybe I should just carry it on a chain around my neck. I pressed the barrel into his spine. I felt him stiffen under my hands.

"You are serious about this."

"Absolutely," I said. "Feet further apart."

He shifted, but it wasn't enough.

I kicked his feet apart until his balance was off-center and started searching him one-handed.

"Dominant, very dominant. Does she like to be on top?"

I ignored him. More surprising, so did Jean-Claude.

"Slower, slower. Hasn't Jean-Claude taught you not to rush?" He drew in a breath at the appropriate moment. "Oooh, that's nice."

Yes, it was embarrassing, but I searched him top to bottom. There wasn't a damn thing to find. But I felt better. I stepped back until I was out of reach and put the gun up.

He was watching over his shoulder. "Do the panties match the bra?"

I shook my head. "You can stand up now."

He stayed against the car. "Don't you need to strip-search me?"

"In your dreams," I said.

He stood, smoothing his coat back into place. "You have no idea what I dream, Anita." I couldn't read the look on his face, but the look was enough. I didn't want to know what Asher saw when he closed his eyes at the break of day.

"Shall we go?" Jean-Claude said.

"Are you so eager to throw your life away?" Asher asked. The anger returned with a rush, chasing out the amused teasing gallant.

"The council will not kill me tonight," Jean-Claude said.

"Are you so sure?"

"It is their own laws that have forbidden those of us in the United States to fight amongst ourselves until the law has passed or failed to pass in Washington. The council wants us to remain legal in this country. If they break their own rules, no one else will obey them."

Asher turned full face into the light. "There are worse things than death, Jean-Claude."

Jean-Claude sighed. "I did not desert you, Asher. What can I say to convince you of the truth? You can taste the truth in my words. I came to you as soon as I knew."

"You have had centuries to convince yourself of what you want the truth to be, Jean-Claude. Wanting it to be true doesn't make it so."

"So be it, Asher. But I would undo whatever you think I have done, if I could. I would bring her back if I could."

Asher held up his hand as if he could push the thought away. "No, no, no! You killed her. You let her die. You let her burn to death. I felt her die, Jean-Claude. I was her master. She was so afraid. To the last she thought you would come save her. I was her master and I know that her last words were your name."

Jean-Claude turned his back on Asher. The other vampire closed the distance between them in two striding steps. He grabbed Jean-Claude's arm and swung him around. The street light showed tears on Jean-Claude's face. He was crying for a woman who had been dead over two hundred years. It was a long time for tears.

"You never told me that before," Jean-Claude said softly.

Asher pushed him away hard enough that he stumbled. "Save your tears, Jean-Claude. You'll need them for yourself and for her. They've promised me my revenge."

Jean-Claude touched the back of his hand to the tears. "You can't kill her. They won't allow that."

Asher smiled, and it was most unpleasant. "I don't want her life, Jean-Claude. I want your pain." He walked around me, circling like a shark. I moved with him and knew he was too close. If he rushed me, I'd never get the gun out in time.

"You've finally given me what I need to hurt you, Jean-Claude. You love someone else at last. Love is never free, Jean-Claude. It is the most expensive emotion we have, and I am going to see that you pay in full." He stood in front of Jean-Claude, hands in fists by his side. He was trembling with the effort not to strike out. Jean-Claude had stopped crying, but I wasn't sure he'd fight back. In that moment I realized he didn't want to hurt Asher. Guilt is a many splendored thing. Problem was, Asher wanted to hurt him.

I stepped between them. I took a step forward. Asher was either going to have to step back or we'd be touching. He stepped back, staring down at me as if I'd just appeared. He'd forgotten me for just a second.

"Love isn't the most expensive emotion, Asher," I said. I took another step forward, and he retreated another step. "Hate is. Because hate will eat you up inside and destroy you, long before it kills you."

"Very philosophical," he said.

"Philosophy's great," I said. "But remember this: don't ever threaten us again. Because if you do, I'll kill you. Because I don't give a fuck about your tortured past. Now, shall we go?"

Asher stared at me for a few heartbeats. "By all means. I cannot wait to introduce you to the council."

He meant it to be ominous, and it was. I didn't want to go and meet the bogeymen of vampirekind, but we were going. One thing I'd learned about master vampires. You can run, but not far enough. You can even hide, but not forever. Eventually, they catch you. And master vampires don't like to be kept waiting.

10

I drove. Asher gave directions. He also hung on the back of the seat. I didn't ask him to buckle up for safety. Jean-Claude sat in the passenger seat next to me, silent, not looking at Asher or me.

"Something's wrong," Jean-Claude said.

I glanced at him. "You mean besides the council coming to town?" He shook his head. "Can't you feel it?"

"I don't feel anything."

"That is the problem." He turned as far as the seat belt would let him and met Asher's eyes. "What is happening to my people?"

Asher sat so his face showed perfectly in the rearview mirror, as if he wanted me to see him. He smiled. His whole face moved when he smiled. The scarred skin had muscles underneath. Everything seemed to work just fine except for the scars. The look on his face was smug, self-satisfied. The kind of joy that cats get from tormenting mice.

"I do not know what is happening to them, but you should. You are—after all—Master of the City."

"What's going on, Jean-Claude? What else is wrong?" I asked.

"I should be able to feel my people, *ma petite*. If I concentrate, it is like . . . background noise. I can feel the ebb and flow of them. In extreme duress I can feel their pain, their fear. Now I am concentrating, and it is like a blank wall."

"Balthasar's master has kept you from hearing the cries of your vampires," Asher said.

Jean-Claude's hand lashed out in a blur of speed that was almost magical. He grabbed Asher's coat collar, twisting it into a choking ring. "I—have—done—nothing—wrong. They have no right to harm my people."

Asher didn't try to get away. He just stared at him. "There is an empty seat on the council for the first time in over four thousand years. Whoever empties that seat takes that seat. That is the law of succession."

Jean-Claude released Asher, slowly. "I don't want it."

"You shouldn't have killed the Earthmover, then."

"He would have killed us," I said.

"Council's privilege," Asher said.

"That's ridiculous," I said. "You're saying because we didn't roll over and die, we're going to be killed now?"

"No one has come here planning to kill anyone," Asher said. "Believe me, that was my vote, but I was the minority. The council just wants to make sure that Jean-Claude isn't trying to set up his own little council."

Jean-Claude and I both looked at him. I had to swing my attention back to the road before I was ready to stop being astonished.

"You are babbling, Asher," Jean-Claude said.

"Not everyone is happy with the current council's rules. Some say they are old-fashioned."

"People have been saying that for four hundred years," Jean-Claude said.

"Yes, but until now there was no alternative. Some see your refusal of the council seat as a blow for a new order."

"You know why I did not take it."

Asher laughed, a low roll that played along my skin. "Whatever do you mean, Jean-Claude?"

"I am not powerful enough to hold a council seat. The first challenger would sense that and kill me, then they would have my council seat. I would be a stalking-horse."

"Yet you killed a council member. How did you manage that, Jean-Claude?" He leaned on the back of my seat. I could feel him. He picked up a curl of my hair, and I jerked my head away.

"Where the hell are we going? You were supposed to give directions," I said.

"There is no need for directions," Jean-Claude said. "They have taken the Circus."

"What?" I stared at him, and the only thing that kept the Jeep from swerving was luck. "What did you say?"

"Don't you understand yet? The Traveler, Balthasar's master, blocked my powers and the powers of my vampires, and kept them from reaching out to me."

"Your wolves. You should have felt something from your wolves. They're your animal to call," I said.

Jean-Claude turned to Asher. "Only one vampire could have kept my wolves from calling out for help. The Master of Beasts."

Asher rested his chin on the back of my seat. I felt him nod.

"Get off my seat," I said.

He raised his head but didn't really move back.

"They must think me powerful indeed to send two council masters," Jean-Claude said.

Asher made a harsh sound. "Only you, Jean-Claude, would be arrogant enough to believe that two council masters came to this country just for you."

"If not to teach me a lesson, then why are they here?" Jean-Claude asked.

"Our dark queen wished to know how this legality is working for the vampires in the States. We have traveled from Boston to New Orleans to San Francisco. She chose what cities we would visit, and in what order. Our dark queen left St. Louis, and you, for last."

"Why would she do that?" Jean-Claude asked.

"The Queen of Nightmares can do anything she likes," Asher said. "She says go to Boston, we go."

"If she said, walk out into the sunlight, would you do it?" I asked. I glanced at him. He was close enough that turning my head was enough, no mirror needed.

His face was blank and beautiful, empty. "Perhaps," he said.

I turned back to the road. "You're crazy, you're all crazy."

"Too true," Asher said. He sniffed my hair.

"Stop that."

"You smell of power, Anita Blake. You reek of the dead." He traced his fingers along my neck.

I swerved the Jeep purposefully, sending him sliding around the back seat. "Don't touch me."

"The council thought we would find you stuffed with power. Bloated with new-found abilities, yet you seem much the same. But she is different. She is new. And there is that werewolf. Yes, that Ulfric, Richard Zeeman. You have him bound to you, as well."

Asher pulled himself back up to the seats, though not so close to me. "It is your servants who have the power. Not you."

"Is Padma anything without his animals?" Jean-Claude asked.

"Very true, though I might not say so in front of him." He leaned on the back of the seats again, not touching me this time. "So you admit it is your servants who have given you the power to take a council member."

"My human servant and my wolf are merely extensions of my power. Their hands are my hands; their deeds, my deeds. That is council law. So what does it matter where my power comes from?"

"Quoting council law, Jean-Claude. You have grown cautious since last we met."

"Caution has served me well, Asher."

"But have you had any fun?" It was a strange question coming from someone who was supposed to hate Jean-Claude.

"Some, and you, Asher, how fares it with you? Are you still serving the council, or did you come along on this mission to torment me?"

"Yes, to both questions."

"Why have you not fled the council?"

"Many aspire to serve them," Asher said.

"You didn't."

"Perhaps revenge has changed my aspirations."

Jean-Claude laid his hand on Asher's arm. "*Ma petite* is right. Hatred is a cold fire, and it gives no warmth."

Asher jerked back, sliding as far back as the seat would let him. I glanced in my rearview mirror. He was huddled in the dark, hugging himself. "When I see you weep for your beloved, I will have all the warmth I need."

"We'll be at the Circus soon," I said. "What's the plan?"

"I am not sure there is a plan. We must assume they have all our people in thrall. So it will be only what the two of us can do alone."

"Are we going to try and take the Circus back, or what?"

Asher laughed. "Is she serious?"

"Always," Jean-Claude said.

"Fine. What are we supposed to do?"

"Survive if you can," Asher said.

"Shut up," I said. "This is what I need to know, Jean-Claude. Do we go in there kicking butt, or crawling?"

"Would you crawl to them, *ma petite*?"

"They have Willie, Jason, and who knows how many others. So, yeah, if it would keep them safe, I'd do a little crawling."

"I do not think you would be very good at it," Jean-Claude said.

"I'm not."

"But no, no crawling tonight. We are not strong enough to retake the Circus, but we go in, as you say, kicking butt."

"Dominant?" I made it a question.

"Oui."

"How dominant?"

"Be aggressive, but not foolish. You may wound anyone you are capable of hurting, but do not kill. We do not want to give them an excuse."

"They think you've started a revolution, Jean-Claude," Asher said from the darkness. "Like all revolutionaries, dead you become a martyr. They don't want you dead."

Jean-Claude turned so he could see the other vampire. "Then what do they want, Asher? Tell me."

"They have to make an example of you. Surely you see that."

"If I had planned on forging a second council in America, yes, I would see their point. But I know my limitations. I cannot hold a council seat against all comers. It would be a death sentence. I want simply to be left alone."

Asher sighed. "It is too late for that, Jean-Claude. The council is here, and they will not believe your protestations of innocence."

"You believe him," I said.

He was quiet for a few seconds, then said, "Yes, I believe him. The one thing Jean-Claude has always done well is survive. Challenging the council is not a good way to do that." Asher slid forward against the seats, putting his face very near mine. "Remember, Anita, that all those years ago, he waited to save me. Waited until he knew he wouldn't be caught. Waited until he could save me at the least risk to himself. Waited until Julianna was dead, because it was too great a risk to take."

"That is not true," Jean-Claude said.

Asher ignored him. "Be careful that he does not wait to save you."

"I don't wait around for anybody to save me," I said.

Jean-Claude stared out the window at the passing cars. He was shaking his head gently, back and forth, back and forth. "I tire of you already, Asher."

"You tire of me because I speak the truth."

Jean-Claude turned and faced him. "No, I tire of you because you remind me of her, and that once, a very long time ago, I was almost happy."

The two vampires stared at each other. "But now you have a second chance," Asher said.

"You could have a second chance, too, Asher. If you would only let the past go."

"The past is all I have."

"And *that* is not my fault," Jean-Claude said.

Asher slid back into the darkness, huddling against the seat. I thought Jean-Claude had won the argument for now. But just call it a feeling; I didn't think the fight was over.

11

The *Circus of* the Damned is in a converted warehouse. From the front it looks like a carnival with posters promoting the freak show, and dancing clowns twirling on top of the glowing sign. From the back, it's just dark.

I pulled the Jeep into the small parking lot reserved for employees. It was small because most of the help lived at the Circus. No need for a car if you never left. Here was hoping we'd be needing our car.

I turned off the engine, and silence swirled into the car. Both vampires had sunk into that utter stillness that made me have to glance at them to make sure they were still there. Mammals can freeze, but a rabbit frozen waiting for the fox to pass is a vibrating thing. It breathes fast and faster. Its heart pounds. Vampires are more like snakes. A snake will put a length of its body out, then freeze. There is no sense of movement stopped. No sense that movement will continue. In that moment of frozen time a snake seems unreal, more like a work of art, something carved rather than something alive. Jean-Claude seemed to have fallen into a well of silence where movement, even breath, was forbidden.

I glanced back at Asher. He sat in the back seat. Utterly still, a perfect golden presence, but not alive.

The silence filled the Jeep like icy water. I wanted to clap my hands, yell, anything to make noise, to startle them into being again. But I knew better. All I'd get would be a blink and a look. A look that wasn't human and maybe never had been.

The sound of my dress against the upholstery was loud. "Will they pat me down for weapons?" My voice seemed flat in the charged silence.

Jean-Claude blinked gracefully, then turned his neck to look at me. The look was peaceful rather than empty. I had begun to wonder if the stillness was a form of meditation for the vampires. Maybe if we lived through the night I'd ask.

"This is a challenge, *ma petite*. They will let us be dangerous. Though I would not flaunt your weaponry. Your little gun is fine."

I shook my head. "I was thinking of more."

He raised his eyebrows. "More?"

I turned to look at Asher. He blinked and raised his eyes to me. I hit the dome light and saw his eyes' true color for the first time. They were blue. But that didn't do them justice. They were as pale a blue as Jean-Claude's were a dark blue. Pale, cold, blue, the startling color of a Husky's eyes. But it wasn't just the eyes, it was the hair. It had looked golden, but the normal gold of a dark blond. In the truer light of the car, I realized it wasn't just illusion and dim light, it *was* gold. His hair was the truest gold I'd ever seen outside of a bottle or a can of metallic paint. The combination of hair and eyes was amazing. Even without the scars he wouldn't have looked real.

I glanced from one vampire to the other. Jean-Claude was the more beautiful, and it wasn't the scars. Asher was just a trace more handsome than he was pretty. "The same vamp made you both, right?" I asked.

Jean-Claude nodded.

Asher just stared at me.

"Where'd she go?" I asked. "Unnaturally-Beautiful-Studs-R-Us?"

Asher let out a harsh bark of laughter. He dragged his fingers down the scarred side of his face, making the skin stretch, drawing it away from his eye so you could see the pale inner flesh of the eye socket. He emphasized everything into a kind of hideous mask. "Do you think I am beautiful, Anita?" He released the skin, and it snapped back into place, resilient, perfect in its own way.

I looked at him. "What do you want me to say, Asher?"

"I want you to be terrified. I want to see on your face what I've seen on every face for the last two hundred years—disgust, derision, horror."

"Sorry," I said.

He leaned into the seats, showing the scars to the light. He seemed to have an innate sense of what any light would do to the wounds, to know just how the shadows would fall. Years of practice, I guess.

I just looked at him. I met his pale, perfect eyes, gazed on the thick waves of golden hair, the fullness of his lips. I shrugged. "What can I say? I'm a hair and eye person, and you have great hair and amazing eyes."

Asher threw himself back into his seat. He gazed at us both, and there was such rage in his eyes. Such horrible rage that it scared me.

"There," he said. "There, you're afraid of me. I can see it, smell it, taste it." He smiled, pleased with himself, triumphant somehow.

"Tell him what you fear, *ma petite*."

I glanced at Jean-Claude, then back at Asher. "It's not the scars, Asher. It's your hatred that's frightening."

He leaned forward, and I think without meaning to, his hair spilled around his face, camouflaging him. It had the look of long habit, long comfort. "Yes, my hatred is frightening. Terrifying. And remember, Anita Blake, that the hatred is all for you and your master."

I knew he meant Jean-Claude, and I couldn't argue with the title anymore, though sometimes I wanted to. "Hatred makes us all ugly," I said.

He hissed at me, and there was nothing human in the gesture.

I gave him a bored look. "Come off it, Asher. Been there, done that. If you want to play big-bad-vampire, get in line."

He stripped his overcoat off in an abrupt, violent movement. A brown tweed

suit jacket ended up crumpled on the seat. He turned his head so I could see that
the scars marched down his neck into the collar of his white dress shirt. He started
unbuttoning the shirt.

I glanced at Jean-Claude. His face was impassive, unhelpful. I was on my own.
So what else was new?

"Not that I don't appreciate the offer, but I don't usually let a man strip down
on the first date."

He snarled at me. He bared his chest to the light, shirt still carefully tucked
into his pants. The scars dribbled down his flesh like someone had drawn a dividing
line down the center of his body. One half pale and perfect, the other half monstrous. They'd been more careful of his face and neck. They had not been careful
of his chest. The scars cut deep runnels. The skin so melted that it didn't even
look real anymore. The scars flowed down his stomach into the belted top of his
pants.

I stared because that's what he wanted me to do. When I could finally meet
his eyes, I had no words left. I'd had holy water poured on a vampire bite before.
Cleansed, they called it. Torture was another word for it. I'd crawled and cursed
and vomited. I couldn't imagine the pain he'd survived.

His eyes were wide and fierce and fearful. "The scars go all the way down,"
he said.

That left a trail of visuals that I'd been trying to avoid. I thought of a lot of
things to say: "Wow," but it seemed too junior high school and cruel; "sorry"
was totally inadequate. I spread my hands wide, kneeling on the seat looking at
him. "I asked you once before, Asher. What do you want me to say?"

He pushed himself as far away from me as he could, back against the Jeep's
door. "Why doesn't she look away? Why doesn't she hate me? Why isn't she
disgusted with this body?"

Like he was disgusted. It hung unsaid on the air, but it was there in his eyes,
in the way he held himself. Unspoken, the words hung in the air with the weight
and push of thunder.

He yelled, "Why don't I see in her eyes what I see in everyone's eyes?"

"You do not see horror in my eyes, *mon ami*," Jean-Claude said.

"No," Asher said, "I see worse. I see pity!" He opened the car door without
turning around. I would have said he fell out of the car, but that isn't true. He
floated upward before he could touch the ground. There was a backwash of wind
that swept over me like a storm, and he was gone.

12

We sat in silence for a few seconds, both of us staring at the open door. Finally, I had to fill the silence. "My, people do come and go quickly here."

Jean-Claude didn't get the movie reference. Richard would have gotten it. He liked the "Wizard of Oz." Jean-Claude answered me seriously, "Asher always was very good at flying."

Someone chuckled. The sound made me reach for the Firestar. The voice was familiar but the tone was new; arrogant, profoundly arrogant.

"Silver bullets won't kill me anymore, Anita. My new master has promised me that."

Liv appeared in the open car door, peering in at us, muscular arms propped on the sides of the door. She smiled broadly enough to flash fangs. When you pass the five-hundred mark like Liv, you only flash fangs when you want to. She was grinning like the Cheshire cat, very pleased about something. She wore a black sports bra and high-cut jogging shorts so that all that body-building muscle gleamed in the street lights. She was one of the vamps that Jean-Claude had invited into his territory recently. She was supposed to be one of his vampire lieutenants.

"What canary did you eat?" I asked.

She frowned at me. "What?"

"The cat that ate the canary," I said.

She continued to frown. Liv's English is perfect, no accent of any kind. Sometimes I forget that it's not her first language. A lot of the vamps have lost their original accents but they still don't understand all the slang. But, hey, I bet Liv knew some Slavic slang that I'd never heard.

"Anita is asking why you are so pleased with yourself," Jean-Claude said, "but I think I already know the answer."

I glanced at him, then back at Liv. I had the Firestar out but not pointed. She was supposed to be on our side. I was getting the feeling that might have changed.

"Did Liv say, her new master?" I asked.

"She did," Jean-Claude said.

I raised the gun and pointed it at her. She laughed. It was unnerving. She crawled into the back seat, still laughing. Very unnerving. Liv may have been six hundred years old and some change, but she wasn't powerful. Certainly not powerful enough to laugh off silver ammo.

"You know I'll shoot you, Liv. So what's the joke?"

"Can you not feel it, *ma petite*? The difference in her."

I steadied my hand on the back of the seat, gun pointed at her impressive chest. I was less than two feet from her, at this distance the bullet would take out her heart. She wasn't worried. She should have been.

I concentrated on Liv. Tried to roll her power in my mind. I'd done her before, knew what she felt like in my head. Or thought I did. Her power beat along my skull, hummed down my bones. I could feel her power like a thrumming note so deep and low it was almost painful.

I took a deep breath and let it out slowly. I kept the gun pointed at her. "If I pull this trigger, Liv, even with the boost in power you'll die."

Liv looked at Jean-Claude. It was a long, self-satisfied look. "You know I won't die, Jean-Claude."

"Only the Traveler could make such an extravagant promise, and hope to keep it," Jean-Claude said. "You are a little too feminine for his tastes, unless he has changed."

Her face was disdainful. "He is above such petty desires. He offered me only power and I accepted."

Jean-Claude shook his head. "If you truly believe the Traveler above the desires of the body, then he has been very . . . careful around you, Liv."

"He is not like the others," she said.

Jean-Claude sighed. "On that I will not argue, Liv. But be careful that his power does not become addictive."

"You seek to frighten me, but it will not work, Jean-Claude. His power is like nothing I have ever felt before, and he can share it. I can be what I was meant to be."

"He can fill you to bursting with his power, Liv, it will not make you a master. If he has promised you that, then he has lied to you."

She hissed at him. "You would say anything to save yourself tonight."

He shrugged. "Perhaps."

"I thought Liv took an oath of loyalty to you," I said.

"*Oui.*"

"Then what's going on?"

"The council will be very careful to observe the rules, *ma petite*. The Circus is a public business, thus the council might have crossed the threshold uninvited. Instead, they found someone to invite them inside."

I stared at the smirking vamp in the back of my Jeep. "She betrayed us?"

"Yes," he said softly. He touched my shoulder. "Do not kill her, *ma petite*. The bullet would enter, but the Traveler would not allow her death. You would simply waste a bullet."

I shook my head. "She betrayed you, all of you."

"If they could not have bribed someone, they would have tortured someone else into betraying us. I much prefer this method," he said.

I stared down the barrel of the gun at Liv's smiling face. I could have pulled the trigger and not worried about it. She'd done all the damage she could do. It wasn't like I'd be killing her to save us. I didn't want, or not want, to pull the trigger. I simply thought she deserved to die for betraying us. Not anger, or even outrage, just good business. It was a bad precedent to allow anyone to betray you and survive. It set a bad example. I realized with an almost physical jolt that killing her meant nothing to me. Just good business. Sweet Jesus. I put up the gun. I didn't want to kill anyone that coldly. Killing didn't bother me, but it should mean something.

Liv leaned back in the seat, grinning, pleased I'd seen the futility of shooting her. If she only realized why I hadn't done it, she might still have been scared of me, but she was hiding behind the power of this Traveler. Confident that it was shield enough against anything. If she pissed me off enough tonight, maybe we'd test the theory.

I shook my head. If I was going to meet the bogeymen of vampirekind I needed more weapons. I had my wrist sheaths, complete with silver knives, in the glove compartment. I often carried them in the Jeep when I wore something I couldn't wear them with, like the dress. Never knew when you'd need a good knife.

"I'll tell them about any weapons I see," she said.

I finished buckling the knives in place. "Yvette and Balthasar know I have the gun. I'm not trying to be subtle here, just prepared." I opened the door and stepped out. I scanned the darkness for more company, though the really old ones could hide almost in plain sight. Some vampires had chameleons beat all to hell when it came to blending with their surroundings. I'd seen one that could wrap himself in shadows, then fling them aside like a cloak. It had been impressive.

Liv scooted out of the car to stand near me. She'd lifted a few too many weights to cross her arms comfortably but she was trying. Trying for that nonchalant bodyguard look. She was six feet tall and built like a brick outhouse; she didn't have to try hard to look intimidating.

Jean-Claude got out of the car on my side, putting himself between the two of us. I wasn't sure who he was protecting; her or me.

He had Asher's long coat in his arms. "I suggest, *ma petite*, that you wear this to cover the weapons."

"I'll tell them about the knives," Liv said.

"If the weapons are in plain sight, it is more of a challenge," Jean-Claude said. "Someone might feel compelled to take them from you."

"They can try," I said.

Jean-Claude handed me the coat, draped across his arms. "Please, *ma petite*."

I took it from him. He didn't say "please" often.

I slipped the black coat on. I was reminded of two things. One, it was too damn hot to wear a coat. Two, Asher was six foot or more, the coat was huge. I started rolling up the sleeves.

"Anita," Liv said.

I glanced at her.

She looked serious now, her strong Nordic face blank and unreadable. "Look into my eyes."

I shook my head. "What do you guys do, sit around watching old Dracula movies and stealing the dialogue?"

Liv took a threatening step forward. I just stared up at her. "Save the big-bad-vampire routine, Liv. We've done this and you can't roll me with your eyes."

"*Ma petite*," Jean-Claude said, "do as she asks."

I frowned at him. "Why?" Suspicious, who me?

"Because if the Traveler's extra power can bespell you through Liv's eyes, it would be better to know here in relative safety than inside among our greater foes."

He had a point, but I didn't like it. I shrugged. "Fine." I stared at her face, into her blue eyes, though the color was a little washed out from the street light.

Liv turned; a spill of yellow light from the open car door hit her eyes and made them that amazing violet-blue, almost purple. Her eyes were her best feature and I'd never had any trouble meeting that flower-petal gaze.

I still could. Not even a twinge.

Liv's hands balled into fists. She spoke, but I didn't think she was talking to either of us, "You promised me. Promised me enough power to roll her mind."

There was a rush of wind, cold enough to make me shiver and huddle into the long coat.

Liv laughed, a loud bray of sound. She raised her arms to the cold wind as if it were wrapping her around like drapes in the breeze.

The cold wind raised the hairs on the back of my neck, but it wasn't the temperature, it was the power in it.

"Now," Liv said, "look into my eyes, if you dare."

"Little better on the dialogue," I said.

"Are you afraid to meet my gaze, Executioner?"

The cold wind that had come from nowhere died, then faded, a last icy caress. I waited until the summer heat slid over me like plastic wrap, waited until sweat trailed down my spine; then I looked up.

Once upon a time I'd avoided looking any vamp in the eyes. I'd had some natural immunity, but even the lesser vamps were dangerous. Their gaze was one trick that almost all of them had to a lesser, or greater, extent. My powers had grown, and the vampire marks had cinched it. I was pretty much immune to vampire gaze. So why was I afraid now?

I met Liv's violet gaze solid, no flinching. At first there was nothing but their extraordinary color. A tension went out of me, my shoulders loosened. They were just eyes. Then it was as if the violet of her eyes was water, and I was something that skated over the surface tension, until something rose from her eyes and pulled me down. Always before it had been like falling, but now something had me, something dark, and strong. It sucked me under like water under ice. I screamed, and lashed out. Lashed out against that cold film of ice, reached for a surface that wasn't physical, wasn't even metaphorical, but I fought to rise. Fought against the pull of that darkness.

I came to myself, kneeling on the parking lot with Jean-Claude's hand grasped in mine. "*Ma petite, ma petite*, are you all right?"

I just shook my head. I didn't trust my voice yet. I'd forgotten how much I hated being rolled by their gaze. Forgotten how helpless I felt. My own power was making me careless around the damn things.

Liv leaned against the side of the Jeep. She seemed tired, too. "I almost had you."

I found my voice. "You didn't have anything. It wasn't your eyes I was being sucked into. It was his."

She shook her head. "He promised me the power to do you, Anita. To take your mind."

I let Jean-Claude help me to my feet, which tells you how shaky I was feeling. "Then he lied, Liv. It's not your power, it's his."

"You fear me now," she said. "I can feel your fear in my head."

I nodded. "Yeah, I'm scared. If that makes you happy, then laugh it up." I started backing away from her. More weapons. I needed more weapons.

"It does make me happy," she said. "You'll never know how happy it makes me."

"His power has left you, Liv," Jean-Claude said.

"It will return," she said.

I was on the other side of the Jeep. I was headed for the back of it, but I didn't want to be within touching range of Liv right this second. I'd broken free, but I didn't want to keep pushing my luck.

"The power may return, Liv, but Anita has broken his bond with you. She has pushed his power aside."

"No," Liv said. "He has chosen to let her go."

Jean-Claude laughed and it chased along my body, and I knew that Liv felt it, too. "The Traveler would have kept *ma petite*, if he could have held her. But he could not. She is too big a fish even for his net."

"Liar!" Liv said.

I left Liv and Jean-Claude to argue between themselves. I'd broken free of the Traveler's power, but it hadn't been pretty, or easy. Though come to think of it, as soon as I started to struggle, it had broken. The sad truth was I hadn't tried to shield myself. I'd stared into Liv's eyes empty and waiting, confident that she couldn't roll me. It had been stupid. No—arrogant. Sometimes there isn't a whole lot of difference between the two.

I walked to the rear of the Jeep. I crawled in the cargo area. Edward, assassin of the undead, had persuaded me to let an acquaintance of his remodel my Jeep. The wheel well on one side was now a secret compartment. Inside was my extra Browning and extra ammo. I'd felt silly when he'd talked me into it. I didn't feel silly now. I opened the compartment and found a surprise. A mini-Uzi complete with shoulder strap. There was a note taped to the gun.

"You can never have too much firepower."

He hadn't signed it, but it was Edward. He'd started his career as a normal assassin, but humans became too easy so he switched to monsters. He did love a challenge. I had another mini-Uzi at home. It had been a gift from Edward, too. He had the best toys.

I took off the coat and slid the Uzi's strap across my chest. When I slipped the coat back on, the Uzi hung at my back. Not perfect but not too noticeable. The second Browning Hi-Power was in the compartment, too. I put it in my pocket and two extra clips of ammo in the other pocket. When I slid to the ground, the coat hung funny, but it was so big on me that it wasn't conspicuous.

The vampires weren't arguing anymore. Liv leaned against the Jeep looking sullen, as if Jean-Claude had had the last word, or won the argument.

I stood watching her. I wanted to shoot her. Not because she'd betrayed us, but because she'd scared me. Not a good enough reason. Besides, it had been my own carelessness that let her scare me. I tried not to punish other people for my mistakes.

"I can't let you go unpunished, Liv," Jean-Claude said. "The council would see it as a weakness."

She just looked at him. "Hit me if it will make you feel better, Jean-Claude." She pushed away from the Jeep and crossed the distance between them with three long strides. She lifted her chin like a bully daring you to take the first swing.

He shook his head. "No, Liv." He touched her face gently. "I had something else in mind." He caressed her face, rubbing his hand along her cheek.

She sighed, rubbing her face against his palm. Liv had been trying to get into Jean-Claude's pants since she hit town. She'd never hidden her plan to sleep her way to the top. She'd been very . . . frustrated that he wouldn't cooperate.

She laid a gentle kiss on his palm. "Things could have been so different if it weren't for your pet human."

I walked up behind them and it was like I wasn't there. They were in some private place that just happened to be in plain sight.

"No, Liv," Jean-Claude said, "it would not have been different. It was not Anita that kept you from my bed, it was you." His hand closed on her throat. His fingers convulsed in her flesh. He made a sharp movement and tore the front of her throat out.

Liv collapsed to the pavement, choking, blood flowing in a crimson wash down her front, out of her mouth. She rolled onto her back, hands clawing at her throat.

I came to stand beside him and stared down at her. I caught a glimpse of her spine deep in the wound. Her eyes were wide, pain-filled, frightened.

Jean-Claude was wiping his hand off on a silk handkerchief he'd pulled from somewhere. He'd flung the gobbets of flesh to the pavement, where they lay looking small and not important enough to die over.

We both watched her writhing on the pavement. Jean-Claude's face was that empty mask he wore, beautiful and distant, like trying to draw comfort from the moon. I didn't have a mirror, and my face would never be his lovely perfection, but it was just as empty. I watched Liv flop on the pavement and felt no pity.

No cold wind came to save her. I think that surprised Liv, because she reached for Jean-Claude. Reached for him, begging with her eyes for him to help her. He was motionless, sunk into that great waiting stillness, as if he was willing himself to vanish. Maybe it did bother him to watch her die.

If she'd been human, it would have been pretty fast. But she wasn't human, and it wasn't fast. She wasn't dying. I wasn't sure it was pity, but I couldn't just stand there and watch anyone in such pain, such terror.

I pulled the Browning out of the coat pocket and pointed it at her head. "I'm going to end this."

"She will heal, *ma petite*. It is a wound that her own vampire body will heal, in time."

"Why isn't her new master helping her?" I asked.

"Because he knows she will heal without his aid."

"No wasted energy, huh?"

"Something like that," he said. It was hard to tell through the blood, but it did look as if the wound was filling in; there was just so much to fill in.

"We offer our throat, or wrist, or the bend of our elbow to each other as a formal greeting. The lesser offer up their flesh to the greater as an acknowledgment of power. It is a pretty thing, a polite thing, but this is the reality, *ma petite*. Liv offered me her throat and I took it."

I stared into her wide, wide eyes. "Did she know this was a possibility?"

"If she did not, then she is a fool. Such violence is never condoned unless the lesser vampire questions the authority of the greater vampire. She questioned my dominance over her. This is the price."

Liv turned onto her side, coughing. Her breath rattled in her throat in a painful gasp. Things were re-forming. She was breathing again. When she had enough air to speak, she said, "Damn you, Jean-Claude." Then she coughed blood. Yummy.

Jean-Claude held his hand out to me. He'd wiped it off, but you never get the blood out from around the fingernails without soap and water. I hesitated, then took his hand. We'd get bloodier before the night was over, it was almost guaranteed.

We walked towards the Circus. The coat billowed behind me like a cape. The Uzi bounced lightly against my back. I'd added one extra thing from the glove compartment. A long silver chain with a cross on it. I'd gotten longer chains when I started dating Jean-Claude. The shorter ones spilled out of my clothing at awkward moments. I was loaded for bear, uh, vampire, and ready to go kill something. Edward would have been proud.

13

The side door of the Circus has no handle. The only way in is if someone opens the door. Security measures. Jean-Claude knocked, and the door swung inward at his touch. Open, waiting, expecting us. Ominous.

The door opened into a small storage room with a bare light bulb hanging from the ceiling. A stark room with a few boxes against one wall. A door to the right led into the main part of the Circus, where people were usually riding the Ferris wheel and eating cotton candy. A smaller door led off to the left. There were no bright lights and cotton candy in that direction.

The light swung back and forth as if someone had just hit it. The naked bulb made the shadows thicker, and the light dance until it was hard to tell shadow from light. Something glinted on the left-hand door. Something attached to its surface. I didn't know what it was, except it glinted dully in the strange light.

I shoved the door flat against the wall just to make sure no one was behind it. Then I put my back to the door and trained the Browning on the room.

"Stop the bulb from swinging," I said.

Jean-Claude reached up and touched the bulb. He had to stand on tiptoe to do it. Whoever had set it swinging was over six feet.

"The room is empty, *ma petite*," Jean-Claude said.

"What's on the door?" It was flat and thin, and my mind couldn't make a shape out of it. Whatever it was, it was hammered to the door with silver nails.

Jean-Claude let out a long sigh. "*Mon Dieu.*"

I crossed the room with the Browning pointed two-handed at the floor. Jean-Claude said the room was empty. I trusted that, but I trusted me more.

Liv staggered to the door. The front of her body was covered with blood, but her throat was perfect. I wondered if the Traveler had helped her after we walked away. She coughed, and cleared her throat so violently it sounded painful. "I wanted to see your faces when you saw the Master of Beasts' compromise," she said. "The Traveler refused to let him and his people greet you in person. This is the Master of Beasts' calling card. How do you like it?" She sounded eager in a predatory, unpleasant sort of way. What the fuck was on the door?

Even standing next to it, I didn't know what it was. Thin rivulets of blood were seeping down the door from it. The sweet metallic scent of blood warmed the stale air. The thing was almost paper thin, but had a consistency more like plastic. It curled at the edges, straining against the five silver nails.

I suddenly had an awful idea. So awful, my eyes couldn't see it even after I'd thought it. I took three steps back from the thing and tried to see the silhouette. There; there; two arms, two legs, shoulders. It was a human skin. Once I found the shape of it, I couldn't stop seeing it. I knew that when I closed my eyes tonight that it would haunt me. That thin stretched thing that used to be a person.

"Where are the hands and feet?" I asked. My voice sounded strange, distant, almost unattached. My lips and fingertips tingled with the pure horror of it.

"It is merely the back of someone's body, not the entire skin, *ma petite*. Besides, it is hard to take the living skin off of fingers and toes when your victim is still struggling," Jean-Claude said. His voice was utterly flat, carefully empty.

"Struggling? You mean whoever this was, was alive?"

"You are the police expert, *ma petite*."

"It wouldn't be bleeding this much if they hadn't been alive," I said.

"Yes, *ma petite*."

He was right. I did know that. But the sight of a human skin nailed to a door had thrown me. It was a first, even for me. "Sweet Jesus, do the silver nails mean the victim was vampire or lycanthrope?"

"Most likely," Jean-Claude said.

"Does that mean they're still alive?"

He looked at me. His look managed to be empty and eloquent all at the same time. "They were alive when the skin was removed. If vampire, or lycanthrope, the mere removal of the skin would not be sufficient to kill them."

A shudder ran through me from head to feet. It wasn't exactly fear. It was horror. Horror at the casualness of it, the callousness of it. "Asher mentioned Padma. Is he the Beast Master?"

"The Master of Beasts," Jean-Claude said. "You cannot kill him for this indiscretion, *ma petite*."

"You're wrong," I said. The horror was there like a coating of ice underneath my skin, but over that was anger. Rage. And under the rage was fear. Fear of anyone that would skin another person alive just to make a point. Told you something about a person. Told you how few rules they had. Told me, in no uncertain terms, that I should kill him as soon as I saw him.

"We cannot punish them for this tonight, *ma petite*. Tonight is about survival for all of us. Remember that and curb your anger."

I stared at the thing on the door. "I am way past anger."

"Then curb your rage. We must save the rest of our people."

"If they're alive."

"They were alive when I came upstairs to wait for you," Liv said.

"Who's skin is it?" I asked.

She laughed, and it was her usual bray. All healed, all better. "Guess," she said. "If you guess right, I'll tell you, but only if you guess right."

It took more control than was pretty not to point the Browning at her. I shook my head. "No games, Liv, not with you. The real games don't even begin until we get downstairs."

"Well said, *ma petite*. Let us go down."

"No," Liv said. "No, you'll guess. You'll guess who it is. I want to see your face. I want to see the pain in your eyes while you think about each of your friends, Anita. I want to watch the horror on your face while you picture it happening to each of them."

"What did I ever do to you, Liv?"

"You stood in my way," she said.

I shook my head and pointed the gun at her. "Three strikes and you're out, Liv."

She frowned. "What are you talking about?"

"Betraying us was one. Trying to roll me with your eyes was number two. That was partly my fault, so I would have let it go. But you took an oath to protect all of Jean-Claude's people. You swore to use that wonderful body, that strength, to protect those weaker than yourself. Whoever belongs to that skin was someone you swore to protect. Instead, you betrayed them. Delivered them over to hell. Strike three, Liv."

"You can't kill me, Anita. The Traveler will heal me, no matter what you do."

I shot her in the right kneecap. She fell to the floor, holding the shattered leg, writhing, screaming.

I felt myself smile, most unpleasant. "I hope it hurts, Liv. I hope it hurts like hell."

The temperature in the room dropped like a stone. It felt cold enough that I half expected to see my breath. Liv's screams stopped, and she stared up at me with her violet eyes. If looks could have killed, I'd have dropped on the spot.

"You cannot harm me, Anita. My master will not allow it." Liv got to her feet with the faintest of limps. She walked to the door with its awful burden. She stretched the edge of the thing, showing holes in the skin that had nothing to do with the skinning process. "I fed on him while they tortured him. I drank his blood while he screamed." Her fingers came away stained with blood. She licked them clean, sliding her fingers in and out of her mouth. "Hmm, tasty."

All I had to do was guess who it was, and she'd tell me. All I had to do was play her game. I shot her in the other knee.

She collapsed to the floor, shrieking. "Don't you understand? You can't hurt me."

"Oh, I think I can, Liv, I think I can." I shot the right knee again. She lay on her back, screaming, grabbing at her shattered knees, and recoiling, because her own touch hurt.

The Traveler's power raised the hair on my body in a shiver of goose bumps. He really was going to heal her. If I wasn't going to kill her, I needed to be somewhere else before she could walk. I knew Liv well enough to know that when she could stand she was going to be pissed. Not that I blamed her. In fact, if I just stood there long enough for her to get to her feet, it'd be self-defense. Of course, it'd be premeditated self-defense.

"Come, *ma petite*, let her be. The Traveler does not give his blessings so easily a second time, or would this be the third? He will heal her at his own pace now. A blessing and a punishment rolled into one. As most of the council's gifts are wont to be.''

He opened the door that led downstairs. His hand came away with blood on it. He held the hand out in front of him like he didn't know what to do with it. He finally walked through the door, wiping his hand along the wall, smearing the blood down the stones in a faint crimson line.

''The longer we delay, the more tortures they will think of.'' With that comforting line he started down the steps. I gave one last glance to Liv. She lay on her side, crying, shrieking. She was shrieking that she was going to see me dead. I should have shot her in the head until her brains leaked on the floor. If I was truly ruthless, I would have. But I didn't. I left her alive and screaming threats. Edward would have been so disappointed.

14

The steps leading underground were taller than normal, as if whatever they were originally designed for wasn't quite human. I kicked the door shut, didn't want to touch the blood. The door cut Liv off in mid scream. I could still hear her very faintly, like the high buzzing of an insect, but the door was almost soundproof. Needed something to muffle the screams from below. Of course, tonight there was only silence on the stairs. A silence so deep that it vibrated in my ears.

Jean-Claude moved in a boneless grace, like a big cat, down the awkward steps. I had to wrap the end of the coat over my left arm to keep from tripping over it. Even then, I didn't glide down the stairs. In three-inch heels I sort of limped.

Jean-Claude waited at the bend of the stairs just before the landing. "I could carry you, *ma petite.*"

"No, thanks." If I took the shoes off, the dress would be so long I'd need to hold it up. I needed one hand free for a gun. If my choices were being slow and having a gun drawn, or being fast and having my hands full of dress . . . I'd be slow.

The stairs stretched empty, wide enough to drive a small car down. The door at the base of the stairs was solid oak, iron bound like the door to a dungeon. Tonight, not a bad analogy.

Jean-Claude pulled on the heavy door, and it swung open. It was usually kept locked. He turned to me. "The council can demand that I greet every vampire within these walls, formally."

"You mean like you did with Liv?" I asked.

He gave a very small smile. "If I do not acknowledge their dominance over me, then perhaps."

"What if you do acknowledge them?" I asked.

He shook his head. "If we had gone to the council for aid of some kind, then I would not fight. I would simply acknowledge their superiority and be done with it. I am not strong enough to be council. I know that." He smoothed his hands down the ruffles his shirt, adjusting the cuffs on his jacket so the ruffles at his wrists showed to best advantage. He often fussed with his clothes when he was nervous. Of course, he fussed with his clothes when he wasn't nervous, too.

"I hear a 'but' coming," I said.

He smiled at me. "*Oui, ma petite*. But they have come to us. They have invaded our lands. Harmed our people. If we acknowledge them as greater than ourselves without a struggle, they may set up a new master in my place. They may take all I have gained."

"I thought the only way to step down as master was to die."

"They would come to that, eventually."

"Then we go in kicking butt."

"But we cannot win by violence, *ma petite*. What we did with Liv was to be expected. She had to be punished. But in a struggle to kill or be killed, the council will win."

I frowned up at him. "If we can't just say they're bigger and badder than we are, and we can't fight them, what can we do?"

"We play the game, *ma petite*."

"What game?"

"The game that I mastered at court so long ago. It is a thing of diplomacy, bravado, insults." He raised my left hand to his lips and laid a gentle kiss on it. "You will be very good at part of the game, and very bad at others. Diplomacy is not your strong suit."

"Bravado and insults are two of my best things."

He smiled, still holding my hand. "Indeed, *ma petite*, indeed. Put the gun away. I am not saying do not use it, but have a care who you shoot. Not everything you will meet tonight can be harmed by silver bullets." He cocked his head to one side as if thinking. "Though come to that, I've never seen anyone try to kill a council member with modern silver ammunition." He smiled. "It might work." He shook his head as if to rid himself of the image. "But if it comes to trying to slay the council by bullets, then all is lost and all that will be left is to take as many of them with us as we can."

"Let's save as many of our people as we can, too," I said.

"You don't understand them, *ma petite*. If we are dead, there will be no mercy for those who are loyal to us. Any good revolution kills the loyalists first." He touched the back of my right hand lightly, reminding. I still had the gun out. Somehow, I just didn't want to put it away.

But I did. I put the safety on. I didn't want them to know the gun was there, so I couldn't keep holding it. I put the safety on because I didn't want to shoot myself in the leg. It would be embarrassing as well as painful and probably wouldn't impress the council one little bit. I didn't understand "the game," but I'd hung around vampires long enough to know that if you could impress them, sometimes you walked out alive. Of course, sometimes they killed you anyway. Sometimes a show of bravado just earned you a slower death, like it did with some American Indian tribes that only tortured enemies they thought worthy of the honor. An honor I could do without. But sometimes in the midst of being tormented you could get away. If they just tore your throat out, all options were over. We were definitely going for impressive. If we couldn't impress them, we'd kill them. If we couldn't kill them . . . they'd kill us. Liv had just been the beginning of the evening's entertainment.

The living room was a bare stone room once again. Jean-Claude's efforts at redecorating lay in piles of black and white cloth and broken wood. The only thing untouched was the portrait above the false fireplace. Jean-Claude, Julianna, and an unscarred Asher gazed down at the ruins. I expected an unpleasant surprise to be waiting for us. There was only Willie McCoy standing in front of the cold fireplace. He had his back to us, hands clasped behind him. His pea-green suit clashed with his slicked-back black hair. One sleeve was torn and bloodstained. He turned towards us. Blood seeped from a gash on his forehead. He dabbed at it with a handkerchief covered in dancing skeletons. It was silk and had been a gift from his girlfriend, a century-old vamp who had recently joined us. Hannah was as tall, leggy, and lovely as Willie was short, badly dressed, and well . . . Willie.

He smiled at us. "So good of you to join us."

"Can the sarcasm," I said. "Where is everybody?" I started walking towards him, but Jean-Claude stopped me with a hand on my arm.

Willie's smile was almost gentle. He stared at Jean-Claude with a look of expectancy. It was an expression I'd never seen on Willie's face.

I glanced at Jean-Claude's perfect mask of a face, closed and careful. No—fearful.

"What's going on?" I asked.

"*Ma petite*, may I introduce the Traveler."

I frowned at him. "What are you talking about?"

Willie laughed, and it was the same irritating bray he'd always had, but it ended in a low, chuckling growl that raised the hairs at the base of my neck. I looked at him and knew the shock showed on my face.

I had to swallow before I could talk, even then I didn't know what to say. "Willie?"

"He can no longer answer your call, *ma petite*."

Willie stood there staring at me. He had been an awkward person alive. Dead, he hadn't been much better. He hadn't been dead long enough to master that otherworldly movement that the others had. He walked towards us in a wave of his own liquid grace. It wasn't Willie.

"Shit," I said softly. "Is it permanent?"

The stranger in Willie's body laughed again. "I am merely borrowing his body. I borrow a great many bodies, don't I, Jean-Claude?"

I felt Jean-Claude draw me backwards. He didn't want to get closer. I didn't argue. We backed up. It was odd being backed up by Willie. Normally, he was one of the least scary vamps I knew. Now, tension sang down Jean-Claude's hand. I could taste his heart beating in my own head. He was afraid, and that made me afraid.

The Traveler stopped, hands on hips, laughing. "Afraid I will use you as my horse, Jean-Claude? If you are truly strong enough to have slain the Earthmover, then you should be strong enough to withstand me."

"I am cautious by nature, Traveler. Time has not lessened the habit."

"You always did have a smooth tongue in your head and so many other places."

I frowned at the double-entendre, not sure I caught the meaning, not sure I wanted to. "Let Willie go."

"He is not being harmed," the vampire said.

"He is still inside the body," Jean-Claude said. "He still feels, still sees. You have only pushed him aside, Traveler, not replaced him."

I glanced at Jean-Claude. His face showed nothing. "You say that like you know from personal experience."

"Jean-Claude was one of my favorite bodies, once upon a time. Balthasar and I enjoyed him very much."

Balthasar walked out of the far hallway as if he'd been waiting for his cue. Maybe he had. He was smiling, but it was more a baring of teeth than pleasure. He strode into the room looking elegant and roguish in his white suit. He stood behind Willie, hands on the shorter man's thin shoulders. Willie, the Traveler, leaned back against Balthasar's chest. The bigger man wrapped his arms around him. They were a couple.

"Will he know what they're doing with his body?" I asked.

"Yes," Jean-Claude said.

"Willie doesn't like men."

"No," Jean-Claude said.

I swallowed and tried to think reasonably, and just couldn't. Vampires could not take over another vampire's body. It wasn't possible. It just wasn't. But I looked at Willie's familiar face with a stranger's thoughts flowing through his brown eyes and knew it was true.

Those brown eyes smiled into mine. I dropped my gaze. If the Traveler could do me through Liv's eyes when he wasn't inside her, then he'd suck me down now for sure. It had been a long time since I had had to practice the trick of staring at a face without meeting the eyes. It was like tag with the vamp trying to capture my gaze, and me avoiding it. It was irritating, and scary.

Jean-Claude had said that violence wouldn't save us tonight. He wasn't kidding. If a vamp had been holding Willie against his will, forcing him sexually, I'd have shot him. But it was Willie's body, and he'd get it back. Shooting it full of holes was a bad idea. What I needed was a good idea.

"Does the Traveler like women?" I asked.

"Are you offering yourself in his place?" the vampire asked.

"No, just wondering how you'd like it if the tables were turned."

"No one else has my ability to share a body," the Traveler said.

"Would you like it if someone forced you to have sex with a woman?"

Willie's face cocked to one side, and the expression was alien to him. The sense of otherness was strong enough to make my skin crawl. "I have never felt the draw of a woman's body."

"You'd find it distasteful," I said.

Willie, the Traveler, nodded. "Yes."

"Then let Willie go. Pick someone who wouldn't mind so much."

The Traveler snuggled into Balthasar's arms and laughed at me. "Are you appealing to my sense of mercy?"

I shrugged. "I can't shoot you. You're council. I was hoping that would mean you had more rules than the rest of them. Guess I was wrong."

He looked at Jean-Claude. "Does your human servant do all your talking now?"

"She does well enough," Jean-Claude said.

"If she seeks to appeal to my sense of fair play, then you have told her nothing about your time with us at court."

Jean-Claude kept my left hand clasped loosely in his, but he stepped away from me. I felt him draw himself straighter as if he'd been hunched just a little, huddled around his panic. I knew he was still afraid, but he had rallied. Brave Jean-Claude. I wasn't that afraid yet. But then, I didn't know any better.

"I do not dwell upon the past," Jean-Claude said.

"He is ashamed of us," Balthasar said, rubbing his face against Willie's. He planted a soft kiss against Willie's temple.

"No," the Traveler said. "He fears us."

"What do you want of me, Traveler? Why has the council invaded my lands and taken my people hostage?"

Willie's body pushed away from Balthasar to stand just in front of the taller man. Willie normally looked smaller than he was, sort of hunched and rabbity, but now he looked slim and certain of himself. The Traveler had given Willie the grace and assurance he never had on his own.

"You slew the Earthmover but did not come to take his council seat. There is no other way to rise to the council except through the death of another. We have a vacancy that only you can fill, Jean-Claude."

"I do not want it, nor am I powerful enough to keep it."

"If not powerful enough, then how did you slay Oliver? He was a frightening force of nature." The Traveler walked towards us with Balthasar in his wake. "How did you slay him?"

Jean-Claude didn't back up this time. His hand tightened on mine, but he stood his ground. "He agreed not to call the earth against me."

The vampire and his servant circled us like sharks. One circling left, the other right, so it was hard to keep an eye on both of them.

"Why would he limit his powers?"

"He had gone rogue, Traveler. Oliver wished to bring back the days when vampires were illegal. An earthquake might have destroyed the city, but it would not have been blamed on a vampire. He wanted to possess my vampires and cause a blood bath that would bring us back to being hunted. Oliver feared we would destroy all the humans eventually, and thus ourselves. He thought we were too dangerous to be allowed legal rights and freedom."

"We received your report," the Traveler said. He stopped by me. Balthasar stopped on the other side, closest to Jean-Claude. They were mirroring each other. I wasn't sure if it was the vampire controlling his servant or just centuries of practice. "I knew Oliver's ideas."

I drew back against Jean-Claude. "Is it just vamps or can he take over humans, too?"

"You are safe from his intrusion, *ma petite*."

"Great," I said.

I stared at the Traveler, and it was frightening how easily I was beginning to think of this body as the Traveler and not Willie. "Why didn't you stop Oliver, then?" I asked.

The Traveler sidled closer and closer until only the barest inch kept us from touching. "He was council. Council cannot fight to the death among ourselves. And nothing short of true death would have stopped him."

"You let him come here, knowing what he planned to do," I said.

"We knew he had left the country but not where he fled to or what his plans were." The Traveler raised a hand towards my face. Balthasar did the same on his side for Jean-Claude. Willie's small hand hovered near my face.

"You had declared him rogue," Jean-Claude said. "Any vampire that found him could slay him without violating our laws. That is what rogue means."

The Traveler traced the barest of touches down my face. A trembling, tentative touch. "So you thought we would not come to your door because you had saved us the trouble of hunting him down ourselves."

"Oui."

Balthasar had stopped caressing Jean-Claude's face. He came to stand by his master. He watched the smaller man slide his hand along my face. Balthasar seemed puzzled, surprised. Something was happening, and I didn't know what it was.

The Traveler cupped my chin in his hand. He turned my face to him. He slid his hand over my jaw, behind my neck, to run fingers in my hair.

I pulled away from him. "I thought you didn't like girls."

"I don't." He stood there, staring at me. "Your power is amazing." His hand lashed out too quick to see, too quick to react. He had a handful of my hair, and his eyes, Willie's eyes, met mine. I was shielding myself this time, prepared, but my heart still fell to my feet. I waited for that cold blackness to pull me under. Nothing happened. We stood there, inches apart, and they were just eyes. I could feel his power beating down his arm like a march of icy fingers, but it wasn't enough.

He laid his hands on either side of my face almost as if he were going to kiss me. Our faces were so close that his next words seemed intimate, even though they weren't. "I could force my gaze upon you, Anita, but it would be an expenditure of power that I might regret before dawn. You have injured Liv twice this night. I am healing her, but that too takes power."

He stepped back from me, hugging himself as if he'd gotten more from touching me than just the feel of skin. He took three gliding steps to put himself face to face with Jean-Claude. "Her power is a heady thing. Something to wrap around your cold skin and warm your heart for all eternity."

Jean-Claude let out a slow breath. "She is my human servant."

"Indeed," said the Traveler. "A hundred years ago I could invade you without touching your fair skin. Now I cannot. Has she given you this power?" He reached towards Jean-Claude's face as he had mine.

I pulled Jean-Claude back, out of reach, and stepped between them. "He's mine, no sharing."

Jean-Claude slid his arm around me, holding me loosely at his side. "If you would leave us in peace, I would let Balthasar and any person you chose use me, but I will not willingly be your horse ever again, Traveler."

Willie's brown eyes stared up at Jean-Claude. There was a shrewdness, a frightening intensity, in those familiar eyes. "I am council. You are not. You will have no choice in the matter."

"Are you saying that if he took the council seat, then you couldn't hurt him?" I asked.

"If he is powerful enough to hold a council seat, then I should not be able to invade his lovely body, even were my lips pressed to him."

"Let me test my understanding here. If he takes the council seat, you'll still try and force yourself on him, because if you can force him, then he's not powerful enough to be council? But if he doesn't take the seat, you'll do it anyway."

The Traveler smiled beautifully at me, delight shining from his eyes, Willie's eyes. "Quite true."

"Why is everything with you people a freaking Catch-22? You don't do business. You just do torture," I said.

"Are you judging us?" he asked. His voice was suddenly lower and deeper than Willie's throat should have been able to hold. He took that last step forward, and I was suddenly touching them both. Their power flared over me; it was like being in the middle of two different fires, but it didn't burn. The Traveler's power was like Jean-Claude's, cool and swimming, a breath of mortality, the touch of the grave.

The power pulled a gasp from my throat and raised every hair on my body. "Back off!" I tried to shove him away from us, but he grabbed my wrist too quick to stop, almost too quick to see. The feel of his bare skin on mine sent a wave of numbing cold through my body, like a spear of ice. He jerked me away from Jean-Claude.

Jean-Claude caught my other wrist. The moment his hand touched my skin, the cold faded. His power swept through me like a flood of warm water, and it wasn't his power. I knew the taste of this warmth. It was Richard. Jean-Claude was drawing on Richard's power as I'd done earlier.

He chased the Traveler's power out of me like summer heat on ice. It was the Traveler who released me. He stepped back rubbing his hand on his coat, as if it hurt. "Jean-Claude, you have been a very naughty boy."

Jean-Claude drew me against him, one hand resting against my neck so that his fingers touched my skin. That electric warmth was still there playing over his skin and mine, and I knew in that moment that Richard had felt our urgency, our need.

15

A noise turned us all to the far hallway. I didn't recognize the man. He was tall, slender, dark-skinned, maybe Hispanic, maybe something more exotic. He wore nothing but a pair of black satin pants with silver embroidery along the legs. He was dragging Willie's lady love, Hannah, by one arm.

Her mascara had run in black tears down her face. Her expensive haircut still framed her face, still brought your eyes to her strong cheekbones and full lips. But her face was like a mask now, black tears, and burgundy lipstick smeared across her lower face like a wound.

The Traveler said, "Why have you brought her here, Fernando?"

"My father is as much council as you are, Traveler."

"I do not dispute that."

"Yet you forbid him come to this first meeting."

"If he is council, then let him bend me to his will." The Traveler's voice was mocking. "We are all council, but we are not all equal."

Fernando smiled. He grabbed Hannah's beaded blue dress and tore it down her back. She screamed.

The Traveler swayed, putting a hand to his face.

"I'm going to fuck her," Fernando said.

Balthasar strode towards them, but two leopards the size of ponies crawled from the hallway. One black, one yellow spotted, both big enough to tear him to pieces. They growled low and deep, moving on huge padded feet between Balthasar and Fernando.

Fernando grabbed Hannah around the waist, pulling her dress over her hips to expose pale blue garters. She turned and slapped him hard enough that he rocked back. She was as feminine as they come, but she was also a vampire and could have thrown him into the solid stone wall so that he stuck there.

Fernando hit her back. Blood spattered from her mouth in shining beads. She sat half-stunned on the floor. Fernando's power boiled through the room as if he'd been holding it in check until now. Shapeshifter. Did he match the leopards that guarded his back? Maybe, but it didn't matter what flavor he was. He picked

Hannah up by the front of her dress, dragging her to her knees. He drew his hand back to hit her again.

I pulled the Browning out of the coat pocket. Willie collapsed to his knees on the floor. He stared up and said, "Angel-fangs." He tried to stand and couldn't. Jean-Claude picked him up under the arms and raised him easily.

Fernando hit Hannah again. A casual slap that rocked her head back and rolled her eyes to white. "He must truly love you to fight off the Traveler's touch every time he sees you abused."

Jean-Claude's hand on my arm brought me back to myself. I had the Browning pointed at Fernando. I had to let out a breath to keep from pulling the trigger. The safety was off, and I didn't remember doing it. Why Fernando and not the kitties? The wereleopards could close the distance in the blink of an eye, but I knew who the alpha was. Take out the leader, and the cats might go play somewhere else.

Jean-Claude supported Willie with one arm, the other still lightly on my arm, as if afraid what I'd do. "Fernando," he said, "you've done what you set out to do. The Traveler is forced out, and it will take him a little time to find a second host. You can let Hannah go."

Fernando grinned at us, white teeth bright in his dark face. "I don't think so." He dragged Hannah to her feet, arms around her waist, pinning her arms to her sides. He tried to kiss her. She turned her head and screamed.

Willie was standing on his own now. He pushed away from Jean-Claude. "No, I won't let you hurt her."

The black leopard dropped to its belly, crawling closer to Willie, to us.

"If we're going to take them out, we have to do it now," I said. Fernando first, then one of the leopards, if I had time. If not . . . one problem at a time.

"Not yet, *ma petite*. Fernando's father, Padma, will not waste precious time tormenting the little ones. The Traveler will return too soon for that."

"The Traveler won't let me taste her once he returns," Fernando said. He kept Hannah pressed to his body with one arm and raised her dress with the other.

"Does he seriously think we're going to stand here while he rapes her?" I asked.

"My father is the Master of Beasts. You won't stop me, for fear of his wrath."

"You just don't get it, do you, Fernando?" I pointed the gun very steadily at his head. "I don't give a fuck who your daddy is. Let go of her, and tell your furry buddies to back off or I'm going to make your daddy a very unhappy vampire."

"You don't want me unhappy." The voice caused my eyes to flick to the hallway beyond, but the gun didn't move.

The vampire in the doorway was Indian, as in from India. He was even wearing one of those long combo coat-tunic things. It was gold and white and shimmered on the edge of my vision as he walked further into the room. I kept my sights on his son. One monster at a time.

Jean-Claude let his hand drop away from my arm. He stepped behind me and to one side, careful not to block my shot. "Padma, Master of Beasts, greetings and welcome to my home."

"Jean-Claude, Master of the City, greetings. Your hospitality has been beyond my wildest expectations.'' He laughed then, but it was just a laugh. Theatrical and annoying, even sinister, but it didn't make my skin jump.

''Tell him to let Hannah go,'' I said.

''You must be Jean-Claude's human servant, Anita Blake.''

''Yeah, nice to meet you. Now tell your son to let go of our vampire, or I'm going to put a really big hole in him.''

''You wouldn't dare harm my son.''

It was my turn to laugh, short, abrupt, and not very funny. ''Your son said almost the same thing. You are both so wrong.''

''If you kill my son, I will kill you. I will kill you all.''

''Fine, let me test my understanding. If he doesn't let her go, what's he going to do with her?''

Fernando laughed, and it was low and hissing. The laugh was enough. Somewhere in that lovely body was black fur and big button eyes; wererat. ''I will have her because the Traveler has forbidden it, and my father has given her to me.''

''No,'' Willie said. He took a step forward but Jean-Claude stopped him.

''No, Willie, this is not your fight.''

Fernando slid his hand over Hannah's groin. Only Jean-Claude's hand on Willie's arm kept him from rushing the shapeshifters.

Hannah said, ''Master, help me.''

''He can't help you, child,'' Padma said. ''He can't help any of you.''

I aimed two inches to the right of Fernando's head. The shot echoed in the big room. The bullet bit into the stone wall. Everyone froze.

''The next bullet goes in Fernando's skull.''

''You wouldn't dare,'' Padma said.

''You keep saying that. Let's get something straight, Beast Master. Fernando is not raping Hannah. No way. I'll kill him first.''

''Then I will kill you,'' Padma said.

''Fine, but that won't bring back your son, now will it?'' I let the breath out of my body and felt that stillness spill through me. ''Decide, Beast Master, decide.''

''I am the Master of Beasts,'' he said.

''I don't care if you're Santa Claus. He lets her go or he dies.''

''Jean-Claude, control your servant.''

''If you can control her, Padma, be my guest. But take great care. Anita never bluffs. She will kill your son.''

''Decide,'' I said softly, ''—decide—decide—decide—decide.'' I wanted to shoot him. I really did, because I knew as surely as I was standing there that if I didn't shoot him now, I'd have to shoot him later. He was too arrogant to leave it alone, too blinded by his own power to leave Hannah alone, and he couldn't have her. That was a line he could not cross and live.

''Let her go, Fernando,'' Padma said.

''Father,'' the man sounded shocked.

''She will pull the trigger, Fernando. She wants to pull it. Don't you, Anita?''

''Yeah, I do.''

''Silver bullets, I assume,'' Padma said.

''Never leave home without them,'' I said.

''Let her go, Fernando. Even I cannot save you from a silver bullet.''

"No, she's mine. You promised."

"I'd listen to your dad, Fernando."

"Do you disobey me, my son?" There was a tone in Padma's voice that sent a rush of warm air through the room. The beginnings of anger. Something was flung over my skin, a backwash of power, but it wasn't vampiric power, not exactly. He wasn't trying to control Jean-Claude. It had a taste of warmer blood, an electric dance that said lycanthrope. Which wasn't really possible. A vampire can't be a lycanthrope, and vice-versa.

Fernando cringed, clutching Hannah to him like a doll, hiding his face in her yellow hair. "No, Father, I would never disobey you."

"Then do as I say."

Fernando flung Hannah backwards. She scrambled to Willie. He took her in his arms, touching the blood on her face, blotting at it with the silken handkerchief.

I lowered the gun.

Fernando pointed a dark hand at me. "Maybe I'll ask for you to be my pet."

"Tough talk, rat-boy. Let's see if you're man enough to back it up." I was baiting him. I realized that I wanted him to rush me. I wanted an excuse to kill him. Not good. Not good. I had to calm down or I *was* going to get us killed.

The black leopard, taller at the shoulders than my waist, started creeping towards me. It was belly to the ground, muscles tensed and rippling. The gun just shifted to it. "Don't try it."

"Elizabeth," Padma said.

The name startled me. I'd seen Elizabeth in human form once, sort of from a distance. She was one of the local wereleopards. I'd assumed, until that moment, that the leopards were part of the entourage that Padma had brought with him. If Elizabeth was local, the other leopard might be, too. The only thing I was sure of was that it wasn't Zane or Nathaniel. Other than that, it could have been anybody. But Zane acknowledging me as his alpha had saved him from being here. If Zane had been alpha, then beating him would have given me all the leopards, and none of them would have been here. Or that was the theory. With me being merely human and not a lycanthrope, the Master of Beasts might still have called the kitties. But I would have tried to keep them safe. I wondered if Elizabeth had tried.

She snarled at him, at me, at everyone. Her fangs were ivory-white, and at less than ten feet, impressive as hell. This close, even a real leopard might have gotten to me before I could fire a killing shot. You aren't supposed to hunt big game with a handgun.

The leopard took another belly crawl forward. "Elizabeth." That one word flung outward burned along my skin and made me gasp. The leopard came up short like she'd hit the end of her leash. She rolled on the floor, struggling, slashing the air.

"She hates you, Anita," Padma said. His voice was normal now, conversational, but whatever he was doing to the wereleopard was still happening. I could feel it like ants marching down my skin. Ants with red hot pokers in their little hands.

I glanced at Jean-Claude, wondering if he could feel it. His face was blank, empty, unreadable. If he felt the pain, it didn't show.

I wasn't sure admitting I could feel it was a good idea. "Stop it," I said.

"She would kill you if I let her. You killed the one she loved, their leader. She would have her revenge."

"You've made your point. Let her go."

"Mercy for one who hates you so?" He glided into the room, slippered feet barely touching the floor, as if he rode always on tiny currents of his own power.

I should have been sensing his vampire powers. But he was almost a blank, as if something was keeping him in check or protecting me. I glanced at Jean-Claude again. Was he powerful enough to keep us safe now? Had the triumvirate helped him that much? His face told me nothing, and I didn't dare ask, not in front of the Master of Beasts.

The leopard lay on its side, panting heavily. It watched me with pale green eyes, and it was not a friendly look.

"When I called them," Padma said. "she tried to bargain with me. They have no alpha and yet she tried to bargain. Elizabeth would bring the leopards without a struggle to do with as I like, if I would let her kill you. Help her kill you." The Beast Master motioned behind him, and a small, slender woman stepped up beside him, like she'd been waiting in the hallway for his call. Like a well-trained dog. She was nude except for a necklace that must have weighed five pounds and burned with diamonds. Her skin was that pale shade of dark that says African-American via Ireland. Bruises decorated her face, running in purple stains down her body. She was one of the most beautiful women I'd ever seen, even with the bruises. She was perfectly proportioned from forehead to slender feet. Her eyes were brown and flicked from the leopard on the floor to Jean-Claude to the rat-man. Back and forth, back and forth, until finally she settled on me.

She pleaded with her eyes, and I didn't need words to know that she was saying, Help me. That I understood, but why me?

"When Elizabeth came, she brought the others with her. I chose Vivian as my present to myself." Padma stroked her hair absently, the way you'd pet a dog. "I will give her a gift for every harm I do her. She will be rich, if she survives."

The air around her trembled like the wash of heat off a summer road. Another wereleopard that I'd never met. How many of them were there? How many people had Elizabeth delivered over to the bad guys?

"What is this, a father-son rape outing?" I asked.

Padma frowned at me. "I grow tired of you, Anita Blake."

"It's mutual," I said.

"We forced the Traveler out of his host body, but his power still shields you. He was to keep you from sensing your vampires' distress. Now he seems to be protecting you from the full rush of my powers. A pity. You would tremble at the feel of them."

Jean-Claude touched my shoulder lightly. The touch was enough. I wasn't here to trade clever repartee with the Master of Beasts. Killing him sounded like a really good idea, but I've met older vamps that you couldn't take out with silver bullets. It would be just my luck that Padma was one of them.

Padma called the leopards to him. The yellow one rolled around his ankles like a big kitty-cat. Elizabeth sat like a well-trained dog.

Willie and Hannah were oblivious to the room. He touched her gently, as if she were glass. They kissed, and that one chaste touch of lips said it all, tenderness, love. Willie and Hannah were just plain gone on each other. It was beautiful.

"You see why I gave her to my son. Such anguish her abuse would have caused them both. But the Traveler needed their bodies."

I stared at him. It was bad enough when I thought the choice was just because Hannah was blond and lovely, but to know it was deliberate cruelty and not just lust—that made it worse.

"You son of a bitch," I said.

"Are you trying to make me angry?" Padma said.

Jean-Claude touched me again. "Anita, please."

He rarely used my real name. When he did, it was either very serious or something I wouldn't like. This time it was both.

I don't know what I was about to say, because suddenly the Traveler lifted his shield. Padma's power crashed over us. It thundered over me, filling my head, scrambling every thought I had. I fell to my knees like I'd been hit by a hammer between the eyes.

Jean-Claude stayed standing, but I felt him sway beside me.

Padma laughed. "He cannot re-enter another host and maintain his shield."

A voice came like a wind easing through the room. I wasn't sure if I heard the voice out loud or if it was just in my head. "He will need his powers in the hallway. I chose to lift the shield. Enough games, Padma. Let him see what lies beyond." There was a scent with the words; fresh turned earth, the smell of roots pulled from the ground. I could almost feel the crumble of rich black soil between my hands. I squeezed my hands around the Browning until they shook, and I still couldn't shake the sense of earth between my hands on the gun. Even staring at the gun, seeing it was clean, didn't make it go away.

"What's happening?" I asked. Surprised and pleased that I could form a coherent sentence.

"They are council," Jean-Claude said. "They have taken off, how would you say, the gloves?"

"Shit," I said.

Padma laughed. He stared at me, and I knew he was concentrating just for little ol' me. His power slammed over me, into me. It was halfway between putting your hand on a live electric wire and shoving the same hand into fire. The electric heat ate through my body. The heat gathered in the center of me. It flexed like a fist growing larger, larger. If he spread his fingers inside me, he'd tear me apart, burst me from the inside out with just his power. I screamed.

16

A cool touch slid over the heat. A wind, cool and easeful as death, swept over my body. The wind blew my hair back from my face. Blessed coolness filled me. Jean-Claude's hands caressed my shoulders. He was kneeling on the floor, cradling me in his arms. I didn't remember falling. His skin was cool to the touch. I knew that somehow he was throwing his hard-won warmth away. His warmth to cool the fire.

That awful pressure inside of me eased, then shrank. It was like Jean-Claude was a wind blowing out Padma's fire. But it cost him. I felt his heart slow. The blood in his veins flowed slow and slower. The warmth that mimicked life was leaving him, and death seeped inside to fill its place.

I turned in his arms so I could see his face. The face was pale and perfect, and you'd never have known, just by watching, what it had cost him to save me.

Hannah turned to us, her battered face set in calm lines. "My apologies, Jean-Claude. My compatriot has let your servant's defiance best his judgment."

Willie stepped away from Hannah, shaking his head. "Damn you, damn you."

Hannah's grey eyes turned to him, angry. "Do not tempt me, little one. You cannot trade insults with me and survive."

"Willie," Jean-Claude said. There was no power to the word, just a warning. It was enough. Willie stepped back.

Jean-Claude looked at the Traveler in his new body. "If he had killed Anita, I might have died with her. Is that why you have truly come? To kill us?"

"I swear it is not." Where he'd made Willie glide, Hannah was awkward on her stiletto heels. He didn't fall, but he didn't glide either. It was almost heartening. He wasn't perfect.

"To prove my sincerity," he said, "take your warmth back from your servant. We will not stop you."

"He thrust me out," Padma said. "How can you allow him to grow strong again?"

"You sound afraid," the Traveler said.

"I do not fear him," Padma said.

"Then let him feed."

I leaned into Jean-Claude's chest, resting my cheek against the mound of silken ruffles on the front of his shirt. His heart had stopped beating. He wasn't even breathing. He'd used too much of himself up.

I watched Padma from the safety of Jean-Claude's arms and knew I would kill him. I knew that Padma wanted us dead. I'd felt it. No one as powerful as he was lost control that badly. He'd nearly killed me, us, and it would all have been a tragic accident. Bullshit.

The Browning lay where I'd dropped it, but I'd tasted Padma's power now. Silver might not be enough to kill him. Wounding him seemed like a really bad idea. Kill or leave him the hell alone, like any big predator. Don't fuck with it unless you can finish the job.

"Feed from your servant," Padma said. "I will not stop you. The Traveler has spoken." That last held a touch of bitterness. Council member or not, Padma feared the Traveler, or he'd have fought him more. Compatriots but not equals.

I knelt, gripping Jean-Claude's arms through the rough lace and the glittering material of his jacket. His arms felt reassuringly solid, real. "What . . ."

He stopped me with fingers on my lips, a delicate touch. "It is not blood that I need, Padma. It is her warmth. It is only a lesser master that must take blood from his servants."

Padma's face had gone empty, blank. "You have not lost your knack of insulting without being insulting, Jean-Claude."

I stared up at Jean-Claude, even kneeling he was taller. His voice eased through my mind. "No questions, *ma petite*, or they will know you are not wholly mine."

Since I had a lot of questions, that pretty much sucked. But if I couldn't ask direct questions, there were other ways. "Does the Beast Master have to sink fang to jump-start his heart?"

"Oui, ma petite."

"How . . . vulgar," I said. It was one of the most civilized insults I'd ever come up with. It worked, too.

Padma hissed at us. "Do not test my patience too far, Jean-Claude. The Traveler is not the head of the council. You have enough enemies here now that a vote might not go your way. Press me too hard and I will force a vote."

"Force a vote to what end?" Jean-Claude asked. "The Traveler has promised that you are not here to kill me. What else would you vote upon, Master of Beasts."

"Get on with it, Jean-Claude." Padma's voice was low with a sound that was almost a growl. It sounded more animal than vampire.

Jean-Claude touched my face gently, turning me to look at him. "Let us show the Master of Beasts how it is done, *ma petite*."

I didn't really like the sound of that. But I knew one thing for certain, Jean-Claude needed his strength back. He'd never be able to repeat the trick of thrusting out a council member when he was so cold, so drained.

"Do it," I said. I had to trust him. Trust him not to hurt me. Trust him not to do something awful or embarrassing. I realized that I didn't trust him. That no matter how much I loved his body, I knew he was other. I knew that what he thought of as okay was not necessarily okay at all.

He smiled. "I will bathe in your warmth, *ma petite*. Roll you around me until my heart beats only for you. My breath will grow warm from your kiss.'' He cupped my face between the chilled skin of his hands and kissed me.

His lips were velvet, his touch light, caressing. His hands slid up the sides of my face, fingers gliding through my hair next to the scalp, kneading, massaging. He kissed my forehead and shuddered.

I tried to kiss him again, and he drew back. ''Remember, *ma petite*, if any of your fair body touches mine too much, it will deaden. Do not be so eager to lose the sweet sensation of your lips for the night.''

I went very still in his arms, thinking about what he'd just said. Bodies touching, bare skin needed, maybe? But if any part touched too long or too forcefully, my skin would deaden, but only for the night. Jean-Claude was really very good at giving information without seeming to. Made me wonder how often he'd had to do it in the past.

He slipped the coat off my shoulders until it hung nearly to my waist. He ran his hands over my skin, kneading his fingers into me. His hands were warm. He slid his hands over the coat, gripping my arms through it, but no bare skin. He kissed my throat butterfly light, his face rubbing up my neck, my cheek.

He drew back from me with a quick rush of breath. I put my hand over his heart, and there was nothing. I caressed his face, touching the big pulse in his throat. Nothing. I wanted to ask what we were doing wrong, but didn't dare. Didn't want the bad guys to know we didn't do things like this much. Sex we did, the otherworldly vampire shit we skipped if I could manage it.

He started unbuttoning his shirt.

I looked at him, eyes a little wide.

He bared a circle of his stomach.

I just looked at that glimpse of pale skin. ''What?'' I asked.

''Touch me, *ma petite*.''

I glanced at the watching vampires. I shook my head. ''No foreplay in front of the bad guys.''

''I could simply take blood, if you would prefer,'' he said softly. He said it as if we did it every night. We'd done it twice voluntarily on my part. Once had been to save his life. The second time had been to save him and Richard. I did not want to donate blood. Sometimes I thought bloodletting was more intimate than sex to a vampire. I didn't want to do that in front of company either.

I stared up at him, getting angry. He was asking me to do very intimate things in front of strangers. I didn't like it, and he knew I wouldn't like it. So why hadn't he warned me? Had he really not thought we'd have to do this tonight?

''She is angry with you,'' Padma said. ''Is she truly that modest?'' He sounded doubtful. ''Could it be that you cannot truly do what you say you can do?''

Hannah's body stood legs apart balancing on the unfamiliar high heels. ''Are you as weak as Padma? Just another bloodsucker?'' The Traveler shook his head, Hannah's hair sliding across the shoulders of her ruined dress. ''What else have you been bluffing about, Jean-Claude?''

''Damn you all to hell,'' I said. I slid my hands inside Jean-Claude's shirt, fingers sliding over his stomach. He was cold to the touch. Dammit. I pulled his shirt out of his pants, none too gently, and ran my hands over his skin. I kneaded my fingers along the muscles of his back, and could feel heat rise up my throat into my face. Under other circumstances, in the privacy of a bedroom, it had possibilities. Now, it was just embarrassing.

He drew my arms out. "Careful, *ma petite*, or your hands will grow cold."

My fingertips were cold as if I'd been outside without gloves. I stared up at him for a second or two. "If I can't touch you with my hands, what do you suggest I use?"

Padma suggested something explicit enough to make me point a finger at him. "You stay out of this."

He laughed at me. "She is truly embarrassed. How terribly precious. Asher said she was a virgin before you. I did not believe him, until now."

I let my head drop to my chest. I was not going to say it. I did not owe the vampire council a rundown on my love life.

Jean-Claude's hand moved into view. He never touched me, but just the movement of his hand brought my face up to meet his gaze. "I would not ask this of you here and now, if it were not necessary. You must believe that."

Looking into his blue, blue eyes, I did believe him. Stupid, but true. "What do you want me to do?"

He raised his fingers and put them just above my lips, so close that if I breathed in, he'd have had to touch me. "Use your lovely mouth over my heart. If our bond is as strong as I believe it to be, there are shortcuts, *ma petite*."

I sighed and pulled his shirt up, baring his chest. In private I loved running my tongue over the cross-shaped burn scar on his chest. But this wasn't private. Hell with it.

I laid my lips against the cool skin of his stomach, and licked a quick, wet line up his chest.

He drew in a sharp hiss of breath. How could he be breathing and not have a heartbeat? No answer to that, but I'd seen it before. Vampires that breathed but did not have a pulse.

I ran my tongue over the smoothness of the cross-shaped burn scar, ending with a kiss over his heart. I felt my lips grow cold. It wasn't the tingling cold of winter, though. It was just as he'd said. His body stealing my warmth. My life seeping away into him.

I knelt back away from him, licking my lips, trying to feel them. "How's that?"

He laughed, and the sound slid down my back like an ice cube, rubbed purposefully and long to the base of my spine.

I shuddered. "You're feeling better."

He lifted me suddenly, hands on my thighs. I let out a surprised yip, putting my hands on his shoulders for balance. He wrapped his arms around my legs and stared up at me. The pupil in his eyes had bled away to a shining blue fire.

I felt his heartbeat in my throat. His pulse raced through my body. He let me slide slowly through his arms. "Kiss me, *ma petite*, as we are meant to kiss. I am warm and safe to touch."

"Warm but never safe," I said. I started to kiss him when I was inches above his forehead and continued the kiss as I slid down his body. He kissed me like he would eat me from the mouth down. Fangs pressed hard and sharp, and he had to draw away or draw blood. The kiss left me breathless, tingling, but not with cold.

I realized that he'd gotten a buzz from drinking in my warmth. That it had felt good in a more than practical way. Trust him to make a virtue out of necessity.

"Now that you have your full powers once again," the Traveler said, "I will be leaving you. You drove Padma out without my aid. Surely you can defend yourself again."

"He bested you, as well," Padma said.

Hannah's face looked at us. "Yes, he did. I would expect nothing less from the master that slew the Earthmover." Hannah turned back to Padma. "And he did what you cannot. He regained his warmth with his human servant without drawing her blood. A trick that any true master can accomplish."

"Enough of this," Padma said. He sounded angry. Having to share blood with your human servant seemed to be a real faux pas. "The night wanes. Now that you are at full strength, Jean-Claude, search for your people. See who does not answer your call."

"I will leave you now, Jean-Claude. I will await you beyond." Hannah suddenly sagged. Willie caught her and lowered her gently to the floor.

"Search, Jean-Claude, search for your people," Padma said. Jean-Claude stood, drawing me with him. His pupils swam through the shining blue of his eyes. His eyes settled into their normal color. He stared past me, past Padma. I didn't think he was seeing anything in the room. His power crept from his hands across my skin. I think if I hadn't been touching him, I wouldn't have felt a thing. The faintest shimmer of energy, as if this was a small thing to do.

He blinked and looked at Padma. "Damian."

Damian was one of Jean-Claude's lieutenants. Like Liv, he was over five hundred, but would never be a master.

In Damian's case it was over a thousand years, but would never be a master. It was a frightening amount of time to have acquired so little power. Don't get me wrong, Damian was powerful. For a five-hundred-year-old he was scary. For a thousand years he was a baby. A dangerous, carnivorous baby, but still Damian had acquired all the power he might ever have. He could live until the sun expanded and swallowed the earth, and he'd be no more powerful than he had been at dusk today.

He was one of the few vamps to ever fool me completely about his age. I'd underestimated his age by over half. I'd judged by power and was just beginning to learn that power was not the only thing to judge by.

Jean-Claude had bargained with Damian's old master for his freedom to come here and play second banana.

"What have you done to Damian?" Jean-Claude asked.

"I, nothing, but is he dead?" Padma smiled and took Vivian's hand. "That is a question only his master may answer." He walked down the hallway, leading the wereleopard by the hand. Vivian looked back at me, watching me with wide, frightened eyes until they were lost to sight. The black leopard lingered, watching me.

I spoke before I thought, instinct almost. "How could you have given them over to that thing?"

She snarled at me, tail twitching.

"You are weak, Elizabeth. Gabriel knew that and despised you for it."

She let out a coughing roar. Padma's voice cut across the sound like a knife blade. "Elizabeth, come to me now or I shall be very angry."

The leopard gave me a last snarl and padded out of sight.

"Did Gabriel tell you she was weak, *ma petite?*"

I shook my head. "She wouldn't have brought them here if she were stronger. He called and she came, but she should have come alone."

"Perhaps she did her best, *ma petite.*"

"Then her best isn't good enough." I looked at Jean-Claude's careful, unreadable face. His body was still, calm. I laid my hand above his heart underneath his shirt. His heart was pounding.

"You think Damian's dead," I said.

"I know he is dead." He stared down at me. "Whether it is permanent, that is the question."

"Dead is dead," I said.

He laughed then and hugged me to him. "Oh, *ma petite*, you above all should know that is not true."

"I thought you said they couldn't kill us tonight," I said.

"So I thought," he said.

Great. Every time I thought I understood the rules, they changed. Why was it that the damn rules always seemed to change for the worse?

17

Willie came over to us, leading Hannah by the hand. "Thank you, master, Anita."

There were gashes in his thin face, part of the initial fight for the Circus, I guess. They were already healing. He looked awful, even more like the walking dead than usual. "You look like hell," I said.

He grinned at me, flashing fang. He hadn't been dead three years yet. It takes a little practice to smile without flashing fang. "I'm okay." He looked at Jean-Claude. "I tried to stop them. We all did."

Jean-Claude had tucked his shirt back in his pants. He smoothed his hands down the front of the shirt and touched Willie's shoulder. "You fought the council, Willie. Win or lose, you did well."

"Thanks, master."

Jean-Claude usually corrected anyone when they called him master, but tonight, I guess we were going formal.

"Come, we must attend Damian." He offered me his wrist, and when I didn't know quite what he wanted, he laid my fingertips over the pulse. "You touch me as if you were taking my pulse."

"Is there some significance to this?"

"It shows that you are more than my servant or my bed partner. It shows I consider you an equal."

"What will the council think about that?" I asked.

"It will force them to negotiate not only with me, but with you. It will complicate things for them and give us more options."

I rested my hand on his wrist. His pulse was steady under my fingers. "Confusion to our enemies, eh?"

He nodded, making it almost a bow. "Indeed, ma petite, indeed."

I walked beside him towards the hallway, my right hand in my pocket on the Browning, which I'd rescued from the floor. When we got a clear view of the hallway, Jean-Claude's pulse sped under my fingers.

Damian lay on his side curled around a sword. Blood had soaked around the blade into the dark material of the vest he wore as a shirt. The point came out his back. He'd been spitted. Hard to be a hundred percent sure, but it looked like a heart blow.

There was a new vampire standing beside him. He held a two-handed sword in his hands, point down, like a cane. I recognized the sword. It was the one Damian slept with in his coffin.

The new vamp was tall, six foot six or more, broad-shouldered. His hair was cut like a bowl of yellow ringlets around his face, leaving his ears bare. He wore a white tunic, white trousers, white on white in layers. He stood rigid, at attention, like a soldier.

"Warrick," Jean-Claude said. "I had hoped you escaped Yvette's tender mercies."

The tall vampire looked at us. His eyes flicked to my hand on Jean-Claude's wrist. He dropped to one knee and held Damian's sword across his hands. He bowed his head and offered the sword to us. "He fought well. It had been too long since I had such an opponent. I forgot myself and slew him. I would not have wished death on such a warrior. His final death is a great loss."

Jean-Claude took the sword from the vampire's hands. "Save your apologies, Warrick. I come to save Damian, not to bury him."

Warrick raised pale blue eyes to us. "But I have pierced his heart. If you were the master that had made him, then there would be a chance, but you did not call him from his grave to his second life."

"But I am Master of the City, and Damian took a blood oath."

Warrick laid the sword on the ground near Damain's still form. "Your blood may call to him. I pray that it will be enough."

I stared at him. I'd never heard a vampire say "I pray." Vampires, for obvious reasons, didn't pray a lot. I mean, who was going to answer? Oh, yeah, there was the Church of Eternal Life, but they were more a humanist religion, sort of New Wavey. I'm not sure they talked much about God.

Damian's hair was nearly blood-red, a startling color against the alabaster whiteness of his skin. I knew his eyes were a green that any cat would envy, but tonight his eyes were closed, and if things went badly, they'd never open again.

Jean-Claude knelt beside Damian. He laid his hand on Damian's chest, near the sword. "If I pull out the sword and his heart does not beat, his eyes do not open, then he is gone. One chance, and one chance only. We could put him in a hole somewhere for a hundred years and until the sword was pulled out of his heart, there would still be a chance. If we do it here and now, we risk losing him forever."

That last bit of lore is why you never ever remove a stake from a corpse's heart no matter how dead it appears to be.

I knelt beside them. "Is there a ritual for it?"

He shook his head. "I will invoke the blood oath he took. That will help call him back, but Warrick is correct. I did not make Damian. I am not his true master."

"No, he's older than you are by about six hundred years." I looked down at the vampire, spitted on the sword, lying in a pool of his own dark blood. He was wearing a pair of dress pants that matched the vest. Without a conservative shirt under the vest it looked strangely erotic. I could still feel Damian in my head. His power, the beat and the pulse of centuries flowed through him. He wasn't dead, or at least not completely dead. I could still feel his aura, something.

"I can still feel Damian," I said.

"What do you mean, *ma petite*?"

I had a horrible compulsion to touch Damian. To run my hands over his bare arms. I wasn't into necrophilia, no matter how close I walked the edge. What was going on?

"I can feel him. His energy in my head. It's like coming on a fresh corpse before the soul has left the body. He's still intact, I think."

Warrick was looking at me. "How can you know that?"

I reached out towards Damian and stopped myself, hands curling into fists. My hands ached to touch him, not sexual exactly but like seeing a really fine sculpture. I wanted to trace the lines of his body, to feel the flow and ebb of him. To . . .

"What is wrong, *ma petite*?"

I touched my fingertips to Damian's arm, as if afraid he would burn. My hand slid over his cool flesh, almost without me wanting it to. The force that animated Damian's body flowed through his cooling skin, flowed over my hand, down my arm, marched in goose bumps across my body.

I gasped.

"What are you doing, *ma petite*?" Jean-Claude was rubbing his arms as if he, too, felt it.

Warrick put out a hand towards me like he was holding his hand in front of fire, not sure if he could or should touch. He pulled back, rubbing his hand on his pants. "It is true. You are a necromancer."

"You ain't seen nothing yet," I whispered. I turned to Jean-Claude. "When you pull out the sword, the trick is going to be to keep the power from leaving with the opening of the wound. To keep, for lack of a better word, his soul from fleeing, right?"

Jean-Claude was watching me, as if he'd never really seen me before. Nice to know I could still surprise him. "I do not know, *ma petite*. I am not a witch or a student of magical metaphysics. I will invoke the oath, speak the ritual, and hope he survives."

"Sometimes when I call a zombie from the grave, it's easier to call them a second time." I slid my hands down to hold Damian's limp hand, but it wasn't enough. My power and the power inside the vampire needed a more immediate touch than mere hands.

"He is not a zombie, *ma petite*."

"Warrick said you hadn't called Damian from the grave, but I have." Once upon a time, nearly by accident I had raised three of Jean-Claude's vampires. It was when he, Richard, and I first invoked the triumvirate. The power had been so overwhelming that I'd raised every true corpse near us as a zombie, but there had been too much power. I'd fed it to the vampires and they'd risen for me. Necromancers were rumored to be able to call all manner of dead to do their bidding. But that was legend. As far as I knew, I was the only living necromancer to pull off this particular trick.

"What are you asking, *ma petite*?"

I crawled around Damian's body. The blood was cool through my hose. My hand trailed up his arm, never losing contact with his body, with that power curled inside of him. The power that animated him had thrust me out once, cast me out, hurt me. But it was like once having brushed each other, we were linked.

"You're linked to Damian, but you're also linked to me. I can feel Damian in my head. I don't know if it's a link, but it's something. Use it," I said.

"You mean draw on your power to help strengthen my hold on him?" Jean-Claude said.

"Yeah." I dragged Damian into my lap, on his side, the sword still spitting him. When Jean-Claude saw what I was doing, he helped me. I cradled Damian on his side, shoulders in my lap, his head resting on my arm. I slid my hand down his chest, searching for his heart, and found the blade instead. It had pierced his heart. Even with my help, even with Jean-Claude's help, if he hadn't been over five hundred, he'd be dead. Five hundred seemed to be an age where vamps gained a great deal of power. Being over a thousand could only help him. I could feel him, through my body, my head. Through the growing power, I realized I'd turned my back to the hallway. It was hard to think, but I said, "Do we have a truce until we raise him?"

"You mean will they attack us while we save him?"

"Yes."

"I will guard you," Warrick said. He stood and took Damian's sword.

"Isn't that a conflict of interest?" I asked.

"If he does not rise, I will be punished for killing him. It is not just sorrow at my own carelessness that prompts me to help you. I fear what my mistress will do."

Jean-Claude stared down at Damian. "Padma wishes to kill us for the power the triumvirate has given us, *ma petite*. Now that he knows you have called Damian from his coffin like a zombie, he will fear you even more."

"Is Warrick going to tell him?"

Jean-Claude gave a gentle smile. "There is no need for Warrick to tell, is there, Traveler?"

A voice sighed around us. "I am here."

I stared up at the air, at nothing. "You little son of bitch, you're an eavesdropper."

Willie stumbled. Hannah jerked back from him. "I am many things, Anita." Willie turned to us with that ancient intelligence burning in his eyes. "Why have you withheld this information from us, Jean-Claude?"

"You see us as a threat without this bit of information, Traveler. Do you blame me for hiding it from you?"

He gave a small smile that was both gentle and condescending. "No, I suppose I don't."

Jean-Claude gripped the hilt of the sword. He put his hand on Damian's chest to brace himself. His fingers brushed my hand. "You might wish to move your hand, *ma petite*. The sword is sharp."

I shook my head. "I'm going to make his heart beat. I can't do that if I'm not touching it."

Jean-Claude turned his head to one side, looking at me. "The magic grips you, *ma petite*, and you forget yourself. At least use your left hand."

He was right. The magic, for lack of a better word, was building. I'd never felt my own power so strongly outside of a blood sacrifice. Of course, there was plenty of blood, just none that I'd spilt myself. But I could sense Damian's heart inside his chest. It was almost as if I could have reached inside and caressed the muscle. Like I was not seeing it, but feeling it, and that wasn't it either. I had no word for it. It wasn't touch or sight, but I could feel it just the same. I pulled my right hand away and slipped my left over Damian's still heart.

"Are you ready, *ma petite*?"

I nodded.

Jean-Claude rose on his knees. "I am the Master of the City. My blood you have drunk. My flesh you have touched. You are mine, Damian. You gave yourself willing to me. Come to me now, Damian. Rise to me now. Come to my hand." He tightened his grip on the blade. I felt Damian's body shift boneless as the dead.

I felt his heart, caressed it and it was cold, dead. "I am master of your heart, Damian," Jean-Claude said. "I will it to beat."

"We will make it beat," I said. My voice sounded distant, strange, not like my voice at all. Power breathed through me, through Damian, into Jean-Claude. I felt it spreading outward and knew that every corpse in the place would feel the rush.

"Now," I whispered.

Jean-Claude looked at me one last time, then turned all his attention to Damian. He yanked the blade out in one harsh motion.

Damian's essence tried to follow the blade out, tried to slip away through the wound. I felt it sliding away. I called to it, pressed it into the dead flesh, and it wasn't enough. I moved my hand over his heart. The sliding blade sliced my hand. Blood, fresh and warm and human, flowed over the wound. The thing inside Damian hesitated. It stayed to taste my blood. It was enough. I didn't caress his heart. I smashed it, filled it with the power that crawled over us.

The heart thudded against his chest so that I felt it in my bones. His spine bowed, raising him out of my lap, throwing his head. His mouth opened in a silent scream. His eyes flew open wide. He slumped back into my lap.

He stared up at me, wide-eyed, frightened. He grabbed my arm. He tried to talk and couldn't speak past the thundering of the pulse in his throat. I could feel the blood in his body, the beat of his heart, the rush of him.

He reached out to Jean-Claude, grabbing the sleeve of his jacket. He finally whispered, "What have you done to me?"

"Saved you, *mon ami*, saved you."

Damian slumped suddenly. His body began to quiet. I began to lose the sense of his pulse, the taste of his heart. It slid slowly away and I let it go. But I was almost sure I could have held it. I could have kept the feel and rush of his body. I could have made it rise and fall to my touch. I was almost sure.

I ran my hand through his thick red hair and knew temptation, and it was only slightly tinged with sex. I raised my still bleeding hand where I could see it. It wasn't much of a cut; two, three stitches and I'd be fine. It hurt, but not enough.

I ran the still bleeding hand through his hair. The thickness of his hair slid across the open wound, abrading it. The pain was suddenly sharper, aching and nauseating. Enough pain to bring me back to myself.

Damian stared up at me, afraid. Afraid of me.

18

"My how terribly impressive." I turned, Damian still in my lap. Yvette was stalking down the hallway towards us. She'd lost the mink stole, and the white dress was very simple, very elegant, very Chanel. The rest of the scene was pure Marquis de Sade.

Jason, werewolf, flunky, sometimes voluntary appetizer to the undead, was with her. He was dressed in a cross between black leather pants and skin-tight chaps. Bare skin showed at his thighs, and what looked like a leather thong covered his groin. Around his neck was a metal-studded dog collar with a leash attached to it. Yvette was holding the leash. Fresh bruises marched down his face, neck, arms. There were cuts on his lower chest and stomach that looked like claw marks. His hands were bound behind his back, arms pulled so tight to his body that that alone had to hurt.

Yvette stopped about eight feet from us, posing. She shoved Jason hard enough in the back for him to let out a small sound, forcing him to his knees. She drew the leash tight so he was almost hanging.

She smoothed her hand through his yellow hair, adjusting it, like he was about to get his picture taken. "He's my gift while I'm here. Do you like the wrapping?"

"Can you sit up?" I asked Damian.

"I think so." He rolled off my lap, sitting up carefully, as if everything wasn't working quite right yet.

I got to my feet. "How you doing, Jason?"

"I'm okay," he said.

Yvette jerked the leash tighter, so he couldn't talk. I realized that the inside of the collar had metal spikes on it, a choke collar. Great.

"He is my wolf, Yvette. Mine to protect. You cannot have him," Jean-Claude said.

"I have already had him," she said. "But I will have him again. I have not hurt him yet. The bruises are not my doing. He got that in defense of this place. In defense of you. Ask him yourself." She eased the collar, and then the leash itself.

Jason took a long breath and looked at us.

"Did she hurt you?" Jean-Claude asked.

"No," he said.

"You have shown great restraint," Jean-Claude said to Yvette. "Or have your tastes changed since last we embraced?"

She laughed. "Oh, no, my tastes are the same as they always were. I will torment him now in front of you and you will be powerless to stop me. This way I torment several people for the price of one." She smiled. She looked better than she had at the restaurant. Not quite so pale.

"Who'd you feed off of?" I asked.

Her eyes flicked to me. "You'll see soon enough." She turned her attention to Warrick. He didn't exactly cringe, but he seemed suddenly smaller, less shining. "Warrick, you failed me."

Warrick stood against the wall, Damian's sword still in his hand. "I did not mean to hurt him, mistress."

"Oh, I don't mean that. You guarded them while they brought him back."

"You said I would be punished if he died."

"So I did, but would you really have used that great sword on me?"

He dropped to his knees. "No, mistress."

"Then how could you guard them?"

Warrick shook his head. "I did not think . . ."

"You never do." She pulled Jason in against her legs, cradling his face against her thigh. "Watch, Jason, watch and see what I do to bad little boys."

Warrick got to his feet, putting his back to the wall. He dropped the sword, clattering on the stones. "Please, mistress, please do not do this."

Yvette took in a deep breath, head back, eyes closed, caressing Jason's face. She was anticipating.

"What's she going to do?" I asked.

"Watch" was all Jean-Claude would say.

Warrick was kneeling close enough for me to touch. Whatever was about to happen, we were going to have a ringside seat. Which was the point, I suppose.

Warrick stared at the far wall, past us, ignoring us as much as he could. A white film spread across his pale blue eyes, until they were cloudy, blind. If I hadn't been standing within arm's reach, it would have been too subtle to see.

His eyes collapsed inward, crumbling with rot. His face was still perfect, strong, heroic, like an engraving of St. George, but his eyes were empty, rotting holes. Thick greenish pus trailed down his cheeks, like thick tears.

"Is she doing that to him?" I asked.

"Yes," Jean-Claude said, almost too soft to hear.

Warrick made a small sound low in his throat. Black fluid burst from his mouth, pouring down his lips. He tried to scream, and all that came out was a deep, choking gurgle. He fell forward onto hands and knees. The pus-filled liquid poured from his mouth, eyes, ears. It flowed in a puddle of liquid thicker than blood.

It should have stunk, but as so often happened with vampires that rotted, there was no odor. Warrick vomited his own rotting internal organs onto the floor.

We all began to move back from the widening pool. Didn't want to step in it. It wouldn't do us any harm, but even the other vampires stepped back from it.

Warrick collapsed onto his side. His white clothes were nearly black with gore. But underneath the mess he was still whole. His body was untouched.

His hand reached out blindly. It was a helpless gesture. A gesture that said better than words that it hurt, and he was still in there. Still feeling. Still thinking.

"Sweet Jesus," I said.

"You should see what I can do with my own body." Yvette's voice dragged our attention back to her. She was still standing there, cradling Jason against her leg. She was a white, gleaming figure, except for her hand. From the elbow down a green rot had started.

Jason noticed it. He started to scream, and she yanked the collar too tight for speech. She caressed his face with her rotting hand, leaving a smear of something thick and dark and all too real.

Jason went wild. He tore away from her. She pulled on the collar until his face turned pink, then red. He fought to stay away from her. Fought like a fish on a hook. His face turned purplish, and still he wouldn't come to her rotting hand.

Jason collapsed to the floor. He was about to choke himself into unconsciousness. "He has tasted the pleasures of rotting flesh before with other vampires, haven't you, Jason? He is so afraid. It is why Padma gave him to me." Yvette started to close the distance between herself and Jason's prone body. "I doubt his mind will survive even a night. Isn't it delicious?"

"We are *so* not doing this," I said. I took the Browning out of my pocket and showed it to her. "Don't touch him."

"You are a conquered people, Anita. Don't you grasp that yet?" she asked.

"Conquer this," I said. I raised the Browning towards her. Jean-Claude touched my arm. "Put away your gun, *ma petite*."

"We can't let her have Jason."

"She will not have Jason," he said. He stared down the hallway at Yvette. "Jason is mine. Mine in every way. I will not share him with you, and it is against the rules of hospitality that you do something to one of my people that will cause permanent damage. Breaking his mind is against council law."

"Padma doesn't think so," Yvette said.

"But you are not Padma." Jean-Claude glided towards them. His power began to fill the hallway like cool rising water.

"You were my toy for over a hundred years, Jean-Claude. Do you really think you can stand against me now?"

I felt her lash out, like a knife striking, but her power met Jean-Claude's and faded. It was like she was striking at mist. His power didn't fight back. It absorbed.

Jean-Claude stepped up, almost touching her, and jerked the leash out of her hand. She touched his face with her rotting flesh, smearing things worse than blood down his cheek.

Jean-Claude laughed, and it was bitter, like swallowing broken glass. It hurt to hear the sound. "I have seen you at your worst, Yvette. There is nothing new you can show me."

She dropped her hands to her side and stared up at him. "There are more delights up ahead. Padma and the Traveler await you." She didn't know that the Traveler was already among us. Willie's body remained quiet, not giving the Traveler away. Interesting.

Yvette held up her hand, and it was smooth and perfect once more. "You are conquered, Jean-Claude. You just don't know it yet."

Jean-Claude hit her, a blur of speed that sent her careening along the floor to end in a not so elegant bundle against the wall. "I may be conquered, Yvette, but not by you. Not by you."

19

Jean-Claude untied Jason's hands and tore the collar from around his neck. Jason huddled into a little ball on the floor. He was making small noises in his throat more primitive than words and more piteous.

Yvette had gotten to her high heels and left us. Warrick was healing, if that was the right word. He sat up, still covered in the remains of his own bodily fluids, but his eyes were clear and blue, and he looked whole.

The Traveler in Willie's body walked up to stand by Jean-Claude. "You have impressed me more than once this night."

"I did none of it to impress, Traveler. These are my people. These are my lands. I defend them. It is not a game." He produced two handkerchiefs from somewhere. He handed me one. "For your hand, *ma petite*." He started to wipe the goop off Jason's face with the other handkerchief.

I stared down at my left hand. Blood was running in a nice steady line down my hand. I'd forgotten about it, watching Warrick rot. Some horrors were worse than pain. I took the bit of blue silk from Jean-Claude. "Thanks." I wrapped the makeshift bandage around the wound, but couldn't tie it one-handed.

The Traveler tried to help me tie the bandage. I pulled away from him.

"I offer you aid, not harm."

"No thanks."

He smiled, and again it was not Willie's thoughts that slid over his face. "It upsets you so much that I inhabit this body. Why?"

"He's my friend," I said.

"Friendship. You claim friendship with this vampire. He is nothing. A power not to be reckoned with."

"He's not my friend because he's powerful or not powerful. He's just my friend."

"It has been a very long time since someone has invoked friendship in my presence. They will beg for mercy, but never on the grounds of friendship."

Jean-Claude stood. "No one else would have thought of it."

"No one else would have been so naive," the Traveler said.

"It is a form of naiveté," Jean-Claude said. "That is true, but how long has it been, Traveler, since someone, anyone, had the courage to be naive before the council? They come before you asking for power, safety, vengeance, but not friendship, not loyalty. No, that they will not ask of the council."

Willie's head did that little turn to one side again, as if the Traveler were thinking. "Does she offer me friendship or ask it of me?"

I started to answer, but Jean-Claude beat me to it. "Can you offer true friendship without asking for it in return?"

I opened my mouth to say that I'd sooner be friends with a hungry crocodile, but Jean-Claude touched my arm gently. It was enough. We were winning. Don't blow it.

"Friendship," the Traveler said. "Now that is indeed something I have not been offered since I took my seat upon the council."

I spoke then, without thinking first. "That must be very lonely."

He laughed, and it was that same eerie mixture of Willie's loud bray and a slithering chuckle. "She is like a wind through a window long closed, Jean-Claude. A mixture of cynicism, naiveté, and power." He touched my face, and I let him. He cupped the side of my face in his hand in an almost familiar gesture. "She does have a certain . . . charm."

His hand trailed down my face, fingertips lingering against my cheek. He dropped his hand suddenly, fingers rubbing against each other as if he were trying to feel some invisible something. He shook his head. "I and this body will await you in the torture room." He answered me before I could even say no. "I do not plan to harm this body, Anita, but I do need it to walk about. I will leave this host if there is one that you would prefer I take."

He turned and stared at the rest of the group. His gaze came to rest at last on Damian. "I could take this one. Balthasar would enjoy that, I think."

I shook my head. "No."

"Is this one also your friend?"

I glanced at Damian. "Not my friend, no, but he's still mine."

The Traveler turned his head to one side, staring at me. "He belongs to you, how? Is he your lover?"

I shook my head. "No."

"Brother? Cousin? Ancestor?"

"No," I said.

"Then how is he . . . yours?"

I didn't know how to explain it. "I won't give Damian to you to save Willie. You said it yourself. You're not hurting him."

"And if I was? Would you trade Damian's safety for your friend?"

I shook my head. "I'm not going to debate this with you."

"I am merely trying to discern how important your friends are to you, Anita."

I shook my head again. I didn't like where this conversation was going. If I said the wrong thing, the Traveler was going to start cutting Willie up. I could see it coming. It was a trap, and everything I thought to say led right into it.

Jean-Claude interrupted, "*Ma petite* values her friends."

The Traveler held up a hand. "No, she must answer this one herself. It is her loyalty that I wish to understand, not yours." He stared at me from less than a foot away, uncomfortably close. "How important are your friends to you, Anita? Answer the question."

I thought of one answer that might not lead where the Traveler wanted to go. "Important enough to kill for," I said.

His eyes flew wide. His mouth opened in amazement. "Are you threatening me?"

I shrugged. "You asked a question. I answered it."

He threw his head back and laughed. "Oh, what a man you would have made."

I'd spent enough time around macho guys to know it was a compliment, a sincerely meant one. They never understood the implied insult. And as long as we weren't cutting up people I cared for, I wasn't going to point it out. "Thanks," I said.

His face blanked instantly, the humor gone like a bad memory. Only his eyes, Willie's eyes, were still alive, glittering with a force that crept along my skin like a chill wind. He offered me his arm like Jean-Claude had done earlier.

I glanced at Jean-Claude. He gave the barest of nods. I placed my still bleeding hand on the Traveler's wrist. His pulse beat hard and fast against my hand. It felt like the small wound had a second heartbeat, pounding in rhythm to his pulse. The blood flowed faster out of the cut, called by his power. It dripped in a tickling line down my arm to the elbow to fall inside the arm of the coat, soaking into the dark cloth. Blood spread over his wrist in crimson rivulets. My blood.

My own heart sped up, feeding the fear, driving the blood faster. I knew in that moment that he could stand there and bleed me to death out of that small wound. That he could waste all the blood in me, all the power in me, to make a point.

My heart was thudding in my ears. I knew I should move my hand, but I just never seemed to get around to moving it, as if something was interfering with the screaming in my head, before it could reach my hand.

Jean-Claude reached out to me, but the Traveler spoke before he could touch us. "No, Jean-Claude. I acknowledge her as a power to be reckoned with if she can break this hold on her own."

My voice was breathy, rushed, as if I'd been running, but I could talk, think, I just couldn't move my hand. "What do I get out it?"

He laughed, pleased with himself. I think I'd finally asked a question he was comfortable with. "What do you want?"

I thought about that as the pulse in my hand beat fast and faster. Blood was beginning to soak the Traveler's sleeve, Willie's sleeve. I wanted Willie back. "Safe passage for me and all my people and friends."

He threw his head back and roared with laughter. The laughter stopped in mid-motion like a badly made film. He turned glittering eyes to me. "Break this hold, Anita, and I will grant you what you ask, but if you fail to break it, what do I gain?"

It was a trap, and I knew it, but I didn't know how to get out of it. If he kept bleeding me I'd pass out from blood loss, and it would all be over.

"Blood," I said.

He smiled. "I have that now."

"A willing drink from me. You don't have that."

"Tempting but not enough."

Grey spots were spreading across my vision. I was sweating and vaguely nauseous. It took a long time to pass out from blood loss, but he was speeding it up. I couldn't think what to offer him. I was having trouble thinking at all. "What do you want?"

Jean-Claude let out a sigh, as if I'd said the wrong thing.

"The truth."

I collapsed slowly to my knees, and only his hand on my elbow kept me upright. My vision was going in large grey-white splotches. I was dizzy, and it was only going to get worse.

"What truth?"

"Who really killed the Earthmover? Tell me that and you are free."

I swallowed hard, and whispered, "Fuck you." I slid to the ground still holding onto him, still bleeding. He bent over me, but through my ruined vision it was just Willie. Willie's sharp-angled face. Willie with his loud suits and worse ties. Willie who loved Hannah with a gentle devotion that made my throat tight. I reached out and touched that face, ran my tingling fingertips through his slicked-back hair, cradled his jaw in my hand, and whispered, "Willie, come to me."

There was a jolt like a shiver of electricity, and I could see. My body still felt numb and distant, but my vision was clear. I looked into those glittering eyes and thought of Willie. There, deep inside was an answering scream. "Willie, come to me." My voice was stronger this time.

The Traveler said, "What are you doing?"

I ignored him. Willie was one of the other vampires I'd accidently called from their coffins, like Damian. And maybe, just maybe, he was mine in more than friendship. "With blood I call you, Willie McCoy. Rise and come to me."

The third heartbeat in my hand slowed. The Traveler was the one trying to get away now, trying to break the hold he had forged, but it was a two-edged blade. It cut both ways, and I wanted to make my point deep and sharp.

"Come to me, Willie. Rise to my voice, my hand, my blood. Rise and answer me. Willie McCoy, come now!" I watched Willie spill into those eyes like water filling a cup. I felt the Traveler forced out. I thrust him out, shoved him away, and slammed a door that I hadn't known I had in my head. In Willie's body. I forced the Traveler out, and he spun shrieking into the darkness.

Willie stared at me, and it was him, but there was a look in his eyes I'd never seen before. "What would you have of me, master?"

I collapsed on the floor, crying. I wanted to say, "I'm not your master," but the words died in my throat, swallowed by a velvet darkness that ate my vision and then the world.

20

I'd fallen asleep with my head in my father's lap. He stroked my hair. I snuggled against his lap, my cheek resting on his bare thigh. Bare thigh? I was suddenly awake, pushing to a sitting position before I could really see. Jason sat leaning against a stone wall. It was his lap I'd woken up in. He gave me a very watered-down version of his usual come-hither smile, but it left his eyes cold and tired. He wasn't up to leering at me tonight. Things are rough when Jason stops teasing.

Jean-Claude and Padma were arguing in French. They stood on either side of a wooden table. A man was bound face-down to the table with silver bands at wrist, ankles, and neck. Bands that were bolted to the table itself. He was nude, but more than his clothes were missing. The entire back of his body was one raw bloody mess. I'd found the owner of the skin on the door. Rafael's darkly handsome face was slack, unconscious. I hoped he stayed that way for a long time.

Rafael, the Rat King, was head of the second-largest and strongest band of shapeshifters in the city. He was no one's toy. What the hell was he doing here like this? "What is Rafael doing here?" I asked Jason.

He answered, voice tired, dragging, "The Master of Beasts wants the wererats. Rafael wasn't strong enough not to come when called, but he was strong enough to not bring any of the other rats. He delivered himself over like a sacrifice." Jason leaned his head back against the wall, eyes closed. "They couldn't break him. They couldn't break Sylvie either."

"Sylvie?" I stared around the room. It was twenty by twenty, not that big. She was across the room chained to the wall. She sagged in the chains, full weight on her wrists, unconscious. Most of her was hidden from view by the table that Rafael was chained to. She didn't look hurt.

"Why is she here?"

"The Master of Beasts called the wolves, too. Richard wasn't here to answer, so Sylvie came. She protected the rest of us, just like Rafael did for his people."

"What are Jean-Claude and the Beastie-Boy arguing about?"

"The Traveler granted us our freedom, but they don't want to include Rafael in the bargain. The Master of Beasts says the Rat King is not our people, nor our friend.''

"He's my friend," I said.

He smiled without opening his eyes. "I knew you'd say that."

I got to my feet, pushing against the wall. I was a little unsteady, but not bad. I walked towards the arguing vampires. The French was hot and furious.

Jean-Claude turned to me. "*Ma petite*, you are awake." His English was heavily accented. It often was after he'd been speaking a lot of French.

Padma held up a hand. "No, do not influence her."

Jean-Claude gave a sweeping bow. "As you like."

I wanted to touch Rafael. I could see his back rising and falling, but I wouldn't really believe he was okay until I touched him. My hands sort of hovered over him, but there was almost no place left to touch that wasn't raw and hurting. I finally touched his hair, then drew back. I didn't want to wake him. Unconscious was better than anything else right now.

"Who is this one to you?" Padma asked.

"He's Rafael, the Rat King. He's my friend."

Hannah walked in through the open dungeon door. The moment she appeared, I knew it was the Traveler. He leaned that very feminine body against the side of the door and managed to look masculine. "You cannot be friends with every monster in the city."

I stared up at him. "Want to bet?"

He shook his head, Hannah's blond hair bouncing back and forth just like in the shampoo commercial. He laughed, and it was girlish. "Oh, no, Anita Blake, I will not bargain with you again this night." He started down the steps. He'd taken off the high heels, and glided down the stairs in stocking feet. "But there will be other nights."

"I asked for safe passage and you gave it," I said. "You can't hurt us anymore."

"I gave safe passage for tonight only, Anita."

"I do not remember a time limit being placed on your promise," Jean-Claude said.

The Traveler waved the objection away. "It was understood."

"Not by me," I said.

He stopped on the other side of the table, by Padma. He stared at me with Hannah's grey eyes and frowned. "Anyone else would have known that I meant tonight alone."

"As you yourself have said, Traveler, she is not anyone," Jean-Claude said.

"He is one council member. He cannot bargain for all," Padma said. "He can force us to let you go tonight, but the rest he cannot do. He cannot free you all without a vote of all represented here."

"Then his promise means nothing," I said.

"If I had dreamt that you meant safety for our entire stay," the Traveler said, "I would have asked for more than merely the truth of the Earthmover's death."

"We made a deal. I kept my end of it," I said.

He tried to cross his arms over his chest, but had to settle for his stomach, arms cradling the breasts. Women are just not designed to look tough. "You have given me yet another problem, Anita. It might be wise to not be so problematic."

"Threaten all you want," I said, "but for tonight you can't touch us."

"Do not let it go to your head." His voice had crawled down a few octaves, dragging out of Hannah's throat.

I moved around to stand at Rafael's head, wanting to stroke his hair and not daring to. Tears pressed like a hand against the back of my eyes. "Unchain him. He goes with us, or your word is worth shit, Traveler."

"I will not give him up," Padma said.

"You will do as you are told," the Traveler said.

I turned away from the sight of Rafael's butchered body. I also didn't want the bad guys to see me cry. Turning away from Rafael gave me a better view of Sylvie. What I saw stopped me in my tracks.

Her pants were down around her ankles, shoes still on. I took a step towards her, then another, and was almost running by the time I got to her. I slid to my knees beside her. Blood stained her thighs. Her hands were balled into fists, eyes squeezed tight. She was whispering something, very softly, over and over. I touched her arm and she flinched. Her voice rose just enough for me to hear the one word, "No, no, no." Over and over and over like a mantra.

I was crying. I'd been talking about putting a bullet in Sylvie earlier today. Now I was crying for her. Some big tough sociopath I turned out to be. I had my problems with Sylvie, but this . . . She didn't even like men under the best of circumstances. It made what they'd done worse somehow, more insulting. Or maybe it was just that I remembered her as so proud, so confident and full of herself. To see her like this was almost more than I could bear.

"Sylvie, Sylvie, it's Anita." I wanted to pull her clothes back in place, but was afraid to touch her again until I was sure she knew it was me. "Sylvie, can you hear me?"

Jason came to stand with us. "Let me try."

"She won't want a man to touch her."

"I won't touch her." He knelt on the other side of her. "I smell like pack. You don't." He very carefully slid his arm in front of her face, trying not to touch her. "Smell the pack, Sylvie. Know the comfort of our touch."

She stopped saying no, but that was it. She wouldn't even open her eyes.

I stood up and faced the room. "Who did this?"

"She could have stopped it at any time," Padma said, "given me the pack and it would all have been over. She could have gone free."

I screamed, "WHO DID THIS!"

"I did," Padma said.

I stared down at the floor, and when I came back up, the Uzi was pointed at him. "I'm going to cut you in half."

"*Ma petite*, you will hit Rafael and perhaps me."

A machine gun was not made for one target in a crowd, but he'd survive the Browning. I shook my head. "He dies. For this, he dies."

The Traveler stepped beside Padma. "Would you slay this body?" He spread his hands wide and stepped in front of Padma. "Would you kill your Willie's lady love?"

Tears hot enough to scald trailed down my cheeks. "Damn you, damn you all."

"Padma did not personally rape your friend," the Traveler said. "Any un-skilled man can rape, but it takes a true artist to skin a live shapeshifter."

"Who then?" My voice was just a little calmer. I wasn't going to use the machine gun, and we all knew it. I dropped the Uzi, letting it slide back under the coat. I wrapped my hand around the Browning and thought about it.

Jean-Claude started walking towards me. He knew me too well. "*Ma petite*, we all walk out of here in safety at least this night. You have given us this. Do not destroy us all for vengeance now."

Fernando walked through the door, and I knew. He might not be the only one, but he'd been one of them. He smirked at me. "The Traveler wouldn't let me have Hannah."

I started to tremble, a fine quivering that started in my arms and spread across my shoulders and down my body. I'd never wanted to kill anyone as badly as I wanted to kill him right that second. He glided down the steps in his bare feet, hands roving across his chest, playing in the line of hair that started on his belly. Rubbing his hands along the silk of his pants.

"Maybe I'll have you chained to a wall," he said.

I felt a smile stretch across my face. I spoke very clearly, very carefully, because if I didn't, I was going to scream, and if I lost control of my voice, I was going to shoot him. I knew that just as surely as I was standing there. "Who helped you?"

Padma stopped his son, drawing him into the circle of his arms. I saw real fear on the master vampire's face. His son was still too arrogant or too stupid to understand.

"I did it myself."

A laugh that was bitter enough to choke me came out. "You couldn't do this much damage on your own. Who helped you?"

The Traveler touched Fernando's shoulder. "Others, unnamed others. If the woman can tell you, let her. If not, you do not need to know. You will not be hunting them, Executioner."

"Not tonight," I said. The trembling was quieting. That cold, icy center of my soul, the place where I'd given up a piece of myself, spread outward. I was calm, deadly calm. I could have shot them all and not blinked. "But you said it yourself, Traveler: there will be other nights."

Jason was talking in a low voice and Sylvie was answering. I glanced at her. She wasn't crying. Her face was pale and strangely stiff, as if everything was held inside, tight and hard. Jason undid the locks on the chains and she slid down the wall. He tried to help her pull up her pants, but she pushed him away.

I knelt beside her. "Let me help, please."

Sylvie tried to pull the pants up herself, but her hands weren't working right. She kept fumbling and finally collapsed to the floor in tears.

I started to dress her, and she let me. She helped where she could, but her hands were shaking so badly, she couldn't do much. Her pants were pink linen. I couldn't find the underwear. It was gone. I knew she'd been wearing some, because Sylvie wouldn't go without. She was a lady, and ladies didn't do that.

When everything was covered, she finally met my eyes. The look in her brown eyes made me want to look away, but I didn't. If she could have that much pain in her face, the least I could do was look at it. No flinching. I'd even stopped crying.

"I didn't give them the pack," she said.

"I know," I said. I wanted to touch her, reassure her, and was afraid to.

She collapsed forward, sobbing; not crying, but sobbing like she'd cry out bits and pieces of herself on the floor. I put my arms around her, tentatively. She sagged against me, holding me. I held her half in my arms, half in my lap, rocking her slowly. I leaned over next to her ear and breathed a sound into it, "He's dead. They're all dead."

She quieted slowly, then looked up at me. "You swear it?"

"I swear it."

She huddled against me and said softly, "I won't kill Richard."

"Good, because I'd hate to kill you now."

She laughed, and it turned it into more crying, but softer now, quieter, not quite so desperate.

I looked up at the others. The men, dead and alive, were staring at me. "Rafael comes with us, no more debating."

Padma nodded. "Very well."

Fernando turned to him. "Father, you can't let her do this. The wolves, yes, but not the Rat King."

"Hush, Fernando."

"He cannot be allowed to live, if he does not submit."

"You weren't rat enough to be dominant to him, were you, Fernando?" I said. "He's stronger than you'll ever be, and you hate him for it."

Fernando took a step towards me. Padma and the Traveler both held him back, a hand on each shoulder.

Jean-Claude stepped between us. "Let us be on our way, *ma petite*. The night grows long."

The Traveler stepped away from Fernando slowly. I wasn't sure who he trusted least, me or the rat-boy. He started unfastening the chains that held Rafael in place. The wererat was still unconscious, oblivious to his fate.

I got to my feet, and Sylvie came with me. She pushed away from me, tried to walk and nearly fell. I caught her, and Jason caught her other arm.

Fernando laughed.

Sylvie stumbled. She looked like she'd been slapped. The laughter cut more than any words. I laid my lips against her cheek, cradled her face against mine with my free hand, lips by her ear. "He's dead, remember that."

She leaned into me for a moment, then nodded. She straightened and let Jason help her walk towards the stairs.

Jean-Claude lifted Rafael in his arms as gently as he could, balancing the man over his shoulders. Rafael groaned, hands spasming, but his eyes stayed shut.

I stared at the Traveler. "You'll need to find another horse to ride," I said. "Hannah comes with us."

"Of course," he said.

"Now, Traveler," I said.

Arrogance spread across his face. It was a look I'd never seen on Hannah's face before. "Do not let one act of magical bravado make you foolish, Anita."

I smiled and knew it wasn't pleasant. It was bitter and arrogant and angry. "My patience is all gone tonight, Traveler. Get out of her now, or . . ." I shoved the Browning into Fernando's groin. They were all huddled that close.

Fernando's eyes widened, but he wasn't nearly as afraid as he should have been. I pressed the barrel in a little harder; makes most men back up. He gave a small grunt but leaned into me, face bending towards me. He was going to try and kiss me.

I laughed. I laughed while his lips hovered over my mouth and the gun pressed into his body. It was the laughter, not the gun, that made him draw back.

Hannah collapsed to her knees. The Traveler had gone. Someone needed to help her to the stairs. I thought of Willie and he came. He helped her to her feet without looking at me. I kept my eyes on the bad guys. One problem at a time.

"Why are you laughing?" Fernando asked.

"Because you are too fucking stupid to survive." I drew back from them, the gun still pointed at him. "Is he your only son?" I asked.

"My only child," Padma said.

"My condolences," I said. No, I didn't shoot him. But staring into Fernando's angry eyes, I knew there'd be other opportunities. Some people seek death through desperation. Some people fall into it out of stupidity. If Fernando wanted to fall, I was more than happy to catch him.

21

Rafael lay on an examining table. We were not in the hospital. The lycanthropes had a makeshift emergency room in the basement of a building that they owned. I'd had my own wounds tended there once. Now Rafael lay on his stomach hooked up to an IV loaded with liquids and painkillers. Painkillers didn't always work well on lycanthropes but hey, they had to try something. He'd regained consciousness in the Jeep. He hadn't screamed, but the small squeezed whimperings that clawed from his throat every time I hit a bump were more than enough.

Dr. Lillian was a small woman with salt-and-pepper hair cut in a no-nonsense style. She was also a wererat. She turned to me. "I've made him as comfortable as I can."

"Will he heal?"

She nodded. "Yes. The real danger with this type of injury once you survive the shock and blood loss is infection. We can't get infections."

"Let's hear it for the terminally furry," I said.

She smiled and patted my shoulder. "I know humor is your way of dealing with stress, but don't try it on Rafael tonight. He wants to speak with you."

"Is he . . . ?"

"Well enough, no, but he is my king and he won't let me put him under until he's spoken with you. I'll go look in on our other patient while you hear whatever he thinks is so important."

I touched her arm before she could move past me. "How is Sylvie?"

Lillian wouldn't look at me, then finally she did. "Physically, she'll heal, but I'm not a therapist. I'm not equipped to deal with the aftereffects of an attack like this. I want her to stay here for the night, but she's insisting that she go with you."

My eyes widened. "Why?"

Lillian shrugged. "I think she feels safe with you. I think she doesn't feel safe here." The older woman was suddenly looking very intently at my face. "Is there a reason she shouldn't feel safe here?"

I thought about that. "Have the wereleopards ever been treated here?"

"Yes," she said.

"Damn."

"Why should that matter? This is a neutral place. We have all agreed to that."

I shook my head. "For tonight you're safe, but anything that Elizabeth knew, the Master of Beasts knows. By tomorrow this may not be a safe haven."

"Do you know that for sure?" she asked.

"No, but I don't know for sure that you will be safe either."

She nodded. "Very well. Take Sylvie with you, then, but Rafael must stay here at least for one night. I will make plans to move him by tomorrow." She looked around at all the medical equipment. "We can't take it all, but we'll do what we can. Now go talk to our king." She left the room.

I was suddenly alone in the hush of the basement. I looked at Rafael. They'd arranged a sort of tent of a sheet over his body, covered but not touching. The naked skin was covered in salve but no bandages. Anything they could put on it would hurt worse than nothing. They were treating it sort of like a burn. I didn't know everything they'd done to treat him because I'd been off getting my hand stitched up part of the time.

I walked around the table so that Rafael wouldn't have to move his head to look at me. Moving was bad. His eyes were closed, but his breathing was fast and ragged. He wasn't asleep.

"Lillian said you wanted to talk to me."

He blinked and looked at me. His eyes rolled at an awkward angle. He tried to move his head, and a sound came from low in his chest. I'd never heard a sound quite like it. I didn't want to hear it again.

"Don't move, please." I found a little stool with wheels on it and brought it over. With me sitting, we were nearly the same height. "You should let her pump you full of drugs. You need to sleep if you can."

"First," he said, "I must know how you freed me." He took a deeper breath, and the pain passed over his face in a flinching wave.

I looked away, then back. No flinching. "I bargained for you."

"What . . ." His hands spasmed, and he closed his full lips into a tight-pressed line. When he spoke again, his voice was lower, more careful, as if even a normal speaking voice hurt.

"What did you give up for me?"

"Nothing."

"He would not . . . have given me up so easily." Rafael stared at me, his dark eyes willing me to tell him the truth. He thought I was lying, that was why he couldn't rest. He thought I'd done something noble and awful to save him.

I sighed and told him a very abbreviated version of the night. It was the easiest way to explain. "See, it didn't cost any extra to throw you in."

He almost smiled. "The wererats will remember what you did tonight, Anita. I will remember."

"Maybe we don't go shopping together or even out to the shooting range, but you are my friend, Rafael. I know that if I called you for help, you'd come."

"Yes," he said. "Yes, I would."

I smiled at him. "I'll go get Lillian now, okay?"

He closed his eyes and some piece of tension flowed out of him. It was almost as if now he could finally give himself over to the pain. "Yes, yes."

I sent Lillian into him and went to find Sylvie. She was in a small room where Lillian had hoped she could get some sleep. Sylvie had been joined by her lady friend, significant other, lover, whatever. Jason had called her. I hadn't known she existed. Gwen's voice came very clearly down the hallway. "You have to tell her, Sylvie, you have to."

I couldn't hear Sylvie's answer, but then the high heels weren't quiet. They knew I was coming. I stepped in through the open door to find Gwen looking at me, and Sylvie decidedly not. The white pillow framed her very short, very curly brown hair. She was three inches taller than me but managed to look fragile in the small bed.

Gwen sat in a straight-backed chair beside the bed, holding Sylvie's hand in both of her own. Gwen had long softly waving blond hair and big brown eyes in a delicate face. Everything about her was dainty, feminine, like a pale, finely made doll. But the intensity in her face, the intelligence in her eyes, was a vibrating thing. Gwen was a psychologist. She would have been a compelling person even without the trickle of lycanthropic energy that trailed around her like perfume.

"What do you need to tell me?" I said.

"How do you know I was referring to you?" Gwen said.

"Call it a hunch."

She patted Sylvie's hand. "Tell her."

Sylvie turned her head but still wouldn't meet my eyes. I leaned against the wall and waited. The machine gun pressed into the small of my back, forcing me to lean mostly shoulders against the cinderblock wall. Why hadn't I taken some of the weapons off? Lay a gun down somewhere, and that's when you'll need it most. I trusted the Traveler to keep his word, but not enough to bet my life on it.

Silence spilled into the small room until the whirr of the air conditioner was as loud as the blood in your own ears. Sylvie finally looked at me. "The Master of Beasts ordered Stephen's brother to rape me." She looked down, then up again, anger spilling into her eyes. "Gregory refused."

I didn't bother to hide the surprise on my face. "I thought Gregory was one of the stars of Raina's porno films."

"He was," Sylvie said softly.

What I wanted to ask was, when did he get to be squeamish? but that seemed crude. "Did he suddenly grow a conscience?" I asked.

"I don't know." She was staring at the sheet, holding onto Gwen's hands like there was worse to come. "He refused to help torture me. The Master of Beasts said he'd punish him. Gregory still refused. He said that Zane had told him that Anita was their new alpha. That all bargains made through Elizabeth weren't binding. That he needed to deal with you for them."

Sylvie withdrew her hand from Gwen's and stared up at me. Her brown eyes were furious, but it wasn't me she was angry with. "You can't be their leader and our lupa. You can't be both. He was lying."

I sighed. "Afraid not."

"But, how . . ."

"Look, it's late, and we're all tired. Let's just do the short version. I killed Gabriel, technically that makes me the wereleopards' leader. Zane acknowledged me after I put a couple of non-silver bullets in him."

"Why didn't you kill him?" Sylvie asked.

"It's sort of my fault. I didn't understand what leaving them without a leader would mean. Someone should have told me that they were meat for anybody without a leader."

"I wanted them to suffer," Sylvie said.

"I was told you wanted them all dead, that if you had your way, the pack would have hunted them down and killed them all."

"Yes," she said, "yes. I want them all dead."

"I know they helped punish you and other pack members."

She shook her head, hands in front of her eyes. It took me a second to realize she was crying. "You don't understand. There's a film of me out there. A film of the leopards raping me." She brought her hands down and stared at me with tear-filled eyes. The rage and pain in her face was raw. "I was outspoken against Raina and Marcus. It was my punishment. Raina wanted to make an example of me for the others. It worked, too. Everyone was scared after that."

I opened my mouth, closed it, then said, "I didn't realize."

"Now do you see why I want them dead?"

"Yes," I said.

"Gregory had raped me once. Why wouldn't he do it again? Why did he refuse to hurt me tonight?"

"If he really believes that I'm his leader, then he knows what I'd do to him."

"Did you mean it in the room? Did you mean it about us killing them all?"

"Oh, yeah," I said, "I meant it."

"Then Gregory was right."

I frowned at her. "What do you mean?"

"He said you were their *léoparde lionné*, their rampant leopard."

"I don't know the term," I said.

Gwen answered. "*Léoparde lionné* is a term from French heraldry. It's a leopard, or even a lion, rampant in action on a crest. It symbolizes brave and generous warriors having done some brave deed. In this case it means a protector, even an avenger. Gabriel was a *lion passant*, a sleeping lion. He led but did not protect. In effect, Gregory did not merely refuse to harm Sylvie, he also told the Master of Beasts that if he was harmed, you would save him."

"How can I be their *léoparde* what-you-call-it if I'm not a leopard?"

"*Léoparde lionné*," Sylvie said. "How can you be lupa and neither be wolf nor our Ulfric's lover?"

She had me there.

Fresh tears streamed down Sylvie's face. "Padma tried to get Vivian, his personal pet while he's here, to do things to me. Said I liked women, and maybe that would loosen my tongue. She refused, and she gave the same reason that Gregory did."

I remembered Vivian staring at me, her frightened eyes pleading for me to help her. "Shit, you mean she really expected me to rescue her tonight."

Sylvie just nodded. Gwen said, "Yes."

"Shit."

"I honestly didn't think of it until after we were in the Jeep. I swear I didn't think of it sooner," Sylvie said. "But I didn't say anything, because I wanted them to suffer. I can't stop hating them just like that. Do you understand?"

I did. "Sylvie, you and I have one thing in common. We are both vindictive as hell. So, yeah, I understand, but we can't leave them there like that, not if they were expecting to be saved."

She wiped at the tears. "You can't go up against them tonight. We can't do anymore tonight."

"I'm not planning to fight anymore tonight, Sylvie."

"But you're planning something." She sounded worried. I smiled. "Yeah."

Gwen stood. "Don't be foolish, Anita."

I shook my head. "Foolish. I'm way past foolish." I stopped in the doorway and turned back. "By the way, Sylvie, don't challenge Richard, ever."

Her eyes widened. "How did you know?"

I shrugged. "Doesn't matter. What does matter is that I'll kill you if you kill him."

"It would be a fair fight."

"I don't care."

"You haven't seen him, Anita. He's on the edge. You can forbid me from challenging him, but there are others, and they won't be nearly as good for the pack as I am."

"Then make it carte blanche," I said. "If anyone kills Richard, I'll execute them. No challenge, no fair fight, I'll just take them out."

"You can't do that," Sylvie said.

"Oh, I think I can. I'm lupa, remember."

"If you forbid fights of succession," Gwen said, "you're undermining Richard. You're saying in effect that you don't believe he can really lead the pack."

"I've been told by two pack members today that Richard is out of control, damn near suicidal. That he's pulled his self-hatred, his loathing of his beast, and my rejection, down around his ears. I won't let him die because I chose someone else. In a few months when he's healthier, then I'll step down. I'll let him take care of himself, but not right now."

"I'll pass the word," Gwen said.

"You do that."

"You're going to try and bring out the leopards tonight, aren't you?" Sylvie said.

I kept seeing the bruises on Vivian's body. The pleading in her eyes. "They expected me to save them, and I didn't."

"You didn't know," Gwen said.

"I know now," I said.

"You can't save everyone," Sylvie said.

"Everyone needs a hobby." I started to walk out again, but Gwen called me back.

I turned in the doorway.

"Tell her the rest," Gwen said softly.

Sylvie wouldn't look at me. She spoke staring down at the sheet. "When Vivian refused to hurt me, they called in Liv." She looked up, tears glittering in her eyes. "She used things on me. Did things to me." Sylvie covered her face with her hands and rolled onto her side, crying.

Gwen met my eyes. The look on her face was frightening in its hatred. "You need to know who to kill."

I nodded. "She won't leave St. Louis alive."

"And the other one? The council member's son?" Gwen asked.

"Him either," I said.

"Promise it," she said.

"I already have," I said. I walked out then, searching for a phone. I wanted to talk to Jean-Claude before I did anything. Jean-Claude had taken everyone else to my house. They were boarding up the basement windows so that the vamps could be tucked safely away before dawn. The Traveler had refused to let them take their coffins. Besides, have you ever tried to rent a truck on a weekend after midnight?

What was I going to do about the wereleopards? Damned if I knew.

22

Jean-Claude's voice floated over the phone, my phone, my house. He'd never been there before. "What has happened, *ma petite*? Jason made it sound urgent."

I told him about the wereleopards.

He was quiet for so long, I had to say something. "Talk to me, Jean-Claude."

"Are you actually thinking of endangering us all for the sake of two people, one of whom you have never met before, and the other who you once described as a waste of skin?"

"I can't leave them there if they expected me to help them."

"*Ma petite, ma petite*, you have a sense of *noblesse oblige* that does you credit. But we cannot save them. Tomorrow evening the council will come for us, and we may not even be able to save ourselves."

"Are they here to kill us?"

"Padma would kill us if he could. He is the weakest of the council, and I think he fears us."

"The Traveler's the one we have to convince," I said.

"No, *ma petite*, the council are seven in number, always an odd number so that a vote may settle a question. Padma and the Traveler will vote against one another, this is true. It has been true for centuries. But Yvette is here to vote in the place of her lord, Morte d'Amour. She hates Padma but she may hate me more. For that matter, Balthasar could persuade the Traveler against us, and we are lost."

"What about everybody else? Do they represent anybody?"

"Asher speaks for Belle Morte, Beautiful Death. It is her line that I am descended from, as is he."

"He hates your guts," I said. "We are sunk."

"I believe the choice of four was very deliberate. They wish me to take a council seat, so I am the fifth vote."

"If the Traveler votes with you, and Yvette hates Padma more than she hates you . . ."

"*Ma petite*, if I act as a voting member of the council, then they will expect me to return to France and take my place on the council."

"France?" I said.

He laughed, and it slithered over the phone like a warm touch. "It is not leaving our fair city that frightens me, *ma petite*. It is holding the seat. If the triumvirate were fully formed perhaps, perhaps, it would be possible to appear frightening enough to force would-be challengers to choose another."

"Are you saying without the fourth mark, the triumvirate is useless?"

Silence on his end, so long and deep, that I said, "Jean-Claude?"

"I am here, *ma petite*. The fourth mark will not make our triumvirate functional unless Richard heals himself."

"You mean his hatred of me."

"His jealousy of us together, yes, that is a problem, but not the only one, *ma petite*. His loathing of his beast is so intense, it weakens him. Weaken any link in a chain and it may snap."

"Did you know about what's been happening in the pack?"

"Richard has forbidden any of the wolves to tell me anything without his permission. I believe you are under the same restriction. It is, and I quote, none of my damn business."

"I'm surprised you didn't force Jason to tell you anyway."

"Have you seen Richard within the last month?"

"No."

"I have. He is on the edge, *ma petite*. I did not need Jason to tell me. It is plain for all to see. His torment will be viewed as a weakness among the pack. Weakness attracts them like blood to a . . . vampire. They will challenge him eventually."

"I've had two lukoi tell me that they don't think Richard will fight. That he'll just let someone kill him. Do you believe that?"

"Suicide by simply not defending himself hard enough. Hmm." He was quiet again, then finally said, "I had not thought of such a thing. If I had, *ma petite*, I would have told you of my concerns. I do not wish Richard harm."

"Yeah, right."

"He is our third, *ma petite*. It is in my own interest to make him healthy and happy. I need him."

"Like you need me," I said.

He laughed low and deep, and even over the phone I could feel it tickling along my body. "*Oui, ma petite*. Richard must not die. But to cure his despair he must embrace his beast. I cannot help him do that. I have tried and he will not hear me. He takes what limited help he needs to keep himself from invading your dreams, or you his, but beyond that he wants nothing from us. Nothing he will admit."

"What's that supposed to mean?" I asked.

"It is your tender mercies that he needs, *ma petite*, not mine."

"Tender mercies?" I made it a question.

"If you could accept his beast, completely, it would mean something to him."

"I can't, Jean-Claude. I wish I could, but I can't. I saw him eat Marcus. I . . ."

I'd only seen Richard shapeshift once. He'd been injured from the fight with Marcus. He half-collapsed with me underneath him. I'd been trapped under him while fur flowed, muscles formed and shifted, bones broke and reknit. Clear liquid had gushed from his power, pouring over me in a near-scalding wave. Maybe if I'd just been watching, it would have been different. But trapped under him, feeling his body do things on top of me that bodies were never meant to do . . . it had been too much. If Richard had handled it differently, if I had seen him change in a nice calm way from a distance, then built up to the whole ride, maybe, maybe. But it had happened, and I couldn't forget it. I could still close my eyes and see his man-wolf shape gulping down a red, bloody piece of Marcus.

I leaned my back against the wall, cradling the receiver. I was rocking ever so slightly. It reminded me of Jason in the hallway. I made myself stand very still. I wanted to forget. I wanted to be able to accept Richard. But I couldn't.

"*Ma petite*, are you all right?"

"Fine, I'm fine."

Jean-Claude let that go. He really was getting smarter, at least about me. "I do not wish to cause you distress."

"I've done what I can for Richard on my end." I told Jean-Claude what I'd told the werewolves.

"You surprise me, *ma petite*. I thought you wanted nothing more to do with the lukoi."

"I don't want Richard to die because I broke his heart."

"You would feel responsible if he died now, is that it?"

"Yeah."

He took a deep breath and let it sigh over the phone. It made me shiver, for no particular reason. "How badly do you wish to help the wereleopards?"

"What kind of question is that?"

"An important one," he said. "What are you willing to risk for them? What would you endure for them?"

"You have something specific in mind, don't you?"

"Padma might give up Vivian in exchange for you. Gregory's freedom could be won if we gave them Jason."

"I notice you're not trading yourself in," I said.

"Padma would not want me, *ma petite*. He is neither a lover of men nor of other vampires in particular. He prefers his companions warm and female."

"Why Jason then?"

"A werewolf for a wereleopard might be an acceptable trade to him."

"Not to me. We are not trading one hostage for another, and I am certainly not giving myself to that monster."

"You see, *ma petite*, you will not endure that. You will not risk Jason to save Gregory. I ask again, what will you risk for them?"

"I'll risk my life, but only if I've got a good chance of getting out alive. No sex, absolutely not. No trading one hostage for another. Nobody else gets skinned alive or raped. How's that for parameters?"

"Padma and Fernando will be disappointed, but the others might agree. I will do the best I can within the limits you have given me."

"No rape, no maiming, no actual intercourse, no hostages, does that really tie your hands that much?"

"When we have survived all this, *ma petite*, and the council has gone home,

I will tell you stories of my time at court. I have seen spectacles that even in the telling would give you nightmares.''

"Nice to know you think we're going to survive."

"I am hopeful, yes."

"But not certain," I said.

"Nothing is certain, *ma petite*, not even death."

He had me there. My beeper went off. It pulled a gasp from my throat. Nervous, who me?

"Are you all right, *ma petite*?"

"My beeper went off," I said. I checked the number. It was Dolph. "It's the police. I need to return the call."

"I will begin negotiations with the council, *ma petite*. If they ask too much, I will let your leopards remain where they are."

"Padma will kill Vivian now that he thinks she belongs to me. He might have killed her before, but it would have been by accident. If we don't get her out of there, he'll do it on purpose."

"One meeting with him and you are so sure of this?"

"You think I'm wrong?" I asked.

"No, *ma petite*, I think you are exactly right."

"Get them out of there, Jean-Claude. Make the best deal you can."

"I have your permission to use your name in this?"

"Yeah." My beeper went off a second time. Dolph, impatient as usual. "I've got to go, Jean-Claude."

"Very well, *ma petite*. I will bargain for us all, then."

"You do that," I said. "Wait . . ."

"Yes, *ma petite*."

"You aren't going to go back to the Circus in person tonight, are you? I don't want you in there alone," I said.

"I will use the phone, if you prefer," he said.

"I do."

"You don't trust them," he said.

"Not hardly."

"Wise beyond your years," he said.

"Suspicious beyond my years, you mean."

"That as well, *ma petite*. If they will not negotiate over the phone?" he asked.

"Then let it go."

"You said you were willing to risk your life, *ma petite*."

"I didn't say I was willing to risk yours."

"Ah," he said. "*Je t'aime, ma petite*."

"I love you, too," I said.

He hung up first, and I dialed the police. Here was hoping whatever Dolph had in mind was some nice straightforward police work. Yeah, right.

23

The victim had been rushed to a hospital by the time I arrived at Burnt Offerings. It's one of my favorites of the newer vampire businesses. It was far from the vampire district. The only other vamp businesses were blocks, miles away. As you walked through the doors there was a poster from the 1970's movie *Burnt Offerings*, Oliver Reed and Bette Davis staring down at you. There was a life size waxwork of Christopher Lee as Dracula in the bar. There was one wall with framed caricatures of horror stars of the sixties and seventies, floor to ceiling, no tables allowed to obstruct the view. It wasn't uncommon to see clusters of visitors trying to identify who was who. At midnight whoever had the most correct guesses got a free dinner for two.

The place was pure schlock. Some of the waiters were real vamps, but others were just wannabes. For some it was just a job, and they specialized in plastic Halloween teeth and jokes. For others it was their chance to pretend. They had dental caps over their canines and worked very hard at being the real thing. Other waiters or waitresses were dressed up as mummies, the wolf man, Frankenstein's monster. To my knowledge the only real monsters were the vamps. If a shapeshifter wanted to come out of the closet, there was better money to be made in more exotic locales.

The place was always packed. I wasn't sure whether Jean-Claude was sorry he hadn't thought of it first or if he was simply embarrassed by it. It was a little déclassé for him. Me, I loved it. From the haunted house soundtrack to the Bela Lugosi burgers, extra rare unless otherwise requested. Bela was one of the few exceptions to the 60's and 70's movie decor. Hard to have a horror theme restaurant without the original movie Dracula.

You haven't lived until you've been there on a Friday night for Scary Karaoke. I took Ronnie. Veronica (Ronnie) Sims is a private detective and my best friend. We had a blast.

But back to the body. All right, not a body, a victim. But if the bartender hadn't been fast with a fire extinguisher, it would have been a body.

Detective Clive Perry was the man in charge. He's tall, slender, sort of Denzel

Washington without the broad shoulders. He's one of the most polite people I've ever met. I've never heard him yell, and only seen him lose his composure once—when a large white cop had pointed a gun at the "nigger detective." Even then I was the one who pointed my gun at the rogue cop. I was the one that was ready to shoot while Perry was still trying to talk the situation down. Maybe I overreacted. Maybe I didn't. No one died.

He turned with a smile, soft voice. "Ms. Blake, good to see you."

"Good to see you, too, Detective Perry." He always affected me this way. He was so polite, so soft-spoken that I fell into the same pattern. I was never this nice to anyone else.

We were in the bar with its life-size waxwork of Christopher Lee as Dracula looming over us. The bartender was a vamp named Harry who had long auburn hair and a silver stud in his nose. He looked very young, very cutting edge, and could probably remember the Jamestown charter, though his British accent showed he was newer to the country than the 1600's. He was polishing the bar like his life depended on it. Even with his nice blank face, I could tell he was nervous. Couldn't blame him, I guess. Harry was part owner as well as bartender.

A woman had been attached in the bar by a vampire patron. Very bad for business. The woman had thrown a drink in his face and lit him with her lighter. Ingenious in an emergency. Vamps burn really well. But the quiet bar in a family-oriented tourist trap didn't seem the place for such extreme measures. Maybe she panicked.

"Witnesses all say she seemed friendly until he got a little too close," Perry said.

"Did he bite her?"

Perry nodded.

"Shit," I said.

"But she lit him up, Anita. He's badly burned. He may not make it. What could she have thrown on him to get third-degree burns so quickly?"

"How quickly?"

He checked his notes. "Seconds and he went up."

I asked Harry. "What was she drinking?"

He didn't ask who, just said, "Straight Scotch. Best we had in the place."

"High alcohol content?"

He nodded.

"That would have been enough," I said. "Once you get a vamp burning, they burn until they're put out. They're very combustible."

"So she didn't come in here with some sort of accelerant?" he asked.

I shook my head. "She didn't need it. What I don't like is the fact that she knew to light the drink. If he'd been human and gotten out of hand, she'd have thrown the drink and yelled for help."

"He did bite her," Perry said.

"If she had that much problem with a vampire sinking fang in her, she wouldn't have been cuddling with him in a bar. Something's off about this."

"Yes," he said, "but I don't know what. If the vampire survives, he's going to be up on charges."

"I'd like to see the woman."

"Dolph took her to the emergency room to get the bite tended. He's got her down at our headquarters. He said to come on down if you think you need to see her."

It was late, and I was tired, but dammit, something was wrong. I walked over to the bar. "Was she trolling for vamps, Harry?"

He shook his head. "Came in to use the phone, then sat down. She's a beauty. Didn't take long for someone to hit on her. Just bad luck it was a vampire."

"Yeah," I said, "bad luck."

He kept polishing the bar in small round circles, while his eyes watched me. "If she sues us, it'll ruin us."

"She won't sue," I said.

"Tell that to the Crematorium in Boston. A woman got bit there and sued them out of business. They had pickets going outside."

I patted his hand, and he went utterly still under my touch. His skin had that hard almost wooden feel that vamps can have when they aren't trying to be human. I met his dark eyes, and his face was as immobile and unreadable as glass.

"I'll go talk to the supposed victim."

He just looked at me. "It won't help, Anita. She's human. We're not. Nothing they do in Washington will change that."

I took my hand away and resisted an urge to wipe it on my dress. I never liked the way vamps felt when they went hard and otherworldly. They didn't feel like flesh then, almost plastic like a dolphin, but harder, as if there was no muscle underneath, nothing but solidness like a tree.

"I'll do what I can, Harry."

"We're monsters, Anita. We'll always be monsters. I've really enjoyed being able to walk the streets like everyone else, but it won't last."

"Maybe, maybe not," I said. "Let's take care of this problem before we borrow another one, okay?"

He nodded and walked away to stack glasses.

"That was very comforting of you," Perry said. Anyone else on the squad would have said it wasn't like me to be comforting. Of course, anyone else would have already given me a hard time about the dress. I was going to have to go down to RPIT headquarters. Dolph would be there and Zerbrowski, probably. They'd know just what to say about the dress.

24

Three o'clock found me at the headquarters for the Regional Preternatural Investigation Team. Another squad had buttons made up for us with the abbreviation RIP bleeding down the front of the button in red or green, your choice. Zerbrowski handed them out, and we all wore them, even Dolph. The first vampire we killed after the buttons arrived came through the morgue with one of the buttons pinned to its shirt. Never did find out who did it. My money was on Zerbrowski.

Zerbrowski met me on the steps leading into the squad room. "If that dress was slit any higher, it'd be a shirt," he said.

I looked him up and down. His pale blue shirt was coming untucked from a pair of dark green dress slacks, his tie so loose, it looked like a bulky necklace. "Jeez, Zerbrowski, is Katie mad at you?"

He frowned. "No, why?"

I motioned at the tie that matched neither shirt nor slacks. "She let you wear this out where people could see you."

He grinned. "I dressed in the dark."

I touched the black-figured tie. "That I believe."

But it didn't faze him. He pushed the door open to the squad room with a flourish. He beamed at me. "Beauty before age."

It was my turn to frown. "What are you up to, Zerbrowski?"

He gave me innocent eyes. "Me, up to something?"

I shook my head and walked through the door. There was a stuffed toy penguin on every desk. Everyone answered phones, filed, worked on their computers. No one paid me any attention. Just the penguins sitting on every desk. It had been almost a year since Dolph and Zerbrowski had seen my penguin collection. The teasing didn't start right away; I thought I was safe. When Zerbrowski got back off sick leave after the new year, the penguins had started showing up at every crime scene. On my car seat, in my trunk. They must have spent a couple of hundred dollars on the things by now.

I still didn't know how to react. Ignore it? Pretend that there weren't a dozen penguins sitting around the room? Collect them as I went through the room and take them home? Get mad? If I could have figured out the reaction that would stop the joke, I'd have given it to them. So far, I'd tried ignoring and collecting. Neither stopped it. In fact, it seemed to be getting worse. I suspected that they were building to some grand climax. I had no idea what and wasn't sure I ever wanted to find out.

"Glad to see everybody's so energetic at three A.M."

"No effort too great, no hour too late," Zerbrowski said.

"Where's Dolph?"

"In the interview room with our victim."

There was something about the way he said it that made me look at him. "Dolph called her the 'supposed' victim over the phone. Why doesn't anyone believe her?"

He smiled. "Dolph would be mad if I spoiled it." He crooked his finger at me. "Come along, little girl. We have someone we want you to meet."

I scowled at him. "If this is some elaborate joke, I am going to be pissed."

He held the door for me. "Did we interrupt your date with Count Dracula?"

"None of your damn business."

A chorus of "ooohs" went through the squad room. I went through the door with everyone calling after me. Some of the suggestions were rude, one physically impossible even with a vampire. Sexual harassment or just being one of the guys, it was always a thin line.

I peeked back through the door and said, "You're all just jealous." That brought more catcalls.

Zerbrowski was waiting on the stairs for me. "I don't know whether you'll flash me more leg if I walk in front of you, looking back, or behind you. I think in front."

"Push it too far, Zerbrowski, and I'll tell Katie on you."

"She knows I'm a lech." He walked down the stairs looking back at me.

I walked down the stairs and let the dress fall where it might. When you wear a dress slit nearly to your hips, even if it is to have a gun handy, you are either comfortable with men looking or you wear something else. "How did you ever convince Katie to date you, let alone marry you?"

"I got her drunk," he said.

I laughed. "I'll ask her next time I'm over for dinner."

He grinned. "She'll give you this cock-and-bull story about something romantic and stupid. Don't believe her." He stopped in front of the first interview room and knocked softly.

Dolph opened the door. He filled the doorway very completely. He isn't just tall, he's bulky like a pro-wrestler. His tie was knotted perfectly, white-starched collar tight to his neck. His grey dress slacks still had a sharp crease. His only concession to the heat and the lateness of the hour was the long white sleeves of his shirt. No jacket. I could count on one hand the times I'd seen Dolph in shirt sleeves.

All cops perfect a bored face or a blank face, some even a mildly amused face. But they all eventually have a face that keeps everything inside. An emptiness settles in their eyes that keeps all their secrets. Dolph gave great blank face when questioning suspects. The look on his face now was angry. I'd never seen him so obviously pissed questioning a suspect.

"What's up?" I asked.

He closed the door behind him, stepping into the hallway. He shook his head. "I don't know why this one's getting to me."

"Tell me," I said.

His eyes flicked to my clothing, as if he'd just noticed. The frown softened into something close to a smile. "Somebody has become a bad influence on your wardrobe."

I frowned at him. "I've got a gun in a bellyband, okay? With the slits, it's easier to get to." I would never have explained my dress to Zerbrowski, but to Dolph . . .

"Ooh," Zerbrowski said. "Flash us, flash us."

Dolph's smile widened enough that his eyes were shiny. "If you're going to flash that much leg, at least it's in a good cause."

I crossed my arms over my stomach. "Is there really a suspect in there or did you call me down here just to yank my chain?"

The smile faded, and the angry frown returned. "She's not the suspect. She's the victim. I know you talked to Perry at the scene, but I want you to hear her story, then tell me what you think." With that, he opened the door. That was Dolph, never liked to influence his people. But frankly, it was a little abrupt. I didn't have time to put my professional face on. I made eye contact with the woman while I still looked sort of surprised.

I had an impression of huge blue eyes, silky blond hair, delicate features, and yet she was tall. Even with her sitting down, I could tell that. Very few women can be both tall and dainty, but she pulled it off.

"Ms. Vicki Pierce, this is Anita Blake. I'd like you to tell her your story."

Ms. Pierce blinked big blue eyes, tears welling in them—not falling, mind you, but glittering. She dabbed at them with a Kleenex. There was a bandage on the side of her neck. "Sergeant Storr, I've told you what happened. I've told you and told you." A single tear slid down her cheek. "I'm so tired, and it's been such a traumatic night. Do I have to tell it all over again?" She leaned towards him in the chair, arms held protectively in front of her, almost pleading with him. A lot of men would have buckled under the sweet pressure of those eyes. Too bad the performance was wasted on Dolph.

"Just one more time for Ms. Blake," he said.

She looked past me to Zerbrowski. "Please, I'm so tired."

Zerbrowski leaned against the wall. "He's the boss."

She'd tried using her womanly wiles, but it wasn't working. She switched to sisterly unity with only a blink of her baby blues. "You're a woman. You know how it is, being so alone among all these—" her voice dropped to a hush—"men." She stared down at the table top, then back up with real tears trailing down her perfect skin.

It was an Oscar-worthy performance. I wanted to applaud, but I'd try sympathy first. There was always time for sarcasm later.

I walked around the table to her and leaned against it without really sitting. I was only inches from her, definitely an invasion of personal space. I patted her shoulder and smiled, though I wasn't a good enough actress for it to reach my eyes. "You're not alone now, Ms. Pierce. I'm here. Please just tell me your story."

"Are you a lawyer?" she asked.

If she asked for a lawyer and was insistent, the interview was over. I knelt in front of her, taking her still trembling hands in mine. I stared up at her. I couldn't manage to look sympathetic but I was interested. I gave her all my attention. I stared at her face like I'd memorize it and said, "Please, Vicki, let me help you."

Her hands had gone very still under mine. She stared at me with her big eyes like a deer that had scented the gun, but thought if it held very still, the gun wouldn't fire. She nodded almost to herself more than to me. She gripped my hands, and her face was utterly sincere.

"I had car trouble, and I went into the bar side of a restaurant to use the phone." She ducked her head, not meeting my eyes. "I know I shouldn't have gone in there. A woman in a bar alone is just asking for trouble. But there weren't any phones anywhere else."

"You have a right to go anywhere you want, anytime you want, Vicki. Being a woman doesn't take away that right." I didn't have to pretend to sound outraged.

She looked at me again, eyes studying my face. I could almost see the wheels in her head turning. She thought she had me. God, she was young.

Her fingers tightened on my hands, a fine tremor going up her arms. "I called a friend of mine to come look at the car. I'm in college and don't have a lot of money, so I didn't want to call a garage right away, not until my friend had seen the car. I hoped he could fix it."

She was volunteering too much information. Already justifying herself. Or maybe she'd just told the story too many times. Naw. "I'd have done the same thing," I said. And I might have.

She squeezed my hands and leaned towards me, a little eager, getting into her story. "There was this man at the bar. He seemed nice. We talked, and he asked me to sit with him. I told him I was waiting for my friend. He said, fine, we'd just talk." Again she looked down. "He said I had the most beautiful skin he'd ever seen." She looked back at me, eyes wide. "I mean, it was so romantic."

It was so rehearsed. "Go on."

"I let him buy me a drink. I know I shouldn't have." She dabbed at her eyes. "I asked if he minded me smoking, and he said no." There was a full ashtray at her elbow. Neither Dolph nor Zerbrowski smoked, which meant little Vicki was damn near a chain smoker.

"He had his arm around me and leaned in to kiss me, I thought." The tears came faster, she hunched over a little, back shaking. "He bit me, on the neck. I swear until that second I didn't realize he was a vampire." She looked at me, from inches away vibrating with sincerity.

I patted her arm. "A lot of people can't tell vampires from humans. Especially if they've fed first."

She blinked at me. "Fed first?"

"If a vampire is full of blood, then he looks more human."

She nodded. "Oh."

"What did you do when he bit you?"

"I threw my drink at him and lit it with my lighter."

"Lit it?" I said, "It, the liquor, or it, the vampire?"

"Both," she said.

I nodded. "Vamps are very combustible. He burned real good, didn't he?"

"I didn't know he'd go up in flames like he did," she said. "A person just doesn't burn like that."

"No," I said, "they don't."

"I started to scream and run away from him. My friend came in the door then. People were shouting and screaming. It was awful."

I stood up. "I bet it was."

She stared up me, blue eyes sincere but not full of horror for what she'd done. There was no remorse. She gripped my arm suddenly, very tight, as if she could will me to understand. "I had to protect myself."

I placed my hand over hers and smiled. "What made you think of lighting the liquor once you'd thrown it?"

"I remembered that vampires were afraid of fire."

"But if you threw a drink in a human's face and lit it, it would only burn until the liquor was gone. A whoosh and it would be all over. A human would leave you alone after that, though they'd be hurt. Weren't you afraid that you'd just make the vampire more angry?"

"But vampires are very combustible, you said it yourself," Vicki said.

My smile widened. "So you knew he'd go up in flames?"

"Yes," she said, clutching me, willing me to understand her plight.

Dolph said, "I thought you didn't know the vampire would go up in flames, Ms. Pierce."

"I didn't, not until he burned like that," she said.

I patted her hand. "But, Vicki dear, you just said you knew he was combustible."

"But you said it first."

"Vicki, you just said you knew he'd go up in flames when you lit him up."

"I didn't."

I nodded. "Yes, you did."

She drew her hands away from me, sitting very straight in her chair. "You are trying to confuse me."

I shook my head. "No, Vicki, you're doing that all on your own." I moved away from her while still maintaining eye contact.

"What's that supposed to mean?" she asked. A little bit of anger peeked through her helpless-damsel act.

"What restaurant was it?" I asked as if I hadn't been there twenty minutes earlier. Interrogations are so often repetitive.

"What?" she asked.

"What was the name of the bar?"

"I don't remember."

"Dolph?" I asked.

"Burnt Offerings," he said.

I laughed. "A notorious vampire hangout."

"It's not in the vampire district," she said. "How was I to know that it was a vampire bar?"

"How about the picture of Christopher Lee as Dracula on the sign outside?"
I said.

"It was quite late and nothing else was open."

"In University City on Delmar on a Friday night? Come on, Vicki. You can
do better than that," I said.

She touched the bandage on her neck with a delicate, trembling hand. "He bit
me." Her voice shook, and more tears trailed down her face.

I walked back to her. I put a hand on either side of her chair and leaned my
face into hers. "You're lying, Vicki."

She burst into tears, hiding her face. I put a finger under her chin and lifted
her face. "Damn, you're good, but not good enough."

She jerked away from me, standing so suddenly, the chair crashed to the floor.
"I was attacked, and you're making me feel like the bad guy. You're a woman. I
thought you'd understand."

I shook my head. "Can the universal sisterhood appeal, Vicki. It don't wash."

She jerked the bandage from her neck and threw it to the floor. "Look, look
what he did to me!"

If she expected me to flinch, she had the wrong girl. I walked up to her, turning
her head to one side. It was vampire fang marks, pretty fresh. A neat, nice bite,
but there was no bruising, no hickey mark spreading across her creamy flesh. It
was just two neat fang marks.

I stepped back from her. "You threw your drink into his face as soon as he
bit you?"

"Yes, I didn't want him touching me."

"A filthy vampire," I said.

"A walking corpse."

She had a point. "Thank you, Vicki, thank you for talking to me." I walked
to the door and motioned Dolph to follow. Zerbrowski stayed behind with Ms.
Pierce.

Dolph closed the door behind us. "What did you see in the bite that I didn't?"
he asked.

"If a vamp plunges fang into you but doesn't have time to feed much, it leaves
a hickey. Just like a human sucking on your neck. The fangs aren't hollow, they
just pierce the skin so that the vamp can suck the blood. One of the reasons they're
so small. If the vamp feeds long enough, he takes blood away from the area and
you don't get marking. No way did a quick bite and suck leave her clean like that.
She had someone else do it ahead of time, and it took a lot more time than a few
seconds."

"I knew she was lying," Dolph said, and shook his head. "But I thought she'd
thrown more on him than a drink. I thought she'd come into the bar with some
sort of accelerant."

I shook my head. "Once you get a vamp burning, they burn until they're put
out or burned to ash. You may get a few bone fragments left, but vamps burn more
completely than any human. Dental records won't even help you."

"The bartender used a fire extinguisher from behind the bar. Witnesses say he
was quick."

I nodded. "Yeah, good ol' Harry. It's a miracle the vamp is still alive. I know there's some hardcore opposition to a vampire business outside the vampire district. There's a petition and some sort of city meeting scheduled. Ms. Pierce will make a great witness to the dangers of vampires being outside the district.''

"The restaurant owner said the bad publicity could ruin him.''

I nodded. "Oh, yeah. It could also be a personal motive against the vampire. Not little Miss Blue Eyes but someone she knows that wanted him dead.''

"She could be a member of Humans First. They'd love all the vamps to burn.''

"A fanatical vampire hater wouldn't let a vamp do their neck like that. No. Humans First might have paid her to discredit the bar. She may be a member of Humans Against Vampires, HAV, or even Humans First, but she doesn't really believe. The bite proves that.''

"Could the vamp have captured her mind?''

"I don't think so, but I've got some better questions for your other witnesses now.''

"Such as?'' he asked.

"Are they sure the vampire in question even got a taste of her? Are they positive that he bit her? Ask them if she smelled of blood when she came in.''

"Explain,'' Dolph said.

"If she came in with the bite, then some of them might have smelled it. Might not, the wound was pretty clean, which was probably why the vamp did it that way. If he'd just bitten her and brought the blood to the surface, the vamps would have all scented it.''

Dolph was writing it all down in his trusty notebook. "So a vamp's involved?''

"He may not know what she was planning to do. I'd check for a vamp boyfriend, maybe, or at least one she's dated. Boyfriend may be too strong a word for Ms. Pierce. I'd see if she has some background in acting. Check out her major in college, maybe.''

"Already done,'' Dolph said. "She's got a background in theater arts.''

I smiled. "Why did you need me? You had it all solved.''

"The bite, the fact that vampires burn that easily . . .'' He shook his head. "None of this shit is in the literature.''

"The books aren't designed for police work, Dolph.''

"Maybe you should do a book,'' he said.

"Yeah, right. Do you have enough to get a warrant for her bank records?''

"If I'm careful what judge I ask, maybe.''

"You know, even if she is charged and convicted, the damage is done. The petition and the meeting are scheduled for next week. All they'll have is rumors of an attack, and it will grow in the telling.''

Dolph nodded. "Nothing we can do about that.''

"You could go down there and tell them what you've learned about Vicki in there.''

"Why don't you do it?''

"Because I'm the whore of Babylon to the right-wingers. I'm boffing the head bloodsucker. They wouldn't believe a damn thing I said.''

"I don't have time to attend civic meetings, Anita.''

"You think the vampire businesses should be segregated?'' I asked.

"Don't go there, Anita. You won't like the answers.''

I dropped it. Dolph thought vampires were monsters that the public needed to be protected from. I even agreed with him to an extent. But I was sleeping with one of the monsters. It made it hard to stay on the same bandwagon as Dolph. We agreed to disagree. It kept the peace and kept us working together.

"If you hate vamps so much, why didn't you buy Ms. Pierce's story?" I asked.

"Because I'm not stupid," Dolph said.

"Sorry," I said. "Sorry that I thought even for a second that personal feelings might interfere with your job. You'd never allow it, would you?"

He smiled. "I don't know. You're not in jail yet."

"If you had proof of wrongdoing, I might be."

"You might," he said. The smile faded from his face. His eyes went empty, cop eyes. "What happened to your hand?"

I glanced down at the bandaged hand as if it had just appeared. "Kitchen accident," I said.

"Kitchen accident," he said.

"Yeah."

"What happened?"

"Sliced my hand with a knife."

"What were you doing?" he asked.

I never cook at home. Dolph knew that. "Slicing a bagel." I gave empty eyes back to him. Once, not long ago, my face showed everything. Every thought plain to see, but not now. I stared at Dolph's suspicious face and knew my face gave him nothing. Only the blankness itself was a clue that I was lying. But he knew I was lying. I wasn't going to waste his time or mine by coming up with a really good lie. Why bother?

We stared at each other. "There's blood on your hose, Anita. That must have been some bagel," he said.

"It was," I said, then couldn't help smiling. "I would have said I was mugged, but you'd want me to fill out a report."

He sighed. "You little shit. You're wrapped up in something else right now. Right this minute." His large hands balled into fists nearly the size of my face. "I'd yell at you, but it wouldn't do any good. I'd throw you in a cell overnight." He laughed, and it was bitter. "For what's left of the night, but I don't have any charges, do I?"

"I haven't done anything, Dolph." I raised the injured hand. "I was doing a favor for a friend, raising some dead. I got cut for more blood. That's it."

"The truth?" he asked.

I nodded. "Yeah."

"Why didn't you just tell me?" he asked.

"Because it was a favor, no money. If Bert finds out I'm raising the dead for free, he'll have a heart attack. He'll believe the bagel story."

Dolph laughed. "He won't ask how you got hurt. He doesn't want to know."

I nodded. "Very true."

"Just in case the kitchen gets any hotter, remember to call if you need help."

"I'll keep it in mind, Dolph."

"You do that." He put up his notebook. "Try not to kill anyone this month,

Anita. Even in clear self-defense you pile up too many bodies, and you're going to get locked up.''

"I haven't killed anyone in over six weeks—hell, nearly seven. I'm cutting down.''

He shook his head. "The last two were the only two we've ever been able to prove, Anita. Both self-defense. One with witnesses out the ass, but we've never found Harold Gaynor's body. Just his wheelchair in that cemetery. Dominga Salvador is still missing.''

I smiled at him. "People say the señora went back to South America.''

"There was blood all over that chair, Anita.''

"Was there?''

"Your luck is going to run out, and I won't be able to help you.''

"I didn't ask for help,'' I said. "Besides, if the new law goes through, I'll have a federal badge.''

"Being a cop, no matter what kind, doesn't mean you can't be arrested.''

It was my turn to sigh. "I'm tired, and I'm going home. Good night, Dolph.''

He looked at me for another second or two, then said, "Good night, Anita.'' He walked back into the interview room and left me standing in the hall.

Dolph had never been this grumpy before he found out I was dating Jean-Claude. I wasn't sure he was aware of how much his attitude had changed towards me, but I certainly was. A little undead nookie and he didn't trust me anymore, not completely.

It made me sad and angry. What was really hard was the fact that less than two months ago I'd have agreed with Dolph. You can't trust anyone who sleeps with the monsters. But here I was, doing it. Me, Anita Blake, turned into coffin bait. Sad, very sad. It wasn't any of Dolph's business who I dated. But I couldn't blame him for the attitude. I didn't like it, but I couldn't bitch about it. Okay, I could bitch, but it wasn't fair of me to do it.

I walked out without going through the main squad room again. I wondered how long they'd keep the penguins on their desks waiting for me to come back. The thought of all those silly-looking toy birds sitting forlornly waiting for me to return brought a smile to my face. But it didn't last. It wasn't just that Dolph mistrusted me. He was a very good cop, a good investigator. If he really started digging, he might get proof. Heaven knew I'd done enough unsanctioned kills to put me in prison. I'd used my animating powers to kill humans. If it could be proved, it was an automatic death sentence. A death sentence for someone who had used magic to kill was not the same sort of sentence as, say, an axe murderer got. A guy could chop up his family and spend the next fifteen years on death row with appeals. There are no appeals for magic-induced murder. Trial, conviction, death within six weeks, usually less.

The prisons are afraid of magic and don't like to keep witches and such around long. There was a sorcerer in Maine who called down demons while in his cell. How anyone left him alone long enough for that particular ritual, I don't know. The people who had goofed all ended up dead, so they couldn't be questioned. They never did find the heads. Even I couldn't raise enough of them as zombies to get them to talk or write down what had happened. It was a mess.

The sorcerer escaped, but was later recaptured with the help of a coven of white witches and, strangely, a group of Satanists. Nobody who performs magic likes it when someone goes rogue. It gives us all a bad name. The last witch burned alive by a mob in this country was only in 1953. Her name was Agnes Simpson. I'd seen the black-and-white photos of her death. Anyone who studied preternatural anything had to have her picture in at least one textbook. The photo that stayed with me was one in which her face was untouched, pale, even from a distance terror plain on her face. Her long brown hair moving in the heat but not yet burning. Only her nightgown and robe had caught fire. Her head thrown back, screaming. The photo won the Pulitzer Prize. The rest of the photos aren't seen as often. A progression of photographs that ends with her burned and blackened and dead.

How anyone could stand there and keep taking pictures, I don't know. Maybe the Pulitzer Prize was a charm against nightmares. Then again, maybe not.

25

I pulled into the lot of the apartment building with its secret hospital in the basement. It was nearly five. Dawn pressed like a cool hand against the wind. The sky was grey, caught between darkness and light. That trembling edge where the vampires are still moving, and you can get your throat ripped out moments from sunrise.

A taxi drew up in front of the building. A tall woman with very short blond hair got out. She was wearing a very short skirt and a leather jacket, no shoes. Zane got out next. Someone had paid his bail, and it wasn't me. Which meant he had been in the Beast Master's tender care. Just luck that he hadn't been part of Sylvie's torment. If he'd refused, he'd have been hurt worse than he appeared to be. If he'd done it, I'd have had to kill him. That would have been damned awkward.

He saw me walking towards them. I put the long coat and its weaponry back on. Zane waved to me, smiling. He was wearing nothing but shiny black vinyl pants, tight enough to be skin, and boots. Oh, and a nipple ring. Mustn't forget the jewelry.

The tall woman stared at me. She didn't look happy to see me. Not hostile exactly, but not pleased. The driver said something, and she got a wad of bills out of her jacket pocket and paid him.

The taxi drove away. Vivian, the Beast Master's pet while he stayed here, hadn't gotten out. Gregory, Stephen's brother with his new conscience, hadn't gotten out either. I was short at least two wereleopards. What was going on?

Zane walked towards me like we were old friends. "I told you, Cherry, she's our alpha, our *léoparde lionné.* I knew she'd save us." He dropped to his knees in front of me. My right hand was in my pocket, gripping the Browning, so he had to settle for my left hand. I'd spent enough time around the werewolves to know that being alpha was a touchie-feelie sort of thing. Like the animals they sometimes were, shapeshifters seemed to need the reassurance of touch. So I didn't fight it, but I did let the safety off the Browning.

Zane took my hand gently, almost reverently. He laid his cheek against my knuckles, then rolled his face from side to side like a cat chin-marking me. His tongue gave one slow lick to the back of my hand, and I gently withdrew it. It took a lot of willpower not to wipe my hand on the coat.

The tall woman, Cherry I presumed, just looked at me. "She didn't save all of us." Her voice was an almost startling low contralto. It purred, even in human form.

"Where are Vivian and Gregory?" I asked.

She pointed back the way they'd come. "Back there, they're still back there."

"The deal was that all my people got out."

Zane bounced to his feet. The movement was so quick it caught my heart and my throat, and my finger went from trigger-guard to trigger. I set the safety on the Browning and eased my hand out. They weren't going to hurt me but if Zane kept bouncing around like a punk version of Tigger I might accidently fire the gun. My nerves were usually better than this.

"The Master of Beasts said that anyone who wished to acknowledge your dominance could leave, if they could walk out. But he'd already made sure that Gregory and Vivian couldn't walk."

Something cold and tight filled my stomach. "What do you mean?"

"Vivian was unconscious when we left." Cherry looked at the ground when she spoke the next words. "Gregory tried to crawl after us, but he was hurt too badly." She raised her eyes, and there were tears trembling in them. She kept her eyes very wide. "He cried after us. Begged us not to leave him." She wiped at the tears with an angry swipe of her hand. "But I left him. I left him screaming, because I wanted out of there more than anything else in the world. Even if it meant leaving my friends to be tortured and killed and raped." She hid her face with both her hands and cried.

Zane came up behind her and hugged her. "Gabriel could never keep us all safe either. She did her best."

"Like hell," I said.

Zane looked at me. He rubbed his cheek against the side of Cherry's neck, but his eyes were serious. He was glad to be alive, but he hadn't wanted to leave them.

"I'm going to make a phone call." I walked into the building and after a few seconds they followed me. I used the same phone I'd called Jean-Claude on earlier. I only had moments before true dawn, and he would be down for the count.

He answered the phone like he'd been expecting the call. *"Oui, ma petite."*

"Gregory and Vivian didn't make it. I thought you negotiated for them."

"The others forced Padma to agree, but he set up one rule, that whoever wished to leave had to walk out. I knew what he meant to do, but it was the best bargain I could make. Please believe that."

"Fine, but I won't leave them. If they can split hairs this finely, so can we."

"What do you plan, *ma petite?*"

"I'm going back and help them walk out. Padma didn't say anything about walking out under their own power, did he?"

"No." Jean-Claude gave a long sigh. "Dawn is frightfully near, *ma petite*. If you must do this thing, wait at least two hours. Time enough for even the most powerful of us to be asleep, but do not wait much longer. I do not know how much sleep the council members need. They may awaken very early."

"I'll wait two hours."

"I will send some of the wolves to you. With Padma asleep they will be useful to you."

"Fine."

"I must go." The phone went dead, and I felt the sun burst above the horizon. I felt it like a great weight, and for just an instant I couldn't breathe, my body felt heavy, so heavy. Then the sensation was gone, and I knew that Jean-Claude was gone for the day. Even with three shared marks, I'd never felt anything like that before. I knew he protected me from things that the third mark would let me feel. He even protected Richard. Of the three of us, Jean-Claude knew more about the marks, how to use them, how not to use them, and what they really meant. Months into it all, and I hadn't asked many questions. Sometimes, I wasn't sure I wanted to know. Richard seemed equally reluctant, according to Jean-Claude. The vampire just seemed patient with us, like a parent with a backward child.

Cherry leaned against the wall, arms crossed over her stomach. She wasn't wearing anything under the leather jacket. Her eyes were cautious, like she'd been disappointed often and badly.

"You're going in after them. Why?"

Zane was sitting by her legs, back against the wall. "Because she's our alpha."

Cherry shook her head. "Why would you risk yourself for two people you don't know? I accepted your dominance because I wanted out of there, but I don't believe it. Why would you go back in there?"

I wasn't sure how to explain it. "They expect me to save them."

"So?" she said.

"So, I'm going to try."

"Why?"

I sighed. "Because . . . because I remember Vivian's pleading eyes and the bruises on her body. Because Gregory cried and screamed for you not to leave him. Because Padma will hurt them worse now than he would have before, because he thinks that by hurting them, he hurts me." I shook my head. "I'm going to find a bed for a couple of hours. I suggest you do the same. But you don't have to come with me. This thing is strictly volunteer."

"I don't want to go back there," she said.

"Then don't," I said.

"I'll come," Zane said.

It almost made me smile. "Somehow I knew you would."

26

I lay in the narrow hospital bed in one of the spare rooms. The evening dress was folded on the room's only chair. The chair was shoved up under the doorknob. Flimsy lock. The chair wouldn't keep out someone truly determined, but it would give me a few seconds to aim. I'd showered and thrown the blood-soaked hose away. I was wearing just my panties. They didn't even have a spare hospital gown. I fell asleep in a strange bed with sheets clutched to my naked breasts, and the Firestar under my pillow. The machine gun was under the bed. I didn't think I'd need it, but where else was I going to stash it?

I was dreaming. Something about being lost in an abandoned house, searching for kittens. The kittens were crying, and there were snakes in the dark, eating the kittens. You didn't have to be Freud to interpret this one. The moment I thought that clearly, that it was a dream and what it meant, the dream melted away and left me awake in the dark. I woke staring upwards, sheets spilled down my body so that I was nearly nude in the blackness.

I could feel my body pulsing. It was like I'd been running a race in my sleep. There was sweat under my breast. Something was wrong.

I pulled the sheet up over me as I sat up, even though I wasn't cold. As a child I'd thought that the monsters in the closet and under the bed couldn't get me if I was covered. After waking from a nightmare I still reached for the sheet, no matter how hot it was. Of course, I was in a basement with air-conditioning. It wasn't hot. So why did my body feel almost fevered?

I reached under the pillow and got the Firestar out. I felt better with it gripped in my hand. If I'd just been spooked by a dream, I was going to feel silly.

I sat in the dark and strained to hear anything before I hit the lights. If there was someone out in the hall, they'd see the light under the door. If they were trying to ambush me, I didn't want them to see the light. Not yet.

I felt something coming down the hallway towards me. A roil of energy, heat, that played over my body like a hand. It was like a storm was rushing towards me, with that prickling brush of lightning growing like weight in the room. I clicked the safety off on the Firestar, and suddenly knew who it was. It was Richard. Richard striding towards me. Richard coming like an angry storm.

I clicked the safety back on but didn't put up the gun. He was mad. I could feel it. I'd seen him toss a solid oak four poster king-size bed around like it was nothing when he was angry. I'd keep the gun, just in case. I didn't like keeping it, but the moral dilemma didn't bother me enough to put it away. I hit the lights. I sat blinking in the sudden brightness, a hard knot forming in my stomach. I did not want to see him. I hadn't known what to say to him since the night I'd first slept with Jean-Claude. The night I'd run from Richard, run from what he was on the night of the full moon. Run from the sight of his beast.

I padded barefoot to the chair and gathered my clothes up. I was struggling into the strapless bra, gun beside me on the bed, when I smelled his after-shave. I felt the air move under the door and knew it was his body disrupting the currents of air. His after-shave wasn't that strong. I shouldn't have smelled it. I knew suddenly as if it had been whispered in my ear that Richard could smell me through the door, that he knew I'd worn Oscar de la Renta parfume for Jean-Claude.

I felt his fingertips press to either side of the door in a small push up motion, felt him draw a breath and scent my body deep into him.

What the hell was going on? We'd been bound for two months, and I'd never felt anything like this, not with Richard, and not with Jean-Claude.

Richard's voice, achingly familiar: "Anita, I need to talk to you." The anger was in his voice; in his body, rage. He was like thunder pressed against the door.

"I'm getting dressed," I said.

I heard him pace in front of the door. "I know. I can feel you in there. What's happening to us?"

That was a loaded question if ever I'd heard one. I was wondering if he could feel my hands as I'd felt his a moment ago. "We haven't been this close at dawn since we were bound. Jean-Claude isn't here to act as a buffer." I hoped that was it. The only alternative I could think of was that the council had done something to our marks. I didn't think that was it, though. But we wouldn't know for sure until we could ask Jean-Claude. Damn.

Richard tried the door handle. "What's taking so long?"

"I'm almost done," I said. I slipped the dress on. It was actually the easiest piece of clothing to get into. The shoes were not comfortable without hose, but I would have felt even less prepared barefoot. Can't explain it, but shoes make me feel better. I moved the chair and unlocked the door. I stepped back, a little too quick, until I was on the far side of the room. I put my hands behind me, still holding the gun. I didn't think he'd hurt me, but I'd never felt him like this. His anger was like a burning knot in my gut.

He opened the door carefully, as if he was having to think before each movement. His control was a trembling line between his rage and me.

He was six foot one, broad-shouldered, with high-sculpted cheekbones, and a wide soft mouth. There was a dimple in his chin, and he was altogether too handsome. His eyes were still perfect chocolate brown; only the pain in them was new. His hair fell in thick waves around his shoulders, a brown so full of gold and copper highlights that there should have been a different word for it. Brown is a dull word, and his hair was not dull. I'd loved running my hands through his hair, grabbing fistfuls of it when we kissed.

He was wearing a blood-red tank top that left his muscular shoulders and arms bare. I knew that every inch of him you could see, and what you could not, was tanned a nice soft brown. But it wasn't really tanned, just his natural skin color.

My heart was beating in my throat, but it wasn't fear. He stared at me in the black dress. Face scrubbed clean of makeup, my hair uncombed, and I felt his body react to the sight of me. I felt it like a twist in my own body. I had to close my eyes to keep from looking at his jeans to see if what I was feeling was visible.

When I opened my eyes, he hadn't moved. He just stood there in the middle of the room, hands balled into fists, breathing a little too hard. His eyes were wild, showing too much white like a horse about to bolt.

I found my voice first. "You said you wanted to talk, so talk." I sounded breathless. It was like I could feel Richard's heart, his chest rising and falling, like it was my own. I'd had moments of this with Jean-Claude, but never with Richard. If we'd still been seeing each other, it would have been intriguing. Now, it was just confusing.

He relaxed his hands, flexing them, fighting not to make fists. "Jean-Claude said he was protecting us from each other. Keeping us from getting too close until we were ready. I didn't believe him, until now."

I nodded. "It's awkward."

He smiled, and shook his head, but the smile never took the anger out of his eyes. "Awkward? Is that all it is to you, Anita? Just awkward?"

"You can feel what I'm feeling, right now, Richard. Answer your own damn question."

He closed his eyes and pressed his hands together in front of his chest. He pressed his palms together until his arms trembled with the effort and the muscles corded, straining against his skin all the way up to his shoulders.

I felt him withdraw from me. Though that doesn't cover how it felt. It was like he built a wall between us. He was raising mental shields between us. Someone had to. I hadn't thought to try. The sight and feel of him in my mind had turned me into a pulsing hormone. It was too embarrassing for words.

I watched his body relax, a muscle at a time, until he opened his eyes, slowly, almost sleepily, his body quiet, at peace. I'd never been that good at meditation.

He lowered his arms and looked at me. "Better?"

I nodded. "Yes, thank you."

He shook his head. "Don't thank me. It was either control it or run screaming."

We stood there, staring at each other. The silence was uncomfortably thick. "What do you want, Richard?"

He gave a choking laugh that brought heat in a rush up my face. "You know what I meant," I said.

"Yes," he said, "I know what you meant. You invoked your status as lupa while I was out of town."

"You mean protecting Stephen?"

He nodded. "You had no right to go against Sylvie's express orders. She was the one I left in charge, not you."

"She'd removed pack protection from him. Do you know what that means?"

"Better than you do," he said. "Without protection of a dominant you're anybody's meat that wants you, like the wereleopards after you killed Gabriel."

I pushed away from the wall. "If you had told me what was happening to them, Richard, I'd have helped them."

"Would you?" he asked. He motioned to the gun in my hand. "Or would you just have killed them?"

"No, that's what Sylvie wanted to do, not me." But I stood there with the gun in my hand and didn't know a graceful way to put it down.

"I know how much you hate shapeshifters, Anita. I didn't think you'd give a damn, and no one else did either or they'd have told you. They all thought you wouldn't care. I mean if you could reject someone you supposedly loved because they turned into a monster once a month, what chance did strangers have?"

He was being deliberately cruel. I'd never seen him do anything just to hurt, just to try and dig the knife in a little deeper. It was petty, and that was one thing Richard was not.

"You know me better than that," I said.

"Do I?" he said. He sat down on the bed, grabbing two handfuls of sheet. He raised the cloth to his face and took a long deep breath. He watched me with angry eyes while he did it. "The smell of you still moves me like some kind of drug, and I hate you for it."

"I just spent a few minutes inside your head, remember. You don't hate me, Richard. It'd be less painful if you did."

He crumpled the sheet in his lap, hands balling the cloth into tight fists. "Love doesn't conquer all, does it?" he asked.

I shook my head. "No, it doesn't."

He stood in an almost violent movement, pacing the room in a tight circle. He came to stand in front of me. There was no "magic" now, just two people. But it was still hard to stand so close to him. Still hard to know I wasn't allowed to touch him anymore. Dammit, it shouldn't have been this hard. I'd made my choice.

"You were never my lover, now you're not even my girlfriend. You are not a shapeshifter. You cannot be my lupa."

"Are you really angry that I protected Stephen?"

"You ordered pack members to guard him and a wereleopard. You told them you'd kill them if they didn't obey you. You don't have that right."

"You gave me that right when you made me lupa." I held up a hand to keep him from interrupting. "And whether you like it or whether you don't, it was a good thing that I had some clout to throw around. Stephen might be dead now if I hadn't been there for him. And Zane would have caused an even worse mess at the hospital. Lycanthropes don't need any more bad press."

"We're monsters, Anita. You can't have good press if you're a monster."

"You don't believe that."

"You believe we're monsters, Anita. You proved that. You'd rather sleep with a corpse than let me touch you."

"What do you want me to say, Richard? That I'm sorry I couldn't cope? I am sorry. That I'm still embarrassed that I ran to Jean-Claude's bed? I am. That I think less of myself for not being able to love you even after what I saw you do to Marcus?''

"You wanted me to kill Marcus."

"He was going to kill you if you didn't. So yeah, I wanted you to kill Marcus. But I didn't tell you to eat him."

"When a pack member is killed in a dominance struggle, we all feed. It's a way to absorb their energy. Marcus and Raina aren't really gone as long as the pack remains."

"You ate Raina, too?"

"Where did you think the bodies went? Did you think your friends on the police force had hidden all the corpses?"

"I thought Jean-Claude had arranged it."

"He did, but it was the pack that did the dirty work. The vampires don't care about a body once it's cold. If the blood isn't warm, they don't want it."

I almost asked if he preferred warm flesh to cold, but didn't. I didn't really want to know. This entire conversation was going nowhere that I wanted to be. I looked at the watch on my wrist. "I've got to go, Richard."

"Go rescue your wereleopards."

I looked at him. "Yes."

"That's why I'm here. I'm your backup."

"Was that Jean-Claude's idea?"

"Sylvie told me that Gregory refused to harm her. Regardless of what they did under Gabriel, they're lycanthropes and we help our own even if they aren't lukoi."

"Do the wereleopards have a fancy name for themselves?" I asked.

He nodded. "They call themselves pard. The werewolves are the lukoi. The leopards are the pard."

I walked past him, shoulder brushing his bare arm. That one touch raised the hairs on my body like he'd touched something much more personal. But I'd get used to it. I'd made my choice, and no matter how confused I was, I wasn't that confused. So I still lusted after Richard, even loved him. I'd picked the vampire, and you can't have your vampire and your werewolf, too.

I got the machine gun out from under the bed and slid the strap across my chest.

"Jean-Claude said that we weren't supposed to kill anybody," Richard said.

"He knew you were coming here?" I asked.

He nodded.

I smiled, but it wasn't happy.

"He didn't tell you?" Richard asked.

"No."

We were left looking at each other again. "You can't trust him, Anita, you know that."

"You're the one who let him give you the first mark voluntarily. What I did, Richard, I did to save your lives, both of you. If you really thought he was so damn untrustworthy, why'd you bind us to him?"

Richard looked away then, and spoke very softly, "I didn't think I'd lose you."

"Go wait in the hall, Richard."

"Why?"

"I've got to finish getting dressed."

His gaze slid to my legs, very white against the blackness of the dress and the heels. "Hose," he said, softly.

"A new holster, actually," I said. "The hose got trashed last night. Now, please get out."

He did. He didn't even make a last cutting remark. It was an improvement. When he closed the door behind him, I sat down on the bed. I did not want to do this. Going back in for the leopards was a bad idea. Going in with Richard as backup was worse. But we'd do it. I couldn't tell him to stay home. Besides, I needed the backup. No matter how emotionally painful it was to be around him, he was one of the most powerful shapeshifters I'd ever met. If he hadn't been crippled by a conscience the size of Rhode Island, he'd have been dangerous. Of course, Marcus would probably have said Richard was plenty dangerous just as he was. And he'd be right.

27

Richard drove his 4 × 4 to the Circus. I sat beside him, but in some ways I might as well not have been there at all. He never looked at me, let alone spoke. But the tension in his body was enough. He knew I was there.

Cherry and Zane rode in the back seat. It had surprised me when Cherry slid into the car. Her eyes flashed white, eyelids fluttering like a nervous tic. She looked like she was going to faint. Zane was his usual self; smiling, eyes secret. His usual self? That was almost funny. I'd known him less than twenty-four hours. I didn't know what the hell was "usual" for him.

Cherry had sunk down on the seat, hugging herself. She was slowly curling into a little ball. I'd known her less time than I'd known Zane, but this wasn't normal for anybody.

I turned as far as the seat belt would allow and said, "What's wrong, Cherry?"

Her eyes rolled to me, then closed, tight. She shook her head and huddled further into herself. There was a fresh bruise forming on her cheek. She might have had it when I first saw her. I just wasn't sure.

"Zane, what's wrong with her?"

"She's scared," he said. His voice was neutral, but there was something in his face that was angry.

"I told her this was strictly voluntary. She doesn't have to come."

"Tell that to Mr. Macho," he said. He was staring at the back of Richard's head.

I turned in the seat until I was staring at his profile. He wouldn't look at me. "What's going on, Richard?"

"She's coming," he said, voice very quiet.

"Why?"

"Because I said so."

"Bullshit."

He glanced at me then. He tried for it to be a cool look, but it was angry. "You're my lupa, but I am still Ulfric. My word is still law."

"Fuck that. You are not dragging her into this because you're mad at me."

The muscle in his jaw clenched tight enough for me to see it. "They both deserted their people. Now they are both going to make it right." His voice was still quiet, low, and careful, like if he wasn't very careful he'd lose control. He spoke like people talk when they want to yell.

"Look at her, Richard. She'll be worse than useless. She'll just be one more victim we have to keep safe."

He shook his head. "You don't leave one of your own behind, not for any reason. It's the law."

"Pack law, but she's not pack."

"Until you stop being my lupa, Anita, what belongs to you, belongs to me."

"You arrogant prick."

He smiled, but it was just a baring of teeth, more snarl than humor. "Everyone has to do something to take the edge off."

It took me a second to realize what he meant, then I was embarrassed. But I'd be damned if I'd sit there and explain that I hadn't meant it literally. He knew I hadn't meant it literally. He was trying to embarrass me. Fuck it. "Did you hit Cherry?"

He was suddenly very interested in the road, but his hands smoothed on the steering wheel. He didn't like that he'd hit her. Neither did I.

"You wanted me to be strong. Well, you got your wish."

"There is a difference between being strong and being cruel, Richard."

"Really? I never could tell the difference."

I think that last was meant for me. But you can only make me feel guilty for so long, and then I just get mad. "Fine, if what belongs to me belongs to you, then it works the other way too."

He glanced at me, frowning. "What do you mean?"

I liked the unease in his face. I enjoyed turning his logic back on him. In my own way, I was just as angry at him as he was at me. I didn't have his moral high ground, but I hadn't turned cannibal either. Maybe I did have some moral high ground, after all.

"If you can force Cherry to go with us, then I can order the pack to guard Stephen. I can order them to do any damn thing I'm dominant enough to make them do."

"No," he said.

"Why not?" I asked.

"Because I said so."

I laughed then, and even to me it sounded bitchy.

He screamed, a long ragged yell of frustration and anger. "God, Anita, God."

"We're going to cut each other up if we don't work something out," I said.

He glanced at me again. His eyes weren't angry anymore. They were almost panic-stricken. "You're sleeping with the vampire. There's nothing to work out."

"The three of us are bound to each other for what could be a very, very long time, Richard. We're going to have to find a way to live together."

He laughed, and it was bitter. "Live together? You want a house for three with Jean-Claude down in the basement and me chained out in the yard?"

"Not exactly, but you can't keep hating yourself like this."

"It's not me I hate. It's you."

I shook my head. "If that were true, I'd leave you alone. But you hate your beast and your beast is you."

He pulled in front of the Circus. "We're here." He turned off the engine and silence filled the car. "Cherry can wait here."

"Thank you, Richard," I said.

He shook his head. "Don't thank me, Anita." He smoothed his hands over his face into his hair, combing his fingers through it. The gesture showed his arms and chest to wonderful advantage. He'd never been aware of how much the simplest thing he did had moved me. "Don't thank me." He got out of the car.

I told Cherry to stay low. I didn't want them to get any ideas about taking her while we were inside rescuing the others. It would sort of defeat the purpose of the entire trip.

Zane kissed her on the forehead the way you'd calm a child. He told her everything would be all right, that I'd keep them safe. God, I hoped he was right.

28

A man had walked up to meet Richard. He'd been waiting for him. I reached in the coat pocket and clicked off the safety on the Browning because I knew him.

Zane, who was very close behind me asked, "Is something wrong?"

I shook my head. "Hello, Jamil."

"Hello, Anita." He was just shy of six feet, wearing a white tank top almost the twin of the one Richard wore. Except that Jamil had cut out the neck, arms, and chopped out the middle of the shirt so that his slender waist and cobblestone abs showed. The white tank top was in startling contrast to the rich solid brown of his skin. His hair was waist-length, worked in thin corn rows intertwined with bright beads. He was wearing white sweat pants and looked like he'd just come from the gym.

The last time I'd seen Jamil he'd been trying to kill Richard. "What are you doing here?" Even to me it didn't sound friendly.

He smiled, a quick baring of teeth. "I'm Richard's enforcer."

"So?"

"They allowed us each one backup, plus the wereleopards," Richard said. He spoke without looking at me, staring at the front of the Circus rising into the bright sunlight.

"I'm short one wereleopard and a backup," I said.

He did look at me then. His face was as closed and guarded as I'd seen it. "I thought Jean-Claude had told you, and you'd just decided against any backup."

"I'd take backup into hell, Richard. You know that."

"Don't blame me if your boyfriend forgot to mention it."

"He probably thought you'd mention it."

He just looked at me with his angry eyes.

"Is there anything else you forgot to tell me?"

"He just said to tell you, don't kill anyone."

"He mention anyone in particular not to kill?" I asked.

Richard frowned then. "As a matter of fact, he did." He said the next in a bad French accent. " 'Tell *ma petite* not to kill Fernando no matter what the provocation.' "

It brought a tight smile to my face. "Fine."

Jamil was staring at me. "The look on your face, babe. That is the most evil little smile I've ever seen. What did this Fernando do to you?"

"To me personally, nothing."

"He raped your Geri, your second in command," Zane said.

Both of the werewolves stared at him, a sudden flash of hostility that made Zane step back. He moved a little behind me, which didn't quite work since he was nearly a foot taller. Hard to cower behind someone who's shorter than you are.

"He raped Sylvie?" Richard asked.

I nodded.

"He has to be punished," Richard said.

I shook my head. "I told Sylvie I'd kill him. That we'd kill them all."

"All?" Richard made it a question.

"All," I said.

He looked away then, not meeting my eyes. He asked without turning around, "How many?"

"Two that she's told me about. There may be more, but if there is, she's not ready to talk about it yet."

"You're sure there was more than just this Fernando?" Richard looked at me, eyes hopeful, almost like he wanted me to tell him it wasn't really as bad as it seemed.

"It was gang rape, Richard. They took great pride in telling me that."

"Who was the second one?" he asked.

He asked. I answered. "Liv."

He blinked at me. "She's a woman."

"I'm aware of that."

He just stared at me. "How?"

I raised eyebrows at him. "You really want me to get that technical?"

Richard shook his head. He looked ill. Jamil didn't. He met my eyes without flinching, his face thinned into tight angry lines. "If they can take one of our highest wolves and use her like that, then the pack's threat means nothing."

"That, too," I said. "But I'm not going to kill someone just to keep the pack's rep in good repair."

"Then why?" Jamil said.

I thought about that for a second. "Because I gave my word I'd do it. They dug their grave when they touched her. All I'm doing is filling in the dirt."

"Why?" Jamil said. "You hated Sylvie." It seemed important to him that I answer, as if the question meant more than it should have, at least to him.

"They didn't break her. All that they did to her, and they couldn't break her. She could have stopped the torture by giving up the pack. She didn't give them up." I tried to put it all into words. "That kind of loyalty and strength deserves the same in return."

"What do you know about loyalty?" Richard asked.

"That's it," I said. I turned to him and poked a finger in his chest. "We can have one knock-down-glorious fight after we save Gregory and Vivian. They gang-raped Sylvie. Do you really think they're doing less to two shapeshifters that they thought had no alpha to protect them?" I was spitting every word into his face, voice squeezed tight and low, because if I let go, I'd be screaming. "We are going to get them out and take them some place safe. When we do all that, then you can go back to being pissed at me. You can wrap your jealousy and self-hatred around us both until we choke. But right this second, we have work to do. Okay?"

He looked at me for a heartbeat or two, then gave the barest of nods. "Okay."

"Great," I said. I'd abandoned my purse at the hospital, but I had the key to the front door in my coat pocket along with ID. What else did a girl need?

"You have a key to the front door?" Richard asked.

"Drop it, Richard," I said.

"You're right. You're right, and I'm wrong. I haven't been paying attention to business for two months. Sylvie told me that. I didn't listen. Maybe if I had, she . . . Maybe if I'd been listening, she wouldn't have gotten hurt."

"Jesus, Richard, don't pull another guilt trip on me. You could be Attila the Hun, and the council would still have come. No show of strength would have kept them out."

"What would have?" he asked.

I shook my head. "They are the council, Richard. The stuff of nightmares. Nightmares don't care how strong you are."

"What do they care about?" he asked.

I shoved the key into the lock. "Scaring you." The big double doors pushed inward. I drew the Browning out of my pocket.

"We aren't supposed to kill anybody," Richard said.

"I remember," I said, but I kept the gun out. I couldn't kill anybody, but Jean-Claude hadn't said I couldn't maim someone. It might not be as satisfying, but when you need to back up your threat, someone writhing on the floor in pain is almost as good as a body. Sometimes it's better.

29

I stood with my back to the closed door, the others fanned out around me. Soft filtered light came down from the high, high windows. The midway looked dark and tired in the morning sunlight. The Ferris wheel towered over the haunted house and mirror maze and the game booths. It was a complete traveling carnival that didn't travel. It smelled like it was suppose to: cotton candy, corn dogs, funnel cakes.

Two men stepped out of the huge circus tent that took up one entire corner. They walked towards us side by side. The taller man was about six foot, square-shouldered, with hair that was somewhere between blond and brown. The hair was straight, thick, and just long enough to trail the edge of his shirt collar. White dress shirt tucked into white jeans, complete with white belt. He wore white loafers, no socks. He looked like he should have been walking along a beach in a credit-card commercial, except for his eyes. Even from a distance there was something odd about his eyes. They were orangish. People didn't have eyes that color.

The second man was about five foot seven, with dark gold hair cut very short. A brownish mustache graced his upper lip and curved back to meet brownish sideburns. Nobody had worn a mustache like that since the 1800's. His white pants were tight and slid into polished black boots. A white vest and a white shirt peeked out from beneath a red jacket. He looked like he should have been riding to the hounds, chasing small furred animals.

His eyes were a nice normal brown. But the first man's eyes just got stranger the closer he came to us. His eyes were yellow—not amber, not brown—yellow with orange spikes radiating from the pupil like a pinwheel of color. They were not human eyes, no way, no how.

If it hadn't been for the eyes, I wouldn't have recognized him as a lycanthrope, but the eyes gave it away. I'd seen pictures of tigers with eyes like that.

They stopped a little distance from us. Richard moved up beside me, Zane and Jamil at our backs. We all stood looking at each other. If I hadn't known better, I'd have said that the two men looked uncomfortable or embarrassed.

The smaller man said, "I am Captain Thomas Carswell. You must be Richard Zeeman." His voice was British and upper-crust, but not too upper-crust.

Richard took a step forward. "I'm Richard Zeeman. This is Anita Blake, Jamil, and Zane."

"I am Gideon," the man with the eyes said. His voice was almost painfully low, as if even in human speech he growled. The sound was so low that it made my spine thrum.

"Where are Vivian and Gregory?" I said.

Captain Thomas Carswell blinked and looked at me. He didn't look happy about the interruption. "Nearby."

"First," said Gideon, "we need your gun, Miss Blake."

I shook my head. "I don't think so."

They exchanged glances. "We cannot allow you to go forward with a gun in your hand, Miss Blake," Carswell said.

"Every time someone wants to take my gun, it means either they don't trust me or they're planning to do something I don't like."

"Please," Gideon said in his gravelly voice. "Surely you must understand our reluctance. You do have a certain reputation."

"Anita?" Richard said, half-question, half-something else.

I clicked the safety on the gun and held it out to Gideon. I had two more guns and two knives left. They could have the Browning.

Gideon took the gun from me and stepped back to stand beside Carswell. "Thank you, Miss Blake."

I nodded. "You're welcome."

"Shall we go?" Carswell said. He offered me his arm as if he were escorting me to dinner.

I stared at him, then back at Richard. I raised my eyebrows, trying to ask what he thought without asking.

He gave a half-shrug.

I slid my left arm through Carswell's arm. "You're being very civilized about this," I said.

"There is no reason to lose all good manners just because things have become . . . somewhat extreme."

I let him lead me towards the tent. Gideon fell into step with Richard. They were almost the same height, and the roil of energy that came off them made the hair on my neck stand up. They were trying each other's power, tasting each other without doing anything at all but lowering their hard-won control. Jamil and Zane brought up the rear like good soldiers.

We were almost at the tent when Carswell stopped, hand tightening on my arm. I slid my right hand behind my back, under the coat, touching the machine gun.

"There is something heavy on your back, Miss Blake. Something that is not a purse." His grip on my left arm grew tighter, not hurting, but I knew he wouldn't let go, not without a fight.

I swung the machine gun around on its strap with my right hand and put the barrel into his chest, not shoving, just there, like his hand on my other arm.

"Everybody be calm," I said.

The other men were suddenly very, very still. "We are going to give you your people, Miss Blake," Gideon growled. "There is no need for this."

"Thomas here asked what I had on my back. I'm showing him."

"You do not know me well enough to call me by my Christian name, Miss Blake," Carswell said.

I blinked at him. There was no fear in him. He was human—one pull on the trigger and he was gone—but there was no fear. I stared into his brown eyes and saw only . . . sadness. A tired sorrow as if he'd almost welcome it.

I shook my head. "Sorry, Captain Carswell."

"We cannot possibly let you go inside the tent with this weapon." His voice was very calm, matter of fact.

"Be reasonable, Anita," Richard said. "If things were reversed, you'd want them without weapons."

The trouble was I had to take off the coat to take off the machine gun. If I took off the coat, they'd see the knives. I didn't want to lose the knives. Of course, I'd still have the Firestar.

I let the machine gun slide back out of sight. "I'll have to remove my coat."

Carswell released my arm cautiously and stepped back, still close enough to grab me. I stared at his careful clothing. The jacket was too tailored for a shoulder holster, the pants had no pockets, but he could have had something at the small of his back.

"I'll remove my coat if you remove yours," I said.

"I have no weapons, Miss Blake."

"Remove your coat and I'll believe you."

He sighed and slid out of the red jacket, then turned in a full circle, arms spread to his sides. "As you see, no weapons." To be really sure I'd need to pat him down, but I didn't want him returning the favor, so I let it go.

I slipped out of the coat and watched his eyes widen at the wrist sheaths. "Miss Blake, I am impressed and disappointed."

I let the coat fall to the floor and slipped the strap over my head. I hated giving up the machine gun, but . . . I did understand. They'd been doing awful things to Gregory and Vivian. I wouldn't necessarily trust me with a gun if I were in their place. I took the clip out of the gun and handed the weapon to Carswell.

His eyes widened a little. "Fearful that I will turn on you and your friends?"

I shrugged. "Can't blame a girl for being cautious."

He smiled, and it almost reached his eyes. "No, I suppose I cannot."

I slid one of the knives out of its sheath and handed it to him hilt-first.

He waved it away. "You may keep your knives, Miss Blake. They will only be protection if someone gets very close, very personal. I think a lady should be allowed to defend her honor."

Damn, he was being nice, gentlemanly. If I kept the second handgun and he found out later, he might not be so nice. "Damn," I said.

Carswell frowned.

"I have one more gun."

"It must be very well concealed, Miss Blake."

I sighed again. "Inconveniently so, yes. Do you want it or not?"

He glanced back at Gideon, who nodded. "Yes, please, Miss Blake."

"Everybody turn their backs."

Amused or bemused looks all around.

"I have to raise the dress and flash the room to get the gun. I don't want anyone peeking." All right, it was stupid and juvenile, but I still couldn't just raise the dress in front of five men. My daddy brought me up better than that.

Carswell turned without being asked a second time. I got some very amused looks, but everyone turned, except for Gideon. "I would be a poor bodyguard if I allowed you to shoot us in the back while we were defending your modesty." He had a point.

"All right, I'll turn my back." Which I did, fishing the gun out for the last time. The bellyband was a good idea, but the Firestar was going in the other coat pocket when I got it back. I was tired of messing with it.

I handed the gun to Gideon. He took it, still looking amused. "Is that everything except for the knives?"

"Yes," I said.

"Your word of honor?"

I nodded. "My word."

He nodded, too, as if that was enough. I knew already that Carswell was someone's human servant. He was the genuine article, a British soldier of Queen Victoria's army. But until that moment I hadn't known that Gideon was as old. Lycanthropes don't age that slowly. He was getting help from somewhere or he was more than just a shapeshifter.

"Lycanthrope," I said, "but what else are you?"

He smiled then, flashing small fangs top and bottom. The only other lycanthrope I'd seen with fangs like that had been Gabriel. You get things like that if you spend too much time in animal form.

"Guess," he said in a whisper so low and rumbling it made me shiver.

Carswell said, "May we turn around, Miss Blake?"

"Sure," I said.

He slid his jacket back on, smoothing it in place, and offered me his arm once more. "Shall we, Miss Blake?"

"Anita, my name's Anita."

He smiled. "Then you may call me Thomas." He said it as if he didn't let a lot of people call him by his first name.

It made me smile. "Thank you, Thomas."

He tucked my arm more securely in the crook of his own. "I do wish . . . Anita, that our meeting could be under better circumstances."

I met his sad eyes and said, "What's happening to my people while you delay me here with your polite smiles?"

He sighed. "I am hoping he will be finished before we walk in upon them." A look almost like pain crossed his face. "It is not a sight fit for a lady."

I tried to pull my arm free, and he gripped it more tightly. His eyes weren't sad anymore. They were full of something I couldn't read. "Know that this is not my choice."

"Let go of me, Thomas."

He let me draw my arm free of him. I was suddenly afraid of what was inside the tent. I'd never spoken with Vivian, and Gregory was a perverted piece of shit, but I suddenly didn't want to see what had happened to them.

Gideon said, "Thomas, should she . . . ?"

"Let her," he said. "She has only the knives."

I didn't exactly run, but I was close when I reached the closed flap of the tent. I heard Richard say, "Anita . . ."

I felt him coming up behind me, but I didn't wait. I flung the flap aside and stepped inside. The tent had just one ring, the center ring. Gregory lay in a naked heap in the center of that ring, hands bound behind his back with thick grey tape. His body was a mass of bruises and cuts. I could see bone glistening in his legs, jagged and wet where they'd broken his legs. Compound fractures are very nasty things. That was why he couldn't walk out on his own power. They'd broken his legs.

There was a small sound that drew me down the aisle to the railing around the ring. Vivian and Fernando were in the ring, too. I'd missed them because they were too close to the side of the railing, hidden from view.

Vivian raised her face up from the ground, tape across her mouth, one eye bloody and swollen shut. Fernando shoved her face back to the ground, showing her hands bound with tape. Showing what he was doing to her. He drew himself out of her, wet and finished at last. He patted her bare butt, giving her a small slap. "That was nice."

I was already walking towards them across the sand of the ring. Which means I'd gotten over the railing in spike heels and a floor-length skirt. I didn't remember doing it.

Fernando stood, fastening his pants, smiling at me. "If you hadn't bargained for her freedom, I'd have never been allowed to touch her. My father doesn't share."

I kept walking. I had one of the knives out, held to the side of the dress. I wasn't sure if he'd noticed, or if I cared. I held my empty left hand out to him. "You're a big man when the lady's tied and gagged. How are you when the lady's armed?"

He smiled, and it was mocking. He touched Vivian with his foot, casually, like you'd poke a dog. "She's beautiful but a little too submissive for my tastes. I like them with a little more fight to them like your wolf-bitch." He finished fastening his pants, running his hands up his chest as if remembering. *"C't'une bonne bourre."*

I knew enough French to know that he'd said Sylvie was a good lay. I balanced the knife. It wasn't made for throwing, but in a pinch it'd do.

There was the faintest shadow in his eyes, as if for the first time he realized that there was no one here to save him; then something leaped over the railings. A blur of speed and motion that hit Fernando hard enough to roll him across the ground. When they came up, Richard was on top of him.

I yelled, "Don't kill him, Richard! Don't kill him!" I ran for them, but Jamil got there first. Jamil knelt by Richard, grabbing his arm, saying something to him. Richard grabbed Jamil by the throat and flung him across the ring. I ran to Jamil, kneeling beside him, but it was too late. His throat was crushed. His eyes were wide, frightened; he tried to breathe but it wasn't working. His legs spasmed, spine bowing, as he fought to breath. He grabbed my hand, his eyes screaming at me. There was nothing I could do. Either he'd heal it or he'd die.

I screamed, "Shit, Richard, help him!"

Richard plunged his hand into Fernando's stomach. He didn't have claws yet. It was only human fingers digging in the flesh, searching for the heart. He was strong enough that he'd dig it out unless we stopped him.

I stood and Jamil's hand slid out of mine. He let me go, but his eyes would haunt me. I ran for Richard, screaming his name: "Richard!"

He looked at me with amber wolf eyes in his human face. He reached towards me with one bloody hand, and the mental shields that kept us safe from one another crashed.

My vision went black, and when I could see again, I was kneeling in the ring. I could feel my body but I could also feel Richard's fingers pushing their way through thick flesh. The blood was warm but there wasn't enough of it. He wanted to use teeth to open the belly and was fighting the urge.

Thomas knelt beside me. "Use your marks to calm him before he kills Fernando."

I shook my head. My fingers were tearing through flesh. I had to press my hands against my eyes to remember what body I was in. I found my voice and that helped separate us. Helped me know who I was, what I was. "Shit, I don't know how."

"Then take his rage, his beast." Thomas touched my hands, gripping them tight, not to hurt but to help me anchor myself in this body. I gripped his hands and stared into his face like a drowning woman.

"I don't know how, Thomas."

He made an exasperated sound. "Gideon will have to intervene until you can calm him." It was almost a question.

I nodded. Sure, I'd been about to kill Fernando myself, but I knew that if we killed him, we would never see another dawn. Padma would kill us. Kill us all.

I kept looking at Thomas's face, but I felt Gideon grab Richard. Felt him pull him off Fernando. Richard twisted and hit Gideon, knocking him to the ground, then leaped on him. They rolled over and over on the ground, each trying to get on top. The only thing that kept it from being a killing fight was that both held onto their human forms and still tried to fight like they had claws. But Richard's beast was growing inside him. If he shifted, short of killing him we'd never keep him from killing someone else.

Thomas touched my face, and I realized that I hadn't been seeing his face. I was seeing Gideon's strange eyes from inches away as my hands tried to crush his throat. But they weren't my hands.

"Help me," I said.

"Just open to his beast," Thomas said. "Simply open and it will fill you. The beast is seeking a channel of escape. Give it one and it will flow into you." I knew in that instant that Thomas and Gideon were part of a triumvirate just like we were.

"I'm not a lycanthrope," I said.

"It does not matter. Do it, or we will have to kill him."

I screamed and did what he said. But it wasn't just opening to it. I reached out to that rage. That power that he called his beast came at my touch. I smelled

like home to it, somehow, and it poured into me, over me, through me, like a
blinding storm of heat and power. It was similar to the times I'd raised power with
Richard and Jean-Claude, but this time there was no spell to use the power on.
Nowhere for the beast to run. It tried to crawl out my skin, tried to expand inside
my body, but there was no beast to call. I was empty for it, and it raged inside
me. I felt it growing until I thought I would burst apart in bloody fragments. The
pressure built and built and had nowhere to go.

  I screamed, one long, ragged shriek after another, as fast as I could get breath.
I felt Richard crawling towards me, felt his hands and legs move over the ground,
felt the muscles in his body that turned crawling into a sensuous art, a stalking
thing. He appeared above me, just his face, staring down. His long hair fell around
his face like a shadowing curtain. Blood glistened at the corner of his mouth. I felt
him want to lick the blood away but stop himself, and bound this closely, I knew
why he stopped. For me. Fear that I would think he was monstrous.

  His power was still trying to find a way out of my body. It wanted the blood,
too. It wanted to lick the blood off his face and taste at his mouth. Wanted to wrap
the warmth of his body around itself and become one. His power cried out like a
frustrated lover for him to open his arms, his body, his mind, to it, and embrace
it. Richard gave it a name apart from himself, his beast, but it wasn't separate. In
that moment I realized why Richard ran so hard and so long from the power. It
was him. Just as the furred shape of him was pulled from the matter of his own
human body, so the rage, the destruction, was pulled from his very human psyche.
His beast was formed of that part of our brains we bury, only dragging into our
consciousness in the worst of our nightmares. Not the dreams where we are hunted
by the monsters, but the dreams where we are the monsters. We raise bloody hands
to the sky and scream, not from fear, but from joy. The pure joy of slaughter. The
cathartic moment when we plunge our hands into the hot blood of our enemies
and there is no civilized thought to stop us from dancing on their graves.

  The power flared inside me like a hand stroking from the inside out, reaching
out towards him as he knelt over me. Fear filled his eyes, and it wasn't fear for
me or of me. It was the fear that the beast was the reality and that all the careful
morals, everything he was or ever had been, was the lie.

  I stared up at him. "Richard," I whispered, "we're all creatures of light and
darkness. Embracing your darkness won't kill the light. Goodness is stronger than
that."

  He dropped from his knees, flat to the ground, only propping himself on his
elbows. His hair brushed my face on either side, and I had to fight the urge to rub
my face back and forth in it. This close I could smell his skin, after-shave, but
underneath that was him. The warm scent that was his body. I wanted to touch
that warmth, to wrap my mouth around it and try and hold it forever. I wanted
him. The power flared at the thought, primitive thoughts excited it, made it harder
to control.

  He whispered, blood still trickling from his mouth, "How can you say goodness is stronger? I want to lick the blood off my own body. I want to press my
bleeding mouth onto yours. I want you to feed off my wound. That is evil."

  I touched his face, the barest trace of fingertips, and even that made power
jump between us. "It's not evil, Richard. It just isn't very civilized." Blood was

building into a single trembling drop on the edge of his face. It fell against my skin and it was burning hot. His power flared upward and took me with it. It wanted to—I wanted to—lick the blood off Richard's face. Part of me was still saying no while I raised my head just enough to run lips, my tongue, and lightly my teeth along his face. I lay back down with the salty taste of him in my mouth and wanted more. The *more* scared me. I was just as scared of this part of him, of me, as he was. That was why I ran from him the night of the full moon. It wasn't that he ate Marcus, though that hadn't helped, or that he'd handled it all so badly. The memory that haunted was the moment I'd been carried away by the pack's power, and for just an instant I'd wanted to drop to my knees and feed with them. I was afraid that Richard's beast would take what was left of my humanity. I was afraid for the same reason Richard was afraid. But what I'd said was true. It wasn't evil, just not very human.

He laid his lips against mine in a trembling kiss. A sound came from low in his throat, and he was suddenly pressing his mouth against mine, until it either bruised or I opened my mouth to him. I opened, and his tongue plunged inside me, his lips feeding on mine. The cut inside his mouth filled my mouth with the taste of him, salty, sweet. I held his face in my hands, my mouth searching his, and it wasn't enough. A small high keening sound crawled out of my mouth into his. The sound was made up of need, frustration, a desire that wasn't civilized and never had been. We'd been playing Ozzie and Harriet, but what we wanted from each other was more Hustler and Penthouse.

We moved to our knees, mouths still pressed together. My hands slid over his chest, his back, and something deep inside me clicked and relaxed. How could I ever be this close to him and not touch him?

His power tried to spill outward, but I held it back. I held it like I could hold my own magic, letting it build until I couldn't hold any longer.

Richard's hands slid up my legs finding the lace top of the black panties. His fingers traced my naked spine and I was undone.

The power spilled upward, outward, filling us both. It flared over us in a rushing wave of heat and light, until my vision swam in pieces, and we both cried out with one voice. His beast slid inside of him. I felt it crawl out of me, pulled like a large, thick string, spilling inside of Richard, coiling into his body. I expected to feel the last bit of it spill between us, like draining the last drop of wine from a cup, but that drop remained.

Somewhere in that rush of power, I'd felt Richard take control of his beast and send that pulsing warmth outward into Jamil. I wouldn't have known how to do it, but Richard did. I'd felt Jamil heal under the thundering rush of power.

Richard knelt with me in his arms, my face pressed to his chest. His heart beat against my cheek like a living thing. Sweat had broken over his body in a light dew. I licked the sweat from his chest and stared up at him.

His eyes were heavy-lidded, dazed. You'd almost have mistaken the look for sleep, but not quite. He cupped his hands on both sides of my face. The wound on his mouth was healed. The rush of power, his beast, had healed it. He lowered his soft lips to mine and just barely brushed my mouth. "What are we going to do?"

I held his hands against my face. "We're going to do what we came to do."

"Then what?" he asked.

I shook my head, rubbing my face against his hands. "Survive first, Richard. Worry about the niceties later."

Something filled his eyes with a sudden rush of panic. "Jamil, I could have killed him."

"You also healed him."

He let that take some of the panic from his face, but he still got to his feet and went to his fallen enforcer. An apology at the very least was needed. I couldn't really argue with that.

I stayed kneeling, not sure I could walk yet, for a variety of reasons.

"Not the way Gideon and I would have done it," Thomas said, "but in a pinch it will do."

I felt heat rush up my face. "Sorry."

"Don't apologize," Gideon growled. "It was a lovely show." He crawled towards us, one arm cradled against his body. Blood dripped down the arm and shoulder. The red showed brilliantly against the white shirt. I had absolutely no desire to lick the blood off his body. I was grateful for that.

"Richard did that?" I asked.

"He was beginning to change form when you called him. You drank his beast and he calmed." He sat leaning to one side, bleeding a little puddle on the floor, but he never asked for help, not by word or expression. But Thomas reached out to him. Touched his shoulder in a neutral, almost brotherly gesture. Their power strengthened in a skin-prickling rush that oozed over me like a cold wind, but if I hadn't been able to sense it, I'd have never known.

"Is this just European reserve?" I asked, "or are Richard and I doing something terribly wrong?"

Thomas smiled, but it was Gideon who answered. "You do nothing wrong. In fact, I feel quite cheated." He patted Thomas's hand and smiled flashing fangs. "There are ways to share power that are quieter, and less . . . showy. But for today you did what needed to be done. It was a desperate thing and called for desperate measures."

I let it go. No need to explain how often being around Richard ended in such "desperate measures." Across the ring Jamil sat up with Richard's help. Zane had untied both the wereleopards. He'd led Vivian over to Gregory. They both knelt by him, Vivian hugging Zane and crying.

I got my feet under me and found that I could walk. Great. Richard got there before I did. He stroked Gregory's tangled hair out of his face until the wereleopard looked up at him. "We have to set these legs."

Gregory nodded, lips in a thin tight line that reminded me of Cherry.

"We need a hospital for this," I said.

Richard looked up at me. "The legs have already begun to reknit like this, Anita. Every minute the bones are out of alignment is another minute that they heal, badly."

I stared down at Gregory's legs. He was totally nude, but the wounds were so fearful that it wasn't embarrassing; it was just piteous. His legs from the knees down bent the wrong way. I had to close my eyes and look away. If it had been a corpse, I could have looked at it, but Gregory was still bleeding, still hurting. Made it worse somehow.

I looked back. "You mean the legs would heal like that?"

"Yes," Richard said.

I stared down into Gregory's frightened eyes. They were still the surprised cornflower-blue of Stephen's. They looked even bluer from the mask of blood that covered his face. I tried to think of something to say, but he spoke first.

His voice was thin, scratchy, as if he'd screamed until he was hoarse. "When you left without me the first time, I thought you were going to let them keep me."

I knelt beside him. "You're not something to keep. You're a person. You deserve to be treated . . ." To say, "better than this" seemed too obvious. I tried to hold his hand the way you'd comfort a child, but two of the fingers were broken so badly, I didn't even know how to touch him.

Vivian spoke for the first time. "Is he dead?" Her voice was breathy, husky, somewhere between that of a little girl and a seductress. She would be great on the phone. The look in her eyes was neither childish nor seductive; it was frightening. She stared past us to where Fernando lay, and her hatred was a hot, scalding thing.

Not that I blamed her. I went to check on our little rapist. Gideon and Thomas got to him first. I noticed that they hadn't gone near him until I did. Why did I think that they didn't like him much better than we did? Fernando just had a way of pissing people off. It seemed to be his only talent.

His bare stomach was a bloody mess where Richard had tried to dig his intestines out, but the wound was healing. Filling itself in like a fast-forward motion picture. You could actually see his body rebuild itself.

"He'll live," I said. Even to me, I sounded disappointed.

"Yes," Thomas said, and that one word sounded as disappointed as I felt. He visibly shook himself, and turned sad brown eyes to me. "If he had died, then Padma would have destroyed the city, seeking you. Make no mistake, Anita, Padma loves his son, but more than that, he is his only son. The only chance he has of having an heir."

"I wouldn't think a vampire would sweat that," I said.

"He comes from a time and a culture where a son is an incredibly important thing. No matter how long we live or what we are in the end, we start out as people. We never quite lose all that we were during life. It haunts us over the centuries, our humanity."

"You're human."

He smiled and shook his head. "Once, perhaps."

I opened my mouth to ask something, but he held his hand up. "If there is time, Gideon and I would enjoy speaking with you and Richard at length on what a triumvirate can be, but now, you must leave before Fernando awakes. During daylight hours he is in charge of us."

My eyes widened, and I looked at Gideon. "But he's not alpha enough to take on Gideon."

"Padma is a harsh master, Anita. We obey or we suffer."

"Which is why," Gideon said, "you must all leave as soon as possible. What the *petit bâtard* would order us to do to you if he awoke now is best left unsaid."

He had a point. Gregory screamed, a high shrieking, that ended in whimpering. Richard had said the legs had begun to heal, bent backwards. I suddenly realized what that meant. "If the legs had healed broken, Gregory would have been crippled," I said.

"Yes," Gideon said. "It was Padma's idea of punishment."

Fernando groaned, eyes still shut. We had to get out of here. "I need my guns back," I said.

They didn't even argue. They just gave them all back. Either they trusted me or they figured I wouldn't shoot Fernando while he was unconscious. They were right, though he'd earned it. I'd killed people for a lot less than what the rat-boy had done, a lot less.

Gregory had mercifully passed out. Richard held him as carefully as he could in his arms. They'd found wood from somewhere and used Richard's shirt to tie the makeshift splints to Gregory's legs. Vivian leaned heavily on Zane as if her legs weren't quite working. She was also trying to cover her lower extremities. So hurt she could barely walk and she was embarrassed about her nudity. We were sort of out of clothes to offer her. The coat I'd brought was in the outer area.

Thomas saved the day by giving her his spiffy red jacket. It was large on her and covered enough. Just making it outside the tent to the midway made my shoulders relax a notch. I picked up the coat and put a gun in each pocket. The machine gun was already across my chest.

Thomas held the door for us. I went through last. "Thank you," I said. We both knew I didn't mean the door.

"You are most welcome." He closed the door behind us, and I heard it lock.

I stood in the hot summer sunlight and felt my body sink into the heat. It was good to be outside in the daylight. But night was coming, and I still didn't know what price Jean-Claude had bargained away to get Vivian and Gregory out of there. But the thought of Gregory's lovely body deliberately crippled forever, and Vivian passed around like so much meat, made me glad we'd bargained. I wouldn't say that whatever the price, it would be worth it, but close. Jean-Claude had said no rape, no actual intercourse, no maiming, no skinning alive. The list had seemed safer and more complete an hour ago.

30

We pulled into the driveway of my rented house with two wounded wereleopards, two unwounded wereleopards, two very silent werewolves, a partridge in a pear tree, and enough equipment for Richard to rig up a pair of traction splints in my bedroom. Gregory needed to be in traction splints for twenty-four hours according to Dr. Lillian. The hospital was being evacuated. If Fernando was in charge for the day, the evacuation wasn't just a precaution, it was a necessity. The rat-boy hadn't wanted to free Rafael, and he'd certainly want revenge on Richard for beating him, so both the wererats and the werewolves were in danger. The thought of what he'd do if he got his paws back on Gregory and Vivian was too scary to think about. The best we could do was keep them with us and try not to be anywhere Fernando would think to go.

I was half-trusting Thomas and Gideon to keep the rat-boy from searching too hard. I don't usually trust people that easily, but Gideon had called him the *petit bâtard*. The little bastard. They didn't like him any better than we did. Hard to believe, but maybe true.

Besides, where could we go where we'd be safe? We couldn't go to a hotel. That would endanger everyone in the place. Same thing with most houses. One of the main things I'd been looking for in a rental was isolation. Frankly, I liked a little city around me, but my life had turned into a free-fire zone lately. No apartments, no condos, no neighborhoods; something with lots of ground and no neighbors to get shot up was what I'd wanted. I got it. Though the isolation was about all I'd gotten that I wanted.

The house was too big for just me. It was a house that cried out for a family with walks in the woods and a dog running circles around the kiddies. Richard had never seen the house. I would have been more comfortable with him seeing it before we'd had our little make-out, oh, umh, make-up session. Before Jean-Claude had interfered, Richard and I had been engaged. We'd been planning the kind of future that went with this kind of house. I don't know if Richard had woken up and smelled the blood-soaked coffee, but I had. The future that included a picket fence and 2.5 children just wasn't in the cards for me. I didn't think it was in the cards for him either, but I wasn't going to burst his bubble. Not as long as his bubble didn't include me. If it did . . . we had a problem.

The house had a medium-sized rectangular flower bed that got full sun almost all day. It had been a rose garden, but the last owners had dug up the plants and tried to take them with them. It looked like the far side of the moon, complete with craters. It had looked so barren that I'd spent a weekend planting the damn thing. Rose moss for the border just because I loved the bright little flowers. Zinnias behind that because the flower colors echoed each other. It was a riot of color, nothing subtle. Butterflies and hummingbirds were attracted to the zinnias. I'd planted cosmos behind the zinnias, towering, feathery and tangled at the same time, with lovely pale open flowers that the butterflies loved and the hummingbirds weren't so fond of. The colors of the cosmos were a little too pastel compared with the other colors, but hey, it still worked. In the fall the cosmos would have seed heads for the goldfinches.

The flower bed had been some sort of admission to myself that I might be here awhile. That I couldn't go back to an apartment or a condo. That my life didn't allow me the luxury of close neighbors.

Richard had remarked as we drove up, "Nice flowers."

"I couldn't just leave it bare."

He made a noncommittal noise. Nearly three months away from each other and even without the marks, he knew me well enough to know when not to say something. It bugged me that I had been unable to leave the flower bed barren and ripped. I hated the fact that I'd been driven to make it pretty. No, I am not comfortable with my feminine side.

Richard and Jamil carried Gregory in on the stretcher that the hospital had loaned us. Lillian had pumped the wereleopard so full of painkillers that he was feeling no pain. I was grateful for that. Awake, he had a tendency to whimper and scream.

Strangely, Cherry turned out to be a nurse. She'd taken one look at Gregory and suddenly turned into a professional. A layer of confidence and competence crawled out of nowhere. She was like a different person. Once Gregory let her touch him, didn't reject her help, Cherry was calm. Though truthfully, it wasn't until Dr. Lillian had seemed to trust Cherry that I did, too. Lillian was confident that she could help us put Gregory into traction and not injure him further. I trusted Lillian's opinion, but I still didn't trust Cherry. I might not have approved of Richard smacking her around, but I agreed that anyone who left you behind to die wasn't trustworthy. No shame in being weak, but I'd never trust her at my back.

Vivian wouldn't let Zane carry her into the house, even though walking was obviously painful. She clung to my arm with both her small hands. Truthfully, her hands weren't any smaller than my own, but somehow she seemed fragile. It wasn't size, or even just the rape, but something about Vivian herself. Even wrapped in the borrowed red coat and a scruffy blue robe that Lillian had loaned her, Vivian looked delicate, feminine, lovely in an almost ethereal sort of way. It's hard to look lovely and ethereal with half your face swollen tight with bruises, but she managed it.

She stumbled on the rock walkway to the house. I caught her, but her knees buckled and I came damn near dropping her on the rocks.

Zane tried to help me, but Vivian let out a small sound and hid her face against my shoulder. Once we hit the car she hadn't wanted any man to touch her. It had been Zane who untied her, but it seemed to be me she looked upon as her rescuer. Or maybe I was just the only female rescuer, and female was safe right now.

I sighed and nodded my head. Zane backed off. If I'd been in jogging shoes or even flats, I'd have just carried Vivian into the house, but I was wearing three inch spike heels. I could not carry someone nearly my own body weight wearing these shoes. If I kicked the shoes off, then the dress would be so long I'd trip. I was beginning to really hate this outfit.

"Vivian." She didn't respond. "Vivian?" She was still sliding towards the ground. I braced my legs far enough apart to get as much leverage as I was going to get in the shoes, and was ready for her when her legs collapsed completely. I might have been able to carry her in a firemen's-carry even with the heels, but I'd seen her body and there were deep bruises on her stomach. Slinging her over my shoulders would hurt. I managed to lift her in my arms, but I knew better than to try and walk.

"Get Cherry," I said.

Zane nodded and went into the house.

I stood there holding Vivian, waiting for help to arrive. The July sun beat down on my back through the black coat. Sweat trickled down my spine. Cicadas filled the heat with their buzzing song. There was a small army of butterflies feeding on the flowers. Don't tell, but I drank at least one cup of coffee every day out here watching the stupid things. It was all very picturesque, but I was getting impatient. How long did it take for Zane to tell Cherry to get her butt out here? Of course, maybe she was busy with Gregory and his fearful injuries. If she was, it could be a while. It wasn't that I couldn't stand there holding her. It was that I felt stupid wearing heels so high that I couldn't carry her into the house. It made me feel girlish in the worst way.

I tried to wait by counting how many different species of butterflies were visible. Tiger swallowtail, spicebrush swallowtail, greater frittilary, giant sulphur, black swallowtail, redspotted purple, and painted lady. A trio of tiny blue hairstreaks spun into the air like glittering bits of sky. Beautiful, but where the hell was Cherry? Enough of this. I started very carefully forward, my ankle twisted and I had to throw myself backward to keep from dumping Vivian to the rocks. I ended up on my butt in the flower bed, crushing the border of rose moss flat and taking a few zinnias with me. The cosmos towered over me, some of them as tall as six feet.

Vivian gave a small moan, blinking her one good eye open. "It's all right," I soothed. "It's all right." I sat there holding her, half rocking her, with my butt in the flowers and my feet almost straight out in front of me. I'd managed to keep my feet through vampires, shapeshifters, human servants, and arsonists, but a pair of high heels had set me back on my ass. Vanity, thy name is woman. Though whoever wrote that had never seen an issue of *GQ*.

A tiger swallowtail nearly as big as my outstretched hand fluttered near my face. It was pale yellow with sharp brown stripes on its wings. It hovered over Vivian, then finally settled on my hand. Butterflies will lick the sweat from your skin for the salt, but usually you have to hold still for it. If you move, they float away. This insect seemed determined. Its proboscis is not much thicker than a straight pin, a long curved tube, but you can feel it like a tickling line.

It was maybe the third time in my life that I'd had a butterfly feed off my skin. I didn't try to chase it away. It was cool. Its wings pulsed up and down very slowly as it fed, its tiny feet almost weightless against my hand.

Cherry walked out the door, eyes widening when she saw me. "Are you hurt?"

I shook my head, still careful not to scare away the butterfly. "Just can't get the leverage to get back up."

Cherry knelt by us, and the butterfly glided away. She watched it for a moment. "I've never seen a butterfly do that."

"It was after the salt in my skin. Butterflies will feed on dogshit or spoiled fruit, too," I said.

Cherry made a face. "Thanks for ruining another idyllic image." She took Vivian out of my arms, wobbling on one knee. Vivian moaned in her arms as Cherry stood, trying to get the balance of it all. Lifting isn't just strength. It's balance, and an unconscious body is not the best thing for balance. "You need a hand up?" she asked.

I shook my head, getting to my knees.

Cherry took me at my word and just walked towards the house. She was smarter than I'd first thought. Of course, if I'd spent the night in Padma's tender care, maybe I wouldn't have made a good first impression either.

I was trying to fluff up the crushed flowers when the butterfly came fluttering back. With it hovering around my face I felt the first prickling brush of power. If it had been dark, I'd have said "vampire," but it was broad daylight.

I stood up and slipped the Browning out of the coat pocket. The bright yellow-and-brown insect batted at my face with paper-thin wings. What had been fun a moment before was suddenly ominous. For the first time in my life I brushed a butterfly away as if it had been something loathsome. And maybe it was.

I am not implying that the butterfly was literally a vampire. They couldn't shapechange, not to my knowledge. Of course, they couldn't be out in full daylight either. They were the council. Did I really know what they were capable of?

The butterfly floated away from me towards the woods on the far side of the driveway. It fluttered back and forth, back and forth, like it was waiting for me. I shook my head. I felt silly holding the gun with just the butterfly there by the woods. But something else was out there. I stood in the summer heat, feeling the sun beat down on the top of my head. I should have been safe. At least from vampires. It wasn't fair that they changed the rules.

I was about to go into the house and yell for backup, when I saw a figure. Tall with a thick hooded cloak pulled around him. Even with the cloak I knew it was a him. Shoulders that broad and that height, and I even knew it was Warrick. Except it couldn't be him. He wasn't even close to powerful enough to be out in daylight.

I stared at that tall shape in the shimmering white cloak. He stood so still, as if he were carved from marble. Even Mr. Oliver, the oldest vamp I'd ever seen had avoided direct sunlight. But there Warrick stood like a ghost that had learned the trick of walking about in daylight. Of course, he wasn't walking. He stood in the wavering shadows of the trees. He didn't try and come out into the direct light of the clearing. Maybe he couldn't. Maybe that thin band of shade was all that kept him from bursting into flames. Maybe.

I walked towards him. I stretched my senses, but his was the only power I felt. It could be a trap, an ambush, but I didn't think so. If they meant to trap me, it wouldn't have been this blatant. But just in case, I stopped a good distance back from the woods. If I saw any movement I'd yell for help and run for the house. Might even get off a shot or two.

Warrick stood with his head bowed so low, the hood completely hid his face. He stood immobile, as if he didn't know I was there. Only the wind making a soft folding line in the white cloth showed any movement. He was like a statue with a cloth thrown over it.

The longer he stood there motionless, the more eerie it seemed. I had to fill the silence. "What do you want, Warrick?"

A shiver went through him and he raised his head slowly. Rot had spread across that strong face. His skin was green and black as if that thin layer of tissue were holding in centuries of death. Even his blue eyes had dulled with a film, like a fish that had been dead too long to eat.

My mouth was hanging open. You'd think after what I'd seen Yvette do to him, it wouldn't have shocked me, but it did. Some sights you don't grow jaded about.

"Is Yvette punishing you?" I asked.

"No, no, my pale mistress sleeps in her coffin. She knows nothing of this visit." His voice was the only thing that remained "normal." The voice was still strong and firm. It didn't match what was happening to his body.

"What's happening to you, Warrick?"

"When the sun rose I did not die. I thought it was a sign from God. That He was giving me permission to end this foul existence. That He had given me the chance to walk into the light for one last time. I walked into the rising sun and did not burn, but this happened." He raised his hands out of the cloak, showing me the greying flesh. The fingernails were blackened, even the ends of the fingers seemed shriveled.

"Will it heal?" I asked.

He smiled and even with that horrific visage, it was a smile full of hope. His rotted face showed a light that had nothing to do with vampire powers. The butterfly hovered above his face. "God will call me to his arms soon. I am after all a dead man."

I couldn't argue with him there. "Why did you come here, Warrick?"

A second butterfly joined the first, then a third. They fluttered above his head like a carousel. Warrick smiled up at them. "I have come to warn you. Padma fears Jean-Claude and your triumvirate. He will see you dead if he can."

"That's not news," I said.

"Our master, Morte d'Amour, has given Yvette orders to destroy you all."

That was news. "Why?" I asked.

"I don't believe that any of the council truly believes that Jean-Claude means to set up his own rival council in this country. But they all see him as a part of this new legal vampirism. They see him as part of a change that may sweep away our old existence. The old ones who have power enough to be comfortable do not want any change in our status quo. When the vote is taken, Anita, there will be two against you.''

''Who else gets to vote?'' I asked.

''Asher has the proxy for his mistress, Belle Morte, Beautiful Death. He hates Jean-Claude with a fine, burning hate like sunlight through glass. I do not think you can count upon his help.''

''So they have all come to kill us,'' I said.

''If they had come merely to kill you, Anita, they would have done so by now.''

''Then I'm confused,'' I said.

''Padma's fear is too strong, but I believe our master would be content if Jean-Claude gave up his seat of power here and joined the council as he was meant to.''

''The first challenger that comes along will take him out,'' I said. ''No thanks.''

''So Jean-Claude keeps saying,'' Warrick said. ''I am beginning to think that he underestimates himself, and you.''

''He's cautious, and so am I.''

A host of butterflies had formed above his head. They fluttered around him in a multicolored cloud. One landed on his hand, bright wings fanning softly as it fed off the rotting flesh.

His power thrummed along my body. It wasn't council-level power, but it was master-level. Warrick was a master vampire, and he hadn't been last night. ''Are you borrowing power from someone else?''

''From God,'' he said.

Of course.

''The longer we are away from our master, the weaker Yvette grows, and the stronger I grow. The Holy Fire of God's eternal light has entered my body once more. Perhaps He will forgive me for my weakness. I feared death, Anita. I feared the punishment of hell more than I feared Yvette. But I walk in the light. I burn with God's power once more.''

Personally I didn't believe God had a private torture chamber, Hell was being cut off from God, cut off from his power, his energy, Him. We walked through his power every day of our lives until it was like white noise, something we ignored or failed to hear. But somehow lecturing Warrick on the fact that he'd let Yvette torture him for centuries because he feared eternal damnation, which I didn't in fact believe existed, seemed pointless. Nay, cruel.

''I'm happy for you, Warrick.''

''I would ask one boon of you, Anita.''

''A boon is a favor, right?'' I asked. Didn't want to agree to something and be wrong.

''Yes,'' he said.

''Ask.''

''Do you have a cross upon you?''

I nodded.

''Show me, please.''

I didn't think this was a good idea, but . . . I pulled the silver chain up until the cross sparkled in the sunlight. It didn't glow. It just dangled.

Warrick smiled. "The Holy Cross does not reject me."

I didn't have the heart to tell him that the cross didn't always glow around all vampires. It seemed to wait for one that meant me harm, though there were exceptions both ways. I, like Warrick, didn't question God's wisdom. I figured He knew what He was doing, and if He didn't, I really didn't want to know.

Warrick walked to the edge of the tree line. He stood there in the white cloak with its black lining, hesitating. I watched the struggle on his face. He wanted to cross into that last band of pure sunlight and was afraid to. I didn't blame him.

He stretched out his hand to the trembling edge of solid golden light, then fell back. "My courage and my faith, they still fail me. I am still not worthy. I should stride into the light and grab the Holy Cross and hold it unafraid." He covered his face with his darkened hands. The butterflies lit on every inch of naked skin, wings fanning. There was nothing to see but the white cloak and the fluttering insects. For a moment the illusion was perfect that the butterflies were all that was inside the cloak.

Warrick spread his hands slowly, carefully, so as not to disturb the insects. He smiled. "I have heard the masters speak of calling their animals for centuries but have never understood until now. It is a wondrous bond."

He seemed happy with his "animal." Me, I'd have been a little disappointed. A butterfly wasn't going to be much defense against the sort of animals that most vamps could call. But, hey, as long as Warrick was happy, who was I to bitch?

"Yvette made me swear an oath to God on some of her secrets. I have not betrayed my word, or my oath."

"Are you saying there are things I should know that you haven't told me?" I asked.

"I have told you all I am free to tell, Anita. Yvette was always clever. She manipulated me all those years ago to betray all I held dear. She bound me with oaths before we arrived on your shores. I didn't understand it at the time, but I do now. She knew I would see you as a person of honor. A person who protects the weak, and does not abandon her friends. You make the council's talk of honor and responsibility seem a pale pretense."

Saying thanks didn't seem enough, but it was all I had. "Thank you, Warrick."

"Even when I was alive there was a vast difference between the nobles that truly led and tended their people's needs, and those who just took from them."

"It hasn't changed that much," I said.

"I am sorry to hear that," he said. He glanced upward, maybe at the sun, maybe at something I couldn't see. "As the sun approaches its zenith I feel weaker."

"Do you need a place to rest for the day?" I asked. The moment I said it, I wasn't sure I should have made the offer. Did I really trust him down in the basement with Jean-Claude and the gang, without me to watch him every minute? Not exactly.

"If this would be my last day in the daylight, then I would not lose it by hiding. I will walk in your delightful woods, then I will dig among the deep leaves. I have hidden among the leaves before. They fall thick and deep in the hollows."

I nodded. "I know. Somehow I figured you for a city boy."

"I have lived in a city for many years, but my first days were among trees thicker and more lush than these. My father's lands were far from any city. Though that has changed. There are no trees now where I fished and hunted as a boy. It is all gone. Yvette allowed me a trip home, in her company. I wish I had not gone. It has tainted my memories, and made them seem like some dreams.''

"The good stuff is as real as the bad stuff,'' I said. "Don't let Yvette take that from you.''

He smiled, then shivered. The butterflies whirled into the air like autumn leaves flung into the sky. "I must go." He moved off through the trees, followed by a line of eager butterflies. I lost sight of the white cloak as he walked down the far side of a hill, but the butterflies trailed after him like tiny vultures marking the line of death.

31

I crossed the yard, the driveway, and was back on the sidewalk when the sound of a car coming down the gravel driveway turned me around. It was Ronnie. Shit. I'd forgotten to call her and cancel our morning jog. Veronica (Ronnie) Sims was a private detective and my best friend. We worked out together at least once a week, usually on Saturday mornings. Sometimes we went to the gym; sometimes we ran. It was Saturday morning, and I'd forgotten to cancel.

I held the gun along my side, hidden in the coat. Not that she'd care. It was just automatic. If you were privileged enough to be allowed a carry permit for your gun, you didn't flash it around. Deliberately flashing your gun in public without just cause is called "brandishment" and can get your permit revoked. It's like a new vampire flashing fangs. It's a sign of an amateur.

I was feeling guilty that I'd made Ronnie come all the way out here for nothing, when I realized she wasn't alone. Louie Fane, Dr. Louis Fane, who taught biology at Wash U. was with her. They spilled out of the car together, laughing, holding hands as soon as the car wasn't between them. They were both dressed for jogging. His shirt was untucked, coming down low enough on his five-foot-six frame that his short-shorts barely showed. His black hair was cut short and neat, and didn't match the oversized T-shirt.

Ronnie was wearing a pair of lavender biker's shorts that showed her long legs to perfection. A crop-top T-shirt in the same color showed flashes of flat stomach as she walked towards me. She never dressed this nicely just to go exercise with me. Her shoulder-length blond hair was freshly washed, blow-dried, and shiny. The only thing missing was makeup, but she didn't need it. Her face glowed. Her grey eyes had that tinge of blue they get when she wears the right color outfit. She'd chosen the color, and Louie had eyes only for her.

I stood there watching them walk hand and hand up the sidewalk and wondered when they'd notice me. They both looked up almost startled, as if I'd appeared out of thin air. Ronnie had the grace to look embarrassed, but Louie just seemed content. I happened to know for a fact that they were having sex, but just watching them together would have been enough. His fingers played lightly over her knuckles as they stood looking at me. I wasn't sure they were in love, but lust, that I was sure of.

Ronnie looked me up and down. "A little overdressed for jogging, aren't you?"

I frowned. "Sorry, I forgot to call. I just got home."

"What happened?" Louie asked. He still held Ronnie's hand, but everything else changed. He was suddenly alert, taller somehow, black eyes searching my face, noticing for the first time the bandage on my hand and other signs of wear. "You smell like blood, and"—his nostrils flared—"something worse."

I wondered if he could smell Warrick's rotted flesh on my shoes, but I didn't ask. I didn't really want to know. He was one of Rafael's lieutenants, and I was surprised he didn't know what had been happening. "Have you guys been out of town?"

They both nodded, and Ronnie's smile was gone now, too. "We were up at the cabin." The cabin had been part of her divorce settlement from a two-year marriage that ended very badly. But it was a great cabin.

"Yeah, it's nice up there."

"What's happened?" Louie asked again.

"Let's go inside. I can't think of a version short enough not to need coffee."

They followed me into the house, still touching, but some of the glow had leaked away. I seemed to have that effect on people. Hard to be bright and shiny in the middle of a kill zone.

Gregory was lying on my couch, still drugged into blissful unconsciousness. Louie stopped in his tracks. Of course, maybe it wasn't just the wereleopard. There was a large Persian rug underneath my white couch and chair. It wasn't my rug. There were bright pillows on the white furniture that echoed the colors of the rug. The colors were like jewels in the early morning sunlight.

Ronnie said, "Stephen." She even went forward as if to touch him, but Louie pulled her back.

"It's not Stephen."

"How can you tell?" I asked.

"They don't smell the same."

Ronnie was just staring. "This is Gregory?"

Louie nodded.

"I knew they were identical twins but . . ."

"Yeah," I said. "I have got to get out of this dress, but let me make one thing clear. Gregory is mine now. He's a good guy. No abusing him."

Louie turned to me, and his black eyes had bled across the pupil so that his eyes were like black buttons, rat's eyes. "He tortured his own brother."

"I was there, Louie. I saw it."

"Then how can you defend him?"

I shook my head. "It has been a long night, Louie. Let's just say that without Gabriel to force the wereleopards to be evil, they've been choosing different paths. He refused to torture one of the wolves, and that's why they broke his legs."

The look on Louie's face said he didn't believe it. I shook my head and made shooing motions. "Go in the kitchen, make coffee. Let me slip out of this damn dress and I'll tell you everything."

Ronnie pulled him towards the kitchen, but her eyes watched me, full of questions. I mouthed, "Later" to her, and she went into the kitchen. I trusted her to keep Louie busy until I got changed. I didn't really think that he'd harm Gregory, but the wereleopards had pissed off so many people. Better to be safe than sorry.

Richard was up on a stepladder drilling holes in the ceiling above my bed. So much for my security deposit. My bedroom was the only one on the first floor. I'd given it up so they wouldn't have to get Gregory up the stairs. Little flakes of ceiling covered his bare torso in a fine white powder. He looked very handymannish in just jeans. Cherry and Zane were on the bed, holding pieces of the traction apparatus for him, helping him measure.

The drill stopped, and I asked, "Where's Vivian?"

"Gwen took her to see Sylvie," Richard said. His eyes were very neutral as he looked at me, voice careful. We hadn't said much to each other since our moment in the ring.

"Nice to have a trained therapist in the house," I said.

Cherry and Zane were both watching me. They reminded me of golden retrievers in the obedience ring, eyes earnest, intent on every word and gesture. I didn't really like people looking at me like that. Made me nervous.

"I just came in to get clothes. I want out of this dress." I moved past them to the chest of drawers. Jean-Claude had been busy in here, too. It just wasn't as obviously not my taste. At the far end was a bay window complete with window seat. It was full to overflowing with my toy penguin collection. There was a new penguin sitting on the bed with a large red bow on its neck and a card leaning against its furry belly. Bits of ceiling had already rained down on its black fur.

The drill stopped, and Richard said, "Go ahead, check the card. That's what he meant for you to do."

I looked up at him, and there was still anger in his eyes and pain, but underneath that there was something else. Something I had no words for, or perhaps didn't want words for. I took the penguin off the bed, dusting it off, and opened the card with my back to him. The drill didn't start up again. I could feel him watching me while I read the card.

It said, "Something to sleep with when I am not with you." It was signed simply with an elegant J.

I shoved the card back in the envelope and turned to face Richard, penguin clutched to my stomach. His expression was very careful, as neutral as he could manage it. He looked at me, fighting to keep his face empty and finally failing. A rawness spilled into his eyes, of need and words and things unsaid.

Zane and Cherry backed off the bed, gliding towards the door. They didn't leave, but they made a point of not standing between us. I didn't think we were going to have a full-out battle, but I couldn't blame them for getting out of the way.

"You can read the note if you want. But I'm not sure it will help."

He made a small abrupt sound, not quite a laugh. "Should you be offering your boyfriend's love letters to your ex-boyfriend?"

"I don't want to hurt you, Richard. I really don't. If seeing the note will make it better, you can see it. Except for that first time, I've never done anything you didn't know about. I don't intend to start now."

I watched the muscles in his jaw clench until the tension swelled his neck and shoulders. He shook his head. "I don't want to see it."

"Fine." I turned around, penguin and card in one arm, and opened the dresser drawer. I grabbed what was on top, not really paying attention. I just wanted out of the suddenly silent room, away from the weight of Richard's eyes.

"I heard someone come in with you," he said, voice quiet. "Who was it?"

I turned, penguin and clothes clutched in a mass. "Louie and Ronnie."

Richard frowned. "Did Rafael send Louie?"

I shook my head. "They were off in a love nest together. Louie doesn't know what's been happening. He seems really pissed at Gregory. Is it personal, or what he did to Stephen?"

"Stephen," Richard said. "Louie is very loyal to his friends." There was something in the way he said that last that seemed to imply that maybe not everyone in the house was as loyal. Or maybe I was just reading things into an otherwise innocent statement. Maybe. Guilt is a many-splendored thing. But meeting Richard's true-brown eyes, I didn't think I was hearing anything he didn't mean for me to hear.

If I'd known what to say to him, I'd have sent the wereleopards out of the room so we could talk. But God help me if I knew what to say. Until I had time to think about things, the talk could wait. In fact, it had better wait. I hadn't expected to still be able to feel something for Richard, or him for me. I was sleeping with another man, in love with another man. It complicated things. Just thinking that made me smile and shake my head.

"What's so funny?" he asked. His eyes were so hurt, so confused.

"Funny?" I said. "Nothing, Richard, absolutely nothing." I fled to the downstairs bathroom to change. This was the biggest bathroom in the house, the one that had a sunken marble tub. It wasn't as big as the one Jean-Claude had at the Circus, but it was close. White candles encircled the head and foot of the tub. Untouched, fresh, new, waiting for nightfall. He'd chosen peppermint candles. He loved scented candles that smelled eatable. His food fetish was showing.

There was a second card taped to the stem of a silver candlestick. There was nothing on the outside of the envelope, but call it a hunch. I opened it.

The note said, "If we were alone, *ma petite*, I would have you light them at dusk. And I would join you. *Je rêve de toi*." The last was French for "I dream of you." This one wasn't even signed. He was such a confident little thing. According to him, I was the only woman in nearly four hundred years to ever turn him down. And even I had finally lost the battle. Hard not to be confident with a track record like that. Truthfully, I'd have loved to fill the tub, light the candles, and been waiting naked and wet for him to rise for the night. It sounded like a very, very good time. But we had a house full of guests, and if Richard was staying the night, we were going to behave ourselves. If Richard had dumped me for another woman, I wouldn't have taken it quite as badly as he was taking it, but I couldn't have stayed in a house and listened to him have sex with the other woman. Even my nerve wasn't that strong. I certainly wasn't going to put Richard into that position. Not on purpose.

I had to make two trips back and forth into the bedroom from the bathroom.

First, I forgot a normal bra. A strapless bra was just not meant to be worn this long. Second, I traded the shorts I'd grabbed first for jeans.

I was very aware of Richard watching me as I came and went. Zane and Cherry watched both of us like nervous dogs that expect to be kicked. The tension was thick enough to walk on and the leopards could feel it. The tension was more than physical awareness. It was like he was thinking very hard, and I could feel it, a building pressure that had a lecture at the end of it, or a fight.

I ended up dressed in a pair of new jeans in that wonderful dark blue color that never lasts, a royal blue tank top, white jogging socks, and white Nikes with a black swoosh. I shoved most of the old clothes into the dirty clothes hamper and folded the dress on top of it. The dress was, of course, "dry clean only." I tucked the Firestar down the front of the jeans. I had an inner pants holster for it, but it was in the bedroom. I didn't want it badly enough to go back in there right this second. I felt like I was tempting fate every time Richard and I passed each other. Eventually, he'd insist on talking, and I wasn't ready. Maybe for this particular talk, I would never be ready.

I folded the borrowed coat over my arm with the Browning hanging heavy in one pocket. The machine gun I kept on my shoulder like a purse. When the bedroom cleared out, I'd put the machine gun in the closet. The trick about having this many loaded guns is that you don't dare leave them lying around. Lycanthropes are great in a fight, but most of them don't seem to know one end of a gun from the other. There's something about a gun just lying around, especially one as nifty as a sub-machine gun that tempts people. There is an almost physical itch to pick it up, point it, go bang-bang. You either make a gun safe, unloaded or locked up, or you keep it on your body where you can control it. Those are the rules. Deviating from the rules is what lets eight-year-old kids blow the heads off their baby sisters.

I went into the living room. Gregory was gone from the couch. I started to assume he'd been carried to the bedroom, then walked into the bedroom to make sure. Be damn silly to let Gregory get snatched from my living room and not notice it.

Cherry and Richard were tucking him into the bed with Zane's help. Gregory had woken enough that he was whimpering. Richard caught me peeking in the doorway.

"Just making sure Gregory was all right," I said.

"No, you were making sure that the bad guys hadn't gotten him," he said.

I looked down, then up. "Yeah," I said.

We might have said more, but Gregory woke up as they put his legs in traction. He started screaming. Lycanthropes metabolized drugs incredibly quickly. Cherry readied a needle full of a clear liquid. I fled. I don't like needles. But truthfully, I didn't want Richard to lecture me over the guns. His being a lycanthrope wasn't our only problem. Richard thought I killed too easily. Maybe he was right, but I'd saved his ass more than once with my quick trigger finger. And he'd endangered me more than once with his squeamishness.

I went back down the stairs, shaking my head. Why did we even bother? We had too many important areas that we disagreed on. It wouldn't work. So we lusted after each other, even loved each other. It wasn't enough. If we couldn't find a way to compromise on the rest of it, we'd just end up cutting each other apart.

Better to just make the break as cleanly as possible. My head agreed with the logic. Other body parts weren't so sure.

I followed the smell of coffee into the kitchen. It was a lovely kitchen, if I ever cooked or entertained. It was all dark wood cabinets with a large island in the middle with hooks above it for cooking pots and pans. I didn't own enough kitchen stuff to fill one whole cabinet let alone the rest of the gleaming expanse. Of all the rooms in the new house this was the one that made me feel most like a stranger. It was so *not* what I would have chosen.

Ronnie and Louie were sitting at my small two-seater kitchen table. It sat on a raised platform in a three-sided bay of windows. The area was meant for a full-sized dining room table. My little breakfast-nook set looked like a temporary measure. Except for the flowers. The flowers took up most of the small table. The flowers were another addition.

I didn't have to count to know that there were a dozen white roses and one lone red one. Jean-Claude had been sending me white roses for years, but ever since we made love for the first time there had been a thirteenth rose. Red, crimson, a spot of passion lost in a sea of white purity. There was no card, because there was no need for a card.

Jamil leaned against the wall near Ronnie and Louie, sipping coffee. He stopped talking when I entered the room, which meant he'd probably been talking about me. Maybe not, but the silence was thick, and Ronnie was very busy not looking at me. Louie looked at me a little too hard. Yep, Jamil had been spilling the beans.

I didn't even want to know before I had some caffeine in me. I poured coffee into a mug that said "Warning: The Surgeon General has determined that bothering me before I've had my first cup of coffee is hazardous to your health." The mug had been at the office until my boss accused me of threatening the clients. I hadn't picked out a new mug yet. I had to find something suitably irritating.

There was a sparkling new espresso machine on the cabinet by the coffee-maker, with another card. I took a sip of coffee and opened this one.

"Something to warm your body and fill this empty *cuisine*." The last was French for "kitchen." He often did that in notes, as if even after a hundred years in this country he still sometimes forgot the correct English phrase. His speech was flawless, but many people speak a second language better than they write it. Of course, it could be his backhanded way of teaching me French. It was working. He'd write a note, and I'd hunt him down and ask what it meant. Having French sweet-nothings whispered in your ear is great, but after a while you wonder exactly what he's whispering, so I asked. There had been other lessons, but nothing much that I could share in public.

"Nice flowers," Ronnie said. Her voice was neutral, but she'd made herself very clear on the subject of Jean-Claude. She thought he was a pushy bastard. She was right. She thought he was evil. I didn't agree on that one.

I sat down at the far end of the octagon, back to the wall, head below the level of the windows. "I don't need any more lectures today, Ronnie. Okay?"

She shrugged and sipped her coffee. "You're a big girl, Anita."

"That's right, I am." It sounded petulant even to me. I settled the submachine gun beside me on the floor with the coat. I breathed in the coffee, black and thick.

Sometimes I added cream and sugar, but for the first cup of the day, black would do.

"Jamil's been filling us in," Louie said. "Did you and Richard actually raise power in the middle of the Circus?"

I took a sip of coffee before answering. "Apparently."

"There is no equivalent among the wererats for the wolves' lupa, but is it common to be able to call power like that?"

Ronnie was glancing back and forth from one to the other of us. Her eyes were a little wide. I'd been telling her what was happening in my life. She'd been hanging around with me and the monsters long enough to meet Louie, but it was still a strange new world for her. Sometimes I thought she'd be better off keeping further away from the monsters, but like she'd said, we were both big girls. Sometimes she even carried a gun. She could make her own decisions.

Jamil answered, "I have been a werewolf for over ten years. This is my third pack. I have never even heard of a lupa that could help her Ulfric raise power outside of the lupanar, our place of power. Most lupas can't even do that. Raina was the first I'd met that could call power within the lupanar. She could do small powers without the full moon to boost her power, but nothing like what I felt today."

"Jamil says you helped Richard raise enough power to heal him," Louie said.

I shrugged, carefully so the coffee wouldn't spill. "I helped Richard control his beast. It raised . . . something. I don't know. Something."

"Richard went into one of his rages, and you helped bring him back?" Louie asked.

I looked at him then. "You've seen him when he loses control?"

He nodded. "Once."

The memory made me shiver. "Once is enough."

"But you helped him control it."

"She did," Jamil said. He sounded pleased.

Louie looked at him and shook his head.

"What's going on?" I asked.

"I've been telling Richard that he won't get better unless he gets you completely out of his system. I thought he had to forget you to heal himself."

"You sound like you've changed your mind," I said.

"If you can help Richard regain control of his beast, then he needs you. I don't care what arrangement you work out, Anita. But if he doesn't do something soon, he's going to end up dead. To stop that from happening, I'd do almost anything."

For the first time I realized that Louie didn't like me anymore. He was Richard's best friend. I guess I couldn't blame him. If he'd dumped Ronnie as badly as I'd dumped Richard, I'd be pissed, too.

"Even encouraging Richard to see me again?" I made it a question.

"Is that what you want?"

I shook my head and wouldn't meet his eyes. "I don't know. We're bound to each other for eternity. That's a long time to bitch at each other."

Richard appeared in the doorway. "A very long time," he said, "to watch you in his arms." He didn't sound bitter then. He sounded tired. His thick hair and muscular upper body were covered in fine white dust. Even his jeans were coated. He looked like something out of a porno movie where the handy-man consoles the lonely housewife. He walked over to stand in front of the roses. "Forever to see white roses with your name on them." He touched the single red rose, and smiled. "Nicely symbolic." His hand closed around the crimson flower; when he opened his hand, red petals scattered across the table. A drop of blood fell to the pale table top. He'd found a thorn.

Ronnie's eyes were wide, staring at the ruined rose. She glanced at me, eyebrows raised, but I didn't even know what expression to give her in return. "That was childish," I said.

Richard turned to me, hand stretched out towards me. "Too bad our other third isn't here to lick the blood off."

I felt an unpleasant smile curl my lips, and spoke before I could stop myself, or maybe I was just tired of trying. "There are at least three people in this room that would love to lick the blood off your skin, Richard. I'm not one of them."

He balled his hand into a fist. "You are such a bitch."

"Woof, woof," I said.

Louie stood. "Stop it, both of you."

"I will if he will," I said.

Richard just turned away, speaking without looking at anyone. "We changed the sheets on the bed. But I'm still a mess." He opened his hand. Blood had spread along the lines in his hand like a river following its banks. He turned to me with angry eyes. "Can I use one of the bathrooms to clean up?" He raised the hand slowly to his mouth and licked the blood very slowly, very deliberately, off his skin.

Ronnie made a small sound, almost a gasp. I managed not to faint; I'd seen the show before. "There's a full bath with shower upstairs. Door across the hall from the bedroom."

He put one finger in his mouth in slow motion, like he'd just eaten some finger-lickin' good chicken. His eyes never moved from my face. I was giving my best blank look, empty, nothing. Whatever he wanted from me, blankness was not it.

"What about the fancy tub downstairs?" he asked.

"Help yourself," I said. I sipped coffee, the picture of nonchalance. Edward would have been proud.

"Wouldn't Jean-Claude be upset if I used your precious tub? I know how much you both like water."

Someone had told him that we'd made love in the tub at the Circus. I'd have loved to know who and hurt them. Heat rose up my face; I couldn't stop it.

"A reaction at last," he said.

"You've embarrassed me, happy?"

He nodded. "Yes, yes I am."

"Go take your shower, Richard, or your bath. Light the damn candles, have a ball."

"Are you going to join me?" There was a time when I'd wanted an invitation like that from Richard more than almost anything in the world. The anger in his voice when he said it brought something very close to tears to my eyes. I wasn't exactly crying, but it hurt.

Ronnie stood, and Louie put a hand on her arm. Everyone stood or sat and tried to pretend they weren't witnessing something painfully personal.

A couple of deep breaths and I was okay. I wasn't about to let him see me cry. No way. "I didn't join Jean-Claude in the tub, Richard. He joined me. Maybe if you hadn't been such a frigging boy scout, it'd be you I was with right now and not him."

"Was one good fuck all it would have taken? Was it just that easy for you?"

I pushed to my feet, coffee sloshing down my hand onto the floor. I set the mug on the table, which put me within touching distance of Richard.

Ronnie and Louie had moved back from the table, giving us room. I think they'd have left the room if they had been sure we wouldn't come to blows. Jamil had set his coffee down as if he was getting ready to jump in and save us from ourselves. But it was too late to save us, far too late.

"You bastard," I said. "It took us both to get where we are, Richard."

"Three of us," he said.

"Fine," I said. My eyes were hot, my throat tight. "Maybe one good fuck would have done it. I don't know. Do your high ideals keep you warm at night, Richard? Does your moral high ground make you less lonely?"

He took that last step that put us almost touching. His anger flowed over me like an electric current. "You cheated on me, but you have him in your bed, and I have no one."

"Then find someone, Richard, find anyone, but let it go. Let it the fuck go."

He stepped back so abruptly, it made me sway. He left the room striding, his rage trailing after him like the smell of disturbing perfume.

I stood there for a second, then said, "Get out, everyone out."

The men left, but Ronnie stayed. I wouldn't have cried, honest, but she touched my shoulders, hugged me from behind, and whispered, "I'm so sorry." I could have withstood anything except sympathy.

I cried with my hands covering my face, still hiding, still hiding.

32

The doorbell rang. I moved as if to answer it, but Ronnie said, "Let someone else get it."

Zane called from the living room. "I'll get it." Which made me wonder where Jamil and Louie were. Comforting Richard, maybe?

I pushed away from Ronnie, scrubbing at my face. "Who could it be out here? We're in the middle of nowhere."

Jamil and Louie were suddenly back in the room. Either they'd heard me, or they were just as suspicious as I was. I picked the machine gun off the floor and stood in the doorway with the gun held at my left side, out of sight. The Firestar was in my right hand, also out of sight. Louie and Jamil moved into the living room to either side.

"Don't cross my line of sight," I said.

They both moved a little farther apart. Ronnie said, "I didn't bring my gun."

"The Browning is in the coat on the floor."

Her grey eyes were just a touch wide, her breathing just a little fast, but she nodded and went for the gun.

Zane was looking back at me with wide eyes. He looked a question at me, and I nodded. He checked the peephole. "Looks like a delivery guy with flowers."

"Open it," I said.

Zane did, blocking my view of the man. The man's voice was too soft to hear. Zane turned back to me. "Says you have to sign for the flowers."

"Who are they from?"

The man peered around Zane, raising his voice to say, "Jean-Claude."

"Just a minute." I laid the machine gun on the floor out of sight and kept the Firestar hidden behind my leg as I moved for the door. Jean-Claude kept me supplied with flowers, but he usually waited for the old ones to start to die, or at least fade. Of course, he had turned on the romantic overtime today.

He was a small man, holding the box of roses in his arm, his left hand on top of the box with a clipboard and a pencil with one of those strings on it.

Zane stepped away from the door to let me move up, but I got my first look in the little plastic window of the box. Yellow roses. I stopped moving forward and tried to smile. "You'll need a tip. Wait there while I get my purse."

The man's eyes flicked around the room, watching Jamil move up to his left and Louie to his right. I stepped to one side trying not to be directly in front of him. He followed me with the box, with his hand under the box.

Jamil had the best angle. I made his name a question, "Jamil?"

"Yes" was all he said, but it was enough.

"I don't need a tip," the man said, "but I'm running behind. Could you just sign for it so I could get going?"

"Sure," I said. Jamil had picked up what was going on, but Zane was still looking puzzled. Ronnie was somewhere behind me. I didn't dare look for her, but I moved just a little more off-line and the man followed me with the hand I couldn't see, with the hand that Jamil had confirmed had a gun in it.

I was almost even with Louie. He'd stopped moving, waiting for me to come to him. He'd figured it out, too. Great, now what?

It was Ronnie who decided it. "Drop the gun, or I drop you." Her voice confident—certain. I spared a glance to see her standing feet apart, Browning in a two-handed grip pointed at the man in the doorway.

Jamil yelled, "Anita!"

I turned and pointed the Firestar in one movement. The man was already raising the hand and the box. I got a glimpse of the gun. He ignored Ronnie completely, pointing the gun at me. If he'd just fired from his hip, he'd have had time for one shot, but he tried for a better shooting stance and that was that.

Zane finally reacted, when what he should have done was stay out of the way, which just goes to show that super strength and super speed are not enough. You got to know what to do with it. He slapped the box and clipboard out of the man's hand, making his first shot ring into the floor.

Ronnie's first shot went wide into the doorjamb. Zane was blocking my line of fire. I watched the gun come back up, pointed towards Ronnie this time.

Zane grabbed for the gun, and the gun went off twice more. Zane's body jerked, falling in slow motion to the floor. I had the gun pointed so that when Zane's body cleared the way, I was ready. Ronnie's second shot took the man in the shoulder, pushing him backwards. He fired at me, slumped in the doorway. His bullet went wide. Mine didn't.

Blood blossomed on his chest. He stared at me, eyes wide and almost puzzled, as if he didn't understand what was happening to him. Even with that first touch of death filling his eyes, he started to raise the gun, trying for one last shot.

Two shots went off like thunderous echoes. My shot took him in the chest. Ronnie's shot took the top of his head off. Glazer Safety Rounds will do that to unprotected flesh.

I walked up to the man, gun pointed at him, ready to shoot him again, but it was over. His chest was a mass of blood, and his head looked like someone had scalped him and gone a little too deep. Heavier fluids than blood were leaking all over my porch step.

Ronnie came up beside me, gun pointed at him. She took one look and stumbled outside, nearly tripping over the dead man's legs. She fell into the grass, retching and crying.

Zane just lay there, bleeding. Louie was checking his pulse. "He's dying." He wiped the blood on his T-shirt and went out into the sunlight to take care of Ronnie.

I stared down at Zane's pale chest. One bullet had taken him low in the lungs. Red bubbles filled the wound, making that horrible sound that sucking chest wounds make that says, without a medic or a doctor, the person is dead. Just a matter of when, not if.

33

We'd called the ambulance and found that they weren't coming right away. Too many other emergencies ahead of us. It was Louie who pried the phone out of my hands and apologized to the nice operator.

Cherry ran to the kitchen. I could hear her opening and shutting drawers, cabinets banging.

I walked into the kitchen.

She was standing in the middle of the room with a drawer pulled all the way out in one hand. Her eyes were almost wild. Before I could say anything, she said, "I need a Ziploc bag, masking tape, and scissors."

I didn't ask stupid questions. I opened the small drawer beside the stove and handed her the tape and scissors. The Ziploc bags were one of the few things in the roomy pantry closet.

Cherry snatched them from my hands and headed for the living room. I had no idea what she had in mind, but she had the medical training. I didn't. If it would give Zane a few more minutes, then I was for it. The ambulance would come eventually. The trick was having him alive for it to matter.

As far as I could tell, she didn't use the scissors. She taped the bag over his chest, plastering it with tape except for one corner. It was very obviously meant to be left that way, but I had to ask. "Why is the one corner untaped?"

She answered without looking up from her patient. "The open corner lets him breathe, but when he sucks in air the bag collapses and seals the wound. It's called an inclusive bandage." She sounded as if she was lecturing. I wondered, not for the first time, what Cherry was like outside the monster stuff. She was almost like two different people. I'd never meant anyone, monster or not, who seemed so divided.

"Will it keep him alive long enough for the ambulance to get here?" I asked.

She finally looked up at me—eyes very serious. "I hope so."

I nodded. It was better than I could have done. I was great at putting holes in people. Not so good at keeping them alive.

Richard brought a blanket and folded it over Zane's legs, letting Cherry take the upper part of the blanket to fix the way she wanted around the wound.

Richard was wearing nothing but a towel around his waist his tanned skin beaded with water as if he hadn't even taken time to dry off. The towel clung in a smooth tight line to his butt as he folded the quilt over Zane. His thick hair hung in heavy strands, so wet that water trickled from it in fine lines down his back.

He stood up, and the towel flashed a lot of thigh.

"I have larger towels," I said.

He frowned at me. "I heard gunshots. I wasn't really worried about the size of the towel."

I nodded. "You're right. Sorry." My anger with Richard seemed to shrink in direct proportion to his clothes. If he really wanted to win the war, all he had to do was strip. I'd have put up a white flag and applauded. Embarrassing, but almost true.

He ran his hand through his hair, smoothing it back from his face and squeezing out the excess water. That small movement showed his arms and chest to wonderful advantage. He arched his back just a little, which stretched the rest of his body in one long muscled line. It was the back arch that did it. I knew he was showing his body off on purpose. He'd always seemed unconscious of the effect his body had on me until now. Now, staring into his angry eyes, I knew he'd shown me his body very deliberately. His way of saying, without words, see what you passed on, see what you lost. If it had just been the great body I'd lost out on, it wouldn't have hurt so much.

I missed Sunday afternoons watching old musicals. Saturday hiking through the woods, bird-watching, or entire weekends of rafting on the Meramec. I missed hearing about his day at school. I missed him. The body was just a very nice bonus. I wasn't sure there were enough roses in the world to make me forget what Richard had almost been to me.

He stalked away towards the stairs and his interrupted shower. If I'd been as strong of will as I liked to think, I wouldn't have watched him walk away. I had a sudden vivid image of licking water off his chest and jerking that tiny white towel away. The image was clear enough that I had to turn away and take a few deep breaths. He wasn't mine anymore. Maybe he never had been.

"I don't mean to interrupt the stud watch," Jamil said, "but who is the dead guy, and why did he try to kill you?"

If I thought I'd been embarrassed before, I was wrong. The fact that I'd let the shit with Richard distract me from the much more vital question of the would-be murderer just proved that I wasn't up on my game. It was too careless for words. The sort of carelessness that can get you killed.

"I don't know him," I said.

Louie lifted the sheet that someone had thrown over him. "I don't recognize him either."

"Please," Ronnie said. She was looking somewhere between grey and green again.

Louie let the sheet fall back, but it was flatter somehow and clung to the top of his head. The blood soaked up the cotton like oil to a wick.

Ronnie made a small sound and ran for the bathroom.

Louie watched her run out. I watched him watch her. He caught me looking and said, "She's killed people before." The implied "why is this worse?" went unsaid.

"Once before," I said.

He stood up. "Did she react like this?"

I shook my head. "I think it was the sight of his brains leaking all over the porch that did it."

Gwen walked into the room. "A lot of people who can take the sight of blood don't like to see other things leaking out."

"Thank you, Ms. Therapist," Jamil said.

She turned to him like a small blond storm, her otherworldly energy spiraling through the room. "You are a homophobic bastard."

I raised eyebrows. "I miss something?"

"Jamil is one of those men who believes that every lesbian is just a heterosexual woman waiting for the right man. He was persistent enough to me that Sylvie kicked his ass."

"Such language from a trained therapist," Jason said. He'd rushed up from the basement where the vampires were stored for the day when the shooting started. When the excitement died down, he'd gone back to check on everybody.

"All quiet down below?" I asked.

He gave me that grin of his that managed to be both mischievous and just a touch evil. "Quiet as a tomb."

I groaned because he expected it. But the smile left my face before it left his. "Could it be the council?" I asked.

"Could what be the council?" Louie asked.

"Whoever sent the hit man," I said.

"Do you really think he was a hit man?" Jamil asked.

"You mean was he a professional assassin?"

Jamil nodded.

"No," I said.

"Why wasn't he a professional?" Gwen asked.

"Not good enough," I said.

"Maybe he was a virgin," Jamil said.

"You mean a first timer?"

"Yes."

"Maybe." I glanced at the sheet-covered lump. "He picked the wrong career."

"If it had been some suburban housewife or an investment banker, he'd have done okay," Jamil said.

"Sounds like you know."

He shrugged. "I've been an enforcer since I was fifteen. My threat's not worth anything unless I'm willing to kill."

"How does Richard feel about that?" I asked.

Jamil shrugged again. "Richard's different, but if he wasn't, then I'd be dead. He'd have killed me right after he killed Marcus. It's standard op for a new Ulfric to kill the old leader's enforcers."

"I wanted you dead."

He smiled and it was tight, but not altogether unpleasant. "I know what you wanted. You're closer to being one of us than he is sometimes."

"I just don't have a lot of illusions, Jamil. That's all."

"You think Richard's morality is an illusion?"

"He nearly crushed your throat earlier today. What do you think?"

"I think he also healed me. Marcus and Raina couldn't have done that."

"Would they have hurt you that badly by accident?" I asked.

He smiled, a quick baring of teeth. "If Raina had gone for my throat, it wouldn't have been by accident."

"On a whim," Gwen said, "but not by accident."

The werewolves all had a moment of perfect understanding. None of them mourned Raina, not even Jamil, who had sort of been on her side.

I shook my head. "I just don't think the council would send out some amateur with a gun. They've got enough daytime muscle to do the job without hiring outsiders."

"Then who?" Jamil asked.

I shook my head again. "I wish I knew."

Ronnie came back into the living room. We all watched her as she made her shaky way back to the couch. She sat down, eyes red-rimmed from crying and other things. Louie brought her a glass of water. She sipped it very slowly and looked at me. I expected her to talk about the dead man. Maybe to accuse me of being a horrible friend. But she'd decided to ignore the dead body and work on the live ones.

"If you had slept with Richard when you first started dating, all this pain could have been avoided."

"You're so sure of that," I said. I let Ronnie change the subject. She needed something else to concentrate on. I'd have preferred the topic to be something besides my love life, but . . . I owed her.

"Yes," she said, "the way you look at him, Anita. The way he looks at you when he's not being cruel. Yeah, I'm sure."

Part of me agreed with her, part of me . . . "There'd still be Jean-Claude."

She made an impatient sound. "I know you. If you'd had sex with Richard first, you still wouldn't be sleeping with that damn vampire. You think sex is a commitment."

I sighed. We'd had this talk before. "Sex should mean something, Ronnie."

"I agree," she said. "But if I had your scruples, I'd still just be holding hands with Louie. We're having a wonderful time."

"But where is it going?"

She closed her eyes and leaned her head against the back of the couch. "Anita, you make your life harder than it has to be." She opened her eyes and moved just her head so she could look at me and still slump. "Why can't a relationship just be what it is? Why does everything with you have to be so damn serious?"

I folded my arms over my stomach and stared at her. If I thought I was going to stare her down, I was wrong. I looked away first. "It is serious or should be."

"Why?" she said.

I was finally reduced to shrugging. If I hadn't been having sex with a vampire out of wedlock, I'd have had some moral high ground to stand on. As it was, I had nothing to fight back with. I'd been virtuous for so long, but when I lost it, I lost it big time. From celibacy to fucking the undead. If I'd still been Catholic, it would have been enough to get me excommunicated. Of course, being an Animator was enough to get me excommunicated. Lucky for me I was Protestant.

"You want some advice from your Auntie Ronnie?"

That made me smile, a small smile, but it was better than nothing. "What advice?"

"Go upstairs and join that man in the shower."

I looked at her, suitably scandalized. The fact that I'd been pretty much fantasizing about doing just that not ten minutes ago only made it more embarrassing. "You saw him in the kitchen, Ronnie. I don't think he's in a co-ed shower sort of mood."

A look came into her eyes that suddenly made me feel young or maybe naive. "You strip off and surprise him, and he won't kick you out. You don't get that kind of anger without heat. He wants you as badly as you want him. Just give into it, girlfriend."

I shook my head.

She sighed. "Why not?"

"A thousand things, but mainly, Jean-Claude."

"Dump him," she said.

I laughed. "Yeah, right."

"Is he really that good? So good that you couldn't give him up?"

I thought about that for a minute and didn't know what to say. It finally boiled down to one thing, and I said it out loud. "I'm not sure there are enough white roses in the world to make me forget Richard." I held up a hand before she could interrupt. "But I'm not sure there are enough cozy afternoons in all eternity to make me forget Jean-Claude."

She sat up straight on the couch, staring at me. A look almost of sorrow filled her eyes. "You mean that, don't you?"

"Yeah," I said.

Ronnie shook her head. "Jesus, Anita, you are screwed."

That made me laugh, because she was right. It was either cry or laugh about it, and Richard had gotten all the tears he was getting from me for one day.

34

The phone rang, and I jumped. Now that the danger was over, I could be jumpy. I went into the kitchen and picked up the phone. Before I could even answer, I heard Dolph's voice. "Anita, you okay?"

"The police grapevine is even faster than I thought," I said.

"What are you talking about?"

I told him what I'd told the 911 operator.

"I didn't know," Dolph said.

"Then why did you want to know if I was okay?"

"Nearly every vampire-owned business or house in the city was hit about the same time this morning. They fire-bombed the Church of Eternal Life, and we've had one-on-one hits on non-vamps all over the city."

Fear rushed through me like fine champagne, useless adrenaline with nowhere to go. I had a lot of friends that were undead, not just Jean-Claude. "Dead Dave's, has it been hit?"

"I know Dave resents being kicked off the force after he . . . died, but we take care of our own. His bar's got a uniformed guard until we find out what the hell is going on. We got the arsonist before he could do more than smoke up an outside wall."

I knew that only the bad vamps were at the Circus, but Dolph didn't. He might find it strange if I didn't ask. "The Circus?"

"They defended themselves against a couple of arsonists. Why didn't you ask about the love of your life, first, Anita? Isn't he home?"

Dolph asked like he already knew, which could mean he knew or it could mean he was fishing. But I was pretty sure the council flunkies wouldn't have told the whole truth. Half-truth, it was. "Jean-Claude stayed over last night."

The silence this time was even thicker than before. I let it build into something thick and unpleasant enough to choke on. I don't know how long we listened to each other breathe, but it was Dolph who broke first. "Lucky for him. Did you know this was coming?"

That caught me off guard. If he thought I'd held out on something this big, no wonder he was pissed at me. "No, Dolph, I swear I had no idea."

"Did your boyfriend?"

I thought about that for a second. "I don't think so, but I'll ask him when he gets up."

"Don't you mean when he rises from the dead?"

"Yeah, Dolph," I said, "that's what I mean."

"You think he could have known about all this shit and not told you?"

"Probably not, but he has his moments."

"Yet you still date him . . . I just don't understand that, Anita."

"If I could explain it so that it made sense to you, Dolph, I would, but I can't."

He sighed. "You got any ideas why someone's hitting all the monsters today?"

"You mean, why monsters or why this date?" I asked.

"Either," he said.

"You've got some suspects in custody, right?"

"Yes."

"They haven't talked."

"Only to ask for a lawyer. A lot of them ended up dead like yours."

"Humans Against Vampires, or Humans First, maybe," I said.

"Would either of them hit shifters?"

My stomach clenched into a nice tight knot. "What do you mean?"

"A man walked into a bar in the loop with a submachine gun with silver ammo."

For a minute I thought Dolph meant the Lunatic Cafe, Raina's old restaurant, but it wasn't an openly lycanthrope hangout. I tried to think what was up there that was openly shifter. "The Leather Den?" I made it a question.

"Yeah," he said.

The Leather Den was the only bar in the country, to my knowledge, that was a hangout for sadomasochistic gay men who happened to be shapeshifters. It was a triple threat to any hatemonger. "Geez, Dolph, if it wasn't happening with every-thing else, I'd say it could be almost any right-wing fruitcake. Did you get the machine gunner alive?"

"Nope," Dolph said. "The survivors ate him."

"Bet they didn't," I said.

"They used teeth to kill him, Anita. That's eating him in my book."

I'd seen shapeshifters eat people, not just attack them, but since most of those were illegal kills, i.e. murders, I let Dolph win the fight. He was still wrong, but hard to show him my proof without getting people in trouble.

"Whatever you say, Dolph."

He was quiet for long enough that I had to say, "You still there?"

"Why do I think you're holding back on me, Anita?"

"Would I do that?"

"In a heartbeat," he said.

His asking about the date had triggered some vague memory. "There is some-thing about today's date."

"What is it?" he asked.

"I don't know—something. Do you need me to come in?"

"Since almost all this shit is preternatural-related, every uniform and his K9 is asking for us. So yeah, we need everybody in the field today. They've been hitting the monster isolation wards of most of the major hospitals."

"Jesus, Stephen," I said.

"He's all right, they all are," Dolph said. "A guy with a 9mm tried for them. The cop at the door got hit."

"He all right?" I asked.

"He'll live." Dolph didn't sound happy, and it wasn't just the hitter or a wounded cop.

"What happened to the shooter?" I asked.

He laughed, an abrupt, harsh sound. "One of Stephen's 'cousins' threw him up against a wall so hard, his skull cracked. Nurses say the shooter was about to put a round right between the uniform's eyes when he was . . . stopped."

"So Stephen's cousin saved the cop's life," I said.

"Yeah," Dolph said.

"You don't sound happy about that."

"Leave it alone, Anita."

"Sorry. What do you want me to do?"

"The detective in charge is Padgett. He's a good cop."

"No small praise coming from you," I said. "Why do I hear a 'but' coming?"

"But," Dolph said, "he gets freaked around the monsters. Someone needs to go down there and hold his hand so he doesn't get carried away with the murderous shapeshifters."

"So I'm a babysitter?"

"It's your party, Anita. I can send someone else. I thought you'd want this one."

"I do, and thanks."

"Don't stay all day, Anita. Make it as quick as you can. Pete McKinnon just called me to ask if he could borrow you."

"Was there another arson?"

"Yes, but it wasn't his firebug. I told you they bombed the Church of Eternal Life."

"Yeah."

"Malcolm is in there," he said.

"Shit," I said. Malcolm was the undead Billy Graham, founder of the fastest-growing denomination in the country. It was the vampire church, but humans could join. In fact, they were encouraged. Though how long they stayed human was debatable.

"I'm surprised his daytime retreat was that obvious."

"What do you mean?"

"Most master vamps spend a lot of time and energy hiding their daytime address so that shit like this doesn't happen to them. Is he dead?"

"You are amusing as hell today, Anita."

"You know what I mean," I said.

"No one knows. McKinnon's going to call you with more details. Hospital first, then his scene. When you get done there call me. I'll figure out where to send you next.''

"Have you called Larry?''

"You think he's up to this much solo action?''

I thought about that for a second. "He knows his preternatural stuff.''

Dolph said, "I hear a 'but' coming.''

I laughed. "We have worked together too damn long. Yeah, but he's not a shooter. And I don't think that's going to change.''

"A lot of good cops aren't shooters, Anita.''

"Cops can go twenty-five years and never clear leather. Vampire executioners don't have that luxury. We go in planning to kill things. The things we're planning to kill know that.''

"If all you have is a hammer, Anita, every problem begins to look like a nail.''

"I read Massad Ayoob, too, Dolph. I don't use my gun as the only solution.''

"Sure, Anita. I'll call Larry.''

I wanted to say, "don't get him killed," but I didn't. Dolph wouldn't get him killed on purpose, and Larry was a grownup. He'd earned the right to take his chances like everyone else. But it hurt something inside of me to know he'd be out there today without me as backup. They call it cutting the apron strings. It feels more like amputating body parts.

I suddenly remembered why today's date was important. "The Day of Cleansing," I said.

"What?'' Dolph said.

"The history books call it the Day of Cleansing. The vampires call it the Inferno. Two hundred years ago the Church joined forces with the military in Germany, England, oh, hell, almost every European country except France—and burned out every vampire or suspected vampire sympathizer in a single day. The destruction was complete and a lot of innocent people went up in the flames. But the fire accomplished their goal, a lot fewer vampires in Europe.''

"Why didn't France join with everyone?''

"Some historians think the King of France had a vampire mistress. The French Revolutionaries put out propaganda that the nobility were all vampires at one point, which wasn't true of course. Some say that's why the guillotine was so popular. It kills both the living and the undead.''

Somewhere during the mini-lecture I realized that I could ask Jean-Claude. If he missed the French Revolution, it wasn't by much. For all I knew, he'd fled the Revolution by coming to this country. Why hadn't I thought to ask? Because it still freaked me out that the man I was sleeping with was nearly three hundred years older than I was. Talk about a generation gap. So sue me if I tried to be as normal in some areas as possible. Asking my lover about events that happened when George Washington and Thomas Jefferson were still alive was definitely not normal.

"Anita, are you all right?''

"Sorry, Dolph, I was . . . thinking.''

"Do I want to know about what?''

"Probably not,'' I said.

He let it go. Not more than a handful of months ago Dolph would have pushed until he thought I'd told him everything about everything. But if we were going to stay co-workers, let alone friends, some things were best left unsaid. Our relationship couldn't survive full disclosure. It never had, but I don't think Dolph understood that until recently.

"Day of Cleansing, okay."

"If you talk to any vampires, don't call it that. Call it the Inferno. The other phrase is like calling the Jewish Holocaust a racial cleansing."

"You've made your point," he said. "Remember while you're out there doing police work that you're still on someone's hit parade."

"Gee, Dolph, you do love me."

"Don't push it," he said.

"Watch your own back, Dolph. Anything happens to you, Zerbrowski's in charge."

Dolph's deep laughter was the last thing I heard before the phone clicked dead. I don't think in the nearly five years I'd known Dolph that he'd ever said goodbye on the phone.

The phone rang as soon as I put it down. It was Pete McKinnon. "Hi, Pete. Just got off the phone with Dolph. He told me you wanted me down at the main branch of the Church."

"He tell you why?"

"Something about Malcolm."

"We've got nearly every human member of his Church screaming for us to make sure their big cheese didn't get toasted. But we opened the floor up to check on some vamps on the west side and they weren't in coffins. Two of them went up in smoke. If we let Malcolm get cooked, trying to save him . . . Let's just say I don't want to do the paper work."

"What do you want me to do?" I seemed to be asking that a lot lately.

"We need to know if it's safe to leave him alone until he can rise on his own, or if we need to figure out how to rescue him. Vampires can't drown, can they?"

I thought the last was a strange question. "Except for holy water, vamps don't have any problem with water."

"Even running water?" he asked.

"You've been doing your homework. I'm impressed," I said.

"I'm big into self-improvement. What about running water?"

"To my knowledge, water isn't a deterrent, running or otherwise. Why do you ask?"

"You've never been to a building after a fire, have you?" he asked.

"No," I said.

"Unless the basement is airtight, it'll be full of water. A lot of water."

Could vampires drown? It was a good question. I wasn't sure. Maybe they could, and that was why some of the folklore talked about running water. Or maybe it was like saying that vampires could shapechange, not true at all. "They don't always breathe, so I don't think they'd drown. I mean, if a vampire woke with his coffin underwater, I think they could just not breathe and get out of the water. But, truthfully, I'm not a hundred percent sure."

"Can you tell if he's okay without going down there?"

"Truth is, I'm not sure. I've never tried anything like that."

"Will you try?"

I nodded, realized he couldn't see it, and said, "Sure, but you're second on my list, not first."

"All right, but hurry. The media is all over this thing. Between them and the Church members, we are not having a good time."

"Ask them if Malcolm is the only vamp down there. Ask them if the basement is steel-reinforced."

"Why would it be?"

"A lot of the basements where vamps sleep have concrete ceilings reinforced with steel beams. The church's basement doesn't have any windows, so it could mean that the lower area was specially designed with vamps in mind. I think you'd need to know that even if you decide to open the floor up."

"We do."

"Take some of the bitching faithful aside and ask them questions. You need to know the answers either way, and it'll at least give them the illusion that something's happening until I can get there."

"That is the best idea I've heard in two hours."

"Thanks. I'll be there as soon as I can, promise." I had a thought. "Wait, Pete. Does Malcolm have a human servant?"

"A lot of the people here have vampire bites."

"No," I said. "I mean a true human servant."

"I thought that was just a human with one or two vampire bites."

"So did I once," I said. "A human with just a couple of bites is what the vamps call a Renfield, as in the character from the novel *Dracula*." I'd asked Jean-Claude what they called them before the book came out. He'd said, "slaves." Ask a silly question.

"What's a human servant, then?" Pete asked. It reminded me of Dolph.

"A human who's bound to the vampire by something called marks. It's sort of mystical and magical shit, but it gives the servant and the vamp a tie that we could use to see if Malcolm is okay."

"Can any vampire have a servant?"

"No, only a master vampire, and not even all of them. I've never heard of Malcolm having one, but he could if he wanted to. Ask the faithful, though I think if he had one, the servant would be yelling louder than the rest. It's still worth a shot. If you solve it before I get there, call. Dolph says there's plenty of other shit to go around."

"He's not kidding. The city is going nuts. So far we've managed to contain the fires to just a few buildings, but if the crazies keep this up, it's going to get out of hand. There's no telling how much of the city could go up."

"We need to know who's behind this," I said.

"Yes, we do," Pete said. "Get here as soon as you can." He sounded so sure I could help. I wished I was as certain. I wasn't sure I could do shit in broad daylight. I'd been told once that the only reason I couldn't raise the dead at high noon was that I thought I couldn't. I was about to put it to the test. I still didn't think I could do it. Doubt is the greatest enemy of any magic or psychic ability. Self-doubt is a self-fulfilling prophecy.

"I'll be there as soon as I can."

"Great. I won't lie. I'm relieved that somebody with vampire experience is going to be on-site. The cops are starting to get some training on how to handle the preternatural, but no one trains firemen for this kind of shit."

It had never occurred to me that firemen have to deal with the monsters almost as much as the police. They don't hunt them down, but they enter their houses. That can be just as dangerous, depending on if the monster in question realizes you're there to help or not.

"I'll be there, Pete."

"We'll be waiting. See ya."

"Bye, Pete."

We hung up. I went for my shoulder holster and a different shirt. The shoulder holster would chafe with just a tank top on.

35

I changed into a navy polo shirt and didn't run into Richard. The water had stopped running, but he hadn't come out. I did not want to see him again, especially not half naked. I wanted away from him. Lucky for me the shit had hit the fan, professionally speaking. Police work, lots of it, maybe enough to keep me out of the house all day. Fine with me. The ambulance arrived, and Zane was loaded in. Cherry went with him. I felt guilty not going with him, but she could do more good than I could. The police had still not shown up for the corpse. I hated leaving the others to talk to the cops without me, but I had to go. The fact that I was relieved to go caused me a few moments of guilt, but not much.

Ronnie had gone back to sitting on the couch. She asked just before I walked out the door, "Am I going to jail tonight?"

I knelt in front of her, taking her strangely cold hands in mine. "Ronnie, you didn't kill him."

"I shot the top of his head off. What kind of ammo do you have in that gun of yours anyway?"

"I shot him twice in the chest. There isn't enough left of his heart to scrape up with a spoon," I said.

She closed her eyes. "His brains are leaking out all over the porch. Don't tell me that wouldn't have killed him all by itself."

I sighed and patted her hands. "Please, Ronnie, you did what you had to do. Maybe it will take a medical examiner to decide which bullet did him in, but when the cops get here, make sure you don't take credit."

"I've been here before, Anita, remember. I know what to say and what not to say." She looked at me and it wasn't an entirely friendly look.

I released her hands and stood. "I'm sorry, Ronnie."

"I've only shot two people and both times I was with you."

"Both times you did it to save my life," I said.

She looked up at me with bleak eyes. "I know."

I touched her face and wanted to pat her on the head or something, comfort her the way you'd comfort a child, but she wasn't a child. "I am sorry this happened, Ronnie. Truly, but what else could you have done?"

"Nothing," she said, "and that makes me wonder if I'm in the right business."

Something inside of me tightened. "Don't you mean, wondering if you have the right friends? This didn't happen because of your business. It happened because of mine."

She gripped my hand tight. "Best friends, Anita, forever."

"Thanks, Ronnie, more than you'll ever know. I don't think I'd ever get over losing you as a friend, but don't decide to stay with me because of loyalty. Think about it, Ronnie, really think about it. My life doesn't seem to be getting any safer. If anything, it's getting more dangerous. You might want to think about whether you want to be in the line of fire." Just making the offer made my eyes burn. I squeezed her hand and turned away before she could see that the scourge of vampirekind was tearing up.

She didn't call me back and profess undying friendship. I'd half wanted her to, but the other half was glad she was really thinking about it. If Ronnie got herself killed because of me, I just might pull the guilt down over my ears and crawl into a hole. I caught Richard watching me from the doorway below the stairs. Maybe he and I could share a hole together. That'd be punishment enough.

"What's happened now?" he asked. He'd dried his hair into a shining mass of waves that slid over the top of his shoulders as he moved into the room. He'd put his jeans back on and found a shirt that fit him. It was a large T-shirt with a caricature of Arthur Conan Doyle on it. I used it for sleeping. It was a little snug on Richard through the shoulders and chest. Not small, mind you, just tight. On me the shirt hung nearly to my knees.

"See you found the blow dryer and the T-shirt drawer. Help yourself," I said.

"Answer my question," he said.

"Ask Jamil. He's got all the details."

"I asked you," Richard said.

"I don't have time to stand here and tell it twice. I've got to go to work."

"Police or vampire?"

"You used to ask that because you worried more if I was out on a vampire execution. You were always relieved if it was just police work. Why the hell do you want to know now, Richard? What do you care?" I walked out without waiting for an answer.

I had to step over the dead man on my porch. I hoped the cops got there soon. It was a typical July day in St. Louis—hot and claustophobically humid. The body would start to smell if it didn't get carried away soon. Just another of the many joys of summer.

My Jeep was in the garage, where it should have been. I'd let Jean-Claude use it to ferry everyone here. Though he hadn't driven. I'd never met an older vamp that drove. The older ones tended to be a bit technophobic. I was actually backing out of the garage when I saw Richard in the rearview mirror. He looked angry. I thought very seriously about just continuing out. He'd move. But just in case he'd be stupid enough not to, I waited for him to come up to the driver's-side window.

I pressed the button and the window whirred down like it was supposed to. "What?" I asked. I let that one word be as hostile as his eyes.

"Three of my pack in danger. Three of my people may be under arrest, and you didn't tell me."

"I'm taking care of it, Richard."

"It's my job to take care of my wolves."

"You want to go down there in person and announce that you're their Ulfric? You can't even go down there and be their friend because that might jeopardize your precious secret."

He gripped the edge of the window hard enough for his fingers to grow pale. "Most pack leaders have secret identities, Anita. You know that."

"Raina was your public alpha, Richard. She would have gone down to the hospital for them. But she's dead. You can't go. Who's left?"

Something popped in the door.

"I will be pissed if you break my car," I said.

He moved his hands slowly as if he needed something to hold just to keep his hands busy. "Don't get too comfortable as lupa, Anita. I am going to replace you."

We stared at each other from less than a foot away. Once he'd have come out to the car for one last goodbye kiss. Now it was one last fight.

"Fine, but until you find someone else, I'm all you've got. Now I've got to go and see if I can keep our wolves out of jail."

"They wouldn't be in police custody if you hadn't put them in harm's way."

He had me there. "If I hadn't put guards on Stephen and Nathaniel, they'd be dead right now." I shook my head and started easing the Jeep back. Richard stepped out of the way so I could do it without risking his toes.

He stood there and watched me drive away. If he'd asked, I would have found him a shirt, but it wouldn't have been that one. One, it was a favorite; two, it reminded me of a particular weekend. There'd been a Sherlock Holmes movie marathon, starring Basil Rathbone. Not my favorite, mainly because they make Dr. Watson out to be a buffoon, but still good. I wore the shirt that weekend even though it was too big to wear outside the house. The fashion police didn't get me, but Richard loved the shirt. Had he just grabbed a shirt and not even remembered? Or had he worn it to remind me of what I'd given up? I think I preferred it as a vindictive gesture. If he could wear the shirt and not remember that weekend, I didn't want to know. We'd managed to spill popcorn all over me and the couch. Richard wouldn't let me get up and dust myself off. He'd insisted on cleaning me up himself. Cleaning up seemed to involve no hands at all and a lot of mouth. If the memory meant nothing to him, then maybe we'd never been in love. Maybe it had all been lust and I just confused the two. God, I hoped not.

36

Another crime scene, another show. At least, the body had been removed. That was an improvement from my house. I'd left three werewolves behind to guard Stephen and Nathaniel. Two of those werewolves were in the hallway. Lorraine was still dressed like the ideal second-grade school teacher except for the handcuffs, which didn't seem to match the outfit. She was sitting in one of those straight-backed chairs that all hospitals seem to have. This one was in a horrid orange color which matched none of the soft pastel walls. She was sobbing with her hands covering her face. Her wrists looked small in the handcuffs. Teddy knelt beside her like a small weightlifting mountain, patting her thin back.

There was a uniformed cop on either side of them, at attention. One of the uniforms had his hand sort of casually resting on the butt of his gun. The strap that held the gun in the holster was already unsnapped. It pissed me off.

I walked up to the cop in question, way too close, invading the hell out of his personal space. "Better snap up the weapon there, Officer, before someone takes it away from you."

He blinked pale eyes at me. "Ma'am?"

"Use your holster the way it's meant to be used or get away from these people."

"What's the problem here. Murdock?" A tall, lanky man with a headful of dark curls walked towards us. His suit hung so loose on his thin body that it looked borrowed. His face was taken up by a huge pair of blue eyes. Except for the height, he looked like a twelve-year-old who had borrowed his daddy's clothes.

"I don't know, sir," Murdock said, eyes front. I was betting that he'd been in the military or wanted to be. He just had that taste to him of a wannabe.

The tall man turned to me. "What seems to be the problem, Detective . . . ?" He left a long blank space for me to put a name in.

"Blake, Anita Blake. I'm with the Regional Preternatural Investigation Team."

He held out a large-knuckled hand to me. He pumped my hand a little too vigorously but he didn't squeeze hard. He wasn't trying to test me, just glad to see me. His touch made my skin tingle. He was psychic. A first among the police I'd met, except for a witch they'd hired on purpose.

"You must be Detective Padgett," I said.

He nodded and dropped my hand, smiling wonderfully. Smiling made him look even younger. If he hadn't been nearly Dolph's height, he'd have had real trouble with being authoritative. But a lot of people mistake height for in charge. I've struggled against the opposite reaction most of my life.

He put a hand across my shoulders and led me away from the werewolves. I didn't much care for the hand on my shoulders. If I'd been a guy, he wouldn't have done it. I let him herd me to one side, then stepped out of the circle of his arm. Didn't make a point of it, just did it. Who says I haven't mellowed?

"Fill me in," I said.

He did. It was pretty much what Dolph had told me. The only addition was that it had been Lorraine who slammed the man into the wall, which explained her tears. She probably thought she'd be going to jail. I couldn't promise she wouldn't be. If she'd been a human female that had just saved a policeman's life by inadvertently killing a bad guy, she wouldn't go to jail, not today. But she wasn't human, and the law isn't even-handed, or blind, no matter what we'd like to believe.

"Let me test my understanding here," I said. "The officer on the door was down. The shooter had the gun pointed at the officer's head and was about to deliver the coup de grâce when the woman dived into him. Her momentum carried them both back into the far wall, where he hit his head. That about right?"

Padgett glanced at his notes. "Yeah, that's about right."

"Why is she in handcuffs?"

His eyes widened, and he gave me his best little boy smile. Detective Padgett was a charmer. Didn't matter that he looked like a scarecrow, he was accustomed to getting by on charm. At least with women. I was betting his act had worked even less well on Lorraine.

"She's a lycanthrope," he said smiling, as if that explained it all.

"She tell you that?" I asked.

He looked startled. "No."

"You assumed she was a shapeshifter because why?"

The smile wilted, replaced by a frown that made him look petulant rather than angry. "She threw a man into a wall hard enough to crack his skull."

"Little old ladies lift cars off their grandchildren. Does that make them lycanthropes?"

"No, but . . ." His face closed down, defensive.

"I'm told you don't like shapeshifters much, Padgett."

"How I feel personally doesn't interfere with my job."

I laughed, and it startled him. "Padgett, how we feel personally always affects our job. I came here pissed because I'd had a fight with an ex-boyfriend, so I got in Murdock's face about his holster. Why don't you like lycanthropes, Padgett?"

"They give me the creeps, okay."

I had an idea. "Literally?" I asked.

"What do you mean, literally?"

"Does being around shapeshifters actually make your skin creep?"

He glanced up towards where the other cops were clustered. He bent forward and lowered his voice, and I knew I was right. "It's like bugs crawling on my skin every time I'm around them." He didn't look twelve now. The fear and the loathing in his face showed lines that put him closer to thirty than twenty.

"You're feeling their energy, their aura."

He jerked back from me. "The hell I am."

"Look, Padgett, I knew you were psychic the second I shook your hand."

"You're full of shit," he said. He was scared, scared of himself.

"Dolph's put the word out for any cops that have talent in this area. Why didn't you apply?"

"I am not a freak," he said.

"Ah, the truth comes out. You're not afraid of lycanthropes. You're afraid of you."

He raised a large fist, not to hit me, but just somewhere for his anger to go. "You don't know anything about me."

"They make my skin crawl, too, Padgett."

That calmed him, a little. "How can you stand to be near them?"

I shrugged. "You get used to it."

He shook his head, almost shivering. "I'd never get used to this."

"They aren't doing it on purpose, Detective. Some shapeshifters are better at hiding what they are than others, but all of them give off more energy during strong emotions. The more you questioned them, the more distressed they got, the more energy they gave off, and the creepier you felt."

"I had the woman in a room alone and I thought my skin was going to crawl off my body."

"Wait, alone? Did you Mirandize her?"

He nodded.

"Did she tell you anything?"

He shook his head. "Not a damn word."

"What about the others?"

"The men didn't do anything."

"Are they free to go?"

"The big one won't leave her and the other one is in the room with the two injured ones. Says he can't leave them unguarded. I told him that we could take care of it. He said, apparently not."

I agreed with Kevin. "You've got witnesses that say she didn't mean to hurt the man. He isn't even dead yet. Why is she still here in handcuffs?"

"She has already killed one man today. I think that's enough," he said.

"Two things, Detective. First, she could snap those cuffs any time she wanted to. Second, if she were human, you'd have let her go home by now."

"That's not true," he said.

I looked at him. He tried to stare me down, but he flinched first. He said, looking at a spot above my head, "The man is dying. If I let her go, she could skip out."

"Skip out on what? She saw a cop about to get his head blown off and jumped an armed man to save him. She didn't cut him up. She pushed him into a wall.

Trust me, Detective, if she'd meant to kill him, it would have been a more thorough job. She risked her life to save one of your own.''

"She didn't risk anything. Bullets don't hurt lycanthropes.''

"Silver bullets do. They work just like real ammo on a human. Every hit that they've investigated today had silver ammo, Padgett. Lorraine could have been killed, but she didn't hesitate. If she had, we'd have a dead cop on our hands. How many citizens would risk their lives to save a cop?''

He finally looked at me, eyes so angry they'd darkened two shades of blue. "You've made your point.''

"Have I?''

He nodded. "Yes.'' He walked back down towards the waiting uniforms and the sobbing werewolf. "Uncuff her.''

Murdock said, "Sir?''

"Do it, Murdock,'' Padgett said.

He didn't question it again, just knelt in front of Lorraine and unlocked the cuffs. His partner on the other side unsnapped his holster and took two big steps back. I let it go. We were winning, no need to fight.

As soon as her hands were free, Lorraine threw herself at me. I knew she didn't mean any harm, but I could hear the leather clearing down the hallway. I raised my voice and said, "It's okay, guys. She's okay. Ease down.''

Lorraine was on her knees, arms locked around my legs, sobbing full out, loud and messy. I held a hand pointed palm out to either end of the hallway. Teddy stood and half the guns swiveled to cover him. We were on the verge of having things go really wrong.

"Padgett, get hold of your men.'' I spared a glanced back at him and found his gun out, pointed at Teddy. Shit.

"Padgett, put up your gun and they'll follow your lead.''

"Have him sit down,'' Padgett said, voice even and very serious.

"Teddy,'' I said softly, "sit back down, very slowly, no sudden moves.''

"I haven't done anything,'' he said.

"Doesn't matter, just do it, please.''

He sat back down under the watchful eyes of half a dozen guns. He put his big hands on his knees, palms down showing he was unarmed. Like he'd had practice trying to look harmless.

"Now put your gun up, Detective,'' I said.

Padgett looked at me for a second. I thought he wasn't going to do it. I looked into those big blue eyes and saw something dangerous. A fear so deep and wide that he needed to destroy the thing he feared. He put the gun up, but that one moment of nakedness in his eyes had been enough. I'd talk to Dolph and see if Padgett had any shapeshifter kills to his credit. I'd almost have bet that he did. Cleared of charges didn't always mean innocent.

I patted the top of Lorraine's head. "It's all right. Everything's all right.'' I had to get them out of here. The good guys were almost as big a threat as the bad ones.

She looked up at me, eyes puffy, nose running. Real crying is like real sex. If you really do it, it isn't pretty. "I didn't mean to hurt him,'' she whispered.

"I know.'' I glanced at the police up and down the hallway. Some of them avoided my eyes. I shook my head and helped her stand. "I'm taking them into Stephen and Nathaniel's room with me, Detective Padgett. Any objections?"

He just shook his head.

"Great. Come on, Teddy."

"I can stand up?" he asked.

I looked at Padgett. "You think you and your people can hold the Rambo routine?"

"If he behaves himself, sure." Padgett wasn't trying to be charming anymore. I think he was embarrassed about the show. I knew he was still angry, maybe at me, maybe at himself. I didn't care as long as he didn't start shooting.

"You got a uniform inside the room?" I asked.

He gave one curt nod.

"Is he as trigger-happy as the rest of you, or can I open the door without being shot at?"

Padgett strode to the door and knocked on it. "Smith, it's Padgett. Detective coming in." He opened the door with a flourish and ushered Lorraine and me in.

I looked at the young uniform seated just inside the door. Kevin was slumped down in a chair across from him, an unlit cigarette in the corner of his mouth. The werewolf looked at me, and one look was enough—not a happy camper. It wasn't just nicotine withdrawal either.

I half-pushed Lorraine into the room, then walked back to Teddy. I held my left hand out to him, and he took it. I helped him stand, though he didn't need the help. "Thank you," he said, and he didn't mean for helping him stand up.

"No problem," I said. I escorted him back to the room. Once they were both safely inside, I turned to Padgett.

"We need to talk. I'd prefer private if I could be guaranteed no one will get shot while I'm gone."

"You okay in here, Smith?" he asked.

The young cop said, "I'm fine. I like animals."

The look on Teddy's face was scary even to me. That otherworldly energy was rising like a warm, stinging tide. "If the nice policeman behaves himself, then so do the rest of you," I said.

Teddy stared right at me. "I know how to follow orders."

"Great, shall we find some place private, Detective Padgett?"

His breath was coming fast, almost a pant. He was feeling the rising energy, too. "We can talk right here. I'm not leaving one of my men alone with these things."

"I'm okay, boss," the young cop said.

"You're not afraid?" Padgett asked. It was a question that cops seldom ask each other. They ask, are you all right. They admit to being nervous. Never scared.

Officer Smith's eyes widened a little, but he shook his head. "I know Crossman. He's a good guy. She saved his life." Smith sat up a little straighter in his chair, said softly, "These aren't the bad guys."

A tic started in Padgett's cheek. He opened his mouth, closed it, then turned abruptly on his heel and left. The door slid shut behind him. We all stood in the suddenly thick silence.

Stephen said, "Anita." He held his hand out to me. His face was flawless, no scars, no marks of any kind. I took his hand and smiled.

"I know you guys heal fast, but it's still impressive. You looked pretty bad last time I saw you."

"I looked worse," a soft male voice said. Nathaniel was awake in the other bed. His long auburn hair hung like a shining curtain around his face, maybe longer than waist-length. I'd never seen a man with hair that long. I couldn't see his face because I was too busy staring at his eyes. They were the color of lilacs, a wonderful pale lavender that was a genuine show-stopper. It took me a few seconds of staring to be able to see the rest of his face. He looked a few years older awake than he had unconscious—nineteen instead of sixteen, maybe. He still looked drawn and tired, ill, but there was a vast improvement.

"Yeah, you looked worse," I said.

Stephen turned to Officer Smith like they were old friends.

"Can we have a few minutes alone?"

Smith looked at me. "Okay with you?"

I nodded.

He stood. "I don't know how Padgett's going to like it, so if you want to exchange secret codes or anything, make it fast."

"Thanks," I said.

"Don't mention it." He stopped in front of Lorraine before he left. "Thank you. Crossman has a wife and two daughters. I know they'd thank you if they could."

Lorraine blushed and nodded, mumbling, "You're welcome."

Smith left, and I walked over to Nathaniel's bed. "Nice to meet you while you're conscious."

He tried to smile, but the effort showed. He held out his left hand to me, the right hand was still hooked up to an IV drip.

I took his hand. His grip was tremblingly weak. He drew my hand towards his mouth as if to kiss it. I let him do it. The effort made his hand shake.

He pressed his lips to my hand, eyes closed, almost as if he were resting. For a second I thought he'd passed out, but his tongue flicked out, a quick wetness.

I jerked back, fighting the urge to wipe my hand on my jeans. "Thanks, a handshake would have been fine."

He frowned up at me. "But you're our *léoparde lionné*," he said.

"So people keep telling me," I said.

He turned his head so he could see Stephen. "You lied to me." Tears trembled in his pale, pale eyes. "She won't feed us."

I looked at Stephen. "I have missed part of this conversation, haven't I?"

"Have you seen Richard share blood with the pack?"

I started to say no, then, "I saw him let Jason feed off of a knife wound once. Jason seemed almost drugged from it."

Stephen nodded. "That's it. Gabriel could share blood."

My eyes widened. "I didn't think he was strong enough to do that."

"Neither did we." This from Kevin. He came to stand near me, cigarette transferred, still unlit, to his left hand. "It's been very interesting listening to

Nathaniel talk about Gabriel. Nathaniel was addicted to heroin and a street whore when Gabriel rescued him, gave him a second life.''

''Bully for him, getting him off drugs, but Gabriel still pimped him out. To a sicker clientele.''

Kevin patted Nathaniel's leg under the sheet, a casual gesture, like you'd pat a dog. ''But Nat here likes it, don't you, boy?''

Nathaniel looked at him and said softly, ''Yes.''

''Please, tell me you didn't enjoy being gutted.''

He closed his eyes. ''No, not that. But until then it was . . .''

''That's all right,'' I said. Something occurred to me. ''Have you told the police who did this to you?''

''He doesn't know,'' Kevin said. He put the ever-present cig back in his mouth, as if just the taste of the paper was sweet.

''What do you mean, he doesn't know?'' I asked.

Stephen answered, ''Zane chained and blindfolded him, then left. That was the deal. Nathaniel never saw them.''

''Them?'' I made it a question.

Stephen nodded. ''Them.''

I took in a deep breath and let it out slowly. ''Do you remember anything unique or different that might help identify them?''

''Perfume like gardenias, and a sickly smell.''

Great, I thought, that was helpful.

He looked full at me, and suddenly his eyes weren't just dull with illness. I realized they were dull with experience. It went beyond jaded, as if Nathaniel had looked into the lower rungs of hell. He'd lived to tell the tale, but he hadn't really survived, not intact.

''I remember the perfume. I'd recognize it again if I smelled it.''

''Okay, Nathaniel, okay.'' In the bottom of the awful emptiness of his eyes was panic. He was scared, unbelievably scared. I patted his hand, and when his fingers curled around mine, I held on. ''No one will ever hurt you like that again, Nathaniel. I promise you that.''

''You'll take care of me?'' He looked up at me with a need in his eyes that was so raw, so primitive, I would have promised him anything to chase that look away.

''Yes, I'll take care of you.''

His whole body relaxed. A tension running out of him like water from a cracked cup. I felt it run down his arm into his hand into me like a jolt of energy. It made me jump, but I didn't pull away.

He smiled up at me, lying back against the pillows. He looked a little better somehow, stronger.

I slid my hand out of his slowly, and he let me go. Great. I turned to the rest of the room. ''We need to get you all out of here.''

''I could go home now,'' Stephen said, ''but Nathaniel still can't be moved.''

''I don't trust the cops without me here to act as a buffer.''

''Padgett is very afraid of us,'' Teddy said.

I nodded. ''I know.''

''Feed me,'' Nathaniel said. ''Give me your strength, and I will go with you.''

I frowned at him, then looked back at Stephen. "He's not seriously suggesting I open a vein for him, is he?"

"Richard could do it," Stephen said.

"Richard couldn't feed one of the leopards," Lorraine said, "only us."

"Raina could have fucked him back to health," Kevin said.

That earned him a long stare from me. "What are you talking about?"

"Raina could share energy without sharing blood," he said. His face registered both distaste and lust, as if he'd enjoyed some of Raina's shows in spite of himself. "She'd run her hands over you, then her body. It always ended with her fucking you. The more hurt you started out, the better she liked it, but you'd be healed when she was finished."

I turned to Stephen, because I didn't believe it. He nodded. "I've seen her do it."

"You're not suggesting that she . . ." Lorraine let the awful thought go unsaid, but I was with her.

"I am not opening a vein, and I am most certainly not going to have sex with him."

"You don't want me." Nathaniel's voice was tear-filled, heartbroken.

"It's nothing personal," I said. "I'm just not into casual sex." This entire conversation was too weird even for me.

"Then Nathaniel has to stay here at least another twenty-four hours," Kevin said. He rolled the cigarette between his fingers while he talked.

Stephen nodded. "That's what the doctor said. We asked when he told me I could go home today."

"Don't leave me, Stephen." Nathaniel reached out across the space between them, as if he could touch him.

"I won't leave you alone, Nathaniel, not without someone to take care of you."

Teddy spoke. "Just because it ended in sex for Raina doesn't mean it has to end that way."

We all looked at him. "What do you mean?" Kevin asked.

"Everything ended in sex for Raina. But it was the touching that healed. I think my injuries were healed before we got down to basics." Just listening to him talk like that with a sixty-inch chest of pure muscle made my brain hurt. It was like finding out your golden retriever talked. You just didn't expect to get brains in such a bulky package.

Kevin shrugged. "I don't know. All I know is she healed me. I don't remember when I was better. I just remember her."

"Is there anyone in this room that didn't sleep with Raina?" I asked.

The only person who raised their hand was Lorraine, and knowing Raina, that had been debatable. "Sweet Jesus."

"I think Anita could heal him without sex, just bare skin," Teddy said.

I started to say no, then remembered sharing energy with Jean-Claude. Bare skin had been important there, too. Maybe it was the same. "Did Raina seem to feel tired after healing you?"

All the men shook their heads. The consensus was it seemed to energize her, not weaken her. Of course, that was Raina and she had been an unusual puppy even for a werewolf.

I didn't want to leave Nathaniel here, not even with werewolves to guard him. I didn't trust Padgett. There was also no guarantee that the zealots, whoever they were, wouldn't try for another hit. Either we all went or we all stayed. I had more crime scenes to visit. I couldn't sit here all bloody day.

"Okay, let's try it, but I don't have the faintest idea how to begin."

Nathaniel settled back into the pillows with something like a smile of expectation on his face. Like a child who's about to get the ice cream he was promised. Trouble was, I was the ice cream.

37

Kevin put a chair under the door handle and we were as secure as we were likely to get. I'd told Smith, who was now manning the door, that I needed to get a feel for things, and I'd be done when I was done. I was being treated like a detective, so the uniforms would stay out. The only worry was Padgett. He'd only stay out until his ego recovered. I half expected him to try and barge in on us. The only thing that might save us from him was the fact that he'd want to break the door in because he'd be sensing what we were doing, and he wouldn't want to admit that.

I stood by the bed. Nathaniel looked up at me with a look that was so trusting, it made me nervous. I turned away and found everyone else looking at me, too. "Okay, guys, now what? I've never even seen this done."

There was an exchange of looks all the way around. Stephen said, "I don't know if we can explain it to you."

I nodded. "I know, magic is like that. You either get it, or you don't."

"Is this magic?" Teddy asked. "Or is it just psychic ability?"

"I'm not sure there is a difference," I said. "Sometimes I think the only difference is that psychic ability is something you do without thinking about it, and magic requires a ritual to get your juices going."

"You do more of this kind of shit than we do," Kevin said. "We're just werewolves, not witches."

"I'm not a witch. I'm a necromancer."

He shrugged. "Same diff to me." He sat down in the chair he'd started out in, crushing the cigarette into the palm of his hand as if it were lit and his flesh were an ashtray. He scowled up at me. I didn't know him well enough to be sure, but he seemed nervous.

Me, too. I only knew two ways to raise energy: ritual or sex. The sex took the place of ritual when I was with Jean-Claude or Richard. But I had no bond with Nathaniel. No marks, no emotion, nothing. I wasn't his *léoparde lionné*, not really. It was all lies. I couldn't do this without some feeling towards him. Pity wasn't enough.

Teddy loomed up behind me. "What's wrong, Anita?"

I would have walked across the room and whispered, but I knew Nathaniel would hear anywhere in the small room. "I need some emotion to work from, something."

"Emotion?" he asked.

"I don't know Nathaniel. I don't feel anything for him except pity, obligation. Neither of those is enough to even get started."

"What do you need?" His eyes were very serious. The intelligence in them was almost touchable.

I tried to put it into words and ended up saying, "I need something to take the place of a ritual."

"Raina didn't use a ritual," Kevin said from the chair.

"She used sex. Sex can take the place of the ritual."

"You raised power at the lupanar that one night with Richard," Stephen said. "You didn't have sex, but you still raised power."

"But I . . . I wanted Richard sexually. It's a sort of energy all of its own."

"Nathaniel is handsome," Stephen said.

I shook my head. "It's never been that easy for me. I need more than a pretty face."

Stephen slid out of the bed in one of those wraparound gowns, but it didn't gape as he moved. It was wrapped around him like a sheet, more cloth than he needed, just like it would have been on me. One size never really fits all.

He tried to take my hand, and I wouldn't let him. "Let me help you."

"Define help." Suspicious, who me?

He smiled, and it was almost condescending. The smile men get around girls when they're doing something sort of cute and girlish. The smile alone pissed me off. "What is your problem?" I asked.

"You," he said softly. "You know I would never hurt you, don't you?"

I looked into his cornflower-blue eyes and nodded. "Never on purpose," I said.

"Then trust me now. Let me help you call the power."

"How?" I asked.

He took my hand in both of his, and this time I let him. He drew my hand to Nathaniel. He rested my fingertips on Nathaniel's forehead. His skin was cool. Just the touch of his skin, and you knew he wasn't well.

"Pet him," Stephen said.

I looked at him, shaking my head. I drew my hand back, "I don't think so."

Nathaniel started to say something, but Stephen put his fingers across his mouth. "No, Nathaniel." It was almost like he knew what the other man was going to say. But he couldn't know, not for sure, could he? I might have believed it if Nathaniel was pack, but he wasn't.

"Close your eyes," Stephen said.

"Uh-huh," I said.

"We don't have time for this," Kevin said.

"He's right," Teddy said. "I understand your natural reluctance, but the police are going to knock on the door eventually."

If Nathaniel couldn't leave with us, that meant leaving people behind to guard him, which put people in danger again. If we were all somewhere together, at least we wouldn't be endangering innocent policemen, though most cops would wince at being called innocent.

I took a deep breath and blew it out. "Fine, what's your idea?"

"Close your eyes," Stephen said.

I frowned at him. He looked patient, long-suffering even, and I closed my eyes. He took my hand in his, and it wasn't until he began to gently open my fist that I realized I'd clenched up. He started to massage my hand.

I said, "Stop that."

"Then loosen up," he said. "It won't hurt."

"I'm not afraid it will hurt," I said.

He moved around to stand in back of me, so close the hem of his gown brushed my legs. "But you're still afraid." His voice had dropped almost to a whisper. "Can you use that fear to call power?"

My pulse was hammering in my throat, and I was afraid, but it wasn't the right kind of fear. The fear that overwhelms you in the midst of an emergency can call power almost without effort. This was the kind of fear that keeps you from jumping out of perfectly good airplanes even though you'd decided to do it. Not an unhealthy fear, but it would hold you back.

"No," I said.

"Then let go of the fear," he said. He touched my arms gently and sat me on the edge of the bed.

Nathaniel made a small protesting sound, as if it had hurt.

I opened my eyes and Stephen said, "Close them." It was the closest thing to an order I'd ever heard him give. I closed them.

He took my hands and laid the tips of my fingers on either side of Nathaniel's face. "The skin just over the temples is so soft." He drew my fingers in a soft feathery line down Nathaniel's face, fingers gliding on either side, as if I were blind and trying to memorize his features.

He slid my hands into Nathaniel's hair. It was silken, unbelievably soft. His hair had the texture of satin. I balled my hands into that soft warmth, lowered my face towards his hair and smelled it. There was a faint medicinal smell. I buried my face in the satin brush of his hair and found his scent under it all. He smelled like vanilla, and under that was the scent of wood and field and fur. He wasn't pack, but the scent was similar. He smelled like home. Something clicked deep inside me, like a switch being thrown.

I opened my eyes and knew what to do, how to do it, wanted to do it. Like a distant thought, I realized that Stephen's hands had fallen away long ago.

I stared down into Nathaniel's lilac eyes and bent towards that amazing gaze. I touched his lips with mine, a chaste kiss, and that one soft brush brought the power in a warm, skin-tingling rush. It spilled out of me like water, warm, soothing, filling. But power alone wasn't enough. It needed direction, guidance, and I knew how to do it, as if I'd done it before. I didn't question it, didn't want to.

I tried to run my hand down his chest, but the gown covered him. He was like Stephen, like me, small. The gown was fastened in front, not in back. My hand sought the opening and slid along bare skin. Slid until I felt the incision.

I straddled Nathaniel's legs. He made another small hurting sound and I liked it. I rose up on my knees so only the sides of my legs touched his body. I slid the sheet down around his body and opened the gown, exposing him. The stitches were a thin dark line across the paleness of his skin that ran nearly from one hip to the other. A fearful wound, a killing wound.

He wore nothing below the waist. Hospitals are always stripping us down, leaving us as vulnerable as possible. The sight of him naked should have stopped me in my tracks. Dimly, it shocked me. I hadn't expected it, but it was too late. The power didn't care. I ran my fingers lightly over the stitches.

Nathaniel cried out, only half from pain. He was half-erect before I lowered my face to the stitches. I licked the wound like a dog would, long, slow caresses. He was more than half-erect when I raised my face to see his eyes staring down at me. I knew in that moment that I could have him, that he wanted me to take that last step.

I could feel the others in the room like a hum of energy, a vibrating backdrop to the energy inside me. I'd never been interested in casual sex, but the smell and feel of Nathaniel's body was almost overwhelming. I'd never been so tempted by a stranger. But temptation is just tempting. You don't have to give in. I rose on my knees over him, placing my hands on the smooth bones of his hips, drawing my hands towards the middle of the incision. When my hands touched, I put one on top of the other and pressed. Not with muscle or flesh but with power. I thrust that warm, rising power into his body.

He gasped, spine bowing underneath me, hands grabbing my arms, fingers convulsing against my bare skin.

It was like smoothing out the imperfections in a zombie except this flesh was warm and alive, and I couldn't see what I was fixing with my eyes. But I could feel it. I could feel his body smooth and firm, caressing places that no hand was meant to touch. Rolling them between my fingers, filling him up with the rising, rushing heat inside me. It spilled down my arms, my hands, into him. The heat spread through his body, through my body, until it was like fever, running over the skin, through the body, forming our bodies into a single thing of heat and flesh, and a rush of power that just kept building. It built until I closed my eyes, but even the darkness was shot with brightness, white flowers exploding on my vision.

My breath came in pants, too quick, too shallow. I opened my eyes and watched Nathaniel's face. His breathing matched mine. I forced us slower, forced his breathing to slow. I could feel his heart as if I caressed it, held in my hands. I could touch any part of him. I could have any part of him. I could smell the blood under his skin and wanted a taste.

He was healed when I lowered myself on top of him, pressed my mouth to his. I turned his face to one side and ate down the side of his neck until I felt the pulse under his skin. I licked the skin, but it wasn't enough. I laid my mouth over the beating pulse, bit gently into the skin until I could hold the throbbing of him in my mouth. I wanted to bite down harder and harder until blood flowed. I wanted it. Dimly, I knew that Jean-Claude had awakened for the day. It was his hunger that I felt, his need. But it wasn't his need that had me straddling Nathaniel's body. It wasn't even mine.

I remembered Nathaniel's body, and I'd never met him before. I knew the taste of him. The feel of him as only an old lover can. Not my memories. Not my energy.

I slid off Nathaniel, tried to crawl out of the bed, and fell to my knees. I couldn't stand, not yet. Richard had said as long as the pack existed, Raina wasn't gone. I hadn't understood what he meant, until now. I was channeling the bitch from hell, channeling her, and having a very good time doing it.

But I knew something else, something that Raina hadn't done. Couldn't blame her for this one. I knew how to heal Nathaniel's body, but I also knew how to tear it apart. Anything that you can fix, you can break. When I held his heart in my metaphysical hand, I'd had a split second, a dark urge, to close that hand, to crush that pulsing, throbbing muscle until blood flowed and his life stopped. A moment, the blink of an eye, of an urge so evil, it scared even me. I'd have liked to blame the bitch from hell, but something told me that this little bit of darkness was all mine. Stephen's hand on my mouth was all that kept me from screaming out loud.

38

Stephen's hand held the screams to a whimper. He held me against his body, hard, as if afraid of what I'd do if I got loose. I wasn't so sure myself. Running seemed like a good idea. Running until I outran the thought of it, the feel of it, all out of me. But like Richard, I couldn't run from myself. That thought made me stop struggling and just sit in the circle of Stephen's arms.

"Are you all right?" he asked softly.

I nodded.

His hand slid away from my mouth, slowly, as if he wasn't sure I'd heard him or understood him.

I sagged against him, almost sliding to the floor.

He stroked my face, over and over, like you'd comfort a sick child. He didn't ask what was wrong. None of them did.

Nathaniel knelt beside us. He didn't just look healed, he looked healthy. He was smiling, handsome in a boyish, unfinished sort of way. If you cut the hair and changed the eyes, he looked like he should have been playing halfback on the high-school football team and dating the homecoming princess.

The fact that I'd almost gone down on him two minutes ago brought a rush of heat that made me hide my face against Stephen's shoulder. I did not want to look into that youthful, handsome face and realize how close I'd come to doing him. The fact that I could still remember his body in details that I'd personally never touched, didn't help. Raina was gone, but not forgotten.

I felt movement. The vibrating energy of the shapeshifters was getting closer. I knew without looking that they were crowding around me. The energy tightened like a circle drawing closed. It was hard to breathe.

I felt someone's cheek brush my face. I moved my head enough to see Kevin inches from me. I'd expected Nathaniel. Teddy's large hands stroked down my bare arms. He brought his hands to his face. "You smell like pack."

Lorraine was on her back staring up at me with eyes gone strange and wolfish. "She smells like Raina." She rolled her face so that her lips brushed the knee of my jeans.

I knew that if I allowed it, we could sleep in one big communal heap like a litter of puppies, that touching was part of what kept the pack together, like the mutual grooming that primates do. Touching, comforting, it didn't have to be sexual. That had been Raina's choice. They were wolves but they were also people and that made them primates. Two animals really, not just one.

Kevin laid his head in my lap, cheek resting on my legs. I couldn't see his eyes, to tell if they'd gone wolf on me. His voice came thick and low, "Now I do need a cigarette."

It made me laugh. Once I started laughing, I couldn't stop. I laughed until tears ran down my face. The werewolves ran their hands up and down me, faces rubbing my bare skin. They were taking my scent, rolling in the lingering scent of Raina. Marking me with their scent.

Stephen kissed my cheek, the way you'd kiss your sister. "Are you all right?" It was hard to remember, but I think he'd asked that before.

I nodded. "Yes." My voice sounded tinny and distant. I realized I was on the edge of shock. Not good.

Stephen shooed the wolves away from me. They moved languorously, as if the energy we'd raised had been some sort of drug, or maybe sex was a better analogy. I didn't know. I wasn't even sure I wanted to know.

"Richard said that Raina wasn't truly gone as long as the pack lived. Is this what he meant?" I asked.

"Yes," Stephen said, "though I've never heard of a non-pack member being able to do what you just did. The spirits of the dead should only be able to enter lukoi."

"Spirits of the dead," I said. "You mean you don't have a fancy name for them?"

"They are munin," Stephen said.

That almost started me laughing again. "Memory, Odin's raven."

He nodded. "Yes."

"What exactly was it, *is* it? It wasn't a ghost. I know what a ghost feels like."

"You've felt one of them," Stephen said. "It's the best explanation I can give you."

"It's energy," Teddy said. "Energy is neither created nor destroyed. It exists. We have the energy of everyone that has ever been pack."

"You don't mean all lukoi, do you?"

"No," he said, "but from the first member of our pack to now, we have them all."

"Not all," Lorraine said.

He nodded. "Sometimes one of us will be lost to accident and the body cannot be recovered and shared. Then all they were, all their knowledge, their power, is lost to us."

Kevin had gone back to the chair, still sitting on the floor, leaning his shoulders against the chair seat. "Sometimes," he said, "we decide not to feed. It's sort of like excommunication. The pack rejects you in death as in life."

"Why didn't you reject Raina? She was a twisted sadistic bitch."

"It was Richard's choice," Teddy said. "By rejecting her body that last time, he thought it would have angered some of the other pack members who aren't wholeheartedly on his side yet. He was right, but . . . now we have her inside us.''

"She's powerful," Lorraine said, and she shivered. "Powerful enough to possess a lesser wolf.''

"Old wives' tales," Kevin said. "She's dead. Her power survives but only when called.''

"I didn't call her," I said.

"We might have," Stephen said softly. He lay back on the floor, hands covering his eyes as if it was too horrible to look at.

"What do you mean?''

"I mean that we've never seen anyone but Raina do what you just did. I was thinking about her, remembering.''

"So was I," Kevin said.

"Yes," Teddy said. He had moved back to the far wall, as if he didn't trust himself near me.

Lorraine had moved back with him, sitting so that their bodies touched lightly. A comforting closeness. "I, too, was thinking about her. Glad she was not here. Happy it was Anita." She hugged her arms as if cold, and Teddy put a muscular arm around her, hugging her close, resting his chin in her hair.

"I wasn't thinking about Raina," Nathaniel said. He crawled towards me.

"Don't touch me," I said.

He rolled onto his back, for all the world like a big pussy cat wanting its belly rubbed. He stretched, straining from toes to finger tips. He laughed and rolled onto his stomach, propped on his elbows. He looked up at me, long, rich brown hair like a curtain across his face. His lilac eyes stared out at me, feral and almost frightening. He lay down in a pool of hair and energy. His gaze stayed on my face, and I realized he was being playful. Not exactly seductive, but playful. It was different and almost more disturbing. Nathaniel managed to be childlike, catlike, and still be an adult. You didn't know whether to pat him on the head, rub his belly, or kiss him. All three seemed to be up for grabs. It was too confusing for me.

I used the far bed to get to my feet. When I was sure I could walk without falling down, I let go of the bed. I swayed just a touch, but not too bad. I could walk. Great, because I wanted out of here.

"What do you want us to do?" Stephen asked.

"Go to my house. Jean-Claude's there, and Richard was there.''

"What about him?" Kevin asked.

Nathaniel raised his head enough to look at us all. He said nothing, asked for nothing, but I could taste his pulse in my mouth. I knew he was scared. Scared to be left alone again. I hoped this empathy with me wasn't permanent. I had quite enough men running around in my head without adding another one.

"Take him with you," I said. "The leopards are mine as you are mine.''

"He is to be protected and treated as pack?" Kevin asked.

I rubbed my temples. I was getting a headache. "Yes, yes. I've given him my protection. Any of the leopards that want my protection can have it.''

"As our lupa that binds us to protect them," Lorraine said, "even to give our life for them. Will they do the same?''

I wasn't getting a headache, I had one.

Nathaniel rolled to his feet in a movement that was too graceful to be real and almost too quick to see. He sat on the foot of Stephen's bed, watching me with bright, eager eyes. He said, "My body is yours. My life, if you want it, is yours to take." He said it almost matter-of-factly—no, joyously, like it was a good thing.

I stared at him. "I don't want anyone's life, Nathaniel, but if the pack is willing to risk their lives to protect you, I expect you to do the same."

"I will do anything you want," he said. "All you have to do is tell me."

He didn't say, "ask me." He said, "tell me." I'd never heard it phrased quite like that. It implied he didn't have the right to say no. I asked, "Does everyone here know they have the right to argue a point with me? I mean, when I say jump, you don't just say how high, right?"

"We don't," Stephen said. His face was guarded, careful.

"How about you?" I asked, turning to Nathaniel.

He rose to his knees, leaning his upper body out towards me, but with both hands still on the bed railing. He didn't try to touch me, just get closer. "How about me, what?" he asked.

"You do understand that you have the right to refuse me? That my word is not like from on high?"

"Just tell me what you want me to do, Anita, and I'll do it."

"Just like that, no questions, you'll just do it?"

He nodded. "Anything."

"Is this a custom among the leopards, the pard?" I asked.

"No," Stephen said, "it's just Nathaniel's way."

I shook my head, literally waving my hands in the air as if I'd just erase it all. "I don't have time for this. He's healed. Take him with you."

"Do you want me to wait in your room?" Nathaniel asked.

"If you need to rest, help yourself to a bed. I won't be there."

He smiled happily and I had the oddest feeling that what I was saying wasn't what he was hearing. I wanted out of the room, away from them all. I'd tell Padgett I was sending them all to a safe house, and he'd buy it because he wanted off this detail. He wanted away from them more than I did.

The doctor was amazed at Nathaniel's recovery. They released him, though they started talking about wanting to run more tests. I vetoed that. We had places to go, people to meet. They all piled into Kevin's and Teddy's cars, and I went for my Jeep. Happy to be rid of them for a while. Happy even if it meant another crime scene. Happy even if I still didn't know how to tell if Malcolm was alive down there in the dark. Nathaniel watched me through the back window of the car, his lilac gaze on me until the car turned a corner. He'd been lost, and now he thought he'd been found. But if he expected me to be more than friends, he was still lost.

39

I felt like shit and didn't have a bruise to show for it. I concentrated on the next problem, pushing what I'd done, and almost done, to the back burner. Nothing I could do about it until I talked to Richard and Jean-Claude. I'd worried about tying myself to the vampire, but I'd never really worried about being tied to the were-wolf. I should have known I'd get shit from both sides.

I got beeped three times in about three minutes. McKinnon first, Dolph second, and an unknown number. The unknown number called back twice in ten minutes. Damn. I pulled off into a service station. I called Dolph first.

"Anita."

"How do you always know it's me?"

"I don't," he said.

"What's up?"

"We need you at a new location."

"I'm on my way to the church site for McKinnon."

"Pete's here with me."

"That sounds ominous."

"We've got a vamp on his way to the hospital," he said.

"In his coffin?"

"No."

"Then how . . . ?"

"He was on the stairs covered in blankets. They don't think he's going to make it. But this is one of the halfway houses for the Church. We've got a two-biter here that says the vamp we took was the guardian for the younger vamps still inside. She seems worried about what the vamps will do when they wake and the guardian isn't there to calm them down or feed them."

"Feed them?" I asked.

"Says that they each take a small drink from the guardian to start the night. Without it, she says the hunger grows too strong, and they may be dangerous."

"Isn't she a font of information."

"She's scared, Anita. She's got two freaking vampire bites on her neck, and she's scared."

"Shit," I said. "I'm on my way, but frankly, Dolph, I don't know what you want me to do."

"You're the vampire expert, you tell me." A little hostility there.

"I'll think about it on the way. Maybe I'll have come up with a plan by the time I get there."

"Before they became legal, we'd have just burned them out ourselves."

"Yeah," I said, "the good old days."

"Yeah," he said. I don't think he got the sarcasm. But with Dolph it was always hard to tell.

I dialed the third number. Larry answered, "Anita." His voice sounded strained, pain-filled.

"What's wrong?" I asked, my throat suddenly tight.

"I'm all right."

"You don't sound all right," I said.

"I've just been moving around too much with the stitches and stuff. I need to take a pain pill, but I won't be able to drive."

"You need a lift?"

He was quiet for a second or two, then, "Yes."

I knew how much it had cost him to call me. This was one of his first times in the field on a police job without me. The fact that he needed my help for anything must have griped his ass. It would have bugged the hell out of me. In fact, I wouldn't have called. I'd have toughed it out, until I passed out. This wasn't a criticism of Larry, it was a criticism of me. He was just smarter than I was sometimes. This was one of those times.

"Where are you?"

He gave me the address, and it was close. Lucky us. "I'm less than five minutes away, but I can't take you home. I'm on my way to another crime scene."

"As long as I don't have to drive, I'll be okay. It's starting to take all my attention just to stay on the road. Time to stop driving when it's this hard."

"You really do have a higher wisdom score than I do."

"Which means you wouldn't have asked for help yet," he said.

"Well . . . yeah."

"When would you have asked for help?"

"When I drove off the road and had to call a tow truck."

He laughed and took a sharp breath as if it hurt. "I'll be waiting for you."

"I'll be there."

"I know," he said. "Thanks for not saying you told me so."

"I wasn't even thinking it, Larry."

"Honest?"

"Cross my heart and . . ."

"Don't say it."

"You getting superstitious on me, Larry?"

He was quiet for a space of heartbeats. "Maybe, or maybe it's just been a long day."

"It'll be a longer night," I said.

"Thanks," he said. "Just what I wanted to hear." He hung up then without saying goodbye.

Maybe I'd trained Dolph never to say goodbye. Maybe I was always the bearer of bad tidings, and everyone wanted to get off the phone with me as soon as possible. Naw.

40

I expected Larry to be sitting in his car. He wasn't. He was leaning against it. Even from a distance I could tell he was in pain, back stiff, trying not to move any more than necessary. I pulled in beside him. Up close he looked worse. His white dress shirt was smeared with black soot. His summer-weight dress pants were brown, so they'd survived a little better. A black smudge ran across his forehead to his chin. The blackness outlined one of his blue eyes so that it seemed darker, like a sapphire surrounded by onyx. The look in his eyes was dull, as if the pain had drained him.

"Jesus, you look like shit," I said.

He almost smiled. "Thanks, I needed that."

"Take a pill, get in the Jeep."

He started to shake his head, stopped in mid-motion and said, "No, if you can drive, I can go to the next disaster."

"You smell like someone set your clothes on fire."

"You look pristine," he said, and he sounded resentful.

"What's wrong, Larry?"

"Other than my back feels like a red-hot poker is being shoved up it?"

"Besides that," I said.

"I'll tell you in the car." Underneath the sulkiness, he sounded tired.

I didn't argue with him, just started walking for the Jeep. A few steps and I realized he wasn't keeping up. I turned and found him standing very still, eyes closed, hands in fists at his sides.

I walked back to him. "Need a hand?"

He opened his eyes, smiled, "A back, actually. Hands work fine."

I smiled and took his arm gently, half expecting him to tell me not to, but he didn't. He was hurting. He took a stiff step, and I steadied him. We made slow but sure progress to the Jeep. His breath was coming in small, shallow pants by the time I got him around to the passenger side door. I opened the door, wasn't sure how to get him inside. It was going to hurt any way I could do it.

"Just let me hold your arm. I can do it myself," he said.

I offered my arm. He got a death grip on it and sat down. He made a small hissing noise between his teeth. "You said it would hurt worse the second day. Why are you always right?"

"Hard to be perfect," I said, "but it's a burden I've learned to cope with." I gave him my best bland face.

He smiled, then started to laugh, then almost doubled over with pain, which hurt more. He ended up writhing on the seat for a few seconds. When he could sit still again, he grabbed the dashboard until his fingers turned colors. "God, don't make me laugh."

"Sorry," I said. I got the aloe-and-lanolin Baby Wipes from the trunk of my car. They were great for getting blood off. They'd probably work on soot. I handed him the wipes and helped him buckle his seat belt. Yes, his wounds would have hurt less if he hadn't had the belt, but no one rides with me without a seat belt. My mom would be alive today if she'd been wearing a belt.

"Take a pill, Larry. Sleep in the car. I'll take you home after this next scene."

"No," he said, and he sounded so stubborn, so determined, that I knew I couldn't talk him out of it. So why try?

"Have it your way," I said. "But what have you been doing that you look like you've been trying to hide your spots?"

He moved just his eyes to look at me, frowning.

"Rolling in soot," I said. "Don't you ever watch Disney movies or read children's books?"

He gave a small smile. "Not lately. I've had three fire scenes where I just had to confirm the vamps were dead. Two of the scenes I couldn't find anything, just ashes. The third one looked like black sticks. I didn't know what to do, Anita. I tried to check for a pulse. I know that was stupid. The skull just exploded into ashes all over me." He was sitting very stiff, very controlled, yet his body gave the impression of hunching from pain, avoiding the blow of what he'd seen today.

What I was about to say wouldn't help things. "Vamps burn to ashes, Larry. If there were skeletal remains left, it wasn't vampire."

He looked at me then, the sudden movement bringing tears to his eyes. "You mean that was human?"

"Probably—I'm not sure, but probably."

"Thanks to me we'll never know for sure. Without the fangs in the skull you can't tell the difference."

"That's not entirely true. They can do DNA. Though truthfully I'm not sure what the fire does to DNA sampling. If they can gather it, they can at least know if it's human or vamp."

"If it's human, I've destroyed any chance they have of using dental records," he said.

"Larry, if the skull was that fragile, I don't think anything could have saved it. It certainly wouldn't have stood up to dental imprinting."

"Are you sure?" he asked.

I licked my lips and wanted to lie. "Not a hundred percent."

"You'd have known it was human. You wouldn't have touched it, thinking it was alive, would you?"

I let silence fill the car.

"Answer me," he said.

"No, I wouldn't have checked for a pulse. I would have assumed it was human remains."

"Dammit, Anita, I've been doing this for over a year, and I'm still making stupid mistakes."

"Not stupid, just mistakes."

"What's the difference?" he asked.

I was thinking that what he'd done to get his back ripped up was a stupid mistake, but decided not to say it out loud. "You know the difference, Larry. When you get over feeling sorry for yourself, you'll know the difference."

"Don't be condescending, Anita."

The anger in his voice stung more than the words. I didn't need this today. I really didn't. "Larry, I'd love to soothe your ego and make it all better, but I am all out of sugarplums and puppy-dog tails. My day hasn't been exactly a barrel of laughs either."

"What's wrong?" he asked.

I shook my head.

"Come on. I'm sorry. I'll listen."

I wasn't even sure where to start, and I wasn't ready to tell anybody about what had happened in the hospital room, least of all Larry.

"I don't even know where to start, Larry."

"Try," he said.

"Richard is being nasty."

"Boyfriend trouble," he said; he sounded almost amused.

I glanced at him. "Don't be condescending, Larry."

"Sorry."

"It's not just that. Before this emergency came up, they wanted me at the Church of Eternal Life. Malcolm is bedded in the basement. His followers want him to be rescued. The firemen want to know if they can leave him until nightfall when he'll rise on his own."

"So?" Larry asked.

"So, I don't have the faintest idea how to find out if Malcolm is alive or dead."

He stared at me. "You're kidding."

"Wish I was."

"But you're a necromancer," he said.

"I raise zombies and an occasional vamp, but I can't raise a master vamp of Malcolm's power. Besides, what if I could? Would that prove he was alive or prove he was dead? I mean if I could raise him, it might just mean he was ready to be a zombie. Hell, Jean-Claude's awake for the day, maybe Malcolm is, too."

"A vampire zombie?" Larry said.

I shrugged. "I don't know. I'm the only person who can raise vamps like zombies, that I know of. There aren't a lot of books on the subject."

"What about Sabitini?"

"You mean the magician?"

"He raised zombies as part of his act, and he had vampires that did his bidding. I've read eyewitness accounts of it."

"First, he died in 1880. A little before my time. Second, the vampires were just dupes who went along with him. It was a way for vampires who would have normally been killed on sight to walk freely among the people. Sabitini and his pet vampires, they called them."

"No one's ever proved that he was a fraud, Anita."

"Fine, but he's dead and he didn't leave any diaries behind."

"Raise him and ask," Larry said.

I stared at him long enough that I had to hit the brakes fast to keep from ramming a car in front of me. "What did you say?"

"Raise Sabitini and find out if he could raise vampires like you can. He's just a little over a hundred years dead. You've raised zombies a lot older than that."

"You missed the case last year where a vaudun priestess had raised a necromancer. The zombie got completely out of control and started killing people."

"You've told me about it, but the priestess didn't know what he was. If you knew going in, you could take precautions."

"No," I said.

"Why not?" he said.

I opened my mouth, closed it, because I didn't have a good answer. "I don't approve of raising the dead for curiosity's sake. You know how much money I've been offered to raise dead celebrities?"

"I'd still like to know what really happened to Marilyn Monroe," he said.

"When her family comes and asks, maybe I'll do it. But I am not raising the poor woman because a tabloid waved money at our boss."

"Waved a lot of money at our boss," Larry said. "Enough money that he sent Jamison out to try it. He couldn't raise her. Too long dead without a bigger sacrifice."

I shook my head. "Jamison is a weenie."

"Everyone else at Animators Inc. turned it down."

"Including you," I said.

He shrugged. "I might raise her and ask how she died, but not in front of cameras. The poor woman was hounded alive. Dead, she's still being hounded. Doesn't seem fair."

"You're a good guy, Larry."

"Not good enough to know that vampires burn to ash and skeletal remains are human."

"Don't start, Larry. It's just experience. I should have told you before you went out today. Truthfully, you're getting so good at the job, I didn't think to tell you."

"You assumed I knew?" he said.

"Yeah."

"I have noticed the daily lectures have been in short supply lately. I used to take more notes at work with you than I ever did in college."

"Not so many notes lately, huh?" I said.

"No, I hadn't really thought about it, but no." He grinned suddenly and it lit up his eyes, chased away the horrors of the day. For a moment he was the bright-eyed, optimistic kid who had first shown up on my doorstep. "You mean I'm finally learning how to do the job?"

"Yeah," I said, "you are. In fact, if you were quicker on the trigger, I'd say you were good at it. It's just hard to learn everything, Larry. Something comes up and you find out you really don't know what the hell's going on after all.''

"You, too?" he said.

"Me, too."

He took a deep breath and let it out. "I've seen you surprised a time or two, Anita. When the monsters get so strange that you don't know what's going either, it usually gets real nasty, real fast.''

He was right. I wished he wasn't, because right now I didn't know what the hell was going on. I didn't understand what had happened with Nathaniel. I didn't know how the marks worked with Richard. I didn't know how to find out if Malcolm was still among the undead, or if he'd crossed into that more permanent state of true death. In fact I had so many questions and so few answers that I just wanted to go home. Maybe Larry and I could both take a pain pill and sleep until tomorrow. Surely tomorrow would be a better day. God, I hoped so.

41

The house was still smoking when we got there. Thin greyish wisps of smoke rose from the blackened beams like miniature ghosts. Some trick of the fire had left the high cupola on top of the building intact. The lower stories were gutted and blackened, but the cupola rose like a white beacon above the wreck. It looked like a black-toothed giant had taken a great bite out of the house.

The fire truck took up most of the narrow street. There was a spread of water seeping along the street like a shallow lake. Firefighters waded through the water rolling up miles of hose over their shoulders. A uniformed police officer stopped us well back from the action.

I eased down my window and flashed my ID. It was a little plastic clip-on card and looked official, but it wasn't a badge. Sometimes the uniforms would let me through, and sometimes they had to go ask permission. Brewster's Law was going around Washington and would give vamp executioners what amounted to federal marshal status. I wasn't sure how I felt about that. It takes a hell of a lot more to make a cop than just a badge, but for me personally I'd love to have had a badge to flash.

"Anita Blake, Larry Kirkland, to see Sergeant Storr."

The officer frowned at the ID. "I'll have to clear this with someone."

I sighed. "Fine, we'll wait here."

The uniform went off in search of Dolph, and we waited.

"You used to argue with them," Larry said.

I shrugged. "They're just doing their job."

"Since when has that stopped you from bitching?"

I looked at him. He was smiling, which saved him from the scathing comeback I had ready. Besides, it was nice to see him smiling about anything right now. "So I'm mellowing—a little. So what?"

The smile widened to a grin, a shit-eating grin, my uncle would have called it. It was like the next thing out of his mouth was almost too funny to say. I was betting I wouldn't think it was funny at all.

"Is it being in love with Jean-Claude that's mellowed you or the regular sex?"

I smiled sweetly. "Speaking of regular sex, how is Detective Tammy?"

He blushed first. I was happy.

The uniform was walking down the wet street towards us with Detective Tammy Reynolds in tow. Oh, life was good.

"Well, if it isn't your little sugarplum now," I said.

Larry saw her then. The red flush brightened to something the color of raw flame, redder than his hair. His blue eyes were a little bulgy with the effort to breathe. The soot had been wiped away, which saved his face from looking like a reddish bruise. "You won't say anything, will you, Anita? Tammy doesn't like to be teased."

"Who does?" I said.

"I'm sorry," he said, speaking very fast before they could get to us. "I apologize. It will never happen again. Please do not embarrass me in front of Tammy."

"Would I do that to you?"

"In a hot second," he said. "Please don't."

They were almost at the car. "Don't pull my leg and I won't pull yours," I whispered.

"Deal," he said.

I eased down the window, smiling. "Detective Reynolds, how good to see you."

Reynolds frowned because I was seldom glad to see her. She was a witch and the first police detective ever with preternatural abilities beyond psychic gifts. But she was young, bright, shiny, and tried just a little too hard to be my friend. She was just sooo fascinated with the fact that I raised the dead. She wanted to know all about it. I'd never had a witch make me feel like such a damned freak. Most witches were nice understanding souls. Perhaps it was the fact that Reynolds was a Christian witch, a member of the Followers of the Way. A sect going back to the Gnostics, who embraced almost all magical ability. They were all but wiped out during the Inquisition due to the fact that their beliefs don't allow them to hide their light under a bushel, but they survived. Fanatics have a way of doing that.

Reynolds was tall, slender, with straight brown hair falling around her shoulders, and eyes that I would have said were hazel but she called green. Greyish-green with a large circle of pale brown around the pupil. Cats have green eyes. Most people don't. She'd tried to be my friend, and when I wouldn't tell her about raising the dead, she'd turned to Larry. He'd been reluctant at first for the same reasons I was, but she hadn't offered me sex. It pushed Larry over the edge and into her arms.

I'd have complained about his choice of sweeties if I'd any moral high ground to stand on. It wasn't the witch part that bothered me or the cop. It was the religious-fanatic part. But when you share the sheets with the walking dead, you don't get a lot of room to bitch.

I smiled sweetly at her.

Reynold's frown deepened. I'd never been this happy to see her before. "Good to see you, too, Anita." Her greeting was cautious, but seemed sincere. Always willing to turn the other cheek. A good little Christian.

I was beginning to wonder if I was still a good Christian. I didn't doubt God.

I doubted me. Having premarital sex with a vampire had shaken my faith in a lot of things.

She bent her five foot ten frame to peer in the window past me at Larry. "Hi, Larry." Her smile was genuine, too. Her eyes sparkled with it. I could feel the waves of lust, if not love, going from her to him like a warm, embarrassing current.

The blush had left Larry's face milk-pale with the sprinkling of freckles like brown ink spots. He turned large blue eyes to her, and I didn't like the way he looked at her. I wasn't sure it was just lust on Larry's part. Maybe it wasn't for Reynolds, either, but I didn't worry about her feelings the way I did Larry's.

"Detective Reynolds," he said. Was it my imagination or was his voice just a touch deeper? Nah.

"Larry." That one word was full of too much warmth.

"Where do you want us to park?" I asked.

She blinked hazel eyes at me, as if for a second she'd forgotten I was there. "Anywhere back here."

"Great."

She stepped back and let me park, but her eyes lingered on Larry. Maybe it was more than lust. Damn.

We parked. Larry undid his seat belt carefully, grimacing. I'd gotten the door for him at the gas station.

"You want me to get the door?"

He turned stiffly towards the door, trying to keep his upper body immobile. He stopped with his hand on the handle. His breath came in little gasps. "Yes, please."

Me, I'd have gotten the door myself, just from pure stubbornness. Larry really was the wiser of the two of us.

I held the door for him and offered him a hand. I pulled, he pushed with his legs, and we got him standing. He started to hunch from the pain, but that bent his back, which made the pain worse. He ended standing as straight as he could, leaning against the Jeep, trying to get his breath back. Pain will leave you breathless.

Reynolds was suddenly beside us. "What's wrong?"

"You tell her. I'll go talk to Dolph."

"Sure," Larry said, voice strained. He needed to be in bed, knocked out on painkillers. Maybe he wasn't that much smarter than me.

It wasn't hard to spot Dolph. Pete McKinnon was standing with them. It was like walking towards two small mountains.

Dolph's dark suit looked freshly pressed, white shirt crisp, tie knotted against the collar. He couldn't have been out in the heat long. Even Dolph sweats.

"Anita," he said.

"Dolph."

"Ms. Blake, nice to see you again," Pete McKinnon said.

I smiled. "Good to know someone's happy to see me."

If Dolph got the dig, he ignored it. "Everyone's waiting for you."

"Dolph always was a man of few words," Pete said.

I grinned at him. "Good to know it's nothing personal."

Dolph frowned at us. "If you two are through, we've got work to do."

Pete and I grinned at each other and followed Dolph across the wet street. I was happy to be back in my Nikes. I could walk as good as any of the men, in the right shoes.

A tall, thin fireman with a grey mustache watched me stride across the street. He was still wearing helmet and coat in the July heat. Four others had stripped down to T-shirts with just the rubbery-looking pants on. Someone had sprayed them down with a water. They looked like an ad for a beefcake wet T-shirt contest. They were drinking Gatorade and water like their lives depended on it.

"Did a Gatorade truck just roll by or is this some arcane post-fire ritual?" I asked.

Pete answered, "It's damned hot in a fire with full gear on. You dehydrate. Water to rehydrate and Gatorade for the electrolytes so you don't pass out from the heat."

"Ah," I said.

The fireman who'd been rolling up the hose came over to us. A delicate triangle of face peered out from under the helmet. Clear grey eyes met my gaze. There was a lift to the chin, a way that she held herself that was a challenge. I recognized the symptoms. I had my own mountain-sized chip on my shoulder. I felt like apologizing for assuming she was a man, but didn't. It would have been insulting.

Pete introduced me to the tall man. "This is Captain Fulton. He's Incident Commander on this site."

I offered my hand while he was still thinking about it. His hand was large, big-knuckled. He shook hands like he was afraid to squeeze too hard, and dropped contact as soon as he could. I bet that he was just pleased as punch to have a female fireperson on his unit.

He introduced the fireperson in question. "Corporal Tucker." She offered her hand.

She had a nice firm handshake and eye contact so sincere it was aggressive. I smiled. "Nice not to be the only woman on the scene for a change."

That brought a very small smile to her face. She gave the barest of nods and stepped back, letting her captain take over.

"How much do you know about a fire scene, Miss Blake?"

"It's Ms. Blake, and not much."

He frowned at the correction. I felt Dolph shift beside me, unhappy with me. His face wouldn't show it, but I could almost feel him willing me not to be a pain in the butt. Who, me?

Corporal Tucker was staring at me, eyes wide, face very still as if she was trying not to laugh.

One of the other firemen joined us. His damp T-shirt clung to a stomach that had required far too many sit-ups, but I enjoyed the view anyway. He was tall, broad-shouldered, blond, and looked like he should have been carrying a surfboard or visiting Barbie in her Malibu dream house. There was a smear of soot on his smiling face, and his eyes were red-rimmed.

He offered his hand without being introduced. "I'm Wren." No rank, just his name. Confident.

He held my hand just a little longer than necessary. It wasn't obnoxious, just interested.

I dropped my eyes. Not out of shyness, but because some men mistake direct eye contact as a come-on. I had about as much beefcake on my plate as I could handle without adding amorous firemen.

Captain Fulton frowned at Wren. "Do you have any questions, Ms. Blake?" He emphasized the *Ms.* so it sounded like three z's at the end.

"You've got a basement full of vampires that you need to rescue without exposing them to sunlight or getting any of your people eaten, right?"

He stared at me for a second or two. "That's the gist of it."

"Why can't you just leave them in the basement until full dark?" I asked.

"The floor could cave in at any minute," he said.

"Which would expose them to sunlight and kill them," I said.

He nodded.

"Dolph said one vamp was covered with blankets, and rushed to the hospital. Is that why you think the others may not be in their coffins?"

He blinked. "There's also a vampire on the stairs leading down. It's . . ." His gaze fell, then came up suddenly to grab mine, angry. "I've seen burn victims but nothing quite like this."

"Are you sure it's a vampire?"

"Yes, why?"

"Because vamps exposed to sunlight or fire usually burn completely down to ash and a few bone fragments."

"We doused it with water," Wren said. "Thought it was a person at first."

"What changed your mind?"

It was his turn to look away. "It moved. It was like third-degree burns down to cartilage and muscle, bone, and it held out its hand to us." His face looked pale, haunted. "No person could have done that. We kept coating it with water, thinking maybe we could save it, but it stopped moving."

"So you assumed it was dead?" I asked.

All three of them exchanged glances. Captain Fulton said, "You mean it might not be dead?"

I shrugged. "Never underestimate a vamp's ability to survive, Captain."

"We've got to go back in there and get it to a hospital," Wren said. He turned as if he'd walk back into the house. Fulton caught his arm.

"Can you tell if the vampire is alive or dead?" Fulton asked.

"I think so."

"You think?"

"I've never heard of a vamp surviving fire. So yeah, I *think* I can tell if it's alive. If I said otherwise, I'd be lying. I try not to do that when it's important."

He nodded twice, briskly, as if he'd made up his mind about me. "The arsonist threw accelerant all over the floor that we're going to be walking on top of, and once we're down in the basement that same floor will be above us."

"So?"

"That floor is not going to hold, Ms. Blake. I'm going to make this a strictly voluntary job for my people."

I looked up into his serious face. "How likely is the floor to fall and how soon?"

"No way of knowing. Frankly, I'm surprised it hasn't caved in by now."

"It's a halfway house for the Church of Eternal Life. If it's like the last basement I saw at a Lifer's place, the ceiling is concrete reinforced with steel beams."

"That would explain why it hasn't fallen in," Fulton said.

"So we're safe, right?" I asked.

Fulton looked at me and shook his head. "The heat could have weakened the concrete, or even weakened the tensile strength of the steel beams."

"So it could still fall down," I said.

He nodded. "With us in it."

Great. "Let's do it."

Fulton grabbed my arm and gripped it too tight. I stared at him, but he didn't flinch and he didn't let me go. "Do you understand that we could be buried alive down there or crushed to death, or even drowned if there's enough water?"

"Let go of me, Captain Fulton." My voice was quiet, steady, not angry. Point for me.

Fulton released me and stepped back. His eyes looked a little wild. He was spooked. "I just want you to understand what could happen."

"She understands," Dolph said.

I had an idea. "Captain Fulton, how do you feel about sending your people in to a potential deathtrap to save a bunch of vampires?"

Something passed through his dark eyes. "The law says they're people. You don't leave people hurt or trapped."

"But," I prompted.

"But my men are worth more to me than a bunch of corpses."

"Not long ago I'd have brought the marshmallows and wieners for the roast," I said.

"What changed your mind?" Fulton asked.

"Kept meeting too many human beings that were as monstrous as the monsters. Maybe not as scary, but just as evil."

"Police work will ruin your view of your fellow man," Detective Tammy said. She and Larry had joined us at last. It had taken Larry a long time to cross those yards. He was far too hurt to insist on going inside the house. Good.

"I'll go in because it's my job, but I don't have to like it," Fulton said.

"Fine, but if we do have a cave-in, we better get dug out before nightfall, because without the vamp chaperone we'll be facing a basement full of new vamps that may not have perfect control over their hunger."

His eyes widened, showing too much white. I would have bet money that Fulton had had a close encounter of the fanged kind once upon a time. There were no scars on his neck, but that didn't prove anything. Vamps didn't always go for the neck, no matter what the movies say. Blood flows near the surface in lots of places.

I touched his arm lightly. Tension sang down his muscles like a string pulled too tight. "Who'd you lose?"

"What?" He seemed to be having trouble focusing on me.

"Who did the vampires take away from you?"

He stared at me, dark eyes focusing on me. Whatever horrible image was floating behind his eyes retreated. His face was almost normal when he said, "Wife, daughter."

I waited for him to say more, but the silence gathered round us in a still, deep pool made up of all the horror in those two whispered words. Wife, daughter. Both lost. No—taken.

"And now you have to go into the dark and save some bloodsuckers and risk yourself and your people. That really sucks."

He took a deep breath through his nose and let it out slowly. I watched him gain control of himself, watched him build his defenses back piece by piece. "I wanted to let it burn when I found out what was inside."

"But you didn't," I said. "You did your job."

"But the job's not done," he said softly.

"Life's a bitch," I said.

"And then you die," Larry finished for me.

I turned and frowned at him, but it was hard to argue. Today, he was right.

42

The two-biter, as Dolph so poetically put it, was a small woman in her thirties. Her brown hair was back in a tight ponytail leaving her neck and the vampire bites painfully visible. Vampire freaks, people who just liked vamps for sexual turn-ons, hid their fang marks unless at one of their hangouts. Human members of the Church of Eternal Life almost always made sure the bites were visible. Hair worn just right, short sleeves if the marks were at wrist or elbow bend. They were proud of the bites, saw them as signs of salvation.

The upper set of fang marks were larger, the skin redder and more torn. Someone hadn't been neat with their food. The second mark was almost dainty, surgically neat. The two-biter's name was Caroline, and she stood hugging herself as if she were cold. Since you could probably fry eggs on the sidewalk, I didn't think she was cold, or at least not that kind of cold.

"You wanted to see me, Caroline?"

She nodded, head bobbing up and down like one of those dogs you used to see in the backs of cars. "Yes," she said, voice breathy. She stared at Dolph and McKinnon, then back at me. The look was enough. She wanted privacy.

"I'm going to take Caroline for a little walk. If that's okay?"

Dolph nodded. McKinnon said, "The Red Cross have coffee and soft drinks." He pointed to a small truck with a camper shell. Red Cross volunteers giving coffee and comfort to the cops and firemen. You didn't see them at every crime scene, but they hit their share.

Dolph caught my gaze and gave a very small nod. He was trusting me to question her without him, trusting me to bring him back any info that pertained to the crime. The fact that he still trusted me that much made the day a little brighter. Nice that something did.

It was also nice to be doing something useful. Dolph had been hot to get me to the scene. Now everything was stalled. Fulton just wasn't eager to risk his people for corpses. But that wasn't it. If there'd been six humans down there, we'd have already been suited up and going in. But they weren't human, and no matter what the law said, it made a difference. Dolph was right, before *Addison v. Clark*, they'd have gotten a fire crew in here to make sure it didn't spread to the other houses, but they'd have let it burn. Standard operating procedure.

But that was four years ago, and the world had changed. Or so we told ourselves. If the vamps weren't in coffins and the roof collapsed, they would be exposed to sunlight, and that would be it. The firemen had used an axe on the wall next to the stairs so I could see the second vamp corpse. It was crispy-crittered but not dust. I had no explanation for why the body had remained so intact. I wasn't even a hundred percent sure that come nightfall it wouldn't heal. *It*—even I still did it. But the body was so badly burned, like black sticks and brown leather, the muscles in the face had pulled away leaving the teeth, complete with fangs, in a grimace that looked like pain. Firemen Wren had explained to me that the muscles contract with the heat enough to break bones sometimes. Just when you think you know every awful thing about death, you find out you're wrong.

I had to think of the body as an ''it'' or I couldn't look at it. Caroline had known the vampire. I think she was having a lot more trouble thinking of the body as an it.

She got a soft drink from the nice Red Cross lady. Even I got a Coke, which meant it was pretty damn hot for me to pass on the coffee.

I led her to the front yard of a neighboring house where no one had come out to check the scene. The drapes were all closed, driveway empty. Everyone gone for the day. The only sign of life was a triangular rose bed and a black swallowtail butterfly floating over it. Peaceful. For a moment I wondered if the butterfly was one of Warrick's pets, but there was no feel of power. It was just a butterfly floating like a tiny tissue-paper kite over the yard. I sat down on the grass. Caroline joined me, smoothing her pale blue shorts down in back as if she was more accustomed to wearing skirts. She took a drink of soda. Now that she had me to herself, she didn't seem to know how to start.

It might have worked better if I'd waited for her to begin, but my patience had been used up long ago. It wasn't one of my cardinal virtues to begin with. ''What did you want to tell me?'' I asked.

She sat her can of soda carefully on the grass, thin hands smoothing along the hem of her shorts. She had pale pink nail polish on her short nails that matched the pink stripes in her tank top. Better than pale blue, I guess.

''Can I trust you?'' she asked in a voice as fragile and pale as she seemed.

I hate being asked questions like that. I wasn't in the mood to lie. ''Maybe. It depends on what you want to trust me with.''

Caroline looked a little startled, as if she'd expected me to just say, sure. ''That was very honest of you. Most people lie without thinking about it.'' Something in the way she said it made me think that Caroline had been lied to often, by people she'd trusted.

''I try not to lie, Caroline, but if you have information that'll help us here, you need to tell me.'' I took a drink of my own soda and tried to appear casual, forced my body not to tense up, not to show how much I wanted to simply scream at her until she told me whatever it was. Short of torture, you can't make people talk, not really. Caroline wanted to tell me her secrets. I just had to be calm and let her do it. If I was overeager or abusive, she'd either fold and tell all, or clam up and let us rot. You never knew which way it would go, so you try patience first. You can always browbeat them later.

"I've been the human liaison for this halfway house for three months now. The guardian who oversaw the younger ones was Giles. He was strong and powerful, but he was trapped in his coffin until true darkness. Then two nights ago he woke in the middle of the day. The first time for him. The one on the stairs has to be one of the younger vampires."

She looked at me, brown eyes wide. She leaned into me, lowering her soft voice even further. I had to lean into her just to catch her voice, close enough that my hair brushed her shoulder.

"None of the younger ones has been dead two years. Do you understand what that means?"

"It means that they shouldn't have risen during daylight hours. It means that the one on the stairs should have been burnt to ashes."

"Exactly," she said. She sounded relieved to finally find someone who understood.

"Was this early waking restricted to your halfway house?"

She shook her head, whispering now. We had our heads together like first-graders talking in class. I was close enough to see the fine red lines in her eyes. Caroline had been losing sleep over something. "Every house and all the churches were suddenly having vampires rise early. The hunger seemed worse on the young ones." Her hand went to her neck and the messy wound. "They were harder to control, even by the guardians."

"Anyone have any theories as to why this was happening?" I asked.

"Malcolm thought someone was interfering with them."

I had several candidates for who might be interfering with the vamps, but we weren't here to get my answers. We were here to get Caroline's answers. "He have any ideas about who?"

"You know about our illustrious visitors?" she asked, voice even lower, as if she were afraid to say the last.

"If you mean the Vampire Council, I've met them."

She jerked back from me then, shocked. "Met them," she said. "But Malcolm has not met them yet."

I shrugged. "They paid their . . . respects to the Master of the City first."

"Malcolm said they would contact us when they were ready. He saw their coming as a sign that the rest of vampirekind was ready to embrace the true faith."

I wasn't about to sit there and tell her why the council had really come to town. If the Church didn't know, they didn't need to know. "I don't think the council thinks much about religion, Caroline."

"Why else would they come?"

I shrugged. "The council has its reasons." See, not a lie, cryptic as hell, but not a lie.

She seemed to accept the statement. Maybe she was used to cryptic bullshit. "Why would the council want to hurt us?"

"Maybe they don't see it as hurting."

"If the firemen go down in there to save the young ones and they wake without a guardian . . ." She drew her knees to her chest, hugging her legs. "They'll rise like revenants, mindless beasts, until they've fed. People could be dead before they come to themselves.''

I touched her shoulder. ''You're scared of them, aren't you?'' I'd never met a human church member who was scared of vampires, especially not one that was donating blood as a human liaison.

She lowered the neckline of her tank top until I could see the tops of her small breasts. There was a bite mark on the pale flesh of one breast that looked more like a dog bite than one made by a vampire. The flesh had bruised badly, as if the vamp had been pulled off her almost as soon as he'd started sucking.

''Giles had to pull him off of me. He had to restrain him. Looking into his face, I knew that if Giles hadn't been there, he'd have killed me. Not to bring me over or embrace me, but just because I was food.'' She let her top slide back over the wound, hugging herself tight, shivering in the hot July sunshine.

''How long have you been with the Church, Caroline?''

''Two years.''

''And this is the first time you've been scared?''

She nodded.

''They've been very careful around you, then.''

''What do you mean?'' she asked.

I unbent my left arm, showing the scars. ''The mound of scar tissue at the crook is where a vamp gnawed on me. He broke the arm. I was lucky not to lose the use of it.''

''What about that?'' She touched the claw marks that trailed down the lower part of the arm.

''Shapeshifted witch.''

''How did the cross get burned into your arm?''

''Humans with a few bites like you thought it was amusing to brand me with the cross. Just amusing themselves until their master rose for the night.''

Her eyes were wide. ''But the vampires in the Church aren't like that. We aren't like that.''

''All vamps are like that, Caroline. Some of them control it better than others, but they still have to feed off humans. You can't really respect something that you see as food.''

''But you are with the Master of the City. Do you believe that of him?''

I thought about that and answered truthfully. ''Sometimes.''

She shook her head. ''I thought I knew what I wanted. What I was going to do for all eternity. Now I don't know anything. I feel so . . . lost.'' Tears trailed out of her wide eyes.

I put my arm across her shoulders, and she leaned into me, clinging to me with her small, carefully painted hands. She cried soundlessly, only the shakiness of her breathing betraying her.

I held her and let her cry. If I took the nice firemen down into the darkness and six newly dead vampires rose as revenants, either the firemen were dead or I'd be forced to kill the vampires. Either way, not a win-win situation.

We needed to find out if the vamps were alive, needed some control over them. If the council was causing the problems, maybe they could help fix it. When big bad vampires come to town to kill me, I don't generally turn to them for help. But we were trying to save vampires lives here, not just human. Maybe they'd help. Maybe they wouldn't, but it couldn't hurt to ask. All right, it could hurt to ask, and probably would.

43

Even over the phone, I could tell Jean-Claude was shocked at my idea of turning to the council for help. Call it a guess. He was literally speechless. It was nearly a first.

"Why not ask for their help?"

"They are the council, *ma petite*," he said, voice almost breathy with emotion.

"Exactly," I said. "They are the leaders of your people. Leadership doesn't just mean privileges. It has a price tag."

"Tell that to your politicians in Washington in their three-thousand-dollar suits," he said.

"I didn't say that we did any better. That's beside the point. They've helped make this problem. They can, by God, help fix it." I had a bad thought. "Unless they're doing it on purpose," I said.

He gave a long sigh. "No, *ma petite*, it is not on purpose. I did not realize that it was happening to the others."

"Why isn't it happening to our vampires?"

I think he laughed. "Our vampires, *ma petite*?"

"You know what I mean."

"Yes, *ma petite*, I know what you mean. I have been protecting our people."

"Don't take this wrong, but I'm surprised you had the juice to keep the council from messing with your people."

"In truth, *ma petite*, so am I."

"So you're more powerful than Malcolm now?"

"It would appear so," he said quietly.

I thought about that for a minute. "But why the early rising? Why the increased hunger? Why would the council want that to be happening?"

"They do not want it, *ma petite*. It is merely a side effect of their proximity."

"Explain," I said.

"Their very presence will give unprotected vampires extra power: early rising, perhaps other gifts. The more voracious appetite and lack of control of the younger ones could mean that the council has decided not to feed while in my territory. I know the Traveler can take energy through lesser vampires without possessing them.''

"So he takes part of the blood they drink?''

"Oui, ma petite.''

"Are the others feeding?'' I asked.

"If all of the Church's members are experiencing this difficulty, I would think not. I think the Traveler has found a way to drain energy for all of them, though I cannot imagine Yvette going for even a night without causing pain to someone.''

"She has Warrick to pick on.'' The moment I said it, I realized I hadn't had a chance to tell Jean-Claude about Warrick's little daytime excursion, or his warning. Jean-Claude had woken from his sleep while I was at the hospital surrounded by wereanimals. Since then I'd been moving from one emergency to another.

"Warrick came to visit me while you were out for the day,'' I said.

"What do you mean, *ma petite?*''

I told him. All of it.

He was silent. Only his soft breathing let me know he was still there. Finally, he spoke. "I knew that Yvette gained power through her master, but I did not realize he was dampening Warrick's abilities.'' He laughed suddenly. "Perhaps that is why I did not realize I was a master vampire while I was with the council that first time. Perhaps my master, too, was preventing my powers from blossoming.''

"Does Warrick's warning change our plans?'' I asked.

"We are committed to a formal entertainment, *ma petite*. If we refuse to pay the price for your wereleopards, then we will give Padma and Yvette the very excuse they need to challenge us. Breaking faith once your word is given is an almost unforgivable sin among us.''

"I've endangered us,'' I said.

"Oui, but being who you are, you could not do less. Warrick a master vampire, who would have thought it? He has been Yvette's plaything for so very long.''

"How long?'' I asked.

Jean-Claude was quiet for a heartbeat or two, then, "He was a knight of the Crusades, *ma petite.*''

"Which crusade? There were several,'' I said.

"So nice to talk to someone who knows their history, *ma petite*. But you have been near him. What age is he?''

I thought about it. "Nine hundred, give or take.''

"Which would mean?''

"I don't like being quizzed, Jean-Claude. The First Crusade in the late 1000s.''

"Exactement.''

"So Yvette was old even then,'' I said.

"Do you not know her age?''

"She's a thousand years old. But it's a soft one thousand. I've met vamps her age that scared the hell out of me. She doesn't.''

"Yes, Yvette is terrifying but not because of her age, or her power. She can live until the end of the world and she will never be a master among us.''

"And that gripes her ass,'' I said.

"Crudely but accurately put, *ma petite.*''

"I'm going to ask the Traveler for help."

"We have bargained for all the aid we will ever get from them, *ma petite*. Do not put yourself further in their debt. I beg this of you."

"You've never begged anything of me," I said.

"Then heed me now, *ma petite*. Do not do this."

"I'm not going to bargain," I said.

He let out a breath as if he'd been holding it. "Good, *ma petite*, very good."

"I'm just going to ask."

"*Ma petite, ma petite*, what have I just told you?"

"Look, we're trying to save vampire lives here, not just human. Vampires are legal in this country. It doesn't just mean you get privileges. It comes with a price. Or it should."

"You are going to appeal to the council's sense of justice?" He didn't bother to keep the incredulity out of his voice. In fact, he played on it.

Put that way it sounded silly, but . . . "The council is partially to blame for what's happening. They've endangered their own people. Good leaders don't do that."

"No one has ever accused them of being good leaders, *ma petite*. They just are. It is not a question of good or bad. We fear them, and that is enough."

"Bullshit. That isn't enough. It isn't even close to enough."

He sighed. "Promise me only that you will not bargain with them. Make your request but do not offer them anything for their aid. You must swear this to me, *ma petite*. Please."

It was the "please" that did it, and the fear in his voice. "I promise. It's their job to do this. You don't bargain to get someone to do what they're supposed to do in the first place."

"You are a wondrous combination of cynicism and naiveté, *ma petite*."

"You think it's naive to expect the council to help the vampires of this city?"

"They will ask what is in it for them, *ma petite*. What will you say?"

"I'll tell them it's their duty, and call them honorless bastards if they don't do it."

He did laugh then. "I would pay to hear this conversation."

"Would it help for you to listen in?"

"No. If they suspect it is my idea, they will demand a price. Only you, *ma petite*, could be this naive before them and hope to be believed."

I didn't think of myself as naive, and it bugged me that he did. Of course, he was nearly three centuries older than I was. Madonna probably seemed naive to him. "I'll let you know how it goes."

"Oh, the Traveler will make very certain that I know the outcome."

"Am I about to get you in trouble?"

"We are already in trouble, *ma petite*. It cannot get much deeper."

"Was that meant to be comforting?" I asked.

"*Un peu*," he said.

"That meant 'a little,' right?"

"*Oui, ma petite. Vous dispose a apprendre.*"

"Stop it," I said.

"As you like." He lowered his voice to a seductive whisper, as if it wasn't already the voice of wet dreams. "What were you doing when I awoke today?"

I'd almost forgotten about my little hospital adventure. Now it came rushing back hard enough to bring heat to my face. "Nothing."

"No, no, *ma petite*, that is not correct. You were most certainly doing something."

"Did Stephen and Nathaniel arrive at the house?"

"They did."

"Great. I'll talk to you later."

"You refuse to answer my question?"

"No, I just don't know a short version that doesn't make me feel like a slut. I don't have time for a longer version right now. So, can you wait?"

"I will wait for all eternity, if my lady asks it."

"Can the crap, Jean-Claude."

"If I wish you luck with the council, would that please you more?"

"Yeah, yeah."

"It is all right to be a lady, Anita. It is not a bad thing being a woman."

"You try being one, then talk to me," I said. I hung up. "My lady" sounded like *my dog*. Ownership. I was his human servant. Short of killing him, I couldn't change that. But I didn't belong to him. If I belonged to anybody, I belonged to me. And that was how I was going to approach the council, as me: Anita Blake, vampire executioner, police liaison for the monsters. They wouldn't listen to Jean-Claude's human servant, but they might listen to me.

44

Thomas answered the phone at the Circus. "They have you doing flunky work?" I asked.

"Excuse me?" he said.

"Sorry, this is Anita Blake."

He was quiet for a second, then, "I'm sorry, we are not open for business until nightfall."

"Is Fernando there?"

"Yes, that's right. Nightfall."

"I need to talk to the Traveler, Thomas. I'm asking this on police business, not as Jean-Claude's human servant. We've got some vampires in trouble, and I think he can help."

"Yes, we do take reservations," he said.

I gave him the number of Dolph's car phone. "We don't have a lot of time, Thomas. If he won't help me, I've got to go in with cops and firemen on my own."

"I look forward to seeing you tonight." He hung up.

Life would be so much easier if Fernando were dead. Besides, I'd promised Sylvie we'd kill him. I always tried to keep my promises.

Dolph was leaning in the door wanting to know what was taking so long, when the phone rang. I looked at him. He nodded and moved away. I picked up. "Yes."

"I am told you needed to speak with me."

I wondered whose lips he was using, whose body. "Thank you for calling me back, Traveler." A little politeness couldn't hurt.

"Thomas was surprisingly eloquent on your behalf. What do you wish of me?" I explained as briefly as possible.

"And what do you wish me to do about this problem of yours?"

"You can stop taking energy through them. That would help."

"Then I must feed on live humans. Is there someone you would offer in their place for each of us?"

"No, no offers, no bargains. This is police business, Traveler. I'm speaking with the authority of human law behind me, not Jean-Claude."

"What is human law to me? To us?"

"If we go down there and they attack us, I'll end up killing some of them. They may kill policemen, firemen. That's bad publicity with Brewster's Law to be decided this fall. The council has stopped all vampires in this country from fighting amongst themselves until the law is finalized. Surely slaughtering policemen is forbidden, too?"

"It is," he said. His voice was so careful. He gave me nothing. I couldn't tell if he was angry or amused or gave a damn either way.

"I'm asking you to help me save the lives of your vampires."

"They belong to this Church of yours. They are not mine," he said.

"But the council is the overall leadership of the vampires, right?"

"We are their ultimate law."

I didn't like the phrasing, but I plowed ahead. "You could find out case by case if the vampires were alive or dead in the burned-out buildings. You could keep the vamps from rising early and attacking us here."

"I think you overestimate my powers, Anita."

"I don't think so," I said.

"If Jean-Claude will supply us with . . . food, I will be more than happy to cease borrowing from the others."

"No, you get nothing for this, Traveler."

"If you give me nothing, I give you nothing," he said.

"Dammit, this isn't a game."

"We are vampires, Anita. Do you not understand what that means? We are apart from your world. What happens to you does not affect us."

"Bullshit. Some fanatics are out here trying to duplicate the Inferno all over again. That affects you. Thomas and Gideon have had to repel invaders while you slept. It does affect you."

"It doesn't matter. We are in your world, but not of it," he said.

"Look, that may have worked in the 1500's or whenever, but the minute vampires became legal citizens, it changed. A vampire got taken to the hospital in an ambulance. They are doing their best to keep him alive, whatever the hell that means for you guys. Firemen are risking their lives to go into burned-out buildings to save vampires. The fanatics are trying to kill you, but the rest of us humans are trying to save you."

"Then you are fools," he said.

"Maybe," I said, "but we poor humans have taken oaths to protect and serve. We honor our promises."

"Are you implying I do not?"

"I'm saying that if you don't help us here, today, then you aren't worthy to be council. You aren't leaders. You're just parasites feeding on the fear of your followers. True leaders don't leave their people to die, not if they can save them."

"Parasites. May I tell the rest of the council your so high opinion of us?" He was angry now. I could hear it like heat across the line.

"Yeah, tell them all. But mark me on this, Traveler, vampires can't just gain privileges with legal citizenship. They also gain responsibilities to the human law that made them legal.''

"Is that so?''

"Yeah, that's so. This mysterious 'in your world but not a part of it' may have worked in the past. But welcome to the twentieth century, because that's what legal status means. Once you're citizens who pay taxes, own businesses, marry, inherit, have children, you can't hide in some crypt somewhere and count the decades. You are a part of our world now.''

"I will think upon what you have said, Anita Blake.''

"When I get off the phone with you, I'm going inside the house. We're going to start bringing out the vamps in body bags to protect them in case the floor caves in. If they rise as revenants while we're doing it, it'll be a bloodbath.''

"I am aware of the problems,'' he said.

"Are you aware that it's the presence of the council that's giving them the energy to possibly rise this early in the day?''

"I cannot change the effect our presence has on the lesser vampires. If this Malcolm wishes to claim the status of master, then it is his duty to keep his people safe. I cannot do it for him.''

"Can't or won't?'' I asked.

"Can't,'' he said.

Hmmm. "Maybe I have overestimated your powers. My apologies if I have.''

"Accepted, and I understand how rare it is for you to apologize for anything, Anita.'' The phone went dead.

I hit the button that turned off the buzzing line.

Dolph walked back as I got out of the car. "Well?'' Dolph asked.

I shrugged. "Looks like we go in without vampire backup.''

"You can't depend on them, Anita, not for backup.'' He took my hand, something he'd never done, squeezing it. "This is all you can count on. One human to another. The monsters don't give a shit about us. If you think they do, then you are fooling yourself.'' He dropped my hand and walked away before I could think of a comeback. Just as well. After talking to the Traveler, I wasn't sure I had one.

45

An hour later I was dressed in a Hazardous Materials suit—Haz-Mat for short. It was bulky, to say the least, and turned into a portable sauna in the St. Louis heat. Heavy tape was wrapped around my elbows and wrists, securing the seal between gloves and sleeves. I'd walked out of the boots twice, so they taped my legs, too. I felt like an astronaut who had gone to the wrong tailor. Insult to injury, there was a Self-Contained Breathing Apparatus, SCBA, strapped to my back. Add Underwater and you got SCUBA, but we weren't planning to go underwater. I was grateful for that.

There was a mask that covered the entire face instead of a mouthpiece with regulator, but other than that, it was damn close to SCUBA gear. I had my diving certification. Got it back in college and keep it updated. If you let it slide, you have to take the whole damn training course over again. Updating was less painful. I was delaying putting on the mask as long as possible. Due to a diving accident in Florida, I've got claustrophobia now. Not bad enough for elevators to be a problem, but enclosed in the suit, with a mask about to cover my face and the Haz-Mat helmet going over my entire head—I was panicking and didn't know what to do about it.

"Do you really think all this is necessary?" I asked for the dozenth time. If they'd just give me a regular fire helmet with the SCBA, I could handle it.

"If you go in with us, yes," Corporal Tucker said. Her three inches of extra height didn't help much. We both looked like we were wearing hand-me-downs.

"There's the possibility of disease contamination if there are bodies floating in the basement," Lieutenant Wren said.

"Will there really be that much water in the basement?"

They exchanged glances. "You've never been in a house after a fire, have you?" Tucker asked.

"No."

"You'll understand once we're in," she said.

"Sounds ominous."

"It's not meant to," she said.

Tucker didn't have much of a sense of humor, and Wren had too much. He'd been entirely too solicitous while we were wriggling into the suits. He'd made sure he taped me up and was even now wasting a brilliant smile on me. But it was nothing too overt. Nothing obvious enough for me to say, look I have a boyfriend. For all I knew, he was always like this and I'd look an ass for taking it personally.

"Put the mask on, and I'll help you fit the hood over it," Wren said.

I shook my head. "Just give me a regular helmet and I'll use the SCBA."

"If you fall in the water without the hood sealed, Anita, you might as well not have the suit at all."

"I'll take my chances," I said.

Tucker said, "You had trouble walking from the Haz-Mat truck to here. You'll get better with practice, but in deep water, even we'll have trouble keeping our feet."

I shook my head again. My heart was pounding so hard, I was having trouble breathing. I put the mask on my face. I took a breath, and that horrible sound began. It was like Darth Vader breathing except it was yours. In the water, in the dark, your breath was the only sound. It could become thunderously loud while you waited to die.

"Strap needs tightening," Wren said. He started to adjust the strap as if I were five and being bundled off to play in the snow.

"I can do it." My voice came over the open radio line in the mask.

He raised his gloved hands skyward, still smiling. He was a hard man to insult, because I'd been trying. He had this sort of cheerful goodwill that seemed to deflect everything. Never trust people who smile constantly. They're either selling something or not very bright. Wren didn't strike me as stupid.

Insult to injury, I couldn't get the strap adjusted on the damned mask. I always hated trying to work with anything bulkier than surgical gloves. I pulled the mask off and my first breath of real air was too loud, too long. I was sweating, and it wasn't just the heat.

I had the Browning and the Firestar lying on the side of the fire truck. There were enough pockets on the outside of the suit to hold half a dozen guns. I had a sawed-off shotgun from my vampire kit in a makeshift pack across my back. Yeah, it's illegal, but Dolph had been with me once upon a time when we went after a revenant vampire. They were like PCP users: immune to pain, stronger even than a normal vamp. A force of hell with fangs. I showed him the shotgun before I got it out. He okayed it. We'd ended with two dead security guards and one rookie officer spread all over the hallway the last time. At least Dolph and his men had silver ammo now. He and Zerbrowski nearly getting killed because they didn't have it was what pushed the paperwork through. I gave them a box of ammo for Christmas before they got official silver ammo. I never wanted to watch any of them bleed their lives away for lack of it.

I'd left the knives in their wrist sheaths. Carrying naked blades in the pockets of a suit that was air-and water-tight seemed sort of defeatist. If I lost both handguns and had to scramble for the knives under the suit, then we were probably toast. No need to worry about it. My silver cross hung naked around my neck. It was the best deterrent I had against baby vamps. They couldn't force their way past a bare cross, not when it was backed up by faith. I'd only met one vamp that could force his way past a blazing cross and harm me. And he was dead. Funny how so many of them ended up that way.

Tucker came over to me. "I'll help you adjust the mask."

I shook my head. "Leave me till last. The less time I'm in this get-up the better."

She licked her lips, started to say something, stopped, then said, "Are you all right?"

Normally, I would have said sure, but they were depending on me, maybe for their lives. How scared was I? Scared. "Not exactly," I said.

"You're claustrophobic, aren't you?" she said.

I must have looked surprised, because she said, "A lot of people want to be firemen, but in the middle of a fire with the mask down and smoke so thick you can't see your hand in front of your eyes, you don't want to be claustrophobic."

I nodded. "I can understand that."

"There's a part of training where they cover your eyes completely and make you do the equipment by touch as if the smoke had blacked out the world. You learn who doesn't like it close."

"I could take the suit without the SCBA. It's the combination of the suit and listening to myself breathe. I had a diving accident just after college."

"Can you do this?" No accusations, just honesty.

I nodded. "I won't leave you stranded."

"That's not what I asked," she said.

We stared at each other. "Give me a few minutes. I just didn't understand what Haz-Mat was. I'll be okay."

"You sure?"

I nodded.

She didn't say anything else, just walked away to let me gather my scattered wits.

Wren had finally wandered over to talk to Fulton. Wren and Tucker were going in because they were both paramedics and we might need their medical training. Also, frankly, I didn't want Fulton in the dark with me and a bunch of vamps. He was simply too freaked. I didn't blame him, but I didn't want him at my back either. Of course, if I'd been watching me sweat and struggle to breathe calmly, I might not want me in there. Dammit. I could do this. I had to do this.

Detective Tammy Reynolds came slogging up in her own suit. They didn't have one big enough to fit Dolph, so she was my armed backup. Oh, joy. I couldn't send them in with Tammy as their only backup.

Tammy had managed to get her shoulder rig over the suit. She had one of those that just rode across the shoulders, no belt to put through straps. When I'd been shopping, all the holsters that just crossed the shoulders moved around on me too much. Part of it is having narrow shoulders. I'd have had to have the holster cut down. I don't buy things that have to be fussed with. Not dresses or holsters.

Reynolds smiled at me. "Larry's really disappointed that he can't come along."

"I'm relieved," I said.

She frowned at me. "I thought you'd want him to back you up."

"Yeah, but a gun can't help him if the ceiling caves in on us."

"You think it will?" she asked.

I shrugged. I'd concentrated on getting suited up, on small details, on Wren's quiet teasing. I'd managed not to dwell on the thought that we were about to walk across a floor that might collapse underneath us, then walk under it and wait for it to collapse on top of us, while wading through water full of coffins and vampires. What could be better?

"Let's just say I'm cautious."

"And you don't want to risk Larry."

"That's right. I don't like the idea of Larry getting hurt, by anything." I stared at her while I said it.

She blinked hazel eyes at me, then smiled. "Neither do I, Anita, neither do I."

I nodded and let it go. I'd done my parenting bit. I wasn't even sure why I didn't trust Tammy, but I didn't. Women's intuition, or maybe I just didn't trust much of anybody anymore. Maybe.

Tucker came back to us. "Time to suit up." She looked right at me.

I nodded. I let her help me adjust the mask over my face. I closed my eyes and concentrated on my breathing—in, out, in, out. In diving if you breathed too fast, you could blow your lungs. Now it was just a way to keep from hyperventilating.

She fitted the suit's hood over my head. I watched her do it and knew my eyes were a little too wide.

Wren's cheerful voice came over the radio in the mask. "Breathe normally, Anita."

"I am breathing normally," I said. It sounded odd to be able to talk normally while my own breathing was wheezing, loud and ominous in my ears. With a regulator in, you couldn't talk, though I'd learned you could scream with a regulator clenched between your teeth. Sounds echo like a son of a bitch under water.

With the helmet over the mask, visibility was not the best. I practiced turning my head, seeing just how big the blind spots were. My peripheral vision was almost gone.

Tammy's voice came over the radio. "It's hard to see in this thing."

"You'll get used to it," Tucker said.

"I hope we're not in this get-up long enough to get used to it," I said.

"If we say 'run,' run like hell," Tucker said.

"Because the floor will be caving in, right?" I said.

I think she nodded, but it was hard to tell through the layers. "Right."

"Fine, but when we get to the stairs, I have to take the lead, and if I say 'run like hell,' it means the vampires are going to eat us."

Wren and Tucker exchanged glances. "You tell us to run," Wren said, "we'll ask how fast."

"Agreed," Tucker said.

"Great," I said. Truthfully, it was a damn relief not to have to argue with anyone. No debate. What a relief. If I hadn't been sweating like a pig, listening to my own breathing echoing horrifically like *The Tell-Tale Heart*, having to relearn how to walk in metal-lined boots, I'd have said working with the fire department was a break. But it wasn't. I'd have rather rappelled down on ropes with Special

Forces into a free-fire zone than shuffle along in the mummy suit trying not to lose it. It was just a phobia, dammit. Nothing was wrong. Nothing was hurting me. My body didn't believe the logic. Phobias are like that. Reason doesn't move them.

Wren stepped onto the floor. It made a noise like a giant groaning in its sleep. He froze, then stomped his feet so hard I thought my pulse was going to spill out my mouth.

"Shouldn't we be quieter?" I asked.

Wren's voice came in my ear. "Walk exactly where I walk. Don't deviate, don't spread out."

"Why?" I asked.

"Just because the floor is solid where I'm walking doesn't mean it's solid anywhere else."

"Oh," I said.

I went right behind Wren, so I got a closeup view of his little stomping dance. It was not comforting. Tucker came behind me, then Detective Reynolds bringing up the rear.

I'd given everybody a cross to put in the pockets of their suits. Why wasn't everyone wearing one like I was? Because Tucker and Wren were carrying a pack of opaque body bags apiece. Plan was to put the vamps in the bags and take them back up. Inside an ambulance in the body bags they'd be safe until nightfall. If we pulled this off and the ceiling didn't collapse before darkness, I was going to be pissed. As long as it didn't fall while we were down here. That I could pass on.

I walked where Wren walked, religiously. Though I did have to say, "Even out of this suit my stride isn't as big as yours. In the suit I'm damned near crippled. Can I take smaller steps?"

"Just as long as the steps are directly in line with mine, yes," Wren said.

Relief. The floor was covered with debris. Nails were everywhere in the blackened boards. I understood the metal insoles now. I was grateful for them, but it didn't make them any easier to walk in.

There was a line to one side going down a hole in the floor. It was a hard suction hose attached to a loud pump some distance away. They were draining the water out of the basement. If the place was watertight, it could be full to the ceiling. Comforting thought.

Fulton had called in a Haz-Mat tanker for the water. He seemed to be treating vampirism like a contagious disease. It was contagious but not in the way he seemed to think. But he was Incident Commander. I was learning that that title equated with God at a fire scene. You couldn't argue with God. You could get mad at him, but it didn't change anything.

I concentrated on moving my feet. Watching for debris. Stepping in Wren's footsteps. I let the world slide away except for moving forward. I was aware of the sun beating down, sweat trickling down my spine, but it was all distant. There was nothing but moving forward, no thinking required. My breathing was normal when I bumped into Wren's back.

I froze, afraid to move. Was something wrong?

"What's up?" I asked.

"Stairs," he said.

Oh, I thought. I was supposed to take the lead now. I wasn't ready. Truthfully,

I wasn't sure how good I could walk on stairs in the damn suit. I just hadn't appreciated how hard it would be to walk in it.

"Stairs are the most dangerous part of a building like this," Wren said. "If anything is going to collapse it'll be the stairs."

"Are you trying to make us feel better?" Reynolds asked.

"Just prepared," he said. "I'll test the first few steps. If it seems solid, I'll move back and let Blake take it." He wasn't teasing anymore. He was all business, and we were suddenly on a last-name basis.

"Watch the body on the stairs," he said. He moved onto the first step, stomping hard enough that I jumped.

The body on the stairs was black, charcoaled. The mouth gaped open in a soundless scream. You had to look close to see the fangs. Real vamp fangs just aren't that big. Tendons were stretched naked looking like they'd snap if you touched them. The body looked fragile, as if one touch and it would be dust. I remembered Larry and the skull that had turned to powder at his touch. This body looked tougher than that, but not by much. Could it be alive? Was there some spark inside it that with nightfall it would move, live? I didn't know. It should have been ash. It should still have been burning in the sunlight, no matter how much water they poured on it.

Wren's voice startled me. "You can take the lead now, Anita."

I looked down the steps and found Wren several steps below, almost halfway. The darkness down below spilled around his feet like a pool. He was far enough down that a really ambitious vamp might have grabbed a leg and pulled him down. I hadn't been concentrating. My fault.

"Come back up, Wren," I said.

He did, and he was oblivious to the possible danger. Damn. "The stairs are concrete, which makes it safer. You should be okay."

"Do I still have to stomp every step?"

"It'd be safer," he said.

"If I feel it going, I yell?"

"Yes," he said. He brushed past me.

I stared down into the Stygian depths. "I need a hand for the railing in this suit. A hand for the gun. I'm out of hands for a flashlight," I said.

"I can try and shine a light in front of you, but it won't be where you need it."

"Don't worry about it, unless I ask." It took me over a minute, maybe two, to fumble the Browning out of its pocket. The gun was definitely going in one hand. I had to use two hands to click off the safety in the bulky gloves. I slid my hand inside the trigger guard on the trigger. I'd never have carried a gun like this normally. But my gloved finger didn't want to fit inside the trigger guard. I was ready to go now. If I put safety first, I'd never get a shot off in time. I'd practiced with winter gloves on, but I'd never dreamed of having to shoot vamps in a Haz-Mat suit. Hell, I didn't know what a Haz-Mat suit was until today.

"What's the holdup?" Fulton's voice. I'd forgotten he was monitoring everything we said. Like being spied on.

"These damn gloves aren't exactly made for shooting."

"What's that mean?" he asked.

"It means, I'm ready to go down now," I said. I kept the Browning pointed up and a little forward. If I fell in the suit and accidently fired a shot, I was going to try very hard not to shoot anyone behind me. I wondered if Detective Tammy had her gun out. I wondered how good a shot she was. How was she in an emergency? I said a short prayer that we wouldn't be finding out, got a death grip on the banister, and stomped the first step. It didn't fall down. I stared ahead into the thick blackness at the middle of the stairs. The sunlight cut across the darkness like a knife.

"Here we go, boys and girls," I said. And down we went.

46

Water lapped at the last few steps. The basement had turned into a lake. Wren's flashlight passed over the dark water like a tiny searchlight. The water was a solid blackness, holding all its secrets close and quiet. A coffin floated about ten feet from the stairs, bobbing gently in the dark, dark water.

Even over the wheezing and whoosh of my own breathing, I could hear the water lapping. There was the sound of wood rubbing together like boats tied up at a dock. I pointed, and Wren's light followed my hand. Two coffins were bumping against one another near the far wall.

"Three coffins visible, but there should be four more. One for the guardian, one for the vamp on the stairs, and two more."

I took that last step into the water. Even through the suit I could feel the liquid like a distant coolness, a liquid weight lapping at my ankles. The feel of the water was enough to speed my breathing, send my heart pounding in my throat.

"You're going to hyperventilate," Wren said. "Slow your breathing."

I took a deep breath and let it out slowly, counting to make it slower. A count of fifteen, then another breath.

"You okay?" he asked.

"What's going on?" Fulton asked.

"Nothing," Wren said.

"I'm okay," I said.

"What's happening?" Fulton said.

"We're missing four coffins. Two could have sunk, but we still have two missing. Just wondering where they are," I said.

"Be careful down there," he said.

"Like a virgin on her wedding night," I whispered.

Someone laughed. Always good to be amusing.

I tried stomping on the next step, knee-deep in water, and my feet went out from under me. I was suddenly sliding down the steps, only my grip on the banister keeping me from going under. I sat in water up to my chin, feeling stupid and scared. A combination I'm not fond of.

Wren came to stand over me, light sliding over the water while he helped me to my feet. I needed the help. I raised the Browning dripping wet into the light.

"Will your gun work now?" he asked.

"I could fire it underwater and it would still work," I said. It still amazes me how many people think a little water ruins a gun. You have to clean it really well afterwards but during the shooting, water is fine. The days of having to keep your powder dry are long past.

I eased down the remaining steps and slid slowly down into the cool water. My breathing grew ragged. Fuck it, I was scared. Flat-footed in the water, I could have gone for the flashlight in one of the pockets, or I could have slid the shotgun out of the bag across my back. But before I started changing guns, I'd let Detective Tammy get down here with her gun to cover me. I still didn't know how good she was, but it was better than nothing.

The water slid around my upper chest, not quite armpit depth, but almost. I slid very carefully out into the water, more swimming than walking, gun held two-handed and ready. Or as ready as you can be half-floating in a borrowed astronaut suit.

I didn't like the fact that we were missing two coffins with vamps inside them. They probably just sank, but my gut was tense, waiting for hands to slide over my ankles, and yank me under. My foot brushed something solid, and I couldn't breathe for a second. My foot scooted against it. Paint can maybe. I guess even vamps have crap in their basement just like the rest of us.

"I've got some debris over here," I said.

"You sound like a real firemen," Wren said.

"Coffin?" Detective Tammy asked from the stairs. She slid into the water last.

"No, just a can of some kind."

The coffin had almost floated to me. No effort. I put a hand out to touch it, keeping it floating gently in the small waves. "When Wren and Tucker get up to the coffin, I'm going to back off. Cover me while I pull out the shotgun."

"You got it," Tammy said. She had her flashlight and gun in two hands, one above the other, so the light moved with the barrel of her gun. She was sweeping the water for movement. Just seeing her do that made the tension in my shoulders ease a bit.

"Don't open the coffin until I'm ready," I said. I had a moment to realize that I wasn't worried about my breathing. The suffocating closeness had receded under the pure adrenaline rush of being chest-deep in water with vampires all around. I could be phobic later, after we survived.

Wren and Tucker took either end of the coffin. Even they were having trouble moving in the water in full suits. "I'm going for the shotgun now, Reynolds."

"You're covered," she said.

I backed off and swung the bag around. I had a moment to decide whether to try to put the Browning back in a pants pocket or in the bag where the shotgun was now. I chose the bag. I kept the bag in front though, where I could put a hand in if I needed the gun. I swung the shotgun around, settling the butt of it against my shoulder. I braced myself as much as I could in the water and said, "Open it."

Tucker steadied it, and Wren swung the lid back. He crossed my line of fire while he did it. "You've crossed my line of sight, Wren."

"What?"

"Move to your right," I said.

He did it without any more questions but that one delay could have been enough to get him hurt or dead. The vampire lay on her back, long hair spread around her pale face, one hand clasped on her chest like a sleeping child.

"Okay to move her?" Wren asked.

"Stay out of my line of fire and you can do anything you want," I said.

"Sorry," he said. Even over the mikes he sounded embarrassed.

I didn't have time to soothe his ego. I was too busy watching for vamps. I kept my attention mainly on the one in the open coffin, but I had no peripheral vision in the suit. My hearing was cut in half or more. I felt totally unprepared.

"Why aren't our crosses glowing?" Reynolds asked from just behind me.

"They don't glow around dead bodies," I said.

Wren and Tucker were having trouble getting the body into the bag. Wren finally threw the body across one shoulder and Tucker started squirming the legs into the bag. The vampire lay utterly limp across Wren's back. Her long hair trailed into the water, turning black as it absorbed the water. When they slid her the last bit into the bag, I got a glimpse of her death-pale face, strands of wet hair clinging to it, like a drowning victim.

Tucker zipped the bag and said, "There's water in the bag. I don't know how to avoid it."

Wren got the body as balanced as he could and started for the stairs. "This is going to take a long time with just two of us carrying," he said.

Fulton's voice came over the radios. "We've got two more suits, Ms. Blake. Is it safe to send more men down?"

"Speaking as one of the sacrificial lambs," I said, "yeah. Why should we have all the fun?"

Wren got to the stairs and started climbing up, one hand on the banister. He tried to do the little stomping routine like we did on the way down and nearly fell back into the water. "I'm just going up the stairs. If they collapse, try not to leave me buried until my air runs out."

"Do our best," I said.

"Thanks," he said, sarcasm traveling just fine over the mikes.

Tucker had isolated one of the other coffins. Reynolds slogged over to steady it while Tucker got the lid. She didn't have enough height to swing it back nicely like Wren had. She just shoved. The lid fell back smacking the other coffin with a loud, echoing thunk. The sound made the tips of my fingers tingle.

"Shit," Reynolds breathed.

"Everything okay?" Fulton asked.

"Yeah," I said, "just a little case of nerves."

"You okay down there, Tucker?" he asked.

"It was me," Reynolds said. "Sorry."

The second vamp was male with short brown hair and a sprinkling of freckles still clinging to his white skin. He was over six foot. He was going to be even harder to bag.

Tucker came up with the idea of dragging the coffin to the stairs and using the stairs to help leverage the body. Sounded good to me. The bottom of the stairs wasn't in sunlight, so the vamp shouldn't mind.

Reynolds and Tucker had dragged the coffin to the foot of the stairs by the time Wren came back down. He laid an unzipped bag over the length of the body. "If Reynolds and Tucker steady the coffin, I think I can just roll him into the bag."

"Sounds like a plan to me," Tucker said. She stepped lower in the water.

Reynolds looked to me, and I said, "Sure." She moved to the other side of the coffin, her gun not pointed at anything anymore, flashlight held beam-down into the water like a distant golden ball of light in the dark pool.

Wren leaned in over the body to roll it on its side. "You're in my line of sight again, Wren," I said.

"Sorry," he said, but his arms were half under the body, rolling it. He didn't move out of the way.

"Move, dammit," I said.

"I've almost got him in the bag."

The vampire's head spasmed. It happens sometimes even in their "sleep," but I didn't like it now. "Drop him and step back Wren, now." My cross and Reynolds's cross flared to life like two small white suns.

Wren did what I asked, but it was too late. The vampire turned on him, mouth wide, fangs straining. It bit into the suit with a loud hiss of released air. They were too close to trust the shotgun. "Reynolds, it's yours," I said.

Wren screamed.

Reynolds's gun made sparks in the near darkness. The vampire jerked back from Wren, a hole in its forehead. But it wasn't dead, not even close. Revenants don't die that easy. I fired into that pale face. The face exploded into blood and bits of meat; small heavy pieces rained down into the water with soft plops. It fell back against the raised coffin lid, head gone, hands still spasming in the white satin interior. Legs kicking. Wren fell to his butt on the stairs.

Tucker was saying, "Wren, Wren, answer me."

"I'm here," he said, voice hoarse. "I'm here."

I came two careful steps closer on the water-covered stairs and put another shell in the vampire's chest, blowing a hole in it and the coffin lid behind it. I pumped another shell in the shotgun and said, "Up the stairs, now!"

I knelt by Wren, hand under his arm, the other full of shotgun. Over the ringing in my ears from the guns I heard Tucker say, "Something brushed my leg."

"Out, now!" I tried to force them up the stairs with my voice. I dragged Wren to his feet and pushed him up the stairs. He didn't need much urging. When he reached sunlight, he turned back, waiting for the rest of us.

Reynolds was almost with us. Two wet, dripping arms came up on either side of Tucker.

I yelled, "Tucker!"

The arms closed and she was suddenly airborne, backwards, under the water. It closed over her like a black fist. There'd never been anything to shoot at.

Her voice was crystalline over the radio, breathing so ragged it hurt to hear it. "Wren! Help me!"

I slid down the steps, falling into the water, letting the blackness close over me. My cross flared through the water like a beacon. I saw movement but wasn't sure it was her.

I felt movement in the water seconds before arms grabbed me from behind. Teeth tore into the suit, hands ripping the helmet off like wet paper. It rolled me in the water, and I let it. I let its eager hands carry me around until I shoved the shotgun against its chin and fired. I watched its head vanish in a cloud of blood by the glow of my cross. I still had the breathing mask on, which was why I wasn't drowning.

Tucker's screams were continuous now. Her screaming was everywhere, in the radio, in the water, echoing and constant.

I stood up, the remnants of the suit sliding down my body. I lost some of the echoes of Tucker's screams. The water was conducting the screams like an amplifier.

Reynolds and Wren were both in the water. A bad idea. He was struggling towards something, and I saw it. Tucker's Haz-Mat suit was floating on the other side of the basement. He threw himself into the water trying to swim to her. Reynolds was trying to stay with him, gun in hand. Her cross was blindingly bright.

I yelled over the radio, "Everyone out! Out, dammit, out!" No one was listening.

Tucker's screams stopped abruptly. Everyone else screamed more. Everyone but me. I went quiet. Screaming wouldn't help. There were at least three vamps down here with us. Three revenants. We were going to die if we stayed down here.

The vampire exploded out of the water in front of me. The shotgun fired before I realized I'd done it. The vampire's chest exploded, and it grabbed for me anyway. I had time to jack another shell in, but not to fire. At moments like this the world goes too fast and too slow. You can't stop anything from happening, but you can see it all in excruciating detail. The vampire's fingers dug into my shoulders, painfully tight, holding me still while he reared back to strike. I had a glimpse of fangs framed by a dark beard. My cross's glow was almost frantically bright, highlighting the vampire's face like a Halloween flashlight. I fired the shotgun straight up under the chin, no time to brace, just to pull the trigger. The head exploded in a red rain all over my face mask. I was blinded by blood and thicker things. The recoil of the shotgun sat me down in the water. I went under without knowing if the thing was still coming or if it was dead.

I struggled to the surface. The water had streaked the face mask clean of blood, but heavier things clung to it, so I was still blind. I jerked the mask off my face, losing the radio but gaining my vision.

The vampire was floating in front of me, not face down, or face up. Faceless. Goody.

When Reynolds's gun fired, the shots sounded strange, and I realized I was deaf in the ear I'd fired the shotgun next to. The vampire's body reacted to the bullets, staggering, but not stopping. She was hitting it full middle body like they teach you on the range.

I yelled, "Head shot."

She raised the gun, and the gun clicked empty. I think she was going for extra ammo in a pocket when the thing jumped her and they both vanished into the water.

I slid out of what remained of the suit. Even with the taped joints it slipped off me like a shed skin. I exchanged hands to keep the shotgun ready and dived into the water. Swimming was faster, and if there was anything to catch, I'd caught it by now. The cross lit my way like a beacon. But it was Reynolds's cross that I swam for. That was my beacon.

I had seconds to reach her or it was all over. I had a sense of movement a second before the last vamp slammed into me. I turned, starting to point the shotgun at it, and it grabbed the gun. I think it was just grabbing anything, but it tore the gun from my hand and grabbed for me.

She was almost pretty with her long pale hair streaming behind her like a mermaid straight out of a fairy story. The cross made her skin glow as she reached for me. I had a knife ready and shoved it up under her chin. It slid in easily but didn't reach the brain. It wasn't a killing blow, not even close. She stood in the water, hands clawing at the knife. I don't think it was pain. She just couldn't open her mouth enough to feed.

I shoved the second blade under her ribs, up into her heart. Her body shuddered, eyes impossibly wide. Her mouth opened enough for me to see my knife blade impaling her. She screamed wordlessly and hit me with the back of her hand. The only thing that kept me from being airborne was the water. It absorbed some of the shock. I fell backwards, and the water closed over me. I had a second of floating, then I tried to breathe, got a mouthful of water and staggered to my feet, coughing, falling down as soon as I stood. I got my feet under me and felt something warmer on my face than water. I was bleeding. My vision was going grey with little white flowers in it.

The vampire was still coming for me with my last two knives in its body. There was no more screaming from across the room. I couldn't see that far, but it could only mean one thing. Reynolds, Wren, and Tucker were gone.

I was backing up in the water. I tripped over something and went down, water pouring over me. It was harder to get up this time, slower. I'd tripped over the Haz-Mat suit, and the bag with the Browning in it. My vision was full of holes. It was like watching the vampire through a strobe light. I closed my eyes, but the white flowers ate the back of my eyelids. I let myself sink into the water and found the bag by my foot. Was I holding my breath, or had I just stopped breathing? I couldn't remember. I got the Browning out without opening my eyes. I didn't need to see to use it.

She grabbed a handful of my hair and dragged me to the surface. I fired as I came up, blowing holes in her body like a zipper until I came to that pale face. She put a hand out, over the muzzle of the gun, and that delicate hand blew into bits of bone, a bloody stump. I fired into that face until it was a red ruin and I was deaf in both ears.

The vampire fell backwards into the water, and I slid to my knees. The water poured over me. I tried to push to the surface again and couldn't. I think I got one last mouthful of air, then the grey and white spots were everywhere. I couldn't see the glow of the cross or the black water. When darkness swallowed my vision, it was smooth and perfect. I had a moment of floating, a dim thought that I should be scared, then nothing.

47

I woke up on the grass where Caroline and I had been sitting. Vomiting water and bile, feeling like shit, but alive. Alive was good. Almost as good was Detective Tammy Reynolds standing over me, watching the EMTs work on me. Her arm was taped to her side, and she was crying. Then nothing, like someone changed the channel, and I woke up to a different show.

Hospital this time, and I was afraid I'd dreamed Reynolds, and that she was really dead. Larry sat in a chair by my bed, head back, asleep or knocked out on painkillers. I took his presence as a sign I hadn't hallucinated Reynolds. If his sweetie had been dead, I didn't think he'd be sitting here, at least not asleep.

He blinked awake, eyes unfocused, from drugs I think. "How are you?"

"You tell me."

He smiled, tried to stand and had to take a deep breath before he could do it. "If I wasn't hurt, I'd be out helping Tammy rescue vamps right now."

Something tight in my chest loosened. "She is alive, then. I thought I'd dreamed it."

He blinked at me. "Yeah, she's alive. So is Wren."

"How?" I asked.

He grinned at me. "A vampire known as the Traveler seems able to inhabit bodies of other vamps. Says he's a member of their council and he's here to help. Says you enlisted his aid." Larry was watching me very closely, the painkillers sliding away from his eyes as he tried to will me to tell the truth.

"That's essentially it," I said.

"He took over the body of the vamp attacking Tammy and Wren. He saved them. She shoved her arm into the vamp's mouth, and it's broken, but it'll heal."

"What about Wren?"

"Okay, but he's pretty broken up over Tucker."

"She didn't make it," I said.

He shook his head. "She was torn up, nearly yanked in half. All that was holding her together was the Haz-Mat suit."

"So you didn't have to stake her," I said.

"The vamps did the job themselves," he said. "They got Tucker's body up but not the vamps you did in. They're still down there."

I looked at him. "Let me guess, it caved in—didn't it?"

"Not five minutes after they pulled Tucker's body out, and laid you on the grass, the whole thing went. The vamp body that the Traveler was using started to burn. I've never seen one of them burn before. It was impressive and scary. The rubble covered the vamp. They couldn't dig him out until dark because that would have exposed him to sunlight again. He dug his own way out while they were still getting started."

"He attack anyone?" I asked.

Larry shook his head. "He seemed pretty calm."

"You were there?"

"Yep."

I let it go. No sense worrying over what might have happened if the vamp had clawed his way to freedom pissed. I also found it very interesting that the Traveler couldn't stand the sunlight, and Warrick could. Surviving sunlight, even dim sunlight, was the rarest of talents among the walking dead. Or maybe Warrick was right. Maybe it was God's grace. Who was I to know?

"Is it my imagination or are you just moving better, with less pain?" I asked.

"It's been another twenty-four hours. I'm starting to heal."

"Excuse me?" I said.

"You've been out for over a day. It's late Sunday afternoon."

"Shit," I said. Had Jean-Claude met with the council without me? Had the "dinner," whatever it was, already happened? "Shit," I said again.

Still frowning, he said, "I've got a message from the Traveler for you. Tell me why you suddenly look so scared and I'll give it to you."

"Just give it to me, Larry, please."

Still frowning, he said, "The dinner is postponed until you feel well enough to attend."

I settled back against the pillows and couldn't keep the relief off my face, my body.

"What the hell is going on, Anita?"

Maybe it was the concussion. Maybe it was the fact that I didn't like to lie to Larry face to face. Whatever it was, I told him truth. I told him all of it. I told him about Richard and the marks. He knew about that, but not what I'd discovered recently. I left out a few things, but not much. When I was done, he sat back in the chair looking stunned.

"Well, say something."

He shook his head. "Sweet Mary Mother of God, I don't know where to start. Jean-Claude had a press conference last night with the Traveler at his side. They talked about vampire and human unity in the face of this awful event."

"Whose body did the Traveler use?" I asked.

Larry shivered. "That is one of the creepiest vamp powers I have ever seen. He used some vamp from Malcolm's Church. Malcolm was at the press conference, too. The Traveler used his powers to help rescue the other vamps, including Malcolm."

"Who acted as intepreter while the sun was up?" I asked.

"Balthasar, his human servant."

"Balthasar as a public servant, that is creepy," I said.

Larry frowned. "He told me he had a thing for men with red hair. Was he kidding?"

I laughed, and it made my head hurt. I was suddenly very aware of a growing headache, as if it had been there all the time, just masked by drugs. Modern chemistry, there is no substitute.

"Probably not, but don't worry. You're not on the menu."

"Who is?" Larry asked.

"I don't know yet. Has Dolph found out who's behind the bombings and stuff?"

"Yes." He said that one word like it was enough.

"Tell me or I will get out of this bed and hurt you."

"It was Humans First. The police raided their headquarters earlier today, got most of the leaders."

"That is wonderful." I frowned, which hurt, then closed my eyes and said, "How did Humans First know where all the monsters were? They hit private homes, secret daytime lairs. They shouldn't have known where everyone was."

I heard the door open a moment before Dolph's voice said, "The vampires had a traitor in their midst."

"Hey, Dolph."

"Hey, yourself. Good to see you awake."

"Good to be awake," I said. "What traitor?"

"Remember Vicki Pierce—and her little scene at Burnt Offerings?"

"I remember."

"She had a boyfriend that was with Humans First. She gave him up when we questioned her a second time."

"Why'd you bring her in?"

"Seems she got paid for her little acting assignment. We threatened to charge her with assault and attempted murder. She folded like a cheap card table."

"What does little Miss Blue Eyes have to do with a vampire traitor?"

"She's been dating Harry, the bartender and part owner of Burnt Offerings."

I was confused. "Then why stage the scene at his business? Why give himself grief?"

"Her human boyfriend wanted to pay her to do it. She didn't want him to know she was seeing Harry. Harry went along with it because he thought it would look funny if his place was the only vamp-owned business not hit by the fanatics."

"So Harry knew what she was using the information for?" I said. I was finding it hard to believe that any vamp would do it, let alone one as old as Harry.

"He knew. He took his cut of the money," Dolph said.

"Why?"

"When we find him, we'll ask."

"Let me guess. He's vanished."

Dolph nodded. "Don't tell your boyfriend, Anita."

"The vampires may be your only hope of catching Harry now."

"But will they turn him over to us or kill him?"

I looked away, not meeting his eyes. "They're going to be pretty pissed."

"I can't blame them for that, but I want him alive, Anita. I need him alive."

"Why?"

"We didn't get every member of Humans First. I don't want them out there with some new nasty surprise waiting."

"You have Vicki. Won't she tell you?"

"She asked for a lawyer, finally, and now she's suddenly developed amnesia."

"Damn."

"We need him to tell us if there's one last big nasty coming our way."

"But you can't find him," I said.

"That's right."

"You don't want me to tell Jean-Claude."

"Give us twenty-four hours to locate Harry. If we fail, then you can put out a vampire all-points. Before they kill him, try to get information from him."

"You say that like I'll be there when he dies," I said.

Dolph just looked at me.

I met his eyes this time. "I don't kill for Jean-Claude, Dolph, no matter what the street says."

"I wish I believed that, Anita. You don't know how much I wished I believed that."

I lay back against the pillows. "Believe what you like, Dolph. You will anyway."

He walked out then without another word, as if what he wanted to say was too painful, too final. Dolph kept pushing against us, against me. I was beginning to worry that he was going to keep pushing until he pushed us apart. We'd be working together but we wouldn't be friends. The headache was getting worse, and it wasn't just the drugs wearing off.

48

I was given a clean bill of health. The doctors were amazed at my recuperative powers. If only they knew. Pete McKinnon called late in the day. He'd found that there were fires similar to those set by our firebug in New Orleans and San Francisco. It took a moment for me to remember why those particular cities were important. When I remembered, I asked, "How about Boston?"

"No, no fires in Boston. Why?"

I don't think he believed me when I said, "nothing," but unlike Dolph, he let it go. I wasn't ready to point the finger at the Vampire Council. Just because the mysterious fires happened in cities they'd been visiting didn't mean it had to be them. There'd been no fires in Boston. Just because there were now mysterious fires in St. Louis, and the council was here, didn't prove anything. Yeah, and the Easter Bunny brings me goodies every year.

I told Jean-Claude about my suspicions. "But why would the council wish to burn empty buildings, *ma petite*? If one of them could call fire to their hands, they would not waste it on empty real estate. Not unless the real estate being burned gained them something."

"You mean a financial motive?" I said.

He shrugged. "Perhaps, though a personal motive would suit them better."

"I can't find out much more information without giving the council up to the authorities as suspects," I said.

He seemed to think about that for a second or two. "Perhaps you could wait upon committing absolute suicide for us until after we have survived this evening."

"Sure," I said.

True darkness found me in a short form-fitting black velvet dress with a V-neck and no sleeves. The waist of the dress was open lace. My skin showed pale and enticing through it. Black thigh-high hose that actually came up a bit higher than mid-thigh, like all the way up until the black lace stretch top brushed against the black satin panties with their lace edgings. The hose were a size too large. Jean-Claude had purchased them, and done it deliberately. I'd tried thigh-highs before and had to agree that the longer length was more flattering for my shorter legs. It sort of framed the right area. If we'd been planning extracurricular activities, I'd have loved to see his face when I was standing in nothing but the stockings. As it was, it was just frustrating, and a little scary.

I'd vetoed the high velvet heels he'd picked out. Instead I used my own black pumps. Not as spiffy. Maybe not even more comfortable, but the heels were low enough that I could run in them, or carry fainting wereleopards if the need arose.

"You are perfection, *ma petite*, except for the shoes."

"Forget it," I said. "You're lucky to have gotten me in the hose. The thought that I'm dressing just in case the rest of the party sees my underwear is just creepy."

"You talked to the Traveler of price and responsibility. Well, tonight we pay the price for your wereleopards. Are you regretting it now?"

Gregory was still trussed up in my bedroom, pale and fragile looking. Vivian was tucked in a guest room speaking in monosyllables.

"No, no I don't regret it."

"Then let us gather the rest of our party and be on our way." But he didn't move. He stayed lying on his stomach on the white couch, head resting on his folded hands. If it had been anyone else, I'd have said they were sprawled on the couch, but Jean-Claude did not sprawl. He posed, he lounged, but he did not sprawl. He lay full length, his long body stretched out, only the tips of his black boots over the edge of the couch.

He was wearing an outfit I'd seen before, but repetition didn't make it less lovely. I loved his clothes; loved watching him dress, and undress.

"What are you thinking?" I asked.

"I wish we were staying home tonight. I want to undress you one piece of clothing at a time, enjoying your body between every unveiling."

Just the suggestion made my body tight. "Me, too," I said, and knelt on the floor in front of him. I folded the short skirt under so it wouldn't wrinkle or ride up. He didn't teach me that, my Grandma Blake did, over a lifetime of Sunday church services where what I looked like seemed more important than the sermon.

I laid my chin on the couch near his face. My hair spilling around me, brushing the sides of his folded hands, curling against his face.

"Do your undies look as nice as mine?" I asked.

"Brushed silk," he said softly.

I had a sensory memory so strong it made me shiver. The feel of him through the thick silk, the almost living texture that the brushed fabric had over the hardness of his body. I had to close my eyes to keep from letting him see it in my face. The image was so vivid it made me clench my hands.

I felt him move a second before he kissed my forehead. He spoke with his lips still touching my skin. "Your thoughts betray you, *ma petite*."

I raised my face upward, sliding his lips down my face. He was utterly passive as I moved against him, until our lips met. Then his mouth pressed against mine, lips and tongue working. Neither of us used our hands, only our mouths touching. Our faces pressed together.

"Can I cut in?" The familiar voice was so heavy with anger that it made me draw back from Jean-Claude.

Richard stood at the end of the couch staring down at us. I hadn't heard him come up. Had Jean-Claude? I was betting he had. Somehow I never thought that even in the throes of passion Jean-Claude would ever let anyone sneak up on him. Or maybe I just didn't think I was that distracting. Poor self-esteem, who me?

I sat back on my heels and looked up at Richard. He was dressed in a black tux, complete with tails. His long hair slicked back into a ponytail so tight it gave the illusion of short hair. You always knew Richard was handsome but it was only when you got rid of the hair that you realized how perfect his face was. The high-sculpted cheekbones, the full mouth, the dimple. He stared down at me with that handsome, familiar face, and he looked arrogant. He knew the effect he had on me, and wanted to turn the knife a little more.

Jean-Claude sat up on the couch, his mouth smeared with my lipstick. The red so vivid against his pale skin it looked like the surprised scarlet of blood. He ran his tongue around the outside of his mouth, then ran his finger across his upper lip, slowly, until it came away red. He put the finger in his mouth and sucked the lipstick off of it, very slowly, very deliberately. His eyes were on me, but the show was for Richard.

I was both grateful for it, and angry about it. He knew Richard was trying to hurt me, so he was hurting Richard. But he was also baiting him, rubbing the proverbial salt in the wound.

The look on Richard's face was so raw I had to look away. "That's enough, Jean-Claude," I said, "that's enough."

Jean-Claude looked amused. "As you like, *ma petite*."

Richard looked down at me again. I met his eyes. Maybe there was something in my face that was too raw to look at, too. He turned abruptly and left the room.

"Go freshen your tasty lipstick, then we must leave." Jean-Claude's voice held regret, the way it sometimes held joy, or sex.

I took his hand, raising it gently to my mouth. "Are you still frightened of them, even after all the good publicity? Surely if they were planning to kill us, they wouldn't have appeared on camera with you." I touched his leg, running my fingers over the cloth, feeling his thigh underneath. "The Traveler shook hands with the mayor of St. Louis, for heaven's sake."

He touched my face, cradling my cheek in his hand. "The council has never before tried to be, what you would call, mainstream. It is their first foray into a very new arena. But they have been the stuff of nightmares for thousands of years, *ma petite*. One day of human politics does not make them into something else."

"But . . ."

He touched fingers to my lips. "It is a good sign, *ma petite*. That I will agree to, but you do not know them as I do. You have not seen them at their worst."

My mind flashed on Rafael's raw, bloody body; Sylvie sagging in the chains, voice small and broken; the sight of Fernando using Vivian. "I've seen them do some pretty awful things since they hit town," I said. "You set up the rules, Jean-Claude. They can't maim us, or rape us, or kill us. What's left?"

He kissed me lightly on the lips, and stood, offering me his hand. I took it, let him pull me to my feet. He was wearing his amused mask, the one that once upon a time I'd thought was his normal face. Now I knew it meant he was hiding things. He looked like that a lot when he was scared and didn't want people to know.

"You're scaring me," I said softly.

He smiled. "No, *ma petite*, they will do that for me, for us all." With that comforting shot, he went off to round up the others. I went for my purse and the tasty lipstick. The council had laid down some conditions of their own. No weapons tonight. Which was why I was dressed like I was; one glance was enough to know I wasn't carrying anything. Jean-Claude thought this would keep them from having an excuse to pat me down. When I asked what the big deal was, all he would say was, "You don't want to give them a reason to touch you, *ma petite*. Trust me on this."

I did trust him. I didn't want any of the council touching me, ever. It was going to be a long night.

49

What had once been Jean-Claude's living room and Nikolaos's throne room before that, had been turned into a banquet room. They'd found a table that was over ten feet long. What you could see of the table was heavy clawed feet with lions' mouths carved in bold relief. A tablecloth so thick with gold embroidery that it shimmered under the lights covered the table. If they had meant for us to actually eat off it, I'd have been worried we'd trash it, but there was no food. There were no chairs. There were no plates. There were white linen napkins with gold rings, crystal wineglasses, and one of those industrial-size warmers with blue gas flames under its gleaming surface. There was a man hanging by his wrists, feet dangling helplessly over the gleaming table. He was hanging directly over the empty warming pan. His name was Ernie. His muscular upper body was bare. A gag cut across his face, trapping part of his long ponytail. His hair was shaved to nothing on either side of his face. The council hadn't done it as torture. He'd done it to himself. He was one of Jean-Claude's newest hangers-on, a human who wanted to be a vampire and was serving his apprenticeship acting as a sort of maid and errand boy. Now, apparently, he was the appetizer.

Richard, Jean-Claude, and I stood with Jamil, Damian, Jason, and surprisingly, Rafael, at our backs. The Rat King had insisted on accompanying us. I hadn't argued too hard. We were allowed one person apiece plus Jason. Yvette had requested him especially. By taking him, we gained a werewolf, but his blue eyes were wide and his breathing a little too quick. Yvette was Jason's idea of hell, and hell had sent out an invitation.

Ernie stared at us all, kicking his feet and struggling, trying to talk through the gag. I think he was trying to say, "Get me down," but I couldn't swear to it.

"What is the meaning of this?" Jean-Claude said. His voice filled the huge room, hissing and tumbling until the shadows gave his words back in harsh, sibilant echoes.

Padma stepped out of the far hallway. He was dressed in a suit that glittered as gold as the tablecloth. He was even wearing a golden turban with peacock feathers and a sapphire bigger than my thumb. He looked like someone had called down to central casting for a maharaja.

"You have offered us no hospitality at all, Jean-Claude. Malcolm and his people have offered us refreshment. But you, the Master of the City, have offered us nothing." He motioned upward at Ernie. "This one walked in without our permission. He said he was yours."

Jean-Claude walked until he stood by the table and could look up into Ernie's face. "You came home two days early from your family visit. The next time, if there is a next time, call first."

Ernie stared at him, eyes wide, making small *hmmm* sounds through the gag. He kicked his legs enough that he started to swing.

"Struggling will just make your shoulders hurt more," Jean-Claude said. "Be at peace." As he said it, Ernie slowly grew limp. Jean-Claude had captured him with his eyes and was lulling him to, if not sleep, peace. The tension drained from him, and he stared at Jean-Claude, brown eyes empty, waiting. At least he wasn't scared anymore.

Gideon and Thomas came up to stand on either side of Padma. Thomas was in full uniform, boots polished like a black mirror. The helmet was white with a long tassel on top that was probably horsehair. The coat was red, the buttons brass, white gloves, even a sword.

Gideon was pretty close to naked. A white thong was all he wore on his body. It barely covered him. A heavy gold collar encrusted with small diamonds and huge emeralds covered almost his entire neck. His carefully combed golden hair fanned over it. A chain led from the collar to Thomas's hands.

Padma put his hand out, and Thomas gave the chain to him. Neither Thomas nor Gideon exchanged so much as a glance. They'd seen the show before.

The only thing that kept me from making some scathing remark was that I'd pretty much given my word to let Jean-Claude do the talking tonight. He thought I might say something to piss someone off. Who me?

Jean-Claude walked around the table. Richard and I fell two steps back, mirroring Padma and his pets. The symbolism wasn't lost on anyone. Thing was, Richard and I were pretending. I didn't think the others were.

"I suppose you mean to slit his throat into the warmer, then serve his blood to all?" Jean-Claude said.

Padma smiled and gave a gracious nod of his head.

Jean-Claude laughed that wonderfully touchable laugh of his. "If you really meant to do that, Master of Beasts, you'd have hung him by his ankles."

Richard and I did exchange glances behind his back. I turned and looked at Ernie's peacefully hanging figure. How had Jean-Claude known you'd have to hang him by his ankles? Ask a silly question.

"Are you saying we are bluffing?" Padma asked.

"No," Jean-Claude said, "merely grandstanding."

Padma smiled, and it almost reached his eyes. "You always did play the game well."

Jean-Claude gave a small bow, never taking his eyes from the other vampire. "I am honored that you think well of me, Master of Beasts."

Padma gave a sharp laugh. "A honeyed tongue, Master of the City." The humor died abruptly, gone, poof. His face was suddenly harsh, empty, except for anger. "But the point remains you have been a poor host. I have fed through my servants." He slid a dark hand caressingly down Gideon's bare shoulder. The weretiger never reacted. It was as if Padma were not there. Or maybe as if he, Gideon, were not there.

"But there are others who are not so blessed as I. They hunger, Jean-Claude. They stand in your territory as your guests and know hunger."

"The Traveler was feeding them," Jean-Claude said. "I thought he was feeding you as well."

"I do not need his cast-off energy," Padma said. "He was sustaining the others until that one"—he pointed at me with his free hand—"told him to stop."

I started to say something, almost asked permission, and thought, screw it. "Asked him to stop," I said. "No one tells the Traveler what to do." There, that was so diplomatic, my teeth hurt.

His laughter entered the room ahead of him. The Traveler's new body was young, male, handsome, and so newly dead he still had a good tan. Balthasar came at his side, hands sliding over the other man's body possessively. A new toy to explore. I'd been told that Malcolm was loaning the Traveler a church member. I wondered if Malcolm really knew what the Traveler and Balthasar were doing with the body.

I would have said they were both wearing togas, but that wasn't quite it. The Traveler wore a rich purple cloth pinned at one shoulder with a ruby-and-gold brooch. His left shoulder was bare, showing the smooth tanned skin to good advantage. The garment was gathered at the waist with two woven red cords. It fell nearly to his ankles, giving glimpses of sandals tied around his ankles.

Balthasar wore red with an amethyst-and-silver brooch at one shoulder. His bare shoulder showed just enough chest to prove he was muscular, as if there'd been any doubt. The red garment was bound at the waist with purple cords.

"You guys look like the Bobbsey Twins," I said.

Jean-Claude cleared his throat.

I stopped talking, but if everyone had such nifty clothes, I wasn't sure I could stop myself from making remarks. I mean, it was just too easy.

The Traveler threw his head back and laughed. It was a joyous laugh with an edge underneath like the hissing of snakes. He turned brown eyes to me, but down in the depths it was him. I'd have known him no matter whose eyes he was looking out of.

Balthasar was actually shorter than the new body by an inch or two. He stood close enough for the Traveler to take him under his arm, like a tall man will walk with a woman, cradled against his body, protected.

"I saved your humans today, Anita. I saved many vampires. Is that not enough for you?"

"Jean-Claude?" I made his name a question.

He let his breath out in a long sigh. "It was pointless to make you promise. Be yourself, *ma petite*, but try not to be too insulting." He stepped back so that we were all even with each other. Maybe he hadn't liked the symbolism either.

"I'm thrilled that you saved my friends today," I said. "I'm ecstatic that you saved all the trapped vampires. But you got a lot of good press out of it without any risk to yourself. I thought you agreed that you guys needed to modernize a little, come into the twentieth century.''

"But I do agree, Anita, I do agree.'' The Traveler rubbed his cheek against Balthasar's face, staring at me hard enough that I was glad he wasn't heterosexual.

"Then what is this medieval shit?'' I jabbed a thumb backwards at Ernie.

His eyes flicked to the man, then back to me. "I would have let it go, but the others voted and it is true that Jean-Claude has been a lax host.''

Jean-Claude touched my arm. "If you had come at my invitation or even requested permission to enter my territory, I would have been more than happy to grant you hunting rights. Though you will find one of the other benefits to legality is an amazing number of willing victims. People will even pay you to quench your thirst on their bodies.''

"It is an old law among us,'' The Traveler said, "not to feed in another's lands without their permission. I sustained the others, but then your human servant showed me that my powers were having serious side effects on your local population.'' He stepped away from Balthasar, coming within touching distance of Jean-Claude.

"But none of your vampires were affected. I could not steal their energy, or give them extra energy. You prevented that. That has surprised me more than anything else you have done, Jean-Claude. It smacks of a power that I would never have credited you with, not now, not a thousand years from now.'' He paced to stand in front of Richard. And the new body was still taller, six foot four at least.

He stood so close that the purple cloth brushed the length of Richard's body. He moved around him so closely that the cloth never stopped touching, sliding over the tailored tux like a cloth hand. "Padma has not gained such power from his joining.'' He ended standing between Jean-Claude and Richard. He raised a hand to stroke Richard's face, and Richard caught his wrist.

"That's enough,'' Richard said.

The Traveler drew his wrist slowly downward so that his hand brushed Richard's. He turned to Balthasar with a smile. "What do you think?''

"I think Jean-Claude is a lucky man,'' Balthasar said.

A red flush crept up Richard's face, his hands curled into fists. He was placed in the position usually reserved for women. If you deny that you're sleeping with someone, they won't believe you. The harder you deny it, the surer everyone is that you're guilty.

Richard was smarter than I was. He didn't try to deny it. He just turned and looked at the Traveler. He stared him nearly eye to eye and said, "Get away from me.''

All the bad guys laughed. None of us did. Us included Gideon and Thomas, strangely enough. What were they doing with Padma? What series of events had trapped them with him? If we all survived, maybe I'd get a chance to ask them, but it was doubtful. If we killed Padma, they would probably die, too. If Padma killed us, well, there you go.

The Traveler walked over to me in a cloud of purple cloth. "Which brings us to you, Anita.'' His new body towered over me, over a foot taller, but hey, you get used to it.

"What?'' I said, staring up at him.

He laughed again. He was so damn happy. I realized what it was—afterglow. He and Balthasar had been polishing the family jewels.

I stared up into that smiling face and said, "Is this new body double-jointed or something, or does Balthasar just like a change of menu?"

The laughter faded from his eyes, his face, like the sun sinking below the horizon. What was left was cold and distant and nothing you could talk to.

Maybe I did talk too much.

Jean-Claude touched my shoulders and moved me back. He started to move in front of me, but I stopped him. "I pissed him off. Don't protect me from him."

Jean-Claude let me stay in front, but at some unseen signal the rest of our entourage moved up, fanning out behind us.

Yvette and Warrick came out of the hallway with Liv. "You all look good enough to eat." She laughed at her own joke. She was dressed in a simple white formal. Her bare shoulders were whiter than the cloth. As soon as I saw her, I knew she hadn't fed. Sleeves that were not attached to the dress covered her from armpit to wrist. The fitted bodice flared into a full white skirt with layers that were mirrored in the layers of the strange unattached sleeves. Her white-blond hair fell in braided loops and whorls around her face. No period costume for Yvette, only the cutting edge of fashion would do. Her makeup was just a little dark against the paper whiteness of her skin, but it was hard to get that understated look when you were so terribly drained.

Warrick wore a white suit with one of those round collars so there was no place to put a tie. It was a lovely suit that matched Yvette's dress so well, they looked like the top of a fashion wedding cake.

Yvette wore the dress like it had been made just for her. Warrick looked chokingly uncomfortable.

Liv glared at all of us impartially. She was dressed in a blue formal that was meant for a woman with softer edges and less muscle. It had been cut down or up for her, and she wore it badly.

This was the first time I'd seen Liv since I learned that she'd helped torture Sylvie. I expected to regret not having killed her when I had the chance. But there was an uncertainity in her eyes, an unease in her body, that said, maybe, she'd seen another side of the council since then. She was afraid. I was glad.

"You look like you're wearing hand-me-downs, Liv," I said. "Like someone's poor relative."

"Has the Traveler given you to Yvette as her handmaiden?" Jean-Claude asked. "Has he given you away so quickly?"

"Yvette merely helped me dress," she said, head high, but her hands were trying to smooth the dress into place. Nothing helped.

"You had much more attractive outfits in your own closet," Jean-Claude said.

"But no dresses," Yvette said. "For a formal occasion you must have dresses for the women." She smiled sweetly.

It made me regret wearing a dress. "I know what you did to Sylvie, Liv. I was regretting not blowing your head off when I did your knees. But you know what, Liv, a few years with the council and you may be regretting it too."

"I regret nothing," she said. But there was a tightness around the eyes, a flicker through those lovely eyes. Something had spooked her good and solid. Part of me wanted to know what had been done to her, but it was enough just to see how scared she was.

"I'm glad you're enjoying yourself, Liv," I said.

Asher walked out in the middle of the scene. His hair had been pulled back in a tight braid. His hair was still nearly the color of the metallic thread in the tablecloth, an unearthly color even if he'd been human. The hair pulled back left the scars on his face naked. It was hard not to look at them, hard not to stare. The rest of the outfit didn't make it any easier.

His naked upper body was a wonderment of contrasts. It was like his face, half angelic beauty, half melted nightmare. His pants were black leather with a line of bare flesh showing from hip to mid-calf, where boots covered the rest. The flesh glimpsed on the right side of his thigh was scarred. The scars seemed to stop about mid-thigh. It left the big question. Had his torturers made him a eunuch or left him whole? It was like a car crash. You wanted to know, and you didn't.

"Jean-Claude, Anita, so good of you to join us." He made the polite words a mockery, filling them with a hissing warmth of threat.

"Your presence is the same pleasure it has always been," Jean-Claude said. Those words were blank, utterly neutral, compliment or snide putdown. It was the listener's choice.

Asher glided towards us, a smile curling his perfect lips. Again both sides of his mouth worked. The muscles were still whole underneath all the scars. He came to stand directly in front of me. He was about two steps closer than was comfortable, but I didn't back up or complain. I just met his smile with one of my own. Neither smile touched our eyes.

"Do you like my outfit, Anita?"

"A little aggressive, don't you think?"

He traced a fingertip down the lace at my waist. The fingertip slid inside the open lace, touching my bare skin. It brought a small gasp from my throat.

"You can touch me, anywhere you like," he said.

I moved his hand. "I can't return the offer, sorry."

"I think you can," the Traveler said.

I looked at him. "No," I said. "I can't."

"Jean-Claude was very clear on your rules," the Traveler said. "Asher needs to feed. It is within the rules for him to feed off of you, Anita. He would prefer to sink something else into you, but he will have to be content with fangs."

I shook my head. "I don't think so."

"*Ma petite,*" Jean-Claude said softly.

I didn't like the way he said my name. I turned, and one look was enough. "You have got to be kidding me."

He stepped close, taking me to one side. "The guidelines you gave me said nothing against sharing blood."

I stared up at him. "Do you really want him to feed off of me?"

He shook his head. "It is not a matter of want, *ma petite.* But if they cannot torture us or rape us, we leave them little else."

"If you wish to trade back one of my wereleopards," Padma said, "Vivian, perhaps, I would grant you safe passage for the return of my so sweet Vivian."

Fernando entered the room as if on cue. He was bruised but walking. More's the pity. He was wearing a jeweled vest and something like harem pants. The Arabian Nights maybe, instead of a *maharaja*.

"Did Fernando tell you he raped her?"

"I know what my son has done."

"That doesn't spoil her for you?" I asked.

Padma looked at me. "What I do with her once she is mine again is no concern of yours, human."

"No way," I said.

"Then you have no choice. You must feed one of us. If there is one among us who would please you more, someone . . . less hideous, we could arrange something. Perhaps I could take you myself. Among our own people only Yvette finds Asher attractive, but then her tastes have always run to the strange and grotesque."

Asher's face betrayed nothing, but I knew he'd heard. He was meant to hear. He'd spent the last two centuries being treated like a circus freak. No wonder he was cranky.

"I'd let Asher sink the whole thing into me before I'd let you touch me."

Surprise showed for a heartbeat on Padma's face, then arrogance. But he hadn't liked the insult. Goody. "Perhaps before the night is over, Anita, you will get your wish."

Not comforting, but Asher was having trouble looking at me, as if he were afraid. Not of me, exactly, but that this was some elaborate game to hurt him. He had that casual tension that victims get when they are slapped too often for too many different things.

Jean-Claude whispered, "Thank you, *ma petite*." I think he was relieved. I think he'd thought I might go down in flames rather than submit. Before Padma had made his little joke, I would have put up more of a fight. I was going to do this. If I drew the line here and refused, that meant we fought them. We would lose. If donating a little blood would keep us all alive come morning, I could spare it.

A leopard screamed. It raised the hairs on my arms. Two leopards padded into the room, jeweled collars sparkling around their necks. The black one, Elizabeth I assumed, snarled at me as they went past. The leopards were just leopard-size, not as tall as a Great Dane but longer. They paced like velvet over muscle, their energy and anger filling the room, prickling along the other shapeshifters like a drug. The leopards sprawled at Padma's feet.

I felt Richard's power swell. It flowed out of him in a soothing wash, willing the leopards quiet, calling them back to human form.

Padma said, "No, no, they are mine. I will keep them in whatever form I choose, however long I choose."

"They will begin to lose human characteristics," Richard said. "Elizabeth is a nurse. She cannot do her job if she has fangs or eyes that do not change back."

"She has no other job than to serve me," Padma said.

Richard took a step forward. Jean-Claude touched his shoulder. "He is baiting us, *mon ami*."

Richard shook his hand off, but nodded. "I don't think the Master of Beasts could stop me if I forced them back to human form."

"Is that a challenge?" Padma asked.

"The wereleopards don't belong to you, Richard," I said.

"These two don't belong to anybody," he said.

"They can be mine if they want to be," I said.

"No," Padma said. "No, I will give up nothing else. No one else to you." He stepped back against the wall, dragging Gideon with him by the jeweled collar. Thomas followed almost as closely. "Asher, take her."

Asher tried to grab my arm, but I backed up. "Hold your horses. Hasn't anyone told you anticipation adds to the experience?"

"I have been anticipating this for over two hundred years, *ma cherie*. If anticipation adds, then it will be wondrous indeed."

I stepped away from his eager eyes and went to Jean-Claude. "Any advice?"

"He will try to make it rape, *ma petite*." He stopped me before I could say anything. "Not actual rape, but the effect is surprisingly similar. Make it a seduction, if you can. Turn necessity into a pleasure. It will be the last thing he expects, and it will unnerve him."

"How unnerve?" I asked.

"That will depend, I think, upon how strong your nerve is."

I glanced back at Asher. The eagerness on his face was frightening. I was sorry he'd been picked on for centuries, but it wasn't my fault. "I don't think it's that good."

Richard had been listening. He came close enough to whisper, "You're donating blood to one vampire, what's one more?"

"*Ma petite* and I do not have to share blood to share power," Jean-Claude said.

Richard frowned at him, then at me. "Still holding back? Don't you know how to give yourself completely to anyone?"

Jean-Claude's face was very neutral, blank and beautiful. I looked from his impassive face to Richard's angry one, and shook my head. "If I could find someone else to fill our third spot, I would, Richard. But we're stuck with each other, so stop being such an ass." I pushed past him hard enough for him to stumble, and it was all I could do not to slap him as I went by. Being nasty in private was one thing. Doing it in front of the bad guys was against the rules.

50

Asher dragged me to a corner, and the others gathered around on the floor like story time in elementary school. Or maybe show-and-tell was a better analogy. He jerked me roughly against him, one hand in my hair controlling my head. He kissed me roughly enough to bruise unless I opened my mouth. I did better than that. I closed my eyes and French kissed him, running my tongue between his fangs. I'd perfected the art of French kissing a vampire without bleeding, and apparently I was good at it because Asher drew back first. There was a look of astonishment, total and complete. He couldn't have looked more surprised if I'd slapped him. No, less surprised. He expected the slap.

Jean-Claude was right. If I could just outmaneuver Asher, be bolder than he was, he might never sink fang into me. It was worth a try. I didn't even let Jean-Claude feed off of me. I wasn't sure it was the lesser evil, but a girl's got to draw the line somewhere.

Asher put his face so near mine, our noses almost touched. "Look at me, girl, look at me. You don't want to touch this."

The startling pale blue of his eyes, almost a white-blue, framed by golden eyelashes, was lovely. I concentrated on the eyes. "Undo your hair," I said.

He pushed me away from him, hard enough that I stumbled. I was pissing him off, stealing his revenge. Can't rape the willing.

I went to him, stalking around him, half wishing for the heels Jean-Claude had wanted me to wear. Asher's back was pure and untouched. Only a few dribbling scars where the holy water had trailed down his side. I ran my hands up that smooth skin, and he jumped as if I'd bit him.

He whirled, grabbing my arms, holding me away from him. He searched my face almost frantically. Whatever he saw, it didn't please him. He moved his hands upward until he held my wrists, then placed one of my hands on the scarred side of his chest. "It's easy to close your eyes and pretend. Easy to touch that which is not spoiled." He pressed my hand against the rough ridges that had been his chest. "This is the reality. This is what I live with every night, what I will live with for all eternity, what he did to me."

I stepped in close, pressing my upper arm against the scars, as well as my hands. The skin was rough, ridged, like frozen, fleshy water. I looked up into his face from inches away, and said, "Jean-Claude did not do this to you. Men who are long dead did this to you." I rose up on tiptoe and kissed his scarred cheek.

He closed his eyes, and a single tear slid from his eye to trail down that rough cheek. I kissed the tear away, and when he opened his eyes, they were suddenly startlingly close. In his eyes I saw a fear, loneliness, a need so overwhelming that it had eaten his heart as surely as the holy water had eaten his skin.

I wanted to take away the hurt I saw in his eyes. I wanted to hold him in my arms until the pain eased. I realized in that moment that it wasn't me. It was Jean-Claude. He wanted to heal Asher's pain. He wanted to take away that awful emptiness. I looked at Asher through a film of emotions that I'd never had for him, a patina of nostalgia for better nights, of love and joy and warm bodies in the cold darkness.

I kissed my way down his chin, careful to touch only the scars, ignoring the perfect skin as I'd ignored the wounded skin earlier. Strangely, his neck was whole, untouched. I kissed his collar bone and its white ridge of scars. His hands eased but didn't release me. I pulled out of his grip as I moved down his body, one soft kiss at a time.

I ran my tongue across his belly where it vanished into his pants. He shuddered. I moved to the open skin on his hip and worked down. When the scars ended at mid-thigh, so did I. I stood, and he watched me, watched me almost afraid of what I would do next.

I had to stand on tiptoe to reach behind him to the braid of his hair. It would have been easier from behind, but he'd have taken it as a rejection. I couldn't turn away from the scars, not even if that wasn't what I was doing at all. I loosened the braid. I separated the strands of hair, then had to lean my body against his just to steady myself while I combed my fingers through the golden strands. There is something very personal to touching a person's hair in the right situation. I took my time, enjoying the feel of it, the extraordinary color, the thick richness of it between my fingers. When his hair fell in waves around his shoulders, I lowered myself flat-footed. My calves were cramped, too long on point.

I put into my eyes what I saw, that he was beautiful.

Asher kissed me on the forehead, a light touch. He held me against him for a moment, then stepped back. "I cannot capture you with my eyes. Without that or the throes of passion, it would only cause you pain. I can feed on anyone. What I saw in your face, no one else could give me." He looked out at Jean-Claude. They stared at each other for a long moment, then Asher stepped out of the circle, and I made my way back to Jean-Claude.

I sat down beside him, knees tucked under, skirt smoothed back. He hugged me and kissed me on the forehead as Asher had done. I wondered if he was trying to taste Asher's mouth on my skin. The thought didn't bother me. Maybe it should have, but I didn't ask him. I wasn't sure I wanted to know.

The Traveler came to his feet as if by magic, just suddenly standing. "I don't think we could be more astonished if Anita had conjured a dragon from thin air. She has tamed our Asher and paid no blood for it." He glided to the open floor space. "Yvette is not so easily sated." He smiled at her as she rose to her feet. "Are you, my dear?"

She ran her hands through Jason's hair as she glided past. He jumped as if she'd stung him, which amused the hell out of her. She was still laughing when she turned with a swoosh of white skirts and held her arms out to him. "Come to me, Jason."

He huddled in on himself, curling into a little ball of arms and elbows and knees. He just shook his head.

"You are my choice, my special one," Yvette said. "You are not strong enough to refuse me."

An awful thought occurred to me. I was willing to bet that Jean-Claude hadn't covered rotting on people as a no-no. Jason might not recover from another embrace from the messily dead. I leaned into Jean-Claude and asked, "You did cover torture, no outright torture, right?"

"Of course," he said.

I stood. "You can feed on him, but you can't rot on him."

She turned cool eyes to me. "You have no say in this."

"Jean-Claude negotiated for no torture. Rotting on Jason while you feed is torture to him. You know that. It's why you want him."

"I want my bit of werewolf blood, and I want it exactly the way I like it best," she said.

Richard said, "You can feed off of me."

"You don't know what you're offering, Richard," I said.

"I know that Jason is mine to protect, and he can't endure this." He got to his feet, splendid in his new tux.

"Has Jason told you what happened to him in Branson?" I asked. Jason had been having a forced tryst with two female vamps when they began to rot. They turned into long-dead corpses while he was still lying naked with them. It was his worse nightmare, almost a phobia now. I'd witnessed the event, even had those dead hands on my body when I waded in to to rescue him. I couldn't blame him for being terrified.

"Jason told me," Richard said.

"Hearing about it isn't the same thing as being there, Richard."

Jason had hidden his face against his knees. He was saying something low. I had to kneel to hear it. He was saying, "I'm sorry, I'm sorry, I'm sorry," over and over and over. I touched his arm, and he screamed, eyes wide, mouth open in astonishment.

"It's okay, Jason. It's okay." Richard was right. Jason couldn't do this.

I nodded. "You're right, Richard."

"No," Padma said. "No, the Wolf King is mine. I will not share him."

"I will take nothing less than a shapeshifter," Yvette said.

Jamil stood.

Richard said, "No, it's my job to protect Jason, not yours, Jamil."

"It's my job to protect you, Ulfric."

Richard shook his head and started undoing the black bow tie. He undid the top few buttons on the pleated shirt, baring the strong, perfect line of his neck.

"No," Yvette said. She stamped her foot, hands on hips. "He is not afraid. I want someone who's afraid."

In my head I thought, he will be afraid. He'll be very afraid. Notice I wasn't jumping up and offering myself in Jason's place. I'd seen this particular show. I had no desire to star in it.

"And I have my own plans for the Ulfric," Padma said.

The Traveler tsked at them like naughty children. "It is a fair offer, Yvette. The Ulfric himself for one of his lesser wolves."

"It is not the potency of the blood I want. It is the terror."

"It is too generous an offer for someone who is not council," Padma said.

"Do they always squabble like this?" I asked.

"*Oui,*" Jean-Claude said.

Near-eternal life, frightening power, and they were petty. How disappointing. How typical. I touched Jason's face, made him look at me. His breath was coming in short gasps. I touched his hands; his skin was cold.

"Jason, if she didn't rot on you, could you let her feed?"

He swallowed twice before he could talk. "I don't know."

A truthful answer. He was terrified. "I'll go with you."

He looked at me then, looked at me and not at the screaming in his head. "She won't like that."

"Fuck her. She can take it or leave it."

That got me the ghost of a smile. He gripped my hands where they lay on top of his. He nodded.

I looked at Jean-Claude still sitting by us. "You're not being much help."

"I too have seen the show, *ma petite.*" He was echoing my thoughts so closely, I wondered whose thoughts were which. But what he was saying was frightening. He wouldn't offer himself to Yvette, not just to save Jason.

I stood up, drawing Jason to his feet. He clung to my hand like a kid on the first day of kindergarten afraid Mommy would leave him alone with the bullies.

"If you give your word of honor that you won't rot on him, you can feed off of him."

"No," Yvette said. "No, that spoils it all."

"It's your choice," I said. "You can have Richard, if Padma will let you, but he won't be afraid. You can rot on him though, but you won't get Jason's horror of you." I moved so she could see him clearly.

Jason flinched but stayed standing, but he wouldn't or couldn't meet her eyes. He stared at me. I think he was actually looking down my dress. But for once I didn't make him stop. Distraction was just what he needed. Knowing Jason, I wasn't surprised that a peek-a-boo show was what he chose.

Yvette licked her lips. Finally, she nodded.

I led Jason towards her. He was dressed for his own peek-a-boo show. He was wearing a pair of leather pants dyed a blue two shades darker than his eyes. The pants looked painted on, sliding seamlessly into boots dyed to match. He wore no shirt, only a vest that matched the pants, fastened with three leather thongs.

He stumbled as we entered the cleared space. Yvette glided towards him, and he hung back. Only my hand kept him from bolting. "Easy, Jason, easy."

He just kept shaking his head, straining against my hold on his wrist. He wasn't exactly struggling, but he wasn't cooperating either.

"It's too much to ask," Richard said. "He is my wolf, and I will not see him tormented."

I looked at Richard, proud, arrogant. "He's my wolf, too." I released Jason's wrist slowly and put a hand on either side of his face. "If this is too much to ask, say so, and we'll do something else."

He gripped my wrists, and I watched him collect himself. I watched his hard-won control fill his eyes, his face. "Don't leave me."

"I'm right here."

"No," Yvette said, "you cannot hold his hand while I feed."

I turned to her, Jason so close our bodies touched without hands. "Then it's over. You don't touch him."

"First you tame Asher. Now you seek to tame me. You have nothing I want, Anita."

"I have Jason."

She hissed at me, all that careful beauty breaking down and showing the beast inside. She snatched at him around me, and he jerked back. She pawed at him like a cat, and I kept my body between them, moving us into the center of the circle. I felt Jason's back hit the wall, and I grabbed Yvette's arm.

"Feel his terror, Yvette. I can feel his heart pounding against my back. My holding his hand won't make him unafraid. Nothing I could do would make him not fear your touch."

Jason hid his face against my back, hands sliding around my waist. I patted his arm. His body was one throbbing beat as his heart, his blood, pumped through his body so hard I could feel it. His terror rode the air like a hot, invisible mist.

"Agreed," she said. She backed away to the center of the cleared floor. She held one pale hand out to us. "Come, Anita, bring our prize."

I slid in his arms until I was leading him by the hand again. His palms were sweating. I led him to stand with his back to her. He gripped my hands in both of his. His hands trembled. He stared at my face as if it were the only thing left in the world.

Yvette touched his back.

He whimpered. I drew him into me until our arms were touching, our faces only inches apart. I had no words of comfort. I could offer nothing but a hand to hold and something else to think about.

Yvette trailed her fingers around his shoulders until she came to the thongs that tied the vest. Her hands brushed the front of my body as she fumbled with the ties. I started to step back, and Jason's hands sang with tension. I stayed where I was, but my own pulse was beating in my throat. I was afraid of her, too, afraid of what she was.

She had to slide her hand around his waist to get the last tie, molding her body against his back. She licked his ear, a quick flick of her pale pink tongue.

He closed his eyes, bowing his head until our foreheads touched.

"You can do this," I said.

He nodded his head, eyes still closed, forehead still touching mine.

Yvette ran her hands up his back under the vest, then curved them around to his naked chest, running her nails down his flesh in a quick rush.

Jason gasped, and I realized in that instant that it wasn't just fear. He had slept with her before he knew what she was. She knew his body, knew how to bring him to passion as only a lover can. She'd use that against him now.

Jason drew his face back from mine. He looked at me, and he seemed lost.

She shoved the vest up around his shoulders and licked a long wet line up his spine.

He turned his face from me, so I wouldn't see his eyes. "It's all right if some of it feels good, Jason."

He turned back to me, and there were other things in his eyes beside fear. I'd been more comfortable with the fear, but he was the one hurting.

Yvette knelt and did something low on his back with her mouth. His knees buckled suddenly, taking us both to the floor. I ended up flat on my back with Jason on top of me. I had one leg free, which was a help and a hindrance, since it put him perfectly on top of me. I could tell his body was happy to be there. I wasn't sure about the rest of him. He was making small sounds low in his throat.

I scooted out from under him enough so that his groin wasn't pressing mine and I could sit up to see what Yvette had done to him. There were fangs marks low on his back near the spine. The blood beaded on the blue leather like it had been Scotch-garded.

His arms locked around my waist. "Don't leave me, please." His cheek was pressed against my waist. The tension in his body made my heart thud.

"I won't leave you, Jason." I stared at Yvette over his body.

She was kneeling with the white skirt pooled around her, as if a wandering photographer would be coming by. She smiled, and it reached her eyes, filling them with a dark, joyous light. She was enjoying the hell out of herself.

"You've fed. It's over," I said.

"That wasn't a feeding, and you know it. I've tasted him, but I haven't fed."

It had been worth a try. She was right. I knew she hadn't fed. "Then just do it, Yvette."

"If you had let me rot, then it would be quicker, but I want his terror and his pleasure. That takes longer."

Jason made a small sound, like a child crying in the dark. I looked out at Richard. He was still standing, but he wasn't angry with me now. There was real pain in his eyes. He'd have rather it be him than Jason. Like a true king he'd have taken the pain.

I smelled forest, rich and green, leaf mold so wet and new it made my throat tight. I stared at Richard and knew what he was suggesting. We'd had our little fight about the munin. He'd truly thought I was safe from them because I wasn't a shapeshifter. He hadn't known the marks I shared with him would put me at risk. But now it had possibilities. Not channeling Raina, I never wanted to do that again, but the power of the pack. Their warmth, their touch—that could help.

I closed my eyes and felt the mark open like curtains parting in my body. Jason raised his head, staring up at me. His nostrils flared, scenting me, scenting the power.

Yvette ripped the vest down his back like it was paper.

Jason gasped.

She licked along his body, then suddenly her mouth closed over his ribs. I saw the muscles in her jaw tense as Jason's body spasmed against me. He collapsed against me, hands scrambling along the floor as if he didn't know what to do with his them, or with his body.

Yvette drew back leaving neat red holes. Blood dripped from the wound. She licked her lips and smiled at me.

"Does it hurt?" I asked Jason.

"Yes," he said, "and no."

I started to raise him up.

Yvette put a hand in the middle of his back. "No, I want him on the ground. I want him below me."

I smelled the sharp musk of fur. Jason tried to look at me, but Yvette forced his head down into my lap. She used him to support her body while she peered into my face. "What are you doing?"

"I am his lupa. I call the pack to his aid."

"They cannot help him," she said.

"Yes," I said, "they can." I slid down, wriggling under Jason's body. The little black dress ended up about waist level. Everyone was getting a great view of the hose and undies. Good that everything matched. But I could see Jason's face. I could feel his body a little more than I wanted to. But it was his eyes I wanted, his face. I wanted him looking at me.

I'd never tried missionary position with a man exactly my height. The eye contact was incredibly intimate. He gave a nervous laugh. "I've had fantasies like this."

"Funny," I said. "I haven't."

"Ooh, too cruel." His spine bowed, body pressing against mine. Yvette had taken another taste. The fear was back in full force, filling his eyes with panic.

"I'm here. We're here."

He closed his eyes and took a deep breath. He drew in the scent of leaves, and fur, and dark places full of bodies that all smelled like pack. And Yvette struck again.

Jason screamed, and I raised myself up enough to see that the vampire had pulled a strip of skin loose so it flapped. Blood poured down his skin.

Jean-Claude came to the edge of the circle. "That is torture, not feeding. It stops here."

"No," Yvette said, "I will feed."

"Then feed," Jean-Claude said, "but do it quickly before our patience is at an end."

She crawled up his body, putting her weight on top of his, grinding me into the floor. The leather stitching over his groin was ground so hard against me that it hurt. His breath came in quick pants, fast and faster. He was going to hyperventilate.

"Look at me," I said.

Yvette jerked his head back by the hair. "No, look at me. Because I will hurt you, Jason. I will haunt your dreams."

"No," I said. The power swelled inside of me, and I spit power into her pale face. Blood flew in a long, shallow cut down her cheek.

Everything froze. Yvette raised a hand to her bleeding cheek. "How did you do that?"

"If I said I wasn't really sure, would you believe me?"

"No," she said.

"Then believe this, bitch. Finish this now or I will cut you up." I believed it when I said it, even though I wasn't sure I could ever repeat the performance. Only master vampires could cause cuts like that from a distance. I'd never even seen Jean-Claude do it.

Yvette believed me. She leaned close enough that the blood from the cut dripped onto Jason's blond hair. "As you like, *putain*, but know this, I will not put him under. For this—" she showed the cut to me by a turn of her face—"he will suffer."

"Ain't it always the way," I said.

She frowned at me, not the response she was expecting apparently. I put a hand on either side of Jason's face, forced his eyes to meet mine. There was puzzlement under the fear now, because Jason knew I'd never done anything like what had just happened to Yvette. But we couldn't say, golly, gee whiz, how'd I do that in front of the bad guys?

Yvette shifted until her body was pressed along the length of Jason's. He moved against me. There was nothing between Jason and me but the leather of his pants and some satin. My body reacted. It was my turn to close my eyes so he wouldn't see. Maybe it was the physical reaction, but I was suddenly drowning in the scent of fur, and the warm, close knowledge of his body. The munin was here in a warm, building rush.

I lifted my face and kissed him. The moment our lips touched, the power flowed between us. It was a binding of a different sort, better than with Nathaniel, and I knew why. Nathaniel wasn't pack.

Jason didn't kiss me back at first; then he sank into my mouth, into the warm power, and the power grew until I could feel it like a small hot wind across my body, across our bodies. The power flowed over Yvette and made her cry out. She plunged fangs into Jason's neck. He screamed into my mouth, body stiffening, but the pain rode on the warm, building power and was washed away.

I could feel Yvette's mouth like a siphon, sucking the power away. I thrust it into her and sent her reeling from us, drunk on more than blood.

Freed of Yvette's body, Jason moved against me. He kissed me as if he'd climb inside and pull me around him, and I kissed him back. I'd welcomed Raina's munin, and I didn't know how to turn it off.

I felt his lower body react, felt him come, and that was enough to help me swim back into control. What a nice embarrassing moment to be driving again.

Jason collapsed on top of me, panting, but not from fear. I turned my face away so that I wouldn't catch a glimpse of anyone gathered around us. Yvette lay on her side near us, curled into a ball, blood trailing down her chin. She licked the blood, almost halfheartedly as if even that small effort were too much. She spoke French to me: *"Je reve de toi."* I'd heard a version of this before from Jean-Claude. She said she'd dream of us.

I heard myself say, "Why do the French always know exactly what to say at times like this?"

Jean-Claude knelt beside us. "It is genetic, *ma petite.*"

"Ah," I said. I had trouble meeting his eyes with Jason still sprawled across my body.

"Jason," I said, tapping his bare shoulder. He said nothing, just rolled off me to lie on the floor, closer to Yvette than I'd have ever thought he'd be willing to get.

I suddenly realized that my skirt was still up around my waist. Jean-Claude helped me sit up while I wiggled the dress down.

Richard knelt with us. I expected a scathing remark. I'd certainly given him enough ammo for one. He surprised me by saying, "Raina, gone, but not forgotten."

I said, "No joke."

"I'm sorry, Anita. When you told me, I didn't realize it was an almost complete melding. I understand why you're afraid of it now. There are things you can do to keep it from happening again. I was too angry at you to believe it was this bad." A look crossed his face, part pain, part confusion. "I am sorry for that."

"If you can keep that from happening again, apology accepted."

Padma was suddenly looming over us. "You and I will dance next, Ulfric. After the show your lupa gave us, I am more eager than ever to taste you."

Richard glanced at me, then at Jason and Yvette, both still lying on the ground as if any movement was too much. "I don't think I'm that good."

"I think you underestimate yourself, wolf," Padma said. He offered Richard a hand, but he stood on his own. The two men were almost the same height. They stared at each other, and I could already feel the power flaring between them, testing each other.

I lay against Jean-Claude's chest and closed my eyes. "Get me out of here before they start. I can't stand to be near this much power so soon." He helped me to stand, and when my legs wouldn't hold me, he scooped me up in his arms, holding me effortlessly. He just stood there holding me, as if expecting me to protest.

I put my arms around his neck and said, "Just do it."

He smiled, and it was wondrous. "I have wanted to do this for a very long time." Was it romantic to be carried in his arms at last? Yes. But when Jason managed to stagger from the floor, the front of his blue leather pants was stained, and that wasn't romantic at all.

51

Padma and Richard faced each other just out of reach. Each was letting his power out like a lure at the end of a line, to see who took the bait first. Richard's power was as it always was, an electric heat. But Padma's power was similar. More than any other vamp I'd been around, his power was warm, alive, for lack of a better word. It did not have the electric shimmer of Richard's, but it had heat.

Their power filled the room as if the very air were charged with their energy. It was everywhere and nowhere. Richard's power bit along my skin, drew a gasp from my throat that Jean-Claude echoed. Padma's power flared along the skin like being too close to an open flame. The two energies combined were almost painful.

Rafael came to stand beside us. Jean-Claude was still holding me in his arms, which lets you know how shitty I was feeling. The Rat King wore a very ordinary navy blue suit, white shirt, understated tie. His black loafers were polished to a gloss, but he could have been going anywhere, from a business meeting to a funeral. Yeah, it had the look of one of those suits that only came out for deaths and marriages.

"They feel evenly matched," he said, "but it is a lie." He said it softly as if just talking to us, but we were close enough that Richard could hear. "He did much the same with me; then he crushed me."

"He didn't crush you," I said. "You won."

"Only because you rescued me."

"No," I said. "You didn't give him the wererats. You won." I touched Jean-Claude's shoulder, and he put me down. I could stand. Yippee.

"Very impressive, Ulfric," Padma said, "but let's see just how impressive you can be, shall we? Thank you, Rafael, for spoiling the surprise. I will return the favor someday." The gloves, as they say, were off. Padma's power thundered through the room. I staggered, and only Jean-Claude's hand kept me from going to my knees.

Richard screamed and did fall to his knees. We were just getting the backwash of Padma's power. Richard was getting the full treatment. I expected him to do with Richard what he'd done with me, but he didn't. He had other plans.

"Change for me, Richard. I like my food with fur."

Richard shook his head. His voice came out strangled, as if the words were being dragged through his throat. "Never."

" 'Never' can be a very long time," Padma said. I felt his power like insects marching over my skin, ants with red-hot pokers taking bites. It was what he'd done to the wereleopard, Elizabeth, when he punished her.

Richard didn't writhe on the floor like she had. He said, "No." He got his feet under him and took a staggering step towards the vampire.

The burning got worse, the red-hot bites closer together like a continuous sheet of tiny fires. I made a small sound, and still Richard stood. He took another staggering step.

The rush of power stopped so abruptly that the absence of pain brought Richard to his knees nearly at Padma's feet. His breathing was loud in the sudden silence.

"Pain will not bring you to me," Padma said. "Shall we dispense with the games, Ulfric? Shall I feed now?"

"Just get it over with," Richard said.

Padma smiled, and there was something in his smile that I didn't like. As if he had everything under control, and everything was going as planned.

He stood behind Richard and dropped gracefully to his knees. He smoothed his hand down the side of Richard's neck, turning his head to the side for a good clean strike. One arm slid across Richard's chest, pinning him to his body; the other hand pressed his face to one side.

Padma leaned over him and whispered something in his ear. A spasm ran the length of Richard's body. He tried to break free of Padma, but the vampire was amazingly quick. He slid both arms under Richard's, fingers clasped behind Richard's neck. A classic full Nelson. Richard's struggles ended with him on the ground and the vampire on top of him. If it had been a wrestling match, Richard would have been pinned, lost. But no referee was coming to say "time."

"What's happening?" I asked.

"I warned Richard," Rafael said, "but he's always been so strong."

"What?" I asked.

"He is calling Richard's beast, *ma petite*," Jean-Claude said. "I have seen him do it before."

Richard's body spasmed so violently, his head hit against the floor with a sharp crack. He rolled on his side, but the vampire stayed on him, whispering, whispering.

"Did he manage to call your beast like this?" I asked Rafael.

"Yes."

I looked at him.

He stared at the show, not meeting my eyes. "He called my beast like water pouring over my skin, then drained it away. He did it over and over, until I passed out. I woke as you found me on the rack, being skinned." His voice was neutral as he told it all, as if it were a story about someone else.

"Help him," I said, turning to Jean-Claude.

"If I enter that circle, Padma will use it as an excuse to challenge me. If it is a duel, I will lose."

"He's baiting you, then," I said.

"He is also enjoying himself, *ma petite*. Breaking the strong is his greatest joy in this existence."

A scream poured from Richard's mouth. A scream that ended in a howl.

"I'm going to help him."

"How, *ma petite*?"

"Padma can't challenge me to a duel, and he can't call my beast. Touch makes the marks stronger, right?"

"*Oui.*"

I smiled and started walking towards Richard. Jean-Claude didn't try to stop me. No one did. Richard had managed to get to his knees with the vampire still molded to his back. Richard's eyes were amber wolf eyes, and he was close to panicking. This near, I could feel his beast like a huge shape just below the surface of some dark lake. When it broke the surface, it would take him with it. Rafael seemed to have accepted his loss, but Richard wouldn't. Richard would take the defeat and beat himself with it.

"What are you doing, human?" Padma asked, staring up at me.

"I'm his lupa and his third. I'm doing my job." I held Richard's face in my hands, and that was enough. The physical touch was all it took to strengthen his control. I felt his heart slow, the pulsing of his body ease. I felt that great shape sink back into the depths. Richard drew on my mark like a drowning man with a rope, coiling it around himself.

"No," Padma said. "He is mine."

I smiled at him. "No, he's mine. Whether we like it or whether we don't, he's mine."

Richard's eyes bled back to their normal brown, and he mouthed the words, "Thank you."

Padma stood in a rush, so quick it was almost like magic. He grabbed my wrist, hard enough to bruise, and I said, "You can't challenge me, because I'm not a vampire. You can't feed off of me, because I can only play victim once tonight, and Asher was my once."

Richard lay on the floor, one arm braced so he wasn't actually lying down, but I had a flash of how bone-weary he was, so tired, so weak.

"You know our rules well, Anita," Padma said. He jerked me close to him, bodies almost touching. "You are not vampire, or food, but you are still his lupa."

"You going to try and call my beast?" I said. "You can't call what's not there."

"I felt your power with the little werewolf." He raised my hand to his face and sniffed along my skin like he was smelling some exotic perfume. "You smell of pack, Anita. There is something in you to call. Whatever it is, I will have it."

"She is not part of the bargain," Jean-Claude said.

"She interfered," Padma said. "That makes her part of this bacchanal. Do not worry. I will not hurt her. Too much."

He leaned into me and spoke low, soft. It was French, and I didn't speak enough French to follow it. I caught the word for wolf, and power, and moon, and I felt the power rise inside of me. It was too soon after Jason. The power was too close to the surface, too near. Padma called to it, and I didn't know how to stop it. The power burst over my skin in a hot wash. My knees buckled and he caught me, as I collapsed against his body.

Richard touched my leg, but it was too late. He tried to strengthen my control, as I'd done for him, but I didn't have any control yet. Padma called and the munin answered. I was channeling Raina for the second time in an hour.

The power filled my skin, and I stood, pressing my body into Padma, staring at him from inches away. The power wanted to touch someone, anyone. It didn't care. I cared, and I had enough control this time to refuse it. I said, "No." I pushed away from him, falling to the ground as I did it.

Padma followed me, touching my hair, my face, as I crawled away from him. "The power is sexual in nature, a mating urge perhaps. How very interesting."

Jean-Claude said, "Leave her alone, Master of Beasts."

He laughed. "What do you think would happen if I kept calling her beast? Do you think she would give in? Do you think she would fuck me?"

"We will not find out," Jean-Claude said.

"If you interfere with my fun, then it is challenge between us."

"That is what you have wanted all along."

Padma laughed again. "Yes, I think you should be killed for the Earthmover's death. But I cannot kill you just for that. The council has voted that down."

"But if you kill me in a duel, then no one will blame you, is that it?"

"That is it."

I huddled on the floor, hugging myself, trying to swallow the power back, but it wasn't going anywhere. Richard crawled to me, touching my bare arm. I recoiled from him as if his touch had burned, because I wanted him, wanted him in a way so raw and primitive it made my body hurt.

"Don't touch me, please."

"How did you get rid of it last time?"

"Sex or violence, the munin leaves after sex or violence." Or healing, I thought. Though that had been sex, too, in a way.

Padma's power rode over us like a tank, a tank with a spiked tread. We both screamed, and Jean-Claude screamed with us. Blood poured from his mouth in a red rush, and I knew what Padma had done. I'd felt him try to do it to me. He'd shoved his power into Jean-Claude and opened it, burst something inside of him.

Jean-Claude fell to his knees, blood spattering the white shirt. I was on my feet without thinking, standing between Padma and Jean-Claude. The power burned along my skin. My anger fed it as if it truly were a beast.

"Get out of my way, human, or I will kill you first, and then your master." It was like standing inside an invisible wall of fire and pain to be this close to Padma now. He'd weakened Richard, then me, done something to the marks. Without us, Jean-Claude could not win.

I stopped fighting the energy inside me. I embraced it, fed it, and it spilled out of my mouth in a laugh that raised the hairs on my arms. It wasn't my laugh. It was a laugh I'd never thought to hear this side of hell.

Padma grabbed me, a hand on each arm, lifting me off my feet. "I am allowed to kill you if you interfere with a duel."

I kissed him, a soft brush of lips.

He was so startled for a second, he just froze; then he kissed me back, locking his arms behind my back, still with my feet dangling off the ground. He raised his face enough to say, "Even if you fuck me here and now, it won't save him."

That laugh spilled from my lips, and I felt a darkness fill my eyes. That cold, white part of me where there was nothing but static and silence, the place where I killed, opened up inside my head, and Raina filled it. I remembered the feel of Nathaniel's heart in my hands, the moment I'd realized I could kill him, that I wanted to kill him, more than I wanted to heal him. So much easier to kill.

I locked my arms around Padma's neck and kissed his mouth. I shoved the power into him like a sword. His body stiffened, arms opening, but I was holding on now. His heart was slick and heavy. It beat against the power like a fish in a net. I crushed the power around it. He fell to his knees and screamed into my mouth. Blood flowed in a warm gush, filling my mouth with the warm salty rush of it.

Hands pulled at me, tried to tear me away from Padma. I clung to him, legs wrapped around his waist, arms around his neck. "Back off or I'll shatter his heart. Back off now!"

Thomas fell to his knees beside us, blood trickling down his chin. "You'll kill me and Gideon."

I didn't want to kill them. The power began to slide away, buried in regret. "No," I said it out loud. I fed the power on my anger, my outrage. The munin swelled and filled me. I squeezed Padma's heart—gently, slowly.

I laid my face against his cheek and whispered, "Why aren't you fighting back, Master of Beasts? Where is that large, burning, power of yours?"

There was no answer but his labored breathing.

I squeezed a little tighter.

He gasped. "We could die together," he said in a voice wet with his own blood.

I rubbed my cheek against his face. The blood from his lips smeared along our skin. I'd always known that blood was a turn-on for lycanthropes but I'd never fully appreciated the appeal. It wasn't so much the feel of the blood as the smell of it. Hot, sweet, flatly metallic, and underneath, the scent of fear. He was so very afraid. I could smell it, feel it.

I raised back from him enough to see his face. It was a mask of blood. Part of me was horrified. Part of me wanted to lick him clean like a cat with a bowl of cream. Instead I gave his heart a little extra squeeze and watched the blood flow faster from his mouth.

His power built in a warm wash. "I will kill you before I die, lupa."

I held him and felt his power begin to build, still weakened, but enough to do the job. "Are you still a good Hindu?" I asked.

His eyes showed confusion.

"How much bad karma have you accumulated this turn of the wheel?" I gave a quick lick over his mouth and had to put my forehead against his and close my eyes to keep from doing what the munin wanted. What Raina would have done if she'd been here. "What would be punishment enough for your evil deeds in the next reincarnation, Padma? How many lives would it take to balance this one turn?"

I drew back enough to see his face. I had enough control again not to clean his face with my tongue. Looking into his eyes, I knew I was right. He feared death and what would come after.

"What would you do to save yourself, Padma? What would you give? Who would you give?" I whispered that last.

He whispered back, "Anything."

"Anyone?" I asked.

He just looked at me.

Jean-Claude was sitting up, cradled in Richard's arms. "It is still a duel until one is dead. It is within our rights to insist on finishing this."

"Are you so eager to die?" the Traveler said. "The death of one is the death of all." He stood above us and a little back as if he didn't want to be too closely associated with us. Too bloody, too primitive, too mortal.

"That is a question for Padma to answer, not me," Jean-Claude said.

"What is your price?" Padma asked.

"No more punishment for Oliver's death. He lost a duel, it is as simple as that." Jean-Claude coughed, and more blood spattered from his lips.

"Agreed," Padma said.

"Agreed," the Traveler said.

"I never wanted them dead because of the Earthmover's death," Yvette said. "Agreed."

Asher said, "The Earthmover earned his death. Agreed."

Jean-Claude held his hand out to me. "Come, *ma petite*. We have our safety."

I shook my head, laying a kiss on Padma's forehead, gentle, chaste. "I promised Sylvie that everyone who raped her would die."

Padma's body jerked, reaction at last. "The woman you can have, but not my son."

"Do you agree to that, Traveler? You, who Liv calls master now. Do you give her up so easily?"

"Will you kill him if I refuse?" he asked.

"I gave Sylvie my word," I said. And I knew that would mean something to them.

"Then Liv is yours to do with as you see fit."

"Master," she said.

"Silence," the Traveler said.

"See, Liv, they're just monsters." I stared down into Padma's bloody face and watched fear fill his eyes like water pouring into a glass. I watched him look into my face and see the emptiness. No, for the first time I wanted to kill. Not for revenge, or safety, or even my word, but just because I could. Because in some dark part of me it would be a pleasure to crush his heart and watch dark blood pour from him. I'd have liked to blame it on Raina's munin, but I wasn't sure. Maybe it was just me. Maybe it always had been. Hell, maybe it was one of the boys. I didn't know and it didn't matter. I let the thought fill my face and eyes. I let Padma see, and fear filled his face, his eyes, because he understood.

"I want Fernando," I said softly.

"He is my son."

"Someone must die for his crimes, Padma. I would rather it were him, but if you won't give him to me, then I'll take you in his place."

"No," Yvette said. "We have been more than generous here. We have let you kill a council member and go unpunished. We have given you back your traitor and our new toy. We owe you nothing else."

I looked at Padma but I spoke for the Traveler's ears. "If you had just insulted the vampires of this city, then it would be over and you would owe us nothing. But we are lukoi and not vampires. You called our Geri to your hand and she came. You tried to break her, and when she would not bend you tortured her. You tortured her when you knew it would not give you the lukoi. You dishonored her for no reason, other than that you could. You did it because you expected no reprisal. The Master of Beasts thought our pack was beneath notice. Pawns in a larger game."

I released his heart, because if I hadn't, the munin would have killed him. I shoved the power deeper into him. I shoved it hard and fast until he screamed. Gideon and Thomas echoed the scream.

Padma collapsed backwards onto the floor with me riding his body.

I rose up, hands flat over his chest, legs straddling his body. "We are the Thronos Rokke, the Throne Rock people, and we are no one's pawns."

Fernando knelt just outside the circle. "Father," he said.

"His life or yours, Padma. His life or yours."

Padma closed his eyes and whispered, "His."

"Father! You can't give me to her. To them!"

"Your word of honor that he is ours to punish as we see fit, even unto death," I said.

Padma nodded. "My word."

Damian, Jason, and Rafael just suddenly appeared around Fernando. He reached out to his father. "I am your son."

Padma would not look at him. Even when I crawled off him, he curled on his side away from Fernando.

I wiped blood off my chin with the back of my hand. The munin was leaving, draining away. I could taste blood all the way down. I rolled onto my side and threw up. Blood does not improve the second time around.

Jean-Claude reached out to me and I went to him. The moment his cool hand touched mine I felt better. Not a lot, but some. Richard's hand touched my face gently. I let them draw me into the circle of their arms. Jean-Claude seemed to gain strength just from my touch. He sat up a little straighter.

I glanced over to find Gideon and Thomas doing much the same with Padma. Blood poured from all of them, but only Padma's eyes were still haunted by fear. I'd pushed him to the edge of the abyss. Pushed us both. I'd been raised Catholic and I wasn't sure there were enough Hail Marys in the world to cover what was happening to me lately.

52

Fernando tried to make a break for it but he was outmanned. Or would that be out-monstered? They bound him with silver chains and gagged him. The last was to stop his constant begging. He just couldn't believe his father had betrayed him.

Liv didn't fight. She seemed to take it almost resignedly. What seemed to surprise her most was the fact that I didn't kill them both where they stood. But I had other plans for them. They'd insulted the pack. It would be pack justice. That was sort of a group activity. Maybe we'd invite the wererats and have a cross species jamboree.

When they were led away, a silence so deep and wide that it thundered in the ears filled the room. Yvette stepped into that silence. She was smiling and lovely, fresh and beautiful on Jason's blood and our mingled power.

"Jean-Claude must still answer for his traitorous ways," she said.

"What are you babbling about?" the Traveler said.

"My master, Morte d' Amour, has accused him of trying to start another council in this country. A council that will steal our power and make us but laughable puppets."

The Traveler waved it away. "Jean-Claude is guilty of many things but that is not one of them."

Yvette smiled, and the smile was enough. She was going to say something bad. "What say you, Padma? If he is a traitor, then we can execute him for it. He can be an example to all others who would dare usurp the council's power."

Padma was still on the ground, cradled in the arms of his two servants. He still wasn't feeling too good. He stared at our little group. We were still huddled on the floor, too. The six of us were not going to be dancing tonight. The look in Padma's eyes said it all. I'd humiliated him, scared the hell out of him, and forced him to give up his only son to sure death. He smiled, and it wasn't pretty. "If they are traitors, then they must be punished."

"Padma," the Traveler said, "you know this is false."

"I did not say they were traitors, Traveler. I said if they were traitors. If they are traitors, then they must be punished. Even you must agree to that."

"But they are not traitors," the Traveler said.

"I use my master's proxy to call a vote," Yvette said. "I think I know what three of the votes will be."

Asher came to stand near Jean-Claude and us. "They are not traitors, Yvette. To say so is a lie."

"Lies are very interesting things. Don't you think . . . Harry?" She held out her hand as if it were a signal and Harry the bartender joined her. I didn't think I could be surprised anymore tonight. I was wrong.

"I see that you know Harry," Yvette said.

"The police are looking for you, Harry," I said.

"I know," he said. At least he had trouble meeting my eyes. Didn't make me feel much better, but a little.

"I knew Harry was one of your line," Jean-Claude said, "but he is truly one of yours."

"*Oui.*"

"What is the meaning of this, Yvette?" the Traveler said.

"Harry leaked the information to those awful fanatics so they would kill monsters."

"Why?" the Traveler asked.

"My question exactly," I said.

"My master is frightened of change, like many of the old ones. Making us legal is the most sweeping change we've ever been threatened with. He fears it. He wants it stopped."

"Like Oliver," I said.

"*Exactement.*"

"But the vampire killings didn't stop it," I said. "If anything, it's given the pro-vamp lobby a boost."

"But now," she said, "we shall have our revenge, a revenge so bloody and awful that it will turn everyone against us."

"You cannot do this," the Traveler said.

"Padma has given me the key. The Master of the City is weak, his link to his servants weaker still. He would be easily killed now if someone would challenge him."

"You," the Traveler said, "you could challenge Jean-Claude, but you could never be Master of the City, Yvette. You will never have enough power on your own to be a master vampire. Your master's power has made you try to rise above your station."

"It is true that I will never be a master, but there is a master here who hates Jean-Claude and his servant. Asher." She said his name like it was planned.

He looked at her, but he seemed startled. Whatever she planned, he didn't know about it. He stared down at Jean-Claude. "You want me to kill him while he is too weak to fight?"

"Yes," she said.

"No," Asher said, "I do not want Jean-Claude's place, not like this. Beating him in a fair duel is one thing, but this is . . . treachery."

"I thought you hated him," Yvette said.

"I do, but honor means something to me."

"Implying I suppose that it doesn't to me?" She shrugged. "You're right. If I could be master of this city, I would do it. But I could live another thousand years and I will never be a master. But it is not honor that stops you. It's her." She pointed at me. "There must be some alchemy in you that I do not see, Anita. You bewitch every vampire that comes near you and every shapeshifter."

"You've had a big taste and don't seem too taken with me," I said.

"My tastes run to things even more exotic than you, animator."

"If Asher will not take the city as Master, then you cannot control the city's vampires. You cannot make them do some terrible deed to the humans," the Traveler said.

"I did not trust Asher's hatred to make our plan work. It would have been useful to have control of the city's vampires but it is not necessary. The carnage has already begun," Yvette said.

We were all silent, staring at her, all of us thinking one thing. I said it out loud. "What do you mean, it's already begun?"

"Tell them, Warrick," she said.

He shook his head.

She sighed. "Fine, I will tell them. Warrick was a holy warrior before I found him. He could call the fire of God to his hands, couldn't you?"

He wouldn't look at any of us. He stood there, this huge figure in shining white, head down like a little boy who's been caught playing hooky.

"You set the fires in New Orleans and San Francisco, and here. Why no fires in Boston?" I asked.

"I told you I began to feel stronger the longer I was away from our shared master. In Boston I was still weak. It wasn't until New Orleans that I felt God's grace return to me for the first time in nearly a thousand years. I was drunk on it at first. I was deeply ashamed that I burned down a building. I did not mean to, but it felt so wonderful, so pure."

"I caught him at it," Yvette said. "I told him to do it other places, everywhere we went. I told him to kill people, but even torture wouldn't make him do that."

He did look up then. "I made sure no one was injured."

"You're a pyrokinetic," I said.

He frowned. "I was given a gift from God. It was the first sign of his favor to return to me. Before, I think I feared the Holy Fire. Feared it would destroy me. But I do not fear my own destruction now. She wishes me to use God's gifts for evil use. She wanted me to burn down your stadium with all the people inside tonight."

I said, "Warrick, what have you done?"

He whispered, "Nothing."

Yvette heard him. She was suddenly beside us, white skirts swinging. She grabbed his chin and forced him to look at her. "The entire point to burning the other buildings was to leave a trail of evidence that would culminate in tonight's little sacrifice. A little burnt offering to our master. You burned the stadium as we planned."

He shook his head, blue eyes wide, but not frightened.

She hit him hard enough to leave her hand in a red outline on his cheek. "You holy-rolling bastard. You answer to the same master that I answer to. I will rot the skin from your bones for this.''

Warrick stood very straight. You could see him preparing for the torment to come. He stood shining and white and he looked like a holy warrior. There was a peace in his face that was lovely to look upon.

Yvette's power surged forward and I got just the faintest backwash. But Warrick stood there untouched, pure. Nothing happened. Yvette turned to all of us. ''Who is helping him? Who is protecting him from me?''

I realized what was happening. ''No one's helping him, Yvette,'' I said. ''He is a master vampire and you can't hurt him anymore.''

''What are you talking about? He is mine. Mine to do with as I see fit. He has always been mine.''

''Not anymore,'' I said.

Warrick smiled and it was beatific. ''God has freed me from you, Yvette. He has finally forgiven me for my fall from grace. My lusting after your white flesh that led me to hell. I am free of it. I am free of you.''

''No,'' she said. ''No!''

''It seems our brother council member was limiting Warrick's powers,'' the Traveler said. ''As he was giving you power, Yvette, he was keeping it from Warrick.''

''This is not possible,'' she said. ''We will burn this city to the ground and take credit for it. We will show them we are monsters.''

''No, Yvette,'' Warrick said. ''We will not.''

''I don't need you for this,'' she said. ''I can be monster enough on my own. I'm sure there is a reporter out there somewhere that I can embrace. I'll rot in front of his cameras, on him. I will not fail our master. I will be the monster he wants us to be. The monsters we truly are.'' She held out her hand to Harry. ''Come, let us go find victims in very public places.''

''We cannot allow this,'' the Traveler said.

''No,'' Padma said. He pushed to his feet with Gideon and Thomas's help. ''We cannot allow this.''

''No,'' Warrick said, ''we cannot allow her to tempt anyone else. It is enough.''

''No, it is not enough. It will never be enough. I will find someone to take your place at my side, Warrick. I can make another of you. Someone who will serve me for all time.''

He shook his head slowly. ''I cannot allow you to steal another man's soul in my place. I will not ransom another man into the hell of your embrace.''

''I thought it was hell you feared,'' Yvette said. ''Centuries of worry that you'll roast in punishment for your crimes.'' She pouted at him, exaggerating her voice. ''Centuries of listening to you whine about your purity and your fall from grace, and the punishment that awaited you.''

''I no longer fear my punishment, Yvette.''

''Because you think you've been forgiven,'' she said.

He shook his head. ''Only God knows if I am truly forgiven, but if I am to be punished, then I will have earned it. As we all have. I cannot allow you to put another in my place.''

She came to him, trailing fingers across his white tunic. I lost sight of her behind his broad back, and when she came back around she was rotting. She trailed decaying hands down his white suit leaving black and green globs, slimy trails like obscene slugs. She laughed at him with a face covered in sores.

Richard whispered, "What is happening to her?"

"Yvette's happening," I said.

"You'll return to France with me. You'll continue to serve me even though you're a master now. If anyone would make such a sacrifice, it is you, Warrick."

"No, no," he said. "If I were truly strong and worthy of God's grace, then perhaps I would return with you, but I am not that strong."

She wrapped her rotting arms around his waist and smiled up at him. Her body was running to ruin, leaking dark fluids over her white dress. Her rich pale hair was drying out before our eyes, turning to crinkling straw. "Then kiss me, Warrick, one last time. I must find your replacement before dawn."

He encircled her with his white robed arms, hugging her against his tall body. "No, Yvette, no." He stared down at her and there was something almost like tenderness on his face. "Forgive me," he said. He held his hands out in front of him.

Blue fire sprang from his hands, a strange pale color, paler even than gas flame.

Yvette turned her rotting face to look behind her at the fire. "You wouldn't dare," she said.

Warrick closed his arms around her. Her dress caught first. She screamed, "Don't be stupid, Warrick! Let me go!"

He held on, and when the fire hit her flesh she went like she'd been doused in kerosene. She burned with a blue light. She screamed, and struggled, but he had her pinned to his chest. She couldn't even beat at the flames with her hands.

The fire bathed Warrick in a nimbus of blue, but he didn't burn. He stood there yellow and white surrounded in blue fire, and he did look like a saint. Something holy and wonderful and terrible to behold. He stood there shining and Yvette began to blacken and peel in his arms. He smiled at us. "God has not forsaken me. Only my fear kept me in thrall to her all these years."

Yvette twisted in his arms, tried to get away, but he held her tight. He dropped to his knees, bowing his head while she fought him. She burned, skin peeling back from her bones, and still she screamed. The stench of burning hair and cooking flesh filled the room, but there was almost no smoke, just heat building. Making everyone in the room move back from them. Finally, mercifully, Yvette stopped moving, stopped screaming.

I think Warrick was praying while she shrieked and writhed and burned. The blue flames roared almost to the ceiling, then changed color. They became pure yellow-orange, the color of ordinary flame.

I remembered McKinnon's story of how the firebug had burned once the fire changed color. "Warrick, Warrick, let her go. You'll burn with her."

Warrick's voice came one last time. "I do not fear God's embrace. He demands sacrifice, but he is merciful." He never screamed. The fire began to eat at him, but he never made a sound. In that silence we heard a different voice. A high-pitched screaming, low and wordless, pitiless, hopeless. Yvette was still alive.

Someone finally asked if there was a fire extinguisher. Jason said, "No, there isn't.'' I looked at him across the room, and he met my gaze. We stared at each other and I knew that he knew exactly where the fire extinguisher was. Jean-Claude, whose hand I was still holding, knew where it was. Hell, I knew where it was. None of us went running. We let her burn. We let them both burn. Warrick I would have saved if I could have, but Yvette—Burn, baby, burn.

53

The council went home. We had the word of two members that we would not be bothered again. I wasn't sure I trusted them, but it was the best we were going to get. Richard and I are meeting regularly with Jean-Claude, learning how to control the marks. I still can't control the munin, but I'm working on it, and Richard is helping me. We're trying to be less nasty to one another. He's gone out of state for the rest of the summer to finish work on his master's degree in preternatural biology. Hard to work on the marks from that big a distance.

He's approached the local pack there for possible lupa candidates. I don't know how I feel about that. I'm not even sure it's Richard that I would miss. It's the pack, the lukoi. You can always find another boyfriend, but a new family, especially one this strange, that's a rare gift. All the wereleopards have come on board my bandwagon, even Elizabeth. Surprise, surprise.

The leopards call me their Nimir-Ra, leopard queen. Me and Tarzan, huh?

I gave Fernando and Liv to Sylvie. Other than a few pieces that Sylvie kept for souvenirs, they're both gone.

Nathaniel wanted to move in with me. I'm paying for his apartment. He seems lost without someone to organize his life. Zane, who recovered from his gunshot wounds, says that Nathaniel needs a master or a mistress, that he's what the S & M crowd call a pet. The term means someone who is a step below slave, someone who can't function alone. I'd never heard of such a thing, but it seems to be true, at least for Nathaniel. No, I don't know what I'm going to do with him.

Stephen and Vivian are dating. Truthfully, I'd begun to assume Stephen liked guys. Shows how much I know.

Asher stayed in St. Louis. Here, strangely, he's among friends. He and Jean-Claude reminisce about things I'd only read about in history books or seen in movies. I suggested Asher see a plastic surgeon. He informed me that the burns could not be healed because they were caused by a holy object. I said, what does it hurt to ask? When he got over the shocking idea that modern technology might be able to do something his own wonderful body could not, he asked. The doctors are hopeful.

Jean-Claude and I did christen the bathtub at my new house. Picture white candles glowing everywhere, the light gleaming on his naked chest. The petals of two dozen red roses floating on the surface of the water. That's what I came home to one morning at about three A.M. We played until dawn, when I tucked him into my bed. I stayed with him until the warmth left his body and my nerve broke.

Richard is right. I can't give myself completely to Jean-Claude. I can't let him feed. I can't truly share a bed. He is, no matter how lovely, the walking dead. I keep shying away from anything that reminds me too strongly of that fact, like blood-drinking and low body temperatures. Jean-Claude certainly has the keys to my libido, but my heart . . . Can a walking corpse hold the keys to my heart? No. Yes. Maybe. How the hell should I know?

BLUE
MOON

This one's for Shawn Holsapple, brother-in-law, police officer, and kindred spirit.

Acknowledgments

To my husband, Gary, who first took me into the hills of Tennessee.

To my writing group, the Alternate Historians: Tom Drennan, N. L. Drew, Deborah Millitello, Rett MacPherson, Marella Sands, Sharon Shinn, and Mark Sumner, and our newest member, W. Agustus Elliot, who missed the critique of this book by a few months. Here's to the best writing group I've ever been a part of.

Here is the correct address to get messages to me online: laurellk@ricia.com It was edited by an overzealous copyeditor in the acknowledgments of the last book.

1

I was dreaming of cool flesh and sheets the color of fresh blood. The phone shattered the dream, leaving only fragments, a glimpse of midnight blue eyes, hands gliding down my body, his hair flung across my face in a sweet, scented cloud. I woke in my own house, miles from Jean-Claude with the feel of his body clinging to me. I fumbled the phone from the bedside table and mumbled, "Hello."

"Anita, is that you?" It was Daniel Zeeman, Richard's baby brother. Daniel was twenty-four and cute as a bug's ear. Baby didn't really cover it. Richard had been my fiancé once upon a time—until I chose Jean-Claude over him. Sleeping with the other man put a real crimp in our social plans. Not that I blamed Richard. No, I blamed myself. It was one of the few things Richard and I still shared.

I squinted at the glowing dial of the bedside clock. 3:10 A.M. "Daniel, what's wrong?" No one calls at ten after the witching hour with good news.

He took a deep breath, as if preparing himself for the next line. "Richard's in jail."

I sat up, sheets sliding in a bundle to my lap. "What did you say?" I was suddenly wide awake, heart thudding, adrenaline pumping.

"Richard is in jail," he repeated.

I didn't make him say it again, though I wanted to. "What for?" I asked.

"Attempted rape," he said.

"What?" I said.

Daniel repeated it. It didn't make any more sense the second time I heard it. "Richard is like the ultimate Boy Scout," I said. "I'd believe murder before I'd believe rape."

"I guess that's a compliment," he said.

"You know what I meant, Daniel. Richard wouldn't do something like that."

"I agree," he said.

"Is he in Saint Louis?" I asked.

"No, he's still in Tennessee. He finished up his requirements for his master's degree and got arrested that night."

"Tell me what happened."

"I don't exactly know," he said.

"What do you mean?" I asked.

"They won't let me see him," Daniel said.

"Why not?"

"Mom got in to see him, but they wouldn't let all of us in."

"Has he got a lawyer?" I asked.

"He says he doesn't need one. He says he didn't do it."

"Prison is full of people who didn't do it, Daniel. He needs a lawyer. It's his word against the woman's. If she's local and he isn't, he's in trouble."

"He's in trouble," Daniel said.

"Shit," I said.

"There's more bad news," he said.

I threw the covers back and stood, clutching the phone. "Tell me."

"There's going to be a blue moon this month." He said it very quietly, no explanation, but I understood.

Richard was an alpha werewolf. He was head of the local pack. It was his only serious flaw. We'd broken up after I'd seen him eat somebody. What I'd seen had sent me running to Jean-Claude's arms. I'd run from the werewolf to the vampire. Jean-Claude was Master of the City of Saint Louis. He was definitely not the more human of the two. I know there isn't a lot to choose from between a bloodsucker and a flesh-eater, but at least after Jean-Claude finished feeding, there weren't chunks between his fangs. A small distinction but a real one.

A blue moon meant a second full moon this month. The moon doesn't actually turn blue most of the time, but it is where the old saying comes from—once in a blue moon. It happens about every three years or so. It was August, and the second full moon was only five days away. Richard's control was very good, but I'd never heard of any werewolf, even an Ulfric, a pack leader, who could fight the change on the night of the full moon. No matter what flavor of animal you changed into, a lycanthrope was a lycanthrope. The full moon ruled them.

"We have to get him out of jail before the full moon," Daniel said.

"Yeah," I said. Richard was hiding what he was. He taught junior high science. If they found out he was a werewolf, he'd lose his job. It was illegal to discriminate on the basis of a disease, especially one as difficult to catch as lycanthropy, but they'd do it. No one wanted a monster teaching their kiddies. Not to mention that the only person in Richard's family who knew his secret was Daniel. Mom and Pop Zeeman didn't know.

"Give me a number to contact you at," I said.

He did. "You'll come down then," he said.

"Yeah."

He sighed. "Thanks. Mom is raising hell, but it's not helping. We need someone here who understands the legal system."

"I'll have a friend call you with the name of a good local lawyer before I get there. You may be able to arrange bail by the time I arrive."

"If he'll see the lawyer," Daniel said.

"Is he being stupid?" I asked.

"He thinks that having the truth on his side is enough."

It sounded like something Richard would say. There was more than one reason why we'd broken up. He clung to ideals that hadn't even worked when they were in vogue. Truth, justice, and the American way certainly didn't work within the legal system. Money, power, and luck were what worked. Or having someone on your side that was part of the system.

I was a vampire executioner. I was licensed to hunt and kill vampires once a court order of execution had been issued. I was licensed in three states. Tennessee was not one of them. But cops, as a general rule, would treat an executioner better than a civilian. We risked our lives and usually had a higher kill count than they did. Of course, the kills being vamps, some people didn't count them as real kills. Had to be human for it to count.

"When can you get here?" Daniel asked.

"I've got some things to clear up here, but I'll see you today before noon."

"I hope you can talk some sense into Richard."

I'd met their mother—more than once—so I said, "I'm surprised that Charlotte can't talk sense to him."

"Where do you think he gets this 'truth will set you free' bit?" Daniel asked.

"Great," I said. "I'll be there, Daniel."

"I've got to go." He hung up suddenly as if afraid of being caught. His mom had probably come into the room. The Zeemans had four sons and a daughter. The sons were all six feet or above. The daughter was five nine. They were all over twenty-one. And they were all scared of their mother. Not literally scared, but Charlotte Zeeman wore the pants in the family. One family dinner and I knew that.

I hung up the phone, turned on the lamp, and started to pack. It occurred to me while I was throwing things into a suitcase to wonder why the hell I was doing this. I could say that it was because Richard was the other third of a triumvirate of power that Jean-Claude had forged between the three of us. Master vampire, Ulfric, or wolf king, and necromancer. I was the necromancer. We were bound so tightly together that sometimes we invaded each other's dreams by accident. Sometimes not so accidentally.

But I wasn't riding to the rescue because Richard was our third. I could admit to myself, if to no one else, that I still loved Richard. Not the same way I loved Jean-Claude, but it was just as real. He was in trouble, and I would help him if I could. Simple. Complicated. Hurtful.

I wondered what Jean-Claude would think of me dropping everything to go rescue Richard. It didn't really matter. I was going, and that was that. But I did spare a thought for how that might make my vampire lover feel. His heart didn't always beat, but it could still break.

Love sucks. Sometimes it feels good. Sometimes it's just another way to bleed.

2

I made phone calls. My friend Catherine Maison-Gillette was an attorney. She'd been with me on more than one occasion when I had to make a statement to the police about a dead body that I helped make dead. So far, no jail time. Hell, no trial. How did I accomplish this? I lied.

Bob, Catherine's husband, answered on the fifth ring, voice so heavy with sleep it was almost unintelligible. Only the bass growl let me know which of them it was. Neither of them woke gracefully.

"Bob, this is Anita. I need to speak with Catherine. It's business."

"You at a police station?" he asked. See, Bob knew me.

"No, I don't need a lawyer for me this time."

He didn't ask questions. He just said, "Here's Catherine. If you think I have no curiosity at all, you're wrong, but Catherine will fill me in after you hang up."

"Thanks, Bob," I said.

"Anita, what's wrong?" Catherine's voice sounded normal. She was a criminal attorney with a private firm. She was wakened a lot at odd hours. She didn't like it, but she recovered well.

I told her the bad news. She knew Richard. Liked him a lot. Didn't understand why in hell I'd dumped him for Jean-Claude. Since I couldn't tell her about Richard being a werewolf, it was sort of hard to explain. Heck, even if I could have mentioned the werewolf part, it was hard to explain.

"Carl Belisarius," she said when I was finished. "He's one of the best criminal attorneys in that state. I know him personally. He's not as careful about his clients as I am. He's got some clients that are known criminal figures, but he's good."

"Can you contact him and get him started?" I asked.

"You need Richard's permission for this, Anita."

"I can't talk Richard into taking on a new attorney until I see him. Time is always precious on a crime, Catherine. Can Belisarius at least start the wheels in motion?"

"Do you know if Richard has an attorney now?"

"Daniel mentioned something about him refusing to see his lawyer, so I assume so."

"Give me Daniel's number, and I'll see what I can do," she said.

"Thanks, Catherine, really."

She sighed. "I know you'd go to this much trouble for any of your friends. You're just that loyal. But are you sure your motives are just friendly in this?"

"What are you asking me?"

"You still love him, don't you?"

"No comment," I said.

Catherine gave a soft laugh. "No comment. You're not the one under suspicion here."

"Says you," I said.

"Fine, I'll do what I can on this end. Let me know when you get there."

"Will do," I said. I hung up and called my main job. Vampire killing was only a sideline. I raised the dead for Animators Inc., the first animating firm in the country. We were also the most profitable. Part of that was due to our boss, Bert Vaughn. He could make a dollar sit up and sing. He didn't like that my helping the police on preternatural crimes was taking more and more of my time. He wouldn't like me going out of town for an indefinite period of time on personal business. I was glad it was the wee hours and he wouldn't be there to yell at me in person.

If Bert kept pushing me, I was going to have to quit, and I didn't want to. I had to raise zombies. It wasn't like a muscle that would wither if you didn't use it. It was an inate ability for me. If I didn't use it, the power would leak out on its own. In college there had been a professor who committed suicide. No one had found the body for the three days that it usually takes for the soul to leave the area. One night, the shambling corpse had come to my dorm room. My roommate got a room switch next day. She had no sense of adventure.

I would raise the dead, one way or another. I had no choice. But I had enough reputation that I could go freelance. I'd need a business manager, but it would work. Trouble is, I didn't want to leave. Some of the people who worked at Animators Inc. were among my best friends. Besides, I had had about as much change as I could handle for one year.

I, Anita Blake, scourge of the undead—the human with more vampire kills than any other vampire executioner in the country—was dating a vampire. It was almost poetically ironic.

The doorbell rang. The sound made my heart pulse in my throat. It was an ordinary sound, but not at 3:45 in the morning. I left my partially packed suitcase on the unmade bed and walked into the living room. My white furniture sat on top of a brilliant oriental rug. Cushions that caught the bright colors were placed casually on the couch and chair. The furniture was mine. The rug and cushions had been gifts from Jean-Claude. His sense of style would always be better than mine. Why argue?

The doorbell rang again. It made me jump for no good reason except it was insistent and it was an odd hour and I was already keyed up from the news about Richard. I went to the door with my favorite gun, a Browning Hi-Power 9mm, in hand, safety off, pointed at the floor. I was almost at the door when I realized I was wearing nothing but my nightgown. A gun, but no robe. I had my priorities in order.

I stood there, barefoot on the elegant rug, debating whether to go back for the robe or a pair of jeans. Something. If I'd been wearing one of my usual extra-large T-shirts, I'd have just answered the door. But I was wearing a black satin nightie with spaghetti straps. It hung almost to my knees. One size does not fit all. It covered everything but wasn't exactly answering-the-door attire. Screw it.

I called, "Who is it?" Bad guys usually didn't ring the doorbell.

"It is Jean-Claude, *ma petite*."

My mouth dropped open. I couldn't have been more surprised if it had been a bad guy. What was he doing here?

I clicked the safety on the gun and opened the door. The satin nightie had been a gift from Jean-Claude. He'd seen me in less. We didn't need the robe.

I opened the door and there he was. It was like I was a magician and had thrown aside the curtain to show my lovely assistant. The sight of him caught my breath in my throat.

His shirt was a conservative business cut with fastened cuffs and a simple collar. It was red with the collar and cuffs a solid almost satiny scarlet. The rest of the shirt was some sheer fabric so that his arms, chest, and waist were bare behind a sheen of red cloth. His black hair curled below his shoulders, darker, richer somehow against the red of the shirt. Even his midnight blue eyes seemed bluer framed by red. It was one of my favorite colors for him to wear, and he knew it. He'd threaded a red cord through the belt loops of his black jeans. The cord fell in knots down one side of his hip. The black boots came almost to the tops of his legs, encasing his long, slender legs in leather from toe to nearly groin.

When I was away from Jean-Claude, away from his body, his voice, I could be embarrassed, scratchy with discomfort that I was dating him. When I was away from him, I could talk myself out of him—almost. But never when I was with him. When I was with him, my stomach dropped to my feet and I had to fight very hard not to say things like *golly*.

I settled for "You look spectacular, as always. What are you doing here on a night that I told you not to come?" What I wanted to do was to throw myself around him like a coat and have him carry me over the threshold clinging to him like a monkey. But I wasn't going to do that. It lacked a certain dignity. Besides, it sort of scared me how much I wanted him—and how often. He was like a new drug. It wasn't vampire powers. It was good, old-fashioned lust. But it was still scary, so I had set up some parameters. Rules. He followed them most of the time.

He smiled, and it was the smile I'd grown to both love and dread. The smile said he was thinking wicked thoughts, things that two or more could do in darkened rooms, where the sheets smelled of expensive perfume, sweat, and other bodily fluids. The smile had never made me blush until we started having sex. Sometimes all he had to do was smile, and heat rushed up my skin like I was thirteen and he was my first crush. He thought it was charming. It embarrassed me.

"You son of a bitch," I said softly.

The smile widened. "Our dream was interrupted, *ma petite*."

"I knew it wasn't an accident that you were in my dreams," I said. It came out hostile, and I was pleased. Because the hot summer wind was blowing the scent of his cologne against my face. Exotic, with an undercurrent of flowers and spice. I almost hated to wash my sheets for fear of losing the scent of him sometimes.

"I asked you to wear my gift so I could dream of you. You knew what I meant to do. If you say other, then you are lying. May I come in?"

He'd been invited in often enough that he could have crossed my threshold without the invitation, but it had become a game with him. A formal acknowledgment every time he crossed that I wanted him. It irritated me and pleased me, like so much about Jean-Claude.

"You might as well come in."

He walked past me. I noticed the black boots were laced up the back from heel to top. The back of his black jeans fit smooth and tight so there was no need to guess what he wasn't wearing under them.

He spoke without turning around. "Do not sound so grumpy, *ma petite*. You have the ability to bar me from your dreams." He turned then, and his eyes were full of a dark light that had nothing to do with vampire powers. "You welcomed me with more than open arms."

I blushed for the second time in less than five minutes. "Richard is in jail in Tennessee," I said.

"I know," he said.

"You know?" I said. "How?"

"The local Master of the City called to tell me. He was very much afraid that I would think it was his doing. His way of destroying our triumvirate."

"If he was going to destroy us, it would be a murder charge, not attempted rape," I said.

"True," Jean-Claude said, then laughed. The laughter trailed over my bare skin like a small, private wind. "Whoever framed our Richard did not know him well. I would believe murder of Richard before rape."

It was almost exactly what I'd said. Why was that unnerving? "Are you going down to Tennessee?"

"The master, Colin, has forbidden me to enter his lands. To do so now would be an act of aggression, if not outright war."

"Why should he care?" I asked.

"He fears my power, *ma petite*. He fears our power, which is why he has made you persona non grata in his territory as well."

I stared at him. "You are kidding, I hope. He's forbidden either of us to help Richard?"

Jean-Claude nodded.

"And he expects us to believe it's not his doing?" I said.

"I believe him, *ma petite*."

"You could tell he wasn't lying over the phone?" I asked.

"Some master vampires can lie to other master vampires, though I do not think Colin is such a power. But that is not why I believe him."

"Why then?"

"The last time you and I traveled to another vampire's lands, we slew her."

"She was trying to kill us," I said.

"Technically," he said, "she had set all of us free save you. You she wished to make a vampire."

"Like I said, she was trying to kill me."

He smiled. "Oh, *ma petite*, you wound me."

"Cut the crap. This Colin can't really believe that we are just going to leave Richard to rot."

"He has the right to deny us safe passage," Jean-Claude said.

"Because we killed another master in her own territory?" I asked.

"He doesn't need grounds for his refusal, *ma petite*. He merely has to refuse."

"How do you vampires get anything accomplished?"

"Slowly," Jean-Claude said. "But remember, *ma petite*, we have the time to be patient."

"Well, I don't, and Richard doesn't."

"You could have eternity if you would both accept the fourth mark," he said, voice quiet, neutral.

I shook my head. "Richard and I both value what little is left of our humanity. Besides, eternity my ass, the fourth mark wouldn't make us immortal. It just means that we live as long as you do. You're harder to kill than we are, but not that much harder."

He sat down on the couch, folding his legs under him. It wasn't an easy position, wearing that much leather. Maybe the boots were softer than they looked. Naw.

He rested his elbows on the couch arm, leaning his chest outward. The sheer red cloth covered his chest completely and left nothing to the imagination. His nipples pressed against the thin fabric. The red haze of cloth made the cross-shaped burn scar look almost bloody.

He raised himself upward with his hands propped on the couch arm like a mermaid on a rock. I expected him to tease or say something sexual. Instead, he said, "I came to tell you of Richard's imprisonment in person." He watched my face very closely. "I thought it might upset you."

"Of course it upsets me. This Colin guy, vampire, whatever the hell he is, is crazy if he thinks he's going to keep us from helping Richard."

Jean-Claude smiled. "Asher is negotiating even as we speak to try and allow you to enter Colin's territory."

Asher was his second banana, his vampire lieutenant. I frowned. "Why me and not you?"

"Because you are much better with police matters than I am." He threw one long, leather-clad leg over the couch arm and slithered over it to his feet. It was like watching a lap dance without a lap. To my knowledge, Jean-Claude had never stripped at Guilty Pleasures, the vampire strip club he owned, but he could have. He had a way of making even the smallest movement sexual and vaguely obscene. You always felt like he was thinking wicked thoughts, things you couldn't say in mixed company.

"Why didn't you just call and tell me all this?" I said. I knew the answer, or at least part of it. He seemed to be as enamored of my body as I was of his. Good sex cuts both ways. The seducer can become the seduced, with the right victim.

He glided towards me. "I thought this was news to be delivered face-to-face."

He stopped just in front of me, so close that the slightly full hem of my nightie brushed his thighs. He gave a small movement of his body and the satin edge of the nightie moved gently against my bare legs. Most men would have had to use their hands to get that kind of movement. Of course, Jean-Claude had had four hundred years to perfect his technique. Practice makes perfect.

"Why face-to-face?" I asked, my voice a little breathy.

A smile curled his lips. "You know why," he said.

"I want to hear you say it," I said.

His beautiful face fell into blank, careful lines, only his eyes held the heat like a banked fire. "I could not let you leave without touching you one last time. I want to do the wicked dance before you leave."

I laughed, but it was tense, nervous. My mouth was suddenly dry. I was having trouble not staring at his chest. The "wicked dance" was his pet euphemism for sex. I wanted to touch him, but if I did, I wasn't sure where it would stop. Richard was in trouble. I'd betrayed him once with Jean-Claude; I wouldn't let him down again. "I need to pack," I said. I turned abruptly and started walking towards the bedroom.

He followed me.

I put my gun on the bedside table beside the phone, got socks out of the drawer, and started tossing them into the suitcase, trying to ignore Jean-Claude. He doesn't ignore easily. He lay on the bed beside the suitcase, propped on one elbow, long legs stretched the length of the bed. He looked fearfully overdressed against my white sheets. He watched me move around the room, moving just his eyes. He reminded me of a cat: watchful, perfectly at ease.

I went into the nearby bathroom to get toiletries. I had a man's shaving kit bag that I kept all the small stuff in. I was traveling out of town more and more lately. Might as well be organized about it.

Jean-Claude was lying on his back, long, black hair spilling like a dark dream on my white pillow. He gave a slight smile as I entered the room. He held a hand out to me. "Join me, *ma petite.*"

I shook my head. "If I join you, we'll get distracted. I'm going to pack and get dressed. We don't have time for anything else."

He crawled towards me over the bed, moving in a rolling glide like he had muscles in places he wasn't supposed to have them. "Am I so unappealing, *ma petite?* Or is your concern for Richard so overwhelming?"

"You know exactly how appealing you are to me. And yes, I am worried about Richard."

He slid off the bed, following at my heels. He glided in a sort of graceful slow motion while I hurried to and fro, but he paced me, matching each of my quick steps with his easy ones. It was like being chased by a very slow predator, one that had all the time in the world but knew in the end it would catch you.

The second time I almost ran into him, I finally said, "What is your problem? Quit following me around. You're making me nervous." Truth was, his body being so close made my skin jump.

He sat down on the edge of the bed and sighed, "I don't want you to go."

That stopped me in my tracks. I turned and stared at him. "Why, for heaven's sake?"

"For centuries I have dreamed of having enough power to be safe. Enough power to hold my lands and finally, at long last, have some sense of peace. Now I fear the very man who could make my ambitions come true."

"What are you talking about?" I came to stand in front of him, arms full of shirts and hangers.

"Richard; I fear Richard." There was a look in his eyes that I'd seldom seen. He was unsure of himself. It was a very normal, human expression. It looked totally at odds with the elegant man in his peekaboo shirt.

"Why would you be afraid of Richard?" I asked.

"If you love Richard more than you love me, I fear you will leave me for him."

"If you haven't noticed, Richard hates me right now. He talks more to you than to me."

"He does not hate you, *ma petite*. He hates that you are with me. There is a great difference between the two hatreds." Jean-Claude stared up at me almost mournfully.

I sighed. "Are you jealous of Richard?"

He looked down at the toes of his expensive boots. "I would be a fool if I were not."

I transferred the blouses to one arm and touched his face. I turned his face up to mine. "I'm sleeping with you, not Richard, remember?"

"Yet, here I am, *ma petite*. I am dressed for your dreams and you do not even offer me a kiss."

His reaction surprised me. Just when I thought I knew him. "Are you hurt that I didn't give you a hello kiss?"

"Perhaps," he said very softly.

I shook my head and tossed the blouses in the general direction of the suitcase. I bumped his knees with my legs until he opened his legs and let me stand, pressing my body the length of his. I put my hands on his shoulders. The sheer red cloth was rougher textured than it looked, not soft. "How can anyone as gorgeous as you are be insecure?"

He wrapped his arms around my waist, snuggling me against him. He squeezed his legs against me. The leather of the boots was softer than it looked, more supple. With his arms around me and his legs squeezing against me, I was effectively trapped. But I was a willing captive, so it was okay.

"What I want to do is go down on my knees and lick the front of this nifty shirt. I want to know just how much of you I can suck through the cloth." I raised my eyebrows at him.

He laughed soft and low. The sound raised goose bumps up and down my body, tightening my nipples and other places. His laughter was a touchable, intrusive thing. He could do things with his voice that most men couldn't do with their hands. Yet he was afraid I'd leave him for Richard.

He rested his face on my chest, cradled between my breasts. He rubbed his cheeks softly back and forth against me, making the satin slide against me, until my breath came faster.

I sighed and leaned my face over him, folding our bodies together. "I don't plan to leave you for Richard. But he's in trouble, and that comes before sex."

Jean-Claude raised his face to me, our arms so entangled that he almost couldn't move. "Kiss me, *ma petite*, that is all. Just a kiss to tell me that you love me."

I laid my lips against his forehead. "I thought you were more secure than this."

"I am," he said, "with everyone but you."

I pulled back enough to study his face. "Love should make you feel more secure not less."

"Yes," he said quietly, "it should. But you love Richard, too. You try not to love him, and he tries not to love you. But love is not so easily slain—or so easily aroused."

I bent over him. The first kiss was a mere brush of lips like satin rubbing against my mouth. The second kiss was harder. I bit lightly along his upper lip, and he made a small sound. He kissed me back, hands sliding to either side of my face. He kissed me as if he were drinking me down, trying to lick the last drops from the bottle of some fine wine, tender, eager, hungry. I collapsed against him, hands sliding over him as if even my hands were hungry for the feel of him.

I felt his fangs, sharp, bruising against my lips and tongue. There was a quick, sharp pain and the sweet copper taste of blood. He made a small inarticulate sound and rolled over me. I was suddenly on the bed with him above me. His eyes were one solid glowing blue, the pupils gone in a rush of desire.

He tried to turn my head to one side, nuzzling at my neck. I turned my face into his, blocking him. "No blood, Jean-Claude."

He went almost limp on top of me, face buried in the rumpled sheets. "Please, *ma petite*."

I pushed at his shoulder. "Get off of me."

He rolled onto his back, staring at the ceiling, carefully not looking at me. "I can enter every orifice of your body with every part of me, but you refuse me the last bit of yourself."

I got off the bed carefully, not sure my knees were steady. "I am not food," I said.

"It is so much more than mere feeding, *ma petite*. If only you would allow me to show you how very much more."

I grabbed the pile of blouses and started taking them off the hanger and folding them in the suitcase. "No blood; that is the rule."

He rolled onto his side. "I have offered you all that I am, *ma petite*, yet you withhold yourself from me. How can I not be jealous of Richard?"

"You're getting sex. He's not even getting dates."

"You are mine, but you are not mine, not completely."

"I'm not a pet, Jean-Claude. People aren't supposed to belong to other people."

"If you could find a way to love Richard's beast, you would not hold back from him. Him you would give yourself to."

I folded the last blouse. "Damn it, Jean-Claude, this is stupid. I chose you. All right? It's a done deal. Why are you so worried?"

"Because the moment he was in trouble, you dropped everything to run to his side."

"I'd do the same for you," I said.

"Exactly," he said. "I have no doubt that you love me in your way, but you love him, too."

I zipped up the suitcase. "We are not having this argument. I'm sleeping with you. I am not going to donate blood just to make you feel more secure."

The phone rang. Asher's cultured voice, so like Jean-Claude's: "Anita, how are you this fine summer evening?"

"I'm fine, Asher. What's up?"

"May I speak with Jean-Claude?" he asked.

I almost argued, but Jean-Claude had his hand out for the phone. I gave the phone to him.

Jean-Claude spoke in French, which he and Asher had a habit of doing. I was glad that he had someone to speak his native tongue with, but my French just wasn't up to following the conversation. I suspected strongly that sometimes the vampires spoke in front of me like you would speak in front of a child that doesn't have enough grown-up talk to follow the conversation. It was rude and condescending, but they were centuries-old vampires, and sometimes they just couldn't help themselves.

He switched to English, talking directly to me. "Colin has refused you entrance to his territory. He has refused entrance to any of my people."

"Can he do that?" I asked.

Jean-Claude nodded. *"Oui."*

"I am going down there to help Richard. Arrange it, Jean-Claude, or I'll go down there without arrangements being made."

"Even if it's war?" he asked.

"Shit," I said. "Call the little son of a bitch and let me talk to him."

Jean-Claude raised his eyebrows but nodded. He hung up on Asher, then dialed a number. He said, "Colin, this is Jean-Claude. Yes, Asher told me what you have decided. My human servant, Anita Blake, wishes to speak with you." He listened for a moment. "No, I do not know what she wishes to say to you." He handed me the phone and settled back against the headboard of the bed as if watching a show.

"Hello, Colin?"

"This is he." His accent was pure Middle American. It made him sound less exotic than some of them.

"My name's Anita Blake."

"I know who you are," he said. "You're the Executioner."

"Yeah, but I'm not coming down there for an execution. My friend is in trouble. I just want to help him."

"He is your third. If you enter my lands, then two of your triumvirate will be within my territory. You are too powerful to be allowed entrance."

"Asher said you also denied access to any of our people, is that true?"

"Yes," he said.

"Why, for God's sake?"

"The Council, the rulers of all vampire kind, itself fears Jean-Claude. I will not have you in my lands."

"Colin, look, I don't want your power base. I don't want your lands. I have no designs upon you whatsoever. You're a master vampire. You can taste the truth in my words."

"You mean what you say, but you are the servant. Jean-Claude is the master."

"Don't take this wrong, Colin, but why would Jean-Claude want your lands? Even if he was planning some sort of Ghengis Kahn invasion, your lands are three territories away from us. If he was going to try conquering someone, he'd pick land next door."

"Maybe there's something here he wants," Colin said, and I could hear the fear in his voice. That was rare with a master vamp. They were usually better at hiding their emotions.

"Colin, I'll swear any oath you want that we don't want anything from you. We just need for me to come down there and get Richard out of jail. Okay?"

"No," he said. "If you come down here uninvited, it is war between us, and I will kill you."

"Look, Colin, I know you're afraid." As soon as I said it, I knew I shouldn't have.

"How do you know what I feel?" The fear rose a notch, but the anger rose faster. "A human servant that can taste a master vampire's fear—and you wonder why I don't want you in my lands."

"I can't taste your fear, Colin. I heard it in your voice."

"Liar!"

My shoulders were beginning to tighten. It doesn't usually take much to piss me off, and he was working at it. "How are we supposed to help Richard, if you won't let us send anyone down there?" My voice was calm, but I could feel my throat tightening, my voice going just a little lower with the effort not to yell.

"What happens to your third is not my concern. Protecting my lands and my people, that is my concern."

"If anything happens to Richard because of this delay, I can make it your concern," I said, voice still quiet.

"See, already the threats begin."

The tightness in my shoulders spilled up my neck and came out my mouth. "Listen, you little pip-squeak, I am coming down there. I am not letting your paranoia hurt Richard."

"We will kill you then," he said.

"Look, Colin, stay out of my way, and I'll stay out of yours. You fuck with me, and I will destroy you, do you understand me? It's only war if you start it, but if you start something, by God I will finish it."

Jean-Claude was motioning for the phone rather desperately. We wrestled for the receiver for a few seconds while I called Colin an antiquated politician, and worse.

Jean-Claude apologized to the empty, buzzing phone. He hung the phone up and looked at me. The look was eloquent. "I would say I am speechless, *ma petite*, or that I don't believe that you just did that, but I do believe it. The question is: Do you understand what you have just done?"

"I am going to rescue Richard. I can go around Colin or over him. It's his choice."

Jean-Claude sighed. "He is within his rights to see it as the beginning of a war. But Colin is very cautious. He will do one of two things. He will either wait and see if you initiate hostilities, or he will try and kill you as soon as you set foot on his lands."

I shook my head. "What was I supposed to do?"

"It doesn't matter now. What's done is done, but it changes the travel arrangements. You can still take my private jet, but you will have company."

"Are you coming?" I asked.

"No. If I arrived with you, Colin would be certain that we had come to kill him. No, I will stay here, but you will have an entourage of guards."

"Now, wait a minute," I said.

He held up his hand. "No, *ma petite*. You have been very rash. Remember, if you die, Richard and I may die, as well. The binding that makes us a triumvirate gives power, but it does not come without a price. It is not merely your own life that you are risking."

That stopped me. "I hadn't thought of it that way," I said.

"You will need an entourage now that befits a human servant of mine, and an entourage that is strong enough to fight Colin's people, if need be."

"Who do you have in mind?" I asked, suddenly suspicious.

"Leave that to me."

"I don't think so," I said.

He stood, and his anger lashed through the room like a scalding wind. "You have endangered yourself and me and Richard. You have endangered everything we have or hope to have with your temper."

"It would have come down to an ultimatum in the end, Jean-Claude. I know vampires. You would have argued and bargained for a day or two, but in the end, it would have come down to this."

"Are you so sure?" he asked.

"Yeah," I said. "I heard the fear in Colin's voice. He's scared shitless of you. He'd have never agreed to us coming down."

"It is not just me he fears, *ma petite*. You are the Executioner. Young vampires are told if they are foolish, you will come and slay them in their coffins."

"You're making that up," I said.

He shook his head. "No, *ma petite*, you are the bogeyman of vampirekind."

"If I see Colin, I'll try not to scare him more than I already have."

"You will see him, *ma petite*, one way or the other. He will either arrange a meeting when he sees you mean him no harm, or he will be there when they attack."

"We have to get Richard out before the full moon. We've only got five days. We didn't have time to do this slowly."

"Who are you trying to convince, *ma petite*, me or yourself?"

I had lost my temper. It had been stupid. Inexcusable. I had a temper, but I was usually better at controlling it than that. "I'm sorry," I said.

Jean-Claude gave a very inelegant snort. "Now she's sorry." He dialed the phone. "I will have Asher and the others pack."

"Asher?" I said. "He's not going with me."

"Yes, he is."

I opened my mouth to protest. He pointed one long, pale finger at me. "I know

Colin and his people. You need an entourage that is impressive without being too frightening, and yet if the worst happens, they must be able to defend you and themselves. I will pick who goes and who stays.''

"That's not fair."

"There is no time for fairness, *ma petite*. Your precious Richard sits behind bars and the full moon is approaching." He let his hand fall to his lap. "If you wish to take some of your wereleopards with you, that would be welcome. Asher and Damian will need food while they are away. They cannot hunt within Colin's territory. That would be taken as an act of hostility."

"You want me to volunteer some of the wereleopards as walking provisions?"

"I am going to supply some werewolves as well," he said.

"I'm lupa for the pack as well as Nimir-ra for the leopards. You need to run the wolves by me, too." Richard had made me lupa of the werewolves when we were dating. Lupa is often just another word for the head wolf's girlfriend, though usually it's another werewolf, not a human. The wereleopards came to me by default. I killed their last leader and found out that everyone else was pretty much beating the hell out of them. Weak shape-shifters without a dominant to protect them end up as anyone's meat. It was my fault, sort of, that they were being hurt, so I extended my protection over them. My protection, since I wasn't a wereleopard, consisted of my threat. My threat was that I'd kill anyone who messed with them. The monsters in town must have believed it, because they left the leopards alone. Use enough silver bullets on enough monsters, and you get a reputation.

Jean-Claude put the receiver up to his ear. "It is getting so that a person cannot insult a monster in Saint Louis without answering to you, *ma petite*." If I hadn't known better, I'd say Jean-Claude was angry with me.

I guess, this once, I couldn't blame him.

3

The private jet was like a long white egg with fins. Okay, it was longer than an egg and more pointy at the ends, but it seemed just as fragile. Have I mentioned I have this little phobia about flying? I sat in my comfy, fully swivel, fully reclinable chair very upright, seat-belted in, fingernails digging into the cushioned arms. I had purposefully turned the seat away from one of the many round windows so I couldn't see out the side nearest me. Unfortunately, the plane was so narrow that I caught glimpses on the opposite side windows of fluffy clouds and clear blue sky. Hard to forget you're thousands of feet above the ground with only a thin sheet of metal between you and eternity when clouds keep floating past the window.

Jason plopped down in the seat next to me, and I let out a little yip. He laughed. "I can't believe you're this scared of flying." He pushed his chair with his feet, making it spin around, slowly, like a kid with Daddy's office chair. His thin blond hair was cut just above his shoulders, no bangs. His eyes were the same pale blue as the sky we were flying through. He was exactly my height, five three, which made him short, especially for a man. He never seemed to mind. He wore an oversized T-shirt and a pair of jeans so faded they were almost white. He wore two hundred dollar jogging shoes, though I knew for a fact he never jogged.

He'd turned twenty-one this summer. He'd informed me that he was a Gemini, and he was now legal for everything. Everything could cover a lot of ground for Jason. He was a werewolf, but he currently lived with Jean-Claude and played morning appetizer or evening snack for the vampire. Shapeshifter blood has a bigger kick to it, more power. You can drink less of it than human blood and feel a hell of a lot better, or so I've observed.

He flung himself up from the chair and fell to his knees in front of me. "Come on, Anita. What's to worry?"

"Leave me alone, Jason. It's a phobia. It has no logic. You can't talk me out of it, so just go away."

He sprang to his feet so fast it was almost magical. "We're perfectly safe." He started jumping up and down on the floor on the plane. "See, solid."

I yelled, "Zane!"

Zane appeared beside me. He was about six feet tall, stretched long and thin as if there wasn't enough flesh to cover his bones. His hair had been dyed a shocking yellow, like neon buttercups, shaved on the sides and gelled into small, stiff spikes on top. He wore black vinyl pants, like a slick second skin, and a matching vest, no shirt. Shiny black boots completed the outfit.

"You rang?" he asked in a voice that was almost painfully deep. If a shape-shifter spends too much time in animal form, some of the physical changes can be permanent. Zane's gravelly voice and the dainty upper and lower fangs in his human mouth said he'd spent a little too much time as a leopard. The voice could have passed for human, but the fangs—the fangs gave it away.

"Get Jason away from me, please," I said through gritted teeth.

Zane looked down at the smaller man.

Jason stood his ground.

Zane moved those last two steps to close the distance between them. They stood there, pressed chest to chest, eyes locked. You could suddenly feel that skin-crawling energy that let you know that human was not what they were.

Shit. I hadn't meant to start a fight.

Zane lowered his face toward the shorter man, a low growl trickling out of his closed lips.

"No fighting, boys," I said.

Zane planted a big, wet kiss on Jason's mouth.

Jason jerked back, laughing. "You bisexual son of a bitch."

"Now, if that isn't the pot calling the kettle black," Zane said.

Jason just grinned and wandered off, though there wasn't a lot of room to wander anywhere. I also have a touch of claustrophobia. I got it from a diving accident, but I've noticed it's worse since I woke up one morning trapped in a coffin with a vampire I didn't like. I got away, but I like enclosed spaces less and less.

Zane slid into the seat beside me. The shiny black vest gaped over his thin, pale chest, giving a glimpse of a silver nipple ring.

Zane patted my knee, and I let him. He was always touching people, nothing personal. A lot of shapeshifters were touchy-feely, as if they were animals instead of people and had fewer physical boundaries, but Zane had turned to casual touch into an art form. I finally realized that he touched others as a sort of security blanket. He tried to play the dominant predator, but he wasn't. Underneath the show of teasing confidence, he knew it. He got really tense if he was in a social situation where he had to stand alone, literally without the touch of other flesh. So I let him touch me when I'd have bitched at anyone else.

"We'll be on the ground soon," he said. The hand left my knee. He understood the rules. I let him touch me when he had no business doing it, but no long, lingering caresses. I was his touchstone when he was nervous, not his girlfriend.

"I know," I said.

He smiled. "But you don't believe me."

"Let's just say I'll relax when we actually land."

Cherry joined us. She was tall and slender, with straight, naturally blond hair cut very, very short and close to a strong, triangular face. The eye shadow was gray, the eyeliner so black it looked like crayon. The lipstick was black. The makeup wasn't the colors I'd have chosen for her, but it did match her clothes. Black fishnet stockings, vinyl miniskirt, black go-go boots, and a black lace bra underneath a fishnet shirt. She'd added the bra for my benefit. Left to her own devices, when she wasn't working as a nurse, she went pretty much topless. She'd been a nurse until they found out she was a wereleopard; then she'd been the victim of budget cuts. Maybe it was budget cuts, but then again, maybe it wasn't. It was illegal to discriminate against someone because they had a disease, but no one wants a were-anything treating the sick. People seem to think lycanthropes can't control themselves around freshly spilled blood. Some of the newer shape-shifters would be in trouble, but Cherry wasn't new. She'd been a good nurse, and now she'd never be a nurse again. She was bitter about it and had turned herself into the slut bride from Planet X, as if even in human form, she wanted people to know what she was now: different, other. Trouble was, she looked like a thousand other teens and early twenties who also wanted to be different and stand out.

"What happens once we land?" Cherry asked in a purring, contralto voice. I'd thought her voice had been the product of too much fur time, like Zane's teeth, but nope, Cherry just had this wonderful, deep, sexy voice. She'd have done good phone sex. She sat on the ground at our feet, knees out, ankles crossed, making the short skirt ride up enough to show the hose were thigh high but still managing to cover the rest. Though in a skirt that short, I was hoping she was wearing undies. I'd have never have been able to wear something that short and not flash.

"I contact Richard's brother and go to the jail," I said.

"What do you want us to do?" Zane asked.

"Jean-Claude said that he made arrangements for rooms, so you guys go to the rooms."

They exchanged a glance. It was more than an ordinary glance.

"What?" I asked.

"One of us will need to go with you," Zane said.

"No, I'm going to go in there flashing my executioner's license. I'm better off on my own."

"What if the master of this city has his people waiting for you in town?" Zane asked. "He'll know you're going to the jail today."

Cherry nodded. "It could be an ambush."

They had a point, but . . . "Look, nothing personal, guys, but you look like the top half of an S and M wedding cake. Cops don't like people who look sort of . . ." I wasn't sure how to say it without being insulting. Cops were meat-and-potatoes people. They weren't impressed by the exotic. They'd seen it all and cleaned up the mess. Most of the exotic that they saw were bad guys. After a while, policemen seem to think anything exotic is a bad guy; just saves time.

If I walked into the police station with Tweedle-punk and Tweedle-slut, it was going to raise the cop's antennae. They'd know I wasn't exactly what I was claiming to be, and that would complicate things. We needed to make things easier, not harder.

I was dressed in vampire executioner casual. New black jeans, not faded, crimson short-sleeved dress shirt, black suit jacket, black Nikes, black belt so the loops of my shoulder holster had something to hang on. The Browning Hi-Power sat under my left arm, a familiar tightness. I was carrying three blades. A silver knife in a wrist sheath on each arm and a blade in a sheath down my spine. The handle stuck up high enough that my hair had to hide it, but my hair was thick and dark enough to do the job. The last blade was like a small sword. I'd used it only once for real to pin a wereleopard through the heart. The tip had pushed out his back. A silver cross under the blouse for true emergencies, and I was packed for were-bear, or almost anything else. I had a spare clip of normal bullets in my fanny pack just in case I met up with a rogue fairie. Silver didn't work against them.

"I'll go with you." Nathaniel slid in behind Cherry, pressing himself against the wall of the plane and my legs. One broad shoulder rested against my jeans in a nice, solid weight. There was actually no way for him to sit there and not touch me. He was always trying to touch me, and he was good enough at it that I couldn't always bitch about it, like now.

"I don't think so, Nathaniel," I said.

He hugged his knees to his chest and asked, "Why not?" He was dressed normally enough in jeans and a tucked-in T-shirt, but the rest of him . . . His hair was a deep, nearly mahogany auburn. He'd tied it back in a loose ponytail, but the hair fell like silken water to his knees.

Nathaniel gazed up at me with eyes the pale purple of Easter egg grass. Even if he cut the hair, the eyes would have given him trouble. He was short for a man, and was also the youngest of us, nineteen. I suspected strongly that he was in the middle of a growth spurt. Someday, that short body was going to match his shoulders, which were broad and very masculine. He was a stripper at Guilty Pleasures, a wereleopard, and once he'd been a male prostitute. I'd put a stop to that. If you're going to be leopard queen, you might as well rule. The rule was that none of the leopards were whores. Gabriel, their old alpha, had pimped them out. Shapeshifters can take a lot of damage and survive. Gabriel had figured out a way to make that pay. He pimped his kitties out to the S and M set. People who liked to give pain had paid a lot of money for Nathaniel, once upon a time. The first time I'd ever seen him was in the hospital after a client had gotten carried away and nearly killed him. Admittedly, this was after Gabriel had been killed. The wereleopards had tried to keep up the client list without anyone to protect them from the clients.

Zane had tried to take Gabriel's place as pimp and bad-ass kitty, but he hadn't been strong enough to fill the bill. He'd let Nathaniel nearly die and hadn't been able to protect him.

Nathaniel could bench-press a grand piano, but he was a victim. He liked pain and wanted someone to be in charge of him. He wanted a master and was trying very hard for me to take the job. We might have worked something out, but being his master—or mistress—seemed to include sex, and that I was not up for.

"I'll go," Jason said. He sat down beside Cherry and laid his head on her shoulder, snuggling. Cherry moved away from him, cuddling closer to Nathaniel. It wasn't sex, exactly, it was that the wereanimals tended to get up close and personal with their own kind. It was considered something of a social gaffe to cuddle up to a different sort of animal. But Jason didn't care. Cherry was female, and he flirted with anything that was female. Nothing personal, just habit.

Jason wiggled his butt until Cherry was pressed between him and Nathaniel. "I've got a suit in my luggage. A nice, normal, blue suit. I'll even wear a tie."

Cherry growled at him. It sounded all wrong, coming from that pretty face. I am not one of those women who wants to redo other women. I don't care much for makeup or clothes. But Cherry made me want to give her hints. If she was pretty in the Bride of Frankenstein makeup, she'd have been a knockout in something that matched her skin tone.

I smiled. "Thanks, Jason. Now, give Cherry some breathing room."

He pressed himself even closer. "Zane gave me a kiss to make me move."

"Move, or I'll bite your nose off." She gave an expression that was half-snarl, half-smile, a threatening flash of teeth.

"I think she means it," I said.

Jason laughed and stood in one of those lightning-fast movements that they were all capable of. He went to stand behind my seat, leaning his forearms on it.

"I'll hide behind you until it's safe," he said.

"Get off the back of my seat," I said.

He moved his arms but stayed standing behind me. "Jean-Claude thought you might have to take some of us into police situations. We can't all look like college students and porn stars."

The porn star comment was sadly accurate for all three of the wereleopards. Another good idea of Gabriel's had been to star his people in porno films. Gabriel did his own share of starring roles. He was never one to ask of his kitties what he wasn't willing—nay, eager—to do himself. He'd been a sick son of a bitch, and he'd made sure that his wereleopards were as sick as he was.

Nathaniel had given me a gift box of three of his movies. He suggested we watch them together. I said thanks, but no thanks. I kept the tapes mainly because I wasn't sure what to do with them. I mean, he'd given me a gift. I was raised not to be rude. They were way in the back of my video cabinet, hidden behind a stack of Disney tapes. And no, I had not watched them once I was alone.

The air slapped against the plane, making it shudder. Turbulence, just turbulence. "You're actually pale," Cherry said.

"Yeah," I said.

Jason kissed the top of my head. "You know you're actually cute when you're scared."

I turned very slowly in the seat and stared at him. I would have liked to say I stared at him until his smile faded away, but we didn't have that kind of time. Jason would grin on his way into hell. "Don't touch me."

The grin widened. His eyes sparkled with it. "Who me?"

I sighed and settled back into the seat. It was going to be a very long couple of days.

4

Portaby Airfield is small. I guess that's why it's called an airfield instead of an airport. There were two small runways and a cluster of buildings, if three could be called a cluster. But it was clean and neat as a pin, and the setting was postcard perfect. The airfield sat in the middle of a wide, green valley surrounded on three sides by the gentle slopes of the Smokey Mountains. On the fourth side, behind the buildings, was the rest of the valley. It sloped sharply down, letting us know that the valley we were standing in was still part of the mountains. The town of Myerton, Tennessee, stretched below us in air so clean it sparkled like someone had dusted the clouds with ground diamonds. Words came to mind like *pristine, crystalline.*

That was the main reason one of the last remaining wild bands of Lesser Smokey Mountain Trolls lived in the area. Richard was finishing up his master's degree in biology. He'd been studying the trolls every summer for four years between teaching full time. Takes longer to get your master's degree part time.

I took a deep breath of the clean, clean air. I could see why Richard would want to spend his summers here. It was exactly the kind of place he'd enjoy. He was into outdoorsy stuff in a big way. Rock climbing, hiking, fishing, camping, canoeing, bird-watching—pretty much anything you could do outside was his idea of fun. Oh, caving, too. Though I guess, technically, you're not outside if you're inside a cave.

When I said that Richard was a Boy Scout, I didn't mean just his moral fiber.

A man walked towards us. He was almost perfectly round in the middle, wearing a pair of coveralls with oil on the knees. White hair stuck out from underneath a billed cap. His glasses were black-rimmed and square. He wiped his hands on a rag as he walked. The look on his face was polite, curious. His eyes flicked from me to the rest of the guys as they filed out of the plane. Then his eyes flicked to the coffins that were being unloaded from the storage compartment. Asher was in one. Damian was in the other.

Asher was the more powerful of the two, but he was several hundred years younger. Damian had been a Viking when he was alive, and I don't mean the

324   BLACK MOON INN

football team. He'd been a card-carrying, sword-wielding, marauding raider. One night he'd raided the wrong castle, and she took him. If she had a name, I've never heard it. She was a master vampire and ruler of her lands, the equivalent to Master of the City when there is no city in a hundred miles. She took Damian on a summer night over a thousand years ago, and she kept him. A thousand years, and he felt no more powerful in my head than a vampire half his age. I'd underestimated his age by hundreds of years, because part of me just couldn't accept that you could exist that long and not be more powerful, scarier. Damian was scary but not a millennium worth of scary. He'd never be more than he was: a third or fourth banana for all eternity. Jean-Claude bargained for Damian's freedom when he came to be Master of the City. He ransomed Damian. I never knew what it cost Jean-Claude, but I knew that it hadn't been cheap. She had not wanted to give up her favorite whipping boy.

The man said, "I'd shake your hand, but I've been working on the planes. Mr. Niley's man is waiting in the building."

I frowned. "Mr. Niley?"

He frowned then. "Aren't you Mr. Niley's people? Milo said you'd be coming in today." He looked back, and a tall man stepped out of the building. His skin was the color of coffee, two creams. His hair was cut in a wedge, leaving his elegant, sculpted face bare and unadorned. He was wearing a suit that cost more than most cars. He stared at me, and even from a distance I felt the dead weight of his eyes. All he needed was a sign over his head that said Muscle.

"No, we're not Mr. Niley's people." That he'd made the mistake made me wonder who Mr. Niley was.

A voice called, "These are the people I've been expecting, Ed." It was Jamil, one of Richard's enforcers. The enforcers were Sköll and Hati after the wolves that chase the sun and moon in Norse mythology. When they catch them, it will be the end of the world. Tells you something about werewolf society that their enforcers were named after creatures that would bring about the end of everything. Jamil was Sköll for Richard's pack, which meant he was head enforcer. He was tall and slender in the way a dancer is slender, all muscles and shoulders planed down to a smooth, graceful machine of flesh. He was wearing a white sleeveless men's undershirt and loose, tailored white pants with a very sharp cuff rolled at the end of the pants legs. Black suspenders graced his upper body and matched the highly polished black shoes. A white linen jacket was thrown over one shoulder. His dark skin gleamed against the whiteness of his clothes. His hair was nearly waist length in cornrows with white beads woven through the braids. Last time I'd seen him, the beads had been multicolored.

Ed flicked a look back at Jamil. "If you say so," he said. He went back to the main building, leaving us to ourselves. Probably just as well.

"I didn't know you were here, Jamil," I said.

"I'm Richard's bodyguard. Where else would I be?"

He had a point. "Where were you the night his body was supposedly attacking this woman?"

"Her name is Betty Schaffer."

"Have you talked to her?"

His eyes widened. "She's already cried rape once on a fine, upstanding white boy. No, I haven't talked to her."

"You could try and blend in a little."

"I'm one of only two black men for about 50 miles," he said, "There's no way for me to blend in, Anita, so I don't try." There was an undercurrent of real anger there. I wondered if Jamil had been having trouble with the locals. It seemed likely. He wasn't just African American. He was tall, handsome, and athletic looking. That alone would have gotten him on the redneck hit parade. The long cornrow hair and the killer fashion sense raised the question that he might violate the last white male bastion of homophobia. I knew that Jamil liked girls, but I was almost willing to bet some of the locals hadn't believed that.

"I assume that is the other African American guy." I was careful not to point at Milo. He was watching us, face expressionless, but too intense. Muscle recognizes muscle, and he was probably wondering about Jamil just as we were wondering about him. What was professional muscle doing out here in the boonies?

Jamil nodded. "Yeah, that's the other one."

"He doesn't blend in, either," I said. "Who is he?"

"His name is Milo Hart. He works for a guy named Frank Niley who is supposed to arrive today."

"You and he sit down and have a talk?"

"No, but Ed is just full of news."

"Why does Frank Niley need a bodyguard?"

"He's rich," Jamil said as if that explained it, and maybe it did. "He's down here doing some land speculation."

"Ed the plane mechanic tell you all this?"

Jamil nodded. "He likes to talk, even to me."

"Gee, and I thought you were just another pretty face."

Jamil smiled. "I'll do my job when Richard lets me."

"What's that supposed to mean?"

"It means if he'd let me watch over him like a good Sköll is supposed to, this rape charge would never have happened. I'd have been a witness, and it wouldn't be just her word against his."

"Maybe I should talk to Ms. Schaffer," I said.

"Babe, you just read my mind."

"You know, Jamil, you're the only person who ever calls me babe. There's a reason for that."

His smile widened. "I'll try to remember that."

"What happened to Richard, Jamil?"

"You mean did he do it?"

I shook my head. "No, I know he didn't do it."

"He did date her," Jamil said.

I looked at him. "What are you saying?"

"Richard's been trying to find a replacement for you."

"So?"

"So, he's been dating anything that moves."

"Just dating?" I asked.

Jamil swirled his jacket from his shoulder to one arm, smoothing the cloth and not looking at me.

"Answer the question, Jamil."

He looked at me, almost smiling, then sighed. "No, not just dating."

I had to ask. "He's been sleeping around?"

Jamil nodded.

I stood there, thinking about that for a second or two. Richard and I had each been celibate for years, separate decisions. I'd certainly changed my lifestyle. Did I really think he'd stay chaste when I hadn't? Was it any of my business what he did? No; no, it wasn't.

I finally shrugged. "He's not my boyfriend anymore, Jamil. And he's a big boy." I shrugged again, not really sure how I felt about Richard sleeping around. Trying very hard not to feel anything about it, because it didn't matter how I felt. Richard had his own life to live, and it didn't include me, not in that way. "I'm not here to police Richard's sex life."

Jamil nodded almost to himself. "Good. I was worried."

"What, you thought I'd throw a fit and storm off, leaving him to his just desserts?"

"Something like that," he said.

"Did he have sex with the woman who's made the accusation?"

"If you mean intercourse, no. She's human," he said. "Richard doesn't do humans. He's afraid they're too fragile."

"I thought you just said he'd been sleeping with Ms. Schaffer."

"Having sex, but not doing the dirty deed."

I wasn't a virgin. I knew there were alternatives, but . . . "Why alternative methods with humans? Why not just . . . do it?"

"Doing the wild thing can release our beast early. You don't want to know what happens when you're with a human who doesn't know what you are, and you shift on top of them, inside them." A shadow crossed his face, and he looked away.

"You sound like the voice of experience," I said.

He looked slowly back at me, and there was something in his face that was suddenly frightening, like looking up and realizing that the bars between you and the lion at the zoo aren't there anymore. "That is none of your business."

I nodded. "Sorry, you're right. You're absolutely right. It was too personal."

But it was interesting information. There had been a point where I'd pretty much begged Richard to stay the night. To have sex with me. He'd said no because it wouldn't be fair until I saw him change into werewolf form. I needed to be able to accept the whole package. I hadn't been able to do that once the package bled and writhed all over me. But now I wondered if part of his hesitation had been simply fear of hurting me. Maybe.

I shook my head. It didn't matter. Business. If I concentrated really hard, maybe I could stay on track. We were here to get him out of jail, not to worry about why we broke up.

"We could use a little help here with the luggage," Jason called.

He had two suitcases under each arm. Zane and Cherry were carrying one coffin. They looked like pallbearer bookends. Nathaniel was lying on his back on the other coffin. He'd taken off his shirt and unbound his hair. His hands were folded across his stomach, eyes closed. I didn't know whether he was playing dead or trying to get a tan.

"A little help here," Jason said, kicking his foot towards the rest of the luggage. Two suitcases and a huge trunk still sat unclaimed.

I walked towards them. "Jesus, only one of those suitcases is mine. Who's the clotheshorse?"

Zane and Cherry put the coffin gently on the Tarmac. "Just one suitcase is mine," Zane said.

"Three of them are mine," Cherry said. She sounded vaguely embarrassed.

"Who brought the trunk?"

"Jean-Claude sent it," Jason said. "Just in case we do meet with the local master. He wanted us to make a good show of it."

I frowned at the trunk. "Please tell me there's nothing in there that Jean-Claude plans on me wearing."

Jason grinned.

I shook my head. "I don't want to see it."

"Maybe you'll get lucky," Jason said. "Maybe they'll try to kill you instead."

I frowned at him. "You're just full of happy thoughts."

"My speciality," he said.

Nathaniel turned his head and looked at me, hands clasped across his bare stomach. "I can lift the coffin, but it's not balanced right for carrying. I need help."

"You certainly do," I said.

He blinked up at me, one hand raised to block the sun. I moved until my body blocked the sun and he could look at me without squinting. He smiled up at me.

"What's with the coffin sunbathing?" I asked.

The smile wilted around the edges, then faded completely. "It's the scene in the crypt," he said as if that explained everything. It didn't.

"I don't know what you're talking about."

He raised just his shoulders and head off the coffin like he was doing stomach crunches. His abs bunched nicely with the effort. "You really haven't watched my movies, have you?"

"Sorry," I said.

He sat up the rest of the way, smoothing his hair back with both hands in a practiced gesture. He slipped a silver clasp around the hair and flipped the tail of auburn hair behind his back.

"I thought silver jewelry burned when it touched a lycanthrope's skin," I said.

He wiggled his hair, settling the silver clasp securely against his neck. "It does," he said.

"A little pain makes the world go round, I guess."

He just stared at me with his strange eyes. He was only nineteen, but the look on his face was older, much older. There were no lines on that smooth skin, but there were shadows in those eyes that nothing would ever erase. Cosmetic surgery for the soul was what he needed. Something to take the terrible burden of knowledge that had made him what he was.

Jason limped over to us, loaded with suitcases. "One of his movies is about a vampire who falls in love with an innocent young human."

"You've seen it," I said.

He nodded.

I shook my head and picked up a suitcase. "You got a car for us?" I asked Jamil.

"A van," he said.

"Great. Pick up a suitcase, and show me the way."

"I don't do luggage."

"If we all help, we can load the van in half the time. I want to see Richard as soon as possible, so grab something and stop being such a freaking prima donna."

Jamil stared at me for a long, slow count, then said, "When Richard replaces you as lupa, I won't have to take shit from you."

"Fine, but until then, hop to it. Besides, this isn't giving you shit, Jamil. When I give you shit, you'll know it."

He gave a low chuckle. He slipped his jacket back on and picked up the trunk. It should have taken two strong men to lift it. He carried it like it weighed nothing. He walked off without a backward glance, leaving me to get the last suitcase. Zane and Cherry picked the coffin back up and walked after him. Jason shuffled after them.

"What about me?" Nathaniel said.

"Put your shirt back on and stay with the coffin. Wouldn't do to have someone make off with Damian."

"I know women who would pay me to take the shirt off," he said.

"Too bad I'm not one of them," I said.

"Yeah," he said, "too bad." He picked his shirt up off the ground. I left him sitting on the coffin in the middle of the Tarmac, shirt wadded in his hands. He looked sort of forlorn in a strange, macabre way. I felt very sorry for Nathaniel. He'd had a rough life. But it wasn't my fault. I was paying for his apartment so he didn't have to turn tricks to make ends meet, though I knew other strippers at Guilty Pleasures who managed to make ends meet on their salary. Maybe Nathaniel wasn't good with money. Big surprise there.

The van was large, black, and looked sinister. The sort of thing serial killers drive in made-for-TV movies. Serial killers did drive vans in real life, but they tended to be pale colors with rust spots.

Jamil drove. Cherry and I rode up front with him. The luggage and everyone else went in the back. I expected Cherry to ask me to sit in the middle because I was at least five inches shorter than she was, but she didn't. She just crawled into the van, in the middle, with those long legs tucked up in front of the dashboard.

The road was well paved, almost no potholes, and if you held your breath, two cars could pass each other without scraping paint. Trees hugged the road on either side. But on one side, you caught glimpses of an amazing drop-off, and on the other side, there was just rocky dirt. I preferred the dirt. The trees were thick enough that the illusion of safety was there, but the trees fell away like a great, green curtain, and you could suddenly see for miles. The illusion was gone, and you realized just how high up we were. Okay, it wasn't like Rocky Mountain high, but it would do the job if the van went over the edge. Falling from high places is one of my least favorite things to do. I don't clutch the upholstery like in the airplane, but I'm a flatlander at heart and would be glad to be in the lower valley.

"Do you want me to drop you at the police station or take you to the cabins first?" Jamil asked.

"Police. Did you say cabins?"

He nodded. "Cabins."

"Rustic living?" I asked.

"No, thank God," he said. "Indoor plumbing, beds, electricity, the works, if you aren't too particular about the decor."

"Not a fashion plate?"

"Not hardly," he said.

Cherry sat very still between us, hands folded in her lap. I realized she wasn't wearing her seat belt. My mother would be alive today if she'd been wearing hers, so I'm picky about it. "You're not wearing your seat belt," I said.

Cherry looked at me. "I'm squashed enough without the seat belt," she said.

"I know you could survive a trip through the windshield," I said, "but having you heal that much damage would sort of blow your cover."

"Am I supposed to be playing human?" she asked.

It was a good question. "For the townsfolk, yeah."

She fastened her seat belt without any more arguing. The wereleopards had taken me to heart as their Nimir-ra. They were so glad to have someone act as protector, even if it was just a human, that they didn't bitch much. "You should have told me we were trying to blend in. I'd have dressed differently."

"You're right; I should have said something." Truthfully, it hadn't occurred to me until just that moment.

The road spilled down into what passed for flatland here. The trees were so thick that it was almost claustrophobic. There was still a gentle swell to the land, letting you know you were driving over the toes of mountains.

"Do you want us to wait for you outside the station?" Jamil asked.

"No, you guys sort of stand out."

"How are you going to get to the cabins?" he asked.

I shook my head. "I don't know. Taxi?"

He looked at me, the look was eloquent. "In Myerton, I don't think so."

"Damn," I said. "Drive us to the cabins then. I'll take the van back into town."

"With Jason?" Jamil said.

I nodded. "With Jason." I looked at him. "Why is everyone so solicitous of me? I mean, I know there may be problems, but you guys are being awful cautious." I sat up straighter in the seat and stared at the side of Jamil's face. He was watching the road like his life depended on it.

"What aren't you guys telling me?"

He hit his turn signal and waited for a pickup truck to go past, then turned left between yet more trees. "It'll take longer to get to the cabins."

"Jamil, what is going on?"

Cherry tried her best to sink into the seat, but when you're model tall and in the middle, it's hard to play invisible. That one body movement told me she knew, too. That they both knew something I didn't.

I looked at her. "Cherry, tell me what's going on."

She sighed and sat up a little straighter. "If anything happens to you, Jean-Claude's going to kill us."

I frowned at her. "I don't understand."

"Jean-Claude couldn't come here himself," Jamil said. "It would be seen as an act of war. But he's worried about you. He told us all that if we let you get killed, and he survives your death, he'll kill us, all of us." He watched the road as he talked, turning onto a gravel road that was so narrow that trees brushed the sides of the van.

"Define *all*," I said.

"All of us," Jamil said. "We're your bodyguards."

"I thought you were Richard's bodyguard?" I said.

"And you're his lupa, his mate."

"If you're a real bodyguard, you can't guard two people. You can only guard one at a time."

"Why?" Cherry asked.

I looked at Jamil. He didn't answer, so I did.

"Because you can't take a bullet for more than one person, and that's what a bodyguard does."

Jamil nodded. "Yeah, that's what a bodyguard does."

"You really think anyone's going to be shooting at Anita?"

"The bullet's a metaphor," Jamil said. "But it doesn't matter. Bullet, knife, claws, whatever it is, I take it." He pulled into a wide gravel turnaround and a huge clearing. There were small, white, boxy cabins scattered around the clearing like a Motel 6 that had been cut into pieces. There was a neon sign, pale in the sunlight, that said Blue Moon Cabins.

"Anita is our Nimir-ra. She's supposed to protect us, not the other way around."

I agreed with her. I'd picked Zane and Cherry not for their bodyguarding ability but because they didn't mind sharing blood with the vampires. Even among the wereleopards, most of them didn't like donating. They seemed to think being a blood cocktail for the vamps was worse than sex for money. I wasn't sure I agreed with them, but I wasn't about to force them to do it if they didn't want to. I didn't donate blood, and I was sleeping with one of the undead.

"No," I said. "I didn't agree to this. I can take care of myself, thank you very much." I opened the door, and Jamil reached across and grabbed my arm. His hand looked very dark against the paleness of my arm. I turned very slowly and looked at him. It was not a friendly look. "Let go of me."

"Anita, please, you are one of the toughest humans I've ever met. You are the most dangerous human female I've ever seen." His hand squeezed just enough for me to feel the immense strength in it. He could probably deadlift an elephant if it didn't wiggle too much. He could certainly crush my arm.

"But you are human, and the things you're up against aren't."

I stared at him. Cherry sat very still between us, half-pinned by Jamil's body. "Let go of me, Jamil."

His hand tightened. It was going to be a hell of a bruise. "Just this once, Anita, stay in the background, or you're going to get us all killed."

Jamil's body was extended across the seat, across Cherry. I was on the edge of the seat, butt half in the air. Neither he nor I were balanced very well. His grip was on the middle of my forearm, not a good place to hold on.

"What you fuzzballs keep forgetting is that strength isn't enough. Leverage, there's the ticket."

He frowned at me, obviously puzzled. His hand tightened just this side of serious injury. "You can't fight this, Anita."

"What do you want me to say? Uncle?"

Jamil smiled. "Uncle, okay, yeah, say uncle. Admit that just this once you can't take care of yourself."

I pushed myself out of the van, tucking my legs so he was suddenly trying to hold my entire body weight with a one-handed grip on my forearm. My arm slipped through his fingers. I let myself fall to the ground, going for the long blade down my back, not worrying about trying to stand. My right hand went for the Browning, but I knew I wouldn't make it in time. I was trusting that Jamil wasn't going to kill me. We were grandstanding. If I was wrong on that, I was about to die.

Jamil spilled over the seat, arms reaching for me, trusting in his own way that I wouldn't blow his head off. He knew I had the gun. He was treating me like a shapeshifter who knew the rules. You didn't kill over small stuff. You bled each other, but you didn't kill.

I sliced his arm open from a nearly prone position. There was a moment of utter surprise on his face. He hadn't known about the third blade or its length, and getting sliced open is always a shock. He jerked backwards out of sight like someone had pulled him, but I knew better. He was just that fast.

I had time to get to one knee before he bounded onto the hood of the van, crouched like the predator he was. I had the Browning pointed at him. I got to my feet, gun nice and steady on the middle of his body. Standing didn't help things. I didn't shoot better standing. But somehow I wanted to be on my feet.

Jamil watched me but made no move to stop me. Maybe he was afraid to try. Not of the gun but of himself. I had hurt him. Blood was splashing all over those pretty white clothes. His entire body vibrated with the desire to close the distance between us. He was pissed, and it was four nights until full moon. He probably wouldn't kill me, but I wasn't going to test the theory. He could break my neck with one blow. Hell, he could explode my skull like an egg. No more chances.

I pointed the Browning at him one-handed, knife still in my left. "Don't do it, Jamil. I'd hate to lose you over something this stupid."

A low growl trickled from his lips. The sound alone raised the hair at the back of my neck.

The others were out of the back of the van. I had a sense of movement. "Everyone stay back," I said.

"Anita," Jason said, voice very calm, no teasing, no jokes. "Anita, what's going on?"

"Ask Mr. Macho there."

Cherry spoke from her seat inside the van. She hadn't moved. "Jamil was trying to explain to Anita how she couldn't handle herself against shapeshifters and vampires." She slid very slowly towards the edge of the seat. I kept my gaze on Jamil, but my peripheral vision was good enough to catch the spots of blood all over the white skin.

"Stay in the van, Cherry. Don't press me."

She stopped scooting along the seat and just sat there. "Jamil wanted her to take a backseat when the action starts."

"She is still human," Jamil growled. "She is still weak."

Cherry's deep, caressing voice said, "She could have sliced your throat open instead of your arm. She could have shot you in the head when you reached for her."

"I still can," I said, "if you don't tone it down."

Jamil lay nearly flat on the hood, fingers splayed. His entire body trembled with tension. Something lurked behind that human body, swimming up through his eyes. His beast pushed against his flesh like a leviathan swimming just below the water, so you caught a dark glimpse of something huge and overwhelmingly alien.

I'd turned my body in silhouette, my left hand with the knife behind my back, the back of my hand resting lightly on the top of my butt. I'd fallen into the stance I used at the shooting range when I was shooting targets. The gun was pointed at his head now, because he'd lowered his body mass until it was the biggest target. I'd saved Jamil's life once. He was a good man to have at Richard's back, even if he didn't always like me. I didn't always like him, so we were even. But I respected him, and until now, I thought he respected me. His little show in the van said he still thought of me as a girl.

Once upon a time, it had bothered me more to kill people. Maybe it was years of killing vampires. They looked human. But somewhere along the way, it just didn't bother me to pull the trigger. I stared at Jamil's face, looked him right in the eyes, and felt that stillness fill me. It was like standing in the middle of a buzzing field of white noise. I could still hear and see, but it all fell away so there was nothing but the gun and Jamil and the emptiness. My body felt light and ready. In my saner moments, I worried that I was becoming a sociopath. But right now, there was nothing but a very calm knowledge that I'd do it. I'd pull the trigger and watch him die at my feet. And feel nothing.

Jamil watched my face, and I saw the tension begin to leak out of him. He stayed very still until that vibrating energy died down and that awful looming presence of his beast slid below the surface once more. Then he very, very slowly sat back on his knees, still watching my face.

I kept the gun pointed on him. I knew how fast they could move, fast as a wolf, maybe faster. Like nothing this side of hell.

"You really would do it," he said. "You'd kill me."

"You bet."

He took a deep breath, and it shuddered down his body, reminding me strangely of a bird settling its feathers. "It's over," he said. "You're lupa. You outrank me."

I lowered the gun carefully, still looking at him, still trying to keep a feel for where everyone else was standing. "Please tell me that this wasn't some sort of dominance crap?"

Jamil gave a smile that was almost embarrassed. "I thought I was trying to make a point, but I wasn't. I've spent the last month down here having to explain to the local pack how we ended up with a human lupa. How I'm outranked by a human woman.''

I shook my head and pointed the gun at the ground. "You stupid son of a bitch. Your pride is wounded that I'm higher in the pack than you are."

He nodded. "Yeah."

"You guys just drive me crazy," I said. I was almost yelling. "We do not have time for macho bullshit."

Zane leaned against the van near Cherry. He was very careful to keep his hands down and move slowly, no sudden moves. "You couldn't have taken Jamil without the knife and the gun. You won't always have them with you."

"Is that a threat?" I asked.

He raised his hands upward. "Just an observation."

"Hey, folks." A man stepped out of one of the cabins. He was tall, thin, with shoulder-length grey hair and a darker mustache. The hair and the lines in his face said he was over fifty.

The body that showed from the T-shirt and jeans looked lean and younger.

He'd frozen in the doorway, hands on the wooden edges of the doorjamb. "Easy there, little lady."

I pointed the gun at him, because under that calm exterior there was enough power to raise goose bumps on my skin, and he wasn't even trying.

"This is Verne," Jamil said. "He owns the cabins."

I lowered the gun to the ground. "He the local Ulfric, or do they have something scarier hiding in the woods?"

Verne laughed and started walking towards us. He moved in an almost clumsy roll like his arms and legs were too long for his body, but it was deceptive. He was playing human for me. I wasn't fooled.

"You spotted me pretty damn quick there, little lady."

I put the Browning up because to keep it out would be rude. I was here as his guest in more than one way. Besides, I had to trust someone enough to put the gun up. I couldn't keep it naked in my hand the entire trip. I still had the naked blade, complete with blood. It needed to be cleaned before I could sheathe it. I'd gummed up a couple of smaller sheaths from not cleaning them well enough.

"Nice to meet you, Verne, but don't call me little lady." I started to wipe the blood on the edge of the black jacket. Black's good for that.

"Don't you ever give an inch?" Jamil asked.

I glanced at him. There was blood all over his nice white clothes. "No," I said. I motioned him over to me.

He frowned. "What?"

"I want to use your shirt to wipe the blood off the blade."

He just stared at me.

"Come on, Jamil. The shirt is already ruined."

Jamil pulled the shirt over his head in one smooth motion. He threw the shirt at me, and I caught it one-handed. I started cleaning the blade with the unstained part of the shirt.

Verne laughed. He had one of those deep, rolling chuckles that matched his gravelly voice. "No wonder Richard's been having such a hard time finding a replacement for you. You are a solid, cast-iron, ball-busting bitch."

I looked at his smiling face. I think it was a compliment Besides, truth was truth. I wasn't down here to win Miss Congeniality. I was down here to rescue Richard and to stay alive. Bitch was just about the right speed for that.

5

The outside of the cabins were white and looked sort of cheap. The interiors weren't honeymoon cabins, but they were amazingly roomy. There was a queen-size bed in the one I was given. There was a desk against one wall with a reading lamp. There was an extra chair in front of a picture window. The chair was blue plush and comfortable. It sat on a small throw rug that looked homemade and was woven in shades of blue. The woods were hardwood and polished to a honeyed gleam. The bed's comforter was royal blue. There was a bedside table, complete with a lamp and a phone. The walls were pale blue. There was even a painting over the bed. It was a reproduction of Van Gogh's *Starry Night*. Frankly, any of Van Gogh's work done after he started going seriously nuts creeps me out. But it was a good choice for a blue room. For all I knew, the other cabins had matadors done on velvet, but this was okay.

The bathroom was standard white with a small window high over the bathtub. The bathroom looked like standard motel issue except for a blue bowl of potpourri that smelled like musk and gardenia.

Verne had informed me that this was the largest cabin left. I needed the floor space. Two coffins take up a lot of room. I wasn't sure I wanted to have Asher and Damian in my room permanently, but I didn't have time to argue. I wanted to go see Richard as soon as possible. We could always argue about who got the vamps as bunk mates after I saw Richard.

I made three phone calls before we went to the jail. The first was to the number that Daniel had given me, to let him know we were in town. No one answered. The second call was to Catherine to let her know I'd arrived safely. I got her machine. The third call was to the lawyer that Catherine had recommended, Carl Belisarius. A woman with a very good phone voice answered. When she found out who I was, she was sort of excited, which puzzled me. She forwarded me to Belisarius's cell phone. Something was up, which was probably bad.

A deep, rich, male voice answered, "Belisarius here."

"Anita Blake. I assume that Catherine Maison-Gillette told you who I am."

"Just a moment, Ms. Blake." He pushed a button and there was silence. I was on hold. When he came back on the phone, I could hear wind and traffic. He'd stepped outside.

"I am very glad to hear from you, Ms. Blake. What the fuck is going on?"

"Excuse me?" I said, tone less than friendly.

"He won't see me. Catherine gave me the impression that he needed a lawyer. I traveled to this godless piece of real estate, and he won't see me. He says he didn't hire me."

"Shit," I said softly. "I'm sorry, Mr. Belisarius." I had a thought. "Did you tell him that I hired you on his behalf?"

"Will that make a difference?"

"Truthfully, I don't know. Either it'll help, or he'll tell you to go to hell."

"He's already done that. I am not cheap, Ms. Blake. Even if he my services, someone has to pay for the day."

"Don't worry, Mr. Belisarius. I'll take care of it."

"Do you have that kind of money?"

"How much are we talking about?" I asked.

He mentioned a fee. I did my best not to whistle in his ear. I counted slowly to five and said, calmly, "You'll get your money."

"You have that kind of money? I took Catherine's word for a lot of things on this. Forgive me if I'm starting to be suspicious."

"No, I understand. Richard's giving you a hard time, so you're giving me one."

He gave a rough laugh. "All right, Ms. Blake, all right. I'll try not to pass the buck, but I want some assurances. Can you pay my fee?"

"I raise the dead for a living, Mr. Belisarius. It's a rare talent. I can pay your fee." And I could, but it sort of hurt to do it. I wasn't raised poor, but I was raised to appreciate the value of a buck, and Belisarius was a little outside of outrageous.

"Send word to Richard that I hired you. Call me back if it makes a difference. He may refuse to see either of us."

"You're paying a great deal of money, Ms. Blake, especially if I take the case. I assumed you and Mr. Zeeman were close in some way."

"It's a long story," I said. "We're sort of hating each other right now."

"A lot of money for someone you hate," he said.

"Don't you start, too," I said.

He laughed again. His laugh was more normal than his speech, almost a bray. Maybe he didn't practice his laugh for the courtroom. I knew he practiced that rich, rolling voice.

"I'll send the message, Ms. Blake. Hopefully, I'll be calling you back."

"Call me even if he says no. At least I'll know what to expect when I come down to the jail."

"You'll come down even if he refuses to see you?" Belisarius asked.

"Yeah," I said.

"I look forward to meeting you, Ms. Blake. You intrigue me."

"I bet you say that to all the girls."

"To very few, Ms. Blake." He hung up.

Jason came out of the bathroom as I hung up. He was wearing the suit. I'd never seen him in anything except T-shirts and jeans or leather and less. It was odd to see him standing there in a navy blue suit, white shirt, and a thin white tie with a tastefully small design running through it. When you looked close, the tie was silk and the print was tiny fleur dis lis. I knew who had picked out the tie. The suit was a better cut than most off the rack, but Jean-Claude had ruined me for off the rack no matter how nice the fit.

He buttoned the first button on the jacket and smoothed his hands through his blond hair. "How do I look?"

I shook my head. "Like a person."

He grinned. "You sound surprised."

I smiled. "I've just never seen you look like a grown-up."

He fake pouted at me, lip pushed out. "You've seen me nearly naked and I didn't look grown-up?"

I shook my head and smiled in spite of myself. I'd changed my clothes in the bedroom while he changed in the bathroom. I found a few dark spots of blood on the red blouse. As it dried, it would turn black and look even worse, which was why the blouse was soaking in the sink. Red shows blood no matter what people say.

The black jeans had escaped unstained as far as I could tell. A few spots of blood are hard to find on black. Black or navy blue hides blood best. I guess a really dark brown would work, but I don't own much brown, so I don't know for sure.

The fresh blouse was a pale, almost icy, lavender. It had been a gift from my stepmother, Judith. When I opened the box at Christmas and saw the pale blouse, I assumed she bought me yet another piece of clothing that would look better on her blond ice princess body than on my darker one. But the pure, clear color actually looked pretty spiffy. I'd even been gracious enough to tell Judith I was wearing it. I think it was the first gift in ten years that I hadn't exchanged. I was still 0 for 8 in the gift department for her. Oh, well.

Black dress pants with a belt wide enough for the Browning and wider than was fashionable, black flats, and I was ready. I'd added just a touch of makeup: eye shadow, mascara, a hint of blush, and lipstick. I tried not to think why I'd dressed up. It wasn't for the local cops. Jason and I were probably both overdressed for the locals. Of course, if we'd shown up in jeans and T-shirts, we'd have been underdressed. The only really good thing to wear to meet police is a uniform and a badge. Anything else and you are not in the club.

There was a law being discussed in Washington, D.C., right now that might give vampire executioners what amounted to federal marshal status. It was being pushed hard by Senator Brewster, whose daughter had gotten munched by a vampire. Of course, he was also pushing to revoke vampires' rights as legal citizens. Federal status for executioners, maybe. Revoking vamps' legal rights. I didn't think so. Some vampires would have to do something pretty gruesome to give the anti-vamp lobby that much push.

In March, vampire executioners had been officially licensed. It was a state license because murder was a state, not a federal, crime.

But I understood the need for federal status for vampire executioners. We didn't just kill, we hunted. But once we crossed out of our licensed area, we were on shaky ground. The court order was valid as long as the state we crossed into agreed to an extradition order. The extradition order was then used to validate the original order of execution. My preference was to get a second order of execution every time I crossed a state line. But that took time, and sometimes you'd lose the vamp to yet another jurisdiction and have to start all over again.

One enterprising vampire crossed seventeen states before he was finally caught and killed. The general run, if they run, is maybe two or three. Which is why most vampire executioners are licensed in more than one state. In our own way, we have territories, sort of like vampires. Within that territory, we kill. Outside of it, it's someone else's job. But there are only ten of us, and that's not a lot for a country with one of the largest vampire populations in the world. We aren't constantly busy. Most of us have day jobs. I mean, if the vampires had been bad enough to keep us hopping, then they'd never have made legal status. But the more vamps you get in an area, the higher your crime rate. Just like with humans.

Having to stop every time you left your licensed area made it harder to do our jobs. Having no real status as a police officer made it impossible to enter an investigation unless invited. Sometimes we weren't invited in until the body count was pretty damn high. My largest body count for a vampire was twenty-three. Twenty-three dead before we caught him. There had been higher body counts. Back in the fifties, Gerald Mallory, sort of the grandfather of the business, had slain a kiss of vampires that took out over a hundred. A kiss of vampires is like a gaggle of geese; it's the group name. Poetic, ain't it?

The phone rang. I picked it up and it was Belisarius. "He'll see us together. I'll try to have something to tell you by the time you get here." He hung up.

I took a big breath in through my nose and let it out in a rush through my mouth.

"What's wrong?" Jason asked.

"Nothing."

"You're nervous about seeing Richard," he said.

"Don't be so dammed smart."

He grinned. "Sorry."

"Like hell," I said. "Let's go."

We went.

6

The drive to Myerton took longer than it had to because I was driving an unfamiliar van on very narrow roads. It made me nervous. Jason finally said, "Can I drive, please? We'll get there before dark."

"Shut up," I said.

He shut up, smiling.

We did finally drive into Myerton. The town consisted of a main street that was paved and looked suspiciously like a two-lane highway with buildings hugging the edges. There was a stoplight with a second, much smaller gravel road spilling red clay dust across the blacktop. The town's only stoplight made you notice the two fast-food restaurants and a mom-and-pop diner that actually had a bigger crowd than the Dairy Queen. Either the food was good, or the Dairy Queen wasn't.

Jamil had given me directions to the police station. He said to drive down the main street, turn right. You can't miss it. Whenever someone says that, it means one of two things. Either they're right and it's obvious, or it's hidden and you'll never find it without a detailed map where X marks the spot.

I turned right at the stoplight. The van hit a pothole and rolled like a great beast treading water. I wished I had my Jeep. The gravel road was the true main street of the town. Buildings with a raised wooden sidewalk in front of them lined one side of the street. I spotted a grocery store and a woodworker's shop selling handmade furniture. They had a rocking chair out in front that still had rough grey bark on parts of the wooden frame. Very rustic. Very nifty. Another shop sold herbs and homemade jellies, though this wasn't the time of year for it. Houses lined the other side of the street. They weren't the newer Midwestern look that has taken over large parts of the South. The houses were mostly one story on cinder blocks or red rock bases. They were covered with side shingles running strongly to off-white and grey. One yard had a herd of ceramic deer and a crop of lawn gnomes so thick, it looked like they should be selling them.

There were mountains at the end of the street and trees like a thick, green curtain. We were about to drive back into the forest, and I hadn't seen anything that looked like a police station. Great.

"It has to be right here," Jason said.

I checked my rearview mirror, no traffic, and stopped. "What do you see that I don't?" I asked.

"Shang-Da," he said.

I looked at him. "Excuse me?"

"On the porch at the end of the street."

I looked where he was looking. A tall man sat slumped in a lawn chair. He was wearing a white T-shirt, jeans, no shoes, and a billed cap pulled low. His tan stood out strongly against the whiteness of the shirt. Large hands held a can of soda or maybe beer. Just an early-morning pick-me-up.

"That's Shang-Da. He's our pack's second enforcer. He's Hati to Jamil's Sköll."

Ah. The light dawned. "He's guarding Richard, so the police station has to be nearby."

Jason nodded.

I looked at the slumped figure. He didn't look particularly alert at first glance. He almost blended into the scene until you realized the T-shirt was spotless and new. The jeans had creases as if they'd been ironed and you realized though he was tanned, the skin coloring wasn't just from the sun. But it wasn't until he moved his head very slowly and looked straight at us that I realized just how good the act was. Even from a distance there was an intensity in his gaze that was almost unnerving. I knew we suddenly had his full attention and all he'd done was move his head.

"Shit," I said.

"Yeah," Jason said. "Shang-Da's new. He transferred in from San Francisco Bay pack. No one fought him when he came in as Hati. No one wanted the job that badly."

Jason pointed across the street. "Is that it?"

It was a low, one-story building made of white-painted cinder blocks. There was a small, gravel parking lot out front but no cars. The van took up most of the parking lot. I parked as close to the side as I could, hearing the soft swish of tree branches along the top of the van. There was probably a police car out there someplace that would be parking beside me. I think they had room.

There was a small wooden sign, elegantly carved, hanging beside the door. It read, Police Station. That was it, the only hint. Couldn't miss it—Jamil had a sense of humor. Or maybe he was still pissed that I'd cut him. Childish.

We got out. I felt Shang-Da's gaze on me. He was yards away, but the power of his attention crept down my skin, raising the hair on my arms. I glanced his way, and for a second, our eyes met. The hair at the back of my neck stood to attention.

Jason came to stand beside me. "Let's go inside."

I nodded, and we walked to the door. "If I didn't know better, I'd say Shang-Da doesn't like me."

"He's loyal to Richard, and you've hurt him—badly."

I glanced at him. "You don't seem mad at me. Aren't you loyal to Richard?"

"I was there the night Richard fought Marcus. Shang-Da wasn't."

"Are you saying I was right to leave Richard?"

"No. I'm saying I understand why you couldn't handle it."

"Thanks, Jason."

He smiled. "Besides, maybe I have designs on your body."

"Jean-Claude would kill you."

He shrugged. "What's life without a little danger?"

I shook my head.

Jason got to the door first but didn't try to open it for me. He knew me better than that.

I opened the mostly glass doors. I guess the doors were also a clue. Everything else on the street had doors like you'd see on a house. The glass doors were modern business doors. The interior was painted white, including the long barlike desk across from the door. There were some wanted posters tacked to a bulletin board to the left of the door and a radio system behind the desk, but other than that, it could have been the reception room for a dentist.

The guy sitting behind the desk was big. Even sitting down, you had a sense of size. His shoulders were almost as broad as I was tall. His hair was very short and still curled in tight ringlets. He'd have had to shave his head to get rid of the curls.

My executioner's license is in a nice fake-leather carrying case. It had my picture on it and looked damned official, but it wasn't a badge. It wasn't even a license good in this state. But it was all I had to flash, so I flashed it. I went in, holding the license out in front, because I was bringing a gun into a police station. Cops tended not to like that.

"I'm Anita Blake, vampire executioner."

The cop moved just his eyes; his hands were hidden behind the desk. "We didn't call for an executioner."

"I'm not here on official business," I said. I stood in front of the desk. I started to put the license away, but he held his hand out for it, and I gave it to him.

He studied the license while he asked, "Why are you here?"

"I'm a friend of Richard Zeeman."

His grey eyes flicked up then. It wasn't a friendly look. He tossed the license back on top of the desk.

I picked it up. "Is there a problem, Officer . . ." I read his nameplate. ". . . Maiden?"

He shook his head. "No problem except that your friend is a damned rapist. I never understand why the meanest son of a bitch in the world always seems to have a girlfriend."

"I'm not his girlfriend," I said. "I'm exactly what I said I was: his friend."

Maiden stood, and he looked every inch of his six-foot-plus frame. He wasn't just tall; he was bulky. He'd probably been a wrestler or a football player in high school. The muscle had started to melt into a general bulk, and he was carrying about twenty pounds around the waist that he didn't need, but I wasn't fooled. He was a big and tough and used to it. The gun around his waist matched the rest of him. It was a chrome-plated Colt Python long barrel with heavy black custom grips. Good for hunting elephants, a little much for scaring drunks on a Saturday night.

"Who are you?" He pointed a thumb at Jason.

"Just a friend," Jason said. He smiled, trying to look harmless. He wasn't as good at looking harmless as I was, but he was close. Beside Officer Maiden we both looked sort of fragile.

"Her friend, or Zeeman's?"

Jason gave a big, good-humored smile. "I'm everyone's friend."

Maiden didn't smile. He just looked at Jason, giving him a cold, hard stare out of those dark grey eyes. Maiden didn't have any better luck staring Jason down than I did. Jason kept smiling. Maiden kept staring.

I finally touched Jason's arm ever so lightly. It was enough. He dropped his eyes, blinked, but the smile never faltered. But it was enough for Maiden to feel he'd won the staring contest.

Maiden lumbered out from behind the desk. He moved like he was aware that he was big, like in his own ears, the earth trembled as he moved. He was big, but he wasn't that big. Of course, I wasn't going to point it out to him.

A second man came out of a small door to the right of the desk. He was wearing a pale tan suit that fit him like an elegant glove. The white shirt was ribbed down the front, and he had one of those string ties with a hunk of gold at his throat. His eyes were large, black, and surprised when they saw me. His hair was cut very short, but stylish. The hand he extended for me to shake had a diamond pinkie ring and a college class ring on it.

"Could this vision of loveliness be the infamous Ms. Blake?"

I smiled before I could stop myself. "You must be Belisarius."

He nodded. "Call me Carl."

"I'm Anita, and this is Jason."

He shook hands with Jason, still smiling, still pleasant. He turned to Maiden. "May we go see my client now?"

"The two of you can go, but not him." Maiden jerked another thumb at Jason. "Sheriff said let the two of you in. No one said anything about anybody else."

Jason opened his mouth. I touched his arm. "That's fine."

"And the gun stays out here," he said. I didn't want to give up the gun, but it made me think better of Maiden that he'd spotted it.

"Sure," I said. I pulled the Browning out from under the jacket. I hit the slide and spilled the clip into my other hand. I jacked the gun open to show the chamber was empty and handed the whole shooting match to Maiden.

"Didn't trust me to unload it for you?"

"I figured the Browning might be too small for your hands. Requires fine motor skills."

"You giving me shit?" he said.

I nodded. "Yeah, I'm giving you shit."

He smiled then. He looked the Browning over before he put it in a desk drawer along with the clip. "Not a bad gun if you can't handle anything bigger." He locked the drawer—another brownie point for Maiden.

"It's not size that counts, Maiden. It's performance."

His smile widened to a grin. "Your friend still has to wait out here."

"I said that was fine. I meant it."

Maiden nodded and led the way back through the door that Belisarius had come out of. There were two doors in the middle of the long, white hallway. One said, Ladies, the other, Men.

"I'd hoped you coming out of this door meant you were visiting Richard."

"I'm afraid not. Mr. Zeeman has not relented."

"Relented," Maiden said, "relented. Now, that's a nice lawyer word."

"Reading improves your vocabulary, Officer Maiden. You should try it sometime. Though I suppose you can get by with just looking at the pictures."

"Ooh, I'm cut to the quick on that one," Maiden said.

"If you cut us, do we not bleed?" Belisarius asked.

Maiden shocked the hell out of me by giving the next line: "If you tickle us, do we not laugh?"

Belisarius clapped softly. "Touché, Officer Maiden."

"Big and well read," I said. "I'm impressed."

He pulled a chain out of his pocket with keys on the end of it. "Don't tell the other cops. They'd think I was a sissy."

I looked up at him, all the way up at him. "It's not reading Shakespeare that makes you a sissy, Maiden. It's that damn gun. Only pansies carry that much hardware."

He unlocked the door at the end of the hallway. "Got to carry something big, Ms. Blake. Balances me out when I run."

That made me laugh. He opened the door and ushered us through. He locked the door behind us and went down a long white stretch of hallway with two closed doors on either side. "Wait here. I'll go make sure your boyfriend is ready to see you."

"He's not my boyfriend," I said. It was becoming automatic, like an involuntary reflex.

Maiden smiled and unlocked the door at the far end. He vanished through it.

"You and Officer Maiden seem to have hit it off, Ms. Blake."

"Cops dish out a lot of shit. Trick is, don't take it personally, and dish back."

"I'll remember that next time."

I looked up Belisarius. "It might not work for you. You're a lawyer, and you're wealthy."

"And I'm not an attractive woman," he said.

"That, too, though that can work against me with policemen."

Belisarius nodded.

Maiden stepped back through the far door. He was smiling like something had amused the hell out of him. I was betting I wasn't going to think it was funny. "I told Zeeman that for a fucking pervert, he had a cute girlfriend."

"I'll bet that's not what you said," I said.

He nodded. "I asked him why, with a nice piece of ass like you for his girlfriend, he had to go out and rape somebody."

"What'd he say?" I asked, face as blank as I could make it.

"He said you're not his girlfriend."

I nodded. "See, I told you so."

Maiden opened the door wide and motioned us through. "Ring the buzzer when you want out." We stepped through, and he said, "Enjoy," as he locked us in.

They must have gotten a deal on white paint because the entire room was white, even the floor. It was like standing in the middle of a blizzard. Two bunks, one on top the other, the bars on a small window, even the toilet and sink were white. The only color was the bars that formed a three-sided cage. Richard sat on the other side of the bars looking at us.

He was sitting on the lower bunk. His hair fell in thick waves, nearly hiding his face. In the stark whiteness of the overhead lights, the hair looked darker than its normal honey brown, almost chestnut. He was wearing a pale green dress shirt untucked, sleeves rolled back over muscular forearms. His dark brown dress slacks were wrinkled from being slept in. He unfolded his six-foot-one-inch body from the bunk. The dress shirt stretched tightly across his shoulders and upper arms. He'd bulked up a little since last I'd seen him, and he'd been pretty muscular to begin with. Once upon a time, it would have been my great pleasure to have peeled that shirt off and seen what was underneath, to have run my hands over that lovely chest and those strong arms. But that was then, and this was a whole new ball game, one that I really couldn't win.

Richard came to stand at the bars, hands wrapping around them. "What are you doing here, Anita?" His voice wasn't as angry as I feared it would be. He sounded almost ordinary, and some tightness in the center of my body relaxed.

Belisarius stepped away from us. He sat at the table outside the cell and began spreading papers out of his briefcase. He tried to look very busy and give us as much privacy as he could. It was a nice gesture.

"I heard you were in trouble."

"So you came to rescue me?" he made it a question. His solid brown eyes stared at me, searching my face. His hair had fallen into his eyes. He smoothed it back from his face in an achingly familiar gesture.

"I came to help."

"I don't need your help. I didn't do it."

Belisarius interrupted. "You've been charged with rape, Mr. Zeeman."

I turned and looked at Belisarius. "I thought it was attempted rape."

"I've been reading the file while I was waiting. Once I had Mr. Zeeman's permission to act as his lawyer, I got access to the records. The rape kit was negative for semen, but there was evidence of penetration. Penetration is enough to constitute rape."

"I never had intercourse with her," Richard said. "It never got that far."

"But you did date her," I said.

He looked at me. "Yes, I did." There was a little anger in his voice now.

I let it go. I'd probably be grumpy, too, if I were in jail on trumped-up charges. Hell, I'd be grumpy even if I had done it.

"The problem, Mr. Zeeman, is that without semen samples, you can't really prove conclusively that you didn't violate Ms. Schaffer. If this is a frame, it's a good one. You dated the woman more than once. She went out with you and came home beaten up." He paged through one of the files. "There was vaginal bruising, some tearing. If she wasn't raped, it was still very rough."

"Becky said she liked it rough," Richard said quietly.

"When did how rough she liked sex come up in conversation?" I asked.

He met my eyes, no flinching, ready to be angry if I was angry. "When she was trying to get me to go to bed with her."

"What exactly did she say?" Belisarius asked.

Richard shook his head. "I don't remember exactly, but I told her I was afraid I'd hurt her. She said if I liked it rough, she was my girl."

I walked away from him to stand looking at the closed door. I didn't want to be here for this. I turned around, and he was already staring at me, already meeting my gaze. "Is this why you wanted to see both of us at once? So I'd hear all the details?"

He gave a harsh sound, almost laughter, but bitter. A strange look passed over his face. Once I could have read his every thought on his face, in his eyes. Now I didn't know him. Sometimes I thought I'd never known him, that we'd both been fooling ourselves. "If you want details, I can give you details. Not about Betty, but there's Lucy and Carrie and Mira. Especially Lucy and Mira. I can give you details on them."

"I heard you'd been a busy boy," I said. My voice was softer than I wanted it to be, but normal. I wasn't going to cry.

"Who told you to come down here, Anita? Who disobeyed me?" That first prickling roil of energy crept through the room. Sometimes you could forget what Richard really was. He was better at hiding it than any lycanthrope I knew. I glanced at Belisarius. He seemed oblivious. Good, he wasn't sensitive to it. But I was. The power crept over my skin like a warm wind.

"No one disobeyed you, Richard."

"Someone told you." His hands flexed on the bars, rubbing over and over. I knew he could have ripped them out of the floor. He could have knocked a hole through the back wall if he wanted to. The fact that he was still in this cage was only because he didn't want out badly enough to blow his cover. A mild-mannered junior high science teacher could not bend steel bars.

I leaned close to the bars, lowering my voice. His otherworldly energy breathed along my skin. "Do you really want to discuss this now, in front of a stranger?"

Richard leaned in so close his forehead pressed against the bars. "He's my lawyer. Doesn't he need to know?"

I leaned in so close I could have touched him through the bars. I wanted to touch him. He didn't seem quite real this way. "You really are a babe in the woods on this one, aren't you?"

"I've never been arrested before," he said.

"No, that was always my job."

He almost smiled. Some of that energy leaked away. His beast sliding away inside that perfect camouflage.

I touched the cool, metal bars, sliding my hands just below his. "I bet you thought you might be visiting me like this someday, but not the other way around."

He gave a small smile. "Yeah, and I'd bake you a cake with a file in it."

I smiled. "You don't need a file, Richard." I slid my hands over his. He squeezed my fingers gently. "You need a good lawyer, and I brought you one."

He stepped away from the bars. "Why do I need a lawyer when I'm innocent?"

Belisarius answered, "You've been charged with rape. The judge has refused you bail. Son, if we can't break her story, you're looking at two to five years, if we're lucky. The pictures are in the file. She was beat up pretty bad. She's a pretty little blond thing. She'll come into court dressed like everyone's favorite second grade teacher. The one you had a crush on that smelled like Ivory soap.'' He stood up and started walking towards us as he talked. ''We'll cut your hair—''

''Cut his hair?'' I exclaimed.

Belasarius frowned at me. ''Cut your hair, dress you up nice. It helps that you're handsome and white, but you're still a big, strong-looking man.'' He shook his head. ''It's not you we have to prove innocent, Mr. Zeeman. It's Ms. Schaffer we have to prove guilty.''

Richard frowned. ''What do you mean?''

''We have to make her look like the whore of Babylon. But first, I'll file a motion that no bail is excessive for a first offense. Hell, you don't even have a traffic ticket. I'll get you bail.''

''How long will it take?'' I asked.

Belisarius looked at me a little too hard. ''Is there a time limit I'm not aware of?''

Richard and I looked at each other as if on cue. Then he said, ''Yes,'' and I said, ''No.''

''Well, which is it, boys and girls, yes or no? Is there something I need to know here?''

Richard looked at me, then said, ''No, I guess not.''

Belisarius didn't like it, but he let it go. ''Okay, kiddies. I'll take your word for it, but if this piece of information that I don't need to know comes up and bites me on the ass, I will not be amused.''

''It won't,'' I said.

He shook his head. ''If it does, I will leave Mr. Zeeman high and dry. You will be finding yourself a new lawyer faster than you can say penitentiary.''

''I didn't do anything wrong,'' Richard said. ''How can this be happening?''

''Why would she cry rape on you?'' I asked.

''Somebody did it,'' Belisarius said. ''If not you, then who?''

Richard shook his head. ''Betty dates a lot. I know of at least three other men, myself.''

''We'll need their names.''

''Why?'' he asked.

''Son, if you are going to argue with me every step of the way, this won't work.''

''I just don't want to drag anyone else into this.''

''Richard,'' I said, ''you are in trouble here. Let Carl do his job, please.''

Richard looked at me. ''You dropped everything to ride to my rescue, huh?''

I smiled. ''Pretty much.''

He shook his head. ''How'd Jean-Claude feel about that?''

I looked away, not meeting his eyes. ''He wasn't thrilled, but he wants you out of jail.''

''I'll just bet he does.''

''Look, kiddies, we don't have a lot of time here. If you two can't curb the personal stuff, maybe Anita here should leave.''

I nodded. "I agree. You're going to have to tell him details about Ms. Schaffer that I don't want to hear. And you need to be able to talk freely about her."

"Are you jealous?" Richard asked.

I took in a deep breath and let it out. I would have liked to have said no, but he could smell a lie. I'd been doing okay until he'd made that crack about Betty being his girl for the rough stuff. That had bugged me. "I have no right to be jealous of you, Richard."

"But you are, aren't you?" he asked. He watched my face while he asked it.

I had to force myself to meet his eyes while I answered. I wanted to dunk my head, and I couldn't stop the rush of color up my face. "Yeah, I'm jealous. Happy?"

He nodded. "Yes."

"I'm out of here." I wrote the phone number of the cabin on Belisarius's notebook and pressed the buzzer to be let out.

"I'm glad you came, Anita," Richard said.

I kept my back turned to the door, hoping Maiden would hurry. "I wish I could say the same, Richard."

The door opened. I escaped.

7

"*Have fun visiting* your boyfriend?" Maiden asked as he followed me down the hall.

I waited at the second locked door. "He's not my boyfriend."

"Everyone keeps saying that." Maiden unlocked the door and held it open. "Maybe it's a case of the lady protesting too much."

"Take your library card and shove it, Maiden."

"Ooh," he said, "that was nasty. Wonder if I can think of a comeback half that good."

"Let me have my gun, Maiden."

He locked the door behind us. Jason was sitting in the little row of chairs across from the desk. He looked up. "Can we go home now?"

"Wasn't Officer Maiden entertaining?" I asked.

"He wouldn't let me play with his handcuffs," Jason said.

Maiden went behind the desk and unlocked the drawer. He brought out the Browning, slipped the clip back in it, and pulled the slide back, which jacked a shell into the chamber. He checked the safety and handed it to me, butt first.

"You think Myerton's dangerous enough to need to carry one in the chamber?" I asked.

Maiden looked at me. It was a long look as if he were trying to tell me something. "You never know," he said finally.

We stood staring at each other for a few frozen moments, then I put the Browning in the holster with the bullet ready to go, though I checked the safety twice. Didn't usually go around with a live round in the chamber. Made me nervous. Made me more nervous that Maiden might be trying to warn me. Of course, he might just be yanking my chain. Some cops, especially small town ones, tended to give me grief. Being a vampire executioner made some of them want to trade macho shit with me, like getting me to carry a live round in the chamber.

"Have a nice day, Blake."

"You, too, Maiden," I said.

I had the door open, Jason at my back, when Maiden said, "Be careful out there."

His eyes were guarded. There was nothing to read on his face. I am not a subtle person, big surprise. "You got something to say, Maiden?" I asked.

"I'm going to be taking my lunch break after you leave."

I looked at him. "It's ten o'clock in the morning. Little early for lunch, don't you think?"

"Just thought you'd like to know I won't be here."

"I'll try and squelch my disappointment," I said.

He flashed a quick grin, then stood. "I gotta lock the door behind you, since I'm leaving the desk unattended."

"Locking Belasarius in with Richard?"

"I won't be gone that long," he said. He opened the door for us, waiting for us to go outside.

"I don't like games, Maiden. What the fuck is going on?"

He wasn't smiling when he said, "If the fancy lawyer gets bail for your boyfriend, I'd leave town."

"You're not suggesting he jump bail, are you, Officer?"

"His family has been here almost from the first night he was taken into custody. Before that, it was the scientists that he's been working with. A lot of nice, upstanding citizens standing around for witnesses. But the nice upstanding citizens won't be here forever."

Maiden and I looked at each other. I stood there for a minute, wondering if he'd stop hinting and just tell me what the hell was going on. He didn't.

I nodded at him. "Thanks, Maiden."

"Don't thank me," he said. He locked the door behind us.

My hand wasn't on the butt of the Browning, but it was sort of close to it. It'd be silly to draw the gun on a nice August morning in a town with a population lower than most college dorms.

"What was that all about?" Jason asked.

"If we don't get Richard out, he's going to get hurt. The only reason he hasn't been yet is that there have been too many witnesses. Too many people to ask questions."

"If the cops are in on it," Jason said, "why would Maiden warn us?"

"He's not happy about being in on it, maybe. Oh, hell, I don't know. But it means that someone wanted Richard in jail for a reason."

A pickup truck pulled across the street in front of the little grey house that Shang-Da was camped out in. Four men jumped out of the back. There was at least one more in the cab. He slid out of sight, and they formed a semicircle at the base of the porch. One of them had a baseball bat.

"Well, well," Jason said. "You think if we bang on the doors and yell for police help, we'll get it?"

I shook my head. "Maiden did help us. He warned us."

"I'm all warm and cozy with the effort," Jason said.

"Yeah," I said. I started walking across the street. Jason followed a couple of steps behind. I was thinking as hard as I could. I had a gun and they might not.

But if I killed somebody, I'd be bunking with Richard. Myerton's legal system didn't seem to take to well to strangers.

Shang-Da stood on the porch, looking down at the men. He'd taken off the billed cap. His black hair was cut very short on the sides and longer on top. The hair was shiny with gel but squashed flat from the cap. He stood balanced on his bare feet, long arms loose at his sides. He wasn't in a fighting stance yet, but I knew the signs.

His eyes flicked to us, and I knew he'd seen us. The thugs hadn't yet. Amateur thugs. Didn't mean they weren't dangerous, but it meant you might be able to bluff them. Professional muscle tended to call a bluff.

A small, elderly woman came through the screen door to stand next to Shang-Da. She leaned heavily on a cane, her back bowed. Her grey and white hair was cut very short and permed in one of those tight hairdos that elderly women seem so fond of. She wore an apron over a pink housedress. Her knee-high hose were rolled down over fuzzy slippers. Glasses perched on a small nose.

She shook a bony fist at the men. "You boys get off my property."

The man with the baseball bat said, "Now, Millie, this has got nothing to do with you."

"This is my grandson you're threatening," she said.

"He ain't her grandson," another man said. He was wearing a faded flannel shirt open like a jacket.

"Are you calling me a liar, Mel Cooper?" the woman asked.

"I didn't say that," Mel said.

If we'd been someplace more private, I'd have just wounded one of them. It would have gotten their attention and called the fight off. But I'd have bet almost any amount of money that if I shot one of them, the mysterious sheriff would ride to their rescue. Maybe the plan was to get more of us in jail. I was too new on the scene to even make an educated guess.

Jason and I walked up onto the grass. Mel was the closest to us. He turned, showing a stained undershirt and a beer gut beneath the flannel shirt. Ooh, charming.

"Who the hell are you?" he asked.

"Well, aren't you just Mr. Smooth."

He took a menacing step towards me. I smiled at him. He frowned at me. "Answer the fucking question, girlie. Who are you?"

"Doesn't matter who she is," the one with the baseball bat said. "This isn't any of her business. Leave it alone, or you'll get what he's going to get." He motioned with his head at Shang-Da.

"I get to the beat the crap out of you, too?" I said. "Oh, goody."

Baseball Bat frowned at me, too. I had two of them puzzled. Confusion to my enemies.

The woman shook a bony fist at them again. "You get off my property, or I will call Sheriff Wilkes."

One of the men laughed, and another said, "Wilkes will be along. When we're finished."

Baseball Bat said, "Come down off that porch, boy, or we're coming up after you."

He was ignoring me. He was ignoring Jason. They weren't just amateur muscle. They were stupid amateur muscle.

Shang-Da's voice was surprisingly deep, very calm. There was no fear in it—big surprise—but there was an undercurrent of eagerness, as if under that calmness he was itching to hurt them. "If I come down off this porch, you will not enjoy it."

The man with the baseball bat wheeled his weapon of choice in a quick, professional circle. He used it like he knew how. Maybe he'd played ball in high school. "Oh, I'll enjoy it, China boy."

"China boy," Jason said. I didn't have to see his face to know he was smiling.

"Not very original is it?" I commented.

"Nope."

Mel turned towards us, and another man moved with him. "Are you making fun of us?"

I nodded. "Oh, yeah."

"You think I won't hit you because you're a girl?" Mel asked.

It was tempting to say, "No, I think you won't hit me because I have a gun," but I didn't say it. Once you pull a gun in a fight, you've pushed the violence level to a height where death is a very real possibility. I didn't want anyone dead with the cops waiting to ride down and sweep us up. Didn't want to go to jail. I have a black belt in judo. But Mel's companion was almost as big as Officer Maiden, and not half as pretty. They both outweighed me and Jason by a hundred pounds apiece, or more. They'd been big most of their lives. They thought it made them tough. Up until this moment, it probably had. In fact, it still might. I wasn't going to stand there and trade blows with them. I'd loose. Whatever I was going to do had to be quick and take my opponent out immediately. Anything less, and I stood a very good chance of getting seriously hurt.

I'd bet on me against any bad guy my size. Trouble was, as usual, none of the bad guys were my size. There was a tightness in my gut, a nervous tremble. I realized with something close to shock that I was more afraid right now than I had been with Jamil in the truck. This wasn't a dominance game with rules. No one was going to say uncle when someone was bleeding. Scared? Who, me? But it had been a long time since I'd stood up to the bad guys without pulling a weapon. Was I becoming too dependent on hardware? Maybe.

Jason and I moved back, sliding a little away from each other. You need room to fight. The thought occurred that I'd never really seen Jason fight. He could have thrown the pickup truck they came in across the street, but I didn't know if he knew how to fight. If you throw human beings around like toys, people can get badly hurt. I didn't want Jason in jail, either.

"Don't kill anyone," I said.

Jason smiled, but it was just a baring of teeth. "Gee, you're no fun." That first prickle of energy that said shapeshifter breathed along my body.

Mel had been moving forward in a flat-footed, untrained movement. No martial arts, no boxing, just big. The other guy was in a stance. He knew what he was doing. Jason could heal a broken jaw in less than a day; I couldn't. I wanted Mel. But he'd stopped moving forward. There were goose bumps on his hairy arms. "What the hell was that?"

He was big and stupid, but he was psychic enough to feel a shapeshifter. Interesting.

"Who the hell are we? What the hell was that? Mel, you need better questions," I said.

"Fuck you," he said.

I smiled and motioned him forward with both hands. "Come and get it, Mel, if you think you're man enough."

He let out a roar and ran at me. He literally ran at me with his beefy arms wide like he was going to do a bear hug. The bigger guy with him rushed Jason. I had a sense of movement and knew Shang-Da wasn't on the porch anymore. There was no time to be afraid. No time to think. Just to move. To do what I'd done a thousand times in practice in the dojo, but never in real life. Never for real.

I ducked Mel's outstretched arms and did two things almost simultaneously: I caught his left arm as he went past and swept his legs out from under him. He fell heavily to his knees, and I got a joint lock on his arm. I really hadn't decided to break the arm. A joint lock on an elbow hurts enough that most people will negotiate after you prove just how much it hurts. Mel didn't give me time. I caught a flash of the blade. I broke his arm. It made a thick wet sound, flopping loose like a chicken wing bent backwards.

He shrieked. Screaming didn't cover the sound. The blade was in his other hand, but he seemed to have forgotten it for the moment.

"Drop the knife, Mel," I said.

He tried to get to his feet, one knee hyperextended to the side. I kicked the knee and heard it give a deep, low pop. A bone breaking is a crisp, sharp sound. A joint doesn't break as clean, but it breaks easier.

He fell on the ground, writhing, screaming.

"Throw the knife away, Mel!" I was yelling at him.

The knife went airborne, lost across the fence into the next yard. I stepped away from Mel, just in case he had another surprise. Everybody else had been busy, too.

The big one that had attacked Jason was lying in a heap by the pickup truck. There was a fresh dent in the side of the truck, as if he'd been thrown into the side of it. He probably had.

A third man lay in a crumpled heap at the foot of the porch steps. He wasn't moving. Another man was trying to crawl away, one leg dangling behind him like a broken tail. He was crying.

Shang-Da was trying to break through the man with the baseball bat's defenses. Jason was fighting a tall, thin man with muscles corded along his bare arms. He was in a low fighting stance, Tae Kwon Do or jujitsu.

Shang-Da took two blows on each arm from the baseball bat, then he took the bat away from him. He broke the bat into two large pieces. The man turned to run. Shang-Da started to stab him in the back with the broken end of the bat.

I yelled, "Don't kill him."

Shang-Da flipped the broken wood in his hand and smashed the unbroken end against the man's skull. He went to his knees so suddenly it was startling.

The tall man fighting Jason crept forward in a fast crab movement that looked sort of silly, but his foot lashed out and Jason had to throw himself back onto the ground. Jason kicked at him, but the tall man leaped over the kick so high and so gracefully that he seemed to float in the air for a moment.

Sirens wailed, coming quickly closer.

Baseball Bat fell forward onto his face. He never tried to catch himself. He was out for the count.

The only one of the bad guys standing was the tall man. Jason scrambled to his feet quickly enough to stay just ahead of the punches and kicks, but not well enough to hurt him back. Super strength does not mean super skill.

Shang-Da started to move in to help.

Jason looked at Shang-Da, and that was all the tall man needed. He landed a kick to the side of Jason's head that stunned him and left him on his knees on the ground. The man turned and I saw the roundhouse kick coming. It was a kick that could snap someone's neck. I was closer than Shang-Da. I didn't even think about it. I moved forward and knew it wouldn't be in time. But the tall man saw the movement. He switched his attention from Jason to me.

I was suddenly in a defensive stance. He reversed the kick, and I managed to avoid it because he was off balance. There were two police cars skidding down the street towards us. Shang-Da stopped moving forward. I think we both thought the fight was over. The tall man thought otherwise.

The kick was just a blur of motion. I got one arm up in a partial block. My arm went numb and the next thing I knew, I was flat on my back staring up at the sky. It didn't even hurt.

He could have moved in and killed me, because for a second, I couldn't move. There was no sound for that frozen second, just me on the grass, blinking upward. Then I could hear my blood pounding in my ears. I took a deep gasping breath and I could hear human voices again.

A man's voice yelled, "Freeze, motherfucker!"

I tried to say, "Colorful," but no sound came out. I could taste blood in my mouth. My face didn't hurt that much yet; I was sort of numb. I opened my mouth just to see if I could. I could. My jaw wasn't broken. Great. I raised one arm upward and managed to say, "Help me up."

Jason said, "They've got guns pointed at us."

Millie came down off the porch with her cane. She looked funny from my angle, like a fuzzy-footed giant. "Don't you be pointing guns at my grandson and his friends. These men attacked them."

"Attacked them?" said a man's voice. "Looks like your 'grandson' and his friends attacked them."

I fumbled my ID out of my jacket pocket and held it up in the air. I could probably have sat up on my own, but since I'd taken a hit, I might as well use it. I was hurt, and the more hurt the cops thought I was, the less likely we'd be going to jail. If only the bad guys had been hurt, then we'd have all ended up in jail on assault charges or worse. I hadn't checked for pulses in at least two of the thugs. They'd been lying awfully still. This way we could all press assault charges. They could put us all in jail, or none in jail. Or that was the plan. As plans go, I'd had better ones. I was lucky my jaw wasn't broken.

"Anita Blake, vampire executioner," I said. The announcement would have had a little more oomph if I hadn't been flat on my back, but hey, you do what you can. I did roll onto one side. My mouth had filled with enough blood that I either had to spit or swallow. I spat onto the grass. Even rolling onto my side made the world spin. I wondered for a second or two if I was going to spit up more on the grass than just blood. The nausea passed, leaving me worried about a concussion. I'd had them before, and they usually made me sick to my stomach.

I couldn't see Millie anymore, but I could hear her. "You put up those guns, Billy Wilkes, or I will tan your hide with my cane."

"Now, Miss Millie," the male voice said.

I repeated who I was and said, "I need some help to stand. Can my people help me up, please?"

The male voice, Sheriff Wilkes I presumed, sounded a little uncertain, but said, "They can move."

Jason grabbed the arm that was holding my ID up in the air. He looked down at me and pulled me to my feet. It was too quick and I didn't have to pretend that the world went spinning. When my knees buckled, I didn't fight it. I slid to my knees and Shang-Da took my other arm. Between the two of them, they got me standing and facing the cops.

Sheriff Wilkes was about five foot eight, and he was wearing a pale blue Smokey the Bear hat and a matching uniform. He looked trim and in shape like he worked out and took it seriously. The gun at his side was a ten mil Beretta. It was holstered. The day was looking up.

He stared at me with eyes a dark, solid, trustworthy brown. He took the hat off and wiped sweat from his forehead. His hair was a pale salt and pepper and made me put his age at over forty. "Anita Blake, I've heard of you. What are you doing in our town?"

I spat another mouthful of blood into the grass and managed to stand more than sag between Shang-Da and Jason. Truth was, I could have stood on my own. But all the bad guys were on the ground. Even the one that had kicked me was down for the count. Shang-Da must have stepped in after I went down. I knew Jason couldn't have taken the tall man.

"I came to see a friend in your jail—Richard Zeeman."

"Friend?" he made it a question.

"Yeah, friend."

There were two deputies behind Wilkes. They were both over six feet tall. One of them had a scar that went from eyebrow to jaw on one side. Jagged; more a broken bottle than a knife. The other deputy had a shotgun in his hands. It wasn't pointed at us, but it was there. Scarface snickered at me. The one with the shotgun just stared with eyes as empty and pitiless as a doll's.

Maiden was standing behind the others, hands in front, one hand clasping his opposite wrist. His face was blank, but there was an edge around his mouth that said he was trying not to smile.

"We've got to run you all in for assault," Wilkes said.

"Great," I said, "I can't wait to press charges."

He looked at me, his eyes just a touch wide. "You're the only ones standing, Ms. Blake. I don't think you have grounds to press charges."

I leaned a little heavier against Jason. A trickle of blood ran from the corner of my mouth. I could feel my eye already starting to swell. I've always been a bleeder if you hit me in the face. I knew I looked pitiful. "They attacked us, and we were forced to defend ourselves." I let my knees slide out from under me. Shang-Da caught me and lifted me easily in his arms. I closed my eyes and curled against his chest.

"Shit," Wilkes said.

"Look at that poor little girl, Billy Wilkes," Millie said. "You going to take her before Judge Henry. What do you think he's going to do to the rest of these hooligans? He's got a daughter about her age."

"Shit," Wilkes said again with more force. "Let's get everybody down to the hospital. We'll sort it out there."

"Ambulance is on its way," Maiden said.

"One won't be enough," Wilkes said.

Maiden laughed low and deep. "There aren't enough ambulances in the county for this many bodies."

"There would have been enough for three," Wilkes said.

I tensed in Shang-Da's arms. He tightened around me, one hand pressed against the side of my head firmly enough that raising up would have hurt my face. I let the breath ease out of my body and concentrated on being still, but I'd remember what Wilkes had said. We'd see who got the ambulance ride next time.

8

It took one ambulance, one pickup truck, two squad cars, Santa's sleigh, and me riding in the van for everyone to get to the hospital. Okay, not Santa's sleigh, but we did look like a parade. Nearly six hours later, we were back in Myerton in the only interrogation room they had. I'd been the only one of the injured that got to leave the hospital.

The guy that Jason had thrown into the truck might have permanent spine damage. They'd know when the swelling went down. Two of the three that Shang-Da had knocked unconscious had regained consciousness. They had concussions but would recover. The third was still out for the count, and the doctors were talking about swelling of the brain and skull fractures. Shang-Da had also done the bad guy with the compound fracture. I only had Mel to my credit, but he was in worse shape than the compound fracture. It takes a hell of a lot of work to heal a joint break. Sometimes you never recover full use of the limb. I felt sort of bad about that, but he had pulled the knife.

Belisarius had been a busy little lawyer. He'd not only arranged bail for Richard, but he'd also been representing us for the last hour or so. Richard was a free man, temporarily. If Belisarius could keep the rest of us out of jail, he was worth the money.

Wilkes didn't want to arrest us, but he wanted to take our fingerprints. I didn't have a problem with that until Shang-Da did. He really didn't want his prints taken, which made both Wilkes and me suspicious. But if Shang-Da wouldn't do it, then none of us would. I told Wilkes if he wanted our prints, he had to charge us with something. He seemed reluctant to do that.

Maybe it was because I'd used my one phone call to contact a cop I knew, who in turn had contacted an FBI agent I knew.

Having a call from the feds made Wilkes jumpy as hell. The bad guys had ambushed us across from the police station. You didn't do a planned attack right next door to the cops unless you were pretty sure they wouldn't spoil the fun. The bad guys had known the police wouldn't help us. They'd said as much during the fight, challenging Millie to call Wilkes, like it wouldn't help. But Wilkes's reaction to the call from the feds sort of clinched it for me. Policemen are very territorial. No federal laws had been broken. The FBI had no business in a simple assault case. Wilkes should have been pissed, and he wasn't. Oh, he made noises like he was angry, and he was, but he should have raised hell, and he didn't. His reaction to everything was just a little bit off—a little bit less convincing than it should have been.

I was betting he was dirty. I just couldn't prove it yet. Of course, it wasn't my job to prove it. I'd come down here to get Richard out of jail, and we'd done that.

Wilkes finally asked to speak with me alone. Belisarius didn't like it, but he left with the others. I sat at the little table and looked at Wilkes.

It was the cleanest interrogation room I'd ever been in. The table was pale pine and looked handmade. The walls were white and clean. Even the linoleum on the floor was hospital bright. I didn't think Myerton got a lot of use for the room. It'd probably started life as a storage closet. It had been almost too small to hold five of us, but there was room for two.

Wilkes pulled a chair out and sat across from me. He clasped his hands in front of him and looked at me. There was a band around his head where the hair had been pressed flat from the hat. There was a plain gold wedding band on his left hand and one of those watches that joggers use, big and black and utilitarian. Since I had the lady's version of the same watch on my left wrist, it was hard to criticize.

"What?" I said. "You going to give me the silent treatment until I scream for mercy?"

He gave a very small smile. "Made some phone calls about you, Blake. There's a lot of talk that you'll bend the law if you need to. That maybe you've murdered people."

I just looked at him. I could feel my face thinning out, blanking. Once upon a time, every emotion I'd felt had played along my face, but that was a while ago. I'd perfected my blank cop stare, and it showed nothing.

"Is there a point to this conversation?" I asked.

The smile this time was bigger. "I just like to know who I'm dealing with, Blake, that's all."

"Good to be thorough," I said.

He nodded. "I got calls from a Saint Louis cop, a fed, and a state cop. The state cop says you're a pain in the ass and will bend the law six ways to Sunday."

"Bet that was Freemount," I said. "She's still pissed about a case we worked together."

He nodded, smiling pleasantly. "The fed sort of hinted that if you were detained, he might find a reason to have the local federal office to come take a look around."

I smiled. "Bet you really enjoyed that."

His brown eyes went hard and dark. "I don't want the feebies down here messing in my pond."

"I'll bet you don't, Wilkes."

His face tightened, letting me see just how angry he was. "What the fuck do you care?"

I leaned across the table on my elbows. "You should be more careful who you do a frame-up job on, Wilkes."

"He's a fucking junior high science teacher. How was I supposed to know he was shacking up with the fucking Executioner?"

"We're not shacking up," I said automatically. I sat back in my seat. "What do you want, Wilkes? Why the private talk?"

He ran his hand through his salt-and-pepper hair, and for the first time, I realized how nervous he was. He was scared. Why? What the hell was happening in this tiny town?

"If the rape charges disappear, Zeeman is free to leave town. You and everybody go with him. No harm, no foul."

A sport's metaphor—ooh, I was all a-tingle. "I didn't come down here to sniff around your mess, Wilkes. I'm not a cop. I came down here to get Richard out of trouble."

"He's out of trouble if he leaves."

"I'm not his keeper, Wilkes. I can't promise what Richard will do."

"Why does a schoolteacher have bodyguards?" Wilkes asked.

I shrugged. "Why do you want the schoolteacher out of the way bad enough to frame him for rape?"

"We've all got our secrets, Blake. You make sure he leaves town and takes his assassins with him, and we can all keep our secrets."

I looked at my hands spread on the smooth tabletop. I looked back up, met his eyes. "I'll talk to Richard, see what I can do. But I can't promise anything until after I've talked to him."

"Make him listen, Blake. Zeeman is so clean he squeaks, but you and I know the score."

I shook my head. "Yeah, I know the score, and I know what people say about me." I stood up.

He stood up. We looked at each other.

"I don't always pay attention to the letter of the law, that's true. One of the reasons Richard and I aren't dating anymore is that he is so fucking squeaking clean it makes my teeth hurt. But we have one thing in common."

"What's that?" Wilkes asked.

"Push us, and we push back. Richard usually for moral grounds, because it's the right thing to do. Me, because I am just that unpleasant."

"Unpleasant," Wilkes said. "Mel Cooper may never walk right again or have the full use of his left arm."

"He shouldn't have pulled a knife on me," I said.

"If there hadn't been witnesses, would you have killed him?"

I smiled, and even to me, it felt like a strange smile, not humorous, unpleasant maybe. "I'll talk to Richard. Hopefully, we'll be out of your hair before tomorrow night."

"I wasn't always a small-town cop, Blake. Don't let the surroundings fool you. I will not let you and your people fuck with me."

"Funny," I said. "I was thinking the very same thing."

"Well," Wilkes said, "we know where we stand."

"I guess we do," I said.

"I hope come dark tomorrow you and your friends are on your way out of town."

I stared into his brown eyes. I'd looked into scarier eyes, blanker, more dead. He didn't have the eyes of a professional killer. He didn't even have good cop eyes. I could see the fear shiny and almost panicked around the edges. No, I'd seen scarier eyes. But that didn't mean he wouldn't kill me if he got the chance. Make even a good man scared enough, and you never know what he'll do. Make a bad man scared, and you are in trouble. Wilkes probably hadn't killed anybody yet or they wouldn't have framed Richard for rape. They'd have framed him for murder or just killed him. So Wilkes hadn't slid completely down into the abyss. But once you embrace the screaming darkness, eventually, you kill. Maybe Wilkes didn't know that yet, but if we pushed hard enough, he'd figure it out.

9

By the time I got back to the cabins, it was after seven. It was August, so it was still daylight, but you could tell it was late. There was a softness to the light, a tiredness to the heat as if the day itself was eager for night. Or maybe it was just me that was tired.

My face hurt. At least I hadn't had to have stitches in my mouth. The EMS guy on the ambulance had said I'd need a couple of stitches. When I got to the hospital, the doctor said I didn't. A very bright spot for me. I'm sort of phobic about needles. But I've taken stitches with no painkiller and that ain't fun, either.

Jamil was standing in front of the cabins. He'd changed into black jeans and a T-shirt with a smiley face on it. The T-shirt was cut across the middle so his abs showed. Though my dance card was full of attractive men, Jamil did have one of the nicest stomachs I'd ever seen. The muscles stood out under the tight smoothness of his skin like shingles on a roof. It didn't even look real. Somehow, I didn't think you needed cobblestone abs to be a good bodyguard. But hey, everyone needs a hobby.

"I'm sorry I missed the fun," he said. He touched my bruised lip gently. It still made me wince. "I'm surprised you let anyone mark you."

"She did it on purpose," Shang-Da said.

Jamil looked at him.

"Anita pretended to faint," Jason said. "She looked really pitiful."

Jamil looked back at me.

I shrugged. "I didn't let someone kick me in the face on purpose. But once I was down, I did play up how hurt I was. This way, we could press our own assault charges."

"I didn't think you lied that well," Jamil said.

"Live and learn," I said. "Where's Richard? I need to talk to him."

Jamil glanced behind him at one of the cabins, then back to me. There was a look on his face that I couldn't read. "He's cleaning up. He's been in the same clothes for two days."

I stared at his so-careful face, trying to figure out what he wasn't telling me. "What's going on, Jamil?"

He shook his head. "Nothing."

"Don't give me grief, Jamil. I need to talk to Richard—now."

"He's in the shower."

I shook my head, and it made my head hurt. "Screw this. What cabin is he in?"

Jamil shook his head. "Give him a few minutes."

"Longer," Shang-Da said, his voice very bland.

Jason looked from one to the other of them, eyes just a touch wide.

"What is going on?" I asked.

The cabin door behind Jamil opened. A woman appeared in the doorway. Richard had her arms and seemed to be trying to push her, gently but firmly, out the door.

The woman turned and saw me. She had pale brown hair in one of those hairdos that seem artless and simple yet actually take hours to do. She pulled away from Richard and stalked towards us. No, towards me. Her dark eyes were all for me.

"Lucy, don't," Richard said.

"I just want to smell her," Lucy said.

It was the kind of comment a dog might make if it could speak. Smell me, not see me. We primates tend to forget that a lot of other mammals consider smell more important than vision.

Lucy and I had time to study each other as she walked towards me. She was only a little taller than me, maybe five foot six. Her walk was an exaggerated sway so that the short, plum-colored skirt bloused around her and you got glimpses of the hose and garters she was wearing underneath. She was carrying a pair of black heels but walked towards us in a graceful, almost tiptoe movement. Her blouse was a paler purple, unbuttoned so that you glimpsed enough of the bra to know it was black and matched the rest of the undies that you could see. And either the bra was a wonderbra or she was, well, stacked. She was wearing more makeup than I ever wore, but it was well-applied and made her skin look smooth and perfect. Her dark lipstick was smeared.

I glanced behind her at Richard. He was wearing a pair of blue jeans and nothing else. Water still beaded on his naked chest. His thick hair clung to his face and shoulders in wet strands. He had her dark lipstick smeared across his mouth like a plum-colored bruise.

We looked at each other, and I don't think either of us knew what to say.

The woman knew exactly what to say. "So you're Richard's human bitch."

It was so hostile, it made me smile.

She didn't like the smile. She stepped into me so close, I'd have to step back to keep the edge of her skirt from brushing my legs. If I'd had any doubt what she was, this close, her power danced over my skin like insects swarming over my body. She was powerful.

I shook my head. "Look, before we get into any arcane werewolf shit or worse, personal shit, I need to talk to Richard about jail and why the local cops went to the trouble of framing him for rape."

She blinked at me. "My name is Lucy Winston. Remember it."

I looked into her pale brown eyes from inches away. I was close enough to see the small imperfections in her eyeliner. Richard had mentioned a Lucy in jail. He couldn't be dating two of them, could he? "Lucy—Richard mentioned you," I said.

She blinked again, but this time she was puzzled. She took a step back from me to glance at Richard. "You mentioned me to her?"

Richard nodded.

She backed up and looked on the verge of tears. "Then why . . ."

I glanced from one to the other of them. Why what, is what I wanted to ask. But I didn't. I'd been enjoying disliking Lucy. If she cried, it might spoil my fun.

I put my hands up like I was surrendering and stepped around her. I walked towards Richard because we had to talk, but seeing Lucy in her garters and hose had taken a lot of the fun out of it.

It was none of my business what he did. I was sleeping with Jean-Claude. I was all out of stones to throw. So why was I having such a hard time not being pissed? Maybe that was a question better left unanswered.

Richard stepped back out of the doorway so I could walk past him. He closed the door behind me, leaning against it. We were suddenly alone, really alone, and I didn't know what to say.

He leaned against the door with his hands behind his back. Water beaded on his naked upper body. He'd always had a nice chest, but he had been lifting weights since last I'd seen him without his shirt. His upper body was almost aggressively masculine, though still short of that overdone look that bodybuilders strive so hard for. He was slumped against the door. It made his stomach muscles bunch. Once upon a time, I could have helped him dry off. His hair was starting to dry in a wavy mass. If he didn't do something soon, he'd have to wet it and start over.

"Lucy drag you out of the shower without a towel?" The moment I said it, I wished I hadn't. I put my hand up and said, "I'm sorry. It's none of my business. I don't have the right to be catty with you."

He smiled, almost sadly. "I think that's the second time I've ever heard you admit you were wrong."

"Oh, I'm wrong a lot. I just don't admit it out loud."

That made him smile again, and it was almost his normal smile. That bright flash of perfect teeth in the permanent tan of his face. Most people thought Richard was tanned. I knew it was skin color because I'd seen the whole package. He was white bread, all Middle American, with a family that made the Waltons look unfriendly, but a generation or so back was something not so white bread.

Richard pushed away from the door. He walked towards me on his bare feet. I was more aware than was polite of the line of hair running down the center of his lower abdomen.

I turned away and said, "Why did they want you in jail?" Business, concentrate on business.

"I'm not sure," he said. "May I get a towel and finish drying off while we talk?"

"It's your cabin. Help yourself," I said.

He disappeared into the bathroom. I was left to look around. The cabin was almost identical to mine except that it was yellow and it was more lived in. The cheerful comforter was pushed onto the floor in a sunny heap. The white sheets were wrinkled. Richard was almost fanatical about making the bed. Somehow Lucy didn't strike me as the neat type. I was betting she had mussed the bed. Of course, there was a wet spot on one side, so maybe she'd had help.

I passed my hand over the damp sheets. Even the pillow was wet as if that thick wet hair had laid across it. My throat felt tight, and if I hadn't known better, I'd have said there were tears in my eyes. Naw, surely not. I mean I'd been the one that dumped Richard. Why should I cry?

The print above the bed was another Van Gogh, *Sunflowers* this time. I wondered if every cabin had a Van Gogh print in a color that matched the decor. Yeah, maybe if I concentrated on the room's furnishings, I wouldn't keep wondering if Lucy had looked up at the melting sunflowers while Richard . . .

I cut that particular visual off. I didn't need to go there—ever. Did I really think that Richard was going to stay chaste while I boffed Jean-Claude? Did I really expect him to just wait around? Maybe I had. Stupid, but maybe true.

The bathroom door was still closed. I could hear water running. Was he taking another shower? Maybe he was just wetting down his hair. Maybe. Or maybe he was cleaning off. Sex was never as neat as the movies made it. Real sex was messy. Good sex was messier.

Three months with Jean-Claude, and I was a sex expert. It was almost funny. I'd been chaste until he came along. Not virginal. My fiancé in college had taken care of that. I'd fallen into my fiancé's arms with the trust that only first love can give you. It was one of the last naive things I ever did.

Richard and I had been engaged, briefly. But we'd never had sex. We'd both been chaste since our first experience in college with other people. Just a personal choice that we both shared. Maybe if we'd given in to that lust, there wouldn't be so much heat left between us. Of course, lately, we'd been mostly fighting.

Richard had been too kindhearted, too tender, too squeamish to rule the wolf pack. He'd had a chance to kill the old Ulfric, Marcus, twice; and twice Richard refused the kill. No kill, no new Ulfric. I urged him to kill Marcus. And after he did it, I dumped him. Unfair, wasn't it? Of course, I hadn't told him to eat Marcus, just to kill him. What's a little cannibalism between friends?

The water was still running in the bathroom. If I hadn't been afraid he'd answer dripping wet in nothing but a towel, I'd have knocked and asked him to hurry. But I'd seen enough of Mr. Zeeman for one day. Less was definitely more.

There were pictures pinned above the desk. I walked towards them. I'd had one semester of Primate Studies: North American. We'd all called it troll class. The Lesser Smokey Mountain Troll is one of the smallest of the North American trolls. They average between three and a half feet to five feet. They are mostly vegetarians but will supplement their diet with carrion and insects. I let all the stats run through my head as I walked towards the pictures. They were covered in blackish fur from head to foot. Crouched in the trees, huddled together, they looked like tall chimpanzees or slender gorillas, but there were pictures of them walking. They were completely bipedal. The only primate except man that walked upright.

The close-up shots of faces were startling. Their faces were more furry than the great apes and more manlike. Some early theories had said trolls were the missing link between man and ape. There had been at least two famous cases of circuses in the early 1900s that toured with trolls but listed them as wild men. American settlers had been killing trolls for centuries. By the early 1900s, they'd been rare enough to be oddities.

Two things happened in 1910 that saved the trolls from utter destruction. One: a scientific article was published that said that the trolls used tools and buried their dead with flowers and personal articles. The scientist very carefully did not project anything beyond the basic findings, but the newspapers did. They declared that trolls believed in an afterlife, that they believed in God.

An evangelical minister named Simon Barkley felt that God spoke to him. He went out and captured a troll and tried to convert him to Christianity. He wrote a book about his experiences with Peter (the troll), and it became a best-seller. Suddenly, trolls were a cause célèbre.

One of my biology profs had kept a black-and-white photo of Peter the Troll up in his office. Peter had his head bowed and his hands clasped. He was even wearing clothes, though Minister Barkley was always distressed that without constant supervision, Peter disrobed.

I wasn't sure how good a time Peter had with Barkley, but he saved his species from almost certain extinction. Peter had been a North American Cave Troll, the only species on this continent smaller than the Lesser Smokey. Barkley had been moved by the spirit of God, but he hadn't been stupid. There had still been Greater Smokey Mountain Trolls in those days, eight to twelve feet tall and carnivorous. Barkley hadn't tried to save one of them. Probably just as well. It would have been a real downer if the troll had eaten Barkley instead of praying for him.

Trolls were the first protected species in America. The Greater Smokey Mountain Troll was not protected. It was hunted to extinction; but then, it pulled up large trees and beat the tourists to death and sucked the marrow from their bones. Hard to get good press that way.

There was still a troll society called Peter's Friends. Even though it was illegal to kill trolls, any trolls, for any reason, it still happened. Hunters poached them. Though staring into those too-human faces, I don't know how they did it. Not just for a trophy.

Richard stepped out of the bathroom in a rush of warm air. He was still wearing the jeans, but now there was a towel on his head and a blow-dryer in one hand. He had rewet his hair, though he seemed to have gotten all of him in the shower to do it. Mercifully, he'd dried his chest and arms off. His arms looked amazingly strong. I knew he could have tossed around small elephants, regardless of how muscular he looked, but the muscles helped remind me. Physically, he was a pleasure to gaze upon. But it made me wonder why he'd been spending the extra time on his body. Richard didn't usually sweat that kind of thing.

I pointed at the pictures. "These are great." I smiled and meant it. Once upon a time, I'd envisioned spending my life in the field doing this kind of work. A sort of preternatural Jane Goodall. Though truthfully, primates hadn't been my main area of interest. Dragons, maybe, or lake monsters. Nothing that wouldn't eat me if it got the chance. But that had been long ago before Bert, my boss, recruited me to raise the dead and slay vampires. Sometimes, even though Richard was older than I was by three years, he made me feel old. He was still trying to have a life amid all the strange shit. I'd given up on anything but the strange shit. You couldn't do both equally well—or I couldn't.

"I'll take you up to see them, if you'd like," he said.

"I'd love to, if it wouldn't upset the trolls."

"They're pretty accustomed to visitors. Carrie—Dr. Onslow—has started allowing small groups of tourists to come and take pictures."

He'd mentioned a Carrie in the same breath with Lucy. Was this the same woman? "Are you guys that hard up for money?" I asked.

He sat down on the side of the bed and plugged in the blow-dryer. "You're always short of money on a project like this, but it's not money we need. It's good press."

I frowned at him. "Why do you need good press?"

"Have you been reading the newspaper lately?" he asked. He removed the towel from his head. His hair was dark and brown with moisture, heavy, as if there was still water to be squeezed from it.

"You know I don't read the newspaper."

"You didn't own a television, either, but you do now."

I leaned my butt against the edge of his desk, as far away from him as I could get and not leave the room. I'd bought the television so that he and I could watch old movies and videos.

"I don't watch much television anymore."

"Jean-Claude not a fan of muscials?" Richard asked, and there was that edge to his voice that I'd heard in the last few weeks: angry, jealous, hurt, cruel.

It was almost a relief to hear it. His anger made everything easier. "Jean-Claude's not much of a watcher. He's more a doer."

Richard's face thinned out, anger making his high, sculpted cheekbones stand out underneath his skin. "Lucy isn't much of a watcher, either," he said, voice low and careful.

I laughed, and it wasn't a happy sound. "Thanks for making this easier, Richard."

He stared down at the floor, his wet hair tucked to one side so his face was in full profile. "I don't want to fight, Anita. I really don't."

"Could have fooled me," I said.

He looked up, and his chocolate brown eyes were dark with more than just color. "If I'd wanted a fight, I could have just given in to Lucy. Let you find us in the bed together."

"You're not mine, anymore, Richard. Why should it bother me what the hell you do?"

"That is the question, isn't it?" He stood and started walking towards me.

"Why did they frame you?" I asked. "Why did they want you in jail?"

"That's you, Anita. All business."

"And you let yourself get distracted, Richard. You don't keep your eye on the ball." Geez, a sports metaphor. Maybe it was contagious.

"Fine," he said, and that one word was so angry that it almost hurt. "The troll band that we're studying has broken into two bands. Their birth rate is so low that they don't do that very often. It's the first recorded offshoot for a North American troll troop in this century."

"This is all fascinating, but what does it have to do with anything?"

"Just shut up and listen," he said.

I did. That was a first.

"The second smaller troop moved out of the park. They've been on private land for a little over a year. The farmer who owned the land was okay with that. In fact, he was sort of pleased. Carrie brought him up to see the first troll baby born on his land, and he carried the picture in his wallet."

I looked at him. "Sounds great."

"The farmer, Ivan Greene, died about six months ago. His son was not a nature lover."

"Ah," I said.

"But trolls are a severely endangered species. And they're not like the snail darter, or the velvet-back toad. They're a big, showy animal. The son tried to sell the land, and we got it stopped legally."

"But the son wasn't happy with that," I said.

Richard smiled. "Not hardly."

"So he took you to court," I said.

"Not exactly," Richard said. "We expected him to do that. In fact, we should have known something was wrong when he didn't keep us tied up in court."

"What did he do?" I asked.

The anger was leaking away as Richard talked. He always had to work really hard to stay angry. Me, it was one of my best things. He retrieved the towel from the bed and started drying his hair while he talked.

"Goats started disappearing from a local farmer."

"Goats?" I said.

Richard peered at me through a curtain of wet hair. "Goats."

"Somebody's been reading too much 'Billy nGoat Gruff,' " I said.

Richard wrapped the towel more firmly around his head and sat down on the bed. "Exactly," he said. "No one who really knew anything about trolls would have taken goats. Even the European Lesser Trolls that do hunt will take your dog before they'll take your goat."

"So it was a setup," I said.

"Yeah, but the newspapers got hold of it. We were still okay until the dogs and cats started disappearing."

"They got smarter," I said.

"They listened to Carrie's interviews where she discussed food preferences," he said.

I'd come to stand at the foot of the bed. "Why are the local cops interested in some land squabble?"

"Wait, it gets worse," he said.

I picked up the spilled comforter and sat on the edge of the bed with it bundled in my lap. "How worse?"

"A man's body was found two weeks ago. It was just one of those horrible hiking acidents at first. He fell off the mountain. It happens," Richard said.

"Having seen some of the mountains, I'm not surprised," I said.

"But somehow the body was listed as a troll kill."

I frowned at him. "It's not like a shark kill, Richard. How did they tell a troll did it?"

"A troll didn't do it," Richard said.

I nodded. "Of course not, but what was their proof, false or otherwise?"

"Carrie tried to get the coroner's report. But it was leaked to the newspapers first. The man had been beaten to death and had bites out of his body from animals. Troll bites."

I shook my head. "Anybody who dies in these mountains is going to have animal bites on the body. Trolls are known scavengers."

"Not according to Sheriff Wilkes," Richard said.

"What does the sheriff get out of this?"

"Money," Richard said.

"Do you know that for sure?" I asked.

"You mean, can I prove it?"

I nodded.

"No. Carrie's been trying to see if there's a paper trail, but so far, nothing. She's been chasing around, trying to get me out of jail for the last few days."

"Is she the same Carrie you mentioned as a girlfriend in jail?" I asked.

Richard nodded.

"Aha," I said.

"Did you just say, aha?" he asked.

"Yes, and I apologize for it, but what better way to keep Carrie from working on the mystery than to put her boyfriend in jail."

"I'm not her boyfriend anymore," he said.

I hurried past that little bit of knowledge. "Is it common knowledge that you're not an item anymore?"

"Not really."

"Then that may explain why they wanted you in jail. They framed you for rape because so far, Wilkes isn't willing to kill."

"You think that will change?" Richard asked.

I touched my swollen lip. "He's already started upping the violence level."

Richard leaned across the bed until his fingertips touched the bruises on my face. It was a tentative touch like a butterfly's wing. "Did Wilkes do this?"

My heart was suddenly beating faster. "No," I said, "Wilkes was very careful to only show up after all the bad guys needed an ambulance."

Richard smiled, fingers tracing the edge of my face, just beyond the bruises. "How many of them did you hurt?"

My pulse was beating so hard, I was afraid he could see it jumping in my throat. "Just one."

Richard scooted just a little closer to me, hand still trailing up and down my cheek. "What did you do to him?"

I didn't know whether to move away or cuddle my aching face against the cool warmth of his hand. "I broke his arm and leg at the joint."

"Why did you do that?" Richard asked.

"He was threatening Shang-Da, and he pulled a knife on me." My voice sounded breathy.

Richard leaned in close, then closer. He pulled the ridiculous towel from his head, and his thick hair fell in chilled, wet strands around his face, against my skin. His lips were so close to my mouth, I could feel his breath.

I stood, stepping back from him, the comforter still bundled in my arms. I let it fall to the floor, and we stared at each other.

"Why not, Anita? You want me. I can feel it, smell it, taste your pulse on my tongue."

"Thanks for that visual, Richard."

"You still want me after months in his bed. You still want *me*."

"That doesn't make it right." I said.

"Loyal to Jean-Claude now?" he asked.

"Just trying not to fuck up any worse than I already have, Richard. That's all."

"Regretting your choice?" he asked.

I shook my head. "No comment."

He stood and started towards me. I put a hand out, and he stopped. The weight of his gaze was almost touchable, as if I could feel what he was thinking, and it was personal and intimate, and things we'd never done before.

"Sheriff Wilkes says get out of Dodge by dark tomorrow, take our bodyguards with us, and he'll just forget everything. The rape charges will vanish, and you can go back to your normal life."

"I can't do that, Anita. They're talking about hunting the trolls down with guns and dogs. I'm not leaving until I know the trolls are safe."

I sighed. "School starts in less than two weeks. Are you going to stay here and lose your job?"

"Do you really think Wilkes will let it go that long?" Richard asked.

"No," I said. "I think he or some of his men will start killing people first. We need to find out why this land is so valuable."

"If it's minerals, Greene hasn't filed the report, which means he doesn't need government permission and doesn't need partners."

"What do you mean permission and partners?"

"If he'd found, say, emeralds on land that bordered the national park, then he'd have to file the claim and try to get permission to placer mine next to the park. If he'd found something that needed blasting and hard mining like maybe lead or something, then he might need partners to help him finance it. Then he'd need to file a claim to show the prospective partners."

"When did you start studing geology?" I asked.

He smiled. "We've been trying to figure out what is on the land that is worth this much trouble. Minerals seemed the logical choice."

I nodded. "Agreed, but either it's not minerals or it's something private, and he doesn't have to share that info, right?"

"Exactly."

"I need to speak with Carrie and the other biologists," I said.

"Tomorrow," he said.

"Why not tonight?"

"You said it outside: arcane werewolf shit."

"What's that supposed to mean?" I asked.

"It means that we're four nights from the full moon, and you're my lupa."

"I heard you've been taking applicants for the job," I said.

He smiled, and it wasn't nearly embarrassed enough. "You may find it strange, but a lot of women find me attractive."

"You know I don't find that strange," I said.

"But you're still with Jean-Claude," he said.

I shook my head. "I'm out of here, Richard. I'll stay around and try to keep you from being killed or getting any of our pack killed, but let's drop the personal stuff."

He closed the distance between us, and I put my hands up to keep him from touching me. My hands ended up pressed to his bare chest. His heart thudded against my hands like a trapped animal.

"Don't do this, Richard."

"I tried hating you, and I can't." He put his hands over mine, holding them against the hard smoothness of his chest.

"Try harder." But it was a whisper.

He leaned over me, and I drew back. "If you don't dry your hair, you're going to have to wet it down again."

"I'll risk it." He kept moving towards me, lips half parted.

I stepped back, pulling my hands out of his, and he let me. He was strong enough that he didn't have to let me, and that still bothered me.

I backed towards the door. "Stop trying to love me, Richard."

"I have tried."

"Then stop trying and just do it." The door was pressed against my back. I grabbed the doorknob without turning around.

"You ran from me that night. You ran from me to Jean-Claude. You pulled his body around you like a shield to keep me away."

I opened the door, but he was just suddenly there, holding it half-closed. I started tugging on the door, and it was like pulling against a wall, immobile. His one hand pressed flat on the door, against the pull of my entire body, and I couldn't budge him. I hated that a lot.

"Damn it, Richard, let me go."

"I think you're more afraid of how much you love me than you are of Jean-Claude. At least with him you know you're not in love."

That was it. I wedged my body in the door enough so he couldn't close it on me, but I stopped tugging on it. I looked up at him, at every gorgeous inch of him. "I may not love Jean-Claude in the same way I love you."

He smiled.

"Don't get cocky," I said. "I do love Jean-Claude. But love isn't enough, Richard. If love were enough, I wouldn't be with Jean-Claude now. I'd be with you." I looked into his big, brown eyes and said, "But I'm not with you, and love isn't enough. Now, get away from this damned door."

He stepped back, hands at his side. "Love can be enough, Anita."

I shook my head and stepped out on the steps. The darkness was thick and touchable but not yet solid. "The last time you listened to me, you killed for the first time, and you haven't recovered from it. I should have just shot Marcus for you."

"I'd have never forgiven you for that," he said.

I gave a harsh sound that was almost a laugh. "But at least you wouldn't be hating yourself. I'd be the monster, not you."

His handsome face was suddenly very solemn; all the light fled from it. "Whatever I do, wherever I go, Anita, I *am* the monster. You left me because of what I am."

I stepped down onto the ground, staring up at him. There was no light inside the cabin, and Richard stood in a darker shadow than the coming night. "I thought you said I left you because I was afraid of how much I loved you."

He looked confused for a second, not knowing how to deal with his own logic thrown back into his face. He finally looked at me. "Do you know why you left me?"

I wanted to say, "Because you ate Marcus," but I didn't. I couldn't say it staring into his face, so ready to believe the worst of himself. He wasn't my problem anymore, so why did I care how hurt his ego was? Good question. I was out of good answers. Besides, maybe there was some truth to what Richard was saying. I didn't know anymore.

"I'm going to go to my cabin, now, Richard. I don't want to talk about this anymore."

"Afraid?" he asked.

I shook my head and answered without turning around. "Tired." I kept walking, knowing he was watching me. The parking area was empty. I didn't know where Jamil and the others had gone, and I didn't care. I needed some alone time.

I walked through the soft, summer darkness. There was a spill of stars overhead, glittering and edged by the dark shapes of leaves. It was going to be a beautiful evening. Somewhere off in the distance, a high, clear howl rode the coming dark. Richard had said something about arcane werewolf shit. We were going to have a moonlight jamboree. God, I hated parties.

10

I leaned against the door of my cabin, eyes closed, breathing in the cool air. I'd turned the air-conditioning on for my two guests. The coffins sat in the middle of the floor between the desk and the bed. Under the Circus of the Damned, deep underground, neither Damian nor Asher slept until full dark. I hadn't been sure if they would aboveground or not. So the air. Though, actually, it had been partly selfish. Vampires in a closed, hot space tended to smell, well, like vampires. They didn't smell like dead bodies. It was like the smell of snakes, and yet that wasn't it, either. It was a neck-ruffling smell. Thick, musky, more reptile than mammal. The smell of vampires.

How could I be sleeping with one of them? I opened my eyes. It was dark in the cabin, but there was still a faint push of illumination through the two windows. A faint touch of light against the gleaming feet of the coffins. Had that small touch of natural light been enough to keep both vampires comatose, dead in their coffins, waiting for true dark? Something had, because I knew that they were still and waiting inside the coffins. A small amount of concentration, and I knew they were still dead to the world.

I strode between the coffins into the bathroom, closed and locked the door. The darkness seemed too solid. I turned on the light. It was white and harsh after the darkness. I was left blinking in the brightness.

Getting a good look at myself in the mirror was almost startling. I hadn't really seen the bruises yet. The corner of my left eye was a wonderful shade of purple black, swollen, puffy. Seeing it made it hurt worse, like seeing blood from a cut that doesn't sting until you notice it.

My left cheek was a wonderful shade of greenish brown. It was that sickly green that usually takes days to accomplish. My lower lip was puffy. You could still see the edge of darkened skin where it had bled. I ran my tongue inside my mouth and could feel the ridge where my cheek had been forced against my teeth, but it was healed. I stared into the mirror and realized as sore and awful as it looked, it wasn't as bad as it should have been.

It took me a few moments of staring to figure it out. When I did finally realize what was happening, a rush of fear ran through my body from my toes to the top of my head. I felt almost faint.

I was healing. I was healing days worth of injury in only hours. At this rate, the bruises would be almost gone by tomorrow. I should have been wearing the fight marks for days, a week at least. What the hell was happening to me?

I felt Damian wake in his coffin. I felt it like a stab through my body. It staggered me against the sink. I knew he was hungry, and I knew that he sensed me near at hand. I was Jean-Claude's human servant, bound by marks that only death would break. But Damian was mine. I'd raised him and another vampire, Willie McCoy, more than once. I'd called them from their coffins during daylight hours, safely underground, but the sun had been burning bright when I did it. One necromancer had said it made perfect sense. We could only raise zombies after the souls had fled the bodies, so I could only raise vamps when their souls had fled for the day.

I wasn't even going to debate the vampires and soul issue. My life was complicated enough without religious discussions. I know, I know, I was just delaying the inevitable. If I stayed with Jean-Claude, I was going to have to face the whole issue. No hiding. But not tonight.

Raising Damian had forged some kind of link between us. I didn't understand it and didn't have anyone to ask advice of. I was the first necromancer in several hundred years that could raise vampires like zombies. It scared me. It scared Damian more. Frankly, I didn't blame him.

Was Asher awake, too? I concentrated on him, sent that power, magic, whatever the hell it was, outward. It brushed him, and he felt me. He was awake and aware of me.

Asher was a master vampire. Not as powerful as Jean-Claude, but a master, nonetheless. That gave him certain abilities that Damian, who was by far the elder of the two, would never have. Without the link between us, Damian wouldn't have sensed me searching for him.

I wanted a few minutes to be alone and think, and I wasn't going to get it. I didn't make them call for me. I opened the door and stood framed in the light, blinking out into the thick darkness.

The vampires stood like pale shadows in the gloom. I hit the overhead light. Asher threw his hand up to protect his eyes from the light, but Damian just blinked at me. I wanted them to cover back from the light. I wanted them to look monstrous, but they didn't.

Damian was a green-eyed redhead, but that didn't really cover it. His hair fell like a red curtain around his upper body, the hair so red it looked like spilled blood against the green silk of his shirt. The shirt was a paler green than his eyes. They were like liquid fire, if fire could burn green. It wasn't vampire powers that made his eyes gleam. It was natural color, as if his mother had fooled around with a cat.

Asher was a blue-eyed blond, but again, that description didn't do him justice. The waves of his shoulder-length hair were golden. I don't mean blond, I mean gold. His hair was almost metallic in its glittering brilliance. His eyes were a blue so pale, they were almost white, like the eyes of a husky.

He was wearing a white dress shirt, untucked over chocolate brown dress pants.

Leather loafers, no socks, completed his clothes. I'd spent too much time around Jean-Claude to call it an outfit.

If you could stop staring at the eyes and hair long enough to see their faces, Asher was the handsomer of the two. Damian was handsome, but there was a length of jaw, a less perfect slope to the nose—small imperfections that might go unnoticed if you hadn't had Asher for comparison. Asher was beautifully handsome like a medieval cherub. Half of him, anyway.

Half of Asher's face was the beauty that drew a master vampire to him centuries ago. The other half was covered in scars. Holy water scars. The scars started about an inch from the midline of his face so his eyes, nose, and those full, perfect lips remained untouched, but the rest was like melted wax. His neck was pale and perfect, but I knew that the scars continued at his shoulders. His upper body was worse than the face, the scars rough and pitted. But like the face, only half of his body was scarred. The other half was still lovely.

I knew that the scars touched his upper thigh, but I had never seen him completely nude. I had to take his word that the scars covered the space between. It had been implied though never stated that he was still capable of sex but was scarred. I didn't know for sure, and I didn't want to know.

"Where are your bodyguards?" Asher asked.

"My bodyguards? You mean Jason and the Furballs?"

Asher nodded. His golden hair fell forward over the scarred side of his face. It was an old habit. The hair hid the scars—or almost hid the scars. He could use the shadows the same way. He always seemed to know just where the light would hit him. Centuries of practice.

"I don't know where they are," I said. "I just finished talking to Richard. I guess they thought we needed privacy."

"Did you need the privacy?" Asher asked. He looked straight at me, using the scars and beauty for a double effect. He didn't look happy for some reason.

"It's none of your damn business," I said.

Damian sat at the foot of the carefully made bed. He smoothed pale, long-fingered hands across the blue coverlet. "Not in this bed, you didn't," he said.

I came to stand beside the bed and stare down at him. "If one more vampire or were-anything tells me they can smell sex, I am going to scream."

Damian didn't smile. He'd never been a real happy camper, but lately was even more serious than usual. He just sat there, looking up at me. Jean-Claude or even Asher would have smiled, teased. Damian just looked at me with eyes that held sorrow the way others' held laughter.

I reached out to touch his shoulder and had to sweep back a lock of his hair to reach it. He jerked back from my touch as if it had hurt. He pushed to his feet and went to stand near the door.

I was left with my hand out, puzzled. "What's wrong with you, Damian?"

Asher came to stand beside me. He rested his hands lightly on my shoulders. "You are quite right, Anita. What you do with Monsieur Zeeman is none of my business."

I slid my hands over his, sliding my fingers to intertwine with his. I remembered the feel of his cool skin against mine. I leaned my back against him, pulling his arms around me, and I wasn't tall enough. It wasn't my memory. It was Jean-

Claude's. Asher and he had been companions for over twenty years, once upon a time.

I sighed and started to pull away.

Asher leaned his chin on the top of my head. "You need someone's arms that you don't feel threatened by."

I leaned against him, eyes closed, and for just a moment let him hold me. "The only reason this feels so good is that I'm remembering someone else's pleasure."

Asher gently kissed the top of my head. "Because you see me through the nostalgia of Jean-Claude's memories, you are the only woman in over two hundred years who doesn't treat me like a circus freak."

I leaned my face against the bend of his arm. "You are devastatingly handsome, Asher."

He smoothed the hair from my bruised cheek. "To you, perhaps." He leaned over me and laid the softest of kisses on my cheek.

I pulled away from him, gently, almost reluctantly. What I remembered of Asher was simpler than anything I was trying to pull off in this lifetime.

Asher didn't try to hold me. "If you were not already in love with two other men, the way you look at me might be enough."

I sighed. "I'm sorry, Asher. I shouldn't touch you like that. It's just . . ." I didn't know how to put it into words.

"You treat me like an old lover," Asher said. "You forget and touch me as if you'd touched me before when it is always the first time. Do not apologize for that, Anita. I enjoy it. No one else will touch me so freely."

"Jean-Claude will," I said. "These are his memories."

Asher smiled and it was almost sorrowful. "He is loyal to you and to Monsieur Zeeman."

"He's turned you down?" I asked and wished I hadn't.

Asher smile brightened, then dimmed. "If you would not share him with another woman, would you truly share him with another man?"

I thought about that for a second or two. "Well, no." I frowned up at him. "Why do I feel like apologizing for that?"

"Because you share with Jean-Claude and myself the memories of Julianna and the two of us. We were a very happy ménage à trois for almost longer than you have been alive."

Julianna had been Asher's human servant. She'd ended up burned as a witch by the same people that had scarred Asher. Jean-Claude couldn't save them both. I wasn't sure that either of them had truly forgiven Jean-Claude for this oversight.

Damian said, "If I'm not interrupting, I need to feed." He was standing by the door, hugging himself as if he were cold.

"You want me to open the door and yell dinner?" I asked.

"I want permission to go feed," he said.

I frowned at the phrasing but said, "Go find one of our walking donors and help yourself. Just our people, though. We can't hunt here."

Damian nodded, standing up straighter as if he'd been hunched in upon himself. I could feel that he was hungry, but it wasn't hunger that made him huddle. "I will not hunt."

"Good," I said.

He hesitated, with his hand on the doorknob. His back was to me, but his voice came low, "May I go and feed?"

I glanced at Asher. "Is he talking to you?"

Asher shook his head. "I think not."

"Sure, help yourself."

Damian opened the door and slipped outside. He left the door slightly ajar.

"What is his problem lately?" I asked.

"I think he must answer that question," Asher said.

I turned and looked at him. "Does that mean you can't answer the question or won't answer it?"

Asher smiled and his face moved freely, even the scarred skin. He was having consultations with a plastic surgeon in Saint Louis. No one had ever tried to repair holy water damage on vamps, so they didn't know if it would work, but the doctors were hopeful. Hopeful but cautious. The first operation was still months away.

"It means, Anita, that some fears are very personal."

"Are you saying Damian's afraid of me?" I didn't try to keep the astonishment out of my voice.

"I am saying that you must speak to him directly if you want answers."

I sighed. "Great, just what I need. Another complicated male in my life."

Asher laughed, and it slid along my bare arms like a touch, raising gooseflesh. The only other vampire that could do that to me was Jean-Claude.

"Stop that," I said.

He gave a low, sweeping bow. "My most sincere apologies."

"Bullshit," I said. "Go get dinner. I think the werewolves are planning some sort of party or ceremony."

"You need one of us with you at all times, Anita."

"I heard Jean-Claude's ultimatum." I looked at him and couldn't keep the surprise off my face. "You think he'd really kill you if something happened to me?"

Asher just looked at me with his pale, pale eyes. "Your life means more to him than mine does, Anita. If it did not, he would be in my bed and not yours."

He had a point, but . . . "It would kill something inside of him to kill you personally."

"But he would do it," Asher said.

"Why? Because he said he'd do it?"

"No, because he would always wonder if I allowed you to die as revenge for his failure to protect Julianna."

Oh. I opened my mouth to say more, and the phone rang. Daniel's voice came low and panicked, backed by country music.

"Anita, we're out at the Happy Cowboy on the main highway. Can you come down?"

"What's wrong, Daniel?"

"Mom's tracked down the woman who accused Richard. She's determined to make her stop lying."

"Are they fighting yet?" I asked.

"Yelling."

"You outweigh her by over a hundred pounds, Daniel. Just toss her over your shoulder and get her out of there. She'll only make things worse."

"She's my mother. I can't do that." .

"Shit," I said.

Asher asked, "What has happened?"

I shook my head. "I'll be there, Daniel, but you're being a wimp."

"I'd rather take on every guy in the bar than my mother," he said.

"If she makes a big enough scene, you may get your chance." I hung up. "I cannot believe this."

"What?" Asher asked again.

I explained as quickly as I could. Daniel and Mrs. Zeeman were staying at a nearby motel. Richard hadn't wanted them at the cabins with so many shapeshifters running around. Now I wished we'd kept them closer to home.

It would have been nice to have changed out of the blood-splattered blouse, but we were out of time. No rest for the wicked.

The real trick was what to do with Richard. He'd want to come along, and I didn't want him anywhere near Miss Betty Schaffer.

Legally, he could enter the bar and sit down beside her. There was no court order to stay away. But if the sheriff realized we weren't getting out of town, he'd look for any excuse to get Richard back behind bars. I didn't think Richard would have nearly as pleasant a second visit as he had a first. Their ambush today had backfired. They'd be frustrated and scared. They'd hurt Richard this time. Hell, they might hurt his mother. Charlotte Zeeman and I were going to have to have a little talk. Come to think of it, I was with Daniel. I'd have rather faced a full-blown bar fight than have a talk with his mother. At least she'd never be my mother-in-law. If I was going to have to punch her out tonight, that was almost comforting.

11

Richard and I compromised. He came along and swore to stay in the car. I brought along Shang-Da, Jamil, and Jason to make sure he stayed in the car, though if push came to shove, I wasn't sure they'd listen to me over Richard, not even if it was for his own good. It was the best I could do. Some nights that has to be enough, because that's all you've got.

The Happy Cowboy, which was one of the worst names for a bar I'd ever heard, was on the main highway. It was a two-story building that was supposed to look like a log cabin and managed not to. Maybe it was the neon horse with its cowboy rider on the sign. The lights gave the illusion that the horse was going up and down, along with the cowboy's arm and hat. He didn't look particularly happy riding the neon horse, but then maybe that was just me. I certainly wasn't happy to be here.

Richard had driven his four-by-four. He'd finally gotten around to blow-drying his hair. It was a thick, wavy foam around his face and shoulders. It looked so soft, you wanted to plunge your hands into it. Or again, maybe that was just me. He'd added a plain green T-shirt, tucked into his jeans, and white jogging shoes.

Jamil and Shang-Da were riding shotgun in the middle seat. Jamil was still wearing his cut-off smiley T-shirt, but Shang-Da had changed. He was all in black from his soft leather loafers to his belted dress slacks, to the silk T-shirt and tailor cut jacket. His short back hair was gelled into a crop of spikes on top of his head. He looked relaxed and at home in the clothes and the hair. He would also look utterly out of place at the Happy Cowboy. Of course, being over six feet tall and Chinese put him behind the game when it came to blending in here. Maybe he, like Jamil, was tired of trying to pass.

That was why Jason, still in his grown-up blue suit, was with us. Nathaniel had wanted to come, but he wasn't old enough to go into a bar. I didn't know how good Zane was in a stress situation yet, and Cherry always made me feel vaguely protective, so Jason it was.

"If you're not out in fifteen minutes, we're coming in," Richard said.

"Thirty minutes," I said. I did not want Richard near Ms. Betty Schaffer.

"Fifteen," he said, voice very quiet, very low, very serious. I knew that tone of voice. I'd gotten all the compromise I was going to get.

"Fine, but remember that if you go to jail tonight, your mom may go with you."

His eyes widened. "What are you talking about?"

"What would Charlotte do if she saw her little boy being dragged away to jail?"

He thought about that for a second, then bowed his head. He laid his forehead on the steering wheel. "She'd put up a fight for me."

"Exactly," I said.

He raised his face and looked at me. "I'll behave for her sake."

I smiled. "I knew it wasn't for mine." I got out of the car before he could answer that one.

Jason settled into step beside me. He'd straightened his tie and buttoned the first button on the jacket. He'd also tried to slick back his baby-fine hair, but it escaped all efforts in tiny wisps. His hair was very straight and very fine, and it would have looked better either much shorter or much longer. But hey, it wasn't my hair.

We were both carded at the door by a muscular guy in a dark blue T-shirt. The crowd was divided almost down the middle. There was the tight jeans, cowboy boots crowd, and the short skirts, business jackets crowd. There was some intermingling. Some of the women in cowboy boots had short skirts. Some of the business jackets were wearing jeans. It was the only alcohol for a twenty-mile radius, and it served food. Where else were you going to go on a Friday night? I'd have rather gone for a moonlit walk, but I didn't drink. Come to think of it, I didn't dance, either, though Jean-Claude was working on both. Corruption at every turn.

There was a live band playing country music so loudly it might as well have been hard rock. A haze of cigarette smoke floated over everything like a late-night fog. The entrance was on a little raised platform so you could look around before plunging into the sea of bodies. Charlotte is actually an inch or two shorter than I am, so I didn't bother scanning for her. I looked for Daniel. How many six-foot-tall, tanned guys with wavy, shoulder-length hair could there be? More than you'd think.

I finally spotted him near the bar because he was waving to me. He'd also tied his long hair back in a very tight ponytail, which was why scanning for the hair hadn't worked. His hair was nearly identical to Richard's except it was a more solid brown, a rich chestnut. His skin was the same tanned shade as his brother's. The same high, sculpted cheekbones, solid brown eyes, even the dimple in the chin. Richard was a little broader through the shoulders and chest, just physically more imposing, but other than that, the family resemblance was almost scary. All the brothers looked like that. The two oldest had cut their hair, one of them was almost a blond, and the father was going a little grey, but the five Zeeman men in one room was a testosterone treat.

And the matriarch of this pile of masculine pulchritude was standing about six feet from her son. Charlotte Zeeman had short blond hair that framed a face that looked at least ten years younger than I knew she was. She was wearing a butter yellow suit jacket over dress slacks. She was also poking her finger into the chest of a tall blond woman.

The second woman had a mane of curled blond hair, but I was betting that neither the color nor the curl were real. It had to be Betty Schaffer, and the name didn't suit her. She looked like someone named Farrah or Tiffany.

I waded into the crowd with Jason behind me. The crowd was thick enough that I stopped saying excuse me about halfway across the room and just started pushing.

A tall man in a plaid work shirt stopped me with a hand on my shoulder. "Can I buy you a drink, little lady?"

I reached back and got Jason's hand. I raised it where it was visible back and got Jason's hand. I raised it where it was visible. "Taken. Sorry." There was more than one reason I'd wanted to bring Jason with me to a bar on a Friday night.

He stared down at Jason, way down, making a show of how very tall he was. "Don't you want something a little bigger?"

"I like them small," I said, my face very serious. "It makes oral sex easier."

We left him speechless. Jason was laughing so hard, he could barely keep his feet. I pulled him through the crowd by the hand. Holding his hand seemed to be hint enough for the rest of the cruising males.

The crowd was clearing around the bar. People had moved back to form a semicircle around Charlotte, Betty, and Daniel. He had stepped up behind his mother, laying a hand on either shoulder trying to pull her back. She shrugged him off rather violently and ignored him. He let her do it.

Charlotte got up in the woman's face. I was close enough to catch a word or two above the band, "Liar . . . whore . . . my son . . . rapist . . ." To hear even that much, Charlotte was screaming at the woman.

Betty was tall, but the spike-heeled boots put her at six feet. The jeans were painted on, the blouse was midriff, and there was no bra. She had small enough breasts that she could get away without, but it was still noticeable and meant to be. She looked like a cowboy hooker. Richard had dated her. It made me think worse of him.

Two large guys wearing T-shirts that matched the guy who had carded us at the door were at the edge of the crowd. I think they were sort of puzzled by Charlotte. She was tiny and female and hadn't hit anyone yet. She also looked older than the general crowd, though not really like anyone's mother.

Betty had finally had enough. She was screaming back words like, "He did, rapist, bastard."

I let go of Jason's hand and stepped up beside them. They both looked at me. Charlotte was the most startled. Her large, honey-brown eyes went wide. She said, "Anita," as if no one had told her I was in town.

I smiled. "Hi, Charlotte. Can we talk outside?" I had to put my face nearly next to hers to be heard.

She shook her head. "This is the whore that's lied about Richard."

I nodded. "I know. Let's take it outside, though."

Charlotte shook her head again. "I am not leaving until she tells the truth. Richard did not rape her."

We were yelling, with our faces almost touching, to be heard. "Of course, he didn't," I said. "Water is wet, the sky is blue, and Richard isn't a rapist."

Charlotte stared at me. "You believe him."

I nodded. "I got him out on bail. He's waiting to see you outside."

Her eyes went even wider, then she smiled, and it was beautiful. It was one of those smiles that made you feel warm down to your toes. Charlotte was like that. When she was happy, everyone around her was happy. When she wasn't happy . . . well, that spilled over, too.

She yelled in my ear, "Let's go see Richard."

I turned to go through the crowd and heard a gasp. I turned to see Betty Schaffer wearing the dripping remnants of a beer. Betty slapped Charlotte. Charlotte returned the favor but with a closed fist.

Betty was suddenly on her butt in the floor, blinking up at us.

The bouncers moved in, as Charlotte moved in to finish the job. I threw Charlotte over my shoulder. She weighed more than she looked like she did, and she was struggling. Unlike most women, she was good at struggling. I didn't want to hurt Charlotte, but she wasn't returning the favor. She kicked me in the knee and I dumped her onto the floor hard.

She lay there for a second, breath knocked out of her, staring up at me. Daniel moved forward to help her up, and I stopped him with a hand on his chest. "No."

The band had fallen silent with a last twangy guitar string. Into the sudden silence, my voice sounded loud, "You can walk out of here on your own, or you can be carried out unconscious, Charlotte. Your choice, but you are leaving."

I went down on one knee, carefully, because Charlotte didn't fight like a girl. I lowered my voice for her ears alone. "Richard will come in here in just a few minutes to see what's wrong. If he gets near her again, the local cops will revoke his bail and lock him up again." It was only partially true. Legally, he had every right to enter the bar, but I was betting that Charlotte didn't know that. Most law-abiding citizens wouldn't have.

Charlotte looked at me for a second longer, then offered me a hand. I helped her stand, still cautious. She had a hell of a temper once it got started. Admittedly, it took a lot to get her this mad, but once she reached it, it was every man for himself.

She let me help her to her feet without trying to slug me. An improvement. We made our way through the crowd with Daniel and Jason trailing behind us. No one crowded us as we went for the door. They stared, but didn't crowd.

The bouncer at the door said, "She doesn't come back in here."

Charlotte opened her mouth to say something, and I gripped her shoulder. "Don't worry. She won't."

He looked at Charlotte but nodded.

I let her get about three good steps ahead of me as we reached the parking lot. Call it an instinct. She whirled, and I think would have hit me, but I was out of reach. She stared at me with those big honey-brown eyes, made somehow paler by the halogen lamps. "Don't you ever lay hands on me again," she said.

"Behave like Richard's mother and not his outraged girlfriend, and I won't."

"How dare you!" she said. She moved closer. I moved away. I didn't really want to have a fistfight in the parking lot of a bar with Richard's mother.

"If anyone should be trying to beat the shit out of Ms. Peroxide Blond, it should be me."

That stopped her cold. She stood straight and looked at me. I could almost see her sanity returning. "But you aren't dating him anymore. Why should you care?"

"That is the sixty-four thousand dollar question, isn't it?" I said.

Charlotte smiled suddenly. "I knew you couldn't resist my boy. No one could."

"If he keeps dating everything in sight, I might."

She frowned. "I can't believe he ever dated that thing," she said.

We both turned and watched Richard walk towards us. There were nearly identical looks on our faces. We disapproved of Ms. Schaffer—a lot.

Her first words were, "I cannot believe you dated that woman. She is a whore."

Richard looked embarrassed, more than I'd gotten from him. "I know what she is."

"Did you have sex with her?"

"Mother!"

"Don't you *mother* me, Richard Alaric Zeeman."

"Alaric," I said.

Richard spared me a frown, then turned back to his mother. "No, I never slept with Betty."

He was saying he'd never had intercourse with her. Charlotte would take it to mean that no sex at all had happened, just like I had. I remembered what Jamil had said about alternatives, but I kept quiet. I didn't want to upset Charlotte, and I didn't want to know.

"Well, at least that shows better sense," Charlotte said. She walked up to him and smoothed the front of his T-shirt, then bowed her head, and I realized she was crying.

I couldn't have been more surprised if she'd bitten him, maybe less.

Richard's entire face crumpled into helpless lines. He looked at me as if for help, and I backed up. I shook my head. I was no better around crying women than he was, maybe less.

He hugged her to him. I heard her murmur, "I was so worried about you in that awful jail."

I backed up out of earshot, and Daniel joined me. He didn't seem eager to join them, either. Of course, Charlotte didn't have to cry to unman Daniel.

"Thanks, Anita," he said.

I looked up at him. He was wearing a red tank top that was almost a twin of one Richard had. For all I knew, it was the same one. He looked tanned and handsome and very grown-up. "You're assertive around everyone but your parents. Why is that?"

He shrugged. "Isn't everyone like that?"

I shook my head. "No."

Jason moved up beside us. He echoed me: "No." Then he laughed. "Of course, my mother would never have gotten into a fight in a bar, no matter what I did. She's much too . . . decorous."

"Decorous," I said.

"My last roommate had a word-a-day calendar," Jason said.

"You've been reading again," I said.

He hung his head, looking abashed, then gave me rolled eyes and a grin. It was such a mix of shame and utter cuteness that I laughed. "I can't donate blood and have sex twenty-four hours a day. There's no television at the Circus of the Damned."

"If there was?" I asked.

"I'd still read, but don't tell anyone."

I put an arm around his shoulders. "Your secret is safe with me."

Daniel put his arm around Jason from the other side and said, "Won't breathe a word of it."

We walked towards the four-by-four, arm in arm. "If Anita was in the middle, this would be perfect," Jason said.

Daniel just stopped in his tracks, staring at Jason. I pulled away from both of them. "You just don't know when to stop, do you, Jason?"

He shook his head. "No."

Richard walked over to us. He sent Daniel to their mother, and Daniel didn't argue with the order. He sent Jason on to the car, and Jason didn't argue. I stood looking up at his suddenly serious face, wondered what my orders were going to be, and bet I would argue with them.

"What's up?" I asked.

"I'll have to go with Daniel and my mother to calm her."

"I hear a *but* coming," I said.

He smiled. "*But* there's a ceremony to meet my lupa tonight. It's customary before two packs share a full moon that they be formally introduced."

"How formally?" I asked. "I didn't pack for formal."

The smile widened into that wondrous smile that was his mother's. It had that same utter good humor to it. Contagious. "I don't mean that kind of formal, Anita. I mean there are rites to observe."

"Rites, as in what?" I asked. I sounded suspicious, even to me.

He hugged me, spontaneously, not girlfriend-boyfriend, but just a happy-to-see-you hug. "I have missed you, Anita."

I pushed away from him. "I make a suspicious comment and you say you've missed me. I don't get that, Richard."

"I love all of you, Anita, even the suspicious parts."

I shook my head. "Stick to business, Richard. What rites?"

The smile faded, the good humor dying from his eyes. He looked suddenly sad and I wanted to take it back, to have him smile at me again. But I didn't. We weren't an item anymore, and he'd been dating little Miss Schaffer, the cowgirl hooker. I didn't understand that at all. She puzzled me even more than Lucy.

"I have to go with my mother for a while. Jamil and Shang-Da can explain what you have to do as my lupa tonight."

I shook my head. "One of the bodyguards stays with you, Richard. I don't care which one it is, but you don't go out there alone."

"Mom will not understand a chaperone that isn't family," Richard said.

"Don't go all momma's boy on me, Richard. I've had enough of that from

Daniel for one night. Explain it any way you like, but you aren't leaving here without backup.''

He stared down at me, and his handsome face was serious, arrogant. ''I am Ulfric, Anita. Not you.''

''Yeah, you're Ulfric, Richard. You're in charge, fine, then do a good job of it.''

''What's that supposed to mean?''

''It means that if the bad guys find you out alone tonight, they might not wait to find out if you're leaving tomorrow. One of them might get a little eager and try to hurt you.''

''If it's not silver bullets, they can't kill me.''

''And how are you going to explain to your mother that you survived a shotgun blast to the chest?'' I asked.

He glanced back at her and Daniel. ''You cut right to the bone, don't you,'' I said.

''It saves time,'' I said.

He turned back to me. Anger had darkened his eyes, thinned out his face. ''I love you, Anita, but sometimes I don't like you very much.''

''It's not me you don't like, Richard, not on this issue. You're terrified that if Mommy Dearest finds out you're a shapeshifter, she'll think you're a monster.''

''Don't call her that.''

''Sorry,'' I said. ''But it's still the truth. I think you're underrating Charlotte. You're her son, and she loves you.''

He shook his head. ''I don't want her to know.''

''Fine, but choose a bodyguard. Why not tell your mom that he's backup in case the police try to make trouble? It's the truth.''

''As far as it goes,'' Richard said.

''The best lies are always at least partially true, Richard.''

''You're much better at lying than I am,'' he said. I looked for anger in the words, but there was nothing. It was just a statement of fact that left his eyes empty and sad.

I was tired of apologizing, so I didn't. ''Do you want to take their car and I can drive the four-by-four back to the cabins?''

He nodded. ''I'll take Shang-Da with me. He doesn't like you much.''

''I thought he might have warmed up to me since the fight this afternoon,'' I said.

''He still thinks you betrayed me,'' Richard said.

I didn't even try to touch that one. ''Fine, I'll take Jason and Jamil with me. They can give me lessons in werewolf etiquette.''

''Jason won't be much help. He's never been part of a healthy pack.''

''What's that supposed to mean?'' I asked.

''It means that because our old lupa was such a sadistic bitch, we were all afraid of each other. A normal pack is much more touchy-feely, more casual with each other.''

''How touchy?'' I asked.

He smiled, almost sadly. ''Talk to Jamil. He'll teach you and Jason, too.'' He seemed to think about that.

"What about the wereleopards, and the vampires?"

"I already asked Verne. They are our guests tonight."

"One big happy family," I said.

Richard looked at me. It was a long, searching look. It took a lot to meet his eyes and not to flinch. "It could be, Anita, it really could be." With that, he turned and walked to his mother and brother.

I watched him go and wasn't sure what to make of his last comment. I used to wonder why he put up with me, but after meeting his mother, I knew. It had taken me three Sunday dinners to realize why Charlotte and I were either in perfect agreement or on opposite ends of any discussion. We were too much alike. A family, like a pack, can only have so many alphas or it tears itself apart. Only Richard's brother, Glenn, is currently married, and his wife and Charlotte butt heads constantly. Aaron is a widower. I'm told the fights between Charlotte and Aaron's deceased wife were legendary. They'd all gone out and married someone like mom. Glenn's wife, though full-blooded Navajo, was still petite, and tough. The Zeeman men seemed to have a weakness for small and tough.

Beverly, as the only girl and the eldest, was wonderfully dominant. She and Charlotte had almost not survived her teenage years, according to Glenn and Aaron. Bev had settled down, gone to college, married, and was pregnant with her fifth child. She had four boys and was trying one last time for a girl.

I'd paid attention to Richard's family because I'd thought they were going to be my in-laws. That didn't seem likely to happen now. Oh, well. I had enough problems with my own family. Who needed a second one?

12

Everyone was in my room getting a lesson in werewolf etiquette. I sat on the foot of the bed with Cherry perched beside me. She'd washed off the black makeup, and her face was pale and young with a dusting of golden freckles across her cheeks. I knew she was my age, twenty-five, but without makeup, she looked younger. Like her own younger more innocent sister. The new clothes added to the illusion. She'd changed into a faded pair of jeans and an oversized T-shirt. Clothes you wouldn't mind shapechanging in. This close to the full moon, sometimes you got carried away and changed early. So I'm told. So I've seen.

Zane leaned against the far wall, wearing nothing but a pair of jeans with the knees worn away to holes. He'd kept the nipple ring. It looked very noticeable against his bare chest.

Jason was wearing shorts that had started life as a pair of jeans. The edges were ragged with strings like he'd picked at them. The only other thing he was wearing was an older pair of jogging shoes, no socks. He lay on his stomach, head pointed towards us, with one of my pillows bundled under his chin, knees bent, feet kicking slowly in the air while he listened to Jamil.

Jamil paced back and forth in front of us in his little smiley shirt. He'd kicked his shoes off by the door and paced on smooth, dark feet. Even just walking he gave off an energy like a low-level current. The moon was nearly full, and energy was easy to come by.

We'd tried to include Nathaniel in the lecture, but we couldn't find him. I didn't like that much. I'd been ready to man a full-scale search, but Zane had seen him going off with one of the female werewolves. The implication seemed to be that they'd gone off for a little one on one. So, no search, but I wasn't happy about it. I wasn't even sure exactly why I wasn't happy about it, but I wasn't.

Nathaniel needed to know some rudimentary greetings because he was mine. No one had ever met a lupa that was also Nimir-ra for a leopard pard, but Verne had decided the leopards would be included because they were mine. So they needed the little greetings lecture. I'd sent Damian and Asher out to find Nathaniel. No one in Verne's pack expected the vampires to be part of the official greeting.

In fact, it had been requested that they not touch any of the werewolves unless offered. Strongly requested.

So it was just the four of us watching Jamil pace. He finally stopped in front of me. "Stand up."

It sounded far too much like an order for my taste, but I stood, looking up at him.

"Richard says you have a degree in biology."

Not the opening I was expecting, but I nodded. "Preternatural biology, yeah."

"How much do you know about natural wolves?"

"I've been reading Mech," I said.

Jamil's eyes widened just a bit. "L. David Mech?"

"Yeah, you seem surprised. He is one of the leading authorities on wolf behavior."

"Why have you been reading him?" Jamil asked.

I shrugged. "I'm lupa of a werewolf pack, but I'm not a werewolf. There are no good books on werewolves, so the best I could do was research real wolves."

"What else have you read?" he asked.

"*Of Wolves and Men*, by Barry Holstun Lopez. A few other books, but those were the two best I've found."

Jamil smiled, a quick baring of teeth. "You have just made my job a lot easier."

I frowned up at him.

"The formal greeting is like one friendly wolf greeting another. The point is to get the nose back here," he touched the hair behind my ear, gently.

"Do you rub the cheek along the other person's cheek like a real wolf would do? I mean in human form, you don't have any glands on the cheek to help you scent mark another wolf."

He looked down at me, solemn almost, nodding. "Yes, you do rub cheeks even in human form. Then you bury your nose in the hair behind the ear."

"How big is Verne's pack?" I asked.

"Fifty-two wolves," Jamil said.

I raised eyebrows at him. "Please tell me that I don't have to rub faces with every single one of them."

Jamil smiled, but it left his eyes serious. He was thinking something. I wanted to know what it was. "Not with all of them, just the alphas."

"How many?"

"Nine," he said.

"Doable, I guess." I looked up into his thoughtful face and just asked, "What are you thinking so hard about, Jamil?"

He blinked at me. "What—"

"Don't tell me it's nothing. You went all solemn and thoughtful about five minutes ago. What gives?"

He stared down at me. The concentration in his dark eyes was almost touchable. "I'm impressed that you bothered to research natural wolves."

"That's the third time you've used the term *natural wolves*. I've never heard it before."

Jason rolled off the bed to his feet. "We are real wolves part of the time. We're just not natural."

I looked to Jamil, and he nodded.

"So calling you guys real wolves is an insult?"

"Yes," Jamil said.

"Anything else to watch for?" I asked.

Jamil looked at Jason. They exchanged a look that made me feel excluded. Like there was some unpleasant surprise coming and no one was telling me.

"What?" I said.

"Let's just do the greeting," Jamil said.

"What are you guys hiding from me?"

Jason laughed. "Just tell her."

A low growl trickled from Jamil's human throat. The sound alone raised the hair on my arms. "I am Sköll, and you have no name among the lukoi. Your voice is only the wind outside our cave."

Jason took a few steps closer. "The trees themselves bow before the wind," he said. It sounded way too formal for Jason.

"Good," Jamil said, "you do know some lukoi phrases."

"We were afraid to touch each other," Jason said, "not to talk to each other."

Zane pushed away from the wall, moving between them, standing close to me. "The moon is rising. Time is passing."

I frowned at all of them. "I feel like you're speaking in code and I don't know how to crack it."

"Apparently, we have some phrases in common," Jamil said, "between the lukoi and the pard."

"Great, the wolves and the leopards share some common ground. Now what?"

"Greet me," Jamil said.

"Uh-uh," I said, "I'm lupa. You're just the Sköll, the muscle. I outrank you, so you offer me your face and throat first."

"She is your lupa, and our Nimir-ra, which is an equivalent rank to your Ulfric, she has the right to ask," Zane said.

Jamil growled at him.

Zane moved behind me, as if using me for a shield. It would have worked better if he hadn't been nearly ten inches taller than me.

"She refuses you," Jamil said. "You stand alone before me."

"No way," I said. "Zane is mine. You aren't going to use him for some macho dominant crap."

Jamil shook his head. "He moved into you, but you didn't touch him."

I frowned up at him. "So?"

Jamil sighed. "All your reading has told you nothing about us."

"Then explain it to me," I said.

Jason said, "When Zane moved in close to you, he was asking for your protection, but you didn't touch him. That's seen as a rejection of his petition for protection."

Cherry was still sitting very still on the bed, hands clasped in her lap. "It's one of the rules that works the same for the wolves and for us."

I glanced behind me at them. "How do the two of you know all this?"

"With Raina and Marcus in charge, we all got to do a lot of petitioning for protection," Jason said.

"Gabriel spent a lot of time with Raina," Cherry said. "We, the wereleopards, got to spend a lot of time with the wolves."

"So when Zane moved up close, what was I supposed to do?"

"Do you want to protect him against me?" Jamil said.

I stared up at that tall, muscular body. Even if he hadn't been a lycanthrope, he'd have scared me in a fair fight. Of course, nature had made sure there would be no fair fight. Jamil outweighed me by a hundred pounds or more. His reach was twice mine. His upper body strength . . . well, enough said. There was no such thing as a fair fight between the two of us. That was why I felt perfectly comfortable using weapons.

"Yeah," I said, "I want to protect Zane against you. If that's what it takes."

"Then touch him," Jamil said.

I frowned again. "Can you be a little more specific?"

"The touch is what's important," Jamil said, "not where or how."

Zane was standing at my back. I moved backwards until my back touched his body. Our bodies made a nice solid line. "Enough?" I asked.

Jamil shook his head. "For God's sake, just touch him." He motioned to Jason. "Ask for my protection."

Jason came to his side with a smile. He stood very close but was careful not to touch. Jamil put an arm across his shoulders, obviously protective, almost a hug. "There, that's it."

"Does it have to be just like that, or can I touch him anywhere that's noticeable?"

Jamil made a small sound between an umph and a growl. "You are making this too complicated."

"No," I said, "you are. Just answer the question."

"No, it doesn't have to be just like this, but it's best if you get in the habit of making the offer look normal to people."

"Why?" I asked.

"What if Zane were running from me in public? He sees you through the crowd, comes up to you. All you have to do is pretend to hug him, or even kiss him. I know you've given him your protection and none of the humans around us know anything is wrong."

I wasn't sure how I felt about not being included with the other humans, but I let it go. I drew Zane out from behind me with a hand around his waist. I'd have been more comfortable if he'd been wearing a shirt, but hey, that was my hang-up, not his. I made it my left arm, leaving my right free. I also moved back enough so that my gun wasn't pressed up against his body. Having my arm around Zane's waist, standing a little apart, made the gun under my arm very obvious. There were a lot of different ways to make threats. "Happy?" I asked.

Jamil nodded once very curtly.

Jason stepped away from him, closer to Zane and me.

"Jamil's just mad that Zane told you he had to do a submissive greeting."

"And you've reminded her," Jamil said.

"Ooh," Jason said, "I'm so scared."

A roil of power prickled through the room. I watched Jamil's brown eyes bleed to a rich yellow. He stared at Jason with wolf eyes. "You will be."

Cherry slid off the bed, kneeling behind me. She reached a hand up to me, and I took it. She licked a quick tongue across my hand, a greeting that only the leopards used, then one slender hand went to my leg, holding onto my pants like a small, shy child. She seemed to think something bad was about to happen.

I half expected Jason to come to me like the wereleopards had, but he didn't. He moved farther into the room, away from Jamil, but he didn't ask for help.

"What's the big deal?" I asked. "Jamil just offers me his cheek first, right?"

"Oh, no," Jason said, "much more fun than that."

That made me frown because I knew what Jason's idea of fun was. "Maybe I asked for something I don't understand."

"But you did ask," Jamil said, "and as our lupa it is your right."

I was beginning to suspect I'd made a faux pas. That I'd asked something of Jamil he didn't want to give and I probably wouldn't like receiving. "If you hadn't been such an asshole when we first got here, Jamil, I'd probably let this go."

"But . . ." he said.

"But I don't back down, not to you."

"Not to anyone," Jason said softly.

That, too.

"If I refuse, it's challenge between us," Jamil said.

"Fine, but remember, you've had your last free pass for the weekend, Jamil."

He nodded. "I see the gun."

"Then we understand each other," I said.

"We understand each other," he said. Jamil closed the distance between us, eyes still an eerie shade of yellow.

"Don't get cute, Jamil."

He gave a quick baring of teeth. "I am doing what you asked, Anita."

Zane moved behind me, hands on my shoulders, but giving me more room to move. Cherry huddled against my legs. Neither of them moved away. I took that as a good sign. I hoped I was right.

Jamil touched my face very lightly with the tips of his fingers. "If we were in public, it would be this." He bent downward and it looked like he was going to kiss me.

He did. A soft brush of lips, fingers still holding my face. He drew back from me. When he opened his eyes, they were still that rich, golden yellow. It was a startling color against the darkness of his skin.

I had just stood there throughout, too startled to know what to do. Neither the leopards nor Jason called foul, so Jamil was doing what I'd forced him to do. Probably. If it had been Jason, I'd suspected some sort of ploy to steal a kiss, but Jamil didn't play those kinds of games.

He stayed with his hands still cradling my face. "But tonight won't be in public. Between ourselves when no one watches . . ." He didn't finish the sentence. He just leaned over me again.

His tongue ran across my lower lip.

I jerked back.

He let his hands fall to his sides. "You read the wolf books, Anita, I am a submissive wolf begging a dominant's attention."

"It's a variation of food begging by pups," I said. "In two adult wolves, it's a ritual of licking and biting gently at the mouth of the dominant wolf by the subordinate."

Jamil nodded.

"You've made your point," I said.

"The greeting I am trying to teach you is like our version of a handshake. You both offer your faces at the same time. It's more like a kiss."

"Show me," I said.

He leaned into me again, but this time he didn't try to touch my mouth. He rubbed his cheek along mine, rubbing his face across my ear until his face was buried in the hair behind my ear. His movement had put my face against his hair. His hair was in cornrows, and the texture was rough and soft at the same time.

Jamil spoke with his mouth still against my hair, "You have to bury your face in the hair and smell the skin."

He burrowed his face into my hair until he had to be touching skin. I heard him breathing in air. His breath was almost hot against my skin.

I tried to return the favor, but had to raise on tiptoe, one hand against his chest for balance. Zane slid away from me, and I used my other hand on his shoulder. The cornrows made it easier to put my face next to the skin of his scalp. The braids moved around my face like small thin ropes.

I could smell his hair straightener, his cologne, and under all that was him. The moment his scent hit me, I felt a rush of power, and it wasn't his. I suddenly knew that Richard was sitting on a bed, holding his mother. I felt him look up as if he'd see me standing at the foot of the bed. But I was miles away, standing at the foot of a different bed. We drew in the rich warm smell of Jamil's skin, and Richard's power broke over me in a march of goose bumps.

Jamil drew back from me, hands still on my shoulders. His nostrils flared while he drew in scent. "Richard—I smell our Ulfric. How?"

Zane pressed against my back, rubbing his face against my hair. Cherry had curled herself around my leg like a fetus. "She is your lupa. Bound to your Ulfric."

Jamil stepped back from me, something very close to fear on his face. "She cannot be bound to Richard. She is not lukoi."

I moved towards him, and Zane went to his knees behind me. Cherry let me go, hands sliding away reluctantly. They huddled together, holding each other.

I spared them a glance and asked, "You guys all right?"

Zane nodded. "I saw you call the power of the marks once before, but I've never been touching you when you called the Ulfric's power. It's a rush."

Cherry just stared at me, eyes gone large in a pale face.

"Don't I know it," Jason said. He was still across the room, hugging his naked chest, hands rubbing up and down his bare arms as if he were cold. He wasn't cold.

I turned back to Jamil. "I am bound to Richard. It isn't the same kind of bonding that he'd have with another lycanthrope, but it is a bond."

"You are Jean-Claude's human servant," Jamil said.

I hated the term, but it was accurate, technically anyway. "Yes, I am, just as Richard is Jean-Claude's wolf to call."

"He cannot call our Ulfric like a dog. Richard does not answer to the vampire's whims."

"Me, either," I said. "Sometimes I think Jean-Claude may have bitten off more than he can drink with the two of us."

The door to the cabin opened, no knock, no preliminaries. Asher stepped through with Nathaniel in his arms. He was bundled into Asher's suit jacket. What I could see of his legs were pale and bare.

I ran forward. "What happened?"

Asher laid Nathaniel on the bed on his back, trapping the jacket under his body. He was nude except for the jacket. Nathaniel tried to curl up onto his side into a ball, but Asher stopped him, trying to smooth his legs down, to make him lie still. "Lie still, Nathaniel."

"It hurts!" His voice was strangled, twisted tight with pain.

I knelt by the bed, touching his face. He looked at me, eyes so wide they flashed white. His mouth opened and a small moan escaped him. His hand clawed at the bedspread as if he needed to hold something, anything. I gave him my hand and his grip was so tight I had to remind him not to crush my hand.

He muttered, "Sorry," then his spine bowed, body twisting. Normally, seeing Nathaniel completely nude would have embarrassed me. Now I was too scared to be embarrassed. There were bleeding cuts on his chest, but they looked shallow. Nothing seemed wrong enough for this kind of pain.

Cherry disappeared into the bathroom. I didn't think you were that squeamish if you were a nurse.

"Who did this?" I asked.

"He is our message from the local vampires," Asher said.

"What message?"

Nathaniel twisted on the bed, his other hand grabbing at my arm. Two slow tears trailed down his cheeks. "They kept asking me why we'd come here." He threw his head back and forth, and I caught a glimpse of something on his neck. I got one hand free and moved all that long, auburn hair so I could see his neck. A vampire bite showed in the smooth flesh of his neck. The bite was clean, neat, but the skin was slightly darker than it should have been.

"Did one of you do this?" I asked.

"I took blood from the bend of his arm," Asher said. "That is Colin's doing."

Nathaniel's body eased against the bed, the spasm or whatever passing. "I told them we were here to rescue Richard. I told them the truth, over and over." His hand convulsed around mine, eyes closing as if he were riding a wave of pain. After a few seconds, he opened his eyes, his hand easing around mine. "They wouldn't believe me."

Cherry came out of the bathroom. She tried to push me gently but firmly out of the way, but Nathaniel clutched at my hand. Cherry settled for making me kneel by the head of the bed. He could still hold my hand, but I was out of the way. She began to explore the wounds on his chest. She was very submissive, almost untrustworthily so, but let someone be injured and it was like a different Cherry rose to the occasion. She became Nurse Cherry, as if the leather-slut-from-hell was her secret identity.

"Do you have a first aid kit in this cabin?" she asked.

"No," I said.

"I've got one in my suitcase in the other cabin," Cherry said.

"I'll get it," Jason offered. He started for the door.

"Wait," I said. "Jamil, go with him. I don't want anyone else taken tonight."

No one argued with me. It was a first. The two werewolves just went for the door. Damian had to move out of the way for them to leave. He shut the door behind them and leaned against it. His eyes had gone a drowning, solid green, like emerald fire. His pale skin was taking on that transluscent, almost glowing quality that the vamps get when their humanity begins to fold away. Strong emotions will do that to the lesser vamps: fear, lust, anger.

I looked at Asher. He was . . . normal. He stood just back from the bed, that handsome, tragic, face blank and empty. It was so like the expression Jean-Claude used when he was hiding something.

"I thought Colin was either supposed to attack us directly or leave us alone," I said. "No one said anything about this kind of shit."

"It was . . . unexpected," Asher said.

"Well, explain it to me."

Damian pushed away from the door, stalking into the room, every movement tight with anger. "They tortured him because they enjoyed it. They're vampires, but they fed off more than just blood."

"What are you saying, Damian?"

"They fed off his fear."

I looked from his glowing face to Asher, then back to Damian. "You mean literally, don't you?"

Damian nodded. "The one who brought me over was like that. She could feed off of fear as if it were blood. She'd go for days feeding off of terror, then suddenly she'd take blood. But she didn't just feed, she slaughtered. She'd come back to the chamber covered in blood, slick with it. Then she'd make me . . ." His voice trailed off. He looked at me, his eyes were beginning to look like naked green flame, as if his power were eating the bones of his eye sockets. "I felt it when we met Colin. I smelled it. He's like her. He's a night hag, a mora."

"What the hell is a night hag or a mora? And what do you mean, you met Colin? I thought you rescued Nathaniel."

"No, they gave him back to us," Asher said. "If we did not see him, the message would not be complete."

Cherry interrupted us. "His pulse is thready, his skin is clammy. He's going into shock. The cuts on his chest are shallow. Even two vampire bites in one night shouldn't put him into shock. We heal better than this."

"There is a third bite," Asher said. Through it all, his voice had been utterly calm, as if nothing touched him.

Cherry looked down the length of Nathaniel's body, then touched his thigh. She moved his legs apart. "Of course, the femoral artery. Why is the skin discolored on both bites?" She touched the skin of his inner thigh. "The skin feels almost cold."

Nathaniel writhed on the bed. He let go of my hand, reaching for me as if he wanted a hug. He grabbed one arm, and a handful of my blouse. His eyes were wild. "It hurts."

"What hurts?" I asked.

"The bites are contaminated," Asher said.

"What do you mean, contaminated?"

"Think of it as a poison."

"He's a wereanimal, they're immune to poisons," I said.

"Not this one," Asher said.

"What kind of poison is it?" Cherry said.

There was a knock on the door. Jason said, "It's us."

Damian looked at me. His eyes had calmed down to a soft glow, his skin almost back to the milky perfection that passed for normal.

I nodded.

He opened the door. Jason came in with a first aid kit bigger than most overnight bags. Maybe Cherry had been a Girl Scout in another life. Jamil followed behind Jason like a dark, solemn shadow.

"The kind of poison that nothing in that little bag will stop," Asher said.

I stared up at him, suddenly realizing what he'd just said. "You mean he's going to . . . ." I couldn't even say it.

"Die," Asher said in that same utterly calm, almost mildly amused voice that he'd been using since they first walked into the cabin.

I stood, Nathaniel's hands clinging to me. I looked at Cherry and she moved in to help me draw free of him. I wanted to say things to Asher that I didn't want Nathaniel to hear. Zane crawled onto the bed on the other side. Nathaniel grabbed his hand and held on. Another spasm threw Nathaniel writhing on the bed. Zane and Cherry held him down, let him use that crushing strength on their hands. The two wereleopards stared at me while Nathaniel thrashed, eyes rolling back into his head. Zane and Cherry watched me. I was their Nimir-ra, their leopard queen. I was supposed to protect them, not drag them into shit like this.

I turned away from their accusing, expectant eyes and moved with Asher to the door. "What do you mean he's going to die?"

"You've seen the kind of vampires that rot and re-form themselves?"

"Yeah. So?"

"One of them bit Nathaniel."

"I've been bitten by one of them. Jason's been bitten by one of them. Nothing like this happened to us." I glanced back and found Jason holding Nathaniel's hand while Cherry started cleaning the chest wounds. Somehow I didn't think bandaging the cuts was going to help.

Jamil and Damian joined us. We stood in a little circle, talking, while Nathaniel screamed. Asher said, "It is one of the rarest of talents. I thought that only Morte d' Amour, Lover of Death, the council member could do this. Colin chose his messages carefully. The slashes are harm from a distance with just a flexing of power."

"Jean-Claude can't cause harm from a distance," I said.

"No, and no one else can spread corruption from their bite. No one else in this country."

"You keep saying corruption," Jamil said. "What does that mean exactly?"

Cherry came to us with white guaze pads in her hands. Her pale freckles stood out like ink on her suddenly pale skin. There was yellow and green puss on the gauze. "This came out of the chest wounds," she said quietly. "What the hell is it?"

We all looked at Asher, even Damian. But I was the one who said it out loud, "He's rotting. He's decaying while he's still alive."

Asher nodded. "The corruption is in his blood. It will spread and then he will rot."

I looked back to the bed. Jason was speaking low and softly to Nathaniel, stroking his head like you'd comfort a sick child. Zane was looking at me.

"There has to be something we can do," I said.

Asher's face was as closed and careful as I'd ever seen it. One of Jean-Claude's memories of Asher went through me so forcefully that my fingertips tingled with it. It wasn't a memory of any one event. I recognized the set of Asher's shoulders. I knew his body language with a familiarity built up of years of observation. More years than I'd been alive.

"What are you hiding, Asher?" I asked.

He looked at me, pale, pale eyes blank, empty, lined with those amazing golden eyelashes like shining lace. He smiled. The smile was everything it should have been: joyous, sensual, welcoming. That smile went through my heart like a knife. I remembered that face whole and perfect. I remembered when that smile had made me catch my breath.

I shook my head. The physical movement helped. I shook off the memories. They faded, but it didn't change what I'd seen, what I knew. "You know how to save him, don't you?"

"How badly do you want to save him, Anita?" His voice wasn't neutral now, it was almost angry.

"I brought him down here, Asher. I put him in danger. I'm supposed to protect him."

"I thought he was supposed to be your bodyguard," Asher said.

"He's walking food, Asher. You know that. Nathaniel can't even guard himself."

Asher let out his breath in a long sigh. "Nathaniel is a *pomme de sang*."

"What the hell are you talking about?"

"It means apple of blood. It is a sobriquiet among the Council for willing food."

Damian finished the thought. "The vampire that feeds from a *pomme de sang* is duty bound to protect them, like a shepherd keeping the wolf from his sheep." Damian looked at Asher while he said it, and it was not a friendly look. They were fighting about something, but there was no time.

I touched Asher's arm. It felt stiff, wooden, not even alive. He was drawing away from me, away from the room, away from what was happening. He was going to let Nathaniel die without even trying. Unacceptable.

I made myself grip that wooden, unalive arm. I hated it when Jean-Claude felt like this. It was a reminder of what he was, and what he wasn't. "Don't let him die, not like this. Please, *mon chardonneret*."

He jumped like I'd hit him when I used the old nickname that Jean-Claude had used so many years ago. It meant literally, my goldfinch, which sounded silly in English. But the look on Asher's face wasn't silly. It was almost shocked.

"No one has called me that in over two hundred years." His arm softened under my hand, feeling warm, alive again.

"I don't beg often, but for this I will."

"He means so much to you?" Asher asked.

"He's everyone's victim, Asher. Someone has to give a damn about him. Please *mon*—" He put his fingers over my lips.

"Don't say it, Anita, don't ever say it again unless you mean it. I will save him, Anita, for you."

I felt like I was missing something. I could remember Jean-Claude's pet name for Asher, but I couldn't remember why Asher was afraid to try to heal Nathaniel. As I watched him walk to the bed, golden hair trailing like a glittering veil across his shoulders, that missing memory seemed very important.

Asher held his hand out to Damian. "Come, my brother, or does the famed courage of the Vikings fail you now?"

"I was slaughtering your ancestors before you were a gleam in your great granddaddy's eye."

"Shit, this is dangerous, isn't it?" I asked.

Asher knelt beside the bed. He looked back at me, the golden hair sliding over the scarred side of his face, hiding it. He knelt, all golden perfection, and smiled, but it was bitter. "We can take the corruption into ourselves, but if we are not powerful enough, it will enter us, and we will die, but your precious wereleopard will be saved either way."

Damian crawled onto the far side of the bed, moving Zane away from his spot by Nathaniel's head. Nathaniel had stopped screaming. He lay very still, skin pale, shiny with sweat. His breath came in shallow pants. The wounds on his chest were oozing pus. There was a smell in the room now, faint but growing. The bite on his neck still seemed solid, but the skin of his neck was a deep blackish green like a bruise that was killing deep.

"Asher," I said.

He looked at me, one hand running along Nathaniel's bare thigh.

"Damian's not a master."

"I cannot save your leopard by myself, Anita. Who would you save? Which will you sacrifice?"

I looked at Damian. His green eyes were human again. He looked very mortal, curled beside Nathaniel.

"Don't make me choose."

"But it is a choice, Anita. It is a choice."

I shook my head.

"Do you want me to save him?" Damian asked.

I met his gaze, and didn't know what to say.

"His pulse is very weak," Cherry said. "If you're going to do something, you better do it soon."

"Do you want me to save him?" Damian asked again.

Nathaniel's fast, gasping breath was the only sound in the sudden silence. They all looked at me. Waited for me to decide. And I couldn't decide. I felt my head nod, almost as if I wasn't doing it. I nodded.

The vampires began to feed.

13

A feeding takes longer in real life than it does in the movies. Either it's too quick or they do a fade like a 1950s sex scene. We all stood around the room and watched. The room was quiet enough that you could hear the vampires making small, wet noises as they fed.

Cherry knelt by the head of the bed. She checked Nathaniel's wrist pulse periodically. The rest of us had moved farther away. I ended up on the far side of the room, leaning my butt on the desk. I was working very hard at not looking at the bed. Everyone moved around the room, restless, embarrassed, I thought.

Jason came to stand beside me, leaning on the desk. "If I didn't know his life was at stake, I'd be jealous."

I looked at him, trying to tell if he was teasing. There was a look in his eyes, a heat, that said he was not. It made me look over at what was happening.

Damian had drawn Nathaniel's body into his arms, his lap, so that he cradled the smaller man almost the full length of his body. Parts of Damian's body were lost to sight behind Nathaniel's naked body. His arm cradled the smaller man's chest against the green silk shirt. The pus had soaked into the cloth in blackening streaks. Nathaniel's face was pressed by one pale hand into the vampire's shoulder. Damian had come from behind for the neck strike. You could see the top of his bloodred hair, his mouth locked over the wound. Even from where I stood, I could see Damian's jaws swallowing.

Asher was still kneeling on the floor, one of Nathaniel's pale legs flung outward so his foot hung in empty air. Asher's face was buried in the man's inner thigh, so close to the groin that Nathaniel's slack genitalia touched the side of his face. Asher moved his head slightly and a spill of golden hair flung over Nathaniel's groin. It didn't hide it so much as have him peeking out through it.

A blush flowed over my face so hard and fast I was almost dizzy. In turning away, I caught a glimpse of myself in the room's only mirror. My face was burning. My eyes looked wide and surprised. It was junior high all over again, stumbling on couples under the bleachers, hearing their laughter chase me into the night.

I stared at myself in the mirror and got a grip. I was not fourteen anymore. I was not a child. I was not a virgin. I could do this with a modicum of grace. Couldn't I?

Jamil had moved to the farthest corner of the room. He was sitting there, arms tucked around his knees, face set in harsh lines, angry. He wasn't enjoying the show, either.

Zane had moved back to lean against the wall, arms crossed. He was looking at the floor as if there was something very interesting on it.

Jason was still sitting against the desk, watching the show. I looked at him without turning around. "You do realize that you're the only one who seems to be enjoying the view."

He shrugged, grinning. "It's a nice view."

I raised my eyebrows. "Don't tell me you're gay."

"Don't tell me you care," he replied.

My eyebrows went up a little farther. "My heart is breaking. I'll have to burn all my lingerie." I kept watching his face. He was smiling but not like it was a joke.

"Are you saying all that teasing is just an act?" I asked.

"Oh, no, I like women. But, Anita, almost none of the vampires in Jean-Claude's inner circle are women. I've been acting as a *pomme de sang* for two years. That's a lot of fangs sinking into your body."

"Is it really that close to sex?" I asked.

The humor left his face and he just looked at me. "You've really never been rolled completely by a vamp, have you? I mean I knew you had partial immunity even before the marks, but I thought someone somewhere would have gotten to you."

"Nope," I said.

"Sometimes I'm not sure, but it may be better than sex, and almost everyone who's been doing me has been a guy."

"So you're bisexual?"

"If what they're doing now counts as sex, yeah. If it doesn't then . . ." he laughed, and the sound was so abrupt in the silence that I saw Zane and Jamil jump. "If this doesn't count as sex, let's just say that 'where no man has gone before' no longer applies."

Damned if I didn't want to ask who it had been. Maybe I would have asked, but Cherry spoke and the moment was gone. "His pulse is stronger. Losing this much blood, he should be getting weaker, but he's not."

Asher drew back from the wound. "We are not so much drinking blood as drawing out the corruption." He stood one hand under Nathaniel's thigh. He moved the leg back onto the bed, straightening his limbs as if he were a sleeping child. A moment before, it had been utterly sexual; now there was something in the way Asher acted that was tender, careful.

Damian pulled away from the wound. There was a spot on his lip, not red, but black. I wondered if it had tasted bad. He wiped the spot away with the back of his hand. If it had been pure blood he'd have licked it off. So it hadn't been pleasant.

He crawled out from under Nathaniel, laying him carefully on his back. He drew covers over Nathaniel as he moved off the bed.

Cherry had her first aid kit open. She recleaned the chest wounds with anti-bacterial antiseptic. The first few sterile cloths came away smeared with pus. We'd all moved next to the bed without realizing it. The smell was stronger here, unpleasant, but fading. When the skin and wounds were completely cleaned, the flesh was whole, and bright red blood welled into the slashes.

Cherry flashed the room a smile so warm and bright that you had to smile back. "He's going to be all right." She sounded surprised, and I wondered how close it had been.

Someone drew a hissing breath. I turned to the sound. Damian was backing up. He was staring at his hands. That pale, milky skin was turning dark, a blackness flowing under the skin. The flesh of his hands began to peel back while we watched.

14

"Shit," I said.

Damian held his hands out to me like a child that had burned its hand. I didn't know which was worse, the terror in his face or the almost resigned look in his eyes.

I shook my head. "No," I said, but my voice was soft. "No," I said it again, louder, stronger.

"You cannot stop it," Asher said.

Damian stared at the darkening flesh of his hands, soft horror on his face. "Help me," he said, and he looked to me.

I stared down at him and didn't have the faintest idea how to save him. "What can we do?" I said.

"I know you are accustomed to riding in on your white steed and saving the day, Anita, but some battles cannot be won," Asher said.

Damian had gone to his knees staring at his hands. He ripped his shirt off in pieces, leaving remnants of the sleeves on his arms. The rotting flesh was halfway to his elbows. A fingernail split and fell to the floor with a burst of something dark and noisome. The smell was back, sweet and sickly.

"I healed Damian once of a facial cut," I said.

Damian made a sound between a laugh and something more bitter. "I didn't nick myself shaving, Anita." He shifted his gaze from the peeling flesh of his hands to me. "Even you can't heal this."

I dropped to my knees in front of him, reaching out to touch his hands. Damian jerked away. "Don't touch me!"

I put my hands over his hands. The skin felt almost hot to the touch, as if the corruption were cooking him from the inside out. The skin was soft as if, if I pressed too hard the skin would give way like a rotted spot in an apple.

My throat was tight. "Damian, I'm . . . sorry." Dear God, it was an inadequate word. A thousand years of "life" and he'd given it up for me. He would never have taken such a risk if I had not asked. It was my fault.

The look in his eyes was grateful, and pain-filled. He pulled his hands gently out from under mine. Careful not to press too hard against my hands. I think we were both afraid my fingers would sink through his skin and into the flesh inside.

His face twisted in pain, and a small sound escaped his lips. I remembered Nathaniel's cries of how it had hurt.

The ends of his fingers burst like overripe fruit, spilling something black and greenish onto the floor. It spattered my arm. The smell was growing in sickening waves.

I didn't swipe at the drops on my arm but I wanted to. I wanted to slap at them like a spider, shrieking. My voice held some of the strain I was trying to keep off my face. "I've got to at least try to heal you."

"How?" Asher asked. "How do, even you, begin to heal this?"

Damian made a low whimpering sound. His body shuddered, face ducking, neck twisting, and finally he screamed. Wordless, hopeless.

"How?" Asher asked again.

"I don't know," and I was screaming, too.

"Only his original master, the one who saved him from the grave, would have any chance of healing him."

I looked at Asher. "I called Damian from his coffin once. It was accidental, but he answered to my call. I kept his . . . soul, whatever, from fleeing his body once. We are bound together, a little."

"How did you call him from his grave?" Asher asked.

"Necromancy," I said, "I am a necromancer, Asher."

"I know nothing of necromancy," he said.

The smell swelled stronger. I breathed through my mouth, but that just put the odor on the back of my tongue. I was almost afraid to look at Damian. I turned slowly like a character in a horror movie, where you just know the monster is right behind you, and you delay looking because you know it will blast your sanity forever. But some things are worse than any nightmare. The rot had moved past his elbows. Naked bone showed through the back of his hand. The smell had driven all but the three of us back. I stayed kneeling in the rotting fluid of Damian's body. Asher stayed close, but only I was still within touching distance.

"If I were his master, what would I do?"

"You would drink his blood, take the corruption into yourself as we did for Nathaniel."

"I didn't think vamps fed on each other."

"Not for food," Asher said, "but there are many reasons to share blood. Food is only one of them."

I stared at Damian, watching the blackness spread under his skin like ink. I could actually see it swimming underneath his flesh. "I can't drink the corruption away," I said.

"But I could," Damian's voice came breathy with pain.

"No!" Asher said. He took a threatening step towards us. I could feel his power flaring out from him like a whip.

Damian flinched, but looked up at the other vampire. He held his hands out to Asher, pleading.

"What is going on?" I asked, looking from one to the other of them.

Asher shook his head, face angry, but otherwise unreadable. I watched his features smooth and grow blank. He was hiding something.

"No," I said, getting to my feet. "No, you tell me what Damian meant." Neither spoke.

"Tell me!" I screamed it into Asher's calm face.

He just stared at me, face as closed and impassive as a doll's.

"Dammit, one of you tell me what Damian meant. How could he drink away his own corruption?"

"If . . ." Damian started.

"No," Asher said, pointing a finger at him.

"You are not my master," Damian said. "I must answer."

"Shut up, Asher," I said. "Shut the fuck up and let him talk."

"Would you have her risk all for you?" Asher asked.

"It does not have to be her. Only someone with more than human blood," Damian said.

"Tell me," I said, "now."

Damian spoke in a rushed whisper, voice edged with pain. "If I drank blood from one powerful . . . enough. I might be able . . ." He shuddered, struggling, then continued in a voice that was weaker than just a moment before. "Might be able to take in enough power to . . . cure myself."

"But if the one he takes blood from is not strong enough mystically to take the corruption into himself, then they will die as Damian is dying now," Asher said.

"I'm sorry," Jason said, "but count me out."

"Me, too," Zane said.

Jamil was across the room hugging his arms. He just shook his head.

Cherry knelt by the bed. She said nothing, eyes huge, face terrified.

I finally turned back to Asher. "It has to be me. I can't ask anyone else to take the risk."

Asher grabbed the back of my hair in a movement so fast I hadn't seen it coming. He twisted my face back to look at Damian. "Is this how you want to die, Anita? Is it? Is it!"

I spoke through gritted teeth. "Let go of me, Asher. Now!"

He released me slowly. "Don't do this, Anita. Please, don't. The risk is too great."

"He's right," Damian's voice came in a bare whisper, so low I was surprised I could hear it at all. "You could cure me but kill . . . yourself."

The rot had spread up his arms and was gliding like some malignant force underneath his collarbones. His chest was like glowing ivory, and I could feel his heart thudding in his chest. I could feel it like a second heartbeat in my own head. A vampire's heart didn't always beat, but it was beating now.

I was so scared I could taste something flat and metallic in my mouth. My fingertips tingled with the desire to run. I couldn't stay in this room and watch Damian melt down into a stinking puddle, but part of my brain was screaming at me to run. Run somewhere far away where I wouldn't have to watch and I certainly wouldn't have to let those rotting hands touch me.

I shook my head. I stared at Damian, not at the rotting flesh, but at his face, his eyes. I stared into those shining green eyes like bits of emerald fire. It was ironic that as parts of him corrupted and slothed away, that what was left had become its most beautiful. His skin was polished ivory with a depth of light like some white jewel. His hair seemed to glow like spun rubies, and those eyes, those emerald eyes . . . I stared at him, made myself see him.

I swept my hair to one side, exposing my neck. "Do it." I dropped my hand, and the hair moved back to hide my neck.

"Anita," he said.

"Do it, Damian, do it. Now, please, before I lose my nerve."

He crawled to me. He swept the hair aside with a hand gone blackened flesh and bone. He left a trail of something heavy and thick on my shoulder. I could feel that thickness sliding down my shirt like a snail. I concentrated on the soft glow of his skin, the imperfect slope of his nose where someone centuries ago had broken that perfect profile.

But it wasn't enough. I turned my head to one side so he wouldn't have to touch me more than necessary. I saw his head tense for the strike and I closed my eyes. It was sharp like needles and it didn't get better. Damian wasn't strong enough to roll me with his eyes. There would be no magic to take away the pain.

His mouth locked against the wound and he began to feed. I thought I'd have to try and force my power into him or lower my shields and let him inside my power, let him drink it away. But moments after his teeth pierced my skin, something flared between us. Power, bond, magic. It raised every hair on my body.

Damian cuddled against the front of me, pressing our chests to one another, and the power burst over us in a rush that filled the room with sighing. Distantly I realized that there was a wind and it was coming from us. A wind forged of the cool touch of vampire and the chill control of necromancy. A wind forged of us.

Damian was like a feeding thing at my throat. The power took the pain, turned it into something else. I felt his mouth at my throat, felt him swallowing my blood, my life, my power. I gathered it all into us and thrust it back into Damian. I fed it into him with my blood.

I visualized his skin whole and perfect. I felt the power spill down his body. I felt us push out the other. I could feel it flowing out of us, not onto the floor but into the floor, past the floor, into the ground below. We were exorcising it, ridding ourselves of it. It was no more.

The two of us knelt bathed in power. A wind trailed Damian's hair across my face, and I knew the wind was us. It was Damian who drew back, trailing power between us like the broken shreds of some dream.

He knelt in front of me, lifting his hands to my face. They were healed, under the remnants of that black ooze, his hands were healed. His arms healed. He cradled my face in his hands and kissed me. The power was still there. It flowed over us, through his mouth, in a line of energy that burned.

I drew back from Damian's kiss. I managed to sit up.

"Anita."

I looked at Damian.

"Thank you," he said.

I nodded. "You're welcome."

"Now," Asher said, "I think it is time for showers all around." He stood, pants covered in black goop. It was on his hands, too, and I couldn't remember when he'd touched Damian or the floor.

I could feel the stuff clinging to my bare back where Damian had touched me. My pants were soaked with it from the knees down. The clothes would have to be burned or at least thrown away. This was one of the reasons I kept a pair of coveralls in my Jeep to put on over my clothes at crime scenes and some zombie raisings. Of course, I hadn't expected to get this messy before I'd even left the damn cabin.

"Showers sound great," I said. "You first."

"May I suggest that you go first. A hot shower is a wonderful luxury, but for Damian and me it is a luxury, not a necessity."

"Good point," I said. My hair had kept the stuff from soaking to my scalp, but I could feel it when I touched my hair.

It. I kept saying, "it." I was shying away from the fact that "it" was Damian's body rotted and leaked out upon the floor. Sometimes when it's too horrible you have to distance yourself from it. Language is a good way to do that. Victims become an "it" very quickly, because sometimes it's too horrible even to say, "he," or "she." When you're scraping pieces of someone's loved one off your hands, it has to be an "it." Has to be, or you run screaming. So, I was covered in black, greenish it.

I washed my hands thoroughly enough so I could dig through my suitcase without contaminating the clothes. I'd picked out jeans and a polo shirt. Asher appeared behind me. I looked up at him.

"What?" I asked. It sounded rude even to me. "I mean, what now?"

Asher rewarded me with a smile. "We will have to meet Colin tonight."

I nodded. "Oh, yeah. He is definitely on my dance card for tonight."

He smiled and shook his head. "We cannot kill him, Anita."

I stared at him. "You mean we can't, as in it's too hard a job or we can't, as in we shouldn't do it?"

"Perhaps both, but certainly the latter."

I stood. "He sent Nathaniel to us to die." I looked into the suitcase, not seeing it, just not wanting to look up. There was a rim of blackness at the base of my fingernails that the scrubbing at the sink hadn't lifted. There had been a moment when the power broke between us, and I knew it would work, but until that second . . . I had tried very hard not to think about it. It was only after I'd gone into the bathroom to clean my hands off that I started to shake. I'd stayed in the bathroom until my hands were steady. The fear was under control, all that was left was anger.

"I do not think anyone was meant to die, Anita. I think it was a test."

"A test of what?" I asked.

"How much power we truly have. In a way it was a compliment. He would never have contaminated Nathaniel if he thought we had no hope of saving him."

"How can you be so sure?"

"Because, to kill a *pomme de sang* of another master vampire is a mortal insult. Wars have begun over less."

"But he knows we can't make war on him without the Council hunting us down."

"Which is why we cannot kill him." Asher held up his hand, which stopped me with my mouth open. I closed it. "The last master you killed was threatening your life directly. You killed her to protect yourself. Self-defense is allowed. But Colin has not offered us personal violence."

"That is cutting it pretty damn close, Asher."

He gave a graceful nod. *"Oui."*

"So if we kill him the Council comes back to town and cleans our clock."

Slight frown lines showed between his eyes. I don't think he understood the slang. "They will kill us," he said.

I'd met some of the Council, and I knew he was right. Jean-Claude had enemies on the Council and now so did I. No, I did not want to give the nightmares of all vampirekind an excuse to come back to St. Louis and wipe us out.

"What can we do? Because, mark me on this, Asher, they will pay for what they did to Nathaniel."

"I agree. If we do nothing to avenge the insult, it will be viewed as a sign of weakness and Colin may come against us and kill us."

"Why is everything so damned complicated with you guys?" I asked. "Why couldn't Colin just believe we'd come down here to rescue Richard?"

"Because we didn't leave town." Nathaniel's voice came thin but steady from the bed. He blinked lilac eyes at me. Cherry had bandaged his chest and the neck wound was covered with a large piece of taped gauze. I assumed the thigh wound was similarly covered, but the bedspread covered him from the waist down.

"When Richard got out of jail, Colin expected us to leave town. When we didn't, he thought we meant to take over his territory."

I went to stand by the bed. "Zane said you went off with one of Verne's werewolves. How did the vamps get hold of you?"

"Mira," he said.

"Excuse me?" I said.

"The werewolf's name is Mira." He looked away from me as if he didn't want to look me in the face while he talked. "She took me home. We had sex. Then she left the room. When she came back the vampires were with her." He looked up at me. I found myself staring down into his eyes and the need in them was so raw it made me flinch.

"There were too many of them for you to fight, Nathaniel," I said. "It's okay."

"Fight?" He laughed, and it was so bitter it hurt just to hear it. "There was no fight. I was already chained down."

I frowned. "Why?"

He let out a long sigh. "Anita, Anita, God." He put one arm across his eyes.

Zane came to the rescue, sort of. "You know that Nathaniel is a submissive?"

I nodded. "I know he likes to be tied up and . . ." The light dawned. "Oh, okay. I get it. Mira invited you home for some S and M sex."

"D and S, dominance and submission," Zane said, "but yeah."

I took a deep breath, mistake. The room still stank of bodily fluids, the unpleasant kind. "So she wrapped you up like a present and gave you to them?"

"Yes," he said, softly. "The sex had been good. She was a good top."

"Top?" I asked.

"Dominant," Zane said.

Ah.

Nathaniel curled onto his side, drawing the bedspread around him. "The master, Colin, paid her to bring one of us to them. Anyone of us. It didn't matter who. It could have been Jason, or Zane, or Cherry. One of their animals, he said." He huddled down into the blankets, eyes fluttering shut, then open, then shut.

I looked at Cherry. "Is he alright?"

"I gave him something to help him sleep. It won't last long. Our metabolisms are too fast, but he'll get maybe half an hour, an hour if we're lucky."

"If you're not going to take a shower, I'd like to," Damian said.

"No, I'm getting in."

"But you can't wear what you've picked out," Asher said.

I frowned at him. "What are you talking about?"

"Jean-Claude sent a trunk of clothes just for this occasion," he said.

"Oh, no," I said, "no more leather and lace shit."

"I agree with you, Anita," Asher said. "If we were simply going to kill them it wouldn't matter what we wore, but we are putting on a show as much as anything. Appearance will matter."

"Well, shit," I said. "Fine, I'll dress up, we won't kill anyone, but you better come up with something that we can do to them. They can't abuse our people like this and just walk away."

"They will expect retribution, Anita. They are waiting for it."

I looked at Nathaniel cuddled so deep in the blankets that only the top of his head showed. "This retribution better be good, Asher."

"I will do my best."

I shook my head. "You do that." I went into the shower without any clothes to put on because the trunk was in the other cabin. I figured with both coffins in my room I didn't need the trunk. I'd really hoped we wouldn't be opening the damn thing. I hated dressing up in normal dressy clothes. Jean-Claude's idea of dressing up was always worse.

15

It took three rounds of shampoo to get my hair clean. The stuff on my body didn't seem to want to come off unless I scrubbed. There is that point in the middle of the back that you just can't do yourself. It is one of the few areas that married people have an edge on us single folk. I finally had to turn the shower on as high as it would go and just let it pound the middle of my back. The stuff finally sloughed off and floated down the drain.

The stuff clung like nothing I'd ever had to clean off before. That included real rotting corpses and zombies. None of it had ever been as tough to get rid of as Damian's . . . fluids.

Cherry was the one who knocked on the door and brought in a pile of clothes. I didn't like any of them. Too much leather for my taste. It took two trips back and forth, wrapped in nothing but a towel, to find clothes that I was willing to wear. There was one red leather bodysuit that seemed to be nothing but straps. It might be interesting for private use just between Jean-Claude and myself, but wearing it in public was definitely out.

I ended up in a short-sleeved, black velvet, midriff top with such a low neckline that it took a special bra under it just so the bra didn't show. Jean-Claude had kindly packed the bra. It was one of those uplifting ones, and if there was one thing my chest didn't need, it was more lift; but it was also the only bra I had access to that plunged low enough that it didn't show with the shirt. There was a velvet dress that would have needed the bra for its neckline, too. Jean-Claude had been a busy little vampire.

Everything fit perfectly, if you were willing to wear it. I picked a leather skirt as the lesser of evils. There was a pair of thigh-high black boots that zipped in the back. The tops of the boots were wide and stiff and open at the back. The fronts of the boots came up to the absolute limit of my legs, brushing my groin at odd moments if I walked wrong. The boots had to have been custom-made for me. I didn't remember Jean-Claude ever measuring me for shoes. He'd held pretty much every inch of me in his hands at one point or another. Apparently, that had been enough.

But the leather skirt had belt loops for my shoulder holster, and the velvet midriff had enough sleeves that the shoulder straps didn't dig into any bare flesh. The side straps felt a little strange against my bare sides when I moved, but it was doable. Of course, there was no way to wear an inner-pants holster in the skirt.

I had added the spine sheath down my back and both wrist sheaths. The spine sheath showed underneath the midriff, but hey, they expected us to be armed. Frankly, I wanted a second gun with me. One of the good things about flying on Jean-Claude's private jet as opposed to an airline was that I had several guns to choose from.

It was a mini-Uzi on a shoulder strap. It had a clip that attached to the back of the skirt so it didn't swing around too much, but you could pull it out into the open with one hand.

When I put it on, Asher's only comment had been, "We can't kill them, Anita."

I looked at the weapons that I'd laid out on one of the last clean spaces of floor. There was an American Derringer, a second Browning Hi-Power, a sawed-off shotgun, and one pump-action shotgun.

I looked up at him. "I didn't bring everything I had."

"So glad to hear it," he said. "But the machine gun is a killing weapon, nothing more."

"The reason I'm in this outfit is because you said we need to make a good show. Well, we can't cause harm from a distance. We can't spread corruption with any of your bites. What the hell are we going to do, Asher? What can we possibly do that will impress them?" I swung the Uzi into my left hand, pointing it at the ceiling. "If there's anyone with him tonight that we can kill, I'll kill them with this."

"And you think that will impress or frighten Colin?"

"Have you ever seen a vampire cut in half by one of these?" I asked.

Asher seemed to think about that for a few seconds as if he'd seen so many horrible things that he just wasn't sure. Finally, he shook his head. "No, I have not."

"Well, I have." I let the gun swing back to the small of my back. "It impressed me."

"Did you do it?" he asked, his voice soft.

I shook my head. "No, just saw it done."

Jamil knelt beside me. He was wearing something that had started life as a black T-shirt but had been cut so severely at the neck, arms, and midriff that it looked more like a wishful thought than a shirt. It covered his nipples, and that was about it. But his upper body was muscular and impressive nearly bare. We were going for impressive tonight. He'd gotten to keep his black jeans and I was jealous. But Jamil didn't belong to Jean-Claude, so there'd been no time to have some piece of leather specially made. Truthfully, I hadn't been a hundred percent certain Jamil was even going to come with us. Not only was Jamil coming but so was Richard. Surprise, surprise. Jamil took an armload of clothes for Richard to choose from. Shang-Da was coming along as well, and he needed to change. Though he, like Jamil, had never belonged to Jean-Claude intimately enough to have specially made clothes. So it was whatever they could find in his suitcase. Happy hunting.

16

Damian had refused to share a shower with Asher, even though they were both dirty and would need someone to help scrape the stuff from the harder-to-reach places. I'd suggested they share a shower because they were both guys. I knew that Asher was bisexual, but I still had a hard time wrapping my Midwestern upbringing around the fact that it didn't matter what sex Asher shared a shower with, he saw both as sexual objects. I knew it, and it didn't really bother me, but every once in a while, the knowledge surprised me. I don't know why.

Asher came out of the shower with nothing but a towel knotted at his waist. Damian went into the shower. The last of the night. Jason had helped Asher scrape the harder-to-reach places. Jason didn't tease the vampire. He just went in, helped him clean up, and got out. I'd actually wondered, after Jason's little confession, if he would tease men the same way he teased women. Apparently not.

The scars on Asher's chest were very visible. As he walked, the scars on his right thigh flashed from the towel. The rest of him was a pale golden perfection. He'd once known what it was like to walk into any room and have people gasp at his beauty. People still gasped, but not for the same reasons.

Zane and Cherry were being very careful not to look at him. They kept their faces blank, but their discomfort screamed how they felt.

Asher's face was bland, as if he didn't notice, but I knew he did.

Jason didn't look away. He'd pulled on a pair of leather pants but waited on the shirt and boots because he still had to help Damian flake the gunk off his skin. He sat on one of the coffins, swinging his bare feet, looking at me. His eyes flicked to the vampire, then back to me.

Oh, hell. Who died and made me den mother? You'd think hanging around with this many preternatural studly guys would mean there was a lot of sex, and sexual tension was in the air a lot, but more than sex, was pain. I don't know if it was because I was a girl, or what, but I ended up doing a hell of a lot more hand-holding than any of the guys. Maybe it was a girl thing. I certainly didn't think of myself as particularly compassionate. So why was it me walking across the floor to the vampire?

Asher was kneeling in front of the trunk. His back was smooth and almost perfect, only a few trailing scars where the holy water had dripped down his side. His golden hair hung thick and wet, water trailing in silver lines down his back. There weren't enough towels, so the guys were forgoing a second towel for the hair.

I took the towel I'd used for my hair from the back of the desk chair. I'd put it there so it could dry. I went to him and put a hand on his shoulder. He flinched, lowering his head, trying to get the wet hair to cover his scarred face. The gesture was automatic, no thinking required, and it hurt my heart to see him do it.

If we'd been lovers, I'd have licked the water off his chest, caressing my tongue down the deep scars, maybe even slid a hand under the towel. But we weren't lovers, and I'd never seen him nude. I didn't know what was under the towel. He'd told me once that he was still fully functional, but that didn't really tell me what he looked like under the towel. And as comfortable as I was with him, I wasn't sure I wanted to know. If it was as bad as his chest, I was almost sure I didn't want to see. Yes, I admit there was a small part of me that did want to know for sheer curiosity's sake.

I did the best I could. I laid my face against the roughness of his right cheek. "What are you going to wear?"

He sighed and leaned his face into me. One hand touched my hand, sliding my arm across his damp chest. "I think we shall need to shock them. I shall wear very little."

I moved back enough to see his face. He kept my hand pressed to his chest, resting on the smooth perfection of his left side. "You sure about that?"

He smiled but blinked at the same time so I couldn't read his eyes. He patted my hand and let me go. "I am accustomed to the effect I have on people, *ma cherie*. I have had centuries to use it to my advantage."

I stood and draped the towel over his shoulders. "You'll need this for your hair."

He grabbed the ends of the towel like a shawl, pressing the cloth to his nose and mouth. "It smells of the sweet scent of your skin."

I touched a strand of that heavy, gold hair. "You say the nicest things." I stared down into that face, into the frosted blue of his eyes, and felt something low in my body tighten. A sudden flexing of lust that made me catch my breath. Sometimes it happens. Sometimes it's just a gesture, a turn of the head, and you catch your breath, your body reacts on a level that you can't control. When it happens, you pretend it didn't, you hide it. Heaven forbid that the object of such instant desire should know what you're thinking. But tonight, I let it show in my eyes. I let him see how he moved me.

He took my hand and laid a gentle kiss against my skin. *"Ma cherie."*

Jason came to stand near us, leaning against the nearest coffin as he'd leaned against the desk. "Damn," he said.

"What?" I asked.

"You've seen me naked, or almost. We've been up close and very personal." He sighed. "And you didn't look at me like that."

"Jealous?" I asked.

He seemed to think about that for a second, then nodded. "Yeah, I think I am."

Asher laughed and it was touchable, caressable, like a feather trailing down your skin held by a knowledgeable hand. "In that smooth, perfect body, in the full bloom of your youth, alive and breathing, and you are jealous of me. How lovely."

A knock on the door saved us from further discussion. I drew the Browning and put my back to the wall near the door. "Who is it?"

"It's Verne."

I parted the drape and looked out. He seemed to be alone. I opened the door and ushered him inside. The moment his back was to me, I pressed the gun barrel into his back and kicked the door closed.

He froze. "What's up?" he asked.

"You tell us," I said.

"Anita," Asher said.

"No, he's the Ulfric. He's supposed to have his pack under solid control."

I felt his ribs expand through the gun barrel. "I can smell the shit in the carpet, the sheets. Colin pay a visit?"

I shoved the barrel tight enough into his back to leave a bruise. "He left a present."

"He gave us one of his presents once," Verne said. "I know what I'm smelling in here because I held Erin's hand while he rotted to death."

"Why should I believe you?" I asked.

"If you have a problem with Colin's people, why pull a gun on me?"

"One of your wolves lured Nathaniel away and delivered him to the vampires."

Again I felt the movement through the gun barrel as he turned his head to look at the bed. "Why isn't he dead?"

"That's our business," I said.

He nodded. "Which of my wolves delivered your cat to Colin?"

"Mira," I said.

"Shit," he said. "I knew she was pissed that Richard had stopped seeing her, but I never thought she'd go over to the vampires."

Asher walked to us. "By rules of hospitality, you can be held responsible for the actions of your pack."

"What can I do to make up for this breach of protocol?" The words sounded way too formal for Verne's down-home drawl.

I leaned into him because the gun couldn't get any closer without going into his body. Had to make my point somehow. "How do I know you didn't tell her to do it?"

"I told you what he did to Erin. Colin said we were getting above ourselves, forgetting that vampires are more powerful than any animal. How the hell did you cure your leopard?"

"His name's Nathaniel," I said.

Verne took a deep breath, let it out slowly. "How did you cure Nathaniel?"

I flicked my eyes past Verne's body to Asher. He gave the slightest of nods, and I backed up enough steps that I'd be out of reach in case Verne was upset about the gun. But I kept the gun pointed at him, because I was still closer than ten feet. Even a normal man armed with just a knife can close that distance quicker than most people can upholster a gun.

"At great risk to ourselves," Asher said.

"How?" Verne asked. He moved towards the bed as if I was of no importance. Asher told him how we'd healed Nathaniel.

"And neither of you were poisoned by it?" Verne asked.

"Damian was affected," Asher said.

Verne searched the room. "You mean the red-haired vampire?"

Asher nodded.

"I can hear him in the bathroom. He should be dead."

"Yes, he should be," Asher said.

Verne turned and looked at me then. "Our vargamor said she felt your power tonight. Said you conjured up some sort of spell."

"I don't know the term *vargamor*," I said.

"A pack's wise woman or wise man, a witch usually, but not always. Sometimes just a psychic. Most packs don't bother with them anymore. How did you save the vampire once he started to rot?"

I holstered the Browning. One, I couldn't keep the gun naked in my hands forever; two, I was beginning to believe Verne. "I'm a necromancer, Verne. Damian's a vampire. I healed him."

His eyes narrowed. "Just like that?"

I laughed. "No, not just like that. We damn near didn't save him, but we did it."

"Could you cure one of my people?"

"Did Colin do one of your people tonight?" I asked.

He shook his head. "No, but if we stand with you against him, he will."

"Why would you stand with us on this?" I asked.

"Because I hate that bloodsucking son of a bitch."

"If that's true, then Mira broke pack law," Jason said.

Verne nodded. "Normally, I'd kick her ass. She disobeyed me, but she injured you. Your grievance takes precedence." He glanced at Asher, then at me, as if he wasn't a hundred percent sure who to ask permission of. "What can my pack do to make this right between us?"

I looked at him, head to one side. I didn't like the idea that one of his wolves had betrayed Nathaniel. It made me not trust him. But I understood why Mira was pissed. Richard had dumped her. A woman scorned and all that.

"First, delay the greeting ceremony," I said. "We're going to be ass deep in vampires; there won't be time for anything else tonight."

Verne nodded. "Done."

"And I want Mira's head in a basket," I said.

"We need a place to meet Colin," Asher said.

"Our lupanar is ready for company," Verne said.

"Most generous," Asher said.

It was generous. Maybe too generous. "You understand that we aren't going to kill Colin for this. That whatever happens tonight—unless he attacks us, forces us to defend ourselves—we'll be leaving in a few days, and Colin will still be Master of the City."

"You mean if I help you hurt him, he may hold a grudge?" Verne said.

I nodded. "Yeah."

"Erin was a good kid. He wasn't even one of the young ones that had gone up against the vampires. They picked him because he was one of my wolves."

"Nathaniel said that Mira had been paid to bring one of our animals to Colin," I said.

"It sounds like him." Verne's hands balled into fists, and his power moved through the cabin like a line of heat. "I've wanted him to pay for what happened to Erin for ten years, but I haven't had the power to go up against him."

"You don't want him dead?" I asked, and I sounded surprised.

"Colin, for the most part, leaves us alone. But better yet, he can't call wolves. If we kill him, a new master will move in, maybe one that can control wolves. Maybe one that is a bigger, meaner son of a bitch. Dead would be great, but not until I know what it would cost my pack."

"The devil you know or the devil you don't," I said.

Verne looked at me for a second, then nodded. "Yes."

"Great," I said, "let's turn up the fire under this particular devil and roast his *cojónes*."

For one of the few times on this trip, everyone seemed to be in agreement. I was used to killing vampires, not punishing them, because I'd learned a long time ago that you either killed monsters or left them the fuck alone. Once you pull on their tail, metaphorically speaking, you're just never quite sure how they're going to react. Sorry, cancel that. I knew exactly how Colin would react. The question was how much blood would be spilled and could we possibly pull this off without getting some of our people killed. I didn't give a damn if we killed some of Colin's people, in fact, I was sort of looking forward to it.

17

I walked through a world of silvered moon shadows and the black outlines of trees. The boots were low-heeled enough and they fit well enough that they actually weren't bad for walking through the woods. It wasn't the fit of anything that made it uncomfortable to be out in the woods; it was the heat and the noise. There was sweat at the bend of my knees underneath the nylons and the leather. I'd added a leather jacket, borrowed from Jason. The jacket hid the mini-Uzi and the big leather purse I had slung over one shoulder. The purse was Cherry's and had a can of aerosol hair spray in it. I had a golden lighter in the pocket of the jacket. The lighter belonged to Asher. It was too hot to be wearing the jacket.

All that leather crinkled and sighed every time I moved. Under other circumstances, it might have been interesting; as it was, it was irritating. Important safety tip: Don't try to sneak up on people in new leather. At least not people with supernatural hearing. Of course, we weren't sneaking up on anybody tonight. The vampires knew we were coming.

Verne's people had delivered the message. Once Richard arrived on the scene, my suspicious nature was ignored. If Verne said he told the vamps where to meet and why, then of course Richard believed him. Truthfully, so did I, but it still bugged me how easily Richard accepted Verne's word.

Of course, Richard had been visiting with Verne's pack for several years every summer. He knew them as friends. I respected friendship; I just didn't always trust it. Okay, I didn't trust other people's friends. I trusted my own, because I trusted my own judgment. Which meant, I guess, that I still didn't trust Richard's judgment. No, I didn't.

Thinking of him was enough. I could feel him off to my left like a warm presence moving through the summer night. I had a moment of feeling him walking. I could feel the rhythm of his body as he moved. I was almost dizzy, stumbling, as I pulled away from the image.

Zane took my arm. "You all right?"

I nodded and pulled away. I didn't know him that well yet. If I had a choice, I wasn't that touchy-feely with people I didn't know. But the moment I pulled away, I felt him shrink back. I knew without any magic at all that I'd hurt his feelings. I was his Nimir-ra, his leopard queen, and I was supposed to like him, or at least not dislike him. I didn't know whether apologizing would make it worse or better, so I said nothing.

Zane moved off through the woods, leaving me to myself. He was wearing the leather pants, vest, and boots he'd worn on the plane. Funny how Zane's personal wardrobe was just fine for tonight.

Richard stopped moving and stared at me across the yards that separated us. He was dressed all in black: leather pants and a silk shirt that clung to his new, improved, muscular upper body. He'd been lifting weights since Jean-Claude last measured him for shirts. He stood there all in black, a color I'd never seen him in. The moonlight was strong enough that I could see his face in bold highlights; only the eyes were lost to shadow, as if he were blind. Even from here, I could feel him like a line of heat in my body.

Earlier, Asher had made things in my body go low and tight. But now, standing in the hot, summer woods, watching the gleam of moonlight reflecting off the silk and leather on Richard's body, seeing his hair slide like a soft cloud around his shoulders, it made my chest tight, closer to tears than to lust, because he wasn't mine anymore. Whether I liked it or not, whether I wanted it or not, I would always regret not having been with Richard. I'd had other opportunities in the past for being with other guys in intimate settings, but I'd never regretted saying no before. In fact, I always felt like I'd dodged a bullet. Only Richard made me regret.

He started walking towards me. It made me look away as if we'd been at a resturant or something, and I'd been caught staring at my ex. I remembered a night just after college when I'd been in a resturant with some friends, and seen my ex-fiancé with his new girlfriend. He'd walked towards us as if he'd introduce me to her. I'd fled to the ladies' room and hid out until one of my girlfriends came and told me the coast was clear. Four years ago, I'd run for cover because he had dumped me and didn't seem to miss me. Now I stood my ground but not because I had dumped Richard. I stood my ground because my pride wouldn't let me hurry away through the trees and pretend I hadn't run away. I wasn't much into running lately.

So I stood there in the silvered dark, my heart beating in my throat, and waited for him to come to me.

Jamil and Shang-Da stood together in the dark, watching but not following him, as if he'd told them to stay put. Even from here, I could tell Shang-Da didn't like it. As far as I could see, Shang-Da hadn't changed clothes. He was still in his all-black, totally monochromed tailored suit, shirt, and accessories.

Richard came to stand about two feet in front of me. He just looked down at me and said nothing. I couldn't read his expression, and I didn't want to read his mind again.

I broke first, babbling. ''I'm sorry about that, Richard. I didn't mean to invade you like that. I'm not very good at controlling the marks yet.''

''That's all right,'' he said. Why is it that voices in the dark can sound so much more intimate?

''You okay with Asher's plan for tonight?'' I asked, more for something to say while he stared down at me than for anything else.

Verne had learned through Mira that Colin believed that Asher was his replacement. Both masters were of an equivalent age. Colin was more powerful, but much of that extra power could have been from the ties that made him Master of the City. It was the first time I'd ever been told that just being Master of the City gave you extra power. Live and learn.

"I understand that Asher has to convince Colin that he doesn't want the job," Richard said.

Asher had decided that the way to do that was to convince Colin he was infatuated with me and with Jean-Claude. I wasn't sure how I felt about the plan, really. But we all agreed, even Richard, that the local vamps wouldn't believe that ties of friendship and nostalgia made Asher happy where he was. Vampires are like people in one respect, they'll believe a sexual explanation before an innocent one. Even death doesn't change the human trait of being willing to believe the worst of a person rather than the best.

"It's none of my business what you do or who you do it with, remember?" His voice was a great deal more neutral than his words.

"I was embarrassed in the bathroom. You caught me off guard."

"I remember," I said. He shook his head. "If we're supposed to flaunt our power tonight, that means we need to use the marks."

"Mira told them that you were interviewing new lupas. They know we're not an item," I said.

"We don't have to show them domestic bliss, Anita, just power." He held out his hand to me.

I stared at it. The last time he'd led me through summer woods had been the night he killed Marcus. The night when everything had gone wrong.

"I don't think I can take another stroll through the woods, Richard."

His hand closed into a fist. "I know I handled it badly that night, Anita. You'd never seen me shapeshift, and I shifted on top of you, while you couldn't get away. I've thought about that. I couldn't have chosen a worse way to introduce you to what I was. I know that now, and I'm sorry I scared you."

Scared didn't quite cover it, but I didn't say it out loud. He was apologizing, and I was going to accept it. "Thank you, Richard. I didn't mean to hurt you. I just . . ."

"Couldn't handle it," he said.

I sighed. "Couldn't handle it."

He held his hand out to me. "I'm sorry, Anita."

"Me, too, Richard."

He gave a small smile. "No magic, Anita, just your hand in mine."

I shook my head. "No, Richard."

"Afraid?" he asked.

I stared up at him. "When we need to draw the marks, we can touch; but not here, not now."

He reached up to touch my face, and I heard the silk of his shirt rip. He lowered his arm and put three fingers in the ripped seam. "That's the third time that's happened." He spread the seam on the other arm, putting his whole hand in it. He turned and showed me his back. The seams at the shoulders had pulled apart on both sides like mouths.

I giggled, and I don't do that often. "You look like the Incredible Hulk."

He flexed his arms and shoulders like a bodybuilder. The look of mock concentration on his face made me laugh. The silk ripped with an almost wet sound. Silk sounds the closest to flesh of any cloth when you tear it; only leather sounds more alive under a blade.

His tanned flesh showed pale through the black cloth, as if some invisible knife were slashing rips in it. He straightened up. One sleeve had ripped so badly at the shoulder that it flapped around his upper arm. The seams at the top of his chest were like twin smiles.

"I feel a draft," he said. He turned and showed me his back. The shirt had peeled off his back, hanging in tatters.

"It's trashed," I said.

"Too much weight lifting since I was measured for the shirt."

"You are perilously close to being too muscular," I said.

"Can you ever be too muscular?" he asked.

"Yes, you can," I said.

"You don't like it?" he asked. He wadded his hands into the front of the shirt and pulled. The silk tore into black shreds, ripping like a soft scream. He tossed the silk at me. I caught it by reflex, not thinking.

He grabbed what was left of the shirt across his shoulders and pulled it over his head, exposing every inch of his chest, his shoulders. He strained his arms upward, making the muscles mold against his skin from stomach to shoulder.

It didn't just make me catch my breath, it made me catch and hold, forgetting to breathe for a few seconds, so that when I did remember, my breath came out in a shaky gasp. So much for being cool and sophisticated.

He lowered his arms and all that was left were the sleeves. He pulled them off like a stripper removing long gloves and let the bits of silk fall to the ground. He stood looking at me, nude from the waist up.

"Am I supposed to applaud or say, 'My, my, Mr. Zeeman, what big shoulders you have'? I'm aware that you have a great body, Richard. You don't have to rub my face in it."

He moved into me until he was standing so close that a hard thought would have made us touch. "What a good idea," he said.

I frowned at him, because I wasn't following. "What's a good idea?"

"Rubbing your face in my body," he said, his voice so low that it was almost a whisper.

I blushed and hoped he couldn't see it in the dark. "It's an expression, Richard. You know I didn't mean it."

"I know," he said, "but it's still a good idea."

I stepped back. "Go away, Richard."

"You don't know the way to the lupanar," he said.

"I'll find it on my own; thanks, anyway."

He started to reach out to touch my face, and I almost stumbled backing up. He flashed me a quick smile and was gone, running through the trees. I could feel the roil of power like wind in a sail. He rode the energy of the woods, the night, the moon overhead, and if I wanted to, I could go along for the ride. I stood there, hugging my arms, concentrating everything I had on blocking him out, cutting the power between us.

When I felt alone and locked within my own skin again, I opened my eyes. Jason was standing so close it made me jump. It also made me realize how careless I'd been.

"Damn, Jason, you scared me."

"Sorry. I thought someone should stay behind and make sure no vampires made off with you."

"Thanks, I mean that."

"You all right?" he asked.

I shook my head. "I'm fine."

He grinned, and there was almost enough moonlight to see the laughter in his eyes. "He's getting better at it," Jason said.

"Getting better at what?" I asked. "Being Ulfric?"

"Seducing you," Jason said.

I stared at him.

"You know how I was jealous of the way you looked at Asher?"

I nodded.

"The way you look at Richard . . ." He just shook his head. "It's something."

I took a deep breath and let it out slowly. "It doesn't matter."

"It matters," he said. "It doesn't make you happy, but it matters."

And to that, there wasn't a damn thing I could say. We started walking through the woods in the general direction everyone else had been going. We didn't need no stinking directions.

18

We found the lupanar, and we didn't need directions. We had Jason's nose and my ability to sense the dead. I'd assumed that all lupanars were the same, but yards away from this one, I knew I was wrong. Whatever lay up ahead had death mixed in with it: old death. It felt almost like a restless grave. Sometimes you'd be out in the woods and find one. An old grave where someone was buried without rites, just a shallow hole in the ground. The dead don't much care for shallow holes. It needs to be deep and wide or they get restless. Cremation takes care of all of it, actually. I'd never met a ghost of someone who had been cremated.

We could see the soft shine of lanterns through the trees when Jason stopped, touching my arm for attention. "I don't like what I'm smelling," he said.

"What do you mean?" I asked.

"A body aboveground for a long time."

"A zombie?" I made it a question.

He shook his head. "No, drier, older than that."

We both looked at each other. I was pretty sure we were both thinking the same thing. Rotting vampire. I realized that I was clutching his arm, and he was clutching mine. We stood in the dark like children wondering if that noise was really a monster or if it was the wind. Neither of us took that next step to find out. If we'd had covers, we'd have been under them.

If we'd gone in there just to kill them, I'd have been all right. A slash-and-burn operation was my style lately. Every time we approached the vamps on their own territory by their own rules, we got hurt. I realized suddenly how much I did not want to walk into that place and negotiate with the monsters. I wanted to press a gun under Colin's chin and pull the trigger. I wanted done with it. I did not want to walk in there and give him power over me through some ancient rules of hospitality among the terminally anemic.

Damian came gliding through the trees. He was dressed in the standard uniform of black leather pants so tight you knew that nothing else was under them but vampire. But he was wearing a black silk T-shirt with a scooped neck. It looked almost like a woman's shirt. His shoulder-length hair helped the illusion of feminity, but the chest and shoulders that peeked out of the shirt ruined the effect: masculine, definitely masculine.

Jason was wearing an almost identical outfit, except the shirt and pants were satin. Though the knee-high boots were identical. For the first time, I realized that Jason was broader through the shoulders than Damian. Had that just happened recently? I looked from the werewolf to the vampire and shook my head. They grow up so fast.

What I said out loud was, "You guys look like backup singers for a Gothic band."

"Everyone's waiting for you," Damian said.

I realized that I still didn't want to go. I felt Jason shake his head. "No," he said.

"You're afraid," Damian said.

Jason nodded. I frowned. Jason and I were both usually braver than this, no matter what nasty things were in the next room—or the next clearing, as the case may be.

"What's up, Damian? What's happening?"

"I told you what Colin was."

"You called him a night hag. He can feed off fear. Was that supposed to be a clue?" I asked.

"He can also cause fear in others," Damian said.

I took a deep breath and forced myself to relax my hold on Jason's arm. He kept his death grip. "That makes sense," I said. "They can always guarantee a meal that way, right?"

Damian nodded. "But he also enjoys it. Fear is like a drug to a night hag. My old master said it was better than blood, because she could walk through a world of fear. If she desired it, she could move through a world that trembled, ever so slightly, at her passing."

"And that's what Colin is doing tonight?" I said.

Jason dropped his hand from my arm. He stayed close enough that our arms brushed, but we weren't huddling in the dark like rabbits.

"I can usually tell when a vamp is doing mind stuff on me. He's good."

"This is different from the other master-level powers, Anita. My first master said it was like breathing to a human, something you did without thinking about it. She could intensify it, but she could never really stop it. A low level dread surrounded her at all times."

"Was she scary in bed?" Jason asked. I think he meant it as a joke.

The look on Damian's face even by moonlight wasn't funny. "Yes," he said. "Yes, she was." He looked at me, and there was an intensity in his face that I didn't like. He actually reached out to me, then let his hand drop.

He finally said. "Some of the masters can feed off of other things, not just fear."

"What else?" I asked.

Asher breathed through my mind, and he must have done the same to Damian, because we both jumped. His voice came like a whisper in a nearby room, almost as if it was sound without words. "Hurry."

There was no more talk. We hurried.

The lantern light shone through the trees like small, yellow moons. Damian glided through that last line of trees into the clearing. I didn't glide. I stumbled over the outer edge of the clearing. There was a power circle in this land so old and walked so often that it was like a curtain waiting to be drawn around the lupanar. It would take almost no power to bring whatever was here alive.

When I quit seeing with that inner vision and looked out into the clearing, I stopped walking. I just stood and stared. Jason stood and stared with me. Between the two of us, we were getting pretty jaded, but the lupanar of the Oak Tree Clan was worth a stare or two.

It was a huge clearing with an oak tree in the center of it, but that was like saying the Empire State Building is tall. The tree was like some great spreading giant. A hundred feet tall, rising up and up. There was a body hanging from one of the lower branches. It was mostly skeleton with dried bits of tendon holding one arm out. The other arm had disintegrated, falling to the ground. There were bones everywhere under the tree. White bones, yellowed bones, bones so old they were grey from being weathered. A carpet of bones stretched out from beneath the tree, filling the clearing.

The wind picked up, hurrying through the forest. It sent the leaves on the oak rustling and whispering. The rope on the skeleton creaked as it swung in the wind. And with that one creak, my eyes went back to the tree, because there were dozens of creaking ropes. Most of them were empty now, broken or eaten to ragged ends, but those ropes creaked and moved with the wind, up and up. I followed the ropes up to the top of the tree as far as I could look in the dark by moonlight. The tree had to be over a hundred years old, and there were ragged bits of rope at its top. They'd been hanging bodies on this tree for a very long time.

The skeleton rotated suddenly in the growing wind, jaw gaping, empty sockets reflecting the lantern light for a second. The tendons at the jaw gave way, and the jaw hung, swinging on one side, like a broken hinge. I had a horrible urge to run across that boneyard and yank the jaw away, or reattach it, anything so that bit of bone would stop waggling in the wind.

"My God," Jason whispered.

All I could do was nod. I wasn't rendered speechless often, but I had no words for this.

Damian had stopped and moved back to stand by us. He seemed to be waiting, as if he were our escort. I finally tore my gaze away from the tree and its awful burden. There were benches forming three sides of a disconnected triangle. There was enough room between each bench that no one was unduly crowded, yet the clearing felt crowded, almost as if the air itself was thick with things unseen, hurrying to and fro, brushing past me in a rush of gooseflesh.

"Did you feel that?" I asked.

Jason looked at me. "Feel what?"

I guess not. That meant whatever was crowding so close in the air wasn't something that a shapeshifter would pick up on. So what was it?

There was a vampire staring at me from where he sat on the near bench. His hair was brown, cut short so his neck was pale and bare. His eyes seemed very dark, maybe brown, maybe black. He smiled, and I felt his power rush over me. He was trying to capture me with his eyes. Usually, I would have tried to stare him down, but I didn't like what I was feeling in this place. Power, and it wasn't vampires. I looked away from his eyes, studying the pale curve of his cheek. His lips were full, with an upper lip that was set in a perfect bow, very feminine. The rest of the face was all points and angles; the chin sharp, the nose too long. It was a face that would be homely except for that mouth and those long-lashed eyes, dark and drowning deep as black mirrors.

I didn't stare too long at those eyes. I was feeling unsteady, as if the ground under my feet wasn't quite solid. Richard should have told me about the lupanar. Someone should have prepared me. Later, I'd be angry that no one had; now, I was just trying to figure out what to do about it. If Verne's clan were practicing human sacrifice, then it had to be stopped.

Damian moved in front of me, blocking my view of the others. "What's wrong, Anita?"

I looked at him. The only thing that kept me from losing it right then in front of the other vampires was Richard. He'd have never tolerated human sacrifice. Oh, he might have come down here once, then never returned, and not called the police, but he would never have returned year after year. He simply wouldn't have approved.

Maybe this was the way Verne's clan treated its dead. If it was anything else, I'd call in the state cops, but not tonight. Not unless they dragged out a screaming victim. If they did that, then all bets were off.

I shook my head. "What could possibly be wrong?" I said. I walked into the clearing, going for our own little group. It looked as if all three groups had the same amount of people. That was pretty typical of a meet between preternatural groups. You always negotiated your entourage.

Richard stood and came to meet me. I took his hand when he offered it, but strangely, right at that moment, I didn't care if he was wearing his shirt or not. I was angry at him. Angry at him for not preparing me for this place. Maybe he thought that nothing shocked me anymore, or maybe . . . oh, hell, I didn't know, but he'd screwed up again.

So I let him hold my hand, and the touch of his flesh meant nothing. I was too confused and working too hard on holding my temper to be seduced right then.

"Take the jacket off, child; let's get a look at what you've got," a voice said.

I turned, slowly, to look at the owner of that voice.

The vampire had hair that I would have called golden if I hadn't had Asher's hair to compare it to. The hair was cut short, all over. His eyes could have been blue or grey in the uncertain light. The face had frozen before he'd ever hit twenty. Still young enough that his face was thin and smooth, as if he'd died before he'd been able to grow a decent beard.

He had the face of a child on a tall, gangly frame, as if he'd been awkward in life. He wasn't awkward as he stood. He came to his feet in a movement so smooth it looked like dancing. He stood, and the black-eyed vamp stood with him, coming to his side in a motion of long practice like they were two parts of a whole.

There was one human woman among the eight of them. She looked like pure Native American with waist-length hair that was as true black as my own. Hers was straight and thick. Her skin was a dark brown, face almost square, with large, brown eyes that had lashes so thick that even from a distance they were noticeable.

If she wore any makeup, I couldn't tell. She was one of those women that is striking rather than beautiful, too strong featured for conventional prettiness, but you wouldn't forget the face once you saw it.

"Come on, girl, strip off," that young face said. "We've seen most everything everybody else has. I will be mighty disappointed if I don't get to see your goodies, too."

The woman's face remained marvelously blank, but there was a tightness to those strong shoulders, a slight turn to that long line of neck. She didn't seem to be enjoying the show.

Richard's hand tightened around mine. I thought at first he was trying to warn me not to get mad, but one glance at his face, and it was the other way around. He was getting pissed. The night would go downhill pretty damn fast if I was supposed to be the calm one.

"Are you always this offensive, or am I getting a special treat?" I asked.

He laughed, but it was just a laugh, ordinary, human. He couldn't do the voice tricks that Jean-Claude and even Asher could do. Of course, Colin had other talents. I'd seen those other talents carved in Nathaniel's chest.

Asher stood. He'd started the evening wearing satin a pale icy blue only two shades darker than his white-blue eyes. The jacket had darker blue embroidery at the sleeves and lapels. It fastened with one of those cloth loops over a large, silk-covered button. The pants matched the jacket perfectly. He'd tried the jacket on with no shirt. His chest had been very visible. The scars had seemed harsher against the soft blue cloth. He'd stared at himself in the room's only mirror for a long time. He'd finally put a white silk shirt on under the jacket.

Now that white shirt was in tatters. It looked like gigantic claws had ripped at it. His chest showed very plainly through the ruined cloth. There was no blood. I'd only seen three vampires that could cause harm from a distance. One of them had been a member of their council. But none of them had had the delicacy of control to shred cloth so close to flesh and not draw blood. We were deep into the pissing contest. So far, Colin was winning.

I looked at Shang-Da and Jamil, standing just behind the bench. They looked untouched, unharmed.

"Some bodyguards," I said.

"We're not here to guard vampires," Shang-Da said.

I looked at Jamil. He shrugged.

Great, just great. Zane was standing even farther behind the wolves. He didn't look any worse for wear, either, but he also looked lost, like the lone teetotaler at a wine tasting.

"Was I supposed to stop him?" he asked.

I shook my head. "No, Zane. Not you." I spared a glance at Richard, wondering why he'd just let everyone stand around. Asher I understood. Asking for help was a sign of weakness.

"Remove the jacket, or I'll remove it for you," Colin said.

"Colin, you've made your point." The woman's voice was surprisingly deep, a rich, smoky alto.

Colin patted her hand, smiled, but his words weren't gentle. "I will tell you when my point has been made, Nikki.'' He moved away from her then, dismissed her, and the pain of that dismissal showed.

For a moment, anger flared in those dark eyes, and I felt her power. Her power, not his. She was a witch or a psychic or something I had no word for. Human in the same way I was human: barely.

The anger vanished behind that dark, stoic face, but I knew what I'd seen. She didn't love him, nor he her. But she was his human servant, bound for all eternity, for better or worse.

"You want to see what's under the jacket," I said, "come over here and help me out of it. It'd be the gentlemanly thing to do."

"Anita," Richard said.

I patted his arm. "It's okay, Richard. Chill."

The look on his face was enough. He didn't trust me to behave. Funny, in our own ways, neither of us trusted the other.

I looked at Asher. We shared no marks. We couldn't read each other's thoughts. But we didn't need to. We were getting our butts kicked because the werewolves weren't helping us.

I looked over at the eight werewolves that were local. Verne sat on the bench with his wolves poised around him. Two of them were in full wolf form, except they were the size of ponies, bigger than any normal grey wolf. Verne was still in his T-shirt and jeans. No one had dressed up but us. Even the other vampires were just in suits and dresses.

I'd never seen this many vampires dressed so . . . ordinarily. Most of them had a sense of style, or at least theater. They put on a good show. Of course, in the presence of the bone-draped tree who needed a better show? Of course, the lupanar was supposed to be our showplace, not Colin's. Again, I wondered if we could trust Verne as far as Richard thought we could.

I walked a little into the center of the triangle made by the three benches. I waited for Colin to join me.

He just stood there next to the black-eyed vamp, smiling. "Now why would I waste the energy to walk even a few yards when I can undress you from here?"

I smiled and I made it mocking. "Scared to get too close?"

"I admit you are a delicate little thing, but appearances are often deceiving. I have used this youthful face of mine more than once to fool the unwary. I am not the unwary, Anita Blake." He extended a pale hand, and I felt the power thrill over my skin before it slashed through the front of the velvet top. The cross spilled out of the velvet like a captive star set free. The cross flared white and I was careful to look sideways from it. It burned like magnesium, so bright it was almost painful. Crosses glow around vamps, but they don't glow like small supernovas unless you are in serious trouble. I'd never had one glow like this when I wasn't afraid yet. I'd always assumed the cross reacted to my level of fear like a holy mood ring. Tonight, for the first time, I realized that it may have been my faith that enabled it to glow, but once the faith was in place, something else took over. Not my will, but thine.

Colin's vampires reacted just as they were supposed to. They cowered, throwing their arms or their jackets or in one case, a skirt, in front of their eyes. Hiding from the light.

Except for Colin and the black-eyed vamp. Why was I not surprised that those two were old enough and powerful enough to face the cross? They weren't happy about it. They were protecting their eyes, squinting against the light, but they weren't cowering.

"Slash me again, fang-boy, see what else falls out."

He did what I asked. I really hadn't thought he'd try. He slashed at me through the air, but the power fell away like water parting around a rock.

"If you want to hurt me, Colin, you're going to have to get up close and personal."

"I could have Nikki rip it from your throat."

"I thought you were hot shit, Colin. Or is that just when you have young men tied up and helpless? Is that what you need to feel like a big bad vampire? Someone tied up and helpless, or is it young men that does it for you?"

Colin said one word: "Barnaby."

The black-eyed vampire moved in front of Colin, closer to the cross. But he stopped, unable to come closer. Then, over the glow of the cross, I watched Barnaby's face begin to rot. That smooth flesh sloughed away, sliding in wet gobbets of flesh down his face, until tendons glistened wetly and bone showed as his nose collapsed, showing his face like a skull covered by rotted things.

He limped towards me, one hand held out, and it reminded me of Damian's hands earlier in the night. The flesh bursting in a stinking wave of blackness. Except there was no smell. The last vamp I'd seen who could rot at will had also been able to control the smell, like a magical deodorant.

If it had been a fight, I'd have drawn a gun and blown him away before he took the cross, but this was a contest of wills more than anything. If he was vampire enough to touch my cross, then I had to be brave enough to let him do it. I hoped he didn't press it between our bodies. I'd had one vampire do that, and a second degree burn on my breast wasn't my idea of fun.

The cross burned brighter and brighter as he came for me. I had to turn my head away from the light; it was so bright it hurt me to look at it. I knew it hurt the vampire more.

I felt that rotted hand slide across my chest, leaving something wet and semi-solid to slide between my breasts. He grabbed the chain and not the cross, smart vampire. He jerked the chain and it broke. The cross swung into his arm, and the silver burned with a flame as white and pure as the light had been.

The vampire screamed and threw the cross, which spun in a glittering arc like a tiny comet until it was swallowed by the dark.

As my eyes adjusted to the dim lantern light once more, I said, "Don't worry about it, Barnaby, I've got extras."

He'd fallen to his knees, cradling his arm. He was still a walking rotted nightmare, but the flesh of his hand had blackened.

"But not everyone has your faith," Colin said. Again, just like in the forest, I didn't feel his vampire powers reach out, but I was suddenly afraid. Now that I knew what it was, it wasn't as bad, but it was different from any other ability I'd ever sensed. Quieter somehow, and more frightening because of it.

"Barnaby, the young blond werewolf is very afraid of you. He's tasted your kind before."

Barnaby got to his feet and tried to move around me. I stepped in front of him. "Jason is under my protection."

"Barnaby won't hurt him, just play with him a little."

I shook my head. "I gave Jason my word that I wouldn't let the vampire that did Nathaniel touch him."

"Your word?" Colin said. "You're a modern American. Your word means nothing."

"My word means something to me," I said. "I don't give it lightly."

"I can taste the truth of your words, but I say that Barnaby shall play with your young friend, and you cannot stop him without breaking truce. Whoever breaks truce first will have the Council to answer to."

I kept moving with Barnaby so that he was slowly backing me up, but I kept getting in his way. "Colin, you can feel fear, so I'm told. You can feel how very afraid he is of your friend here."

"Oh, yes, I will feast tonight."

"You could break his mind," I said. Someone touched my back and I jumped. It was Asher. I'd been backed up all the way to the bench.

Richard and his bodyguards had moved around Jason. They might not protect Asher, but they would protect Jason. Barnaby moved to one side, trying to get around me. I was forced to jump on and over the bench to put myself in his way again.

I put my left hand against that decaying chest. The right was on the butt of the Browning. I made sure he saw it.

Colin spoke. Though Barnaby's body should have blocked his view, it was almost as if he could see through the other vampire's eyes. "If you shoot one of my vampires, then you will have broken truce."

"You sent Nathaniel back to us dying. Asher said it was a compliment of sorts, that you truly thought we could cure him."

"And you did, didn't you?" Colin said.

"Yeah," I said. "Well, let me pay you the same compliment. I think if I shoot Barnaby point-blank, he'll survive it. I've shot rotting vamps before, and their clothes took more damage than they did."

"You can taste the truth in her words," Asher said. "She believes he'll live, which means it is not a breach of truce."

"She believes it, but she hopes for his death," Colin said.

"Breaking the mind of one of our entourage," Asher said, "will break the truce, as well."

"I do not agree," Colin said.

"Then we've got a stalemate," I said.

"I think not," Colin said. He turned to Verne. "Verne, earn your keep. Strip the young one of his protectors."

Verne stood and his wolves flowed around him. They moved into the clearing on a roil of energy that made the nape of my neck dance and my hand go for a gun.

Richard said, "Verne."

But Verne wasn't looking at Richard. He was looking at me. He was carrying a small covered basket in his hands. I didn't wait to find out what he had in the basket. I pointed the gun at his chest.

19

"Ease down, girl," Verne said. "It's a present."

I kept the gun nice and steady on the center of his body. "Yeah, right."

"When you see what it is, you'll know that we aren't on his side."

"Don't pick the wrong side, puppy dog," Colin said. "Or I will make you very, very sorry."

Verne looked at the vampire. I watched his eyes bleed from human to wolf while he held that basket out to me. But he kept those angry, frightening eyes on Colin.

"You have no animal to call," Verne said, in a voice gone rough and growling low. "You dare to stand in our place of power and threaten us. You are less than the wind outside our cave. You are nothing here."

"She is not one of you, either," Colin said.

"She is lupa of the Thronnus Roke Clan."

"She is human."

"She stands between you and a werewolf. That's lupa enough for me."

Barnaby had backed off. I don't know if he thought I'd jump the gun and shoot him or if Colin had whispered a new plan in his rotting skull. I wasn't sure I even cared. There was a glob of something heavy and wet sliding down into the bra. It was like feeling a tear slide down your cheek but worse, so much worse. I'd resisted the urge to wipe it away with Barnaby staring me down. As soon as he crept back to Colin, I used my left hand to scoop the leftover part out and fling it on the ground.

"What's the matter, Anita? Too up close and personal for you?"

I wiped my hand on the leather skirt and smiled. "Fuck you, Colin."

Verne stepped into the center of the triangle alone. His wolves stayed huddled in front of the far bench. He came to stand a couple of yards in front of our bench with that basket in his hands.

I glanced at Asher. He shrugged. Richard nodded like I was supposed to go meet him. A present, Verne had called it.

I went to meet him. He knelt, setting the basket on the ground between us. He stayed kneeling. I knelt, too, because he seemed to expect it. He just kept looking at me with those wolfish eyes. He still looked like an aging Hell's Angel, but those eyes . . . I wondered if I would ever get used to seeing wolf eyes in a human face. Probably not.

I raised the hinged lid of the small basket. A face, a head, looked up at me. I scrambled to my feet. The Browning just appeared in my hand. I pointed it at Verne, then the ground, then pressed the flat of the barrel to my forehead.

I found my voice, finally. "What is that?"

"You said you wanted Mira's head in a basket. That if we gave you that, it would make it right between our two clans."

I took a sharp breath and blew it out. I looked down into the basket, still standing, still holding the gun like the comfort object it was. The mouth was open in a soundless scream, the eyes half closed as if they'd caught her napping, but I knew they hadn't. Someone had simply closed the eyes after they took her head. Even dead, like this, the bones of the face were delicate, and you knew at least the face had been pretty.

I forced myself to put up the gun. It couldn't help me now. I dropped back to my knees, staring at it. I finally looked up at Verne. I was shaking my head over and over. I looked into his face and tried to read something in it that I could yell at or talk to. But the expression was alien, and it wasn't just the eyes.

You'd think after all this time, I would stop forgetting that they weren't human. But I had. I'd been pissed, and I'd spoken as if I was talking to another human being, but I hadn't been. I'd been speaking to werewolves, and I'd forgotten that.

I heard someone whispering, and it was me. I was whispering, "This is my fault. This is my fault." I started to put my left hand in front of my face, and I caught a whiff of Barnaby's rotted flesh. It was enough.

I crawled to one side and vomited. I knelt on all fours, waiting for it to pass. When I could speak, I said, "Don't any of you people understand the term? It's just a fucking expression!"

Richard was there, kneeling by me. He touched my back gently. "You told him what you wanted, Anita. She had betrayed the pack's honor. It can carry a death penalty. All you helped them choose was the method of execution."

I glanced sideways at him. I had a horrible urge to cry. "I didn't mean it," I whispered.

He nodded. "I know." There was a look in his eyes of such sorrow, of a shared knowledge of how many times you never really meant what you said, but the monsters were listening, and they always took you at your word.

20

"*I thought you* were tough, Miss Blake."

Richard helped me stand and I let him. I leaned against him for a second, my forehead against the smooth skin of his arm. I pushed away from him and stood on my own. I met Colin's eyes. They were definitely grey, not blue.

"I know we're supposed to go through all the protocol and waltz for a while, Colin. But the last of my patience is sitting in that basket. So state your grievance and let's all get the fuck out of here."

He smiled. "So tenderhearted, maybe your reputation is just talk after all."

I smiled then and shook my head. "Maybe it is, but since we're not supposed to kill each other tonight, Colin, it doesn't matter."

Colin walked away from me. He went to stand closer to his own people but faced Asher. I had been dismissed as his own human servant had been dismissed.

"I will not be replaced, Asher."

"I have not come to replace you," Asher said, voice empty, neutral.

"Why would Jean-Claude send a master almost exactly my age into my lands against my express orders?"

"I could have hidden what I was," Asher said. "But Jean-Claude thought you would misinterpret that. I came in hiding nothing."

"But still you came," Colin said.

"I cannot change what has happened," Asher said. "What would satisfy us all?"

"Your death," Colin said.

Everybody went very still, as if we'd all caught our collective breaths. I started to say something and Richard touched my shoulder. I closed my mouth and let Asher talk, but it was hard.

Asher laughed that wonderful touchable laugh. "Breaking the truce, aren't you, Colin?"

"Not if I kill a rival sent to supplant me. Then I am merely protecting myself and making an example for other ambitious vampires."

"You know I have not come to supplant you," Asher said.

"I know nothing of the kind."

"I am content where I am."

"Why?" Colin asked. "You could be the master of a city somewhere far from their triumvirate. Why would you be content with less?"

Asher gave a very small smile. "I prefer gentler persuasions over power."

Colin shook his head. "I have been told you are in love with her, and with Jean-Claude himself. I have been told that you are bedding them both and that is why the Ulfric seeks a new lupa."

"If he would only cooperate, it could be a happy foursome," Asher said.

Richard, startled beside me, stiffened. It was my turn to touch his arm and keep him from saying what he was thinking.

"I have been told many things," Colin said. "My people have watched you from afar. We believe you are enamored of the girl and of Jean-Claude. We are aware of your history together. We even believe that a lover of men like yourself would do their Ulfric if he would let you. What we do not believe is that you are bedding any of them. We believe that this is a pathetic story to save yourself."

I started walking to Asher. The plan was that we would put on a mild show of petting. I'd warned him it better be mild, but I never got the chance.

There was movement in the dark. Dozens of vampires appeared out of the darkness, encircling the clearing. Colin had been distracting us while the vampires moved up to flank us, and neither Asher nor I, nor any of the wereanimals had sensed them.

"Let us have Asher and the rest of you may go free."

"You are breaking the truce now," Asher said. He sounded calm, empty, as if Colin hadn't just demanded his death.

Verne strode forward. "This is our lupanar. We can close it to all strangers."

"Not without your vargamor. You left her safe at home just in case things went wrong. So protective of your human pet. I counted on it." He raised an arm as if summoning his people. "No one you have with you is witch enough to invoke the circle."

"If you kill Asher it will break truce."

"I will not harm Jean-Claude's triumvirate. I merely remove a rival."

The vampires moved up through the trees. They didn't hurry. They moved like solid shadows, slow, as if they had all night to tighten the circle and take us. "Asher?" I asked without taking my gaze from those slowly menacing figures.

"*Oui.*"

"Does this break truce?"

"*Oui.*"

"Great," I said.

I felt him move towards me, but I had eyes only for the outer dark and that ever-shrinking circle. I picked one vampire out. Male, slender, youngish in appearance. He wore no shirt. His chest was a pale, almost glowing whiteness in the darkness.

"What is it, *ma cherie*?" Asher was standing very close to me now. I moved him to one side with my left arm and brought the mini-Uzi out with my right, swinging it around my body, shooting before I'd actually pointed so the bullets cut across the vampire's legs, making him jerk. I grabbed it with both hands and fought the gun to spray it back and fourth across his body. I was screaming as I did it, wordless, not to sound menacing. You couldn't hear the screams over the machine gun. I screamed because I couldn't help myself, because the tension, the horror, something came up my hand from the gun and out my mouth.

The blood that sprayed from his body was black from distance and night. It looked like his body was torn in half by some giant hand. His upper body fell slowly to one side. His lower body collapsed to its knees.

The circle of vampires had frozen or had dived for cover. The silence was thunderous. My own labored breathing seemed painfully loud. My voice came breathy, but clear, a shout, "Nobody move, nobody fucking move!"

No one moved.

Asher's voice broke the stillness. "We can all walk away from here tonight, Colin."

"Impressively violent," Colin said, "but I think you are mistaken. Poor Archie will not be walking anywhere."

"My apologies to Archie," I said.

"I must have payment for him, Miss Blake."

"You can bill me."

"Oh, I intend to, Miss Blake. I intend to take it out of your hide."

"How many of your people do you want me to kill tonight, Colin? I've got lots more bullets."

"You cannot kill them all, Miss Blake."

"Yeah, but I can kill about a half dozen and wound twice that many. I don't see them lining up for it, Colin."

I badly wanted to see his face, but I kept my attention on the vamps in the trees. They hadn't moved. The vampires already inside the lupanar were someone else's problem. My job was keeping the others at a distance. I think Asher knew the division of labor. I just hoped Richard did.

"I don't know how Jean-Claude runs his territory, but I know how I run mine. What you fail to appreciate, Miss Blake, is that nothing you can do to them will make them fear you more than they already fear me."

"Death is the ultimate threat, Colin, and I don't bluff."

"Neither do I."

I felt something move out through the trees. Power moving from Colin to those waiting figures. I started to turn the gun from the darkness to Colin, but Asher touched my arm. "He is mine. Watch the others."

I slid the gun a fraction back to the still forms. "You get the Master of the City and I get all the rest. Sounds fair."

Richard moved up beside me. "You don't get all of them," he said.

I wanted to ask if he would kill them. If he would use that preternatural strength to snap spines and tear their bodies apart with his bare hands as I had done with the machine gun. But I didn't ask. How good Richard's threat was was between him and his conscience. The only thing that bothered me about Richard's conscience was that I couldn't count on him for a single kill tonight. He'd hurt people and toss them around, but if he wouldn't kill, that meant that he couldn't account for any of them. There were over a hundred bad guys, vampires, and only eight of us. Sixteen if I could count Verne, but I didn't know if I could count on him and his people. It would have been nice to be able to trust Richard at my back, but I didn't.

The vampires out in the dark began to rot. Not all of them, but damn near half. I'd never seen so many. For a vampire to rot, it means that the vamp that made them was the same kind of creature. Which meant that Barnaby had made half of Colin's people. No Master of the City would allow any subordinate to have such power. But the proof was staring me in the face with eye sockets gone to black dripping ruin.

"You have been very bold, Colin, to share your power with your second to this degree," Asher said.

"Barnaby is my right hand, my second eye. Together we are a stronger master than either of us would be apart."

"As are Jean-Claude and I," Asher said.

"But Barnaby is a corruptor. He brings that to the dance," Colin said. "What do you bring to Jean-Claude's dance, Asher?" Fear breathed through the lupanar. I shivered as it prickled down my skin, tightened my chest, and tried to stop my breath in my throat.

"Night hag," Damian spoke, his voice a hiss. He spit on the ground in the general direction of Colin, but he didn't walk any closer.

"I smell your fear, Damian. I can taste it like rich, nutty ale on the back of my tongue," Colin said. "Your master must have been a fine piece of work."

Damian moved back a step, then stopped. "You ask why Asher is content to remain with Jean-Claude when he could go elsewhere and be his own master. Maybe he is tired as I am tired of the struggle. The in-fighting. The fucking politics. Jean-Claude ransomed me from my master. I am not a master vampire, nor will I ever be. I have no special powers. Yet, Jean-Claude bargained for me. I serve him not out of fear but out of gratitude."

"You make Jean-Claude sound weak. The Council does not fear weaklings, yet they fear him," Colin said.

"Compassion is not weakness," Richard said. "Only those without compassion think otherwise."

I glanced at him, but he was looking at the vampires, not me. The fact that I felt it was a personal remark to me was just me being overly sensitive.

"Compassion." Colin shook his head. He threw back his head and laughed. It was sort of unnerving. I kept my attention on the outer darkness and the waiting vamps, but it was hard not to watch the laughing vampire. Hard not to ask what was so funny.

"Compassion," Colin said again. "Now that is not a word I would have used for Jean-Claude. Has he fallen in love with his human servant? I do not think love is the path to Jean-Claude's heart. Is it sex?" He raised his voice and called to me. "Is that it, Miss Blake? Has the seducer finally been seduced? Are you that good a piece of ass, Miss Blake?"

That made my shoulders hunch. But I kept my eye on the other vampires, the machine gun held in both hands. "A lady doesn't kiss and tell, Colin."

That made him laugh again. "Jean-Claude would never forgive me if I killed the best piece of ass he's found in centuries. I say again, give me Asher, and the blond wolf. Asher's life and the wolf's fear at Barnaby's hands. That is the price for safe passage through my lands.''

It was my turn to laugh, a soft, harsh sound. "Fuck you."

"I take it that is a no," he said.

"No," I said. I watched the vampires out in the dark. They hadn't moved, but somehow there was a sense of movement, an increased energy. It was nothing I could start shooting about, but I didn't like it.

"Does Miss Blake speak for all of you?" Colin asked.

"You can't have Jason to torture," Richard said.

"I would not willingly give up my life," Asher said.

"The human servant speaking for all. How very strange. But if the answer is no, then the answer is no."

Asher yelled, "Anita!"

I started to rotate the gun back towards them, but something slashed down my face, over one eye. It made me hesitate, one hand going over my eye, holding it. I had time to think, stupid, and start to lower my hand, start to raise the gun back up, and a vampire slammed into me, taking us both to the ground.

I was flat on my back with a woman on top of me, mouth wide, fangs snapping at my face like a dog. I pulled the trigger with the muzzle pressed to her body. The bullets exploded out her back in a rain of blood and thicker bits. Her body danced on top of mine, twitching, jerking. I had to push her body off of me, and when I could sit up, it was too late. The vampires were inside the lupanar and the fighting was joined.

I couldn't see out of my right eye. It was too full of blood, and more kept pouring down. A figure appeared in front of me and I fired up the length of its body until the bullets exploded its head in a burst of splattering rain. I closed my right eye and did my best to ignore it. Nursing the wound was going to get me killed.

I looked around for the others. Verne tore the head off a vampire and sent it spinning into the dark. Richard was at the center of a mob, almost lost to sight with bodies hanging off him. Asher was covered in blood, facing Colin. There were werewolves everywhere in wolf or manwolf form. Two vamps came for me and sight-seeing was over.

One of them was rotting down to bones, the other was solid. I shot the solid one first because he, I was sure, I could kill. Rotting vamps don't also die from bullets. The solid one fell to his knees in a spray of blood, face split in half like a ripe melon.

The rotting vamp jumped me in a blur of speed and we went tumbling across the ground as I tried to bring the gun up. The mouth stretched above my face, naked tendons straining between the bones of his cheeks, fangs came for my face. I fired into the body, but the gun was at a bad angle and missed anything vital. All I got for my troubles was the scream of a wolf, and I knew that I'd shot someone that was on our side. Shit.

I turned my head and the fangs sank through the leather jacket into my shoulder. I screamed, my hand fumbling for the jacket pocket and my backup cross. A rotted hand caressed my face, sliding over the wound above my eye. The leather jacket acted as a sort of armor, keeping the fangs from getting a good lock on my shoulder. The mouth worried at my shoulder like a dog with a bone, trying to dig through the thick leather into the flesh beyond. It hurt, but not as much as it was going to hurt if I didn't do something.

The cross flared to life like a captive star, but the vamp had its face buried in the leather. It couldn't see the cross. I swung the cross by the chain into its bare skull. Smoke rose from the bone, and the vampire jerked its face back from me, naked teeth opened in a scream. I shoved the cross in its face, and those teeth snapped at it like a dog telling you to stay away. But those teeth caught the chain, and bit through it. There was a moment where even without most of the flesh left on the skull I could see surprise on its face. I flung my arms across my face and heard the dull explosion, the spatter of debris. There was a sharp pain in my hand, and when I could look, I had a bone shard in my left hand. I pulled the shard out, and only then did I bleed.

The vampire was just so much mess scattered around me. The cross lay on the ground still glowing, smoke rising off its surface as if the metal had been freshly made and quenched in the blood of the vampire. I started to pick it up by the chain, and Nikki, Colin's human servant, was standing over me. I caught the dull flash of her knife and rolled away, coming to one knee with the Browning in one hand. She was right above me waiting for an underhand strike, but I wasn't standing, and she didn't have time to change her strike. I started to pull the trigger and a werewolf barreled into her, took them both off into the dark. Shit. What was I supposed to do, yell "mine" like in a volleyball game?

I heard Jason yelling. He was standing only about a yard away with both arms stuck through the chest of a rotting vampire. He was pulling desperately on his arms, but they seemed trapped, caught on the ribs. The vampire didn't seem to mind. It licked his face, and he screamed. Another rotter was on his back, riding him, head back for a strike. I sighted down my arm at the head and fired. The head jerked back, and brains spilled out a hole on the other side in a dark gush, but the vampire turned its head slowly and looked at me. I fired into that calm face three more times in a tight cluster before the head collapsed in upon itself like an empty eggshell. The vampire fell away from Jason.

I walked towards Jason and the other vampire. Now it was the vampire who was struggling to get free of Jason, but they were entwined like bumpers after a car wreck. I put the gun barrel under the vampire's chin, my other hand over Jason's eyes to protect them, and fired. It took three shots for the brain to be destroyed and the body to go limp.

I moved my hand from Jason's eyes, and he looked past me, eyes widening. I was already turning before he could yell, "Behind you!"

The blow came before I'd finished the turn. My shoulder and arm went numb. My hand opened and the Browning slipped out while I was still trying to see what had hit me. I dived for the ground, rolling on my good shoulder and came up to my knee to see Nikki holding a very big stick. I was lucky she'd lost the knife somewhere.

I started to draw the big knife down my back, but I was using my left hand, because my right still wasn't working. Left-handed I was slower, and Nikki was unbelievably fast. She moved in a blur of motion that was beyond human. She was on me, slashing the air with the club, and I gave up trying to draw a knife, and worked just at not being hit. The attack was so quick, so savage, that I didn't have time to stand. All I could do was roll on the ground barely ahead of each blow.

The jagged end of the branch sank into the ground next to my face. She struggled for a second to free it, and I kicked her in the knee. It made her stagger, but didn't dislocate it, or she'd have screamed. It did force her back from the club. I rolled away, trying to get to my feet. She grabbed me, and lifted me over her head like she was bench-pressing me. The next thing I knew I was airborne. I hit the ground just short of the oak, falling into the bones beneath the tree hard enough that some of them shattered. The jolt of power that ran through me from hands to knees drove what air I had left from my body. I lay there half-stunned, not just from being thrown across the clearing, but from the power roaring across my body from the bones. It was death magic, and though different from mine, it recognized me, recognized my power. I knew as I lay in the bones that I could bring the circle to life? But what would happen when the wards flared to life? This pack worshipped Odin. If I set the circle of power would it count as a holy place? Would it suddenly be like standing inside a church? It had possibilities if I could warn Asher and Damian.

I got painfully to my knees and found that we were losing. Everywhere I looked our people were buried under piles of vampires. Asher and Damain were still standing free, but both were bleeding and Colin and Barnaby were pressing the attack. Richard was completely lost to sight except for one arm gone long with claws. Verne was standing with another werewolf in human form. It was a woman shorter than I was with short dark hair that touched her shoulders, dressed in a thigh-long T-shirt and pants. She looked small beside Verne, but she was the only one of his people still standing. The others were dead or dying on the ground.

My right hand was working again, just stunned not dislocated. Lucky me. I drew a knife from one of the wrist sheaths. It wasn't a blade consecrated to ritual, but it would have to do.

I wanted to whisper to Asher and Damian for them to fly, but it was too far away to whisper, and I didn't know how to talk directly to either of their minds. I did the only thing I could think of, I yelled. I yelled, "Asher, Damian!"

They turned startled faces to me.

I raised the knife so they could see it, and screamed, "Fly, damn it, fly!"

Nikki was almost to the bone circle. I screamed, "Fly!" Asher grabbed Damian's wrist, and I had to turn away before I could see them safe. I had moments to try and make this work. Nikki had a power similar to mine. If she figured out what I was trying to do she'd stop me if she could.

I pressed my hands to the tree trunk and the power breathed through me. It was magic that had been built with death, and that was my speciality. The moment I touched the tree I knew that it wasn't human sacrifice, but that this was where their munin gathered. The spirits of their dead were here in the bones, the tree, the ground. They filled the air with a whispering, tittering, noise that only I could hear.

The lukoi consume their dead, at least part of them, and the eating of their flesh puts them into some sort of ancestral memory. Munin they call them after Odin's raven, Memory. They aren't ghosts, but they are the spirits of the dead, and I was a necromancer. The munin liked me. They eased around me like a cool caress of wind, entwining like phantom cats. I could channel the munin, sort of like a medium at a séance, but more, and worse. The only munin I'd ever channeled had been Raina, the wicked bitch of the east. But when she came, it was like a battering ram. Standing there in the middle of hundreds, thousands of munin, I knew I could open to them. But it would be like opening a door, an invitation. I could wallow in the past, live other lives. It was a whisper of seduction. Raina came like a rapist, an overwhelming force. Not a sharing, but a taking.

However they'd tied their munin to this place it was blood magic, death magic. I cut the palm of my hand and pressed it to the tree. I prayed, and sprinkled blood on the bones at my feet. The circle of power snapped into place with a rush that raised my skin as if it would crawl off my flesh. I invoked the circle. I called the wards. I worshipped, and it was enough.

Shrieks, screams filled the night. The vampires went up in flames. They ran, burning, for the edge of the ward and all who made it across exploded in a rain of burning bits and pieces.

I felt Damian above me, and Asher. None of the vampires left behind tried to do anything but run. Most fell into burning heaps on the ground without taking another step. Anyone under a hundred died where they stood.

The Indian woman had come to stand on the edge of the bone circle. She stared at me while the vampires screamed and died, and the stink of burning flesh and hair was thick enough to choke. Her face showed nothing. She'd rescued the club.

Finally she said, "I should kill you."

I nodded. "Yes, you should, but your allies are dead and your master has flown away. I'd get out while the getting's good, if I were you."

She nodded and threw the club to the ground. "Colin and Barnaby live, and we will see you again, Anita."

"I look forward to it," I said. I was hoping that she wouldn't notice that my back was pressed against the tree, because I wasn't sure I could stand on my own.

Nikki nodded, and started to walk away into the dark, past the tree and the bones. She spoke something then stepped through the ward. When she stepped through, the magic quenched, swallowed back into the earth.

She looked at me from the dark on the other side of the quieted circle. We stared at each other for a long moment, and I knew that if we met again she would kill me if she could. She was Colin's human servant. It was her job.

I slid down the tree until I was sitting in the bones. My legs were too weak to hold me and a fine trembling had started in my hands. I gazed out into the lupanar, gazed out over my handiwork. Some of the bodies still burned, but no vampire moved within the circle. The vampires were dead. All of them.

21

Another fight, another shower. Rotting vampire was not an odor you wanted to wear to bed. My hair was still damp when I called Jean-Claude to fill him in on what we'd done. Okay, on what I'd done.

I told him the shortest version possible. His response, "You did *what?*"

I repeated it.

Silence on the other end of the phone. I couldn't even hear him breathe.

"Jean-Claude, you still there?"

"I am here, *ma petite.*" He sighed. "You have surprised me once again. I did not see this coming."

"You don't sound happy," I said. "You know the news could be worse. We could all be dead."

"I did not think Colin would be so foolish."

"Live and learn," I said.

"Colin was right to fear you, *ma petite.*"

"I told Colin what would happen if he messed with us. He pushed the button, not me."

"Who are you trying to convince, *ma petite*, me or yourself?"

I thought about that for a moment. "I don't know."

"Are you admitting you were wrong?" His voice held mild amusement.

"No." I tried to think how to say it. Finally, I said, "We were losing, Jean-Claude. They were going to kill us. I had to do something. I wasn't even sure it would work." I held the phone, and wished that he were here to hold me. I hated the thought that I wanted him like that. That I wanted anyone like that. I hated needing people. They all had a tendency to die on me. But I'd have given a great deal for a pair of comforting arms right at that moment.

"*Ma petite, ma petite*, what is wrong?"

I motioned Asher over to the phone. "Talk to your second banana. Ask Asher if there were other options. If there were other options, I couldn't see them."

"There is something in your voice, *ma petite.* Something fragile." He whispered the last word.

I just nodded, and handed the phone to Asher. I walked away from it hugging myself tight. Fragile, he said. Scared, more like. I'd scared myself tonight. Something in the power I released had extinguished the torches around the lupanar. Those of us still standing had moved by the light of burning corpses. It had been a scene right out of Dante's *Inferno*, and I had done it. The power inside of me had done this thing. Yeah, scared about covered it.

Damian came up to me. He whispered, "Jason's crying in the shower."

I sighed. *Great, just what I needed, another crisis.* But I didn't ask questions. I just knocked on the door of the bathroom. "Jason, you all right?"

He didn't answer me. "Jason?"

"I'm all right, Anita." His voice, even over the shower sounded strained. I'd never really heard him cry before, but that's what it sounded like, a voice thick with tears.

I pressed the top of my head to the door and sighed. I did not need this tonight. But Jason was my friend, and who else was I going to send in to comfort him? Damian had come to me with it. Zane didn't seem the hand-holding type, and Cherry, well . . . if I was going to send another woman into comfort him, it seemed cowardly. Asher? Naw.

I knocked on the door again. "Jason, can I come in for a minute?"

Silence. If he'd been feeling anywhere near okay, he'd have made some kind of joke about me finally seeing him in the shower. That he didn't tease me at all was a bad sign.

"Jason, can I come in . . . please?"

"Come in," he said finally.

I opened the door and the warm air fogged around me. I closed the door behind me. The room was soft and thick with warmth. It was hot, the moisture beading on every surface as if he'd cranked the shower up to as hot as it would go. Hot as it would go was enough to scald the flesh from your bones, if you were human.

The light left his shadow on the white shower curtain. He wasn't standing. He was sitting on the floor of the shower, huddled.

I moved the towel from the lid of the stool and sat down with it in my lap. "What's wrong?"

He took a deep sobbing breath, and even over the shower I could hear him weeping. Crying didn't cover it, weeping.

I wanted to see him while I talked to him, and I didn't want to see him naked. Choices, choices.

"Talk to me, Jason. What's wrong?"

"I can't get it off me. I can't get clean."

"You mean metaphorically speaking or literally?" I asked.

"It's all over me and I can't get it off."

I was being a coward and a prude. I reached a hand for the curtain and slowly drew it back until I could see him without splashing the entire bathroom with water.

Jason had his knees drawn up tight to his chest, arms locked around them. The heat from the water was enough to make me draw back. His skin had turned a nice cherry pink but that was it. I'd have had blisters or worse by now.

There were clinging patches of black goo on his back. The back of one arm had a patch on it. He'd scrubbed and boiled himself nearly raw and couldn't get clean.

He stared straight ahead at the faucets, rocking ever so slightly. "I was okay until I got in the shower and it wouldn't come off. Then I kept seeing those two vampires in Branson. I thought about Yvette, watching her rot. But it's the two in Branson. I can still feel their hands on me, Anita. Sometimes I still wake up in the middle of the day in a cold sweat, remembering."

In Branson, Missouri we'd taken on the local Master of the City. She'd had two young women that she was going to torture unless we gave her some of us to torture. They'd suggested that if Jason made love to two of the female vamps they would let one of the girls go. I think he'd enjoyed it, at first, but then they'd started to rot.

Jason had struggled away from them, crawling against the wall. His bare chest was covered in bits of their flesh. A strand of something thick and heavy slid slowly down his neck onto his chest. He batted at it like you would swat at a spider that you found crawling along your skin. He was pressed into the black wall with his pants nearly to his thighs.

The blond rolled off her back and crawled towards him, reaching a hand out that was nothing but bones with bits of dried flesh. She seemed to be decaying in dry ground. The brunette was wet. She lay back on the floor, and some dark fluid rushed out from her to pool beneath her body. She'd undone her own leather shirt, and her breasts were like heavy bags of fluid.

"I'm ready for you," the brunette said. Her voice was still clear and solid. No human voice should have come out of those rotting lips.

The blond grabbed Jason's arm and he screamed.

I shook my head trying to clear the memory. It had haunted my dreams for a while just witnessing it. But for Jason it had become his private phobia. One of the Council's flunkies had been one of the rotting ones. She'd tortured him, too, because she liked how very, very afraid he was of her. Yvette's little torment had only happened about two months ago. Tonight's fun and games had been far too close to home.

I took off the wrist sheaths and laid them on the back of the stool. The fact that I was wearing the wrist sheaths when I should have been getting ready for bed said something about my own paranoia. The heat from the water as I reached for the knob was almost frightening. Years of being told, don't touch, hot. I knew that fire killed wereanimals, but apparently heat didn't. I turned the knob until the temperature was something I could touch.

Jason started to shiver almost as soon as the water began to cool. Frankly, I was amazed that the cabin's hot water heater had kept up this long. The floor was wet and the water soaked into the legs of my jeans. I had another pair I could change into.

I found the bar of soap but the washrag was black. I threw it into the sink and got the last clean one. I'd have to remember to ask for extra towels. I should have done that anyway.

Jason finally looked at me, a slow turning of his head. His blue eyes looked almost glassy, as if he were slipping into his own version of shock. "I can't go through it again, Anita. I can't."

I soaped the clean washrag until it squished white suds. I touched his back and he flinched. I would have given almost anything in that moment if he had grabbed for me, or teased, or even made a pass. Anything to let me know he was okay. Instead he sat there naked and wet and miserable. It made my throat tight, but damn it if I cried, I was afraid I wouldn't stop. I was in here to comfort Jason not to make him comfort me.

Worse yet, I couldn't get it off his back. It had been hard enough to get off my own skin, but the extra hour Jason had sat around waiting for me to finish my shower had turned the fluid into glue. I finally resorted to using my fingernails, glad that I'd refused Cherry's offer of fingernail polish. I would have chipped it all to hell. I scraped it off a piece at a time with my fingers while the hot water ran and Jason shivered. But it wasn't the cold that made him shiver. I was so hot in the moist heat, I didn't feel well.

I'd cleaned everything but one last patch low on his back, very low. It was like the fluid had soaked into the band of his pants, low enough that the curve of buttocks started just below the patch. I was squeamish about that one. Because, though Jason seemed unaware that he was nude, I was very aware of it.

I was also having trouble keeping the oversized T-shirt I'd put on for bed from getting wet. Normally I wouldn't have cared but I'd forgotten to pack a second nightshirt. I finally turned the shower off and adjusted the temperature on the faucets so I had water without having to try and dodge the shower.

I moved back to Jason and started peeling that last patch off his skin. I tried talking to get my mind off of where my hands were. "We killed all the vampires, Jason. It's okay."

He shook his head. "Not Barnaby. We missed him, and he was their creator. I can't stand the thought of him touching me, Anita. I can't do this again."

"Then go home, Jason. Take the jet and get out."

"I won't desert you," he said. His gaze stayed on my face for a moment. "And it's not just because Jean-Claude wouldn't like it."

"I know that," I said. "But all I can do is swear to you that if it is within my power to protect you from Barnaby, I will."

I was leaning very close to him, my arm down the length of his back. I'd finally gotten over the embarrassment with the sheer concentration of prying the dried bits from his body. It was like dissecting that frog in high school. It was gross until the teacher told me to cut out the brain. Then I got so interested in scraping the skull away, ever so carefully, so as not to damage the brain, that I forgot the smell, the poor pitiful frog, and just concentrated on getting the brain out in one piece. My lab partner and I were the only pair to get the brain out whole.

Jason turned his head towards me, brushing my hair with his face. "You smell like Cherry's base makeup."

I spoke without looking up. "I don't own any base so she put some of hers on me earlier. She wears base that is way too pale for her, so it works for me. I thought I got all of it off."

"Hmm," he said. His mouth was very close to my ear.

I froze in mid-movement. My body pressed against his back, my hand touching the smooth skin just above his buttocks. There was a tension now that hadn't been there. My pulse sped up with the awareness of his body, because I suddenly knew he was aware of me. I got the last piece of dried goop off his skin and took a deep breath. I started to lean back and knew that he was going to try something. Part of me was nervous about it and part of me was relieved. It was Jason after all, and he was naked, and I was close, and it was Jason. If he'd let the opportunity pass, I'd have known he was hurt beyond anything I could fix.

His arm slid around my waist, and he used that incredible speed that they were capable of. I felt him lift me and we were just suddenly on the floor with him on top. It was his legs on my legs that pinned me. He used his arms to keep his body raised enough that his groin didn't press into me, which of course meant my view of his body was unobstructed. A mixed blessing. He began to lean his face down for a kiss.

I put a hand on his chest and stopped the movement. "Stop it, Jason."

"The last time I did this you shoved a gun in my ribs and said you'd shoot me if I stole a kiss."

"I meant it," I said.

"You're armed," he said, "I'm not holding your hands down."

I sighed. "You know my rule. I don't point a gun at anyone unless I plan to shoot them. You're my friend now, Jason. I'm not going to shoot you for stealing a kiss. You know it, I know it."

He smiled and leaned in closer. My hand was on his chest but my hand just kept getting closer to my own chest. "But I also don't want you to kiss me. If you're really my friend, you won't do it. You'll just let me up."

His face was just above mine so close it was hard to focus on his eyes. "What if I tried for more than a kiss?" He moved his face so his mouth was hovering over my chest. I could feel his breath just above the soft line where my breasts began.

"Don't push it, Jason. If I shoot you in the right spot, it won't kill you, you'll be hurt, but you'll heal."

He raised his face back up to me. He grinned, and started to roll off of me. The door opened and Richard was just suddenly standing there staring down at us. Perfect, just perfect.

22

"*Would you believe* I slipped?" Jason asked.

"No," Richard said. That one word was very cold.

"Get off of me, Jason."

He rolled to one side but made no move to grab for a towel. Richard threw the towel at him. Jason caught it, and his eyes sparkled with the effort not to smile. Jason had a streak in him that made him enjoy yanking someone's chain. He liked to stir the pot and see what happened. Someday he was going to do it with the wrong person, and he was going to get hurt. But not tonight.

"Get out, Jason. I need to talk to Anita."

Jason stood and wrapped the towel around his waist. I'd sat up but hadn't stood up. Jason offered me his hand. I almost never let a man help me stand, sit, or do much of anything. I took Jason's hand, and he gave it that little extra pull that made me bump into him when I got to my feet.

"You want me to go?" he asked.

I moved a step back but let him keep my hand. "I'll be all right," I said.

Jason grinned up at Richard as he walked out the door. Richard closed the door, leaning against it. I was effectively trapped and he was angry enough that the room filled with prickling energy.

"What was all that about?" he asked.

"It's none of your business anymore, is it?" I asked.

"Earlier today I thought you turned me down because you were being loyal to Jean-Claude."

"I turned you down because it was the right thing to do." I went to the sink and started trying to clean the bits of black crud out from under my fingernails.

"If Jean-Claude finds out you're doing Jason, he'd hurt him, maybe kill him."

"Are you going to tell on us? Run home tattling to our master?" I looked at him in the mirror when I said it. My reward was that he flinched. A little too close to home, that comment.

"Why Jason?" he asked.

"Do you really believe that I'm having sex with Jason?" I turned and used the slightly damp towel to dry my hands.

Richard just looked at me.

"Jesus, Richard, just because you're jumping everything in sight doesn't mean I am." I sat down on the closed stool and tried to blot my jeans dry with the towel.

"So you're not sleeping with him?"

The towel was not helping the jeans. "No, I'm not." I threw the towel in the corner. "I can't believe you'd even ask."

"If you'd found me on the floor with a naked woman on top of me, you'd have thought the same thing," he said.

Hmm, he had me there. "All the women I'd find you with would be strangers who are either dating you, fucking you, or both. What you saw on the floor was Jason being Jason. You know how he is."

"You used to threaten to shoot him if he touched you."

I stood. "Do you really want me to shoot him because he made a pass? I thought one of our main problems was that you thought I shot first and asked questions later. I think you called me bloodthirsty." I pushed past him and where our skin touched power flared like an invisible flame.

He moved back clutching his arm like it had hurt. But I knew it hadn't hurt. It had felt wonderful, a rush of power to make your hair stand on end. It was little touches like that that let us both know what it could be between us.

I walked out. So there was power between us, so there was heat, so what? It didn't change the fact that I was sleeping with Jean-Claude. It didn't change the fact that Richard was sleeping around. The fact that I was jealous of his girlfriends and he was jealous of any man he thought I might be having sex with was just a nasty cosmic joke. We'd get over it.

23

There were three people in my bed; none of them were me. Cherry and Zane had curled up around Nathaniel like fleshy security blankets. I'd been informed that the physical closeness of your group, whatever the animal flavor, was healing both emotionally and physically. Richard had backed up this bit of werelore, so the wereleopards got the bed, because Nathaniel had hysterics at the thought of being without me.

So the wereleopards got the bed, and I got the floor. I managed to get a blanket and a pillow to go with my bit of carpet. We were in a new cabin. Verne was going to try to clean the old cabin, but the bed and carpet were probably a lost cause.

I apologized for that, but Verne seemed to think I could do no wrong. He was tickled pink, purple, and blue that I'd fried Colin's vamps. I was not so happy. Revenge can be a very scary thing. If someone had done to Jean-Claude's vamps what I did to Colin's vamps, I'd . . . we'd have killed them.

The bathroom door opened and closed quietly.

I sat up, hugging the blanket around me. Jason threaded his way between the two coffins. He was wearing a pair of silk boxers. He'd put them on last night in the bathroom and come out without a word. I'd still been trying to convince the wereleopards that they couldn't all sleep naked.

Jason had wanted to sleep with them, adding his otherworldly energy to theirs, but they refused him. Not because he was wolf instead of leopard, but because Cherry didn't trust him to keep his hands to himself.

Jason paused in front of the bed, staring down at the pile of sleeping wereleopards. He ran his hands through his sleep-tousled hair. His hair was straight enough and baby fine enough that his hands could smooth the hair into place. He stayed near the foot of the bed, staring down.

I finally stood, wrapping the blanket around me. I was wearing an oversized sleeping shirt that hit me at midcalf. One size does not fit all, but it was still nightclothes, and I wanted something between me and anyone else. At heart, I am a prude. I went to stand next to Jason, covered shoulder to foot in the blanket. It wasn't Jason I didn't trust. It was everyone else who made me uncomfortable.

Cherry lay on her back, sheets tangled around her knees. She was wearing a pair of red bikini underwear stretched tight across narrow hips. Her waist was very long so that she got height from there as well as those long legs. Her breasts were small and firm. She sighed and rolled one shoulder, making the flesh of one breast move, settling closer to the bed. The nipple tightened as if something in the movement or the dream was exciting. Or maybe she was just cold.

I glanced at Jason. He was gazing at her like he was memorizing every curve, the way her breast spilled to the side. His eyes were almost soft as he looked at her. More than lust, maybe? Or the way you look at a really fine work of art, admiring it because you're not allowed to touch.

Neither of the others were giving nearly as good a show. Nathaniel was wrapped in a ball, head pressed to Cherry's waist. He was so bound in covers that all you could see was the top of his head. He whimpered in his sleep, and Cherry's hand touched the top of his head, her other arm flinging out into space, eyes still closed, still asleep. But even in her sleep, she reached for him, comforted him.

Zane lay on the other side of Nathaniel, spooning his body against the smaller man's. But the covers had been dragged off him, showing the blue bikinis he was wearing. The underwear looked suspiciously like Cherry's, as if she'd had to give him something to wear to bed.

Jason had eyes only for Cherry's slender form. I was surprised that she couldn't feel the weight of his gaze, even in her sleep.

I held the quilt in place with one hand and touched his wrist with the other. I crooked my finger at him and led the way to the far corner of the room, as far away from the bed as we could get.

I leaned against the wall to the side of the window. Jason leaned against the wall close enough that his shoulder brushed the edge of the quilt. I didn't protest because we were whispering. Besides, after awhile, complaining about everything that Jason did just got tiresome. It wasn't really personal. He pushed his luck with everyone.

"Did you sense anyone the last watch?"

He shook his head, leaning so close that I could feel his breath against my cheek. "They're afraid of you after last night."

I turned to look at him and had to move my head back a little to be able to focus on his eyes. "Afraid of me?"

His face was very serious. "Don't be coy, Anita. What you did last night was impressive, and you know it."

I hugged the blanket around my shoulders and looked at the ground. After the rush of power had faded last night, I'd been cold. I'd been cold all night. It was nearly ninety degrees outside. The air conditioner was whirring, and I was cold. Unfortunately, it wasn't the kind of cold that blankets or heat or even another warm body could chase away. I'd scared myself last night. Lately, that took a lot.

I'd seen the burning vampires in my dreams. They'd chased me with flame-covered arms. Their mouths opened in screams, fangs leaking fire like dragon's breath. The burning vamps had offered me Mira's head. The head had talked in its basket, asking, "Why?" Because I was careless didn't seem like a good enough answer. I ran from the dying vampires all night long, one dream after another, or maybe it was just one long, broken dream. Who knows? Either way, it hadn't been restful.

Richard had turned to me last night with the vampire bodies still glowing like banked fires. He'd looked at me, and I'd felt his revulsion, his horror at what I'd done, like a knife through my heart. If things had been reversed and I'd been the werewolf and he'd been the human, he'd have been just as sickened after the show with Marcus as I had been. No, more so. The only reason Richard hung around with monsters was the fact that he was one.

Richard had gone off to his cabin with Jamil and Shang-Da. Shang-Da and Jamil hadn't been horrified; they'd been impressed. Though Shang-Da had said, "They'll kill us all for this."

Asher had disagreed. "Colin is a lesser master than Jean-Claude, yet he demanded the life of Jean-Claude's second, me, and the sanity of one of his wolves, Jason. He overstepped his bounds. Anita merely reminded him of that."

Shang-Da had looked at the blackened corpses, slowly turning to piles of ash. "You think any master vampire will allow this to go unanswered?"

Asher shrugged. "It is no disgrace to lose against someone who has met the Council and survived."

"Besides," Jamil said, "he'll be scared now. He won't come against Anita face-to-face again."

Asher nodded. "Exactly; he fears her now."

"His human servant, Nikki, could have enabled the wards just like I did," I said.

"I believe," Asher said, "that if his servant had power so similar to your own, she would not have merely warned him."

"She'd have tried to keep me from setting the magic free," I said.

"Yes," Asher said.

"She lied," I said.

Asher smiled and touched my cheek. "How can you be so cynical and be surprised when people lie?"

To that, there was no answer. What I'd done was just beginning to sink in then. Now, in the light of midday, not morning—we'd managed to sleep the morning away—I was cold with the knowledge that what I'd done last night hadn't used power from either Richard or Jean-Claude. What I'd done last night had been all me. I'd have been able to do it without a single vampire mark or a drop of extra power.

I hated it when I did something so inhuman and couldn't blame anyone else for it. Made me feel like a freak.

Jason touched my shoulder. I looked at him. There must have been something in my face, because the grin faded from his. His eyes held that world-weary sorrow that peeked through every once in awhile.

"What's wrong?" he asked.

I shook my head. "You saw what I did last night. I did it. Not Jean-Claude. Not Richard. Me. Just little old me."

He put his hands on my shoulders and turned me to look at him full face.

"You saved me last night, Anita. You put yourself between me and those things. I'll never forget that, ever."

I tried to look away, and he shook me gently until I looked at him. We were exactly the same height, so it wasn't like looking up at him, just at him. All the teasing was gone. What was left behind was something more serious, more grown-up, less Jason. "You killed to save us last night. None of us will forget that. Verne and his wolves won't forget that."

"Colin won't forget it, either," I said. "He'll come after us."

Jason shook his head. "Asher and Jamil are right. He's scared shitless of you now. He won't come near you."

I grabbed his arms, letting the quilt slide to the floor. "But he'll hurt the rest of you. He'll try and take you, Jason. He'll give you to Barnaby. He'll break you just to hurt me."

"Or he'll kill Asher," Jason said. "I know." He smiled, and it was almost his usual grin. "Why do you think we both stayed in here with you last night? I, for one, wanted your protection."

"You know you have it," I said.

The smile softened. "I know." He touched my face gently. "What's wrong? I mean really wrong? Why do you look so . . . tormented today?"

"What I did last night wasn't very human, Jason. I felt Richard's horror. I felt him think of me as a monster, and he's right."

Jason hugged me. I stiffened at first, and he started to let me go, then I relaxed against him. I let him hold me, wrapping my own arms around his back. I buried my face against his neck and had a horrible urge to cry.

There was a soft sound from behind us. I raised my head to look. The wereleopards were climbing off the bed, gliding towards us on human feet but moving as if there were muscles in their legs and hips and torsos that didn't exist in mine. Zane and Cherry writhed and glided, nearly naked, towards us. Cherry held Nathaniel's hand, leading him like a child. But he didn't look like a child as he padded towards us, naked. Undies would have hurt the upper thigh wound. Now, as he came towards us, it was clear that he wasn't completely unhappy to see me. Or maybe it was waking up next to Cherry, or maybe it was just a guy thing. Either way, I didn't like it.

I pushed away from Jason. He didn't fight it, just stepped back. He watched the wereleopards come, but I don't think he was worried about it. In fact, I could feel his energy prickle along my skin. Strong emotions like lust will make a shapeshifter's energy rise. The moment I thought it, I looked without thinking. Jason was happy to see Cherry, very happy.

I looked away, blushing. I turned my back on all of them, arms hugging my sides.

Someone touched my shoulder. I flinched.

"It's me, Anita," Jason said.

I shook my head.

He hugged me from behind, arms very carefully across my shoulders and no lower. "I'm not sorry you killed them, Anita. I'm just sorry you didn't kill Barnaby."

"Someone else is going to pay for my bravado, Jason. Like Mira last night. I do things, say things, around you guys, and it all goes wrong."

Zane moved around in front of me. I stared up at him with Jason's arms still around my shoulders like a bulky necklace. Zane's brown eyes were as serious as I'd seen them on this trip.

He reached out to touch my face, and only Jason's arms tightening ever so slightly kept me from backing away or saying, "Don't." Touching didn't mean the same thing to lycanthropes as it did to the rest of American society. I would say *human*, but there were a lot of countries that were more into casual touching than ours.

Zane's fingers trailed down my cheek while he studied my face, frowning. "Gabriel was our whole world. He and Elizabeth made us, chose us. As bad as you think he was, Gabriel saved most of us. I was a junkie, but he didn't allow drugs in his pard."

He leaned into me, sniffing along my skin, rubbing his cheek so that I could feel the fine stubble along his jaw. "Nathaniel was a street whore. Gabriel pimped him out but not to just anybody, not to everybody."

Cherry was on her knees. She took my hand, rubbing her face against my skin like a cat scent-marking. "I lost a leg in a hit-and-run accident. Gabriel offered me my leg back. He cut it off above the stump, and when I shifted, the leg grew back."

Zane laid a gentle kiss on my forehead. "He did care for us in his own, twisted way."

"But he never risked his life for us," Cherry said. She started licking my hand, again for all the world like a cat. She stopped licking me seconds before I told her to stop. Maybe she sensed my tension. "You risked your life to save Nathaniel. You risked the lives of your vampires for him."

Zane cradled my face in his hands, leaning back so he could see my face. "You love Asher. Why would you risk him for Nathaniel?"

I drew back gently from their hands until I was standing alone near the door. I wasn't going to make a break for it, I just needed some room.

Nathaniel crouched in the middle of the room. He was the only one who hadn't touched me.

"I don't love Asher," I said.

"We can smell your desire for him," Zane said.

Oh, great. "I didn't say I didn't think he was cute. I said I didn't love him." My eyes slid to the coffin. I knew he couldn't hear me, but . . .

Jason was leaning against the wall, grinning at me, arms crossed over his chest. The look on his face was enough.

"I don't love him."

Cherry and Zane stared at me, wearing almost identical expressions, neither of which I could read. "You care for him," Cherry said.

I thought about that, then nodded. "Okay, I care for him."

"Why would you risk him for Nathaniel?" she asked. She was still on her knees. She went to all fours as she spoke. Her breasts hung down, moving as she crawled towards me. I'd never had a naked woman crawl towards me, ever. Naked men, but not naked women. It bothered me. Homophobic? Who me?

"Nathaniel is mine to protect. I'm his Nimir-ra, right?''

Cherry kept crawling towards me. Zane had dropped to all fours and was joining her. Muscles moved under the skin of their shoulders, their arms, muscles that shouldn't have been there. They moved forward in a wave of grace and muscled potential, like violence contained inside skin. Except for Nathaniel. He stayed crouched and immobile, as if waiting for some signal.

I looked past the oncoming wereleopards to Jason. "What's going on?"

"They want to understand you."

"There's nothing to understand," I said. "Colin hurt Nathaniel because he could, like you'd abuse a dog you didn't like. No one abuses my friends. It's not allowed."

Cherry had waited for Zane so that they moved in tandem towards me, a nearly matched pair. They were almost to me, almost within touching range, and I didn't want them to touch me. Something was going on, and I didn't like it.

"Nathaniel isn't your friend," Jason said. "It wasn't friendship that made you risk Asher."

I frowned at him. "Stop helping me."

Zane and Cherry looked up at me, and I think they would have touched me but weren't sure of their welcome. "Gabriel said he cared for us," Zane said, "but he risked nothing. He sacrificed nothing." He raised up on his knees, close enough that his otherworldly energy pressed like a warm wind against my bare legs. "You risked your life for one of us last night. Why?"

Cherry raised up on her knees, and again it was like an echo. Their power pressed against me like a great, warm hand. Their intensity, their need, filled their eyes. And I realized for the first time that it wasn't just Nathaniel that was needy. It was all of them. They had no home, no love, no care.

"It wasn't friendship," Zane said. "The wolf is right."

"You aren't having sex with Nathaniel," Cherry said.

I stared at them, at those eager faces. "Sometimes you do things just because it's the right thing to do," I said.

"You risked Asher and Damian, then you risked yourself," Zane said. "Why? Why?"

"Why did you protect me last night?" Jason asked. "Why did you stand between me and Barnaby?"

"You're my friend," I said.

Jason smiled. "Now, I am, but that wasn't why you protected me. You'd have done the same for Zane."

I frowned at Jason. "What do you want me to say, Jason?"

"The real reason why you protected me. The same reason you risked so much for Nathaniel. Not friendship, or sex, or love."

"Then why?" I asked.

"You know the answer, Anita."

I looked from him to the two kneeling wereleopards. I hated putting it into words, but Jason was right. "Nathaniel is mine now. He's on the list of people that I'll protect. He's mine, and no one can hurt him without answering to me. Jason's mine. You're all mine, and no one hurts what's mine. It's not allowed."

It sounded so arrogant saying it out loud. It sounded medieval, but it was still true. Some things just are true; you don't have to voice them, they just are. And somewhere along the way, I'd started collecting people. My people. It used to mean friends, but lately, it meant more than that, or less. It meant people like Nathaniel. We certainly weren't friends, but he was mine, just the same.

Staring down into Zane and Cherry's faces, it was like I could see all the disappointments, the small betrayals, the selfishness, the pettiness, the cruelty. I watched it fill their eyes. They'd seen so much of it that they simply couldn't understand kindness or honor; or worse, they just didn't trust it.

"If you mean that," Zane said, "we're yours. You can have all of us."

"Have?" I made it a question.

"They mean sex," Jason said. He wasn't smiling now. I wasn't sure why. He'd been enjoying the show a moment before.

"I don't want to have sex with either of you, any of you," I added hastily. Didn't want to have any misunderstandings.

"Please," Cherry said, "please choose one of us."

I looked at them. "Why do you want me to have sex with one of you?"

"You love some of the wolves," Zane said. "You feel true friendship for them. You feel none of that for us."

"But you feel lust," Cherry said. "Nathaniel disturbs you because you find him attractive."

That cut a little too close to home. "Look, guys, I don't sleep with people just because I find them attractive."

"Why not?" Zane asked.

I sighed. "I don't do casual sex. If you don't understand that, I'm not sure I can explain it to you."

"How can we trust you if you don't want anything from us?" Cherry said.

I didn't have an answer for that one. I looked at Jason. "Can you help me out here?"

He pushed away from the wall. "I think so, but you may not like it."

"Explain," I said.

"The problem is that they've never really had a Nimir-ra, not for real. Gabriel was an alpha, and he was powerful, but he wasn't a Nimir-raj, either."

"One of the werewolves described Gabriel as a *lion passant*, a passive leopard, one that had power but didn't protect," I said. "The pard called me a *léoparde lionne*, one that protects, before they promoted me to Nimir-ra."

"We called Gabriel *léopard lionne*," Zane said, "because he was all we knew, but the wolves were right, he was a *lion passant*."

"Great," I said, "so it's settled."

"No," Cherry said. "If Gabriel taught us anything, it was that you can't trust anyone unless they want something from you. You don't have to love us, but pick one of us for a lover."

I shook my head. "No. I mean thanks for the invitation, but no thanks."

"Then how can we trust you?" Cherry asked, voice almost a whisper.

"You can trust her," Jason said. "It's Gabriel that you couldn't trust. He's the one that convinced you that sex was so damned important. Anita isn't even sleeping with our Ulfric, but Zane saw her last night. He saw what she did to protect me."

"She did it to protect her vampire. The one she cares for," Zane said.

"I don't feel for Damian the way I feel for Asher, but I risked my life for him last night," I said.

The leopards frowned up at me. "I know," Zane said, "and I don't understand that. Why didn't you let him die?"

"I'd asked him to risk his life to save Nathaniel. I try never to ask of others what I'm not willing to do myself. If Damian was willing to risk his life, then I couldn't do less."

The leopards were lost. It showed in their faces, the tension that flowed through their power, as it breathed along my skin.

"Am I yours?" Nathaniel asked. His voice sounded small and lost.

I looked past the others to him. He was still crouched, huddled in the middle of the floor. He was huddled in around himself. His long, long hair had spilled around him, across his face. His flower-petal eyes stared out at me through that curtain of hair, like he was staring out through fur. I'd seen other lycanthropes that did that, hid behind their hair, and stared. Crouched there, he was suddenly feral and vaguely unreal. He brushed the hair back from one side, revealing a line of arm and chest. His face was suddenly young, open, and raw with need.

"I won't let anyone else hurt you, Nathaniel," I said.

A single tear slid down his face. "I'm so tired of not belonging to anyone, Anita. So tired of being anyone's meat that wanted me. So tired of being scared."

"You don't have to be scared anymore, Nathaniel. If it's within my power to keep you safe, I will."

"I belong to you now?"

I didn't like the phrasing, but watching him cry, one crystalline tear at a time, I knew that now wasn't the time to quibble over semantics. I hoped I wasn't signing up for more up-close-and-personal care than I wanted, but I nodded. "Yes, Nathaniel, you belong to me." Words alone rarely impressed shapeshifters. It was like part of them didn't understand words.

I held out my hand to him. "Come, Nathaniel, come to me."

He crawled to me, not in that wild, muscular grace, but head down, crying, face hidden by his hair. He was sobbing full out by the time he reached me. He held one hand up to me blind, not looking at me.

Zane and Cherry had moved to either side, letting him come close to me.

I took Nathaniel's hand and wondered what to do with it. Shaking it wasn't enough, kissing it seemed wrong. I racked my brain for anything on leopards and just blanked. The one thing that the leopards did most often was lick each other. I couldn't think of anything else.

I raised Nathaniel's hand to my mouth, bending over to press my mouth to the back of his hand. I licked his skin, one quick movement, and the taste of him was familiar. I knew in that moment that Raina had licked this skin, ran lips, tongue, teeth, down this body.

The munin welled up inside of me, and I fought it. The munin wanted to bite his hand, to draw blood and lap it like a cat with cream. The imagery was too repulsive to me. My own horror helped me chase Raina away. I pushed her down inside me and realized that she never really left me anymore. That was why she came so quickly and so easily. I felt her hiding inside me like a cancer waiting to spread.

I stood there with the taste of Nathaniel's skin in my mouth and did what Raina had never done: I gave comfort.

I raised Nathaniel's head gently until I could cradle his face between my hands. I kissed his forehead, I kissed the salty taste of tears from his cheeks.

He fell against me with a sob, arms locked around my legs, pressed against me. There was a moment when Raina tried to flare to life as Nathaniel's groin pressed against my bare legs.

I reached out to Richard, drawing on the mark between us. His power came to my call like a warm brush of fur. It helped chase away that awful, stinging presence.

I offered my hands to the other leopards. They pressed their faces to my skin, chin marking me like cats, licking me as if I were a kitten. I stood there with the three wereleopards pressed to me, borrowing Richard's power to keep Raina at bay. But it was more than that. Richard's power filled me, washed through me into the leopards.

I was like the wood in the center of a fire. Richard was the flame, and the wereleopards warmed themselves against that heat. They took it into themselves, bathed in it, wrapped it around themselves like a promise.

Standing there, caught between Richard's power, the wereleopards' needs, and that awful touch of Raina, like some foul perfume, I prayed: Dear God, don't let me fail them.

24

The greeting ceremony that had been interrupted last night was back on for tonight. One thing about the monsters: You have to observe the rules. The rules said we needed a greeting ceremony, well, by golly, we'd have one. Vengeful vampires, or crooked cops, or hell freezing over, if there was a rite to be performed, or a ceremony to be had, you went ahead with it. The vampires were worse about being cultured while they tore your throat out, but the werewolves weren't far behind.

Me, I'd have ordered takeout and said, "Hell with it; let's try to solve the mystery." But I wasn't in charge. Even crispy-crittering over twenty vamps last night didn't make me top dog or top anything else, though Verne's invitation had been very, very polite. Colin wasn't the only one who was scared of me now.

Executing almost all of Colin's vamps meant that Verne's pack was in charge now. They had the personnel to keep Colin from making more vamps. Apparently, if there was no tie between vampires and wereanimals in an area, then whoever had the strength could rule over the others. Until last night, Colin had kept the wolves in line; now the shoe was on the other foot, and from the look in Verne's eyes, the shoe was going to pinch.

It was one of those hot August nights that is utterly still. The world sits in the close, hot darkness as if holding its breath, waiting for a cool breeze that never comes.

But there was movement under the trees. No wind, but movement. People crept among the trees. No, not people, werewolves. Everyone was still in human form, but you wouldn't have mistaken them for human. They eased through the trees like gliding shadows, moving through the scattered underbrush almost soundlessly. If there had been even the smallest breeze to stir the trees, they would have been soundless. But a brush of twig, a crunch of leaf, a rustle of green leaves, and you heard them. On a night like tonight, even the small sounds carried.

A twig snapped off to my left, and I jumped. Jamil touched my arm, and I jumped again.

"Damn, babe, you're jumpy tonight."

"Don't call me babe."

His smile flashed in the darkness. "Sorry."

I rubbed my hands along my arms.

"You can't be cold," he said.

"I'm not." It wasn't cold that was trailing up and down my skin like insects marching.

"What's wrong?" Jason asked.

I stopped in the dark woods, knee-deep in some tall, leggy weed. I shook my head, searching the darkness. Yeah, there were several dozen werewolves slinking around, but it wasn't the shapeshifters themselves that were freaking me out. It was . . . it was like hearing voices in a distant room. I couldn't understand what they were saying, but I could hear them—hear them in my head. I knew what it was; it was the munin. The munin in the lupanar. The munin called to me, whispered across my skin. They were eager for me to come, waiting for me. Shit.

Zane stared out into the dark. He was standing close enough that I heard him draw a breath and knew he was scenting the wind. They were all turned out into the night, even Nathaniel. He seemed more confident than I'd ever seen him, more comfortable in his own skin, no pun intended. Our little ceremony this afternoon had meant something to all three of the leopards. I still wasn't sure what, exactly, it meant to me.

They were all wearing old jeans, T-shirts, things you wouldn't mind shapeshifting in, because one night closer to the full moon, accidents happened. No, not accidents. I would get to watch some of them lose their human shapes tonight. I realized that I really didn't want to see it. Not really.

Asher and Damian were not here. They had gone to spy or negotiate with Colin and his remaining vamps. I'd thought this was a really bad idea, but Asher had assured me that it was expected. That he as Jean-Claude's second would carry the message that I, we, had spared Colin and his second in command, Barnaby. We had allowed his human servant to walk from the circle. We had been generous, and we didn't have to be. By their laws, Colin had overstepped his bounds. He was the lesser vampire, and we could have taken everything from him.

Of course, the truth was that Colin and Barnaby had escaped. The only person we allowed to escape was Colin's human servant. But Asher assured me that he could lie to Colin and that the Master of this City would never realize it was a lie.

There was a tightness in my gut at the thought of Damian and Asher out there alone with Colin and company. The vamps had rules for everything, but they had a tendency to bend the rules until they were just this side of breaking. Close enough to get Asher and Damian hurt. But Asher had been so confident, and tonight I was playing lupa. One monster at a time, I guess.

Another thing that was making me nervous was no guns. Knives were okay, they substituted for claws, but no guns. Marcus had been the same way. No Ulfric worth his salt would let you bring a gun into their inner sanctum. I understood it, but I didn't have to like it. After what I'd done for Verne last night, I thought the request for no guns was downright rude.

Richard had informed me that my killing of Colin's vamps inside the lupanar would be our gift, the gift that the visiting Ulfric and lupa gave to the resident pack.

The gift was usually a freshly killed animal, jewelry for the lupa, or something mystical. Death, jewelry, or magic; it sounded like Valentine's Day.

I'd put jeans on to protect my legs from the underbrush, even though it was hot enough for my knees to sweat. The only one of us wearing shorts was Jason. If his legs were getting scratched up, he didn't seem to mind. He was also the only one not wearing a shirt of some kind. I'd put on a royal blue tank top so at least the top of me would be cool. It did leave the knives sort of visible, though.

The big knife down my spine was still invisible unless you looked really hard at my back. The tank top was thin material, and you could see the sheath, though not in the dark. I had my usual wrist sheaths and silver blades on my forearms. They were very visible against my skin. I had a new knife in my pocket. It was a four-inch switchblade with a safety lock. Didn't want to sit down and stab myself. This is one of those blades that comes straight out. Yes, it is illegal. It had been a gift from a friend who didn't sweat legalities much. So why have a four-incher that is illegal to carry in most states? Because at six inches, it wasn't comfortable to sit down with it in my pocket. So nice to have friends that know your size.

I was also wearing a silver crucifix. I didn't plan on meeting any bad vamps tonight, but I didn't trust Colin not to try something. If he knew enough about the greeting ceremony to know I wouldn't be allowed a gun, now is when he would jump me.

There were soft grey shadows under the trees. The moon and stars were bright somewhere overhead. But where we stood, the trees were a solid darkness between us and the sky. I felt almost claustrophobic standing there in the dark.

"I don't smell anything but other lukoi," Jason said.

Everybody agreed. Nothing but us shapeshifters tonight. No one but me seemed to be able to feel that whispering echo. I was the only necromancer in the bunch, so the spirits of the dead liked me better.

"We need to be at the meeting place before the ceremony goes any further," Jamil said.

I looked at him. "You mean they've started the ceremony already?"

"The call has been given," Jason said.

He said it like *call* should have been in capital letters. "What do you mean the call has been given?"

"They've sacrificed an animal and smeared blood on the tree, sort of what you did last night," Jason said.

I rubbed my arms. "I wonder if that's why I'm sensing the munin."

"When we smear blood on the rock throne, our spirit symbol, it doesn't make the munin come," Jason said.

I shook my head. "I've been in your lupanar, Jason; this one is different. Their magic is different from yours."

I felt something creeping through the trees. A roil of energy that made my heart skip a beat, and then beat faster, as if I'd been running. "Jesus, what was that?"

"She's feeling the call," Jason said.

"That's impossible," Jamil said. "She isn't lukoi." He stabbed a finger at Cherry, Zane, and Nathaniel. "They don't feel it. They're shapeshifters, and they don't feel the call to the lupanar."

Cherry looked at us, then shook her head. "He's right. I feel something like a vague buzz through the woods, but it's nothing big."

Nathaniel and Zane agreed with her.

My skin rushed across my body like it was going to try to crawl away under its own power. It was creepy as hell. "What is happening to me?"

"She is feeling the call," Jason said.

"That is not possible," Jamil said.

"You keep saying that about her, Jamil, and you keep being wrong," Jason said.

A low, growling snarl trickled from Jamil's mouth.

"Stop it, both of you," I said. I looked behind me farther into the trees until there was nothing but a wall of darkness shot by faint moonlight. Jason was right. I could feel the magic. It was ritual magic, and it was death magic. Lycanthropes' power comes from life. They are the most alive preternatural creatures I've ever been around, more like fairies than humans, sometimes. But this lupanar ran on death as well as life; it called to me twice. Once through Richard's marks; second through my necromancy. I wished Richard were here.

He'd gone to have dinner with his family. Shang-Da had gone with him at my insistence. Sheriff Wilkes had to know we weren't leaving town by now. It wasn't just the local vampires we had to worry about. Richard had called on the telephone, saying they were running late, to start without him. His mother just hadn't understood why he couldn't stay longer. All of the Zeeman men were so pussy whipped—ah, henpecked, sorry.

I started through the trees, and they followed me. I climbed on top of a fallen log. You never step directly over a log. You never know if there's a snake on the other side. Step on the log, then over. Tonight it wasn't snakes I was worried about. I moved slowly, picking my way through the trees. My night vision is excellent for a human, and I could have gone faster. I wanted to go faster. I wanted to fling myself through the trees and run. I didn't, but it was force of will alone that kept me walking.

It wasn't just the death I was picking up on. It was that warm rising energy that was pure lycanthrope. I knew I could sense some of this with Richard holding my hand. We'd done it before on a full moon, but never with me alone. Never just me moving through the darkness trying to breathe past the beating of my heart and the rush of someone else's power.

I whispered, "Richard, what have you done to me?" Maybe it was his name, maybe it was just thinking of him, but I suddenly felt him sitting in the car. I had a moment of seeing Daniel driving. I could smell Daniel's aftershave. I could feel the warm tightness of Richard's chest. I pulled away and was left staggering. If I hadn't had a tree to hug, I'd have fallen to my knees. If that moment of sharing hit Richard as hard as it hit me, I was glad he wasn't driving.

"Anita, are you all right?" Jason touched my shoulder. And power flowed between us in a hot, skin-creeping rush. I turned to him and it felt like I was moving in slow motion. I couldn't breathe past the power and the sensations that filled my mind. Images, flashes, like watching a room through strobe light. A bed, white sheets, the smell of sex so fresh it was hot and musky. My hands resting on a smooth chest. A man's chest. That warm, rolling power that was pure lycanthrope, pure beast, filled my body, like the man underneath me. Sharp, pleasant, exciting. The power spilled out my fingertips, pulling claws from my hands like knives unsheathing. The beast pushed at the smooth skin of my body, tried to slip out and overwhelm me. But I held it, tightened my body around it, and let only my hands turn monstrous. Claws sliced that smooth chest. Blood, hot and fresh enough to taste on our tongues.

Jason stared up at me from the bed, still pinned by my body, our body, and he screamed. He'd wanted this. Chosen it. And still he screamed. I felt his flesh give under claws. Those hands struck again and again, until the white sheets were spongy with blood and he lay motionless underneath us. If he survived, he would be one of us. I remembered not caring if he lived or if he died, not really. It was the sex, the pain, the joy of it all that mattered.

When I could feel my body again, Jason and I were kneeling in the leaves. His hands were still on my arms. Someone was screaming, and it was me. Jason stared at me with a face almost blank with horror. He'd shared the ride, but it wasn't his memory.

It wasn't Richard's memory, or mine. It was Raina's. She was dead but not forgotten. She was why I feared the munin. I was a necromancer with ties to the wolves. The munin liked me. Raina's munin liked me best of all.

"What's wrong?" Cherry said. She touched me, and it opened something inside of me again. It welcomed Raina back with a rush that left me screaming. But I fought it this time. Fought it because I did not want to see Cherry the way Raina would see her. Jason wouldn't care. Cherry would care. I would care.

There was a rush of sensations: skin damp with sweat, hands with long, polished nails on my breasts, those grey eyes staring up at me, mouth open, slack, shoulder-length yellow hair against a pillow. Raina on top again.

I screamed and pulled away from them both. The images died as if a plug had been pulled. I scrambled through the leaves on all fours, eyes shut tight. I ended sitting, hugging my knees to my chest, face buried against my legs. I squeezed my eyes so tight that I began seeing white snakes against my eyelids.

I heard someone move through the crunching leaves. I felt them hovering over me.

"Don't touch me," I said. It was almost another scream.

I heard whoever it was kneel in the dry leaves before Jamil's voice came. "I won't touch you. Are you still getting the memories?"

He didn't ask if I was seeing the memories. I found the phrasing strange. I shook my head without looking up.

"Then it's over, Anita. Once the munin leave, they're gone until called again."

"I didn't call her." I raised my face slowly and opened my eyes. The summer night seemed blacker somehow.

"It was Raina again?" he made it a question.

"Yes."

He knelt as close as he could get without touching me. "You shared the memories with Jason and with Cherry."

I wasn't sure if it was a question or a statement, but I answered it: "Yeah."

"It was a full visual," Jason said. He was sitting with his bare back against a tree.

Cherry had her hands pressed to her face. She spoke, face hidden. "I cut my hair after that night, after what she did to me. One night with her was the price for not having to do one of their porno movies." She jerked her hands away from her face, crying. "God, I can smell Raina's scent." She rubbed her hands against her jeans, over and over, as if she'd touched something bad and was trying to wipe it away.

"What the fuck was that?" I asked. "I've channeled Raina before, but it wasn't like that. I've got glimpses of memories, but not a full-blown movie. Nothing like that, ever."

"Have you been trying to learn to control the munin?" Jamil asked.

"Just to get rid of it, them, whatever."

Jamil moved closer to me, studying my face as if looking for something. "If you were lukoi, I'd tell you, you can't just turn the munin off. If you have the power to call them, then you must learn to control them, not just shut them out. Because you can't shut them out. They'll seek a way into you, through you."

"How do you know so much?" I asked.

"I knew a werewolf who could call the munin. She hated it. She tried to shut them out. It didn't work."

"Just because it didn't work for your friend doesn't mean I can't do it." I could feel his breath warm against my face. "Back off, Jamil."

He scooted back, but he was still closer than I wanted him to be. He sat back in the leaves. "She went crazy, Anita. The pack had to execute her." His eyes went past me into the darkness. I turned to see what he was looking at. Two figures stood in the darkness. One was a woman with long, pale hair and a long, white dress like something out of a 1950s horror movie. If you were playing the victim. But she stood very straight, very certain, as if she were anchored to the ground like a tree. There was something almost frightfully confident about her.

The man with her was tall, slender, and tanned dark enough that he looked brown in the dark. His hair was short and a paler brown than his skin. If the woman seemed calm, he seemed nervous. He gave off energy in a roiling bath that breathed along my skin and made the night seem hotter.

"Are you well?" the woman asked.

"She shared the munin with two of us," Jamil said.

"By accident, I take it," the woman said. She sounded faintly amused.

I was not amused. I got to my feet, a little unsteady, but standing. "Who are you?"

"My name is Marianne. I am the vargamor for this clan."

I remembered Verne and Colin talking about a varga-something last night. "Verne mentioned you last night. Colin said he'd left you at home to keep you safe."

"A good witch is hard to find," she said, smiling.

I looked at her. "You don't feel Wiccan."

Again, I knew she smiled at me. Her peaceful condescension grated on my nerves. "A psychic then, if you prefer the term."

"I'd never heard the term vargamor before last night," I said.

"It's rare," she said. "Most packs don't have one anymore. Considered too old-fashioned."

"You aren't lukoi," I said.

Her head cocked to one side, and the smile was gone, as if I'd finally done something worthwhile. "Are you so sure?"

I tried to get a sense of what had made me so sure she was human, or at least not lukoi. She had her own energy. She was psychic enough for me to notice. We'd have recognized each other without any introductions. We might not have known the exact flavor of each other's abilities, but we'd have recognized a kindred or rival spirit. Whatever power moved her, it wasn't lycanthropy.

"Yeah, I'm sure you're not lukoi," I said.

"Why?" she asked.

"You don't taste like a shapeshifter."

She laughed then, and it was a rich, musical sound that managed to be wholesome and earthy all at the same time. "I like your choice of senses. Most humans would have said I didn't feel right. Feel is such an imprecise word, don't you think?"

I shrugged. "Maybe."

"This is Roland. He is my bodyguard for this night. We poor humans must be watched over for fear that some overzealous shapeshifter might lose control and harm us."

"Somehow I don't think you are that easy a prey, Marianne."

She laughed again. "Why, thank you, child."

Her calling me child made me add about ten years to her age. She didn't look it. It was dark, but she still didn't look it.

"Come, Anita. We will escort you to the lupanar." She held out her hand to me like I was supposed to take it and be led like a child.

I looked to Jamil. I hoped somebody knew what was going on, because I was lost.

"It's all right, Anita. The vargamor is neutral. She never fights or takes sides in challenges. That's how she can be human and run with the pack."

"Are we involved in a challenge or a fight that I don't know about?" I asked.

"No," Jamil said, but he sounded uncertain.

Marianne interpreted for me without being asked. "Introducing two outside dominants to a pack can lead to fighting. Having someone as powerful as Richard is raising the hackles on our younger wolves. Having him sleeping with our pack's only two dominant females makes it worse."

"You mean we may get into a pissing contest," I said.

"A colorful phrase, but accurate enough," she said.

"Okay, now what?" I asked.

"Now, Roland and I escort you all to the lupanar. The rest of you may go ahead. You know the way, Jamil."

"I don't think so," I said.

"No to what?" Marianne asked.

"Do I look like Little Red Riding Hood?" I said. "I'm not taking a stroll in the woods with two strangers. One of them a werewolf and the other a . . . I don't know what you are yet, Marianne. But I don't want to be alone with the two of you."

"Very well," she said. "Some or all may stay. I was thinking that you might like privacy to speak with another human tied to the lukoi. Perhaps I was wrong."

"Tomorrow in the light of day, we can talk. Tonight, let's just take it easy."

"As you like," she said. Again, she held out her hand to me. "Come. Let us talk as we all troop to the lupanar as one big, happy family."

"You're making fun of me now," I said. "That won't put you on my A-list."

"I make fun of everyone a little," she said. "I mean no harm by it." She waggled her hand at me. "Come, child, the moon is passing above us. Time wastes away."

I walked towards her with my five bodyguards at my back. I didn't take her hand, though.

I was close enough to see the condescending smile clearly now. Anita Blake, the famous vampire hunter, afraid of some backcountry wisewoman.

I smiled. "I'm cautious by nature and paranoid by profession. You've offered me your hand twice now within just a few minutes. You don't strike me as someone who does anything without a reason. What gives?"

She put her hands on her hips and tsked at me. "Is she always this difficult?"

"Worse," Jason said.

I frowned at him. Even if he couldn't see it in the dark, it made me feel better.

"All I want, child, is to touch your hand and get a sense of how powerful you are before we let you inside the boundaries of our lupanar again. After what you did last night, some of our pack fear you within the boundaries of our lupanar. They seem to think you will steal our power."

"I can tap into it," I said, "but I can't steal it."

"But the munin already reach out to you. I felt you call your munin. It traveled through the power we have called tonight in the lupanar. It disturbed it like plucking on a thread of a spider's web. We came to see what we had caught, and if it were too big to eat, we would cut it loose and not take it home."

"The spider metaphor worked for maybe two sentences, then you lost me," I said.

"The lupanar is our place of power, Anita. I need to get a sense of what you are before you enter it this night." The laughter was gone from her voice. She was suddenly very serious. "It is not just our protection I am thinking of, child. It is yours. Think, child, what would happen to you if the munin within our circle rode you one after another? I need to make sure you can control at least that well."

Just hearing her say it made my stomach tight with fear. "Okay." I held out my hand to her like we were going to shake hands, but I gave her my left hand. If she didn't like it, she could refuse it.

"Offering the left hand is an insult," she said.

"Take it or leave it, vargamor. We don't have all night."

"That is more true than you know, little one." She put her hand out as if to touch mine but stopped with her hand just above mine. She spread her hand above my skin. I mirrored her. She was trying to get a sense of my aura. Two could play at that game.

When I raised my hands up in front of my body, she mirrored me. We stood facing each other, hands spread wide, not quite touching. She was tall, five-foot-seven or five-foot-eight. I didn't think there were high heels under that long dress.

Her aura was warm against my skin. It had a weight to it, as if I could have wrapped her aura in my hands like dough. I'd never met anyone with such weight to their aura. It confirmed my first sense of her. Solid.

She pushed forward suddenly, wrapping her fingers around my hand. She forced my aura back in upon itself like a knife thrust. It made me gasp, but again, I knew what was happening. I pushed back and felt her waver.

She smiled, but it wasn't condescending now. It was almost as if she were pleased.

The hair at the back of my neck tried to crawl down my spine.

"Powerful," she said. "Strong."

I spoke around a tightness in my throat. "You, too."

"Thank you," she said.

I felt her power, her magic, move over me, through me, like a rush of wind. She pulled away so abruptly it staggered both of us.

We were left standing a foot away from each other, breathing hard like we'd been running. My heart thudded in my throat like a trapped thing. And I could taste her pulse on the back of my tongue. No, I could hear it. I could hear it like a small ticking clock. But it wasn't her pulse. I smelled Richard's aftershave like a cloud that I had walked through. When the marks were working through Richard, it was often scent that let me know what was happening. I didn't know what had caused them to act up. Maybe the power of the other lycanthropes or the closeness of the full moon. Who knew? But something had opened me to him. I was channeling more than the sweet smell of his body.

"What is that sound?" I asked.

"Describe it," Marianne said.

"Like a clicking, soft, almost mechanical."

"I've got an artificial valve in my heart," she said.

"It can't be that."

"Why not? When I lean forward to the mirror to apply eyeliner, I can hear it through my open mouth, echoing against the mirror."

"But I can't hear it," I said.

"But you are," she said.

I shook my head. I was losing the sense of her. She was pulling away from me, putting up shields. I didn't blame her, because, for just a second I could feel her heart beating, limping along. The sound hadn't made me sorry for her or empathetic. The sound excited me. I felt it pull things deep inside my body. It was almost sexual. She'd be slow, an easy kill. I looked at this tall, confident woman, and for a split second all I saw was food.

Fuck.

25

We followed Marianne and her guard, Roland, through the darkened trees. I'd have caught that damn dress on every twig and deadfall. Marianne floated through the woods as if the trees themselves let her and the dress pass gently through. Roland paced at her arm, gliding through the woods like water down a well-worn channel. Jamil, Nathaniel, and Zane moved just as gracefully. It was the rest of us that were having trouble.

My excuse was that I was human. I didn't know what Jason and Cherry's excuse was. I tried to step on a log and missed. I ended up on my stomach, arms scraping along the rough bark. I straddled it like a horse and couldn't seem to get my leg over the other side. Cherry tripped on something in the leaves and fell to her knees. I watched her get to her feet and trip over the same damn thing. This time she stayed on her knees, head down.

Jason fell in a tangle of dry tree roots at the end of the log I was sitting on. He fell on his face and cursed. When he got to his feet, there was a scrape on his chest deep enough to show blood, black in the moonlight. It reminded me of what Raina had done to him. She'd cut his chest to rags, and there wasn't a scar on him from it.

I closed my eyes and leaned over the log, resting my forearms on it. My arms hurt. I raised myself slowly and looked at them. I'd scraped them up enough so that blood was slowly filling the wounds in spots. Great.

Jason leaned against the end of the log, far enough away that we wouldn't touch. I think we were all still afraid of that. Didn't want a repeat.

"What's wrong with us?" Jason asked.

I shook my head. "I don't know."

Marianne was just suddenly there. I hadn't heard her come up. Was I losing time? Was I that out of it?

"You cast out the munin before it was ready to release you."

"So?" I said.

"So, that takes energy," she said.

"Fine, that explains me stumbling around. What about them? Why do they feel like shit?"

She gave a very small smile. "You are not the only one who fought the munin, Anita. It was you who called it, and if you had not been willing to fight it, then the other two would have been helpless before it, but they fought it as well. They struggled against the memories. That costs."

"You sound like you know," I said.

"I can call the munin. These chaotic flashes are what happens when you have a munin that hunts you, and that you do not want to embrace."

"How did you know it was chaotic?" I asked.

"I caught a glimpse or two of what you saw. The merest touch," she said.

"Why don't you feel awful?" I asked.

"I did not struggle. If you simply allow the munin to ride you, it passes much more quickly and relatively painlessly."

I half-laughed at her. "That sounds like the old advice of lie back, close your eyes, and it'll be over soon."

She turned her head to one side, long hair sliding over her shoulders like a pale ghost. "Embracing the munin can be pleasant or unpleasant, but this munin hunts you, Anita. Most of the time, a munin that tries to bond with a pack member does so out of love or shared sorrow."

I just looked at her. "It isn't love that motivates this one."

"No," she said, "I felt both the strength of her personality and her hatred of you. She chases you out of spite."

I shook my head. "Not just spite. What little is left of her enjoys the game. She's having a really good time when I channel her."

Marianne nodded. "Yes. But if you would embrace her instead of fighting, you could pick and choose among the memories. Strong ones will come easiest, but you could control more of what comes and how strongly it comes. If you would truly channel her, as you put it, then the images would be less like a movie and more . . . like wearing a glove."

"Except that I'm the glove," I said, "and her personality overwhelms mine. No thanks."

"If you continue to fight this munin, it will get worse. If you will cease struggling and meet her even partway, the munin will lose some of its strength. Some feed off of love. This one feeds off of fear and hatred. Was this the old lupa? The one you killed?"

"Yeah," I said.

Marianne shivered. "I never met Raina, but even that small touch of her makes me glad she's dead. She was evil."

"She didn't see herself that way," I said. "She saw herself as more neutral than evil." I said it like I knew, and I did know. I knew because I'd worn her essence like a dress more than once.

"Very few people see their own actions as truly evil," Marianne said. "It is left to their victims to decide what is evil and what is not."

Jason raised his hand. "Evil."

Cherry echoed him. "Evil."

Nathaniel and Zane and even Jamil, raised their hands.

I raised my hand, too. "It's unanimous," I said.

Marianne laughed, and again, it was a sound equally at home in the kitchen or the bedroom. How she managed to be both wholesome and suggestive in the same breath puzzled me. Of course, a lot of things puzzled me about Marianne.

"We'll be late," Roland said. His voice was deeper than I thought it would be, low and careful, almost too old for his body. He looked peaceful enough, but I could look at him with things other than my eyes. You couldn't see it, but you could feel it. He was a mass of nervous energy. It danced along his skin, breathing out into the dark like an invisible cloud, hot, almost touchable, like steam.

"I know, Roland," she said. "I know."

"We could carry them," Jamil said.

A thrill of power flowed through the trees. It caught at my heart as if some invisible hand had touched me.

"We must go," Roland said.

"What is your problem?" I asked.

Roland looked at me with eyes that were a nice, solid darkness. "You are," he said. He spoke in a low voice, and it sounded like a threat.

Jamil moved between us so that my view of Roland was almost completely blocked, and I assumed, his view of me.

"Now, children," Marianne said, "play nicely."

"We will miss the ceremony entirely if they do not hurry," Roland said.

"If you were a true lupa," Marianne said, "you could draw energy from your wolves and give it in return like a great recycling battery." It sounded like she'd given this lecture before. I guess every pack needs a teacher. I know ours needed one sorely. I was beginning to realize that we were like children that had been raised by neglectful parents. We were grown-up, but we didn't know how to behave.

"You're psychic enough that you might be able to do it in a small way without being lukoi," Marianne said.

"I don't think I'd call being a necromancer the same thing as being psychic," Jamil said.

Marianne shrugged. "It's all much more alike than most people wish to acknowledge. Many religious groups are comfortable with psychic ability but not with magic. But call it what you will, it's either that or we call some more wolves and throw you across our shoulders."

The real trouble was that I only knew two ways to call power. One was ritual, the other was sex. I'd realized a few months ago that sex could take the place of ritual for me. Not always, and I had to be attracted to the person involved, but sometimes. I didn't really want to admit to strangers that sexual energy was one of the ways I performed magic. Even though no actual sex was involved, it was still embarrassing. Besides, doing anything sexual seemed like putting out the welcome mat for Raina's munin.

How could I explain all this to Marianne without sounding like a slut? I couldn't think of a way to explain it that didn't make me sound bad, so I wasn't going to try.

"Go on without us, Marianne. We'll get there on our own. Thanks, anyway."

She stamped her foot under that flowing gown. "Why are you so reluctant to try, Anita?"

I shook my head. "We can discuss magical metaphysics tomorrow. Right now, why don't you take your wolf and go. We'll get there, slow but sure."

"Let's go," Roland said.

Marianne looked to him, then back to me. "I was told to see if you were a danger to us, and you are not, but I don't like leaving you out here like this. The three of you are weak."

"We'll get over it," I said.

She cocked her head to one side again, hair sweeping like a white veil to frame her face. "Are you planning some sort of magic that you don't wish me to see?"

"Maybe," I said. Truth was, no. No way was I voluntarily touching Jason or Cherry again, not tonight. But if Marianne thought we were going to do something mystical but private, she might go away. I wanted her to go away.

She stood looking at me for nearly a full minute, then finally smiled, dim in the moonlight. "Very well, but do hurry. The others will grow impatient to greet Richard's human lupa. You have everyone's curiosity piqued."

"Glad to hear it. The sooner you go, the sooner we can start."

She turned without another word and started off through the trees. Roland trailed her, then took the lead. We all stood around waiting for Marianne's white dress to grow distant and ghostlike through the forest.

Finally, Jason said, "Start what?"

"Nothing," I said. "I just wanted them gone."

"Why?" Jamil asked.

I shrugged. "I don't want to be carried like a sack of potatoes." I started walking, slow but sure, towards the lupanar.

Jamil fell into step beside me. "Why not try what she was suggesting?"

I walked carefully, paying a lot more attention to my feet than I usually did. "Because outside of raising the dead, I'm still an amateur. It will probably take less time for us to walk to the lupanar than for me to do something mystical."

Jason agreed with me, which made me frown at him, but it was still true. I was like someone with a loaded gun that didn't know how to shoot. I would be struggling to figure out how to undo the safety while the bad guys shot me a million times. About two months ago, the only other necromancer I'd ever met had offered to teach me real necromancy, not this voodoo dabbling I was doing. He'd ended up dead before he could teach me much of anything. Funny how many people ended up dead after they met me. No, I didn't kill him.

Cherry stumbled and went down again. Zane and Nathaniel were just suddenly there, one on either side of her. They helped her stand, hugging each other for a moment. Cherry slipped a hand around the waist of both men, leaning her head for a second on Zane's shoulder. They walked this way through the treacherous dark, Cherry leaning heavily on her fellow wereleopards. There was a camaraderie between them that hadn't been there before. Had I done that? Had just having someone to protect them forged some sort of bond? Or had it been Richard's prickling energy? I had a lot of questions and didn't even know if there was anyone who would know. Maybe Marianne would know, if I decided I could trust her.

Jamil offered me his arm. I waved him away. I knew that Raina had slept with him, and I did not want the memory. "Help Jason," I said.

Jamil looked at me for a second, then went and offered his arm to Jason, who refused the offer. "If Anita doesn't need help, neither do I."

"Don't be a hard case," I said.

"Now, that's the pot calling the kettle black," Jason said.

"If I offered you my arm, you'd take it," I said.

"An excuse to hang all over a pretty girl? Sure." Then he seemed to think about it. "But maybe not tonight. I can't call the munin, but there's something in the air tonight." He shivered, rubbing his hands along his bare arms. "Of all the memories Raina had of me, why that one?"

We were both slowly walking as we talked. "The three things Raina liked best were sex and violence and terrorizing people. Making you lukoi hit all her buttons."

Jason stumbled, fell to his knees, and just stayed that way for a second or two. I waited with him, wondering if I should offer to help him up. "I know you wondered why I never did any of her porno movies."

"I guess. I mean you're not exactly the shy type."

He looked up at me, and even by moonlight, there was a sorrow in his face that was deeper and wider than most people ever saw. He was too young for the look in his eyes, but there it was. Innocence lost.

"I'll always remember the look on her face when she killed me."

"She didn't kill you, Jason."

"She tried. It didn't matter to her whether I lived or died. It really didn't."

That one shared memory, and I couldn't argue with him. Raina's pleasure had been more important to her than his life. Like a serial killer.

Jason hunched in upon himself. "But she was my sponsor, and I had to stay with her until my probation period was over. When I could, I got away."

"Is that why you went to stay with Jean-Claude, as his lapwolf? To escape Raina?"

Jason nodded. "Partly." He looked up suddenly and grinned. "Of course, Jean-Claude is way cool."

I shook my head and offered him my hand.

"Think we can risk it?" he asked.

"I think so. I'm not feeling particularly muninish right now."

He took my hand and it was just a hand. His hand in mine. I helped him stand, and he staggered just a bit on his feet, which made me wobble. We clung to each other for a second like two drunks leaving a party. I hugged him, and he hugged me back. It was quick. He pulled away first, and looked almost embarrassed. "Don't tell anyone I didn't take my chance to grope you when it was your idea."

I patted him on the back. "Not a soul."

He gave me his usual grin, and we started through the woods, walking close enough to catch each other if we fell. A breeze blew through the trees, rustling everything. The woods were suddenly alive with sound. I turned my face to the wind, hoping it would be cool, but it was hot like the air from an oven.

Jason's baby fine hair moved gently in the breeze. I heard him take a deep breath, then he touched my arm. He spoke low. "I smell the man that I threw into the truck yesterday."

We kept walking as if nothing were wrong. "Are you sure?" I asked.

I saw his nostrils flare as he tested the air. "He smelled like peppermint Life-savers and cigarettes."

"A lot of people smell like peppermint and cigarettes," I said.

We kept moving, his hand on my arm now. "I also smell gun oil."

Great.

Jamil was waiting for us just up ahead. The three wereleopards waited among the trees. Jamil came back to us, smiling, and enveloped both of us in a big, hearty hug. "You guys are so damned slow tonight." He hugged us against him and whispered, "I smell two, maybe three, to our left."

"One of them is a guy I beat up yesterday," Jason said, smiling as if we were talking about something else entirely.

"Revenge maybe?" He made it a question.

"How far away are they?" I asked.

He drew back with a big very un-Jamil grin. He whispered, "A few yards. I can smell the guns."

I encircled his slender waist with my arm and whispered against his chest. "We don't have any guns. Any suggestions?"

Jason leaned in, laughing, and said, "I don't feel good enough to outrun them."

I patted his arm. "Me, either."

"If they're here for revenge," Jamil said, "then maybe, they'll settle for just the two of you."

I drew back from him. I wasn't sure I liked his reasoning. "So?"

"You stay here and make out. They move up to get you, and I get them."

"They've got guns. You don't."

"I'll send Zane and Cherry to the others. They'll bring reinforcements. But we can't let them follow us to the lupanar. We can't take danger there."

"Some werewolf rule?" I asked.

"Yes," he said.

"All right," I said. "But don't let them kill me, okay?"

"What about me?" Jason said.

"Sorry. Him either."

Jamil leaned into both of us. "I suggest the two of you get a lot more cozy, fast, or they're not going to buy it."

I transferred my arm to Jason's waist, but said, "How long have they been watching?"

"Make them think you're drunk, just in case they saw the screaming. Make out, but get on the ground as soon as possible in case they just decide to shoot you." With that comforting thought, Jamil went back to the others. He walked away into the dark with the wereleopards. Zane looked at me as they walked away, but I nodded once, and that seemed to satisfy him. He turned and let Jamil lead him away. I really was going to have to find the leopards a true alpha. They were all so damn submissive.

Jason pushed me up against a tree.

"Watch it," I said.

He grinned at me. "We want it to look real, don't we?"

"I thought we had a moment of real friendship bonding back there," I said.

Jason leaned in towards me as if he were going to kiss me. "Just because we're friends doesn't mean that I don't want to sleep with you." He kissed me, a soft brush of lips.

I frowned at him, not kissing back. "Please tell me that you don't want to sleep with all your female friends."

He put a hand on either side of my head, propping himself against the tree. "What can I say? I'm a guy."

I shook my head. "That's not an excuse."

He leaned his whole body into me in a sort of standing push-up. The muscles in his arms swelled with the effort. "How about because it's me."

I smiled. "That I'll buy." I put my hands on his waist. He was leaning against me but not too hard. He could have been taking a lot more advantage of the situation than he was. I realized that he was being a gentleman. There was a time not long ago that Jason wouldn't have made the effort. We were friends. But we needed to get down on the ground, and this wasn't getting us there.

I glanced, as casually as I could, at the others. I could still see Zane, and Cherry's hair gleamed through the trees. I had a sense that Jamil and Nathaniel was still with them, but it was all that blond hair that made them so visible. If the bad guys had a high-powered rifle, they could shoot us both through the tree. Once the others got out of sight, they might do just that.

I slid my hands up Jason's chest. The skin was soft, but underneath, he was very firm. I knew what that smooth flesh felt like shredding under claws. It wasn't the munin coming back. It was just me flashing on the vision. I balled my hands into fists and forced my hands to his face. I didn't want to do anything that would remind either of us of what we'd just shared. There was always the extra danger that it could bring Raina back. No, I didn't want to be channeling Raina with armed goons in the woods.

I cradled Jason's face in my hands, moving just my head towards him. As I leaned into him, he leaned more into me. I was suddenly very aware that his body was pressed down the length of mine. It made me hesitate, but when his lips brushed mine, I kissed him. I ran my hand back through his hair, until I had a handful of it.

I whispered into his mouth, "We need to get on the ground as soon as possible."

He kissed me harder, hands dropping to my belt. He slid his fingertips inside the belt, and knelt in front of me, pulling me down with him. I let him. He fell back into the leaves and pulled me down on top of him. I propped myself on my scraped forearms against his chest, sort of startled. I just wasn't a good enough actress for this.

I could feel his heart thudding under my hands. He rolled me suddenly, and I let out a little yip of surprise. He ended very firmly on top, and I didn't like it.

"I want on top," I said.

He put his lips next to my cheek. "If they shoot us, I can take a bullet better than you can." He rubbed his cheek along my face, and I realized he was doing the werewolf greeting. Maybe it was their version of a handshake, but I'd never been tempted to shake hands while making out.

I whispered into his ear, which was very close to my mouth, "Do you hear them?"

"Yes." He raised his face enough to kiss me.

"How close?" I kissed him back, but we were both listening, straining to hear. Here we were, lying on top of each other, bodies perfectly matched up, and we were both tight enough that I could feel the muscles along his back knotting.

"A few yards," he said. "They're good." He rested his cheek against mine. "They move quietly."

"Not quiet enough," I whispered.

"Can you hear them?" he asked.

"No."

We were both just staring at each other. Neither of us was making much of an effort to kiss or anything else. I could feel that his body was happy to be pressed up against mine, but it was all secondary. Men with guns were coming. Men who didn't like us very much.

I stared up into his eyes from inches away. I knew they were pale blue, but by moonlight they looked almost silver. "You're not going to do anything stupid like shield my body with yours."

He pushed just a little with his hips and grinned. "Why do you think I'm on top?" The grin and the hip movement were to distract me from how very serious his eyes were.

"Get off of me, Jason."

"Nope," he said. He propped himself up on his arms, pressing into me, leaning over like we were kissing. "They're almost here."

I slid a knife out for either hand.

He whispered against my mouth. "We're supposed to look helpless, remember? Bait doesn't go armed."

I could feel how very smooth his cheek was, smell his cologne. I stared past the pale halo of his hair. "We just trust that Jamil and the rest will save us, is that it?"

He licked my chin, then my mouth. I realized he was doing the submissive greeting. He was begging me to go along. His tongue was very wet and very warm.

"Stop licking me, and I'll do it," I said.

He laughed, but it was high with an edge of tension to it. I couldn't resheath the knives with him pressed on top of me, so I laid them down in the leaves. I kept my hands on them, lightly, but tried to relax and look harmless. With Jason pressed on top of me, kissing down my neck, it was easy to look helpless. The relaxed part wasn't going to happen.

I heard them now, moving through the dry leaves. They were quiet. If I hadn't been listening for it, I might have thought it was wind, an animal moving through the undergrowth. But it wasn't. It was men moving heavy and secretively through the forest. Hunting. They were hunting. They were hunting Jason and me.

I saw the first one round the tree, and I wasn't a good enough actress to look surprised. I just stared up at him with Jason on top of me, still kissing the side of my neck.

He'd looked big yesterday. From flat on my back, he was enormous, like a two-legged tree. The rifle in his hand looked long and black and hostile. He didn't point it at us, just held it in the crook of one arm. A big smile split his pale face.

I heard the second man before he touched Jason's shoulder with the tip of a double-barreled shotgun. The moment I saw the shotgun, I knew they'd come to kill us. You didn't go after people with shotguns if you just meant to scare them, not as a general rule, anyway.

If it were silver shot at this range, he could have killed both of us. I wasn't scared yet. I was pissed. Where the hell was our backup?

Jason raised his face slowly. The shotgun tapped his cheek almost gently. "My brother Mel sends his regards."

I rolled my eyes to look past the shotgun. The man was wearing a black T-shirt with a Harley logo on it. His belly hung out over his belt. There was a family resemblance.

I said very calmly, each word careful but not scared, "What do you want?"

Mel's brother laughed.

The first man joined him.

They stood over us with the guns and laughed. Not a good sign. Where the fuck was Jamil?

"Get off of her real slow," the first man said. The rifle was at his shoulder now, snuggled against his chin like he knew what he was doing.

Jason leaned over me until I was as hidden as I could get under his body. Being short made it hard for him to shield me completely.

I told him. "Get off of me."

"No," he said. He'd seen the shotgun, too. And I realized he understood what it meant. I was not going to let him die a hero. I was certainly not going to let him die by spattering his brains all over me. Some things you recover from. Some things you don't. Wiping Jason's brains off my face might be one of the latter.

I let go of the knife in my right hand, letting the blade lie in the leaves. It took everything I had not to tighten my grip on the one in my left. I tried to keep my hand very still. In the dark, they might not notice. They hadn't, so far.

"Get off of her," the man repeated, "or I will shoot you both where you lay."

"Off, Jason," I said softly.

He moved enough so we could see each other's eyes. I looked to my right at the rifleman. Then I touched my chest and looked at Mel's brother. I was trying to tell him that the rifle was his problem and the shotgun was mine. I hoped he understood. Either he did, or he had his own plan, because he raised very slowly and got to his knees. I sat up, not too fast, not too slow. I kept my left hand in the leaves, knife gripped tightly.

The rifleman said, "Hands on your head, boy."

Jason didn't argue. He just clasped his hands on his head like he'd done it before.

No one told me to put my hands on my head, so I didn't. If we were lucky, they'd treat me like a girl. The rifleman had been unconscious when I hurt Mel. The one with the shotgun hadn't been there. What had Mel told them?

The rifleman said, "Remember me, asshole?"

"Is he asking you or me?" I asked. I scooted in the leaves a little closer to the guy with the shotgun.

"Don't get cute, chickie," the rifleman said. "We came here for both of you, but I want my piece of this one first."

Jason flicked his eyes to me. "You must be losing some of your charm, Anita. He wants a piece of me instead of you."

The rifleman had the rifle aimed very steadily at the middle of Jason's chest. If it were silver ammo, he was gone. The rifleman said, "Chuck."

Chuck, the one with the shotgun, grabbed my left arm. I opened my hand and let the knife fall before he raised my hand free of the leaves. The rifle was too steady on Jason for me to try stabbing Chuck. If I were lucky, I'd get another chance. If I wasn't, I was going to come back and haunt Jamil.

Chuck's hands were big and meaty. Thick fingers dug into my arm enough that if I lived, I'd be bruised.

"If you don't do exactly what I say, your girlfriend gets it."

I wanted to say, "Who writes your dialogue?" but I didn't. The shotgun hovered about an inch from my cheek. Pretty clear what it was. I could smell the oil in the gun barrels. It had been cleaned recently. Nice to know ol' Chuck took care of his weapon.

The rifleman did two things almost at once: He stepped forward and reversed his gun. The rifle butt smashed into Jason's chin. Jason swayed but didn't fall.

The rifle stabbed at him again, catching him high on one cheekbone. Blood spilled in a black line.

I must have moved, because the shotgun was suddenly pressed against my cheek. "Don't do it, bitch."

I swallowed and spoke very carefully with the cool metal against my face. "Do what?"

"Anything," he said. He jerked my arm for emphasis, grinding the shotgun into my cheek.

The rifleman said, "The doc said you could have broken my spine. Said I was lucky. I am going to hurt you, asshole, then I'm going to kill you. If you take it like a man, I'll let the girl go. You wimp out, and I do you both." He smashed the rifle into Jason's mouth. Blood and something heavier flew shining in the moonlight. The beating began in earnest.

I'd seen people hurt on the judo mat. I'd gone to martial arts tournaments. I'd even been knocked out a couple of times for real by bad guys. But I'd never seen a real beating, not like this. It was methodical, thorough, professional.

Jason made no move to protect himself. He never cried out. He just knelt in the leaves and took it. His face was covered in blood. His eyes fluttered, and I knew he was close to passing out. I had to do something before he lost it.

Through it all, Chuck had kept the shotgun pressed to my face so hard I knew I'd have the imprint of it on my skin. He never wavered, never gave me any chance to do anything. I was beginning to think that Chuck wasn't an amateur. I'd given up on Jamil or anyone else. It was just the four of us in the darkened woods. Just the smack of the rifle hitting flesh. The sound of the rifleman's grunt of effort as he tried to make Jason cry out.

Jason finally slipped to his side. He tried to keep his hands up, but he couldn't.

He leaned on his arms in the leaves. There was a fine, visible trembling in his upper body. He was fighting to stay upright.

"Beg me to stop," the rifleman said. "Beg me, and maybe I'll just shoot you. Beg me to stop, or I will fucking beat you to death."

I believed him. I think Jason did, too, because he just shook his head. He knew if he gave the man what he wanted, he would finish it.

I felt something, a prickling rush of warmth. It was Richard. He was out there somewhere. He opened the mark inside my body. It flowed over my skin and across Chuck's hand. "What the fuck was that?" he asked.

I didn't move or say anything.

"Answer me, bitch, you trying some magic shit on me?" He pushed the shotgun in even harder. If he kept it up, he was just going to shove it through my cheek.

"Wasn't me," I said.

He jerked me to my knees, and the shotgun wasn't pressed into me anymore. It was pointed out into the darkness for just a second. It was one of those moments. Everything slowed down, as if I had all the time in the world to draw the big knife down my back. The knife cleared the sheath. The shotgun and Chuck turned back towards me. I used the momentum of drawing the blade to swing it down and across. I felt the tip catch Chuck's throat, and knew it wasn't a killing blow. Something fell from the trees above us. A shadow only a little more solid than the rest. The shotgun's barrels were like two dark tunnels pointed at my face.

I heard the rifle behind me, but there was no time to look for Jason. There was just the gun pointed at my face, the shadow that I didn't have time to look up and see.

The shadow fell between us. The shadow had fur. The shotgun exploded on the other side of that furred shadow. The lycanthrope staggered backwards but didn't fall. The shotgun exploded again, both barrels. Before the echoes died, I was scrambling through the leaves, around the lycanthrope. Chuck's eyes were wild, showing white, but he had the shotgun broken down across his left arm. The two spent shells were gone and two more were being shoved into the breech. He was good.

I shoved the blade just under his big shiny belt buckle. A shudder ran through him, but he slid the shells inside the breech. I shoved the blade in until it grated on bone, spine or pelvic girdle, who knew. He slapped the breech closed against his arm like he was skeet shooting. I pulled the blade out of his body in a gout of blood.

He fell in slow motion, straight down to his knees. I lifted the newly loaded shotgun from his hands, and he didn't fight me. He knelt in the leaves and blinked out into the darkness. He didn't seem to be seeing me now.

Someone was screaming, high and wild. I glanced behind me, and it was the rifleman. He was sitting on the ground with one arm pointed up in the moonlight. The arm was missing from the elbow down. Jason was lying very still in the leaves. Zane was sitting beside him with blood on the back of his yellow T-shirt.

I stood and moved away from Chuck. He fell face forward into the leaves. He was alive enough to put his face to one side, but not to catch himself with his hands. The werewolf that had saved me was lying on his back, gasping for air.

There was a hole in his gut bigger than my two fists. There was a bitter smell almost like vomit but ranker. His intestines had been perforated. The smell told me that. The gut wound wouldn't kill him. Even if it was silver shot, it wouldn't kill him right away.

The second wound was higher up in the deep, broad chest. His black fur was wet to the touch, soaked with blood. I could have shoved my hands in the dark, wet hole, but I couldn't see shit. I couldn't see if the heart was damaged.

His breathing was wet, sloppy, almost strangled. I could hear bubbling coming from the wound. At least one lung had been compromised, that's what I was hearing. He was still struggling to breathe, so his heart had to be working, didn't it?

Real werewolves look sort of like movie wolfmen, but the movies never quite capture it. He, very definitely a he, lay on his back, gasping. It was like watching a dream breathe, except this dream was dying. I thought it was one of Verne's wolves, that I didn't know him. Then I saw the remnants of a white T-shirt caught on one shoulder like a bit of forgotten skin. I pulled gently on the cloth, and saw the smiley face on it. I stared into yellow wolf eyes. Stared down at Jamil. He'd done what a bodyguard is supposed to do. He'd taken my bullet. I took off my shirt and packed it into the hole in his chest. It took both my hands to cover the wound, to try and make a seal so he could breathe again. So he wouldn't bleed to death.

I whispered, "Don't die on me, damn it," then I started screaming for help.

26

My hands were wet with blood. The shirt had soaked up what blood it could, but more was pouring out. It was soaking into my jeans, covering my forearms. He stared at me with yellow eyes, mouth open, trying desperately to keep breathing. Long-clawed hands made small convulsive movements in the leaves. A prickling warmth spread under my hands. His skin moved under my hands like warm, furry water.

Shapes appeared out of the darkness. They looked like people, but I knew it was a lie. Werewolves—I was eyeball deep in werewolves.

"He needs a doctor," I said.

A dark-haired man with small, round glasses knelt on the other side of Jamil. He opened a large brown satchel and pulled out a stethoscope. I didn't question it. Most packs had a doctor. Never knew when you'd need some confidential medical care.

He pushed my hands from the wound. "It's healing. It wasn't silver shot." He shone a penlight into the wound. "What the hell is in there?"

"My shirt."

"Get it out before the skin heals around it."

The wound was healing. My hand barely squeezed into the opening. I got a handful of blood-soaked shirt and pulled. It came out in a long wet sloppy mess. Blood poured in a steady stream from one corner of the shirt. I let the shirt fall to the leaves. I would not be wearing it tonight. I had a thought that I was wearing nothing above the waist except a black bra. I didn't care.

"Is he going to live?" I asked.

"He'll live."

"Promise," I said.

He stared at me and nodded. Stray moonlight made his glasses look like blank silver mirrors. "I promise."

I looked down into Jamil's wolfish face. I stroked the fur across his forehead. The fur was both rough and thick and soft. "I'll be right back."

There were other people with Jason and Zane. Cherry with Zane, cradling him.

Nathaniel was kneeling by them, but his eyes were for me. There was even a man leaning over the rifleman. He was tying a belt off on the stump of his arm. Good. I wanted him alive. I had questions for him but not yet.

I knelt by Jason. He lay in the leaves on his side. A woman was tending his wounds. She was dressed in short shorts and a halter top, dark hair tied back in a loose ponytail. It wasn't until she turned her head that I realized it was Lucy. She held a penlight between her teeth and was searching Jason's wounds with sure hands, as if she knew what she was doing.

She answered my question before I asked. "He'll heal, but it's going to take a couple of days." Which meant if Jason had been human, the beating would have been fatal.

She looked at me then. Our eyes met from inches away. The makeup was a little less severe, but the face was still pretty by moonlight.

I turned away from her first. I didn't want to see what was in her eyes. I just didn't want to know. I knelt over Jason, started to touch his face, then stopped because the blood was still wet on my hands.

He said something very soft. I had to lean over him to hear it. "Let me lick the blood," he said.

I stared down at him, eyes just a little wide. "You're not dying, Jason," I said. "Don't get cute."

Verne said, "It's fresh blood, Anita. It's pack blood. It will help him heal."

I stared at him. The local Ulfric stood off to one side, tall and straight and slender, letting his medical personnel do their jobs. I started to ask him where the hell he had been while we got cut up, but Zane made a sound.

Zane seemed to be healing just fine from a rifle blast that would have cost a human his arm. But it hurt, and he made small pain sounds while the doctor worked on him.

"The blood will help them heal," Verne said. "Especially blood from someone as powerful as you are. Marianne feeds the pack sometimes."

Lucy said, "It really will help him." Her face was neutral as she said it.

I looked down at Jason. His face was a mask of blood. One eye was swollen completely shut. He tried to smile at me, but his lips were so badly swollen that the smile didn't work. It was like part of his face just didn't work right now.

I touched those wounded lips with my fingertips, brushed the fresh blood across his lower lip. He rolled his lip under, tasting the blood. But the movement made him wince. It hurt.

I laid two fingers against his lips and slid them gently into his mouth. He tried to suck them, but his mouth wouldn't work right. He licked the blood, swallowing almost convulsively. I drew the fingers out, and his hand came up to grab my wrist. I let him guide two new fingers into his mouth.

Richard spilled into the clearing, going to his knees in the leaves. Shang-Da was at his back like a good bodyguard. Richard's gaze met mine, and just the glance opened me up to him a little more. Without Jean-Claude to act as a buffer, the marks between Richard and I were stronger. He knelt there, his breathing coming in near-painful gasps. I could feel his chest rising and falling, almost as if I were breathing for him. I felt him look at the woman beside me. I saw Lucy for a second as he saw her. I saw the rise of her breasts swelling under the halter top.

The line of her cheek half in shadow, half in moonlight. She raised her face to meet my eyes like she could feel me looking.

"He still wants you," I said.

She gave a very small smile. "But not as much as he wants you."

The marks between Richard and I quieted. I couldn't feel him breathe or what he was thinking. He had cut me off. Afraid of what I'd see, maybe. "What happened, Verne? They were supposed to be safe in your lands," Richard said.

Cherry answered, "Jamil sent the three of us for help. He"—she pointed to a shadowy figure on the other side of the clearing—"wouldn't let us pass into the lupanar. He wouldn't take our request for aid to Verne."

The man stepped forward so a patch of moonlight showed him: tall, muscular, dark-haired, pale. "They are not pack. They have no right to demand passage."

Verne was just suddenly there, and the tall werewolf was on the ground. I hadn't seen him move. It was a speed that was dreamlike, impossible. But I'd almost seen it.

"I am Ulfric. I decide who is worthy and who is not, Eric. You are only Freki, third in the pack. You have one more battle before you can even challenge me."

Eric touched his hand to his face and came away with something dark and liquid. "I am not challenging you."

There was movement behind me in the leaves. Zane was crawling towards me, the wounded arm held close to his chest with a makeshift sling. "I came back to help while Cherry and Nathaniel argued with their watchwolf." I could feel an intensity to his gaze, even in the dark. "The blood's going to dry before he gets to it all." He stayed there in the leaves, just out of touching distance. His shirt had been ripped off one side of his slender chest. It hung in rags to one shoulder. He stared at me and even by scattered moonlight, I could see the need, not in his face but in his body, the way he held himself. He was asking for more than the healing of his body. If he hadn't been there, Jason would be dead now. Even a lycanthrope has a limit to the damage he can take.

Jason held the palm of my hand to his mouth, licking with long, lingering movements.

"You need the other hand?" I asked.

"It will be dried before he can use it," Lucy said.

I stared at her and hated her just a little. Hated her for having been in Richard's bed. Hated her for doing things with him that I'd never allowed myself to do.

"The wereleopard doesn't need the blood," Richard said. "He'll heal without it."

I just stared at him and held my hand out to Zane. He crawled to me on his knees and his good arm. I stared at Richard while Zane took my fingers into his mouth. He sucked on them like a hungry child licking the last bit of cake from a spoon.

"He's mine, Richard, mine as much as Jason is. I am Nimir-ra and lupa."

Richard stood. "I know what you are, Anita."

I shook my head. "You have no idea what I am." The moment I said it, I felt that warm, growing presence. Munin rising inside of me like a pool of warm water, spilling upward. Richard's mark seemed to bring it on sometimes. Or maybe it was just the way he made me feel. Lust or anger or both. I didn't fight the munin.

Marianne had said if I stopped fighting, that it would lose some of its control over me. I wasn't even sure I could fight it off completely. The best I could do was control it. I let it flow over me, down my arms into the two men.

Jason had worked his way to my wrist, tongue moving over the veins there. He'd been hesitating over the smell of fresher blood so very close to the surface. Now his good eye stared up at me, wide, a little scared.

I smiled down at him, and I knew that it wasn't just my smile. I was still here, but I wasn't exactly alone. Raina's thoughts lay over mine like a veil. I could see out, but it colored everything I saw. Her body, our body, wanted things, craved things that made me want to run screaming. But if I were careful, I could use her as she used me. It was like walking up a flight of steep, narrow stairs with a cup of scalding coffee filled to the brim. Careful, oh, so careful or it spills over the edge and you get burned.

The alternative to letting the munin have a little fun was what happened in the woods earlier. I did not want another full-blown memory with Jason and Zane hanging onto me. Not tonight, not ever. Jason couldn't handle it, and neither could I.

I looked down at Jason. "It's all right, Jason. Enjoy the blood while it lasts. I don't think you're going to get this offer twice."

He ran his tongue up my arm, working hard against the skin like a cat washing its own fur. Zane had sucked my fingers clean and had raised my hand up in front of his face, cradled in his good hand. He was licking very slowly, very thoroughly up my palm.

There was a sound behind us. I turned to see the rifleman. He was conscious and in some pain. The doctor with the round glasses was about to give him a shot.

I called, "Bring him to me."

The doctor and the werewolf with him looked across the clearing to Verne and Richard. Richard had moved across to the other Ulfric. They were discussing how everything had gone wrong. They could discuss things all night. I wanted answers.

"Don't look at them. Look at me. And bring him to me!" Raina's munin swelled outward and burst over me, over Jason, over Zane. It spilled over Lucy and brought a gasp from her throat. Everyone in the clearing got a taste, a preview if you like. It was getting harder to hold together. Harder to think.

They dragged the rifleman over to me. I knew what I looked like. I was wearing a black underwire bra that hid more than most bathing suits, but it was still a bra. I was still covered in blood. Jason and Zane were licking blood from my naked skin. It was strange and macabre and would work as a threat very nicely.

The doctor and the other werewolf threw the rifleman down in front of me. Jason and Zane ignored him, mouths on my skin. Zane slid his mouth along the edge of my skin, teeth grating ever so gently on the skin. His eyes slid to the rifleman, and I knew we would put on a show for him.

I felt Raina's munin like a warm glow. She, it, whatever, wanted to cover Zane's mouth with ours and taste Jamil's blood. Wanted to rip the bandage off his shoulder and lick the wound. With the thought came the knowledge that licking the wound would make it heal faster. Surely not.

The rifleman stared at me, his eyes showing mostly white. I could feel his breath, smell his fear. I could smell his fear like a miasma of sweat. I could taste in his scent how injured he was. I knew his skin would be cool to the touch from blood loss. All this from a smell. Shit.

"What's your name?"

The question seemed too hard for him.

"We can check your wallet. What's your name?"

He made an involuntary move to his back pocket with a hand he didn't have anymore.

"If we get him to a hospital soon," the doctor said, "they might be able to reattach the arm."

"If he answers my questions truthfully, you can take him to the hospital."

"What's your name?" I asked.

"Terry, Terry Fletcher."

"Okay, Terry. Who sent you to kill us?"

"I wanted to pay you back for making us look bad. That's all. Nobody was supposed to die."

Jason had cleaned my arm to the elbow. I could feel the passage of his tongue like a cool line running over and over my skin. Hot where he still touched me, cool where he'd just been.

"Lies won't get you to a hospital, Terry. Lies won't save your arm. Who paid you to hurt us?" I asked.

"He'll kill me."

I looked at him and laughed. The laugh was rich and thick enough to hold. It rolled out of my mouth and it wasn't my laugh. The sound raised the hairs on the back of my neck and made Jason hesitate, mouth pressed to my arm.

"Do you really think I won't kill you?"

A breeze had finally come up, hot and stale. Jason's mouth was cooler.

His mouth had healed enough to suck at my skin, but there was an edge of swelling to the side of his mouth. I wanted to kiss the wound, lick it, see if what I was being told was right. Could I really heal him?

I looked at Terry. "Tell me who paid you to hurt us. Tell me who sent you to kill us. Tell me everything I want to know, and the good doctor will take you to a hospital where they may save your arm. Lie to me, and your arm is just so much meat. Lie to me, and you die tonight, here, in this clearing. You think it over, Terry. I've got all night."

I leaned over Jason, drawing his mouth away from my arm. We kissed, and I could taste Jamil's blood, my skin, the faint remnant of the perfume on my wrist, and Jason's blood. His mouth had bled, and I could taste that, too. But it wasn't bleeding now. It was healing, and I could make it heal faster. It took everything I had not to press my mouth hard against his and force that warmth into him, everything I had not to press Jason's wounded body into the leaves and ride him.

I drew away from him, eyes closed. I opened my eyes and looked at the man. Jason moved to my stomach, licking along the top of my jeans. They were soaked in blood, and wouldn't really dry while I was still wearing them. Zane curved around to my back, licking along my spine. There was no blood there, and he had to stop at the spine sheath, but it looked good for our captive audience.

"Talk to me, Terry. Once I start fucking one of them, I really don't want to be interrupted." I leaned towards him just a little, and he flinched. I drew away from Jason and Zane and crawled towards Terry. I made the movement everything it was supposed to be: fluid, dangerous, sexual. Even now, his eyes kept flicking to my breasts so white against the blackness of the lingerie. Even now, he was still a man. I felt Raina's utter disdain of men. All that sex, and it was mostly hate. How terribly odd.

She was enjoying terrorizing the man. His wide eyes, the quick breath, the pounding of his heart. I could hear it. Hell, I could almost taste his skin on my tongue. Food, he smelled like food.

"Who sent you, Terry?" I made it a whisper, intimate, for his ears only. I reached out to him, and when I trailed my finger down his cheek, he whimpered. I leaned forward and licked a quick line the length of his face. "You taste like food, Terry."

I could feel the others at our back. Verne's pack responding to Raina's call. To my call. Through Richard, I was more lupa than I wanted to be. But now, tonight, it had possibilities. They came from every side, moving like shadows. Creeping closer, nearer, drawn by my desire and the man's terror.

He stared at them, watched them coming closer with wide eyes. He turned his head to watch them moving in. I kissed his cheek while he wasn't looking, and he screamed.

"Oh, God, please don't."

Raina's laugh fell from my lips. "Names, Terry, names."

"Niley, Franklin Niley. He paid us to run you off, said the cops wouldn't be a problem. Then he said kill you. You especially. He said kill that bitch before she queers my deal."

"What deal?" I whispered. Frank Niley was the employer of the muscleman Milo Hart. I hadn't seen him since. He was here for land speculation. Was he the buyer for Greene's land?

Terry's eyes flicked around to the waiting werewolves. "I don't know, honest to God. I don't know. He paid us five hundred apiece to hurt you. He made it five thousand for Chuck and me to kill you."

"Five thousand apiece?" I asked.

He nodded.

"It wasn't enough," I said.

"We didn't know you was a werewolf. We didn't know what you were." One of the shadowy throng was sniffing his leg. Terry's voice rose a little higher with every word. His next "I didn't know" was almost a scream.

Raina's munin was like a warm pulse behind my eyes. I leaned into the man, as if I'd kiss him. He backed away but bumped into the good doctor. My mouth hovered over the man's, but it wasn't a kiss I wanted. I stayed there, hovering over his mouth, frozen, fighting not to lower my mouth to his neck. Fighting not to sink teeth into his throat and tear. Fighting not to draw first blood and let the pack feed.

I started crawling back from him, as if I were the one that was afraid. "Take him to the hospital."

"You can't let him live," Zane said.

"I promised him if he talked, we'd take him." I caressed Zane's face. We stayed kneeling in the leaves, close enough to embrace when I didn't remember moving that close. "Take him, take the arm. And Terry," I said.

The man wasn't looking at me. He was staring at the waiting wolves.

"Terry," I said again. I was still caressing Zane, one hand buried in his short, white hair.

The man looked at me, eyes flicking back and forth madly as if he were trying to keep all of us in sight at once. "What? What do you want? You said I could go to the hospital."

"If you tell Niley about tonight, about what I am and what happened, I'll kill you." I lowered Zane's face until I planted a gentle kiss on his forehead.

"I won't tell. I won't tell anyone. Niley'd kill me if he knew I gave him up. He'd fucking kill me."

"Good," I said. I cradled Zane against me. He began to lick down my neck. He passed over my shoulder, licking a small line down my collarbone. He went lower, and I pushed him away, rough enough that he fell on his wounded shoulder. The world was narrowing down. I was losing the fight with Raina.

"Get him out of here—now!" I felt like I was going blind. I could see, but it was all different. I was fighting her and she didn't like it. She'd asked for violence, and I'd refused. She'd asked for sex, and I'd refused. Even dead, she was a hard lady to say no to.

I covered my eyes with my hands. I heard someone moving towards me. "Don't touch me."

"It's Marianne, child. Tell me what's happening."

I lowered my hands until I could see Marianne. She was still in the white dress with her long, pale hair. "You never met Raina, did you?"

"No, child."

I reached for her hand, and it was just a hand. There was no memory attached to it. No horror that the munin could share. "Help me."

She gripped my hand with both of hers. "It's too late to force the munin out. It must be made to want to leave."

I shook my head. "She won't leave."

"She's left you before."

I shook my head harder until my hair slapped my face. "You don't know what she wants. You don't understand what she wants. I can't. I won't."

Richard was there. He started to touch my shoulder, and I fell back into the leaves. One hand raised as if to ward off a blow. I did not want to know what Raina had done with him or to him. That was one image I did not need.

"What's wrong?"

"The munin will not leave until Anita does something it wants."

"You knew Raina," I said. "Tell her the kind of thing Raina enjoyed." It was rising inside me. I couldn't stop it. It rose higher and higher until the power spilled out of my mouth in a shriek.

He started to touch me and I crawled away from him. "No, no, no, no."

Marianne caught me, held me against her. She smelled like Ivory soap and lilacs. I knew I could have broken her hold, but I didn't want to. I wanted to be held. I wanted help. I needed help.

She smoothed my hair, rocking me like I was a child. "Anita, you must give in to the munin in part. You've done it before. Richard has discussed past events with me. When the munin leaves you this time, we will work together to make sure this does not happen again.''

I raised up enough to see her face. "Can you really stop this?"

"I can teach you how to stop it."

I stared into her pale eyes for a space of heartbeats. I could hear the strange click of her artificial heart valve. The munin was hinting that food would do as well as sex. Not as well, but it would do.

I pushed gently away from Marianne. "You're just food to her." I crawled back from her, slowly.

Marianne just watched me, kneeling in the leaves in her white dress. She was the only one in the clearing that was more than a shadow. All that whiteness caught the moonlight and glimmered. She looked like a target.

I stood, my breath coming in ragged gasps. I could taste my heart in my throat like a ball that I could have touched and played with. I looked around the clearing, desperate for a way out. Something that Raina would be content with and I could live with.

Zane was staring at me. Raina wanted him. But what she wanted had very little to do with sex. I went to him. He knelt in the leaves, staring up at me with large eyes gone silver with moonlight.

I fell to my knees in front of him and ripped the sling off his shoulder. He made a small grunt of pain, and Raina liked it. The problem with doing something to get the munin out was that the munin had to be in control enough for me to be willing to do what it wanted. Giving her more control seemed like a bad idea. But what she wanted was to plant our mouth over the wound in his shoulder, and I couldn't do it sober. There wasn't enough Raina in me yet to put my tongue in an open wound.

I crawled away from Zane and found Jason. I stared at him. He was almost a safety zone for me when the munin had me. The munin liked him, and I wasn't afraid of him.

I went to him, kneeling on all fours in the leaves, but knew if I touched him and I was still fighting the munin, we'd get another rush of horror. If I went to him, it had to be for real. I had to be willing to give in, at least a little.

His mouth was almost completely healed. The swelling in his eye was better. The blood or the munin—it really was working. He was healing. I knew the munin could be used for healing on lycanthropes. I'd done it once before, but not like this. That was back when Raina first made an appearance, and I hadn't realized how much trouble I was in. Now I knew, and I was scared and hated it. Raina thought that was hilarious, that dead, she scared me more than she had when she was alive.

I could feel her pleasure like a line of warmth through my body. The echo of her laughter chased through my mind and made gooseflesh on my arms. Being possessed by anyone would have scared me. Being possessed by a sociopathic nymphomaniac sadomasochist that I had killed personally was too frightening and too ironic for words.

Jason lay back in the leaves. I was very careful not to touch him as I crawled over his body on all fours. I knelt there on hands and knees and stared down at him, legs and arms wide so that we didn't accidentally touch.

His voice came hoarse, rough, as if something in his throat were still hurting. "You have a plan?"

"If I don't fight the munin, Marianne says no memories, just power."

He stared up at me. "You going to kiss it and make it all better?"

I nodded, my hair sliding over his face. "All better." I leaned my face towards his in a sort of push-up motion. Our lips brushed in a trembling line, and what not an hour before had been chaste and a little uncomfortable was suddenly changed. I broke the kiss and held my body off of his with fingertips and toes, my body above his. I could feel the trembling energy of his aura underneath me, pushing against the power of my aura, the power that was munin. I stayed above him, not touching, staring into his face. When we kissed again, the power poured from my mouth into his in a warm breath that burned through our bodies.

I let my body drop against his in an abrupt, violent movement that brought a cry of pain from him. The sound fell into my mouth and was swallowed in a wave of heat and power. I poured the munin into Jason. I poured me into him. I poured in through his mouth, down through my pores. Everywhere that skin touched skin, I seeped into him. I felt as if I were draining away into his body.

He behaved himself at first, hands at his sides, but the power rode us both. His arms locked behind my back. His mouth searched mine as if he were climbing inside. I straddled his body and felt him hard and ready even through our jeans.

He rolled me over suddenly so that he was on top. My body did nothing to protect itself. I locked my legs around his waist, and felt him pumping against me. Each thrust made things low in my abdomen jerk and tighten.

I swam upward through the power and started pushing at his chest. We were not doing this again. I was not doing this. "Off. Get off." My voice was strangled, hoarse. I swallowed the munin back enough to struggle inside and out.

Jason froze over me, then collapsed on top of me. His heart beat frantically against my chest. His breathing was rushed. He swallowed and managed to say, "If I said it was too late to stop, would you believe me?"

I started crawling out from under him. "No," I said.

He rolled onto his back, freeing me to stand. The bruises were gone. His face stared up at me as clean and innocent as it started. If I could only get this shit to work without the sex.

"My turn?" Zane asked. I turned, and he was kneeling in the leaves. He'd stripped off the remains of his shirt. I never really thought of Zane as a guy, not like that. But now he was kneeling in a splash of moonlight so that the shadows and light showed the muscles in his chest and stomach. His arms were lost in darkness. His face was a pattern of strong, clean flesh, gleaming pale, one half caught in shadows, like pieces of darkness. His nipple ring glinted silver, like a wink of an eye, an invitation. And that was all it took.

I stood in front of him, staring down, and did what the munin wanted. I grabbed his wounded arm and jerked it upward, forcing the shoulder to its fullest extension. He cried out in pain. The skin had closed over the wound, but it was there below the surface. I pressed my mouth to the wound and felt the muscles torn. The bone, already knitting, broken. I bit him, sinking teeth in enough to leave a mark and blew power into his skin. I healed it and fought Raina. She wanted to take a chunk out of his skin. A sort of joke, heal him and hurt him at the same time.

I pushed away from him before I could give in. I stumbled to my feet and realized that each time I used it, the power was growing. It was filling me like another person, something growing inside of me, pushing at my skin.

I staggered to Jamil and fell beside him to my knees. He'd changed back to human form, which meant he had been very hurt. I stared down at his nude body and fought with Raina not to touch him. Not to do what she wanted. Or not to do everything she wanted.

I ran my hands over Jamil's chest until I touched the wound. The skin was closed, but soft. I knew I could force my fingers inside him. I knew I could reach in and snatch his heart. Instead, I lowered my face to his chest and kissed the wound, gently, softly. I closed my eyes and took in the scent of him, the feel of his soft skin. Healing skin was always so soft, like a baby's flesh, tender and smooth. I put my hands over the wound and thrust that warm building power into him like a sword.

Jamil's eyes flew wide, and his spine bowed. He tried to scream, and I stole it with a kiss. I rode his body, straddling not his groin but the second, lower wound. I drew back from his lips and forced my hands low on his body. I healed him. I felt it leave my body in a warm rush. My hands slid lower. I brushed him and he was beginning to grow hard. I threw myself off of him. She'd healed him. Raina felt somebody owed her something for the healing.

I fought it until I fell back into the leaves and screamed. My body writhed and it was like my left side wasn't talking to my right. Like something was breaking inside me. That large, warm presence, that second body was trying to rise to the surface, trying to break the surface. Raina's beast was trying to come out. Trying to make me lupa in truth, but my body couldn't hold it. Couldn't give it a home. I was human, and no matter how much power you shoved into me, that didn't change.

Hands held me down. Richard's voice as if from a great height. "What's happening to her?"

"She's fighting the munin." It was Marianne's voice. I heard her voice close to my face, but I couldn't see her. It was like the world was vanishing into the dark. "Don't fight, Anita. Whatever happens tonight, tomorrow I can help you. Give in and live, or the munin will kill you."

"Anita, please, please!" Richard again.

"She will kill you if she can. She will kill you from the grave itself, Anita. Stop fighting. Embrace it, or it will destroy you."

I screamed, *"No!"* Then, suddenly, I could see again. I stared up into the tree-lined darkness. There was a sparkle of moonlight through the leaves. It seemed as bright as sunlight, only softer. I lay very still, blinking up at them all. Richard had my shoulders pinned. Verne had my legs. Shang-Da had my right arm. Lucy had my left. I'd been having convulsions. I remembered that.

Marianne was kneeling near my face, keeping my face still between her hands. "Anita?" she made it a question.

"I'm here." My voice was quiet but clear. I felt light and empty, but not alone. I wasn't fooled. The munin hadn't left. It wasn't finished.

"Is the munin gone?" Richard asked.

Marianne shook her head. "It's still here."

It made me think better of her that she wasn't fooled.

"Do we let her up?" Verne asked.

"Anita?" Marianne asked me.

"Let me up."

They let me go, slowly, as if almost afraid. Afraid of me or for me, I wasn't sure which. They moved away from me. Only Richard stayed kneeling. I leaned my back against him and let him hold me in his arms. I closed my eyes and let him take it all away for just an instant. I'd never had anyone's arms feel as safe as his. No one's.

My leg brushed something in the leaves. I pulled away from him enough to find my knife. I sheathed it.

From across the small clearing, Jason said, "Here's the other one." He held it up by the blade.

I went to him, taking the blade from his hand. I could feel all of them watching me. Like I was something new and uncertain that had just appeared. I sheathed the second blade.

Jason grinned up at me. "Don't take this wrong, Anita, but someday I'd like to do that for real."

"Why not tonight?" I said.

Jason stared up at me. "What did you say?"

I walked back across the clearing. I felt their eyes following me as I moved. I smelled of blood and power and flesh, and there was nothing better than that for attracting werewolves.

Richard stood there in his jeans and T-shirt. His hair foamed around his shoulders, a soft, rich brown in the moonlight.

I grabbed a fistful of his T-shirt and forced his face low enough for me to kiss. The kiss was long and full, and he tasted all the blood I'd had. Every skin I'd touched. I pulled his shirt out of his pants in a long motion, running my hands across his bare stomach, across the smooth hardness of his chest.

He grabbed my arms and pulled my hands away. "What's wrong with you?"

"Is she not good enough for you either?" It was Lucy striding towards us. Her impressive breasts strained against the white material of her halter top. Either she had very large nipples or she was cold, because the outline of her nipples was clear, even in this dim light.

I stared up at Richard. I'd been sleeping with Jean-Claude. He'd been sleeping with Lucy and Mira—mustn't forget Mira. It was fair that he had other lovers. Really. But I hated it and hated me for minding. Hated me for wanting him. Hated me for being with Jean-Claude and not being happy with it. Hated me for knowing that even if I'd been with Richard instead, I'd have been missing Jean-Claude. I was fucked no matter what I did.

I knew as I stared at her that the hands that held my arms with such tender strength had cupped those large, round breasts. I knew that she'd touched him, all of him. That she'd held him naked inside her. And I knew jealousy so strong that the only word for it was hate.

I pulled away from Richard and unsheathed one of the knives.

Shang-Da moved forward as if to step between us, but Richard stopped him and made him step back. He just stared at Shang-Da until he stepped out of reach, but you could tell from his face that he was really unhappy about it. I didn't blame him. Richard turned back to me, stared at me, but made no move to protect himself. I don't know if he didn't believe I'd hurt him or was sure I couldn't. I was sure I could.

My hand was already on the downward stroke before I could stop myself. I sliced through his shirt, not deep, but the wound bled.

He winced, eyes so lost, hurt. Fuck him.

Shang-Da was there, and it was Richard who struggled with him. Richard who kept him from grabbing me, disarming me, hurting me.

I put the tip of the blade against my chest and drew downward over my heart. The pain was sharp and immediate, but it was shallow. I wasn't hurt. The blood trickled down between my breasts like tickling fingers. The blood was very dark against the whiteness of my skin.

Richard started towards me, and Verne caught him. "It's her choice," Verne said.

"It's not her. It's Raina," Richard said.

But in a way he was wrong. Raina had finally found something that called to both of us. We both wanted him to suffer. We both felt betrayed. And neither of us had a right to it. We'd both betrayed him in our own ways.

Words that I didn't know spilled from my lips. "Your heart to mine, mine to yours. Lupa to your Ulfric. But not to your bed, nor you to mine." I threw the knife into the ground so it stuck, thrumming. I could feel the blade in the earth as if I'd disturbed some large, sleeping beast. The power burst over me from the ground, from me, and something let loose in a liquid rush inside me. I was dizzy and on my knees without meaning to fall.

I stared up at Richard, still struggling, and said, "Help me." But it was too late. I felt the munin blow outward like a wind. And every man it touched caught the scent. I could almost feel their bodies react. I knew what Raina had done, and if it were to be her last night in the driver's seat, she couldn't have chosen better. Short of killing me, it was the perfect revenge.

I fell to my knees, fighting not to finish the ritual, but I could feel them in the dark, eager. I was giving off scent, and it wasn't just the blood. The words were pulled from my throat as if by a hand. Each word squeezed out until it hurt to speak.

"Claim me again if you can, my Ulfric." I stared up at him and saw the look on his face. It was wild, and part of me was pleased. God help me. My own jealousy had given her the keys to me. I stared around at the shapes in the dark. I could feel them like a growing tension in the air. It was like the air before a storm, so heavy it was hard to breathe through the growing power. You could feel the lightning growing in the air, coming closer, but this storm was waiting for me. Waiting for me to move.

Marianne was beside me. "Get up," she said.

I struggled to my feet, and she helped me.

"Now, run," she said.

I stared at her. "What are you talking about?"

"You've declared yourself Frejya. Now, run, before they lose patience and take you here."

I knew what she meant, but I had to have her say it out loud. "Take me?"

"If the munin does not come to the front, it will be rape, but it will still happen. Now, go!" She pushed me towards the dark. I stumbled and stared around the clearing one last time. Richard's face was tormented, horrified. Shang-Da was at Richard's shoulder, and he was angry. Angry with me. Jason's face was as neutral as I'd ever seen it, as if afraid to show me what he was feeling. I caught Roland's face, too. I'd met him an hour or two before, but his face wasn't neutral. His face was hungry, anticipatory. And I knew that they'd do it. That someone, somewhere would have me unless I killed them. Two silver blades and an entire pack of werewolves. Not good odds. And Richard would do everything he could to save me—everything.

"Shang-Da," I said.

The tall bodyguard stared at me. I could feel the weight of his gaze in the moonlit dark.

"Richard's life means more to me than my own safety, Shang-Da. Don't let him die," I said.

He stared at me, then gave one sharp nod.

Marianne grabbed my arm and said, "Go!"

I went. I flung myself into the trees, into the dark beyond, and ran. I ran as if I could see in the dark. Flinging myself into half-perceived openings, trusting to the forest the way you trust to water, knowing it will part before you without question. I gave myself over to the night woods like I'd learned to do as a girl. You don't run in the dark in the forest with your eyes. You run with the same part of your brain that makes the back of your neck prickle. I ran and leaped and dodged, and knew it wouldn't be enough.

27

A *howl cut* the night in a long, mournful line. There were growls and a sharp whimper, cut so short I knew someone was hurt, maybe dead. Would they really kill each other for the privilege? Real wolves didn't do this shit. Only people could take a nice, sane animal and screw it up this badly.

I slipped going over a log that was bigger around than a small car. I fell, sprawling. I lay there for a moment on the ground, catching my breath, and I didn't have the faintest idea what to do. I didn't so much hear the werewolves as feel them in the ground under my hands. I knew they were out there in a way I hadn't before the munin invaded. I pressed myself against the huge log, and my hands found an opening. It was partially hollow. I crawled into the black opening, hand with knife in front of me, half expecting to meet a raccoon or snake, but there was nothing but the feel of the cool, rotted wood under my bare stomach and the weight of the great fallen tree above me.

I knew they'd find me. That wasn't the point. It would take them a little time to get me out of the hole. I was trying to buy time. I wasn't even sure time for what. I needed a plan, and I didn't have one. The munin thought that Richard might save us. That thought scared me all on its own. Richard was sort of squeamish when it came to killing. The thought that he might get himself killed trying to save me was almost worse than me getting caught. I would probably survive being raped. I wasn't at all sure I'd survive Richard's death. Of course, having never been raped, maybe I was jumping to conclusions. Maybe I wouldn't survive.

I heard them moving around the log. More than one, more than two. Three, four? Shit.

Claws ripped at the rotted log, and I screamed, one of those short yips that is almost exclusively a girl sound. I heard one of them rolling around on the ground. I felt the rush of energy as he shifted into wolf form. And just like that, he was out of the running. If you lost human form before the lupa you were chasing, you couldn't mate with her. You went furry, you lost. The rules about going Frejya had never been written for a human who had no other shape. We'd lose the lesser wolves to their beasts, this close to full moon with sex and violence in the air.

We'd maybe lose half a dozen, maybe a dozen, to their beasts. Fifty wolves in Verne's pack altogether, a dozen helped.

Something heavy hit the side of the log. I managed not to scream. At least that was an improvement. I heard the sounds of scuffling. At least two of them were fighting. But I was almost sure there was a third.

The fighting stopped, and there was a loud crack as if something brittle and wet had broken. The silence was so heavy, my heartbeat was thunderous.

The log moved. I froze as if just holding very still would save me.

The end of the log near my feet lifted into the air. The cavity that had hidden me kept me trapped as that one end raised slowly into the air. The fallen tree was at least six feet around. I didn't know how much it weighed, but it was heavy. A tall, bearded man was lifting it. He pushed it overhead, palms flat against the wood. He smiled down at me, his teeth white against the beard.

His voice was more growl than words, "Come out, little one."

Little one? I crept very carefully out from under the huge log. It was a crushing weight. A fine trembling ran through his body all the way to his feet. It was not effortless to hold the fallen giant up. I stayed crouched just beside his leg. He'd have to put the log down before he could touch me. His smile widened, as if not moving away from him was a good sign for him.

I shoved the knife into his belly and rolled away from him, tearing the blade along the meat of his stomach as I moved. He looked surprised as he fell to his knees and the tree fell on top of him. It pinned him to the ground, and I didn't wait to see if he could get out from under it. There were two bodies on the ground. One man's skull was smashed open, and thicker things than blood licked onto the ground. In the dark, everything was grey and black. The second guy might have had a pulse, but I didn't check. I ran.

I felt the rushing of air and looked in time to see a blur of motion. A man hit me from the side in a flying tackle. I was on my back with him on top of me, one arm pinned between us. I had a second to recognize Roland, then I slashed at him with the knife. He jerked back too fast to see, and his fist was suddenly connecting with my chin.

I didn't pass out, but my body went limp. The knife fell from my fingers, and I couldn't stop it. Part of me was screaming silently. The other part was saying, "Oh, what pretty trees." When I could move again, my jeans were halfway down my thighs. The only thing that kept me that much dressed was the jeans were tight and wet with blood. Wet jeans peel slowly.

"Roland, don't do this."

He kept pulling on my jeans like I hadn't said anything. I didn't want him to hit me again. If I passed out, it was all over. He was having trouble getting my jeans over my Nikes, because the jeans won't go over my Nikes.

I raised up on my elbows and tried to be friendly, reasonable, and wondered where the hell my knife was. "Roland, Roland, the shoes have to come off first." Maybe if I were helpful, I'd get brownie points. At least maybe I could stall. Where was Richard?

Roland wrapped my jeans in one hand, effectively trapping my feet. "Why help me?" he said. His voice was still too deep for his slender chest, his words still carefully spoken. That nervous energy still crawled along his skin, vibrating like summer heat on a road. He was no different, but everything else had changed.

"Maybe I just don't want you to hit me again," I said.

"I don't want to be stabbed, either," he said.

"Fair enough."

We stayed that way, staring at each other, me propped on my elbows, him kneeling at my feet. It was almost as if he didn't know what to do next. I think he hadn't expected me to be calm. Crying, anger, maybe even eagerness, he was ready for, but I gave him nothing. I was friendly, helpful, as if he'd asked me directions to a restaurant I knew. I even felt calm, strangely. It had a faintly surrealistic air, as if it wasn't really happening. If he touched me, it was going to seem all too real, but as long as he stayed where he was, I was fine.

He pinned my jeans with his knee and started taking off his shirt. The shirt was okay. I was fine with that. He had a nice chest, pleasant to look at. As long as his pants stayed on, I was fine. Where the hell was Richard?

He undid the snap to his pants, and my nerves just weren't that good. I didn't want to try and contact Richard in case he was fighting. Using the marks was distracting. But I wanted some help. I was betting that Roland didn't wear underwear. I won my bet.

I sent out a call to Richard, and he was fighting. I saw through his eyes for one dizzying second. He was fighting Eric. Great. I broke contact as quickly as I could, but I knew it cost him a second of concentration. I was on my own.

Roland pushed his jeans to his knees and seemed to think that was sufficient, because he started to crawl up my legs. Oh, this was romantic.

It wasn't Richard who came to the rescue. It was a man I didn't know. He tackled Roland, much as Roland had tackled me. They rolled off me and down a small incline into a hollow. I started pulling my pants up as fast as I could.

There was a movement behind me, and I turned, pants just above my knees and no weapon in sight. It was Zane, one arm held tight to his chest. Nathaniel came out of the dark behind him. Nathaniel held out his one good hand to me. "Hurry."

I hurried. Nathaniel took my hand and pulled me into the trees. He ran like liquid spilling through every crack and shadow. I tried to stay behind him, trusting that if his body could go through the openings, so could mine. I jumped when he jumped, weaved when he weaved, even if I couldn't see the obstacle. His night vision was better than mine, and I didn't question it. I had a sense of Zane behind us, following like smoke in our wake.

A chorus of howls broke out to our right. Nathaniel pulled me faster through the trees until I fell headlong, and a jagged branch sliced my cheek open. It missed my eye by a wish. "Shit, Nathaniel."

"They're coming," he said.

"I know." I touched my hand to my cheek and came away with blood. "Fuck."

"I won't let them take you," Nathaniel said.

I stared up at him. He was only three inches taller than I was. He couldn't have outweighed me by thirty pounds. It was muscle, but he was small. Size counts if everyone you're fighting can lift large trees.

"They'll kill you, Nathaniel."

He didn't look at me, just kept staring out into the dark as if he could hear things I couldn't.

Zane leaned against a tree, looking at me. His good hand was rubbing his bound arm like it hurt. I bet it did.

"If they take you, you'll fight," Zane said. "They'll kill you." He closed his eyes. "This is one time when you can't protect yourself, but maybe we can."

"You'll both die," I said.

Zane shrugged with his one good shoulder, casual, like it didn't matter.

The thought came that it would all be over if I had sex. It would end then, and only then. Raina came back in full force, spilling through me. She wanted Nathaniel, and that she could not have, not with my body. Fucking Nathaniel would be like child molesting. I wouldn't do it.

Zane. Zane would do. Raina had always been fickle. I got a sudden visual so strong it made me blush. Was there anyone that Raina hadn't slept with? I wasn't going to do either of them. No way.

Then they'll die. I wasn't sure if it was my thought or the munin. Either way, we were right.

Jason limped into sight. I knew him just by the shape of his shoulders and his hair. Either I hadn't healed him completely, or he'd been in a fight. Maybe both. I'd broken contact before I finished. The munin was saving the deeper healing for sex. For her it was the toll to be paid for services rendered. No payment, no healing. Like a drug dealer giving just a taste.

Jason gave me a very strange smile as he entered the trees near Nathaniel and Zane. He slid down until he was sitting with his back against a small tree trunk. He let out a sigh.

We all looked at him. A scream tore our gaze back to the woods. Out there, close, they were fighting. Another howl rode the still, hot air. The sound was close enough to make my scalp prickle.

The trees we had stopped at were at the bottom of a hill. It was familiar. "Are the cabins just up there?"

"Yes," Zane said.

"If you go to the cabins, they'll follow," Jason said. "Can't have the tourists seeing it."

"Fuck that," I said, "Some of them won't follow to the cabins because of the tourists. I say we go and board ourselves in."

"It won't end until someone wins," Jason said. He sounded tired or maybe discouraged.

"And up there are two vampires who are on my side." I started up the hill. Nathaniel and Zane followed at my heels. Jason just sat there. We were a quarter of the way up the hill before he pushed to his feet to follow. When all this shit was over, I'd ask what was wrong. Right now, there was no time.

Figures appeared through the trees. Zane gave a little push to my back. "Run," he said, "I'll delay them."

Nathaniel turned with him, facing down into the dark and the danger.

"No," Zane said, "you go with her, Nathaniel." He looked at me. "I'm learning what it means to be an alpha. Nathaniel doesn't know how to fight."

Nathaniel looked from one to the other of us. He finally settled on me. "What do you want me to do?"

I thought about that for a second, studying Zane's so-careful face. "I'd say come with me, but I'm not leaving Zane behind."

I reached back and touched Zane's hand. "I won't leave you to die."

"Damn it, Anita, if you're not here, they won't kill us. They'll just hurt us and go after you," Zane said.

"I'm sort of bait," I said.

"Yes."

"Don't die on me, okay?"

"I'll do my best," Zane said.

I squeezed his hand. "Don't do your best, just don't die. You, either," I said to Jason.

He shook his head. "I have to stay with you. Richard's orders."

"Why?"

He shook his head and glanced back at the dark figures moving through the trees. Closer, always closer. "Later. Now, we move."

He had a point. We moved and left Zane alone in the dark with at least five figures gliding through the trees. They put on a burst of speed as we neared the crest of the hill. I cleared the hill on my knees, and we were at a flat-out run across the gravel parking lot.

I thought, *Damian*. He opened the door as if I'd spoken. He was standing there with a surprised look on his face. It isn't often you see a thousand-year-old vampire shocked. I had a moment to think how we must look. Me bloody, in just the black bra and blood-soaked jeans. Jason running with a noticeable limp. Nathaniel running full out behind us.

We cleared the doorway. Damian shut the door behind us. He locked it without being told. Smart vampire.

"What—" he started to say.

"Block the windows and door," I said.

Asher grabbed the heavy wooden desk like it weighed nothing and shoved it over the window. "Do we have nails, or am I forced to hold it in place."

Something struck the window, shattering glass around the edges of the desk like glittering rain. Asher was staggered backwards. Damian joined him, and they shoved the desk against the window. The door shuddered as something heavy threw itself against it.

"He's not going to make it in time," Jason said.

Nathaniel stood in the center of the room like he was lost. "What now?"

The door shuddered again.

Jason went to the door, leaning against it. "Nathaniel, help me!" Nathaniel joined him, putting his shoulder against the quaking wood.

Hands pushed past the edge of the table. Asher took one hand off the table to break the wrist like match wood. There was a scream, and the hand pulled back.

He spoke as if he wasn't using almost all his strength to hold the table against the broken window. "May one ask why the local werewolf pack is trying to kill us?"

"They're not trying to kill us," Jason said. "They're trying to fuck her." He leaned his entire back against the door. Whatever was at the door left abruptly, and Jason almost fell against the suddenly quiet door.

The window cleared, too. It was suddenly terribly quiet, too quiet, as the old saying goes.

"What is going on?" Damian said.

"Later," Jason said. His eyes looked almost wild. "Ask me why Richard told me to stay with you."

I stared at him. "Okay, why did Richard tell you to stay with me?"

"This ends when you have sex with any of the lukoi."

I stared at him harder. "Come again."

"If it looks like someone else will get there first, he told me to do it."

"Do it?" I said. I walked around to the nightstand. "You mean, do me."

Jason had the grace to look down. He nodded.

I opened the drawer and took out the Firestar. I tucked it down the front of my jeans. I took the Browning out next and clicked off the safety. "Nothing personal, Jason, but I've got a different plan."

"I didn't say I liked the plan," Jason said. "I may joke about it, and I would love to be with you, but Jean-Claude is my master, too. He'd kill me."

I glanced at Asher. He gave a very small nod. "Probably."

"And if you let someone else get to me because you were squeamish?" I let it be a question.

"Richard doesn't kill easily," Jason said, "but if I let someone rape you, for that he'd make an exception."

I waggled the gun in the air, barrel pointed at the ceiling. "Lucky for you I'm armed."

Jason nodded.

Glass broke in the bathroom. "Shit!" We'd been stupid. "Stay at the doors," I said. I kicked the bathroom door in, already sighting down my arm. I had a glimpse of a man trying to squeeze a large body through the small window. I hit the wildly swinging door with one hip and fired into the mass of the man. He screamed and fell back through the opening.

I yelled, "I've got this window covered."

Sounds of fighting came from outside the cabin. Screams turned into growls. I felt the rising energy and knew that people were losing human form. I could feel them slipping away, slinking through the trees. I could almost smell the musk of their fur. The munin swam back up so suddenly and so purely that I staggered against the door that I was using to steady my aim.

I turned away from the window to stare across the room at Jason. Raina was fine with that. She didn't care who. If it caused Jean-Claude distress or cost Jason his life, that was dandy. I slid down the door slowly, eyes closed, the flat of the gun barrel pressed to my forehead.

"Someone else needs to do this window," I said. I hoped I'd spoken aloud. I was having trouble telling.

Jason must have filled them in because no one asked what was wrong. I felt Damian brush my legs as he went into the bathroom. The feel of his passing caused things low in my stomach to clench. I glanced up at him, and he was frozen in the doorway as if he'd felt my body's reaction.

He stared down at me with his cat green eyes, and I knew as surely as I knew anything that if I told him to come to me, he would have done it. What I didn't know for sure was why.

"Damian," Asher said, "the window."

Damian stayed where he was, staring down at me. "I can't."

"Order him to watch the window, Anita," Asher said.

I went to my knees, free hand sliding up Damian's pants leg. I slid my hand up his thigh and shook my head. I grabbed a handful of his green silk shirt and pulled him down to me. He stayed on the balls of his feet, knees on either side of my body. I went to my knees and kissed him.

I slid my tongue between the delicate points of his fangs. I'd perfected the art of French kissing a vampire. Practice, practice.

He tried not to kiss me back. He drew back enough to whisper, "You taste like blood, other people's blood." Then he locked his mouth to mine like he would breathe me into himself. His long, pale hands cupped my face, slid behind my head in the warmth of my hair.

I pressed my body against him. The Firestar was still in front of my pants. The gun pressed into his groin. I ground it into him until he made a small pain sound. The Browning was lost on the floor.

There was a sound at the bathroom window. I drew back from the kiss, and Damian began to run his lips down my neck. I saw the man crawling through the window as if down a long crystalline tunnel.

I tugged the Firestar from my pants and pointed it. I sighted at the center of his forehead. His eyes widened, and he suddenly spilled backwards into the night. Not so far gone that he didn't want to live. The question was, how far gone was I?

Damian's mouth hovered over the big pulse in my throat. His tongue curled over it, caressing. He was asking for permission. But it wasn't that kind of blood I wanted to donate tonight. Raina had no interest in just opening a vein.

I wrapped my free hand in his long, blood-red hair and jerked his face up to me. "Don't bleed me, fuck me."

Asher yelled, "Jean-Claude will kill him."

"I don't care." The moment I heard myself say it, I swam back up. It was like pushing aside a wet curtain that clung to my face, suffocating, trying to mold itself to my body and keep me, drown me.

I crawled away from Damian into the room. I said, "Watch the damn window, Damian, and stay away from me."

He stood in the doorway, uncertain.

Asher said, "You heard your mistress. Do as you're told."

I heard him walk into the bathroom. Heard his boots crunch on the broken glass. I stayed on all fours, my head hanging down, my breath coming in gasps. The Firestar was still gripped in one hand. I squeezed it tight until my hand ached. I ground the feel of the gun butt into my skin. This was real. This was real. Raina was dead. She was just another kind of ghost, damn it.

I heard someone crawling towards me. I raised my head to find Nathaniel staring at me with lilac eyes. I screamed and scrambled back from him. He was a victim and Raina liked victims. I held my hand out to him as if to ward off a blow.

I ended with my back against the bed, gun squeezed in both hands, rocking back and fourth.

Nathaniel crawled towards me. He crawled like he had muscles in places he shouldn't have, in a graceful roll that was almost snakelike, as if his spine had too many parts. He put his face so close to mine that when he spoke, I could feel his breath on my face. "I'm yours, Anita. You are my Nimir-ra. My queen." He was very careful not to touch me. He stayed that last fraction of an inch away, so that it was my decision. But it wasn't mine.

I tried to tell him to get away from me, but my voice wouldn't work. I couldn't speak. I couldn't move. All I could do was hold onto that last ragged edge of control and not move my mouth that last space. I fought with all I had left not to kiss Nathaniel. Because whoever I fell on next was it. The munin was wearing me down. Even my self-control wasn't limitless. I didn't want it to be Nathaniel. That helped me hold on.

There was a knock at the door. It was so unexpected that I screamed. The scream pushed Nathaniel back to his knees, a little farther out of reach, but still too close.

Asher asked, "Do you open it?"

I shook my head, not as a no, but I couldn't say. I couldn't think. I was fighting too hard to not throw my clothes off and fuck something in the room. That was taking about all my concentration.

Maybe Asher figured that out for himself, because he said, "Who is it?" Very civilized.

The answer shocked us all, I think. "It's Richard."

Jason was on his feet, opening the door, before anyone could tell him to do it. The outer surface of the door was clawed and broken. Richard stood there in the doorway. His T-shirt was in rags, still clinging to his shoulders but so ripped apart that you could see the bloody wounds in his tanned skin. He walked through the door a little unsteadily. Zane and Shang-Da came behind him.

Zane looked unhurt, but Shang-Da's face had been opened from forehead to chin. His eye sat in a mask of blood. He closed the door and looked at me with cool eyes.

I was glad to see all of them. But I couldn't move. If I moved, it was over. I was putting everything I had into just staying where I was. If I moved anything, the control was gone. A tear squeezed out of one eye and fell in a hard, hot line down my cheek. I stared up at Richard and wanted to say so many things and couldn't say any of them. Words would break me into a million glittering pieces.

Richard walked to me. He stood over me, staring down. I didn't look up. He didn't so much kneel as collapse to his knees in front of me.

I put out a hand to steady him, and the munin spilled across my skin like a flame. The Firestar fell to the floor with a thunk. I grabbed a handful of the torn T-shirt, balled it into both my fists, and pulled him those last few inches into a kiss.

His lips were dry. I licked his mouth, running my tongue over his lips until they were like wet, rubbed velvet to kiss. I slid my hand inside one of the tears to trace the cut I'd made over his heart.

His breath came out in a sharp hiss as if it hurt. He grabbed my wrist. I slid my other hand inside the tear and found another wound to probe. He grabbed both my wrists in his hands. You forget how large Richard is. He doesn't seem intimidating physically, but he could have held both my wrists in one hand. He forced my arms back at my sides. I tried to pull my hands free, and his grip tightened. He leaned over me, but not for a kiss.

He licked the edge of the knife wound on my chest.

I gasped, half in pain, half in pleasure.

He ran his mouth down the wound until he came to the soft upper part of my breast. He bit gently into my flesh, not hard enough to leave a mark, just hard enough that I felt his teeth. I made a small moan.

He raised his face to look at me. He let go of my wrists and put a hand on either side of my face. He trapped my face between the strength of his hands and forced me to stare into the perfect chocolate brown of his eyes.

"Anita, can you hear me?"

I tried to move forward for a kiss, but his hands held me trapped. My hands found his chest, explored the smooth flesh, the torn wounds. I tried to press my body forward against his, but his hands held my face, and I couldn't go closer.

"Anita, Anita, talk to me. Are you in there?" The grip on my face was almost painful.

I didn't push the munin aside. It fell back. I felt Raina leave me enough for me to answer. "I'm here." It was a whisper.

"Do you want this?" he asked.

I started to cry; huge, silent tears slid down my face.

"Do you want me now, like this?" He shook my face between his hands, as if he could shake me back to myself.

I slid my hands over his, cupping him against me while I cried. Did I want him? "Yes," it was a whisper.

"Now, like this?"

The question was too hard for me. I curled my fingers against his hands, trying to move them from my face. I started tugging at his hands. "Kiss me, please, kiss me. Please, Richard, please!" I was crying again and couldn't have said why.

He leaned into me, hands still on either side of my face. He kissed me. His lips pressed against mine like heat. His tongue parted my lips, and I tried again to move forward, but his hands held me. He leaned into me, pressing his mouth against mine. He kissed me like he was tasting me, as if he'd reach into my mouth with his tongue and his lips and pull me inside out.

I shuddered in his hands from the feel of his mouth. Eyes closed, my hands limp at my sides, letting him do it all. His hands slid, very slowly, from my face. He never stopped kissing me as his fingertips slid down my bare shoulders. His hands hesitated over the shoulder straps for the spine sheath, as if he didn't know what to do with it.

I opened my eyes, started to lift my hands up to help him. He grabbed my hands and held them down at my sides. "I'll figure it out," he said softly.

I stared up at him. I could barely breathe around the need. I wanted his naked skin pressed against mine. I grabbed one of the tears in the T-shirt and ripped it wider. "Off."

He shook his head. "Not yet."

I wanted to fall on him like a ravening wolf, and he was so controlled. I could feel his need. Feel his need as great as my own, and yet he could kneel there, so close, so very close.

"Everyone out," Richard demanded.

I'd forgotten that we still had an audience. I hid my forehead against Richard's chest. My hands slid behind his back, trying to press myself against him.

Asher said, "What of the other wolves?"

"I made a pact with Verne. It's over except for this."

I stared past Richard's broad shoulder into Asher's scarred face. His face was carefully blank, empty, unreadable. I had a thought: what was he hiding? But most of my thoughts were the scent of Richard's skin. The smell of fresh blood. The clinging scent of earth and pine and leaves. The light, salty dew of sweat on his body. There was no room for regrets. There was only the warmth of his body pressed against mine.

"If you take her like this, it will be very like rape," Asher said.

"I'm going to try very hard for it not to be," Richard said.

Asher gave a small sound that might have been a laugh. *"Bon heur,"* he said, and left. Good luck, he'd said. He'd said it in French, and it made me think of Jean-Claude.

So close to the warmth of Richard's body I could feel him hard and ready, and I thought of Jean-Claude. I wanted to wrap myself in Richard. I wanted to pull him around me like a blanket, but what would my other lover say? That thought pushed the munin away better than anything else had.

Months in Jean-Claude's bed, and I still wanted Richard. *I* wanted Richard, not Raina, not munin. *I* wanted him. I wanted him so badly I couldn't think about anything but the feel of him in my arms. But it wasn't fair, not like this. Not with Raina riding me.

She poured over me like a warm bath. This was her price. This. That she be here with us for the first time. That even this would always be part hers. My skin ached to be touched. My body hurt with a need I'd never known.

When the door closed behind them, Richard pulled me away from his body. He held me away from him with his hands on my forearms while I struggled to get closer. I needed him. Needed him.

I reached for him, crying, "Richard, please, please."

He spun me around until I fell against the foot of the bed. He put a hand in the middle of my back, keeping me turned away from him. He slipped the shoulder straps of the spine sheath off, sliding them down my arms. He threw the sheath across the room to bang into the wall. Then he leaned over me, a hand on either side of the bed. He leaned his face over until his hair brushed my face. He molded his body against mine, arms wrapping my arms against my chest. He held me with his body and his arms, pressing us so close I could feel his heart beating against my back.

He whispered against my cheek. "If at any time you want to stop, say so, and it's over. I'll go."

I made a small sound very like a whimper, and said, "Fuck me, Richard, fuck me, please."

A shudder ran through his body from toes to head, and his breath fell out in a long sigh. He pulled back enough to undo the back of my bra, then he slid it slowly off my shoulders. He used the bra straps to lower my arms to my sides again. He pushed the bra off my arms, and it fell to the floor.

His hands slid over my waist. His hands felt hot. He slid upward slowly, so slowly that I wanted to cry out. His hands spilled over my breasts, cupping them, kneading them. His fingers rolled my nipples, and I did cry out.

He turned me to face him, almost throwing me against the bed. His arms locked under my buttocks, and he lifted me, still on his knees. His mouth found my breasts. His tongue flicked across my nipple, fast, quick, wet.

I leaned into him, and his mouth slid over my breast, sucking it. The feel of his mouth on me was almost too intense. It made me want to cry out, to squirm, to say stop, and never stop. I made a small sound like a sob as he released my breast in one long pull so that the nipple stretched between his teeth. He moved to the other breast, harsher this time, using more teeth. He bit gently around the soft tissue of my breast, then licked the nipple, rolling it with his tongue. He gave one quick bite that hurt, and I was suddenly on the floor looking up.

He knelt over me and put his hands into the tears in his T-shirt and ripped it open, exposing the hardness of his chest, his arms. There were two slashing claw wounds, one high and one low. The high one had gone over his nipple, and blood had dried on the tip of it.

I sat up and reached for him. He didn't stop me. I ran my tongue over his chest, over the wounds, and he gasped. I licked a quick tongue over the bloody nipple, and when he didn't chase me away, I locked my mouth around it and fed. I sucked the wound clean, pulling hard enough that I reopened the wound.

It was his turn to cry out. He pushed me back to the floor, gently. He took off my shoes and socks, and I let him. My heart was beating so fast it hurt, pounding in my throat like a trapped thing.

His hands went to the tops of my jeans. When the top button went, it made my stomach jerk. He unzipped my pants and started sliding them down my hips. I helped him push the drying cloth down my legs. He pulled the jeans off in one last motion, and I was left lying, wearing nothing but the black panties that had matched the bra.

He was on his knees, staring down at me. His hands went to his own jeans, unsnapping them. He hesitated. "I've wanted this for so long, Anita. Wanted you like this, but not . . ."

As much as Raina and I hated each other, her essence and I had a moment of perfect understanding. I went to him, kneeling.

"Oh, no, you don't. Don't go all Boy Scout on me now." My hands finished unzipping his pants.

He caught my hands, eyes searching my face. "It's you again."

"Yes," I said, "it's me." I pulled my hands out of his, and he let me. "Undress for me, Richard; let me see you naked."

"You've seen me naked before," he said softly.

"Not like this," I said. "No stopping, no questions."

He stood up. "This will change everything for me, Anita. It has to change some things for you, too."

I covered my eyes with my hands and gave a little scream. "Oh, for God's sake, Richard, stop talking. I want your hands on my body. I want you inside me so badly I can't think. How can you stand there and be reasonable?''

Something fell across my hands and face. It was his jeans and underwear. I sat up and found Richard naked. I just looked at him. The perfect golden brown of his skin was uninterrupted from the curve of his calves to the narrowness of his hips, the swelling of his groin, the flat hardness of his chest, and the sweep of his shoulders. His hair fell across one side of his face in a golden brown mass that left half his face in shadow.

I stood and walked towards him. I was scared. Nervous didn't cover it. Scared and eager. I put my hands on his chest and rose on tiptoe to offer him my lips. We kissed, and the movement made my body fall full against his. The feel of him hard and naked with nothing between us but the black lace panties made me shudder and fall back from the kiss.

His hands caught me around the waist and kept us pressed together. Then he was suddenly on his knees, hands pulling down my panties in a motion so quick, it was violent. I was suddenly naked, with him kneeling in front of me, staring up. There was a look in his eyes that made things all over my body tighten.

He put his large hands on the insides of my thighs and spread my legs. He slid his hands along my thighs until they cupped my buttocks, bringing my groin against his face. He laid his cheek against me, licking a quick line along my hip. My heart was beating so hard, I couldn't get a good breath, but I could talk. "Please, Richard, please. Please."

He slid one hand between my thighs. One finger slid inside me. I shuddered, head back, eyes closed.

"You're wet," he said.

I opened my eyes and stared down at him. "I know." My voice sounded breathy.

"Raina was like that."

"She still is," I said. "Make her go away."

He licked the inside of my thigh, forcing me to spread my legs just by licking, nuzzling his mouth against my skin. The first touch of his tongue between my legs made me gasp.

He kissed me there like he'd kissed my mouth, all tongue and exploring. He licked me in long, sure strokes, then he found just the right spot and sucked. I could see his eyes staring up at me while he did it. There was a dark light in his eyes, something more primitive than we have words for. It had nothing to do with being a werewolf and everything to do with being a man. It was waves pulsing along my body. The sensations were overwhelming. It felt so good it was almost too much, a pleasure so great it was almost pain. He pulled me into his mouth until the warmth spread from my groin upward in a golden rush that left the world hazy and edged with white gauze like I was seeing through a mist. With the last drop of pleasure, I felt Raina leave. The munin was gone when he lowered me to the floor.

His mouth was glistening. He used the remains of his shirt to wipe his mouth. He said, "I could always go brush my teeth."

I just shook my head. "Don't you dare." I held my arms out to him.

"Is she gone?" he asked.

I nodded. "Just me, just us."

"Good," he said. He moved over me and laid his naked body the length of mine. He was too tall for missionary position. I'd have suffocated against his chest. He propped himself up on his arms in a sort of push-up position. He slid inside me, and it was tight and wet and I could feel every inch of him working its way inside of me. When he was sheathed inside of me, he stared down at me. His eyes had gone that startling amber of a wolf. They were almost orange gold in the tan of his face.

He worked in and out, once, twice, three times, gently, as if making room. Then his hips caught the rhythmn. I slid my hands to his buttocks until I could cup them while he pushed himself inside me. I dug my fingernails into the smooth hardness of his flesh. He pumped faster, harder, still holding most of his weight on his arms and shoulders.

I raised my hips to meet his body. Without his body trapping me under him, I could move. A rhythm began between us, a wave of movement and heat and muscles moving together.

Something opened inside of me, inside of him. I felt the mark that bound us open like a door. What fell through that door was a warm, golden, rush of power. It spilled over me, into me. It raised every hair on my body as if it were an electric current.

Richard lifted me in his arms, still sheathed inside me. He half-carried me, half-flung me to the bed. He collapsed on top of me, and I was lost under the warmth of his skin and the weight of his chest. It was as if his power rode my skin; every thrust sent a line of warmth pouring inside of me. It was as if I were bathing in the golden warmth of his body inside and out. It grew in golden pulses with every thrust. The pulses turned to waves that made my body tighten around him.

He cried out, but didn't come. He raised back up on his arms, only his hips and legs pinning me to the bed. His eyes were still amber, still not human, and I didn't care. I watched his beast ride up through those alien eyes. I watched it look down at me from Richard's face. I watched thoughts slide across that handsome face that had more to do with food than sex, and nothing to do with love.

His hands flexed in the bed on either side of me. I heard the cloth tear, ripping. I turned my head and saw his hands lengthening, turning into human claws. Those claws ripped the mattress with a thick, tearing sound.

I stared up at Richard and couldn't keep the fear off my face. "Richard," I said.

"I would never hurt you." He whispered it, and when his hands convulsed in the bed, bits of white bedding sprang in the air.

I said, "Richard!" My voice was high, not panicked, but close.

He sliced claws down the length of the bed and pulled out, rolled off me. He rolled onto his side into a tight ball. His hands, his claws were long and thin with his fingernails turned into something monstrous, dangerous.

Shit.

I smoothed my hands down his back. "I'm sorry, Richard. I'm sorry."

"I won't change during sex, Anita, but this close to the full moon, it's hard." He turned his head to look up at me, and his eyes were still amber. His hands began to re-form, shrinking back to human. I watched them change, felt the rush of energy like a wave of dancing insects on my skin.

I knew that if I left him like this, he'd never recover. It wasn't my loss, not really. It was that this would confirm his deepest fears: that he was a monster and only fit to be with other monsters. Richard was not a monster. I believed that. I trusted him not to hurt me. I trusted him more than I trusted myself sometimes.

"Roll over," I said.

He just looked at me.

I rolled his hips over, and he let me. He wasn't completely hard now. Nothing like having your lover scream for help to take the fun out of it. I touched him, and he shuddered, eyes closing. I held him in my hands and stroked him until he grew warm and hard.

I slid over him, and he was almost too big from this angle, almost too much. It was more intense with me on top, sharper somehow. A small moan escaped him.

"I love you, Richard. I love you." I moved above him with him so deep inside me, it felt like I should be able to taste him.

His hands slid around my waist, then to my breasts. The feeling of his hands on me while I rode his body was almost too much. I moved my hips gently at first, then faster. I forced him into me, hard and fast and deep, until I wasn't sure if it felt good or hurt.

I felt the orgasm growing. I felt it filling me up like warm water in a cup, filling from the bottom up. I felt it flow over me in small spasms.

Richard's breathing changed, quickened, and I knew he was close. "Not yet," I whispered, "not yet."

He dug his hands into the bed on either side of me. I felt his hands go. I felt them slip their skin. I felt it like the small release it was, like an echo of what his body was doing inside of me. The claws tore into the bed like nails. I heard the mattress material make that heavy ripping sound, and it was too late.

The orgasm caught me in a burst that bowed my spine and made me cry out. It washed over me in a skin-shifting, nerve-jumping dance as if every part of me were trying to leave every other part behind. For a shining second, I felt skinless, boneless, nothing but the warm roll of pleasure and the feel of his body underneath me. Only his body anchored me, only the feel of him going inside me in one great release reminded me where I was, who I was.

I opened my eyes and found his eyes brown and human. He raised his hands to me, and I fell against his body. I laid my head on his chest and felt his heart beating against my cheek. I lay there feeling his body pulse underneath me. His arms holding me.

He laughed, and it was joyous. He raised my face to his and kissed me lightly and carefully. "I love you, too," he said.

28

Warm. He was so warm. He? My eyes were wide open, and sleep fell away like a crash of glass. I was left lying in bed with my heart pounding and a tanned arm flung across my stomach. I stared up that arm and found Richard on his stomach, hair flung over his face like a curtain. I was lying on my back, sheets down past my waist, trapped under Richard's arm.

I raised my head back and found Van Gogh's *Sunflowers* above the bed. Richard's cabin. We'd done too much damage to mine.

I had a very strong urge to pull the sheets up and cover my breasts. Okay, okay, Richard had seen the whole show last night, but this morning, I wanted to cover up. I was embarrassed. Not big, awful embarrassed, but little, confused embarrassed.

I realized I was lying there with my arms tucked across my chest, as if I was hiding. Richard's arm looked very dark against the pale white skin of my stomach. Jean-Claude had remarked that my skin was almost as pale as his. I'd had enough moral problems with premarital sex with the undead. My one comfort had been that I was monogamous. Now I didn't even have that. Whoredom had finally arrived just as my Grandmother Blake had always warned. In a way, she was right. Once you have sex with anyone, sex becomes more of a possibility with others.

The drapes in the cabin hadn't been pulled completely. Morning sunlight fell through the white sheers and spilled over the bed. I'd never seen a man's body by morning light. I'd never slept with a man and awakened beside him. Oh, once with Stephen, but fully clothed with guns and bad guys about to come through the door isn't quite the same thing.

I reached out towards Richard's arm, tentative. You'd think after what we did last night, I'd be braver, but I was almost afraid to touch him. I'd had sexual fantasies about Richard, but this—this was the big one. To wake up beside him, warm and alive. God forgive me, but I valued that.

I touched his arm lightly so that all I really touched were the small golden hairs, no skin. I brushed upward just above the skin until there was nothing but the bare skin of his upper arm and shoulder. I drew my fingertips over the warmth of his skin. He was incredibly warm. Warmer than skin temperature, almost fevered.

I felt him wake, a tension in his shoulder and back that hadn't been there before. I turned my head, and his brown eyes were staring at me through the thick curtain of his hair.

He rose up on one elbow and smoothed his hair back from his face. He smiled, and it was the same smile that had melted me into my socks a hundred times. "Good morning," he said.

"Good morning," I said. I had pulled the sheets up over my breasts without thinking about it.

He wiggled closer, which made the sheets at his waist slide down to reveal the smooth expanse of his buttocks. He kissed me, soft, tender, then rubbed his face along my cheek until his breath was warm against my ear, then farther back into my hair. He was giving me a wolf greeting. He kissed lightly down my neck and stopped at my shoulder, which was about all that was uncovered.

"You seem tense," he said.

"You don't," I said.

He laughed, and the sound made me shiver and smile at the same time. It was a laugh I'd never heard from Richard. It was very masculine, very . . . something: possessive, satisfied maybe.

I felt heat creep up my face. Being that embarrassed made me feel silly for being embarrassed. "Oh, hell."

"What?" he asked. He stroked the side of my face.

"Cuddle with me, Richard. Sex is great, but when I thought of this moment, I thought of you holding me, spooning me."

His smile was gentle, pleased. He turned on his side and even spilled the sheets back over his waist. He raised his upper arm.

I rolled onto my side so my back faced him and snuggled against his warm body. He was a little tall for spooning, but we wiggled around with much giggling and stupid comments until we found a position that felt right. I wrapped his arm around me, sinking into the warm curve of his chest and all the rest, and let out a sigh. The feel of his naked groin pressed against me wasn't so much exciting as it just felt right. I felt possessive of his body, of him. I wanted to hold him like this forever.

His skin was almost hot. "You feel like you've got a fever," I said.

"It's the full moon," he said. "By tomorrow night when the moon is completely full, my base temperature will be over a hundred and one."

He pushed my hair aside until he could nuzzle the back of my neck. It made me break out in gooseflesh. I squirmed. "That tickles."

"Yes," he said, "it does." I could feel him growing larger against my body.

I laughed and rolled over on my back. "Why, Mr. Zeeman, you seem happy to see me."

He leaned in for a kiss. "Always."

The kiss grew, becoming more. I moved my body against his and had one leg wrapped around his buttocks when he scooted back, going onto his knees.

"What's wrong?" I asked. We'd already established last night, after it would have been too late, that I was on the pill. He'd been nicely horrified when he thought of it. Since werewolves can't get or carry disease, once the pregnancy issue was addressed, you were safe. Which also explained why I wasn't worried about licking blood off of the lycanthropes last night. Gross, but not dangerous.

"I can't," Richard said.

I looked down the length of his body. "Oh, I'd say you're ready."

He blushed for me. "You saw me last night, Anita. One day closer to the full moon, my control will be worse, not better."

I lay back on the bed. "Oh." I was disappointed. Minutes before, I'd been worried that we'd given in to our lust, and now I was sad that we couldn't do it again. Trust me to be logical about my men.

"I'm glad you're disappointed, too," he said. "For a minute there, I thought you were going to get up out of bed, say it had all been a terrible mistake, and go back to Jean-Claude."

I covered my eyes with my hands, then made myself look at Richard while I said it. He sat there looking too scrumptious for words, but I couldn't let it slide. If he was thinking this meant I'd dump Jean-Claude, I couldn't let it slide. But I wanted to. "What do you think last night meant, Richard?"

The smile faded around the edges but didn't disappear completely. "It meant something to me, Anita. I thought it meant something to you."

"It did. It does. But . . ."

"But what about Jean-Claude." Richard said it softly, but it had to be said by someone.

I nodded, hugging the sheet to my chest. "Yeah."

"Can you go back to just dating him after last night?"

I sat up and reached for his hand. He gave it to me. "I've missed you so much, Richard. The sex is nice, but . . ."

He raised eyebrows. "Nice, just nice?"

I smiled. "It was wonderful and you know it. And you know that's not what I meant."

He nodded, hair swinging into his eyes. He brushed it back. "I know. I've missed you, too. I'm lost on weekends without you."

I pressed his hand to my cheek. "Me, too."

He sighed. "So you're going to be with us both?"

I let his hand fall to my lap, still holding it. "You'd go along with that?"

"Maybe." He leaned in and kissed my forehead, ever so gently. "Notice I didn't ask you to give him up and just date me."

I touched his face. "I know, and I'm both relieved and surprised. Thank you for not asking."

He pulled back enough to see my face clearly. He looked very serious. "You don't like ultimatums, Anita. If I push you, I'll lose."

"Why do you want to win, Richard? Why don't you just dump me?"

He smiled. "Now she gives me the choice."

"I've given you the choice before," I said. "I mean, I know why Jean-Claude puts up with me. I help his power base. You'd be better off if you picked out a nice, safe werewolf for your lupa. I hurt your power base."

"I'm in love with you," he said simply.

"Why do I feel like apologizing for that?" I asked.

"I've been doing a lot of thinking about why I couldn't hate you. Why I couldn't let you go."

"And?" I had pulled the sheets around me like a nest so I wouldn't be naked. If somewhere in this conversation he did dump me, I didn't want to be naked. Silly but true.

Naked didn't seem to bother Richard. Frankly, it was distracting to me. "I need a human girlfriend. I need someone who isn't a monster."

"A lot of humans would be happy to be your snuggle bunny, Richard."

"I found that out," he said, "but I didn't have sex with any of them."

"Why not?"

"Farther away from the full moon I have better control. The eyes don't go, let alone the hands. I can pass for human, but I'm not human. You know what I am, and even you almost couldn't accept it."

There was nothing I could say to that, so I didn't try.

He looked down at the bed, fingers playing along the edge of the sheet. His voice grew very soft. "My first year in the pack, one of the other new wolves had a human girlfriend. He crushed her pelvis while they were making love."

My eyes widened. "A little too rough," I said.

Richard shook his head. He let his hair fall this time, hiding most of his face. "You don't understand, Anita. Strength is strength. We can pick up small cars and throw them. If you don't realize your own strength, you can't control it." He looked at me suddenly, staring out at me through his hair. It was a gesture that Gabriel had been fond of, as if the hair were comforting or reminded them of fur. "You're the first nonlycanthrope I've ever had sex with since I became one."

"I'm flattered, I guess."

"I was still scared I'd hurt you like my friend had hurt his girlfriend or in a thousand other ways. During sex you lose control. That's part of the fun. I can never lose control, not completely, unless I'm with another lycanthrope."

I looked at him. "What are you trying to say, Richard?"

"I'm saying you date both of us. Have sex with both of us. I will hate it, but . . ."

I stared at him. I didn't like that he didn't want to finish the sentence. Made me nervous. "What, Richard?"

He brushed his hair back with both hands until his face was clean and tight. "You date both of us, and I'll keep dating other lycanthropes."

I just kept staring at him.

"Say something," he said.

I opened my mouth, closed it, tried again. "You mean you'll keep having sex with Lucy."

"Not Lucy, she's . . . You've met her. She could never be lupa of our pack."

"So you're going to keep auditioning lupas?"

"I don't know if I am or not, but I know if you sleep with Jean-Claude, I have the right to sleep with other people."

I couldn't exactly argue with him, but I wanted to. "You're still trying to get me to give up Jean-Claude."

"No," he said. "I'm just saying that if you're not monogamous to me, then why should I be monogamous to you?"

"No reason, I guess. Except . . . I thought we loved each other."

"We do. I do." He stood and picked up his jeans from the floor. "But you don't love me enough to give up Jean-Claude. Why should I love you enough to give up everyone else?"

I stared at him and felt tears begin to fill my eyes. "You bastard."

He nodded. He slipped into his pants without underwear, zipping carefully. "The real bitch is that I do love you enough to give up everyone else. I just don't know if I can share you with Jean-Claude. I just don't know if I can stand the thought of you in his bed. The thought of him being with you like that drives me . . ." He shook his head. "I'm going to take a shower. I've still got trolls to study."

I couldn't even begin to think about what he'd just said. It was too much all at once. When confused, concentrate on business.

"I need to come with you and talk to the biologists. We need to find out if Franklin Niley is the buyer for the land. The guy who lost his arm last night was afraid of him. It takes someone pretty scary to make a man hesitate when he's surrounded by werewolves. Your normal real estate types don't have that kind of juice."

Richard strode back to the bed. He picked me up around the waist and kissed me. He crushed me against him, like he'd crawl in through my mouth and pull me around him. I was breathless when he sat me back down on the bed.

"I want to touch you, Anita. I want to hold your hand and do silly, goofy grins. I want us to act like people who are in love."

"We are in love," I said.

"Then for today, let's throw all the doubts out. Just be with me the way I've always wanted you to be. If I want to touch you today, I don't want to be afraid not to. I want what happened last night to change things."

I nodded. "All right."

"You don't look sure," he said.

"I'd love to go around holding your hand, Richard. I'm just realizing that . . . Oh, hell, Richard, what am I going to tell Jean-Claude?"

"I asked Jean-Claude how much difference the marks made to you, how much harder you were to hurt physically. He figured out why I was asking. I ended up telling him the whole sad story about my friend and his dead girlfriend."

I looked at him. "What did he say?"

"He said, 'Trust yourself, *mon ami*. You are not your friend with his so-sad tale. And Anita is not human. Through us she is more than that. Both of us huddle around her humanity like it is the last candle flame in a world of darkness. But by our very love, we make her less human, and more.' "

My eyebrows went up. "You remembered all that?"

Richard looked at me, and it was a long, considering look. He nodded. "I remembered because he's right. He's right. We both love you in our ways for similar reasons. It isn't just power that draws him to you. You saw him as a monster. The fact that you don't anymore makes him feel less like one."

"It sounds like you guys have been having some long conversations."

"Yeah, it's been a real male bonding experience." He sounded bitter, tired.

"It also sounds like you discussed whether you were going to make love to me with Jean-Claude before you discussed it with me."

"Never directly," he said. "Never word for word."

"It still sounds an awful lot like asking permission," I said.

Richard was back in the bathroom doorway. "What would you have done if we'd made love and Jean-Claude had tried to kill me afterwards? Would you have killed him protecting me?"

I just looked at him. "I don't know. I . . . I wouldn't have let him kill you."

Richard nodded. "Exactly. Whether Jean-Claude killed me or I killed him or whether you killed one of us, even if we survived the death with the marks dragging us down to the grave, even if you and I survived, you'd never forgive yourself for killing him. You'd never recover from it. We'd never have a life together. Even dead and gone, Jean-Claude would haunt us."

"So you tested the waters," I said.

Richard nodded. "I tested the waters."

"You asked his permission," I said.

He nodded, again. "I asked his permission."

"And he gave it," I said.

"I think that Jean-Claude knows if he kills me, you would kill him. That you'd sacrifice all of us for one of us."

It was true. It sounded sort of stupid put that way, but it was still true. "I guess I would."

"So if I can stand it, and you want to do it, you date both of us. You share both of our beds." His hands balled into fists at his sides. "But if I can't have monogamy from you, you can't have it from me. Fair?"

I looked at him and gave the barest of nods. "It's fair, but I hate it. I hate it a lot."

Richard looked at me. "Good," he said and closed the door. A moment later, I heard water running. And I was left naked in his bed with everything I'd ever wanted offered to me on a silver platter. So why was I sitting there, hugging my knees to my chest and fighting not to cry?

29

I wanted to get dressed. I'd brought my suitcase over from my cabin for just that reason, but I needed a shower. I'd had too much fighting, too much sweating, too much blood, too much sex last night not to shower. So I sat huddled in a nest of sheets that smelled of Richard's cologne, my perfume, the sweet scent of his skin, and sex. I had managed not to cry. In fact, if Richard had just admitted undying monogamy to me, I'd have joined him in the shower. But he hadn't, and I was confused.

There was a knock on the door. It startled me, and I almost just ignored it. Almost pretended we were still asleep or otherwise occupied, but the second knock was more insistent. The third was so firm, the door shook.

"Police, open up."

Police? "I'm not dressed. Just a minute." I really hadn't packed a robe. But I also had a sudden bad feeling. If he just wanted us out of town, why come this early? Why wouldn't he give us time to pack and get out? Unless he didn't care if we left anymore, at least not on our own. Maybe he'd known about the hit last night. Maybe he meant to kill us. I'd dealt with rogue cops before, once. It made everything harder. If I met them at the door with a gun, it would give them an excuse to shoot me. If I didn't protect myself and they shot me anyway, I'd be pissed.

"Open the fuck up, Blake."

I didn't pick up my gun, I picked up the telephone. I didn't call a lawyer. Carl Belisarius was good, but not good enough to help me stop a bullet. I called Dolph. What I wanted was another witness that couldn't be shot. A cop in another state seemed a good bet.

The phone was near my pillow. The pillow had the Browning under it, but if I had to go for the gun, I was dead.

Dolph answered with "Storr."

"It's Anita. Wilkes and his deputies are about to break down my door."

"Why?"

"Don't know yet."

"I'm putting a call through on the other line for the state cops there."

"Why? Because the cops broke down my door when I didn't open it?"

"If you don't want help, why are you calling, Anita?"

"I want to be on the phone to another cop when they come through the door."

I could hear Dolph breathe for a second or two, then, "Don't have your gun in your hand. Don't give them an excuse."

And the door burst open. Maiden was first through the door. He cleared the door going low. The tall deputy with the scar took high. They both trained guns on me. Maiden's big forty-five looked right at home in his big hands.

I just stood there, one hand clutching the white sheet to my chest, the phone in my other hand. I was very careful not to move. I stood frozen with my heart beating so hard it filled my throat like air.

Dolph's voice was in my ear: "Anita?"

"I'm here, Sergeant Storr." I didn't yell it, but I made sure my voice carried.

Sheriff Wilkes came in behind his deputies. His gun was holstered. "Put down the phone, Blake."

"Why, Sheriff Wilkes, fancy meeting you in Richard's cabin on such a lovely morning."

He strode across the room to me. He yanked the phone from my hand, and I didn't fight him. I didn't think he was here to kill anyone, but he was here to hurt. I was going to try very hard not to give him an excuse to do it. Whatever he did today, I wouldn't make it easier for him.

He put the phone to his ear just long enough to hear Dolph, then hung it up. "A phone call won't save you this time, Blake."

I looked up at him and gave him big brown eyes. I did everything but flutter my lashes at him. "Do I need saving, Sheriff Wilkes?"

The phone rang. We stood there, letting it ring. Seven rings and Wilkes picked it up and hung it up again without putting it to his ear. He was so angry, he was shaking. A fine tremor ran through his hands, his arms. His face was flushed with the effort not to do something violent or regrettable.

I stood there as neutral as I could manage. Looking as harmless as I could manage. With my long hair tousled from sleep, wearing nothing but a sheet, it wasn't hard to look harmless.

The bathroom door opened, and Richard just stood there in nothing but a towel. Guns turned and pointed at him. He froze in the doorway with steam curling around him, spilling out into the room like clouds.

There was a lot of screaming. Cops yelling, "Hands up! Get on the floor!" Richard laced his fingers on top of his head and took it all pretty calmly. He'd heard them. He'd stepped out of the shower, knowing they were out here. He could have gone out the window, but he hadn't.

Of course, if they really thought we were dangerous, they'd have gone in after him. But they'd let him come out to us. They weren't treating us like criminals. They were acting like the criminals.

Richard was on his stomach with Maiden's gun pressed to his back. Handcuffs went on. The scarred deputy pulled him to his knees, using his long, wet hair. The towel stayed on. Tough towel.

The phone rang. It rang three times. Each one seemed louder than the last.

Wilkes grabbed the entire phone and jerked it out of the wall. He threw it against the far wall, where it lay silenced. He stared down at me, breathing so hard it looked painful.

He spoke very carefully, as if afraid to yell, afraid that if he lost control of even his voice, it would be over. "I told you to get out of my town."

I kept my voice very soft, very unthreatening. "You gave me until sundown today, Wilkes. It's not even nine o'clock in the morning. What's the rush?"

"Are you going today?"

I opened my mouth to lie. Richard said, "No."

Shit.

Wilkes grabbed me by the arm and pulled me towards Richard. I tripped on the sheet, and he dragged me the last few feet. I put most of my effort into clutching the sheet to my chest. Bruises were okay; being naked in front of them was definitely not okay.

Wilkes half-threw me, half-dropped me on the floor beside Richard. Richard tried to get to his feet, and the scarred deputy hit him in the shoulder with the butt of the shotgun.

I touched Richard's arm. "It's all right, Richard. Everyone just be calm."

The scarred deputy said, "God, you are a cold bitch."

I just looked at Wilkes. He was the one in charge. He was the one who would dictate how bad this was going to be. If he stayed calm, so would the others. If he lost it, we were in deep shit.

Wilkes just stared down at me. His breathing had eased, but his eyes were still wild. "Leave town, Mr. Zeeman. Leave town today."

Richard opened his mouth, and I squeezed his arm. He'd tell the truth unless I made him shut up. The truth was not what we needed right now.

"We'll leave, Wilkes. You've made your point," I said.

Wilkes shook his head. "I think you're lying, Blake. I think Richard here is planning to stay. I think you'd say anything to get us out of this room right now."

It was the truth, and that made it hard to argue. "We'd be fools to stay, Wilkes."

"I think Richard is a fool. A softhearted, tree-hugging liberal. It's not you we have to convince, Anita. It's your boyfriend."

I didn't argue with the boyfriend part. I couldn't anymore. I leaned a little into Richard. "How do you plan to convince him?"

Wilkes said, "Thompson."

The scarred deputy gave up his place in back of Richard to Maiden. Maiden looked uncertain, as if things were moving too fast for him, but he kept his gun out, not pointed at Richard, sort of resting against his face.

"Thompson, we never patted Ms. Blake down for weapons."

Thompson smiled, a big, good-humored smile. "No, we did not, Sheriff." He grabbed two handfuls of sheet and dragged me to my feet. He jerked hard enough that I stumbled into him. He locked one arm behind me, holding me against him. His Sam Brown belt pressed into my stomach but kept the rest of him from touching me.

I felt more than heard Richard behind me. I looked back. Maiden had traded his gun for his baton. He had the baton underneath Richard's chin, pressed against his throat above the Adam's apple so he wouldn't accidentally crush his windpipe. It looked like Maiden had had training.

Thompson said, "Don't struggle yet, lover. You ain't seen nothing to get excited about yet."

I didn't like the sound of that at all. He grabbed the sheet and tried to tear it out of my hands. I fought him. He stepped back from me, holding the sheet, and yanked. It was hard enough I stumbled, but I kept the sheet.

"Thompson," Wilkes said, "stop playing goddamn tug-of-war and do it."

Thompson slid his fingers down the front of the sheet and gave it all he had. It pulled me to my knees in an ungraceful heap, but I won. I kept the sheet. I was pissing him off, not my best idea, but I'm not good naked. I never feel nude. I feel naked.

He grabbed me by the back of the head and used my hair to throw me up against the bed. I could have pulled away if I wanted to leave a handful of hair and blood in his hands, but it would hurt, and unless I was willing to start killing people, this was going to happen. The more I fought it, the worse it was going to be.

As long as it was just a little slap and tickle for Richard's benefit, I could handle it. That's what I told myself while Thompson yanked me half across the bed by my hair.

He held me down by my head, putting enough weight on that one arm that it almost hurt. The sheet had pulled down from my back to my waist. He jerked it down farther, exposing my butt.

I struggled just a bit then. He pressed down so hard on my head that my face was pressed into the bed enough that it was difficult to get a full breath. The mattress wasn't firm enough for this shit. I lay very still. I did not want him to push my face down into the mattress. Passing out would be bad. You never wake up better off than you started.

"Stay," Thompson said, "or I'll put handcuffs on you."

I did what he said. Richard could break a pair of handcuffs. I couldn't. As much as I loved Richard, I didn't want him to be the only person free in a room full of cops gone bad. If it really came down to having to fight our way out, it would mean killing. To my knowledge, Richard had never killed a human being. He was squeamish enough about killing other shapeshifters.

Thompson pulled my arms out from under my chest and spread my arms to either side on the bed. He slid his hands over my hands, my arms, as if bare skin could hide any weapons. His hands slid down my bare back, sloping along my waist and lower. His hands slipped over my buttocks and between my thighs, spreading my legs. It was too reminiscent of last night with Richard, too intimate.

I raised up. "What is this, a rape theme down here?"

Thompson slapped me on the back of the head. "Be still, or I'll make you be still." But his hands weren't playing with my thighs. He could hit me more and harder if his hands didn't wander lower.

"This can all stop, Richard," Wilkes said. "This can all be over. Just leave."

"You'll kill the trolls," Richard said.

I turned to look at Richard. I wanted to scream at him, "Just lie!" We'd figure it out later, but I wanted him to just lie now. I couldn't say that out loud. I stared at him and did something I had rarely attempted. I tried to open the bond between us. I reached out to him not with my hands or with my arms, but it felt like reaching. I moved out towards him with things I couldn't see but could feel. I opened something inside him. I felt it give. I saw the widening of his eyes. I felt the beat of his heart.

Thompson grabbed my shoulder and shoved me back to the bed. It broke my concentration.

There was a knock on the door. The other deputy, who had been with Thompson that first day, stepped into the doorway. He gave the room a once-over, eyes lingering on me on the bed, but his face stayed neutral. "There's a crowd gathering, Sheriff."

"A crowd?" Wilkes said. "The tree-huggers are out studying their precious trolls. If it's just the bodyguards, fuck them."

The deputy shook his head. "It's a shit load of people, Sheriff."

Wilkes sighed. He looked at Richard. "This is your last warning, Zeeman." He walked over to me, and Thompson backed off. He squatted so we'd be eye to eye. I gathered the sheet and turned to meet his gaze.

"Where are Chuck and Terry?" he asked.

I blinked and kept my face neutral. Once, not long ago, I wouldn't have been able to do it. Now my face gave nothing away. I was as blank and empty as the white sheet around my body.

"Who?"

"Thompson." Wilkes stood.

I felt Thompson move in from behind me.

"Does he do all your dirty work, Wilkes? You aren't man enough to abuse an unarmed woman?"

Wilkes hit me a backhanded slap that rocked me against the bed. I tasted blood. I probably could have blocked the slap, but that would have made the second blow harder. Besides, I'd asked for it. I don't mean I deserved it. I mean I preferred Wilkes to Thompson for abuse. I never wanted to be at Thompson's mercy without Wilkes there to rein him in. Thompson wasn't a cop. He was a goon with a badge.

The second blow was a slap, the third was another backhand. The blows were quick and hard and left my ears ringing. I saw spots of light against my vision. The proverbial stars, and he hadn't even closed his fist.

Wilkes stood over me, breathing too hard, hands in fists at his side. That fine trembling was back again, as if he was fighting not to close his fists. We both knew if he did, he wouldn't stop. If he hit me even once with his fist, it would be over. He'd hit me until someone pulled him off. I wasn't a hundred percent sure that there was anyone in the room who would pull him off.

I stared up at him with a trickle of blood at the corner of my mouth. I licked at the blood with my tongue and stared into Wilkes's brown eyes. I saw the abyss down at the end of his gaze. The monster was there, barely caged. I'd underestimated how close to the edge Wilkes was. I knew in that moment that this last warning was just that: a last warning. A last chance, not just for us, but for Wilkes. A last chance for him to walk away without any actual blood on his own lily-white hands.

The deputy by the door said, "Sheriff, we've got over twenty people outside here."

"We can't do this with an audience," Maiden said.

Wilkes kept staring down at me, and I held his gaze. It was almost like we were both afraid to look away, as if even that small movement would uncage the monster. Maybe it wasn't Thompson I should be afraid of.

"Sheriff," Maiden said softly.

"In twenty-four hours," Wilkes said, voice squeezed down until it was almost painful to hear, "we'll file a missing person's report on Chuck and Terry. Then we'll be back, Ms. Blake. We'll be back, and we'll take you in for questioning regarding their disappearance."

"What are you going to write down in the report as to why you thought I might know where they are?"

He went back to staring at me, but at least the fine trembling had stopped.

I kept my voice neutral but said, "I'm sure some of the tree-huggers called the cops last night. But no one came. You're the law in this town, Wilkes. You're all these people have between them and the bad guys. Last night, you didn't come because you thought you knew what was happening. You thought Chuck and Terry had gotten carried away. So you come by this morning to pick up the bodies, but there aren't any bodies."

"You killed them," he said, his voice soft and tight.

I shook my head. "No, I didn't." Which was technically true. I hadn't killed *them*. I'd killed Chuck but not Terry.

"You're saying you never saw them last night."

"I didn't say that. I just said I didn't kill them."

Wilkes glanced behind at Richard. "The Boy Scout didn't do them."

"Never said he did."

"That little guy you were with, Jason? Schuyler? He couldn't have taken both of them."

"Nope," I said.

"You are pissing me off, Blake. You don't want me angry."

"No, I don't, Sheriff Wilkes. I really don't want you angry. But I am not lying. I did not kill them. I don't know where they are." That at least was totally true. I was beginning to wonder if Terry had ever made it to the hospital, and I was beginning to think he probably hadn't. Did Verne's pack kill him after I promised him we wouldn't? I hoped not.

"I've been a cop for longer than you've been alive, Blake. You make my bullshit meter go off. You're lying to me, and you're good at it."

"I didn't kill your two friends, Sheriff. I don't know where they are now. That's the truth."

He hunkered back down beside me. "This is your last warning, Blake. Get the fuck out of my town, or I am going to drop-kick you into the nearest hole. I've lived here a long time. If I hide a body, it stays hid."

"A lot of people go missing around here?" I asked.

"Missing people are bad for tourism," Wilkes said. He stood. "But it happens. Don't let it happen to you. Get out now, today. If you're not gone by dark, it's over."

I stared up at him and knew he meant it.

I nodded. "We're history."

Wilkes turned to Richard. "What about you, Boy Scout? You agree? Is this enough? Or does it have to get worse?"

I looked across the room at Richard and urged him to lie. Maiden still had a baton stretched across his throat. The towel had slipped down, and he was naked, with his wrists still in cuffs behind his back.

Richard swallowed, then said, "It's enough."

"You're out by dark?" Wilkes made it a question.

"Yes," Richard said.

Wilkes nodded. "I can't tell you how happy I am to hear that, Mr. Zeeman. Come on, boys."

Maiden very slowly took his baton away from Richard's throat and stepped back. "I'll take the cuffs off if you promise to behave yourself."

"It's over, right, Richard?" Wilkes said. "Take the cuffs off. They won't give us any more trouble."

Maiden didn't look as convinced as Wilkes seemed to be, but he did what he was told. He took the cuffs off.

Richard rubbed his wrists but didn't bother grabbing at the fallen towel. Without clothes, Richard was nude, not naked. He was comfortable. Most lycanthropes were.

Maiden followed Wilkes to the door, but he kept an eye on both of us, as if still expecting trouble. A good cop never turns his back completely.

Thompson was the last to move towards the door. He said, "Lover's thing is almost as big as you are."

Nothing else he'd done had made me blush, but that did. I hated it but couldn't stop it.

He laughed. "I hope you don't leave town. I hope you stay, because I really do want another chance to be alone together."

"My new goal in life, Thompson, is to never be alone with you."

He laughed again. He laughed while he walked out the door. The deputy that kept complaining about the crowd left. Only Maiden waited in the door for Wilkes.

The sheriff said, "I hope we never meet again, Blake."

"Ditto, Sheriff," I said.

"Mr. Zeeman." He gave a nod as if he'd just pulled us over for a traffic stop and let us go with a warning. His entire body language changed as he moved through the door. Just a good ol' boy talking to some strangers about that disturbance last night.

When the door closed behind them, Richard crawled to me. He started to touch my face, then stopped, fingers hovering helplessly around my face. "Are you hurt?"

"A little."

He hugged me, pulling me gently in against his body. "Go home, Anita. Go back to Saint Louis."

I pulled away enough to meet his eyes. "Oh, no. If you stay, I stay."

He cradled my face in his hands. "They'll hurt you."

"Not if they think we really left. Can Verne's people hide us?"

"Who do you think is outside in the crowd?"

I looked up into his open face. "Did they kill the other man? Did Verne's people kill Terry after they left?"

"I don't know, Anita." He hugged me again. "I don't know."

"I promised him he'd live if he told us what he knew."

He pulled back, holding my face in his hands. "You could have killed him during the fight last night and not blinked, but because you promised him safety, you're upset."

I pulled away from Richard, standing, tugging the sheet out from under his knees. "If I give my word, it means something. I gave my word that he'd live. If he's dead now, I want to know why."

"The cops are on the other side. Don't piss Verne and his pack off, Anita. They're all we have."

I knelt by the suitcase on the other side of the bed and started getting out clothes. "No, Richard, we have each other and we have Shang-Da and Jason and Asher and everyone we brought with us. If Verne's people went behind my back last night and killed Terry, we don't have them. They have us. Because we need them, and they know it."

I stood with an armful of clothes and shuffled towards the bathroom with the sheet still around me. For some reason, I just didn't want to be naked in front of anyone right now, not even Richard. I made one stop on the way. I got the Browning out from under my pillow and piled it on top of the clothes. No more going unarmed for the rest of the trip. If someone didn't like it, they could lump it. That included my nearest and dearest. Though, to Richard's credit, he didn't say a word about the gun or anything else as I closed the door.

30

I wanted a long, hot shower. I settled for a brief, hot shower. I'd called Dolph back first to let him know I wasn't dead. But all I managed to do was leave a message. I was hoping to give him the name Franklin Niley and see if there was any criminal connection. Dolph didn't usually share police info with me unless we were involved in a case together, but I was hoping he'd make an exception. Dirty cops are one of Dolph's least favorite things. He might help just to spite Wilkes.

I put on white jogging socks, blue jeans, and a royal blue tank top. I'd put a short-sleeved dress shirt over the tank top to camouflage the Browning. The holster would chafe a little around the edges, but when it comes to summer wear for concealed carry, the options are not limitless. I'd have worn shorts if I hadn't planned on tramping through the woods after trolls and biologists. I was trading being cooler for protection from the underbrush.

I smeared hair goop through my curls while they were still damp, combed it, and the hair was done. Since I didn't bother with makeup, it was a quick shower. I stared into the oval of mirror that I'd cleaned off with the towel. The rest was still lost to steam. The bruises from the original beating were gone, swallowed into my skin as if they'd never been. But my mouth was slightly puffy on one side, and a spot of red sat on my skin near my mouth like a wound. At this rate, I could have a beating a day and be healed in time for the next one.

There were voices on the other side of the door. One of the voices was Richard. The other voice had a low bass rumble to it that sounded like Verne. Good; I needed to talk to him. There were more voices. I heard Nathaniel's voice, high and clear: "I didn't know what else to do."

The gang was all here. I wondered what the topic of conversation was. I had a few ideas.

I put the Browning down the front of the jeans. As long as I didn't sit down, I was okay. The barrel was too long for comfortable sitting. I opened the door, and the conversation stopped like I'd pulled a switch. Guess I was the topic of conversation.

Nathaniel was standing the closest to me. He was wearing silky jogging shorts and a matching tank top. His long hair was in a thick braid down his back. He looked like an ad for an upscale gym. "I was on guard, Anita, but they're cops. I didn't know what to do." He looked away, turned away, and I had to catch his arm to turn him back to me.

He turned those big lilac eyes to me.

"Next time, just yell a warning. That's all you could have done differently."

"I suck as a bodyguard," he said.

This was sort of true, but I didn't want to say it to his face. There really wasn't much he could have done.

I looked across the room at Shang-Da. He was sitting with his back to the wall, balanced effortlessly on the balls of his feet. He was dressed in black slacks and a white, short-sleeved shirt. The claw marks on his face had turned to angry red welts. What should have been scars that he would carry for the rest of his life would be healed in a couple of days.

"If you'd been on duty, Shang-Da, what would you have done differently?" I kept hold of Nathaniel's arm while I asked it.

"They would not have gotten past me without your permission."

"Would you have fought them if they tried to handcuff you?"

He seemed to think about that for a second or two, then looked up at me. "I don't like being handcuffed."

I pulled Nathaniel into a half-hug. "See, Nathaniel, there are bodyguards who would have given them an excuse to start shooting. Don't worry about it." But secretly, I planned on Nathaniel never doing guard duty alone again. I also planned on the same for Shang-Da. For very different reasons, I didn't trust either of them alone.

Verne sat in the big chair by the window. Except for the T-shirt being different, he was dressed as I'd first seen him. Maybe that was all he had. Jeans and an endless supply of different T-shirts. He'd tied his long, greying hair in a loose ponytail.

Richard had put on a pair of jeans and blow-dried his hair, but that was it. He'd go an entire day wearing nothing but jeans or shorts, slipping on shoes only if he had to go outside. The shirt only appeared when he was going out. Richard is comfortable with his body. Of course, when you've got a body like his, why wouldn't you be?

"Are you okay?" Verne asked.

I shrugged. "I'll live. Speaking of living, how is ol' Terry? Did the hospital get his arm reattached?"

Richard reached his hand out to me. I hesitated, then took his hand. I let him draw me to my knees beside him. I took the Browning out from my jeans so I could sit between his legs. He folded me back against his bare chest, jean-clad knees on either side of me. His arms were warm and very solid. I leaned my head back against his chest. I kept eye contact with Verne the entire time.

It didn't hurt that I had the Browning naked in my hand.

Richard kissed my damp hair. He was trying to remind me to be a good girl. To not start another fight. He was right, in a way. We certainly had enough fights on our plate without starting another one.

"Answer me, Verne," I said.

"Most of my pack passes for human, Anita. Do you really think some shithead would have kept his mouth shut?" He leaned forward in the chair, hands clasped together. Mr. Sincere.

"He was our only link to the other bad guys, Verne. The only one that was willing to talk to us."

Richard's arms wrapped just a little tighter around my arms. I realized that if he squeezed, I wouldn't be able to point the gun. "I'm not going to shoot him, Richard. Chill, okay?"

"Couldn't I just be hugging you?" he asked, voice so close to my ear I could feel his breath.

"No," I said.

His arms slid to either side, loosely around my waist, which put his hands almost in my lap, since I had my knees up. Under other circumstances, it would have been an interesting position, but when I have a point to make, I don't distract.

"The pack is my priority, Anita. It has to be."

"I would never do anything to endanger your pack, Verne. But I gave my word that if he told us what he knew, we'd take him to the hospital and let them try to reattach his arm. I gave my word, Verne."

"You take your word that seriously," he said.

"Yes."

"I respect that," he said.

"You killed him, didn't you?" I asked.

"Not personally, but I gave the order."

Richard's arms tightened around me. I felt him struggling to relax against me. He rubbed his chin against my wet hair, hands rubbing up and down my bare arms like you'd soothe a dog that you were afraid was going to bite someone.

"And I gave my word," I said.

"What can I do to make this right between us?" Verne asked.

I wanted to say, "Nothing," but Richard was right. We needed them. Or we needed someone, and they were all we had. What could he do to make this right? Raising the dead was my department, and bringing him back as a zombie wouldn't be the same thing, anyway.

"Truthfully, Verne, I don't know. But I'll think of something."

"You mean, I'll owe you a favor," he said.

"A man's dead, Verne. It would have to be one hell of a favor."

He looked at me for a long, measuring moment, then nodded. "I guess so."

"Okay," I said, "okay. We'll leave it there for now, Verne, but when I come up with something to ask for or of you, disappointing me again would not be a good idea."

He gave a quick smile. "I don't know if I'm looking forward to you and Roxanne meeting or dreading it."

"Who's Roxanne?" I asked.

"His lupa," Richard said.

Verne stood. "Richard said you and Roxanne would like each other if you didn't kill each other first. I know what he meant now." He walked over to us. He held his hand down, as if offering to help me off the floor. But call it a hunch, I thought it was more than that.

Richard's arms opened, and I took Verne's hand. He didn't so much pull me to my feet as just hold my hand while I stood. The other hand still held the Browning.

"If you ask for something that harms my pack, I can't promise that. But short of that, you have my word. Ask it of me, and it's yours." He grinned suddenly, then looked past me to Richard. "God, she is a tiny thing."

Richard, wisely, did not comment.

Verne knelt in front of me. "To seal my word, I'm going to offer you my neck. You understand the symbolism?"

I nodded. "If I were a wolf, I could tear your throat out. It's an act of trust."

He nodded and bent his head to one side so the big vein in his neck was just below the surface stretched tight under the skin of his throat. He kept hold of my hand the entire time.

I glanced back at Richard. "What am I supposed to do?"

"Kiss the big pulse in his neck, or bite gently over it. The harder you bite the less you trust the person, or the more dominant you see yourself to them."

I stared down at Verne. He was being very good. No trickle of power escaped him, and I was holding his hand, skin to skin. I'd felt how powerful he was; he could have made my skin crawl if he'd wanted to.

I squeezed his hand and moved to stand behind him. I tossed the Browning on the bed. I ran my hand along his neck, finding the big pulse with my fingertips.

I looked at Richard. You could almost see the "no" on his face—the near-warning not to do what I was thinking of. Which in a way made it all the more tempting.

Verne drew me down towards him, pulling my hand across his chest like I was hugging him. It brought my mouth down to his neck, as if he'd done this before.

He smelled warm, as if he'd been out in the sun. The scent of trees and the ground itself clung to his skin. I ran my nose just above his skin. I could smell the blood. It was as if the skin on his neck was growing thinner and thinner, until there was nothing between the smell of sweet blood but a pliable warmth, as if the skin itself almost didn't exist.

My mouth hovered over that pulsing warmth. I was drowning in the smell of his body. The need to place my mouth over that pulsing, living thing was almost overwhelming. I didn't trust myself to do it, or rather, didn't trust myself not to do too much. Did Richard go through life tasting other people's blood? Could he feel their life like something fragile and touchable?

Maybe I hesitated too long. Maybe Verne felt the power that was trying to overwhelm me. His power broke over my body in a shivering rush that made me gasp. And it was too much. Too tempting a drink to offer a starving man.

My teeth closed over that evaporating warmth. The meat of his neck filled my mouth. My tongue found his pulse, and I bit down, trying to carve that jumping, beating thing out of the flesh.

His power roared over me, and something inside of me poured back like two tidal waves crashing, churning, destroying. Far below, there was a land and a beach, and it was all washed away in the pounding, drowning depths.

I felt eyes open, and they weren't my eyes. Jean-Claude opened his eyes all those miles away, surprised from a sleep that should have lasted hours yet. Shocked awake by his hunger, my hunger, our hunger, being fed.

Hands dragged me off of that pulsing warmth. Hands prying me away. I came to myself with Richard pulling me into the air, completely helpless. Verne still had my hand. He was holding on, trying to drag me back. His neck was bleeding. A near perfect imprint of my teeth sat in his flesh. His hand fell away as Richard pulled me off of him.

Verne's eyes looked heavy-lidded. He drew in a large, shaking breath and laughed. The low chuckle made my body react. "God, Jesus, girl, what the hell was that?"

I didn't fight to get back to him. I didn't fight to finish it. I lay passive in Richard's arms, blinking in a spill of morning light, staring at what I'd done to Verne's neck and not understanding.

When I could talk, I asked, "What the hell was that?"

Richard cradled me in his arms like I was a child. Since I wasn't sure I could stand, I wasn't bitching about it. I felt distant and light and horrible.

He hugged me against him, kissing my forehead. "Us being together has strengthened the marks. Jean-Claude thought it might."

I stared up at Richard. I was still having trouble focusing. "Are you saying that us having sex strengthened his hold on both of us?"

Richard seemed to think about that for a second or two. "It strengthened our hold on each other."

"Put me down."

He did what I asked. I slid to my knees, unable to stand, and pushed his hands away when he tried to help. "You knew and you didn't tell me."

"Would it have made a difference last night?" he asked.

I stared up at him, tears threatening, and I wanted to say yes, but I didn't lie. "No," I said, "no." Last night it would have taken a hell of a lot more than the knowledge that the marks would strengthen to keep me out of Richard's bed. Of course, last night I hadn't understood what it meant. Last night I hadn't just tried to eat my way through a man's throat.

I got to my feet and fell a second time. It wasn't lack of energy. It was almost like being drunk. But it wasn't a downer. It was defiantly an upper. "What is wrong with me?"

Shang-Da answered, "I've seen vampires do this. If they drink someone powerful or drink too much . . . power."

"Shit."

"I'm feeling pretty damn good, myself," Verne said. He touched the bite on his neck. "I've never let a vampire do me before. If it feels that good, maybe I've been missing out."

"Better," Nathaniel said. "It can feel much better than that."

"It wasn't vampire," Richard said, "it was power. Verne's power, mine, Anita's, and Jean-Claude's."

"Sort of a preternatural suicide cocktail," I said and giggled. I lay on the floor, hiding my face behind my hands and fighting an urge to roll in the afterglow. I wanted to take the feeling and wrap it around my body like a blanket. And down the long, glowing warmth, I felt a darkness. I felt Jean-Claude like a black hole sucking in all our warmth, all our life. And in that moment, I knew two things. One, that he'd known when Richard and I made love. That he'd felt it. Two, that as he ate from our lives, we ate of his darkness. We drank that still, cold death as surely as he tasted the sun-warmed flesh and pulse of our bodies. And we all drew power from it. The light and the dark. The cold and the hot. Life and death. As the marks drew us closer, the lines between life and death would blur. I felt Jean-Claude's heartbeat earlier than it had ever beat in over four hundred years. I felt his gladness, his joy in it. At that moment, I hated him.

31

Two hours later, Richard, Shang-Da, and I were tramping through the woods in search of biologists and trolls. We had until dark to get out of town, and since we really weren't getting out of town, we might as well continue with our original plans. We left everyone else behind scurrying like ants, packing, packing, packing. We would pack and leave. In fact, we were supposed to call the sheriff when we were ready to leave. Wilkes had kindly offered us an escort out of town—before dark. After dark, I think the offer was a bullet and a hole somewhere.

I followed Richard through the woods. He moved among the trees like he could see the openings or as if, as he moved forward, the trees moved around him. I knew that wasn't true. I'd have felt the presence of that much preternatural energy, but Richard made it look easy. It wasn't being a werewolf. It was being Mr. Outdoorsman. His hiking boots were nicely broken in. His T-shirt was blue green with a picture of a sea cow, a manatee, swimming on front and back. I had the identical T-shirt at home, a gift from Richard. He'd been disappointed that I hadn't packed mine. Even if I had, I wouldn't have worn it. I wasn't much into the Bobbsey Twin look for couples. Besides, I was still angry with him in a vague sort of way. I should not have been the only one of the three of us who didn't know what it would mean for Richard and me to have sex. I should have been told that it would bind us all closer.

Of course, it was hard to be mad at him when the T-shirt clung to his body like a thin, second skin. His thick hair was tied back in a loose ponytail. Every time he passed through a bar of sunlight, his hair glowed with streaks of copper and gold. It was hard to be angry when the sight of him made my chest tight.

Richard moved smoothly ahead of us. I followed in my Nikes, not doing too bad a job. I'm okay in the woods. Not as good as Richard, but not bad.

Shang-Da, on the other hand, was not a woodsman. He moved through the woods almost daintily, as if afraid of stepping in something. His black dress slacks and fresh white shirt seemed to catch on things that didn't bother either Richard or me. Shang-Da's shoes had started the trip black and polished to a fine sheen. They didn't stay that way. Dress shoes, even men's dress shoes, aren't meant for walking in the woods. I'd never met a city werewolf before, but no amount of physical grace made up for his total lack of familiarity with the out-of-doors.

There was a breeze today. The trees rustled and hushed with the wind. It was a cool sound high up in the trees, but the wind never came near the ground. We moved through a world of green heat and solid brown tree trunks. Sunlight glittered on the leaves, hitting the ground in shining yellow patches before we moved into heavier shade. The shade was a few degrees cooler but still heavy with heat. It was almost dead-up noon, and even the insects had fallen quiet with the heat.

Richard stopped just ahead of us. "Do you hear that?" he asked softly.

Shang-Da said, "Someone crying. A woman."

I didn't hear a damn thing.

Richard nodded. "Maybe a woman." He eased through the trees in a movement that was almost a run. Crouched, hands almost touching the ground. His power spilled back from him like the bubbling wake of a ship.

I followed him. I tried to look where I was going, but I stumbled and fell. Shang-Da helped me to my feet. I jerked away from him and ran. I stopped looking at my feet or the trees. I stared only at Richard's back, his body. I mimicked his movements, trusting that if he could make the openings, so could I. I leaped over logs that I didn't see until he moved over them. It was almost hypnotic. The world narrowed down to his body speeding through the trees. Again and again I almost careened into trees, pushing my body to move too fast. I was moving faster than my mind could work. If Richard had jumped off a cliff, I'd have followed, because I was just moving. It was like I'd given up everything to my body. I was just muscles working, legs running. The world was a blur of green and light and shade and Richard's body sliding at a run through the trees.

He stopped like a switch had been thrown. One minute running, the next stopped, no in between. But I didn't bump into him. I was stopped, too. It was like a part of my brain I couldn't access had known he would stop.

Shang-Da was at my back. He stepped close enough for me to smell his faint, expensive aftershave. He whispered, "How did you do that, human?"

I glanced at him. "What?"

"Run."

I knew that *run* meant more to the lukoi than the word said. I stood there, covered in a light dew of sweat, barely breathing hard, and knew that something had happened that hadn't before. Richard and I had tried to jog together before, and it hadn't worked. He was two inches shy of being an entire foot taller than me. A lot of that was leg. His speed for jogging was running to me, and even then, I couldn't keep up with him. Add the fact that he was a lycanthrope, and, well, he was too fast for me. The only other time I'd kept up with him had been with him holding my hand, with him pulling me along with the marks and his power.

I turned to look at Shang-Da. There must have been something on my face, some soft astonishment, because his expression softened to something almost like pity.

Richard moved away from us, and we both turned back to follow his progress. As my pulse slowed, I could hear what they had heard ages ago: crying—though that was too soft a word for it. Someone was sobbing as if their heart were breaking.

Richard moved toward the sound, and we followed him. There was a huge sycamore in the middle of a clearing. On the other side of the tree's large, (patchy) trunk, a woman huddled. She had squeezed herself down into a small, tight ball, her arms hugging her knees. Her face was thrown up to the sparkling sunlight, eyes squeezed shut, blind.

She had brunette hair so dark it could have passed for black, cut very short. She was white with a fringe of dark lashes pasted to her pale cheeks. Her face was small and triangular, but beyond that I couldn't describe it. Her face was ravished with tears, eyes swollen, skin reddened. She was small, dressed in heavy khaki shorts, thick socks, hiking boots, and a T-shirt.

Richard knelt in the leaves beside her. He touched her arm before he said anything, and she screamed, eyes flying wide. There was a moment of utter panic on her face, then she threw herself against his chest, wrapped her arms around him, and fell into a fresh bout of sobbing.

He stroked her hair, murmuring, "Carrie, Carrie, it's all right. It's all right."

Carrie. Could it be Dr. Carrie Onslow? It seemed likely. But what was the head biologist on the troll project doing having hysterics in the woods?

Richard had slid completely down into the leaves. He'd pulled her into his lap like she was a child. It was hard to judge, but she seemed tiny, smaller than I was.

The crying eased. She lay cuddled in his lap, held in his arms. They'd dated. I tried to feel jealous, but I couldn't manage it. Her distress was too extreme.

Richard stroked the side of her face. "What's wrong, Carrie? What's happened?"

She took a deep breath that shuddered as it escaped her lips, then she nodded and blinked up at Shang-Da and me.

"Shang-Da." Her eyes turned to me. She seemed embarrassed that we'd seen her lose control. "I don't know you."

"Anita Blake," I said.

Her cheek rested against Richard's chest, so all she had to do was roll her eyes upward to look at him. "You're his Anita?" She made it a question.

He looked up at me. "When we're not mad at each other, yes."

I watched her rebuild herself, gathering her personality back around her like layering clothes against winter weather. Her eyes filled while I watched until her face burned with intelligence, with a force, commitment, a determination that shone so fiercely it seemed to thrum through her skin. I watched her and knew instantly why Richard had dated her. Staring down at her, I was glad she was human, glad he wouldn't be having sex with her. Because just a few moments in her presence, and I knew that this one, this one could be trouble. That was the real danger with not being monogamous. It wasn't really the sex, though that bugged me a lot. It was the fact that it meant the other person wasn't satisfied, that they were still looking. If you're still looking, sometimes you find it, whatever it is.

I didn't like staring down at this woman who was obviously in pain and thinking about my own problems. I didn't like the fact that I was a little afraid of her. I mean, I was human, and he'd had sex with me. I hated that this was what I was thinking before anything. Hated it a lot.

She started to push away from Richard's arms.

I said, "Don't move on my account." It came out dry and sarcastic. Good, better than wounded and confused.

Richard looked up at me. I couldn't read his expression, and I made sure mine was pleasant and gave him nothing.

Dr. Carrie Onslow glanced up at Richard, frowned, then finished pushing away. She slid out of his lap to lean against the tree trunk. Small frown lines had formed between her eyes, and she kept glancing from Richard to me, as if she were confused and didn't like it.

"What's happened, Carrie?" Richard asked again.

"We went out today just before dawn, as usual." She stopped talking, staring at her lap, then took a deep, shaking breath. Three breaths and she seemed better. "We found a body."

"Another hiker?" I asked.

Her eyes flicked to me, then back to her lap, as if she didn't want any eye contact for the story. "Maybe, it was impossible to tell. It was a woman, beyond that . . ." Her voice failed her. She looked up at us, small eyes shimmering with fresh tears. "I have never seen anything so horrible in my life. The local police are saying that our trolls did it. That this is proof that that hiker was a troll kill."

"Lesser Smokey Mountain trolls don't hunt and kill humans," I said.

She looked at me. "Well, something did. The state police wanted my expert opinion on what could have done it if it wasn't trolls." She buried her face in her hands, then raised her face like someone coming out of deep water. "I looked at the bites. They were made by something with a primate jaw structure."

"Human?" I offered.

She shook her head. "I don't know. I don't think so. I don't think a human mouth could do that kind of damage." She hugged herself, shivering in the heat. "They'll use this to try and call in some bounty hunters and kill our trolls, if they can prove that the trolls did this. I don't see how we can stop them from either killing them all or shipping them to zoos."

"Our trolls did not kill a human being," Richard said. He touched her shoulder when he said it.

"Something did, Richard. Something that wasn't a wolf or a bear or any large predator that I've ever seen."

"Did you say that the state cops are on site?" I asked. She looked up at me. "Yes."

"Did you call them?"

She shook her head. "They arrived shortly after the local police."

I'd have loved to know who called them, though if the local cops suspected it was either a homicide or a preternatural kill, it was standard op for them to call either the staties or the local vampire hunter, though admittedly only if they thought the kill was some form of undead.

"Was the body found near a cemetery?" I asked.

Dr. Onslow shook her head.

"Why?" Richard asked.

"It could have been ghouls. They're cowards, but if she'd fallen and knocked herself unconscious, ghouls would have fed on her. They are active scavengers."

"What's that mean?" Dr. Onslow asked. "Active scavenger?"

"It means if you're wounded and reduced to crawling, you don't want to be in a ghoul-infested cemetery."

She stared up at me, then finally shook her head. "No graves. Just in the middle of our land. In the middle of the trolls' territory."

I nodded. "I need to go see the body."

"Do you think that's a good idea?" Richard asked. He kept his voice as neutral as he could.

"They're expecting her," Dr. Onslow said.

It surprised us all. "What do you mean?" I asked.

"The state police found out you're in the area. Evidently, your reputation is good enough that they wanted you to see the body. They were trying to reach you at your cabin when I left."

How convenient. How weird. Who had called the staties? Who had put my name in front of them? Who, who, who?

"I'll go look at the body then."

"Take Shang-Da with you," Richard said.

I looked up at the tall man's face. The claw marks were still red and sort of gruesome looking on his face. I shook my head. "I don't think so."

"I don't want you going alone," Richard said.

Funny how he wasn't offering to come with me himself. He was going to stay here and comfort Dr. Onslow. Fine. I was a big girl.

"I'll be okay, Richard. You stay here with the good doctor and Shang-Da."

Richard stood. "You're being childish."

I rolled my eyes and motioned him over away from Dr. Onslow. When I was sure she couldn't overhear us, I said, "Look at Shang-Da's face."

He didn't glance back. He knew what it looked like. "What about it?"

I stared up at him. "Richard, you should know as well as I do that if you have someone eaten to death by a mysterious critter, werewolves are always top of the hit list to blame."

"They try to blame a lot of things on us," he said.

"So far, Wilkes and his men don't know what you are. If we show up with Shang-Da cut up like this and then he turns up healed, they'll figure it out. With a body on the ground, you don't want them to figure it out."

"Shang-Da won't be healed by nightfall," Richard said.

"But he'll be more healed than he is right now. It isn't human to heal that fast. If Wilkes finds out that we haven't really left town, he'll use everything he has. He'll out you or charge you with this crime."

"What could have killed this woman?"

"Won't know until I see the body."

"I don't want you going there alone. I'll go with you."

"The police don't like it when you bring your civvie boyfriends to crime scenes, Richard. Stay here; comfort Dr. Onslow."

He frowned at me.

"I'm not being catty, Richard." I smiled. "All right, not very catty. She's shook. Hold her hand. I'll be okay."

He touched my face gently. "You don't need much hand-holding, do you?"

I sighed. "One night with you and I nearly eat Verne's neck. One night, and I just ran through the woods like . . . like a werewolf. Just one lovemaking session, and you say you knew it was a possibility. You should have at least tried to tell me last night, Richard.''

He nodded. ''You're right, I should have. I don't have any excuse good enough. I'm sorry, Anita.''

Staring up into his so-sincere face, it was hard to be angry. But it wasn't hard to be distrustful. Maybe Richard had been learning more from Jean-Claude than just how to control the marks. Maybe lying by omission was contagious.

''I need to go see a body, Richard.''

Dr. Onslow pointed me in the right direction. I started off through the woods. Richard caught up with me. ''I'll walk you.''

''I'm armed, Richard. I'll be okay.''

''I want to go with you.''

I stopped and turned and stared up at him. ''I don't want you with me. Right this moment, I need you to be somewhere else.''

''I didn't mean to hide things from you. Everything happened so fast last night. I just didn't have time. I didn't think.''

''Tell it to someone who cares, Richard. Tell it to someone who cares.'' I walked away into the trees, and he stayed where I'd left him. I felt him watch me as I moved through the trees. I could feel the weight of his gaze like a hand on my back. If I looked back, would he be waving? I didn't look back. I loved Richard. He loved me. I was sure of those two things. The one thing I wasn't sure of was whether that love would be enough. If he slept with other women, it wouldn't be. Fair or not, I wouldn't survive it.

Richard said he hadn't asked me to give up Jean-Claude. He hadn't. But as long as I shared my bed with Jean-Claude, Richard would sleep with other women. As long as I wasn't monogamous, he wouldn't be, either. He hadn't asked me to give up Jean-Claude. He'd just made sure that I wasn't going to be happy in either bed. I could have them both as long as Richard slept around. I could have Richard all to myself, as long as I gave up Jean-Claude. I wasn't ready to make the second choice, and I couldn't live with the first. Unless there were a third choice, we were in trouble.

32

The murder scene was in the middle of the woods. Five miles from the nearest road good enough to take even a four-wheeler, according to Dr. Onslow. It was a great place for trolls, but not for conducting a police investigation. They were going to have to hike everything in, and when the time came, hike the body out. Not pleasant, not fast.

One good thing about the isolated location was no gawkers. I'd been to a lot of murder scenes, but the only ones without an audience were either at really odd hours or in the middle of nowhere. The odd hours weren't enough if there were people nearby. People would climb out of their beds before dawn to see a corpse.

Even without the civvies, there was a crowd. I spotted the uniforms of Wilkes and one of his men. I was really looking forward to seeing them again today. The state troopers were thick on the ground along with some plainclothes state detectives. I didn't have to be introduced to them to know they were cops. They moved around the scene with little plastic gloves on, squatting on the balls of their feet rather than kneeling on the evidence.

Yellow crime scene tape wrapped around it all like a ribbon on a package. There was no uniform on this side of the tape because no one expected company from the direction opposite the road. I was wearing the Browning and the Firestar and the knife down my spine, so I dug out my license and held it aloft as I ducked under the tape. Eventually, someone would see me and some uniform would get yelled at for letting me cross the perimeter without being spotted.

A state trooper spotted me before I'd come down the hill very far. They'd made a wide circle of tape, and he'd been standing near the upper edge of it. He had brown hair and dark eyes and a sprinkling of freckles across his pale cheeks. He walked towards me, hand out, "I'm sorry, miss, but you can't be in here."

I waggled the license at him. "I'm Anita Blake. I heard you guys were looking for me. Something about a body you want me to take a peek at."

"A peek," he said. "You want to take a peek at the body." He said it sort of soft, not like he was teasing me. His dark eyes stared past me for a second, then he seemed to remember where he was. He held his hand out for my license.

I let him take it, look at it, read it twice. He handed it back to me. He looked down the hill to the knot of people. He pointed. "The short man in the black suit, blond hair, that's Captain Henderson. He's in charge."

I just looked at him. He should have taken me to the man in charge. No way would a cop who didn't know me let me walk a crime scene unaccompanied. Vampire executioners aren't civilians, but most of us aren't detectives, either. I'm one of the very few who deals so intimately with the police. In Saint Louis where most of the cops knew me by reputation or on sight, I could see it. But here, where no one knew me, no way.

I read the trooper's nameplate. "Michaels, is it?"

He nodded, and again his eyes weren't looking at me. He wasn't acting like a cop. He was acting scared. Cops don't spook easily. Give them a few years on the job, and they perfect jaded indifference: been there, done that, wasn't impressed, didn't bother to get a T-shirt. Michaels had sergeant bars on his uniform. You didn't get sergeant stripes in the state troopers by getting shook at every crime scene.

"Sergeant Michaels," he said. "Is there something I can do for you, Ms. Blake?" He seemed to be rebuilding himself before my eyes. It reminded me of the way Dr. Carrie Onslow had recovered. His eyes lost that vague, glassy look. He looked at me straight on, but there was still a tightness around his eyes, almost like something hurt. What the hell was down at the bottom of this hill? What could make a seasoned cop look like this?

"Nothing, Sergeant, nothing. Thanks." I kept my license out because I was almost sure to be stopped again without a police escort. A woman was throwing up by a small pine tree. She and the man holding her forehead wore Emergency Medical Services uniforms. It's a bad sign when the EMS techs are throwing up. A very bad sign.

It was Maiden who stopped me. We stood there for a second or two just looking at each other. I was standing uphill, looking down at him.

"Ms. Blake," he said.

"Maiden," I said. I left off the officer on purpose, because as far as I was concerned, he wasn't an officer. He'd stopped being a cop when he became a bad guy.

He gave a small, odd, smile. "I'll take you through to Captain Henderson. He's in charge."

"Fine."

"You might want to prepare yourself, Blake. It's . . . bad."

"I'll be all right," I said.

He shook his head, looked at the ground. When he looked back up, his eyes were empty, cold cop eyes. "Maybe you will, Blake, maybe you will. But I won't be."

"What's that supposed to mean?"

"Who the hell is she?" It was Captain Henderson. He'd spotted us. He came up the hillside in his dress shoes, sliding just a bit. But he was determined and knew how to walk in the leaves even in the wrong shoes. He was about five-eight, with short, blond hair. He had odd eyes that changed color as he moved through the dappled sunlight. One moment pale green, the next grey. He came up to stand between the two of us. He looked at Maiden. "Who is this, and why is she inside my perimeter?"

"Anita Blake, Captain Henderson," Maiden said.

He looked straight at me, and his eyes were cool and grey with swirling flecks of green. He was handsome in a clean-cut, ordinary sort of way. He might have been more than that, but there was a harshness to his face, a sourness, that robbed him of something likeable and pleasant.

No matter how funky the eye color when he looked at me, the eyes were distant, judging, cop eyes. "So you're Anita Blake?" His voice was almost angry.

I nodded. "Yes." I didn't let the anger get to me. He wasn't angry at me. Something was wrong. Something beyond the crime itself. I wondered what.

He looked me up and down, not sexual, but as if he were taking my measure. I was used to that, though it was usually a little less blatant. "How strong's your stomach, Blake?"

I raised eyebrows at that, then smiled.

"What in the hell is funny?" Henderson said.

"Look, I know it's bad. I just left your sergeant at the top of the hill so spooked he wouldn't come near it a second time. Maiden here's already told me it's awful. Just take me to the body."

Henderson stepped up, invading the hell out of my personal space. "You that confident that you can take it, Blake?"

I sighed. "No."

The no seemed to take some of the anger away. He blinked and took a step back. "No?" he said.

"I don't know if I can take it, Captain Henderson. There's always the chance that the next horror will be something so awful, I'll never recover. Something that stains my mind and sends me screaming. But so far, so good. So, take me to see the grisly remains. The foreplay is getting tiresome."

I watched the emotions play over his face: amusement, then anger, but finally, amusement won. Lucky me. "The grisly remains. Are you sure you're not a reporter?"

That made me smile. "I'm guilty of a lot of sins, but that's not one of them."

That made him smile. When he smiled, he looked ten years younger and was more than just ordinarily handsome. "Okay, Ms. Blake, follow me. I'll take you to see the grisly remains." He laughed soft, low, and deeper than his speaking voice, as if when he sang he might be a bass. "I hope you're as amusing after you've seen the show, Ms. Blake."

"Me, too," I said.

He gave me a strange look, then led the way down the hill. I followed because it was my job. An hour ago, I'd have said the day couldn't get much worse. I had a sinking feeling it was about to get worse—much worse.

33

The body lay in a small clearing. I knew it was human because they told me it was. It wasn't that the body didn't look human, exactly. The shape was there enough that I could tell it was lying on its back. It was more that my mind refused to acknowledge that this could have been a human being. My eyes saw it, but my mind kept refusing to put the pieces together, so it was like looking at one of those pictures where you stare and stare until the hidden shapes spin out in 3-D relief. It looked as if there had been an explosion of blood and flesh, and the body had been at the center of it. Dried blood spread out from the body in every direction, as if when the body were moved there'd be a body-shaped clean spot, like an ink blot.

I could see all that, but still my eyes couldn't make sense of it. My mind was trying to protect me. It had happened before—once or twice. The smart thing would be to turn and walk away. Let my mind have its confusion because the truth was going to be one of those mind-blasting moments. I'd jokingly told Henderson at the top of the hill that some things stain the mind. It wasn't funny now.

I forced myself to look at it, forced myself not to look away, but the summer heat wavered around me in a sickening rush. I wanted to cover my eyes with my hands, but I settled for turning away. Covering my eyes would look silly and childish, like blotting out the worst of a horror movie.

Henderson turned when I did. If I wasn't going to look at the body, then he wouldn't, either. "You okay?"

The world stopped spinning like a ball that had slid to a stop. "I will be." My voice sounded breathy.

"Good," he said.

We stood that way for a few seconds more, then I took a shallow breath. I knew better than to take a deep one this close to the body. I had to do this. Trolls didn't do this. No natural animal did this. I turned slowly around to face the body. It hadn't gotten any better.

Henderson turned with me. He was the man in charge. He could take it if I could. I wasn't sure I could, but since I was out of other choices . . .

I'd borrowed surgical gloves. Someone had offered me heavier plastic gloves to go over. AIDS, you know. I declined. One, my hands would sweat. Two, if I had to feel the body for clues, I wouldn't be able to feel shit. Three, with three vampire marks on me, I didn't sweat AIDS anymore. I was free from blood-borne disease, so I'd been told. I believed Jean-Claude on this one because he wouldn't want to lose me. I was a third of his triumvirate. He wanted me safe. In the back of my head a voice said, *He loves you.* The voice in the front of my head said, *Yeah right.*

"Can I track up the blood pattern?" I asked.

"You can't get close to the body unless you step in the blood," Henderson said.

I nodded. "True. So you've videotaped it, gotten all your pictures?"

"We know how to do our job, Ms. Blake."

"I'm not questioning that, Captain. I need to know if I can move the body around, that's all. I don't want to fuck up the evidence."

"When you're done with it, we'll be bagging it up."

I nodded. "Okay." I stared down at the body and suddenly could see it. All of it. I hugged my arms across my stomach to keep my hands from covering my eyes. The nose had been bitten off so that it was just a bloody hole. The lips were torn away until teeth and the bones of the jaw were visible under the drying blood. The muscles of the jaw were missing on the side facing me. Whatever had done this hadn't just taken a quick bite. It had sat down and fed.

So many bites, so much missing flesh, but most of it too shallow to kill. I said a short prayer that most of the bites were postmortem. Even as I prayed, I was pretty sure I wouldn't get a good answer; there was too much blood. She'd been alive through most of it. Intestines spilled out of the ripped jeans in a dried nest covered in thicker things than blood. The outhouse smell of her lower intestines being ripped would have faded by now. One smell dies, but there's always another. Her body had started to ripen in the summer heat. It is a smell that is hard to describe, both overwhelmingly sweet and bitter enough to gag. I took shallow breaths and stepped onto the dried splatter.

Something moved through me like a phantom blow. The hair on the back of my neck tried to crawl down my spine. That part of my brain that had nothing to do with cars or indoor plumbing and everything to do with running and screaming and not thinking at all, was whispering now. It was whispering that something was wrong. Something evil had been here—not just dangerous, evil.

I waited to see if the feeling would grow stronger, but it faded. It faded like a bad memory, which probably meant I'd walked through the edge of some kind of spell—or rather, the remnants of one, a nasty one.

You didn't call something this evil without a circle of protection either for the sorcerer to stand in or for the beastie to be put inside of. I searched the ground, but there was nothing but blood. The blood didn't form a circle of protection. It was just splatter, mess, no pattern.

I should have known there wouldn't be anything that obvious. The police aren't practitioners of the arts, though that is beginning to change, but you can't be a cop long and not look for signs of magic when the shit is this strange.

The scene looked undisturbed, but that didn't mean it was undisturbed. If someone were really good at magic, they could make you *not* see something. Not true invisibility. Humans don't do that. Physics is physics. Light hits a solid object and bounces. But they can make the eye reluctant to see, so that you keep looking past something and your mind doesn't register it. Like looking for a set of car keys that is sitting in plain sight, lost for two days.

I squatted beside the body. I didn't have the coveralls I usually wore at murder scenes and didn't want the blood to soak into my jeans. I was still hugging myself. There were things here that someone didn't want us to see. But what?

Henderson called, "We found the wallet. Do you want the ID?"

"No," I said. "No." I wasn't being clever. I just didn't want a name, an identity for the thing at my feet. I'd done the trick of turning the body into an it. It wasn't real. It was just something to be studied, examined. It had never been real. To think anything else at that moment would have had me vomiting all over the evidence. I'd done that only once, years ago. Dolph and the gang had never let me live it down.

The eyes had been clawed out and left to dry into blackened lumps on the cheeks. Long hair was plastered along the side of the face, stuck to one shoulder. Maybe blond hair from the color. But it was hard to tell with all the soaked blood. The long hair made me think female. My eyes traveled down and found the remains of clothing. The blouse had been reduced to a lump of cloth under one arm. The chest was bare. One breast torn completely off. The other deflated like a balloon as if something had eaten the flesh out of the middle, like a kid sucking the jelly out of a donut.

It was an unfortunate choice of metaphors, even in my own head. I had to stand up. I had to walk away, blowing air out very fast and too shallow. I went to stand beside one of the trees that edged the clearing. I had to take deep breaths, but that meant the odor went down strong. That sweet, sweet smell slid along my tongue and coated the back of my throat until I couldn't stand the thought of swallowing but didn't know what else to do. I swallowed, and the smell slid down, and my morning coffee inched up.

I had two comforts. One, I'd managed to get outside the blood pattern to vomit. Two, I didn't have much in my stomach to come up. Maybe this was one reason that I've stopped eating breakfast. I get a lot of early-morning body viewing.

I knelt in the dry leaves and felt better. I hadn't thrown up at a crime scene in a long time. At least Zerbrowski wasn't here to rib me about it. I wasn't even embarrassed. Was that a sign of maturity?

Male voices behind me. Sheriff Wilkes saying, almost yelling, "She's just a civvie. She shouldn't be here. She isn't even licensed for this state."

"I'm in charge here, Sheriff. I say who stays and who goes." Henderson wasn't yelling, but his voice carried.

I grabbed the tree trunk to help me stand, and my arm tingled so hard it almost went numb. I stood, pushing away from the tree, nearly falling, but I kept my feet. I looked up the smooth trunk. About eight feet up was a pentagram carved into the bark of the tree. The cut had been darkened with blood. With the dried blood rubbed into it, it was almost invisible against the dark grey bark, but there was also a spell of reluctance on it. So that no one had looked, not even me. Only when

I touched the tree did I sense it. Like all illusion, once you see it, you know it's there.

I looked at the other trees and found a bloody pentagram carved into each one. It was a circle of power, of protection. A circle formed of blood and the land itself. Wiccans—witches—can use their power for evil if they're willing to pay the price in karma. Whatever you do, good or ill, comes back to you threefold. But even a wiccan gone bad wouldn't carve up a tree. Had the trees, the land, themselves, been invoked? That might mean an elemental. They could be nasty. But they didn't feel evil. They felt angry if you messed with their land, but they weren't evil, more angry-neutral. I'd gotten that whiff of evil as I passed through the circle. Evil with a capital *E*. There just aren't that many preternatural critters that trip that particular wire.

"Captain Henderson," I said. I had to say it twice before they stopped arguing and looked at me.

They both looked at me. Neither looked friendly, but at least I knew who they were mad at: each other. Local cops don't like anybody horning in on their turf. It was normal for the local police to resent outsiders. But I knew that Wilkes had more to protect than his turf. He must be frantic having real cops here now. But now wasn't the time to spill the beans. I had no proof. Accusing a policeman of corruption tends to upset the other cops.

"Did you see the pentagrams on the trees?"

The question was strange enough that they both stopped being angry and paid attention. I pointed the pentagrams out, and like all good illusion, once I showed them, they could see it. The emperor has no clothes.

"So?" Wilkes said.

"So, this was a circle of protection, of power. Something was called here to kill her."

"The marks on the trees could have been here for days," Wilkes said.

"Test the blood on the pentagrams," I said. "It won't be hers, but it will be fresh."

"Why isn't it the victim's?" Henderson asked.

"Because they used the blood to seal the circle. They had to have the blood before the death."

"It was a human sacrifice then," Henderson said.

"Not exactly," I said.

"This was a troll kill," Wilkes said. He didn't sound sure; he sounded desperate.

Henderson turned to him. "You keep saying that, Wilkes. You keep saying it was trolls."

"That biologist herself said it looked like primates. It sure as hell wasn't a person. There aren't that many primates running around the Tennessee hills."

"She said humanoid," I said.

They both looked at me again.

"Dr. Onslow said humanoid. A lot of people assume humanoid means primate, but there are other options."

"Like what?" Wilkes said. His beeper went off. He checked the number, then looked at me. "Excuse me, Captain Henderson."

Henderson looked at me. "Do you and the sheriff have some sort of history, Ms. Blake?"

I frowned. "History? How?"

"He was very certain that you shouldn't be anywhere near this body. He was also very certain that this was a troll kill. Very certain."

"Who called you guys then?"

"An anonymous tip."

We looked at each other. "Who suggested I get to join the fun?"

"One of the EMS crew. The man's usual partner met you last night."

I shook my head. "I don't know him."

"His regular partner is a girl. Lucy something."

That explained Lucy's medical knowledge, and why she wasn't working on the day of the full moon. Don't want to be around fresh blood with the moon almost full. Too tempting. Too chancy.

"I remember her vaguely, I guess." I remembered her more than vaguely, but the last time I'd seen her was just after I'd murdered someone, so I was going to be fuzzy on the details. For one awful moment, I wondered if Henderson had been trying to trick me and the body was really Lucy. But the height was wrong. The woman had been tall, not my size. Most of the women that Richard dated were short. I guess if you've got a body type you like, you stick to it. My choice of victims seemed to be a lot wider.

"Why did they need a power circle, Ms. Blake?" Henderson asked.

"To keep in what they called."

He frowned at me. "Like you said before, the foreplay is getting tiresome. Just tell me what the fuck you think it was."

"I think they called a demon."

His eyes widened. "A what?"

"A demon," I said.

Henderson just looked at me. "Why?"

"When I crossed the circle, I got that feeling of evil. No matter how monstrous the critter, it doesn't feel the same as something dedicated to evil and no other purpose."

"You see many demons while you're out slaying vampires, Ms. Blake?"

"Once, Captain, just once. It was . . ." I stepped out of the circle of power, and I felt better. They'd done their best to hide the traces, but things like this have a tendency to cling. "I was called into a case that they thought was a vampire, but it was demonic possession. The woman . . ." I stopped again because I didn't have words for it, or no words that wouldn't seem silly, melodramatic. I tried to tell the story by sticking to the facts. Me and Sergeant Friday.

"The woman had been an ordinary housewife, mother of two. She'd been a diagnosed schizophrenic, Captain. Her particular brand of craziness was almost a multiple personality disorder, but not that clear-cut. She was like the little girl with a curl in the middle of her forehead. When she was good, she was very, very good. A model churchgoer, teacher of Sunday school. She canned her own vegetables, sewed doll clothes for her girls. But when she was bad, she slept around, abused the kids, hung the family dog from a tree."

Henderson raised an eyebrow at that. For a cop, it was pure shock. "Why wasn't she in a hospital?"

"Because when she took her medicine, she was the good mother, the good wife. I talked to her when she was 'well,' and she was a very nice person. I saw why the husband tried to hold on to her. It was tragic in the true sense of the word that her own brain chemistry was destroying her life."

"It's sad, but it's not demonic," Henderson said.

"Neighborhood pets were vanishing, showing up drained of blood. I traced it to the woman. Her history of mental illness had raised flags with the cops. So far, just sad, right." I stared off up the hill at the cops and the techs and everyone. They were not looking down the hill. No one wanted to hang around this one. Even if you aren't truly sensitive to the psychic, we all have survival instincts that work better than we do. Everyone would be reluctant on this one, and they wouldn't know why.

"You still with me, Blake?" Henderson asked.

"Sorry. The night we arrested her, two uniforms had had to drag her out of another man's bed, handcuffed. They didn't have another female on site that night, so I rode in back with her. She was loud and boisterous, flirting with the men, being snotty with me. I don't even remember what I said, but I remember the look on her face when she turned to me. We're riding in this dark police car, and as she turns her head to look at me, the hair on my body stood up. There were no glowing eyes, no smell of sulfur, Captain Henderson, but I felt evil rise off of her like some disturbing perfume." I looked at him, and he was scrutinizing my face like he was trying to memorize it. "I don't scare easy, Captain, but for that instant, I was scared. Scared of her, and it showed on my face, and she laughed, and the moment was gone."

"What did you do?"

"I recommended they do an exorcism."

"Did they?" he asked.

"Not the police, but her husband signed the papers for it."

"And?" Henderson said.

"And it worked. If she stays on her medication, the mental illness is under control. The possession didn't cause the schizophrenia."

Henderson nodded. "We all get the lecture in training that mental illness can open a person up to demonic possession, Ms. Blake. It's like PCP but weirder."

"Yeah," I said. "PCP doesn't cause people to levitate."

He frowned at me. "Did you witness the exorcism?"

I shook my head. "I won't talk about it. I especially won't talk about it here and now. Words have power, Captain. Memories have power. I won't play into it."

He nodded. "Are you positive humans didn't do this?"

I shook my head. "They ate her to death. It ate her to death. A person might be able to bite your throat out and do some of this damage, but not all of it."

"If you told me this was a possession, I'd call my chain of command and start looking for a priest; but Blake, do you know how rare overt demonic attacks are?"

"Probably better than you do, Captain. I get called in for all sorts of weird shit."

"Have you ever seen a demon kill a person by straight attack, not trickery?"

"No."

"Then how can you be so sure?" he asked.

"I told you why I'm sure, Captain. Once you've been in the presence of the demonic, you don't forget what it feels like." I shook my head and fought the urge to take another step away from the body.

"But I'm not an expert on demons, Captain Henderson. I suggest you contact a priest. I'm also not an expert on this kind of magic. Call a local witch to look it over. They may be able to give you more information. The best I can do is general stuff."

"Could you have called a demon and made it kill her?"

I frowned at him. "What are you talking about?"

"Just answer the question, Ms. Blake."

"I raise the dead, Captain. I don't do demons."

"A lot of people don't see that big a difference between the two."

"Great, just great. You call me down here. I tell you it's black magic, and now you're going to blame me. I don't feel like being the toasty end of a witch hunt, Captain Henderson."

He smiled. "Just answer the question. Could you do it?"

"No, I could not do this. Trafficking with the demonic taints the soul. I may not be a perfect Christian, but I am trying."

"Fucking vampires taints the soul, too, Blake."

I stared up at him. I looked at him for several long seconds, because what I wanted to do was hit him or scream at him. No, hit him. But I couldn't do that. I settled for one of those smiles you get sometimes when what you really want to do is hurt someone.

"Fine, Captain, fine. This was powerful magic, and I have a reputation for powerful magic. It's not your fault that you don't understand the vast difference between the two schools of magic. Lack of education, can't hold that against you." My voice said plainly that I wanted to. "But if I were going to kill someone, I'd probably just shoot them. That would at least put me near the middle of the suspect list, not the top."

"I heard that about you. That you were a shooter."

I looked at him. "Heard from whom?"

"Cops talk to one another, Ms. Blake. If she'd shown up with a bullet in her head, then I might believe you did it."

"Why would I kill some unknown woman?"

"But she isn't unknown, Ms. Blake." He was watching me very closely.

I glanced back at the body. I looked down the length of it. There was nothing that I recognized. Of all the women I'd met since I came here, none were tall enough for the body. Except one.

I turned back to him and felt the blood drain from my face. "Who is it?"

"Betty Schaffer, the woman who accused your lover boy of rape."

The world swam in stripes of color and heat. Someone was holding my elbow, and only that kept me standing. When my vision cleared, Henderson had my arm, and Wilkes was back. "Are you all right, Ms. Blake?" Wilkes asked.

I looked him right in the eyes and didn't know what to say. Betty Schaffer had been worse than murdered. If the ritual was done right and the person was in jeopardy, not pure, like being a traitor or a liar or lecherous, then the soul could be taken with the life. I'd only seen one body that had been killed in ritual for a demon, and it had been nothing like this. The sacrifice had been killed with a knife, but the soul had been taken. And I couldn't raise the body. If a demon was involved with the death, then the body was just so much clay. I had no power here.

Wilkes couldn't have called a demon. None of his men had the power. Who could have done it? No one I'd met since I arrived had that kind of power and that kind of taint.

Before I could think of anything to say, Wilkes spoke first. "You've got a call. I think you should take it."

He was afraid I'd talk. Trouble was, I didn't have any proof of anything. Hell, I didn't even know what was going on. What was on this ordinary looking land that was worth killing over? Why did the trolls have to be gotten rid of? Was it just so the land could be sold? Or was there a darker purpose? Someone had called a demon to try to make it look like a troll kill. I knew why they'd done it, but not who. I even knew why it was Betty. She'd compromised herself, put herself at risk for that kind of ceremony.

Movies try to give us shit about needing virgins and purity for sacrifice, but true evil doesn't want to kill and send purity to heaven. True evil wants to corrupt good, and once the good are dead, they are beyond the devil's reach. But the impure, to sacrifice them, to kill them—well, the devil gets his due.

Wilkes took my arm as if to help me.

"Don't touch me, Wilkes. Don't ever touch me again."

He let his hand fall. Henderson was watching us like he was seeing more than we were telling. Cops are good about that. Give them anything suspicious, and they'll put two and two together and make ten to twenty-five to life.

Wilkes looked at me. "Could it be werewolves?" His voice was quiet.

I couldn't keep the shock off my face. I fought to regain my nice, blank face, but it was enough. Wilkes knew what Richard was—somehow he knew—and he'd try to blame Betty's death on Richard. Werewolves were a good scapegoat, and a lot more fun to believe in than demons.

He pulled a cell phone from his pocket. He punched up a number. "She's right here." He handed the phone to me.

Henderson was watching us like we were entertaining. I took the phone. The voice on the other end was a man, and I didn't know him.

"I am Franklin Niley, Ms. Blake. I think it is time we meet face-to-face."

"I don't think so," I said.

"Wilkes told me that you have spoiled our little plan about blaming those pesky trolls for the death. But it is not too late to blame your lover. How many people will believe his innocence once they find out he is a werewolf?"

"I don't know what you're talking about," I said.

I had to turn my back on Henderson's alert eyes. His attention was a little too intense. Wilkes wasn't watching me. He was watching Henderson. Unfortunately, turning around put me back to staring at the corpse. I turned to the side and stared off through the trees.

The voice on the phone was cultured, almost too well-mannered for comfort.

"Come, Ms. Blake, let us not play games, the two of us. I know what Mr. Zeeman is, and once he's accused, a simple blood test in the jail will prove me right. He'd lose his job, his career, and perhaps be executed. You have hired an excellent attorney; my congratulations. But if he is convicted, then it is an automatic death sentence. Juries have a strong tendency to convict monsters.''

"I'm listening.''

"Meet me at the diner in town. A public place, so you'll feel safe.''

"Why do you want to meet?'' My voice was growing progressively lower, whispering.

"To beg you one last time to leave town, Ms. Blake. I have no wish to come against you. The spirits say that to come against you is death.''

"Spirits?'' I whispered.

"Meet me, Ms. Blake. You and Mr. Zeeman. Meet me, and I promise you it will all be over. You will leave town and all will be well.''

"I don't trust you.''

"Nor should you,'' Niley said. He laughed, deep and rich. "But meet me at the diner, Ms. Blake. I'll answer your questions. I'll tell you why I want the land. Once my people have made sure you're not wearing a wire, I'll answer any direct question you have. Surely that tempts you.''

"You sound like a man who knows a lot about temptation, Mr. Niley.''

He laughed again. "Money tempts many people, Ms. Blake, and I have a great deal of it.''

I'd been walking slowly away from Henderson. "You going to offer me money?''

"No, Ms. Blake, that is what won a certain officer of the law to my camp— and his men. I do not think money is the key to your soul.''

I didn't like the way he said that. "What do you want, Niley?''

"To talk, that is all. I would swear to you or promise you your safety, but I do not think you would believe me.''

"You got that right.''

"Come to me, Ms. Blake. Let us talk. After I have answered your questions, then you can decide whether to leave or stay. Now, would you be so kind as to put the sheriff back on the phone?''

I turned back to the waiting men and held up the phone. "He wants to talk to you again.''

Wilkes came for the phone. It was just the two of us by the body when he tried to take the phone. I held onto it. I leaned in close to him and said, "Money doesn't spend in hell, Wilkes. The devil deals in a different coin.''

He jerked the phone from my hand and walked away into the trees, listening to the voice in his ear. The voice that had offered him money to sell out everything he was or might have been. The motive I understood least of all for murder or betrayal was greed. But damned if it wasn't a popular motive for both.

34

Richard hadn't said a word since we started the drive to the diner. He'd pulled the rubber band out of his hair and played with it, stretching it wide, letting it relax, open, close, open, close. He didn't usually have nervous habits. It wasn't a good sign. I pulled into the parking lot and shut off the engine. Richard was sitting in the middle with his long legs drawn up. He'd wanted me to drive. Something about being more easily distracted this close to the full moon. Shang-Da sat on the other side, his face calm. Every time I looked at him, the horrible claw marks seemed to be smoothing out. By nightfall tomorrow, he'd be clean. It was impressive, and it would mark him in everyone's eyes who saw him as what he was: a shapeshifter.

We sat there a moment, listening to the engine tick. "You're not going to do anything stupid, are you?" I asked Richard.

The rubber band broke with a snap, jumping for the floorboard. "Whatever makes you think that?"

I touched his arm. He looked at me. His eyes were perfect chocolate brown, human, but there was something in the depths of those human eyes that was other. His beast crawled just behind those true, brown orbs.

"Can you sit through this without losing it?" I asked.

"I can."

"Will you?" I asked.

He gave me a tight smile, and I didn't like the look on his face. "If I let this much anger out in public with the moon overhead, I might shift. Don't worry, Anita. I know how to deal with my rage." He seemed very self-contained, as if he'd pulled back into himself, behind walls of careful construction. But behind those walls was a vibrating, menacing thing. If Niley's sorcerer were inside, he or she would recognize something was wrong. Of course, they knew what Richard was, so it was all right, I guess.

Shang-Da handed Richard a pair of black wraparound shades. He took them and slipped them on, running his hands through his hair, fluffing it around his shoulders. Another nervous gesture.

"I've never seen you wear sunglasses," I said.

"It's in case my eyes change," Richard said.

I glanced at Shang-Da and his naked eyes. "What about you?"

"I didn't date the girl. I didn't even like her."

Ah. "Great, let's go."

The men walked at my back like bodyguards. Their energy swirled behind me like some kind of psychic wall. It made the skin along my back tight and itchy. I pushed through the glass doors of the diner and stood there for a moment, searching for Niley.

The diner was a 1950s throwback, long and narrow in front, with a wider area to one side that looked like a later addition. There was a long counter with little, round stools. The place was full of locals and families that matched the out-of-state license plates in the parking lot.

The waitresses wore pink uniforms and small, useless aprons. A blond waitress came up to us, smiling. "Richard, Shang-Da, haven't seen you in here all week. Knew you couldn't stay away from Albert's hash browns."

Richard flashed her that smile of his that has been known to melt women into little quivering puddles. The fact that he's unaware of the effect makes it all the more devastating.

Shang-Da nodded at her, which for him was a rousing hello.

"Hi, Aggie," Richard said. "We're meeting someone. Frank Niley."

She frowned, then nodded. "They're over there at the big table around the corner. You know the way. I'll bring water and menus in just a sec."

Richard led the way through the crowded tables. We went around the L-shape, and at the end of it, against a bank of windows that overlooked a very pretty mountian view, was our party.

The African American bodyguard, Milo, was one of three men at the table. He stood when he saw us. He was still tall, leanly muscled, with square-cut hair, handsome in a cold sort of way. He had a long coat on, and it was too hot for long coats.

I grabbed Richard's arm, slowed him. "Please," I said.

Richard stared down at me from behind black lenses, his eyes lost. I'd never realized how much of his expression was in his eyes. I couldn't read what he was thinking. With some effort, I might have found out, but the last thing I wanted to do was activate the marks in front of Niley's people.

Richard let me walk a little ahead of him. Shang-Da had put a sport jacket on over the white shirt and black slacks. He'd surprised me by having a snub-nosed thirty-eight, chrome-plated. It had a paddle holster and fit at the small of his back without breaking the line of his jacket. When I'd questioned the gun, he'd said, "These are not policemen."

The logic was sound, and he'd checked the gun automatically to see it was loaded. He handled the gun like it was habit. He was the first lycanthrope I'd ever met who carried and seemed comfy with it.

It was actually nice to not be the only person on our side with a gun.

There were two men still sitting. One was under twenty-five, with curly brown hair cut short and a wide, almost surprised face. Not Niley. The other one was well over six feet and must have weighed close to three hundred pounds. He gave the impression of size without being exactly fat. His hair was black and receding sharply in front. He'd done nothing to hide this fact. Rather, the rest of his hair had been buzzed very close to his head, making it all the more obvious. The lack of hair made his face seem too small for his broad shoulders.

The dark pin-striped suit sat over his white shirt, smooth and costly. He wore a vest but no tie. The wide, white collar showed a curl of greying chest hair. He smiled as he watched us move through the tables of tourists and their screaming children.

His eyes were pleasant and empty like an amused snake. He waved large blunt-fingered hands. Gold rings glittered from every finger. "Ms. Blake, so good of you to come." He didn't stand for me, which made me wonder what was in his lap. A sawed-off shotgun, maybe. Or maybe his overly mannered speech was an affectation, and he didn't know the actions that went with it. Or maybe he didn't consider me a lady. Maybe.

Shang-Da had moved to one side so that he and Milo were facing each other. I narrowed my focus to Niley and the younger man. He looked benign, like he should have been sitting at one of the other tables, surrounded by normal people doing normal things.

Niley offered me his hand. I took it. His handshake was too quick, barely touching. "This is Howard."

Howard didn't offer me his hand, which made me offer my hand to him. His big brown eyes got even bigger. And I realized that Howard was afraid of me. Interesting.

"Howard doesn't shake hands," Niley said. "He's a rather powerful clairvoyant. I'm sure you understand."

I nodded. "I've never met a strong clairvoyant that would willingly touch a stranger. Too much crap to pick up."

Niley nodded, small head bobbing on his wide shoulders. "Exactly, Ms. Blake, exactly."

I sat down. Richard slid into the chair beside me.

Niley's eyes moved from me to Richard. "Well, Mr. Zeeman, we meet at last."

Richard stared at him from behind dark glasses. "Why did you kill her?"

The abruptness of it made even me wince.

I must have made some movement, because Richard said, "I didn't come here to play games."

"Nor did I," Niley said. "If you will accompany me to the men's room, I will check you for listening devices. Milo will check your bodyguard."

"Shang-Da," Richard said. "His name's Shang-Da."

Niley smiled even more broadly. If his smile kept getting wider, soon his face would just split open.

"Of course."

"Who gets to search me?" I said. "Howard?"

Niley shook his head. "My other associate is running a little late today." He stood and there was nothing in his lap. Paranoia. "Shall we, Mr. Zeeman? May I call you Richard?"

"No," Richard said, voice deep and low, as if he wanted to say more.

I touched his arm as he moved past me. I looked up into his face, trying to tell him with a look not to do anything stupid.

Niley took Richard's other arm, slipping it through his like you'd walk arm and arm with your lover. He patted Richard's arm. "My, aren't you a handsome fellow."

Richard gave me a look as Niley led him away. I'd have given a great deal to see his eyes at that moment. Usually the bad guys make moves on me.

Shang-Da moved back so Milo could come out from behind the table. They moved off together, not touching, the tension between them thick enough to swing on.

I was left with Howard and my back to the door. I changed chairs, sitting where Milo had been, so I could see the entrance. It put me closer to Howard, and he didn't like that much. I smelled a weak link.

"How good are you?" I asked.

"Good enough to be scared of you," he said.

I frowned at him. "I'm not one of the bad guys, Howard."

"I can see your aura," he said in a voice that I could barely hear above the murmur of voices and silverware.

The waitress came with glasses of water and menus. I assured her the others were coming back to the table, but I wasn't sure if all of us were ordering. She left with a smile.

I turned back to Howard. "So you can see my aura. So what?"

"I know how powerful you are, Anita. I can feel it."

"I can't see your aura, Howard. I can feel a little of your power, but not much. Dazzle me. Show me what you can do."

"Why?"

"Maybe I'm bored."

He licked his lips. "Give me something benign. No weapons, nothing magic."

That sort of cut down on my options. I finally took the cross around my neck off and handed it to him. I pooled the chain into his hand. "Don't touch my skin with your hand," he said.

I let the last of the chain spill into his hand and was careful not to touch him. He closed his hand over the cross. He didn't close his eyes, but he wasn't seeing the restaurant. He looked past it all, and I felt his power ripple over me like a tiny electric current.

"I see a woman, older, your grandmother." He blinked and looked at me. "She gave you this when you graduated high school."

I nodded. "Impressive." I'd started wearing this particuliar cross just recently. I valued it, and I'd had a lot of crosses taken from me over the years. But lately, I'd felt the need of something special. Grandmother Blake had given it to me with a note that said, "May your faith be as strong as this chain and as pure as this silver." Lately, I needed all the purity I could get.

Howard's eyes went past me, staring at something at the end of the room. His breathing had stopped for just a second, like an inaudible gasp.

I turned to see what had captured his attention so thoroughly. The man was close to seven feet tall and had to weigh over five hundred pounds. His face was totally hairless, not just clean shaven. He had no eyelashes, nothing; smooth and unreal. His eyes were a nearly colorless grey too small for his large face. He wore a black shirt untucked over black slacks, black shoes. The skin of his arms and face were unbelievably white as if the sun never touched him.

The man didn't make my skin creep with power. In fact, he was too empty, walking towards us, as if he were shielding himself.

I stood up. Partly it was his size. Partly it was the lack of anything from him, like he wasn't there. I didn't like it when someone worked that hard to shield themselves. It usually meant they had something to hide. If this was the sorcerer that had killed Betty, I knew exactly what he was hiding.

The man stopped in front of us. Howard hugged himself and made introductions. "Linus, this is Anita Blake. Anita, this is Linus Beck." Howard's voice was higher than it should have been, like he was scared. He seemed to be afraid of a lot of people.

Linus Beck smiled down at me. His voice, when it came, was shocking, a delicate soprano of a voice. "So happy to meet you, Anita. So seldom do I meet a fellow practitioner of the arts."

"We don't practice the same brand, Linus."

"Are you so sure?" he asked.

"Positive." Even standing, I had to crane my neck upward to see his face. "Why does Niley need a first-rate clairvoyant and a sorcerer?"

Linus Beck smiled, and it looked genuine. "You know the correct term. I am pleased."

"Glad to hear it. Now, answer the question."

"When I have checked you for wires, then all will be answered."

I looked at those large, white hands and didn't want him to touch me. There was almost no hair, even on his arms. It was like a golden down, like the arm of small child. Something clicked in my head, and I stared up at him. Maybe it showed on my face. Maybe he read my mind, though I don't think so.

"My manhood was sacrificed many years ago so I could better serve my master."

I blinked at him. "You're a eunuch."

He gave a small nod.

I wanted to ask why but didn't. There was no answer that would make sense, so why bother? "What flavor are you, sociopath, psychopath, or schizophrenic?"

He blinked small eyes, the smile fading. "Misguided people have told me I was crazy, Anita. But I did hear voices, my master's voice."

"Yeah, but were the first voices your master or just bad brain chemistry?"

His frown deepened. "I don't know what you mean."

I sighed. He probably didn't. Sorcerers were people who got their magic through demonic—or worse—power. They bargained for what they got and bartered their souls for money, comfort, lust, power. But some were a version of possession. People weakened by some flaw: mental illness or even a flaw of character. The right kind of flaws can attract evil.

Niley led the other men back around the corner. He and Richard were not holding hands anymore. Richard's face was tight and angry. Shang-Da and Milo's faces gave nothing away as if nothing had happened. Niley looked happy, pleased with himself. He clapped Linus Beck on the back, and the eunuch raised the other man's hand to his mouth and kissed it.

Maybe I didn't know as much about eunuchs as I thought I did. I thought it meant sexless. Maybe I was wrong.

"Linus will search you for wires, then we can talk."

"I don't want him touching me. Nothing personal, Linus."

"You fear my master," he said.

I nodded. "You bet."

"I must insist it be Linus, in case you have some magic or other about your person that would disturb us."

I frowned at him. "Like what? The holy hand grenade?"

Niley waved the comment away. "Linus must search you, but if you like, you can have one of your men accompany you."

I didn't like it, but it was probably the best offer we were going to get. The waitress came to take our order, and I realized I was hungry. You learn to be able to eat in the midst of disaster and gore, or you get another line of work. They served breakfast all day. I ordered pancakes and maple-cured bacon.

Richard looked shocked. "How can you eat?"

"You either learn to eat in the middle of disaster and gore, or you get another day job, Richard."

"Very practical, Ms. Blake," Niley said.

I looked at him and felt a small, unpleasant smile curve my lips. "Just of late, Mr. Niley, I've become very, very practical."

"Good," he said, "very good. Then we understand each other."

I shook my head. "No, Mr. Niley, I don't understand you. I know what you are, and what you'll do, but I don't understand why."

"And what am I, Ms. Blake?"

The smile grew. "A bad guy, Mr. Niley; you're a bad guy."

He nodded. "Yes, I am, Ms. Blake. I am a very, very bad guy."

"Guess that makes us the good guys," I said.

Niley smiled. "I know what I am, Ms. Blake, and I am content with it. Are you content?"

We looked at each other for a long moment. "My state of mind isn't really any of your business."

"Answer enough," he said.

"Let's order," I said.

Everyone ordered, finally even Richard. When the waitress walked away, Linus, Richard, and I headed for the rest room so he could search me for listening devices and magical booby traps.

I only had one question. "Which bathroom are we going to use?"

35

We used the men's room. Linus's hands felt strangely soft as if there were no muscles under his skin, just bones and flesh. Maybe he'd given up other things to serve his master. He was creepy, but he was thorough. He even ran his fingers through my hair, which most people forget to do. He behaved himself, even when his hands were on delicate areas. He didn't give Richard any reason to grump at him. Me, either.

We all trooped back out to the table. The food hadn't arrived yet, but my coffee had. Everything goes down better with coffee.

We were again in the chairs with our backs to the door. If we'd gotten there first, they'd have had these chairs, so it was hard to bitch. Linus sat on Niley's right. I realized why we weren't in a booth. Linus wouldn't have fit.

"You wanted to talk, Niley. Talk." I sipped coffee. It was bitter and had been on the burner too long, but there's no such thing as undrinkable coffee. I did hope the food was better.

"I want you to leave town, Anita."

"Wilkes and his men already covered that. We told them we were leaving by sundown," I said.

"I know what you told the good sheriff," Niley said. He wasn't smiling now. His eyes were cool, the humor dying from his face like the sun sinking away, leaving the world to darkness.

"I don't think he believes we're leaving, Richard," I said.

"I don't care what he believes," Richard said.

I glanced at Richard. He was sitting with his arms crossed, staring at Niley. It would have been more unnerving without the manatee T-shirt, but he got the point across. So much for Richard playing clever repartee with me. I left him to his quiet anger and plowed ahead alone.

"Why is it so important that we get out of town, Niley?"

"I told you. The spirits say to come against you is death."

I shook my head. "What spirits?"

"Howard uses the Ouija board as well as his other gifts. The spirits warned of a Lady Death. A woman that would be my undoing. We were warned of this in connection to this purchase. When I heard your name mentioned, I suddenly knew who Lady Death was. The spirits say that if I come against you directly, you will slay me.''

"So you sent Wilkes and his bully boys around to scare me off.''

"Yes, and I hired two locals to kill you. Are they dead?''

I smiled. "I didn't search you guys for wires, now did I?''

He seemed to find that amusing. "I suppose not. But I assume the two men will not be coming back for the second half of their payment.''

"You can assume that,'' I said.

The waitress came with our food. We were all utterly quiet as she set the plates down. She put syrup in front of me and asked if we wanted anything else. We all shook our heads, and off she went.

I stared down at my pancakes and bacon and wished I hadn't ordered them. I wasn't in the mood to spar anymore. I just wanted this over.

"If you're not supposed to confront me directly, then why the change of plans? Why this meeting?''

He smiled and cut a piece of his country omelet. "Anita, do not be coy. I think we both know that Wilkes does not have the stomach for this work. He may work himself up to shooting you, but he is not up to truly scaring you away. His threat, shall we say, lacks a certain fright factor.'' He took his bite of omelet and chewed.

"Is the threat next?'' I said, pouring syrup on my pancakes.

He smiled, dabbed at his mouth with a napkin, and shook his head. "Let us save that for last. Now, ask your questions.''

"Why do you want this piece of land?''

Richard shifted in his chair, leaning forward. He'd been wondering about that particular question longer than I had.

"There is a relic on that land somewhere. I need to own the land so I can tear it up and search for the relic.''

"What relic?'' I asked.

He smiled. "The lance that pierced Christ's side.''

I stared at him. I stared at him longer. He didn't seem to be kidding. "That is a myth, Niley.''

"You don't believe in Christ?''

"Of course I do, but a Roman lance doesn't last for thousands of years. It was lost long ago.''

"Do you believe in the Grail?'' he asked.

"The Grail is a historical fact. It's been found and lost twice in recorded history. The spear has never been authenticated. It's passed around like the bones of some saint, but it's just bait for the gullible.''

"Do I look gullible, Anita?''

"No,'' I said. "How did it get to the mountains of Tennessee?''

"The spear was given as a private gift to President James Madison.''

I frowned at him. "I don't remember that from history class.''

"It is listed among the gifts from a certain Mideastern principality. One spear, Roman. Unfortunately, it was one of the items that went missing after the British burned and sacked Washington, D.C., in 1815.''

"I remember reading about the burning of the White House during the War of 1812. Valuables went missing. So, say you're right. How did it end up here?" I asked.

"Howard has chased it here through his psychic gifts. The spirits have led us to this place. We hired a diviner, and he traced off the boundaries of our search area. That area lies within Greene's land."

"Search the land," Richard said. "You don't have to buy it to do that. You don't have to disturb the trolls to search for a spear."

"It could be buried anywhere on the land, Richard. I don't think Greene would appreciate us tearing up his property unless we owned it."

"I'm amazed that Greene is still alive," I said.

"We looked into his father's will. Did you know that if the man's son dies, the land becomes an animal preserve? He was enamored of your trolls, Mr. Zeeman, was the late Farmer Greene."

"I didn't know that," Richard said.

"Why should you? John Greene, the man's son, is trying to sell to us. He told us all the provisions of his father's estate. He was complaining about them, but it saved his life. So we must buy the land, and the trolls must be gone for that— unless you will simply stop fighting the sale in court." Niley smiled at Richard. "Would you do that for me, Richard? Would you just let us buy the land? I promise we will disturb your trolls as little as possible."

Richard leaned over to me and whispered, "Are you running your foot up and down my leg?"

I looked at him. "No."

Richard scooted his chair back with a loud scrape. He moved closer to me, one arm going around the back of my chair. "Once you own the land, Niley, you can bulldoze it, and we can't stop you. The only thing we can do is stop your purchase."

"Richard, you disappoint me. After our little tête-à-tête in the bathroom, I thought we were friends."

Richard blushed almost purple from his neck to the roots of his hair. "Why did you kill Betty?"

"Why, to frame the trolls for the death of a person. I thought you would have figured that out by now."

"Why Betty?"

Linus answered in his high, musical voice. "She was a liar, a traitoress, and a wanton thing. She opened herself to evil."

Power breathed off of Richard from the arm against my back. An almost visible aura of heat rose around him. It clicked with something deep inside of me. I put a hand on his thigh. He jumped until he realized it was me, then settled back. I thought soothing thoughts at him. But what he was thinking of was Betty, and the thought was strong enough that he made me flash on her body. I had one quick visual of her torn breasts, and he stood so abruptly his chair fell to the floor. His hands were on the table, and he swayed softly. I thought he might faint.

I started to touch him, but was afraid to, afraid he'd see more. Shang-Da came to take his arm.

The voices around us had quieted, hushed. Everyone was looking. "Please, Richard, sit down," I whispered.

Shang-Da helped him sit. We all waited quietly, watching each other until the voices around us rose and everyone went back to eating. Howard whispered, "Your auras converged for a moment. They became one piece and flared. What are you to each other?"

Richard's voice squeezed out, "Betty wasn't perfect, but she didn't deserve to die like that." He leaned his face down toward the table, and I realized he was crying.

I touched his back, tentatively, rubbing it in small circles. "Your plan to blame her death on the trolls is a bust. Now what?"

"It doesn't matter what we're going to do next, Anita. You will be out of town."

"We told Wilkes we were leaving," I said.

Richard took off the sunglasses and wiped at his eyes with his palms.

"Look at me, please, Richard," Niley said.

Maybe it was the please; for just an instant, Richard looked across the table. For an instant, Niley saw his eyes. "Such pretty brown eyes. You are a lucky woman, Anita."

Richard started to push to his feet. I laid a hand on his arm. His muscles were hard and so tense they thrummed with, I think, a desire to jump across the table and hurt Niley.

"I want to make sure that you are gone. Lately, the spirits have told Howard of a beast that will aid the lady. I think I am looking at the beast."

"How did you find out?" I asked.

Richard slid the glasses back in place and slid his chair back into the table. His shoulders were hunched so hard, the T-shirt was straining at the seams.

"The local vampires don't like you much," Niley said. "I approached them, trying to gather information about the spear. Some of them have been in this area for long enough to have witnessed the event. Sadly, they had not, but they told me interesting things about you and Richard and the Master of the City in Saint Louis. They said you were a ménage à trois, though Richard seems reluctant to admit an interest in men."

"Don't believe everything that you're told, Niley, especially from people who don't like us. Your enemies always make up better rumors than your friends."

Niley pouted. "Oh, dear. Then my advances have been very unwanted indeed." He laughed. The smile faded. "I think it is time for the threat."

"Knock yourself out," I said.

"I think a tranquillizer dart from a distance for Richard. When he wakes, he will be bound by silver chains and on his stomach, naked. I will rape him, and I will enjoy it. Then I will let Linus slit his throat, and Linus will enjoy that." He turned cold eyes to me. "You, Anita, I will give to Linus for his master."

Linus turned to me. He looked the same, but the skin on my back tried to detach itself and crawl away and hide. Every hair on my arm stood up in nervous rows. Evil whispered through that bright diner.

Howard gasped, hugging himself.

I stared at Linus and didn't try to hide it. I was scared of him and what lay inside him.

Niley laughed, deep and pleasant. "I think we understand each other at last, Anita."

Richard turned and looked at Linus. The hair on his arms was standing at attention, too. He spoke, looking directly at the sorcerer. "How you are fallen from Heaven, O Day Star, son of Dawn!"

At the first line, that awful power receded, the skin creeping a little less. Linus's face was no longer pleasant.

Richard said, "How you are cut down to the ground, you who laid the nations low! You said in your heart, 'I will ascend to Heaven; Above the stars of God I will set my throne on high.' Isaiah." With the last line, the scent of evil retreated. It lingered like perfume in an empty room, but it was closed down for now.

"Impressive, Richard," Niley said. "So you are a true believer."

Richard rose slowly from his chair. He put a hand flat on the table and leaned across it. I felt the prickling rush of energy like a hot thread pulled across my skin. He lowered his sunglasses just enough for Niley to see his eyes, and I knew what he was doing. I knew that Niley was watching those brown eyes change to wolf amber.

Richard spoke low and carefully. " 'And the light shineth in darkness; and the darkness comprehended it not.' " He slid his glasses back over his eyes, stood, and stepped away from the table. He held his hand out for me. I took it. I let him lead me out of the restaurant. Shang-Da followed at our backs.

I risked a glance back. I didn't turn to a pillar of salt, but I saw Niley's face. And I knew, knew without doubt, that he would see us dead.

36

I didn't even ask Richard if we were leaving town for real. I knew the answer, and frankly, I was with him. On the off chance that Niley was right and the spear was here, we couldn't let him have it. But it was more than that. Richard had drawn a line in the sand; good versus evil. Good can't tuck tail and run. It's against the rules.

It took about three hours for us to pack and pretend to leave town. We put Jamil in the back of the van with a coffin on either side of him to keep the stretcher from sliding around. Nathaniel had managed to get his lower back sliced up defending my honor. Though he admitted that he hadn't been fighting so much as getting in the way of an eager werewolf. However it happened, he got to ride in the back with the injured, probably stretching on top of a coffin, for all I knew. Cherry rode in back with them—I think to act as a peace officer. Jamil didn't seem to like Nathaniel much. I drove the van. Richard followed in his four-by-four with Shang-Da, and all the equipment he'd brought for an entire summer of camping and studying large primates. Everybody else rode with me.

Sheriff Wilkes sent Maiden and Thompson to escort us out of town in a black and white, or in this case, a blue and white, but the effect was the same. Thompson waved merrily as we drove past them out of the city limits. It would have been childish to give him the finger, so I didn't do it. Zane did it for me. Jason blew them a kiss.

We drove for over an hour to a prearranged rendezvous with Verne. We couldn't all stay at one house. Too many new people might raise suspicions, so we divided up. I didn't like it, but I had to agree that all together we made too good a show.

I ended up driving to Marianne's house. I rode in the back of her truck with Zane, Cherry, and the coffins. Nathaniel got to ride in the truck cab because of his claw wound. Zane's gunshot wound seemed to be healing a lot faster than the claw marks. I wasn't sure if it was because Nathaniel was a slow healer or if bullet wounds just healed faster than claws.

The open bed of the truck was a very rough ride. I wedged myself in the corner near the cab, with Damian's coffin pressed against my ribs. If I pressed my head back against the truck to brace my neck, my teeth rattled. If I sat up more, my neck snapped with every pothole. It was like an endless beating, until my bones thrummed with it and I had a headache the size of Idaho in the middle of my forehead. The sun was like a smear of yellow fire in the sky. It beat down unblinking, unrelenting, until sweat ran down my face and arms.

Zane was in the corner opposite me, shoved against Asher's coffin. His black T-shirt had molded to him like a sweaty second skin. Cherry had chosen a white T-shirt today. The reddish dust of the road clung to the white material and mingled with the sweat until it was like dried blood.

My hair had turned into a mass of sweaty ringlets. Not those cute Shirley Temple ringlets. Nothing that neat, just a curled mess. Zane and Cherry's hair just lay slick and flat against their heads.

The three of us made no effort to talk. We settled into the heat and bone-jarring ride like it was a kind of coma, something to be endured rather than shared.

The road spilled onto a paved road, and the sudden smoothness was almost startling. I could hear again.

"Thank God," Cherry said.

Marianne yelled back to us, "Car coming, hide."

We all wiggled under the top layer of the tarp covering the coffins. There was a second tarp and ropes underneath me. The tarp smelled musty and dry. It was a toss-up whether it was cooler because of the shade or hotter because of the lack of air. I thought I heard a car go by in a spill of gravel, but Marianne didn't tell us to get up, so I didn't. I could see Zane through the hot dimness. We looked at each other with dull eyes; then I smiled. He smiled. It all started to be funny. You just reach a level of discomfort where you either scream or laugh.

The truck lurched to a rattling stop. In the sudden silence I could hear Zane laughing. Cherry's voice came clearly, "What in hell is so funny?"

"We're home, boys and girls," Marianne said. "You can come out now."

Zane and I crawled out into the open air, still giggling. Cherry frowned at both of us. "What is so funny?"

We both shook our heads. You either got the joke, or you didn't. It could not be explained, not even to ourselves.

Marianne came to stand near me. "I'm glad to see you're in a better mood."

I ran my hands through my hair and could almost squeeze the sweat out of it. "Might as well be in a good mood. The day's not going to improve."

Marianne frowned. "Pessimism is unbecoming in one so young."

She stood there, looking cool and collected, wearing a sleeveless white shirt tied off at the waist. It wasn't a midriff but gave the illusion of one. A pair of pale blue shorts and flat, white tennis shoes completed the outfit. Her pale hair was in a bun. The hair was all streaks: silvery grey, pale blond, and white. Fine lines showed at her eyes and mouth that hadn't been visible last night. Over fifty, but like Verne, her body was still thin and firm. She looked cool, comfortable, and far too clean.

"I need a shower," I said.

"I second the motion," Cherry said.

Zane just nodded.

"Welcome to my home," Marianne said.

The truck was parked in a gravel driveway of a two story white house. The house had yellow shutters and a pink climbing rose up one side of the front porch. There were two tubs of white and pink geraniums at the bottom of the wide porch steps. The flowers were lush and well watered. The yard was brown and dying in the summer heat. Actually, I approved. I didn't believe in watering grass. A small flock of speckled hens pecked in the dry dirt of the yard.

"Nice," I said.

She smiled. "Thank you. The barn is over that way, hidden by the trees. I've got some dairy cows and horses. The garden's behind the house. You'll be able to see it from your bedroom."

"Great, thanks."

She smiled. "Why do I think you don't care about my tomato crop?"

"Let me take a shower, and I'll care," I said.

"We can unload the coffins, then your two wereleopards can take a bath. I hope there's enough hot water for three baths. If two of you could double up, it would conserve water."

"I'm not sharing," I said. I looked at Cherry.

She shrugged, "Zane and I can share."

It must have shown on my face, because she added, "We aren't lovers, Anita. Though we have been. It will be . . . a comfort to touch each other. It's not sexual. It's . . ." She looked at Marianne, as if for help.

Marianne smiled. "One of the things that binds a pack or a pard into a unit is touch. They touch each other constantly. They groom each other. They care for each other."

I shook my head. "I'm not sharing a bathtub."

"No one is asking you to," Marianne said. "There are many ways to forge a pack bond, Anita."

"I'm not part of the pack," I said.

"There are many ways to be part of the pack, Anita. I have found my place among them, and I am not lukoi." She left Zane, Cherry, and me to unload the coffins while she took Nathaniel off to lie down. Cherry and Zane helped stow the coffins in the basement, then went off to take their communal bath.

The entrance to the basement was outside, like an old-fashioned storm cellar. The back door was all screen and wood. It clanged loudly as the wereleopards went inside. Marianne met me at that door, stepped through that door, and blocked my way.

She was smiling and calm and seemed at peace in the center of her universe. Just seeing that content look on her face made me itchy and uncomfortable. Made me want to scream and lash out until her universe was as messy as my own. How dare she be content when I was so confused?

"What is so very wrong, child? I can hear your confusion like bees buzzing in the walls."

There was a stand of pine trees near the back of the house like a line of soldiers. The air smelled like a perpetual Christmas. I usually like the smell of pine, but not today. I just wasn't in a Christmas mood. I leaned against the weathered boards of the house, while she stayed on the small back porch looking down at me.

The Firestar dug into my back. I pulled it out and shoved it down the front of my jeans. Fuck it if somebody saw.

"You saw Verne," I said.

She looked at me, grey eyes calm, unreadable. "I saw what you did to his neck, if that is what you mean."

"Yeah, that's what I mean."

"Your mark on his neck proves two things to all of us. That you consider yourself his equal—no small boast—and that you are not happy with his hospitality to date. Are either of these untrue?"

I thought about that for a moment, then said, "I don't acknowledge anyone as dominant to me. Maybe they can beat the shit out of me or kill me, but they're not better than I am. Stronger doesn't mean better or more dominant."

"There are those who would argue with you, Anita, but I am not one of them."

"And no, I'm not happy with the hospitality to date. I destroyed most of Colin's vampires for you guys. Verne was pleased as punch, but he still didn't let me have my guns last night. If I'd had my guns last night, then the bad guys wouldn't have nearly killed Jamil and Jason and Zane—hell—and me."

"Verne regretted last night or he would not have offered himself to you."

"Great, fine, but I didn't mean to mark him. I didn't mean to do it. Do you understand, Marianne? I didn't do it on purpose. Just like last night with the munin, this morning I wasn't in control. I was seduced by the scent of blood and warm flesh. It was . . . creepy."

She laughed. "Creepy? Is that the best word you can come up with, Anita? Creepy. You are the Executioner and a force to be feared, but you are still so . . . young."

I looked up at her. "You mean naive."

"You are not naive in the sense that it is usually meant. I am sure you have seen more blood and death than I have. It stains your power, this violence. You both attract it and pursue it. But there is something about you that stays fresh and somehow perpetually childlike. No matter how jaded you grow, there will always be a part of you that would be more comfortable saying 'golly' than 'goddamn.' ' "

I wanted to wiggle under the intensity of her gaze, or run. "I am losing control of my life, Marianne, and control is very important to me."

"I would say that control is one of *the* most important things to you."

I nodded, my hair catching on the peeling paint of the house. I pushed away from the boards to stand in front of her in the dusty yard. "How can I get back control, Marianne? You seem to have all the answers."

She laughed again, that wholesome-bedroom sound. "Not all the answers, but the answers you seek, perhaps. I know that the munin will come for you again. It may be when you least expect it or when you need your precious control the most. It may overwhelm you and cost the lives of people you hold dear as it could have last night. All that saved Richard from having to kill to get to you was Verne's intercession."

"Raina would love that, to drag one of us down to the grave."

"I felt the munin's pleasure in destruction. You are attracted to violence, but only as it serves a greater purpose. It is a tool that you use well. Your old lupa was attracted to violence for its own sake, as a destructive thing. Destroying was what she was about. It is nicely ironic that someone so dedicated to negativity was also a healer.''

"Life is just full of little ironies," I said. I didn't try to keep the sarcasm out of my voice.

"You have a chance to make her munin, her essence, into something positive. In a way, you might help her spirit work through some of its karma.''

I frowned at her.

She waved her hands. "My apologies. I'll keep the philosophy to a minimum. I believe I can help you call and tame the munin. I believe that together we can begin to harness all the different kinds of power you are being offered now. I can teach you to ride not just the munin but this master vampire of yours, and even your Ulfric. You are their key to each other, Anita. Their bridge. Their feelings for you are part of the binding that has been wrought between the three. I can make you the rider and not the horse.''

There was a fierceness in her face, a force that made my skin react. She meant what she said; she believed it. And strangely, so did I.

"I want to control it, Marianne, all of it. I want that more than almost anything right now. If I can't stop it, I want to control it.''

She smiled, and it made her eyes sparkle. "Good; then let's begin with our first lesson.''

I frowned at her. "What lesson?''

"Come into the house, Anita. The first lesson is waiting for you if your heart and mind are open to it.'' She went back inside without waiting for me.

I stood there for a moment in the summer heat. If my heart and mind were open to it. What the hell did that mean? Well, as the cliché goes, only one way to find out. I opened the screen door and walked inside. Lesson number one was waiting for me.

37

Marianne led me to the room where she'd settled Nathaniel. It was a large bedroom downstairs. Hours earlier, the room would have been filled with morning light, but now, at nearly three o'clock in the afternoon, the room was dim, almost dark. The window was open, and a breeze had finally found us, spilling the white lacy curtains into the room. A small oscillating fan sat on a kitchen chair so the fan could cool the bed. The wallpaper was off-white with a fine line of pink flowers. There was a large brown water stain in the corner of the ceiling like a giant Rorschach ink blot.

The bed was a brass four-poster that had been painted white. The bedspread was quilted and looked homemade with a lot of purple- and pink-flowered fabric. Marianne had folded the bedspread and placed it on top of a large cedar chest that was under the window. "Too hot for quilts," she'd said.

Nathaniel lay naked on the pink sheets. Marianne tucked the sheets to the tops of his thighs, patting his shoulder in a motherly sort of way. I would have protested his state of undress, but I could see the wounds clearly for the first time.

Something with claws had swiped him wide and deep, starting about the middle of his back and slashing downward across the right side of his buttocks. The wound was deep and ragged on his back, growing more shallow as it worked down his body. It must have hurt to have clothes over it, hurt a lot.

I was surprised that Nathaniel hadn't flashed me his wounds earlier. He usually went to great lengths to show me his body. What had changed?

Marianne pointed to the phone beside the bed. "In case your police friend calls you. I've got a cordless phone for normal calls, but I use the bedside phone for pack business."

"So no one can accidentally monitor the cordless phone," I said.

Marianne nodded. She walked to the vanity, which had a heavy oval mirror and marble knobs on the drawers. "When I was a little girl and I was hurt or lonely, especially when it was so hot, my mother would unbraid my hair and brush it. She'd brush it until it lay like silk down my back." She turned with a brush in her hands. "Even now, when I am low, one of my greatest pleasures is for some friend to brush my hair."

I looked at her. "Are you suggesting I brush your hair?"

She smiled, and it was bright and charming, and I didn't trust it. "No, I am suggesting you brush Nathaniel's hair."

I kept staring at her. "Come again?"

She walked towards me, offering me the brush, that too-cheery smile on her face. "Part of what makes you vulnerable to Raina is your own squeamishness."

"I'm not squeamish."

"Prudishness, then," she said.

I frowned at her. "What's that supposed to mean?"

"It means that every time one of the lycanthropes disrobes, you get embarrassed. Every time one of them touches you, you take it sexually. That isn't always what they mean. A healthy pack or pard is built up of a thousand gentle touches. A million small comforts. It's like building a relationship with a boyfriend. Every touch builds and strengthens it."

My frown deepened. "I thought you said it wasn't sexual."

It was her turn to frown. "A different metaphor then. It is like building your relationship with a newborn baby. Every touch, every time you feed him when he's hungry, change him when he's wet, comfort him when he's frightened—the everyday intimacies forge a bond between you. True parenthood is built over years of interdependency. The bond between the pack is built much the same way."

I glanced back at the bed. Nathaniel was still lying there naked except for the sheets on his legs. I turned back to Marianne. "If he was a newborn baby, I'd be fine with him being naked. I might be afraid I'd drop him, but I wouldn't be embarrassed."

"And that is precisely my point," she said. She held the brush out to me. "If you could control the munin, you could heal his wounds. You could take his pain."

"You're not suggesting that I purposely try to call Raina?"

"No, Anita. This is the first lesson, not the graduation exercise. Today, I simply want you to begin to try and be more comfortable around their nudity. I believe that if you can desensitize yourself to the more casual sexual situations, that Raina will have less hold on you. You draw away from situations like this, and that leaves a void, a place where you will not go willingly. So Raina spills into that void and forces you to go much farther than you would have gone on your own."

"And what good will brushing Nathaniel's hair do?"

She held the brush inches from me, arms folded. "It is a small thing, Anita. A thing to give him comfort while we wait for Dr. Patrick to come. Patrick will give him a local for the pain, but sometime before he is finished stitching him up, the painkiller will wear off. Their metabolism is too fast for a local, and giving more than that can be tricky. It can be deadly in one with such a low aura of power as Nathaniel."

I stared up at her, meeting those calm, serious grey eyes. "You're saying that he'll be stitched up without a painkiller."

She just looked at me.

"And that's my fault because I could heal him if I could control the munin."

Marianne shook her head. "It is not your fault, Anita, not yet. But the munin is a tool like your guns or your necromancy. Once you learn how to control it, it can do wonderful things. You must look at the ability to call the munin not as a curse but as a gift.''

I shook my head. "I think you've exceeded the lesson for the day, Marianne."

She smiled. "Perhaps. But take the brush, do this one small thing. Not for me. Not for Nathaniel, but for yourself. Take back that piece of you that looks away from his body. Give Raina less ground in your heart."

"And if I can't help being embarrassed or thinking sexual thoughts and Raina comes up and tries to eat me, what then?''

Marianne's smile widened. "Then I will help you, child. We will all help you. That is what a pack is for."

"Nathaniel isn't lukoi any more than I am," I said.

"Lukoi or pard, it makes no difference to you, Anita. You are queen of both castles. Growing comfortable with one will help with the other."

She actually took my hand and pried it out from under my elbow. She put the hairbrush in my hand and closed my fingers over it. "Be with him, child. Wait for your phone call. Answer only the bedside phone. Only pack will call that number. You can't possibly answer my other phone because you are in another state. Do not answer the door, either.''

"You sound like you're going somewhere," I said.

"You must learn to be comfortable around your people, Anita. That means without me looking over your shoulder."

She pulled me towards the bed by the arm. She tried to make me sit on the bed, but I just didn't bend with it. Short of pushing me onto the bed, she had to leave me standing.

She tsked at me. "Stand here and do nothing. It is your choice, child, but at least stand here." She left.

I was left standing in the middle of the room where I'd followed her, like a child not wanting to be left alone on the first day of school. The brush was still in my hand. The brush looked as antique as the rest of the room. It was wooden but painted white with a shine of varnish. The varnish had a webbing of cracks but held. I ran the pale bristles over the back of my other hand. They were as soft as they looked, silken like a baby's brush. I had no idea what the bristles were made out of.

I glanced back at Nathaniel. He was watching me out of those eyes of his. His face was neutral as if it didn't matter, but his eyes weren't neutral. They were tight, waiting for the rejection, waiting for me to leave him alone in the strange room, naked and waiting for a doctor to come and stitch him up. He was nineteen, and lying there with that raw look in his eyes, he looked it. Hell, he looked younger. The body was great. When you're a stripper, you've got to take care of yourself. But the face . . . the face was young and in the same gaze old. Nathaniel still had the most jaded eyes of anyone I'd ever met under the age of twenty. No, not jaded, lost.

I walked around to the far side of the bed. I laid the hairbrush on the pillow on the empty side of the bed.

Nathaniel moved just his head, turning to look at me. No, to watch me. He watched me like every movement was important. It was a level of scrutiny that made me want to squirm or blush or run. It wasn't exactly sexual, but it wasn't exactly not sexual, either.

No matter what metaphors Marianne used, this was not the same thing as caring for an infant. Nathaniel was young, but he was definitely not a child. At least not childlike in the way that would have made this comfortable.

I slipped off the short-sleeved shirt. There was no one to see the shoulder holster, and it would be cooler. Of course, it would really be cooler if I took off all the guns and the spine sheath, but I wasn't that hot. I did lay the Firestar under the pillow. It had a short enough barrel to sit or lie down with it, but there is no such thing as a truly comfortable gun to wear if you're lounging around. Guns aren't designed for comfort. It's one of the few things that are worn, mostly by men, that are as uncomfortable as a pair of high heels.

I crawled onto the bed, kneeling, still not within touching distance. He was so easily hurt that I had to say it out loud. "I'm not upset with you, Nathaniel. I just don't like playing student."

"You like Marianne, but you resent her," he said.

That made me blink a couple of times and stare at him. He was right, and it was more perceptive than I'd ever expected from Nathaniel. Hearing him say something that smart made me feel better. If there was a brain in that body, then he wasn't just a submissive mess. And maybe, just maybe, he was salvageable, save-able. It was the most positive thought I'd had all day.

I crawled to Nathaniel's side, brush in hand. I stared down at him stretched across the bed, eyes watching me. The look in his eyes stopped me. It was too intense.

Maybe he sensed it, because he turned his head back so that I couldn't see his face. All I could see was all that long, auburn hair. Even in the dim light, it was an incredibly rich color. The darkest auburn I'd ever seen that was still truly auburn and not brown.

I smoothed my hand through his hair. It was like heavy silk, warm to the touch. Of course, that could have just been the room. The fan swept over the bed, ruffling the sheets, passing like a cool hand over my back. Nathaniel's long hair stirred in the fan's caress, the sheet over his thighs blowing like a hand had moved them. He shifted as the fan passed over his bare body. Then stillness. His hair, the sheet, everything utterly still while the fan made its circuit. It swept back, spilling over everything in reverse; the pink sheets, Nathaniel's hair, my chest this time, blowing my own hair back from my face, then past us, and the heat wrapped around us like a suffocating hand.

The breeze from the window had died. The white curtains lay like a painting until the small fan spilled over them. I knelt in the hot room with the only sound the whir of the fan and the small tick it made every time it came to the end of its cycle.

I stroked the hairbrush through his hair, and the stroke ended long before I got to the end of the hair. I'd had hair down to my butt once upon a time when I was about fourteen. But Nathaniel's hair was knee length. If he'd been a woman, I'd have said his hair fell like a dress around him. The hair lay in a soft, silken pile beside his body so it wouldn't brush the wound. I lifted the hair in my arms, and it was like holding something alive. The hair poured through my hands with a sound like dry water, a rushing noise.

I had enough trouble taking care of shoulder-length hair. I couldn't imagine the amount of effort that just washing it must take. I was either going to have to divide the hair to either side and actually get up and move from side to side, or sweep the hair back behind his head so it spilled across the bed. I voted for that.

I pulled his hair behind his back and spilled it behind his head. He moved his head as if snuggling into the pillow, but other than that made no movement and said nothing.

"How you doing?" I asked.

"I'm fine," he said. His voice was soft, neutral, almost empty.

"Talk to me, Nathaniel," I said.

"You don't like it when I talk to you."

I leaned over him, smoothing the hair back so I had a clear view of his face. "That's not true."

He turned his face enough to look up at me. "Isn't it?"

I leaned back from that direct gaze. "It's not you talking I mind, Nathaniel. It's your choice of topics."

"Tell me what you want me to say, and I'll say it."

"I can tell you what not to say," I said.

"What?" he asked.

"Don't talk about pornographic movies, sadomasochism, sex in general." I thought about it for a second or two. "That hits the usual things you say to piss me off."

He laughed. "I don't know what else to talk about."

I started combing his hair across the bed. The stroke was firm and flowing, then I actually had to pick the hair up to finish the stroke. The fan hit me with an armful of hair, and the hair spilled around my face in a vanilla-scented cloud that tickled my face and neck.

"Talk about anything, Nathaniel. Talk about yourself."

"I don't like to talk about myself."

"Why not?" I asked.

He raised up enough to look at me. "You talk about yourself."

"Okay." Then I didn't know what to say. I just suddenly couldn't think of where to start. I smiled. "Good point, forget I said it."

The phone rang, and I gave a little yip. Nervous? Who me? It was Dolph. "Anita?"

"Yeah, it's me."

"Franklin Niley, unless it's a different guy with the same name, is an art dealer. He specializes in mystical artifacts. He's not picky about how he gets them, either."

"How not picky?" I asked.

"He's based out of Miami. The cops there would like to tie him to at least half a dozen homicides but don't have enough proof. Every town he visits on business, people disappear or turn up dead. Chicago P.D. nearly got him on the death of a wiccan high priestess last year, but the witness went into a mysterious coma and hasn't come out yet."

"Mysterious coma?" I made it a question.

"The doctors think it was magic of some kind, but you know how hard that is to prove."

"What do you have on his associates?"

"One hasn't been with him long, a psychic named Howard Grant, young, no criminal record. There's a black bodyguard, Milo Hart. He's got a second-degree black belt in karate and has been in the pen once for attempted murder. He's been beating people up for Niley since he got out of prison five years ago. The third is Linus Beck. He's been in twice. Once for assault with a deadly, second time for murder."

"Lovely," I said.

"It gets better," Dolph said.

"Better?" I asked. "How much better can it get?"

"Beck's murder conviction was a human sacrifice."

I let that sink in for a second or two. "How was the victim killed?"

"Knife wound," Dolph said.

I told him about the body I'd just finished seeing.

"Direct attack by demons went out with the middle ages, Anita."

"They wanted to make it look like a troll attack."

"You've talked to them," he said.

"Yeah."

"Why?"

"They wanted to threaten me," I said.

I heard papers rustling on the other end. "Why did they want to threaten you?"

I told Dolph almost everything. I also told him I couldn't prove a damn thing.

"I talked to a cop in Miami. He said that Niley admitted two murders to him, told him details, but not under Miranda and not useable in court. He likes to taunt."

"He thinks he's untouchable," I said.

"But the spirits say you're going to kill him."

"So his pet psychic says."

"When I put out the name and asked for info, police all over the country and out of it are willing to give me anything they got, if we can just nail this guy," Dolph said.

"A bad guy's, bad guy," I said.

"He's not above doing his own killing, Anita. At least two of the dead men down in Miami, they think were Frank's personal kills. You watch your ass like a son of a bitch. If you have anything that even looks like proof of a crime, call me."

"You don't have any jurisdiction here," I said.

"Trust me on this, Anita. You come up with some proof, and I can get you somebody down there with jurisdiction, ready and willing to put this guy away."

"He on the blue hit parade?"

"He's made a career out of breaking the law and has never seen the inside of a jail cell for more than twenty-four hours. A lot of people in a lot of states would like to see him gone."

"I'll see what I can do," I said.

"I don't mean dead, Anita. I mean arrested."

"I knew what you meant, Dolph."

He was quiet for a second. "I know you knew what I meant, but I thought I should say it, anyway. Don't kill anyone."

"Would I do something so illegal?"

"Don't start, Anita."

"Sorry. Thanks for all the info. It's more than I'd hoped for. After meeting him, I'm not exactly surprised by any of it. He is a very creepy guy."

"Creepy—Anita, he's a hell of a lot more than creepy."

"You sound worried, Dolph."

"You're down there without a safety net, Anita. The cops are not your friends."

"That's an understatement," I said. "But the state cops are down here on the murder now."

"I can't come down there," Dolph said.

"I would never ask you to."

He was quiet so long that I said, "Dolph, you still there?"

"I'm here." He didn't sound happy. "You know how I told you not to kill anyone?"

"Yeah," I said.

"I'll deny this in court, but don't hesitate, Anita. If it comes down to him or you, make the right choice."

My mouth was hanging open. "Dolph, are you telling me to murder him if I get the chance?"

Dolph was quiet again. Finally, he said, "No, not murder, but I am saying don't let him get the drop on you. You do not want to be at this man's mercy, Anita. Some of the bodies they've found have been tortured. He's real creative about it."

"What's in that file that you haven't told me about, Dolph?"

"They found one man's head floating in his pool. There were no marks of a weapon, like the head had been pulled off. They never found the body. It all reads like that, Anita. Not just violent but weird shit."

"You going to post bail if I nail him and get caught?"

"You get caught, we never had this conversation."

"Mum's the word," I said.

"Watch your back, Anita. Niley doesn't have any limits. That's what all this paperwork means. He's a total fucking sociopath, Anita, and Beck and Hart are the same thing."

"I'll be careful, Dolph. I promise."

"Don't be careful, be ruthless. I don't want to be identifying what's left of your body after he gets through with it."

"You trying to scare me, Dolph?"

"Yeah," he said, then he hung up.

I hung the phone up and sat on the bed in the hot, hot room, and I was afraid. I was suddenly more afraid than I had been since we got here. Dolph didn't spook easily. I'd never heard him like that, not about anything or anybody.

Nathaniel touched my leg. "What's wrong?"

I shook my head. I couldn't shake the bad feeling. Dolph, Mr. Law and Order, had encouraged me to kill someone. Unprecedented. The police were telling me to break the law. Too weird. But underneath the wonderment of it was the fear, a fine, trembling sense of unease. Demons. I didn't like demons. They didn't give a shit about silver bullets or much of anything else. Richard felt strong in his faith. I envied him that. *I* was having a crisis of faith right now. I mean, I was sleeping with the undead and had cheated on one lover with another. I also had a few more kills to my credit than the last time I'd been touched by the demonic. I wasn't feeling particularly pure and holy right now. You needed that against demons. You needed surety.

Nathaniel laid his head on my thigh. "You look like you've seen a ghost."

I stared down at the naked man with his head in my lap. No, if I ran up against a demon now, my house was made of glass, and nothing throws stones like the demonic. They know just where to hit so that the whole damn thing comes crashing down around your ears. I was really not in the mood to find out how far from grace I'd actually fallen.

38

Cherry came into the room. She'd slipped into a pair of jean shorts, and a white midriff tank top. Her small breasts were pressed against the thin material. I was a little too well-endowed to ever dream of going without a bra, but small or not, in that top she needed a bra. I was a prude.

Her short yellow hair was still damp. She stalked into the room on those long legs, managing to look both slutty casual and unnaturally graceful.

Just watching her walk into the room made me want to move Nathaniel's head out of my lap. Force of will alone kept me from scooting away from him. We weren't doing anything wrong. But it bothered me.

"Your turn," Cherry said. "I'll wait with Nathaniel."

"Is Zane out yet?"

I caught movement in the hall, and it was Zane. He was wearing jean shorts, too, and nothing else. The ever-present nipple ring was the only thing on his pale, thin chest.

"Don't you ever take that thing out of your chest?" I asked.

He smiled. "If I take the ring out, the hole will close up and I'll have to get it pierced all over again. I might get the other nipple pierced, but I don't want to have to redo the first one."

"I thought you liked pain," I said.

He shrugged. "In some situations with naked women, yeah." He touched the ring, pulling on it until the nipple stretched just a little. "The actual piercing hurt like a son of a bitch."

I looked at the slender, too-thin chest, especially the part right next to his right arm. There was a dark area where the shoulder attached to the chest, but that was all.

"Is that all that's left of the bullet wound?" I asked.

Zane nodded and sat down at the foot of the bed, crawling onto the covers so he was beside Nathaniel and far too close to me. "You can touch the wound if you want."

I frowned. "No, thanks." I started to back off the bed on all fours, spilling

Nathaniel's head gently to the covers. I stopped myself. Marianne said that Raina fed on my embarrassment, my prudishness, that if I could be more comfortable around small stuff, Raina would lose some of her power over me. Was it true?

I wasn't attracted to Zane. That moment last night had been pure Raina. She seemed to have been attracted to anything that had a pulse and some things that didn't. I gritted my teeth and reached out towards Zane.

He went very still, face suddenly serious, as if he had some clue how much it cost me to reach out to him. I ran my fingertips over the wound. The skin was smooth, shiny like a scar but softer and more pliable. I found myself running my hand over the wound, exploring it. It felt strangely plastic, and at the same time soft, like baby's skin.

"This feels . . . cool."

Zane grinned. It reminded me of Jason and that one thought relaxed a tension in my shoulders that I hadn't even known was there.

Cherry came up behind him to slide her hands over his shoulders, massaging them. "I never get over being amazed at how we heal."

I wanted to take my hand back, just because Cherry had touched him, too. I forced myself to keep my hand on the wound, but I'd stopped exploring it, just touching it was all I could manage.

"The muscles can get tight when it's healing," Cherry said. "You get spasms around it, like the body heals too fast for the muscles to keep up."

I took my hand away slowly. I sat on the bed watching Cherry massage Zane's shoulders. Nathaniel nuzzled my leg, rolling his eyes up to me. I didn't move away from him, and he seemed to take that as permission to roll his head onto my thigh. He nestled against me with a contented sigh.

Zane rolled onto his back on the other side of me, not touching me, but watching me. His eyes were very careful.

Cherry stayed kneeling on the foot of the bed, watching my face. They all watched me like I was the center of their world. I'd seen dogs in obedience trials watch their owners that way. In dogs it was a good thing. In people it was unnerving. I didn't have a dog because I didn't feel responsible enough to take care of one. Now I suddenly had three wereleopards, and I knew I wasn't responsible enough for them.

I laid my hand on Nathaniel's warm hair. Zane stretched his full six-foot frame, fingers and toes straining, spine bowing like a big cat.

I laughed. "What am I supposed to do, rub your tummy?"

Everyone laughed, even Nathaniel. I realized with a shock that it was the first time I'd ever heard him laugh. The laughter was young, high-schoolish. Lying naked in my lap with claw marks on his butt, and he was laughing, a full-throated, happy sound.

I was happy to hear it, and nervous. They were trying to make me their home. Because that was what an Ulfric was supposed to be, and a Nimir-ra, or Nimir-raj, for a guy, was the equivalent. Strangely, there didn't seem to be a werewolf equivalent of a queen wolf. Sexism? Or some arcane shit I didn't understand yet? I'd ask Richard later.

"I've got to go take my bath, guys."

"We could help," Zane said. He licked my arm, grimaced. "I like the taste of sweat, but the gravel dust . . ."

Nathaniel raised his face enough to lick my other arm. His tongue ran down my arm in a long slow glide. "I don't mind the dust," he said, voice low and soft.

I slid off the bed, calmly, slowly. I did not go yuck, or scream. I was very calm and very relieved to be standing on the floor. The bed had suddenly become crowded. "Thanks, but the bath will be fine. Don't answer any phone but the one by the bed, and don't open the door to anyone but Dr. Patrick."

"Aye, aye, Captain," Zane said.

I slid the Firestar down the front of my jeans and picked up my suitcase from against the wall. I glanced back at the three of them from the doorway. Zane had lain down on the other side of Nathaniel, only propped on his elbow, one hand touching Nathaniel's back. Cherry had curled at the foot of the bed. She was running her hand up and down his thigh. Either the sheet had slid off or she'd moved it so she could touch him. There was nothing sexual on their faces, nothing overt.

They looked like the opening scene for a porno movie to me, but I was sure that when I left the room, nothing would happen. There was no anticipation between them, no eagerness to have me gone so they could be alone. Their eyes still followed me. They touched each other for comfort, not for sex. The discomfort was mine, not theirs.

"I'm sorry I went with Mira," Nathaniel said suddenly.

That stopped me in the doorway. "You're a big boy, Nathaniel. You had every right to find someone. It was just your choice of partners that was bad."

Zane began to rub his hand up and down Nathaniel's back, like you'd pet a dog. Nathaniel lowered his head so his hair slid around him like a veil, hiding his face. "I thought you were going to be my mistress, my top. I thought for a long time that you understood the game. That you were telling me not to have sex with anyone. I was so good. I didn't even touch myself."

I opened my mouth, closed it, opened it, and didn't have a damn thing to say.

"When you finally gave me permission to have sex with you, it could have been straight vanilla. It was the waiting, the buildup, the teasing that would have made it enough."

I found my voice. "I don't know what vanilla means, Nathaniel."

"Staight sex," Zane said, "normal stuff."

I shook my head. "Whatever, I am not playing with you, Nathaniel. I would never do that."

He looked at me sort of sideways as if afraid to look me full in the face. "I know that now. It was this trip that I realized you didn't even know we were playing a game. You aren't teasing me. You don't think about me at all."

That last sounded sort of pitiful, but I couldn't help that. "I keep having to apologize to you, Nathaniel. Half the time I don't even know what I'm apologizing for."

"I don't understand how you can be my Nimir-ra and not be my top, but I know now that you see it as two separate things. Gabriel didn't."

"What is a top?" I asked.

Zane answered for him again. "A dominant to Nathaniel's submissive. A submissive is called a bottom."

Ah. "I am not Gabriel," I said.

Nathaniel laughed, but it wasn't a happy sound. "Would you get mad if I said sometimes I wish you were?"

I just blinked at him. "I'm not mad, Nathaniel, you just puzzle the hell out of me. I know I'm supposed to be taking care of you, but I don't know how to do it." He was like some exotic pet that I'd been given as a gift, but the instructions didn't come in the box.

He lay back down on the pillow, head turned so he could see me. "I went with Mira when I realized you weren't there for me."

"I am there for you, Nathaniel, but not in that way."

"Is this where you tell me we can still be friends?" He laughed, and it was harsh.

"You don't need a friend, Nathaniel, you need a keeper."

"I thought you were going to be my keeper."

I looked at Cherry and Zane. "How about you guys?"

"Nathaniel is the most . . ." Cherry hesitated, "the most broken of us. Gabriel and Raina made sure we were all bottoms; it was all we were trained for. They were the tops, always, but . . . but Nathaniel . . ." She finally shrugged.

I knew what she meant. Nathaniel was the weakest of them. The one who needed the most care.

I set the suitcase down and went to kneel by the bed. I brushed his hair from his face so I could see his eyes. "We'll all be there for you, Nathaniel. We are your pard. Your people. We'll take care of you. *I'll* take care of you."

Tears filled his eyes. "But you won't fuck me."

I took a deep breath and stood. "No, Nathaniel, I won't fuck you." I shook my head and picked up my suitcase. I'd had all I could take for one afternoon. If Marianne wasn't happy with this little lesson, then screw her. Maybe it wasn't supposed to be sexual, but thanks to the way Gabriel and Raina had treated the wereleopards, sex did keep coming up. I was almost afraid to hear what Marianne's solution to that one would be.

39

I ran out of hot water before I filled the tub, and I didn't care. The small white-tiled room was hot enough that a truly hot bath seemed a bad idea. The single window was set high in the wall, so if I was careful, I wouldn't flash. So I kept the window open, even the drapes, hoping for a stray breeze. I sank down into the lukewarm water without a bubble in sight. There was nothing but Ivory soap and a partially burned white candle on the corner near the faucet. I put the Firestar on the small corner beside my head. I'd tried the Browning there, but it was too big and kept trying to slide into the water.

I was completely underwater, rinsing off my hair, when I heard the door crash open. I surfaced, sputtering, groping for the Firestar. I had the gun pointed before I even saw what was coming through the door. Even when I could see, it didn't make any sense.

There was a woman in the doorway. Physically, she was small, about my size, but she seemed to fill the room as if she took up more space than the eye could see. Her hair was long and brown. The bangs had been allowed to grow and were thinned until the hair covered her face past her nose like a veil. The hair was tinted ever so slightly blue. She wore a jean jacket with no sleeves. One bare, muscular, tatooed arm was holding the door so that the force of its being kicked in didn't send it flying back in her face. Under other circumstances, I'd have been sort of disdainful, except for the roil of power pouring from her. She looked like she'd gotten lost on her way to a punk biker bar. Psychically, she felt like a wind from the mouth of hell, hot and unfriendly.

There was so much power in the tiny room, I felt like the bathwater should start to boil. I kept the gun very steadily pointed at her chest. I think it was the only thing that kept her just inside the door. The look on her face was pure rage.

Water dripped down my face from my hair, tangling in my eyelashes. I blinked, resisting the urge to wipe the water away with my hands. "One step, just one, and I will pull this trigger," I said.

Roland appeared behind her in the doorway. This just got better and better. He was still tall, tanned, with his short, curly hair. His brown eyes swept the room and stayed on me, crouching naked in the tub. I kept the gun on the woman, but it was tempting.

He touched the woman's shoulders. He spoke in that low, rolling voice of his. "Roxanne, trust me, she will kill you."

It made me not want to shoot him after all.

A second man peeked into the room. He was taller than Roland, which made him over six feet. I had enough of a glimpse to know he was Native American and had long, black hair. Then he ducked back, eyes averted, a gentleman. He said, "Roxanne, this is not appropriate."

Roxanne shook off Roland's hands and started to walk farther into the room.

I fired the gun inches from her head. The sound was thunderous. The bullet took a bite out of the door and buried into the wall behind. It was a Glazer Safety Round, so the wall stopped it. I wasn't afraid of it going through the wall.

My ears rang with the shot in this tiny, tiled room. For a second, if someone spoke, I couldn't hear it. I kept my eyes on Roxanne. She had stopped moving. I had the barrel of the gun sighted in the middle of that pretty face. It took a second or two of staring to realize that under all the tatoos, the funky hair, and the power, she was pretty. It was a traditional, girl-next-door pretty. Maybe it was the reasons for the tatoo and the hair. When nature makes you look wholesome, there are ways to cheat.

"Come on, Roxanne," Roland said, "back away."

She just stood there. Her power breathed around me like a warm cloud. It was continuous and nearly suffocating. I'd never been around any shapeshifter that had this kind of raw power. Or never around one this powerful who didn't even try to pass for human. Roxanne didn't vibrate with power. She was power. And I was about two seconds away from snuffing it out.

"You would really kill me," she said.

"In a heartbeat," I said. I was getting tired of crouching in the water. Made it hard to be tough. Of course, being naked didn't help, either.

"Why didn't you kill me just now?"

"You're the lupa for Verne's pack. Killing you would rain all sorts of crap down. But I will do it, Roxanne. Now, back out of the room, close the door, and let me get dressed. If you still want to talk, fine, but don't ever, ever pull shit like this again."

"Without that little gun you wouldn't be so confident."

"Yeah, it's a real confidence booster. Now, get the fuck out of the room, or I will shoot you."

Marianne was suddenly in the doorway. "Roxanne, let's go have some tea and let Anita get dressed." I don't know what Marianne did, but even I felt calmer. It was like she projected calm and peace into the room.

Roxanne let Roland and Marianne drag her back through the door. Roxanne pointed a finger at me. "You insulted my Ulfric, and you will pay for that, with or without the gun."

"Fine," I said.

The door closed behind them. The lock had shattered in a pile of splinters. Cherry's voice came through the door. "I'll stay outside the door until you're out. I can give you a warning if any more bad guys come."

Bad guys. Was Roxanne a bad guy or just psycho? I was betting on the latter.

40

I got dressed in record time. Black jean shorts, red short-sleeved knit top, white jogging socks, black Nikes. Normally, I'd have left off the shoulder holster inside a house, but I threaded it through the belt and slipped it on. The black holster looked very stark against the red shirt. I put the Firestar down the front of the shorts in the Uncle Mike's Sidekick holster that it usually rode in. I left off the spine sheath. The leather was beginning to smell like sweat. I was going to have to let it dry out before I could wear it again.

I smeared hair goop on the hair and let it go. It'd dry on its own. Call it a hunch, but I didn't think Roxanne was the patient type. If I took the time for makeup or blow-drying my hair, she might come looking for me. I don't normally fuss, anyway. In truth, the only reason I'd planned on it was the fact that Richard was coming with Dr. Carrie Onslow, and I was feeling insecure. Me, insecure. How sad.

Richard had spent a great deal of the day with Dr. Carrie Onslow. I was jealous and hated it.

Of course, first I needed to go confront a pissed-off werewolf. I could figure out what the hell I was going to do with Richard after I talked to Roxanne. One thing I was pretty sure of, if I killed her, it would be war between the two packs. I did not want to bring that on our people, not if it could be avoided. Anita, the politician—now, *that* was sad.

I opened the door. Cherry looked up at me from her seat on the floor. There was something on her face, a hesitation, that made me say, "What?"

She pushed to her feet, using the wall. "You just look . . . aggressive."

"You mean the guns?"

"The guns, the red and black. It's all very stark and out there."

"You think I should be wearing pink and something frilly to cover the guns?"

Cherry smiled. "I think that Roxanne is almost psychotically dominant, and if you go down there dressed like that, she'll take it as a sign that she's got to be just as aggressive."

"You don't even know her," I said.

She said, very simply, "Do you think I'm wrong?"

Put that way . . . "I don't have anything pink and frilly in my suitcase."

"How about something not black, not red?"

I frowned at her. "Will purple do?"

"It would be better," she said.

I went back in and changed into a top that was identical cotton knit, scoop necked, but royal purple. I had to admit that the purple was softer. I kept the shoulder holster on but transferred the Firestar to the small of my back. Theoretically, I could draw it from there, but it was not my favorite position. The only shirt I could find to match the purple and cover the shoulder holster was thin and black and nylon, which half defeated the point of wearing the cotton shirt to begin with, but I had to admit that it looked better. It was still black and not cheery, but it wasn't so aggressive. You couldn't see the guns. I could have walked into any mall in the country and not gotten a second glance. Of course, if I moved fast, the shirt would blow back and flash, but hey, I wasn't planning to go jogging.

I opened the door a second time and said, "Better?"

Cherry nodded, smiling. "Much better. Thank you for listening to me. I know it's not one of your best things."

"I am not going to drag Richard's pack into a war because I couldn't tone it down a little."

The smile widened into something gentle and almost heart-warming. "You are a good lupa, Anita, a good Nimir-ra. For a human, you're positively excellent."

"Yeah, but the human part is still true."

She touched my shoulder. "But we don't hold it against you."

I looked at her to see if she was kidding me, but I just couldn't tell. "I think Roxanne will hold it against me."

Cherry nodded. "Probably. They're all waiting in the kitchen."

The kitchen was tiled in black and white with some cracks starting in the high-traffic areas, but the floor was mopped within an inch of its existence. The tile gleamed softly in the indirect light that touched the windows. Like the bedroom Nathaniel was staying in, it would get morning light but not afternoon. Roxanne sat with her back to the door. The edges of the white tablecloth trailed in her lap. There was a stiffness to the way she held herself that said she knew I was there, but she didn't turn around.

Marianne sat across from her with a china teacup and saucer in front of her. She looked at me like she was trying to tell me something with her eyes, but I didn't know what that something was.

Roland stood in the corner next to a hutch that held the china that matched the cup. He had his arms crossed and looked very bodyguardish.

The other man I'd glimpsed stood in the opposite corner like a second bookend. His arms were crossed, and he looked very bodyguardish.

That was the only thing that was similar. Okay, one other: They both had great tans. But I suspected, like Richard, that the new guy wasn't just tanned. His skin was a rich brown, his brown eyes almost perfectly almond shaped. They were almost too small for the rest of that face. It was all angles, high cheekbones, broad forehead, hooked nose. Every feature he had was aggressively male and ethnic. His hair was long and black and moved like silky water as he looked at me. The hair was a solid blackness like my own, that black that has blue highlights in the sun.

He was also at least six foot two, maybe an inch taller, with shoulders to match. He leaned against the wall, exuding a sort of easy physical energy like someone who knew his potential and didn't sweat proving it.

"That's Ben. He's your replacement Sköll until Jamil is healed."

I wanted to turn down the offer of putting my life in a stranger's hands, but was almost sure it would be considered an insult. I nodded. "Hi."

He nodded back. "Hello."

Roxanne turned in the chair, sliding her legs so she was sitting sideways in the chair. "Verne meant our wolf to be an apology for allowing your people to be injured on our lands." She looked full at me and those brown eyes were not friendly. "I think it is you who owes us an apology."

"Apology for what?" I asked.

She stood, and that energy spilled through the room like water, swirling around the ankles, rising to the knees. Her power spilled outward, upward, as if she would fill the room with the breathing warmth of her presence.

She was so powerful, it made my throat tight just standing this close to her. "Shit," I whispered.

"You marked Verne as if he were the least of us and not the greatest."

"You mean the neck thing," I said.

She slammed the chair back into the floor. It fell with a loud crash.

I didn't go for a gun, but it was an effort.

Roxanne stood there breathing far too fast and far too shallow. Strong emotion makes the energy spill worse, and her anger made the power bite and dance over my skin in a tight, electric dance.

Cherry moved up a little behind me. Zane appeared in the doorway and flanked her. They stood to either side and a little back like bodyguards. They'd do their best, but I didn't want to test them against Roland and Ben. I was pretty sure who would win, and it wouldn't be us.

"I am sorry that I marked Verne," I said.

"Lies," Roxanne said.

"I truly didn't mean to do it."

She took a trembling step forward. I didn't step back, but maybe I should have. She was too damn close. At this range, I might get the Browning out, but if I did, I'd have to use it, because she'd be on top of me in seconds.

"Can someone please explain why she's so pissed, and what we can do about it that won't end with one of us dead?"

Marianne stood slowly. Roxanne's head pivoted, and the intensity in that gaze, even turned to another, made my skin jump. Marianne held her hands palm out and advanced slowly around the table towards her lupa.

"Roxanne sees the marking as an insult to Verne and the entire pack," Marianne said.

"I got that," I said. "I didn't mean it to be insulting. I didn't mean to do it at all."

Roxanne's head turned slowly until she was staring at me. Her eyes bled from brown to a rich, startling yellow while I watched.

I put my hand on the butt of the Browning. "Ease down, wolf-girl."

A low, rumbling growl crawled out of that slender throat.

Marianne said, "If you truly didn't mean to be insulting, then would you be willing to make amends?"

I kept my gaze on Roxanne but answered, "How would I make amends?"

"We could fight," Roxanne said.

I looked into her nearly glowing yellow eyes. "I don't think so."

Marianne was standing sort of between us without actually standing between us. "You could offer your neck to Roxanne in a public ceremony."

My eyes slid to Marianne, then back to the werewolf. "I am not letting her near my neck in public or private, not on purpose."

"You don't trust me," Roxanne said.

"Nope."

She took another painfully slow step forward. Marianne did step between us then. If Roxanne moved forward another inch, her shoulder would bump Marianne.

"There is another ceremony," Marianne said.

"I am not offering Roxanne my neck," I said.

"No neck offering, but you do exchange blows."

I felt my eyes widen. I stared at the nearly snarling woman across from me. "You must be joking. She'd kill me."

"I'll let you hit me first," Roxanne said.

"I've read this story. No thanks."

Roxanne frowned. "Story?"

"*Sir Gawain and the Green Knight*," I said. She still looked puzzled. "The Green Knight lets Sir Gawain have the first blow. Gawain cuts off his head. The Green Knight picks up his head under one arm and says, 'My turn, a year from now!' "

"Haven't read it," she said.

"It's not top twenty reading list, I guess. Anyway, the point is the same. I can hit you as hard as I can, and it won't hurt you. You can flick your fingers in my direction and break my neck."

"Then we fight," she said.

My hand was still resting on the Browning. "I'll kill you, Roxanne, but I won't fight you."

"Coward!"

"You bet," I said.

I felt Richard brush over me, through me, like wind. He'd recognized Roxanne's car and was letting me know he was about to bring a human into the mess. A human who didn't know who the monsters were.

I looked away to see his shape outside the kitchen door, and I shouldn't have. I didn't so much see Roxanne's fist as sense the movement. My hand was already on the Browning, only seconds to pull it, but that blur of movement caught me in the chin. I had the sensation of falling, but I didn't remember hitting the floor or didn't feel it.

I was on the floor looking up at the white ceiling. Marianne was beside me. Her lips were moving, but no sound came out. Sound finally came through with an almost audible pop like a small sonic boom.

Screaming. Everyone was screaming. I heard Richard's voice and Roxanne's and others. I tried to sit up and couldn't.

Marianne touched my shoulder. "Don't try to move."

I wanted to see what was happening, but I couldn't make my body move. I could feel it, but it was like a great weight along my body, as if what I really wanted to do was sleep.

I flexed my right hand, and it was empty. I'd dropped the Browning somewhere. Frankly, I was just happy to be able to move my hand. I wasn't joking when I'd told Roxanne she could break my neck without trying hard.

I kept flexing things, waiting to be able to stand up. I was finally able to move my head enough to see the rest of the room. Richard had Roxanne around the waist, feet completely off the ground. Roland and Ben were trying to pull Richard off of her. Shang-Da was trying to get Dr. Carrie Onslow to go back outside the kitchen door.

Roxanne squirmed out of Richard's arms. She strode over to me, and Zane and Cherry moved like a wall between us. She shoved between the two of them, screaming, "Your turn, bitch! Your turn!"

She was standing there, sideways, with the two wereleopards trying to hold her without hurting her. Her right leg was flexed forward. I think only Marianne heard me say, "My pleasure."

I kicked Roxanne just below the kneecap, aiming up. The kneecap popped out of its socket, and she went down shrieking. I kicked her twice in the face. Blood blossomed from her nose and mouth.

I got to my feet. No one tried to help me. The room had suddenly fallen so quiet, you could hear Roxanne's breathing, too loud, too fast. She spat blood on the floor. I walked around her and the wereleopards until I was close to the table. Ben and Roland still held Richard, but it was like they'd forgotten why they were doing it. Shang-Da picked Carrie Onslow up and carried her out the door with her yelling, "Richard!"

It was one of those moments when time seems to slow and stretch and happen too fast all at the same time. I heard Roxanne say, "I will kill you for that!" But I don't honestly remember whether I picked the chair up before or after she said it. I only remember having the chair and when she leaped at me, I smashed the chair into her like you'd use a baseball bat, taking the arms way back, throwing my shoulders and back muscles into it. The shock of the blow left my fingers and hands tingling, but I kept the grip on the chair.

Roxanne was on all fours on the floor, but she wasn't down. I raised the chair for another blow as her power flowed over me like a scalding wind. I smashed the chair down with everything I had. She caught it and tore it out of my hands.

I backed up and pulled the Firestar.

Roland yelled, "No guns!"

I glanced at Richard. He said, "No guns." The look on his face was enough. He was scared for me. So was I.

No guns. Were they kidding? Roxanne tried to get to her feet, but the knee wouldn't hold. She fell, and the chair thudded into the floor. She screamed and threw the chair at me. I had to dive for the floor to avoid it.

She came for me on hands and one leg in a movement almost too fast to follow. I had plenty of time to shoot her, but I wasn't supposed to shoot her. I crab walked backwards, trying to stay away. The Firestar was still in my hand. I yelled, "Richard!"

The marks suddenly opened between us like a floodgate. I was bathed in the scent of his skin and the distant musk of fur.

Roxanne hesitated in that maniac, skittering crawl. Her pretty face began to stretch outward as if a hand were pushing out from the inside. A muzzle bloomed in the middle of that human face, covered in human skin with a line of lipstick where lips used to be.

I reached down that line of power between Richard and myself. I wrapped the scent of him, the feel of him, the jittering play of energy. I could suddenly feel the moon in the daylight sky, and knew—knew in every cell of my body—that tomorrow night was it, tomorrow night I would be free. And for an instant, I wasn't sure whose thought that was, Richard's or his beast's.

I left the Firestar on the floor and got to my feet with the window behind me. I knew Richard wouldn't let her kill me, but I also knew she was going to hurt me. I'd thrown a werewolf through a window once upon a time. It had stopped the fight. It was all I could think of. Of course, Roxanne had to cooperate and run at me like a maniac to set herself up for the throw. If she came at me slower, it wouldn't work.

She came at me slower, in a limping run. I was out of ideas. One thing I knew: If she touched me with those claws or that mouth, I might be a lupa for real next month. Time was in that crystalline run, slow and fast, slow and glitteringly fast. I thought of several things to do and wouldn't be fast enough to do any of them. But I'd go down trying.

Richard was yelling, "No claws, Roxanne, no claws."

I don't think Roxanne heard him. She swiped at me with those monstrous claws, and I ducked under the swinging arm. I ducked blows that were too fast to see, avoided her like I knew where she'd be. It was Richard, the marks, but it was too confusing, too new for me to be able to fight with it. I could use it to avoid her, but only for so long.

I ended up on my back, on the floor, pointing the Firestar up at her. She was coming with claws and teeth, and I was out of options.

The door burst open, and Verne yelled, "Roxanne, no!" I felt his power crash through the room like the lid on a boiling pot, something thrown over the heat, to hold it, contain it, but it didn't stop it.

Ben and Roland were suddenly hanging onto Roxanne, dragging her back from me. If Verne had given an order to them, I hadn't heard it. Roxanne was cutting them up, slicing their arms open, and they were taking it.

Verne was still yelling, "I lied, Roxanne. I lied. She didn't proposition me."

Roxanne went very still in their arms. She spoke around that only partly human mouth, "What did you say?"

Lucy came in behind Verne, through the still-open door. She shut the door and leaned against it, smiling, enjoying the show.

"I said, I lied," Verne said. "I'm an old man, and you are beautiful and powerful and thirty years younger than I am. I told you when she marked my neck that she propositioned me. She didn't."

Roxanne relaxed in the grip of her bleeding bodyguards. You could feel the tension seep away, and with it her flesh. Her face, her hands, flowed until she stood human again. Her nose was bloody where I'd kicked her.

"You can let me go," she said. "I won't hurt her."

They didn't let her go. They looked at Verne.

"How about me, darling?" he said. "You going to hurt me?"

"When we get home, I'll kick the shit out of you, but not here, not now."

Verne smiled. Roxanne smiled. And both smiles were the same. It was more than lust, though that was mixed in with it. It was a look that couples have, like a secret language, a look that excludes everyone else and cannot be explained.

I looked at Richard. "They be crazier than we are."

He smiled at me, and the smile warmed me down to my Nikes. I smiled back, and realized with a jolt that tingled through my entire body that we had our own secret look. God, I'd missed him.

Lucy stalked into the room on a pair of platform shoes, purple short-shorts, and what looked like a lavender bra but probably wasn't. She sashayed up to Richard, slipping both of her arms through one of his.

"He's rejected me for you, sweetie," she said in a voice that was too pleasant for the anger in her eyes.

I looked at Richard. "I don't think he dumped you because of me."

She pushed away from Richard to stand in front of me. I had the gun in my hand. I figured I was safe. The marks with Richard faded, pulled back, replaced with the knowledge that we were a couple again. I valued that a hell of a lot more than the marks.

"I can do things for him in bed that your human body could never do. I can take every ounce of strength, every thrust, and it just feels good. It doesn't have to be gentle with me, careful with me."

Which hit a little close to home, which is my only excuse for what I said next. "Gee, Lucy, I don't know. He spends one night with me and drops you like yesterday's news. Either you're not that good a lay, or I'm better."

Her face narrowed down, eyes wide; for a second, I thought she might cry. I didn't want her to cry. That would spoil it and make me feel like a shit.

Lucy turned away from me, bringing her hands to cover her face. Damn.

I looked past her to Richard. The look on his face was not happy with me. I couldn't blame him on this one.

I didn't see Lucy turn, I felt it. I felt the air move as she whirled. Her hand caught me across the face. I had the sensation of falling, but if I hit the ground, I didn't remember it.

41

I woke to darkness and the smell of clean sheets. I blinked at the strange windows and the spill of moonlight on the floor. I didn't recognize the room. Once I realized I wasn't anywhere I'd ever been, tension filled me like water. I heard someone behind me, and that raised the tension another notch. I tried to lie still, but I knew my breathing had changed. If they were human, they might not have noticed, but I just didn't know that many humans right now.

"Anita, it's Damian."

I rolled over onto my right side, and it hurt. My right arm was bandaged from my palm to about the middle of my forearm. It didn't hurt that much, but I couldn't remember how I'd injured it. The vampire was sitting in a chair by the door. His long, red hair looked a strange pale brown in the dark. He was wearing the vest and pants of a very nice, probably tailored, business suit. It might have been black or navy or even dark brown. His skin glowed pale against the darkness of the cloth.

"What time is it?" I asked.

"You're the only one wearing a watch," he said.

I raised my left hand in front of my face and hit the little button that made it glow. The glow seemed brighter than it should have because of the darkness. "God, it's after eleven. I've been out for hours." I lay back on the bed. "Did it occur to anyone to take me to a hospital?"

"The sun's only been down for a little over two hours, Anita. I don't know what choices were made. When Asher and I woke, we were in the basement here. We fed, then I took Richard's place here by your bed."

"Where is Richard?"

"I think he's at their lupanar, but I'm not certain."

I glanced at him. He seemed somehow distant. "You didn't ask any questions?"

"I was told to stay here and guard your rest. What more did I need to know?"

"You aren't a slave, Damian. You're allowed to ask questions."

"I got to sit here in the dark and watch you sleep. What more could your pet vampire ask?" That last had a bitter edge to it.

I sat up slowly because I still felt wobbly. "What's that supposed to mean?" I tried to prop my back against the heavy wooden headboard but needed more pillows under me. I tried to push them under me with my right hand, and it hurt. It was a nice, sharp ache.

"I remember Lucy hitting me, but what happened to my arm?"

Damian put one knee on the bed and helped prop the pillows under my back. He even found an extra one for me to lay my right arm on. "Richard said Lucy tried to pull your arm off."

That bit of knowledge left me cold and scared. "Jesus, a woman scorned."

"Pillows better?" he asked.

"Yeah, thanks."

He got to his feet and started to move back to the chair.

I said, "Don't." I held my left hand out to him.

He took my hand. His skin was warm to the touch. There was a light dew of sweat on his palm. Vampires can sweat, but they don't do it often. I squeezed his hand, staring up into his face. The moonlight was strong, so I could see his face. His skin was pale, almost luminous. Those brilliant green eyes were just liquid darkness by moonlight. I drew him to sit beside me.

"You've fed tonight or your skin would be cold, so why the sweat?"

He drew his hand out of mine, turning his face away. "You don't want to know."

"Yeah, I do." I touched his chin with my fingertips, turning his face back to me. "What's wrong?"

"Don't you have enough to worry about without bothering with me?"

"Tell me what's wrong, Damian. I mean it."

He let out a long, shaking breath. "There; you've done it. A direct order."

"Tell me," I said.

"I was happy to sit here in the dark and watch you sleep. I think if Richard had known just how happy, he would have made Asher do it."

I frowned at him. "You've lost me."

"You feel it, too, Anita. Not as strongly as I do, but you feel it."

"Feel what, Damian?"

"This." He placed his hand against my face, and I wanted to rub my face against his skin. I had a momentary urge to pull him down on the bed beside me. Not for sex, necessarily, but to touch him. To run my hands over that pale skin, to bathe in the power that animated his flesh.

I swallowed hard and drew back from his hand. "What is going on, Damian?"

"You're a necromancer, and I'm the walking dead. You've raised me from the dead twice. You've called me once from my coffin and once back from the edge of true death. You've healed me with your powers. I am your creature. I have made vows of loyalty to Jean-Claude as my Master of the City, and I honor them, but you I would follow into hell itself. Not out of duty, but out of desire. I can think of nothing better than to be by your side. Nothing pleases me more than doing what you ask. When I'm near you, I find it very hard to do almost anything large, like feeding or leaving your presence, without asking your permission."

I just stared at him. I didn't know what to say, not uncommon for me today. But with him sitting so close in the dark room, I had to say something. "Damian,

I . . . I didn't mean for anything like this to happen. I don't want you to be some sort of undead servant.''

"I know," he said. "But I also understand why the vampire council made it a habit to kill necromancers. I don't serve you out of fear. I want to do it. When I am with you, I am happier than without you. It's a little like being in love, but . . . much more frightening.''

"I knew we had a connection. I even knew why we had it. I just didn't have any idea it was this strong for you," I said.

"I didn't realize you felt drawn to me as I am to you until last night. You could have chosen Asher. He adores you, and you remember being in his bed. But you chose me to kiss. Me to hold. I don't think it was an accident.''

I shook my head. "I don't know. I don't remember everything clearly from last night. The munin is sort of like being drunk.''

"Do you remember what you said to me?''

"I said a lot of things." But my voice was soft, and I was very afraid I did remember the phrase he was searching for.

"You said, don't bleed me, fuck me.''

Yep, that was the phrase. Just remembering it was so embarrassing, I squirmed. It was my turn to look away. "It was the munin talking," I said. "You're one of the few males that I hang around with that Raina never had sex with. Maybe she wanted something different.''

He touched my face, turned me back to meet his eyes. "That isn't it, and you know it.''

I pulled back from his hand. "Look, my plate is like full to overflowing with guys right now. I'm flattered, thanks for the offer, but no thanks.''

"And how happy are you with the two men in your bed right now?'' he asked. "You've had sex with Richard now, and the marks are binding you tighter than ever.''

"Did everyone know that was a possibility but me?'' I asked.

"Jean-Claude forbade me from telling you. I thought you had a right to know.''

"I felt Jean-Claude wake this morning before ten. I felt him wake, Damian. I felt the fierceness of his joy, his triumph." I tried to cross my arms over my chest, and the right one wouldn't cooperate. "Damn it to hell.''

"I was the servant of my original mistress for a very long time, Anita. The thought of being your servant, anyone's servant, terrifies me." He touched the bandages on my right arm. "But I see them using you, Anita. I see them withholding information from you." He cradled my bandaged hand in both of his. "I swore oaths to Jean-Claude, but it's your power that makes my heart beat, your pulse I can taste like cherries on my tongue.''

I drew my hand out of his. "What are you saying, Damian?''

"I'm saying that you shouldn't be the only one of the three that doesn't know what's going on.''

"And you can tell me," I said.

He nodded. "I can answer your questions. In fact, if you make them orders, I can't refuse to answer them.''

"You're handing me the keys to your soul, Damian. Why?''

He smiled, teeth a dim whiteness in his face. "Because I serve you before I serve anyone else. I tried fighting it, but I can't. So I'm through fighting. I give myself to you willingly, even eagerly."

"If you mean what I think you mean, didn't Asher say something last night about if I had sex with you, Jean-Claude would kill you?"

"Yes," he said.

I looked at him. "I may be good, Damian, but no one's worth dying for."

"I don't think he'd kill me. Jean-Claude has questioned me about the bond I feel with you."

"He has, has he?"

"Yes, and he's pleased. He thinks it's another sign of your increasing powers as a necromancer. He's right."

"Jean-Claude knew you were obeying me without wanting to, and he didn't tell me?" I said.

"He thought it would upset you."

"When was he going to mention this little fact to me?"

"He's the Master of the City. He doesn't answer to me. I don't know what he plans to tell you or when."

"Okay, what other powers can I expect to gain through the marks?"

He lay down on the other side of the pillow he'd gotten for my injured arm. He propped himself up on one elbow, long legs stretched out the length of the bed. "Their physical strength, their sight, hearing. You could gain almost every power they have without giving up your humanity. Though you'd probably have to take the fourth mark to gain the full powers."

"No, thanks," I said.

"Eternal life without having to die for it, Anita. It's tempted many over the centuries."

"I've had too many surprises in the last two days, Damian. I'm not tying myself any closer to Jean-Claude."

"You say that now, but let a few more years pass, and you may change your mind. Eternal youth, Anita. It's not a small offering."

I shook my head. "What else can I expect from the marks?"

"Theoretically, any power they possess."

"That's not typical for a human servant, is it?"

"They all gain some strength, stamina, healing, resistance to injury, immunity to disease and poison. Though again, without the fourth mark, I'm not sure how much of that you've gained. I'm not sure Jean-Claude or Richard know, either, until you pull another rabbit out of your hat."

"Was the munin a surprise to them?"

"Oh, yes," Damian said. He lay his head on the edge of the pillow I wasn't using. He rolled onto his back so he was looking up at me. "Jean-Claude knew of the munin, but hadn't really thought that they were the spirits of the dead and what that would mean for you. Even necromancers of legend don't control the munin."

"The necromancers of legend don't have a bond with an alpha werewolf," I said.

"That's what Jean-Claude thinks, too."

I settled lower in the nest of pillows. "It's so great that he's talking about me to everyone but me."

Damian rolled so that he was staring up at me. "I know how much you value honesty, and in all honesty, Jean-Claude could not have known that you would gain these powers. A human servant is a tool to be used, so it is good if it is a powerful tool, but you seem to be gaining such power that it may, at some point, be questionable who is master and who is servant. Perhaps it is the fact that you are a necromancer."

"Jean-Claude told me before I took the marks that he wasn't sure who would be master and who would be servant because of my necromancy. But he didn't really explain it. I guess I should have asked."

"If he'd told you all this before the marks were offered, would you have taken them upon yourself?"

"I took the marks to save both their lives, not to mention my own."

"But if you'd known, would you have done it?" He rolled onto his side, face so close to my arm, I could feel his breath against my skin.

"I think so. I couldn't let them both die. One, maybe, I could have lost one of them, but not both. Not both, if I could have saved them."

"Then Jean-Claude has kept all this from you for nothing. He's angered you for nothing."

"Yeah, I'm pissed."

"It makes you not trust him." Damian moved that one inch closer until his cheek rested against my upper arm.

"Yeah, it makes me not trust him. Worse yet, it makes me not trust Richard." I shook my head. "I never thought he'd keep anything from me, let alone things this important."

"It makes you doubt them," Damian said.

I stared down at the vampire. Just his cheek rested against my arm. The rest of his body stretched down the length of the bed but didn't touch me. "This doesn't seem like you, Damian."

"What doesn't seem like me?" he asked. His hand slid from where it rested on his side to the sheets. That one pale hand lay between our bodies, not touching, just . . . waiting.

"This, all this, it's not you."

"You don't know anything about me, Anita. You don't know what I'm like, not really."

"What do you want from me, Damian?"

"Right now, to put this hand around your waist."

"And if I said yes?"

"Is that a yes?" he asked.

What would Richard say? What would Jean-Claude say? Fuck them. "Yes," I said.

He slid his hand over my waist until his arm rested across my stomach. It would have been natural to cuddle the body after the arm, but he didn't. He kept that artificial distance between us.

I ran my left hand up and down that pale arm, playing over the small hairs on his arm. It felt terribly right to touch him, as if I'd been wanting to do it for a very long time. I didn't want him to hold me. I wanted to hold him. It was a very different feeling than what I felt for Richard or Jean-Claude. Damian was right; it was the necromancy. It wanted to touch him, explore the edges of the power that bound us, the power that animated him.

My own personal power is closer kin to Jean-Claude's than to Richard's. It is a cool power, like an unfelt wind that plays over the mind and body. I let that cool thread spill out through my hand, down Damian's arm. I thrust it into him like an invisible hand, shoved it into that pale body and felt an answering spark deep inside him. I felt my power flare and recognize a piece of itself. Whatever had animated Damian before was gone. I animated Damian now. He was truly mine, which, of course, was not possible.

He slid his body that last inch so that the length of him lay against me from my waist to my feet. He slid one leg over my legs, pressing himself against me.

"You're trying to seduce me," I said. But my voice was too soft, too private.

He laid a soft kiss on my arm. "Am I seducing you, or have you already seduced me?"

I shook my head. "Get up and get out, Damian."

"You want me. I can feel it."

"The power wants you, not me. I don't want you the way I want Richard or Jean-Claude."

"I'm not asking for love, Anita, just to be with you."

I wanted to run my hands down his body. I knew that I could explore that body, touch every inch of it, and he wouldn't stop me. It was both inviting and frightening.

I slid off the bed, letting Damian have the whole thing to himself. I could stand, no dizziness; great. "We are not doing this Damian. We are so not doing this."

Damian propped himself up on his elbows, watching me. "If you give me a direct order, I must obey you, Anita. Even if that order contradicts one that Jean-Claude has given me."

I frowned at him. "What are you saying?"

"Don't you wonder what else he's forbidden me to tell you?" Damian asked.

"You little bastard."

He sat up, swinging his long legs off the side of the bed. "Don't you want to know?"

I stared down at him for a heartbeat. "Yes, damn you, yes, I want to know."

"You have to order me to tell you. I can't do it otherwise."

I almost didn't do it. I was afraid of what he would say. Afraid of what else Jean-Claude had been hiding from me. "I order you, Damian, to tell me all the secrets that Jean-Claude has forbidden you to tell me."

His breath came out in a long sigh. "Free at last. Jean-Claude, Asher, and even my master are all descended from the line of Belle Morte, Beautiful Death. She is our council master. Have you ever wondered why hundreds of years ago, most personal accounts of vampires said they were hideous monsters, walking corpses?"

"No, and what does that have to do with anything?"

"I've waited a long time to tell you this, Anita. Let me tell it."

I sighed. "Fine, tell me."

"No one thought of a vampire as a sexual object in the seventeen hundreds.

There were a few tales of beautiful vampires, but they were all tricks, not real. But then things changed. Most personal accounts speak of beauty and great sexual allure.'' He slid off the bed, and I backed up. I didn't want him too close. I wasn't sure who I trusted less: him or me.

When I backed up, he stopped moving and just stood there, looking at me. ''The Council decides which of them will send their vampires out to make more. For thousands of years, it was the Queen of Nightmares, our leader; or Morte d' Amour, the lover of death, and the Dragon; but they grew tired of the games and retreated inside the council chambers. You rarely see them. She-Who-Made-Me took me to court with her more than once. It's where I met Jean-Claude. Belle Morte, Beautiful Death, sent forth her people to populate the world with vampires. Jean-Claude, Asher, and I descend from her line. Even her blood cannot make the ugly beautiful, though all is improved by her touch, but it is more than that. Some in her line have the power of sex. They live on it, breathe on it. They feed on it like Colin and my old master fed on fear. They can gain power through sex and use it as a second lure for mortals.'' He stopped and looked at me.

''Finish it, Damian,'' I said.

''Jean-Claude is one of these. In another time, he would be considered an incubus. Asher and I are not like him. It is a rare power, even among those who descend more directly from Belle Morte.''

''So Jean-Claude can feed off of sex like Colin can feed off fear. So what?''

Damian moved towards me, and I let him touch my shoulder. ''Don't you understand? Jean-Claude gains power through sex, not just intercourse, but sexual energy, lust. It means that every time you have sex, it is power. That every intimate act between the three of you binds the marks tighter and increases your power.''

I felt almost faint. ''When was he going to tell me?''

''In Jean-Claude's defense, he says it didn't work this way the first time he marked you. The sex wasn't such a strong power focus. You were three marks deep before you broke away, and it didn't work like this between you. He thinks it's the addition of Richard that's pushed it over the edge.''

''What do you get out of this, Damian? What do you get out of telling me all this?'' I stared up at him in the dark.

''My mistress controlled me for centuries with her fear and her sex. You deserve the truth, all of it.''

I pulled away from him, turned my back on him. It made perfect sense. Jean-Claude gave off sex like other people wore cologne. It explained why his first business was a stripper club—lots of sexual energy to feed off. Did it change anything? I wasn't sure. I just wasn't sure.

I stared out the window, forehead pressed to the cool glass. The curtains blew gently in the night breeze. ''Does Richard know that Jean-Claude is some kind of incubus?''

''I don't think so,'' Damian said.

Power breathed on the wind. I could almost smell it like ozone in the air. It raised the hair at the back of my neck. It wasn't vampire or shapeshifter. I recognized it for what it was: necromancy. Somewhere close by, someone was using a power very similar to mine.

I turned to Damian. ''Colin's human servant, is she a necromancer?''

He shrugged. "I don't know."

"Shit." I cast outward, searching for Asher. My power touched him and was thrown backwards, out, away. I ran for the door.

Damian followed me, asking, "What is it? What's wrong?"

I had the Browning naked in my hand when I hit the yard. Damian saw them before I did, and he pointed at them. Colin's human servant stood at the edge of the trees, almost lost in shadows and darkness. Asher stood a few yards in front of her. He was on his knees.

I fired at her as I ran. The shots went wild, but it broke some of her concentration and I could feel Asher again. His life was being pulled out of him like a fish on a string. I could feel his blood thundering against his skin. His heart leaped in his chest like a caged thing struggling to get out, and it was her his heart was trying to get to, as if she could pull his heart from his chest from a distance.

I forced myself to stop running. I stood there and sighted down my arm. I felt movement from above. I looked up in time to see Barnaby's pale face coming at me like some giant bird of prey, then Damian was off the ground and the two vampires rolled into the sky, struggling.

I was close enough to see Asher's face now. He was bleeding from every opening; eyes, mouth, nose. He was a mask of blood; his clothes were soaked in it. He fell forward onto all fours.

I shot the woman. I shot her in the chest twice. She fell slowly to her knees, looking at me. She looked surprised. I heard her say, "We're not allowed to kill each other's human servants."

"If Colin hadn't known I'd kill you, he'd have come himself."

That made her smile for some reason. She said, "I hope he dies with me." Then she collapsed facedown on the ground. Even by moonlight I could see the exit holes in her back like great gaping mouths.

Asher stayed on all fours, blood dripping from his mouth. I knelt by him, touched his shoulder, and the shirt was blood-soaked. "Asher, Asher, can you hear me?"

"I thought it was you," he said, in a voice thick with things that should never be in a living throat. "I thought it was you calling me." He coughed blood onto the ground.

I looked up into the sky, and there was no sight of Damian and Barnaby. I screamed for help, and no one answered.

I put my arms around Asher, and he collapsed into my lap. I cradled as much of him into my lap as I could get. I had to lean over him to hear his voice.

"I thought you had called me out into the night for a rendezvous. Isn't that ironic?" He coughed so hard that it was hard to hold him. Thicker things than blood spilled from his mouth. I held him while he bled his life away on the ground and screamed, "Damian!"

I heard a distant scream, but that was all. "Don't die, Asher, please, don't die."

He coughed until something dark and black came out his mouth. Blood poured out of his mouth in a near steady stream. I touched his skin, and it was cool to the touch.

"If you fed off of one of the lycanthropes, would it be enough to save you?"

"If it's soon, perhaps." His voice was soft and thick.

I touched his forehead and came away with chill sweat. "How badly are you hurt?"

He ignored me, speaking very softly, "Know this, Anita, that seeing myself through your eyes has healed my heart."

My throat was tight with tears. "Please, Asher, don't."

A drop of pure blood slid out of his eye. "Be happy with your two beaus. Don't make the same mistakes that Jean-Claude and I made all those long years ago." He touched my face with a hand that was slick with blood. "Be happy in their arms, *ma cherie*."

His eyes fluttered. If he passed out, we might lose him. There was nothing in the night but the sounds of cicada and the wind. Where the hell was everyone?

"Asher, don't pass out."

His eyes fluttered open, but he was having trouble focusing. I felt his heart hesitate, skip a beat. He could live without his heart beating, but I knew that this time, when the heart went, it was over. He was dying. Nikki had broken him inside too badly for healing.

I put my right wrist, encased in white bandages, in front of his mouth. "Take my blood."

"To drink from you is to give you power over any of us. I do not want to be your slave any more than I already am."

I was crying, tears so hot they burned. "Don't let Colin kill you. Please, please!" I held him against me and whispered, "Don't leave us, Asher." I felt Jean-Claude all those miles away. I felt his panic at the thought of losing Asher. "Don't leave us, not now, not now that we've found you again. *Tu es beau, mon amour. Tu me fais craquer*."

He actually smiled. "I shatter your heart, eh?"

I kissed his cheek, kissed his face, and cried, hot tears against the harsh scars of his face. "*Je t'embrasse partout. Je t'embrasse partout.* I kiss you all over, *mon amour*."

He stared up at me. "*Je te bois des yeux*."

"Don't drink me with your eyes, damn it, drink me with your mouth." I tore the bandages away from my right wrist with my teeth and put my bare, warm flesh against his cold lips.

He whispered, "*Je t'adore*." Fangs sank into my wrist. It was sharp and deep. His mouth locked against my skin. His throat convulsed, swallowing. I stared into his pale eyes and felt something in my head part like a curtain, some shield shattered. One moment it was one continuous ache almost nauseating, then there was nothing but the spreading warmth. I didn't even have time to panic. Asher rolled over my mind like a warm lip of ocean, pleasurable, caressing. It burst over me in a skin-tingling, breath-stealing rush that left me gasping and wet. Then Asher was kneeling above me, laying me gently on the ground.

I lay, staring at nothing, riding the sensations up and down my body. I'd never let any vampire do me like this, never let them steal my mind while they stole my blood. I hadn't even known he could do it. Not to me.

He kissed me on the forehead. "Forgive me, Anita. I did not know that I could embrace your mind. I did not know that any vampire could." He stared down at my face, searching for some reaction. I couldn't give him one yet. He drew back enough to see my face clearly. "I feared you would possess me as you possess Damian if I fed from your blood without using any of my powers. I did try to scale your shield, break your barriers, but I did it to protect myself from your power. I did not dream that I could breach such impenetrable walls." He started to touch my face, then stopped, his hand falling to his lap. "The marks that bind you to Jean-Claude protect you from him embracing your mind. But he was never as good at this as I was. I should have thought of that before."

I just lay there, half-floating. Nothing was real yet. I couldn't think, couldn't speak.

He raised my hand and pressed it against his scarred cheek. "I drew back as soon as I realized what I had done. It was just, how do you say, a quickie. It was only a small taste of what it could have been, Anita. Please, believe me." He stood, and I couldn't follow the movement. I lay on the ground and tried to think.

Jason knelt beside me. I was aware enough to wonder where the hell he'd come from. He wasn't staying at Marianne's. Or was he? "It's your first time?" he asked.

I tried to nod but couldn't.

"Now you know why I stay with them," he said.

"No," I said, but my voice was distant as if it wasn't my voice at all. "No, I don't."

"You felt it. You rode him. How can you not love it?"

I couldn't explain it. It had felt wondrous, but as the glow began to fade, the fear welled up big and black enough to swallow the world. It felt amazing, and that had been a "quickie," as he put it. I never wanted anything more from Asher. Because if it was much better than this, I might chase the rest of my days for another taste. And Jean-Claude could not give it to me. The marks prevented him from rolling my mind. It was one of the things that made the difference between servant and slave. I would never get this with Jean-Claude, never. And I wanted it. I hadn't wanted Asher to die. Now I wasn't so sure.

Asher came back to stand over me. We stared at each other. There were people in the dark now. Someone had a flashlight. They flared it over me. I was left staring in the brightness, nearly blind. The light stood harsh on Asher's face, highlighting the reddish tracks of tears. "Don't hate me, Anita. I could not bear it if you hated me."

"I don't hate you, Asher." My voice still sounded thick and heavy with that golden edge of pleasure. "I fear you."

He just stood there, tears sliding down his face. The tears slid in reddish lines down the smooth skin of his left side. The tears got lost in the scars on the other side, and were beginning to collect in a reddish stain on the stiff skin. "Worse," he whispered, "worse, I think."

42

I kicked everyone out except Jason. He got to stay because they started arguing that I couldn't be left completely alone. Had I forgotten that people were trying to kill me? Had I forgotten that Jean-Claude had said he'd kill them all if I died? That last did not win friends and influence people with me. My comment had been, "If we all died, I guess that'd solve everything." Which sort of put an end to the arguments.

Jason lay on the bed propped in the nest of pillows. He tried to roll onto his side, then stopped in midmotion with a small sound of pain. He moved stiffly, like things hurt, which was what had gotten him a place on the bed instead of the chair.

I was pacing the room. I had a little circuit mapped out. Foot of the bed, windows, far wall, near wall with the door.

"You know that you've walked past the foot of the bed twenty times, and that's just since I started counting," Jason said.

"Shut up," I said. I'd put all my guns back on, not because I thought I needed them, but because they were familiar. The tightness of the shoulder holster, the digging of the Firestar in its inner-pants holster made me feel more like myself. I was the only one of the three of us who carried guns. It was one thing I knew that I hadn't gotten from either of them. It was mine. Guns, this particular brand of violence, was all mine. I needed something that was all mine right now.

Jason moved over on his side, slowly, an inch at a time. It took him until I'd made the circuit and was back at the foot of the bed before he made it to his side with a look of relief. He and Jamil had been moved to this house so that all the injured could be in one place. Roxanne was just down the hall with Ben sitting guard. Apparently, I'd been channeling enough of Richard's power that they thought she might have a concussion. I wasn't sure if Ben was supposed to be guarding her from me or the other way around. Dr. Patrick was down in the kitchen, stirring the stew that Marianne had left us. Zane and Cherry were here, but all the other shifters had gone to the lupanar. They were going to finish the ceremony that had been interrupted last night. Bully for them.

Asher was somewhere in the house. I didn't know where and didn't want to know. Too much was happening too damned fast. I needed some time to regroup. And I wasn't going to get it.

There was a knock on the door.

"Who is it?" I asked.

"It's Damian."

"Go away."

"There's a vampire down here with one of Sheriff Wilkes's deputies. They say they have to talk to you or Richard. They aren't treating this like police business."

That got my attention. I stopped pacing and went to the door. Damian stood there, still wearing the vest that Barnaby had ripped all the buttons off of. When Colin's human servant died, Barnaby had given up the fight and flown away. Damian's suit was black in bright light and made his skin look unbelievably white.

"What did they say exactly?" I asked.

"Just that they had a message for the two of you from Frank Niley."

"Fuck," I said, softly.

"They're sitting in the kitchen with Dr. Patrick and Asher."

"Tell Roxanne and Jamil that the bad guys are here. I'll go down and talk to them."

"The man has a gun," Damian said.

"So do I," I said. I walked down the hall, and Damian fell in step behind me.

Jason called from the door. "Wait for me."

"Follow at your own pace, Jason. I'm not waiting for you to trip down the stairs."

"Don't let her get killed, Damian," he said.

I called back over my shoulder, "He'll do what I tell him to do." An hour or so of thinking about everything I had learned had not improved my mood.

I clattered down the stairs. Damian followed like a soundless shadow at my back. Why hadn't Wilkes and his men stormed the place? I'd really expected them to just start shooting if they found out we hadn't left town. What message could they have from Niley? And where did the vampire come in? Dolph hadn't mentioned anything about Niley traveling with a vamp. Dolph hated vamps enough that he would have mentioned it. So many questions, and for once, I was going to get them answered almost as soon as I thought of them. How refreshing.

The kitchen looked normal. They'd scrubbed the blood off the linoleum and placed a fresh lace tablecloth on the table. Deputy Thompson sat in one of the kitchen chairs. He was in civvie clothes, no uniform. A tall, thin vampire that I'd never seen before sat in the chair beside him. Dr. Patrick sat in the chair facing them with his back to the hallway, to us. Nathaniel took up the last chair. He was staring at the vampire.

Zane stood with his back against the sink. Asher leaned against the china cabinet close enough to Thompson that he could have touched him and certainly could prevent him from pulling the gun. The gun in question was a Berretta 10 mil in a shoulder holster. Same gun as on duty, just in a different holster. Letting Asher that close was careless, but Thompson didn't seem to think that.

He smiled at me, and the smile was confident, arrogant, like he had me where he wanted me, and I couldn't do anything about it. What was going on?

"How'd you find me?" I asked.

He stuck a thumb in the vampire's direction. "The local Master of the City told us he could still feel you in town. They helped us hunt you down. Evidently, you're easier to find than your boyfriend. Something about your power attracts them."

I stared at the vampire. His face was unreadable, pale and empty. His eyes were dark grey, his hair straight and black. It was cut short and smoothed back over his forehead in a pompadour. That was what they'd called it in the fifties. The hairdo matched the feel of him in my head. He wasn't fifty years dead yet.

"What's your name?"

"Donald."

"Hi, Donald, missed you at the wienie roast."

Anger flared across the vampire's face. He wasn't old enough to hide it. "You told my master that you were here just to get your third out of jail. Once you had accomplished that, you should have gone home. You pretended to leave town but did not. If you had simply left, we would have accepted the murder of our people. By staying, you show that you intend to possess our lands and my master's power."

"Have you talked to your master lately?" I asked. "Or more importantly, has he talked to his human servant lately?"

The vampire glared at me, but there was no power to it. "Colin is injured but not yet dead. But the Council will slay you for . . . killing his servant."

Asher said, "A human servant gives up their safe conduct if they attack another vampire directly. That is Council law. Anita did nothing that the Council will hunt her for. If Colin persists in trying to harm us, it is he the Council will hunt down and destroy."

"Enough of the vampire crap," I said. I turned back to Thompson. "So, what's the message? I thought if we were still here after dark, Frank was going to do us all personally."

"Ol' Frank seems scared shitless of you. Howard keeps mumbling that the signs are real bad, that they need to leave town now. That if they stay, you'll kill them all."

I raised an eyebrow. "Having met Niley and his crew, I'm flattered at being their bogeyman. Now, what the fuck is the message?"

Thompson brought a small white box out of his pocket. It was like something you'd buy an inexpensive necklace in. He held it out to me with a smile that was so unpleasant, it made me afraid to take the box.

"It won't bite," he said.

I glanced at Asher. He shrugged.

I took the box. It was tacky on the bottom. I raised it to see a brownish stain on the white cardboard. The box was light but not empty. "What's in here?"

"Don't want to spoil the surprise," Thompson said.

I took a deep breath and lifted the lid off. There was a lock of hair, curled over some cotton. The hair was long and thick and chestnut brown, tied with a bit of red ribbon like you'd use on a present. I lifted the lock of hair and it fell across my palm. The cotton it had been resting on was stained at one corner. Stained reddish brown.

I fought to keep my face blank. "So?" I said.

"Don't you recognize it? Zeeman's baby brother donated that."

"You didn't get blood cutting Daniel's hair," I said.

"No," he smiled, laughed, squirming in his chair like a kid who couldn't wait for the rest of the joke, "There's another little present in the box. Lift up the cotton."

I laid the hair on the table. It lay there curled and gleaming. I didn't want to lift the cotton. I didn't want to see what else they'd cut off of Daniel. The one consolation I had was that of the many awful possibilities that flashed through my mind, most of them were too big to fit into the box.

I lifted the cotton and fell to my knees like someone had struck me. I knelt there, staring down at the tip of a little finger that was far too delicate to be Daniel's. The nail polish on the finger was still perfect, smooth, pale. Nothing déclassé about Richard's mother.

Dr. Patrick had to leave the table and throw up in the sink. Soft touch for a doctor and a werewolf.

"What is it?" Cherry asked.

I couldn't speak.

Asher answered because he could see over my shoulder into the box. "It's a woman's finger."

Jason had just entered the room. "What did you just say?"

The vampire, Donald, said, "What have you done, human?"

"We have Richard's brother and his mother," Thompson said. "I thought we'd just kill you, but Niley's paying the money. He wants to give you a way out besides killing. He seems to think if he doesn't try to kill you, you won't try and kill him. Funny, ain't it?"

I finally looked up, away from Charlotte Zeeman's finger. "What do you want?"

"You leave town tonight. We release Richard's mother and brother tomorrow morning, when we're sure you really are gone. If you don't leave this time, Niley will keep trimming pieces off of Zeeman's family. Maybe an ear next time, maybe something bigger." He was grinning as he said it. Thompson was a sadistic brute, but he didn't understand me at all, or he wouldn't have been smiling.

There was a look on Donald the vampire's face that said he did understand me.

I stood up very slowly. I laid the box on the table beside the lock of hair. My voice was amazingly calm, almost empty of inflection. "Where are they?"

"We left them safe and sound," Thompson said.

"I did not know what they had done," the vampire said. "I did not know they had mutilated your third's family."

I shook my head. "You see, that's the problem, Donald. When you play with bad guys, you can't control how bad they are. You both just left Daniel and Charlotte, just left them there."

"Yeah," Thompson said. "Ol' Don here picked me up in his car."

I was staring at the finger. I couldn't seem to not look at it. I raised my eyes to Donald the vampire. "So, you both know where they are," I said.

Donald's eyes went wide. He whispered, "I didn't know."

Asher moved forward and laid hands on Thompson's shoulders.

Thompson wasn't worried. "If anything happens to us, they'll do worse to both of them. Richard's mom is a real attractive woman. Be a shame to change that."

Donald said, "I am sorry about what they did, but my orders are the same. You must leave our territory tonight."

"Use the kitchen phone. Tell them we give. Tell them don't hurt them, and we're out of here."

Thompson smirked. "No, no phone calls. They're giving us two hours. Then, if we're not back, they'll start cutting things off that will affect a lot more than her typing."

I nodded and pulled the Browning. I pointed it and shot it in one motion. I didn't even remember aiming. The vampire's head exploded in a cloud of blood and brains. The body rocked back and fell, taking the chair with it.

Asher held Thompson in his seat. Some of the blood had splattered Thompson's face. A glob of something thicker than blood was trailing down his forehead. He was trying to bat at the piece of flesh, but Asher held him.

I took the gun out from under his arm and pointed the Browning at his forehead.

Thompson stopped fighting and glared up at me. I had to give him credit. Covered in blood and brains, held down by a vampire, staring at the barrel of a gun, and he was putting on a brave show. "Kill me, it won't get you anything but them cut to pieces."

"Tell me where they are, Thompson, and I'll go get them."

"Fuck you! You're going to kill me, anyway."

"I give you my word that if you tell us where they are, and we get them out alive, you get to live."

"I don't believe you, bitch."

"Problem with being a traitorous, untrustworthy, wretch, Thompson, is you begin to believe everyone else is the same way." I put the safety on the Browning and reholstered it. He watched me do it, puzzled. "I keep my word, Thompson. Do you want to live or not?"

"Niley and Linus Beck are a hell of a lot scarier than you will ever be, chickie."

He'd called me bitch and chickie. He was either stupid, or . . . "You're trying to get me to kill you."

"If I talk, my life is over. And Niley won't just shoot me." Thompson stared up at me, and there was a knowledge in his eyes that he was already dead. It was only a matter of how and who. And he preferred me, now, to Niley, later.

"He doesn't fear death," Asher said softly.

I shook my head. "No, he doesn't."

"We could call the cops," Jason offered.

"If he's not scared of you guys, he won't be scared of the state cops." I stood staring down at Thompson. "I don't know what I'm going to do with you, Thompson, but I'll tell you what I won't do. I won't sit here for two hours and watch the time tick away. I won't let Daniel and Charlotte die."

"Then leave town," Thompson said.

"I've met Niley, Thompson. Do you really expect me to believe that he's going to let them go?"

"He said he would."

"You believe him?" I asked.

Thompson just looked at me.

"I didn't think so."

Asher's fingers kneaded the man's shoulders almost like he was massaging them. "There are other things to fear besides death, Anita. If you have the stomach for it."

I looked into that beautiful, tragic face and couldn't read it. "What do you have in mind?"

"An eye for an eye, I think," the vampire said.

I stared into crystalline blue eyes and let the idea grow in my head like a horrible flower. A lot of people who could face being shot, quick death, blanched at torture. I was one of them. And that's what we were talking about.

"I believe the deputy will tell us where they are within the next half hour, if we are ruthless," Asher said. "I will do the dirty work, as it were. You need only permit it."

Thompson looked worried. "What the fuck are you talking about?"

"Jason," I said.

He came to stand beside me. He stared down at what lay on the table. He didn't say anything, but tears slid silently down his face. He'd been over at the Zeeman house for a lot of Sunday dinners.

"Help hold Thompson," I said.

Jason went to stand on the other side, pinning one arm to the top of the table. Asher still held his shoulders.

I looked at Asher and nodded. "Do it."

"Damian, if you would be so kind as to fetch me a knife. One with a serrated edge would be best. It will go through bone better."

Damian just turned and walked across the kitchen. Zane and he started opening drawers.

"What are you going to do?" Thompson said.

"Guess," I said.

"I didn't cut anything off of that bitch. I didn't touch them. It was that strange goon that Niley has. Linus Beck. He cut the finger off. He did it. I didn't do anything."

"Don't worry, Thompson. We'll get to Linus. But right now, you're all we've got."

Damian had a big serrated butcher knife. He stalked towards the table with it.

Thompson was struggling now. It was hard to hold him sitting. "Better take him to the floor," I said.

Nathaniel helped. They held him facedown, one on each arm, Nathaniel pinning his legs. Thompson was a big, strong man, but he couldn't fight them. They were too strong. Far too strong.

Thompson was screaming. "Fuck you!"

Damian held the knife out to Asher. "I'll hold him."

I touched Damian's arm and shook my head. "No, I'll do it."

Damian looked at me.

"The rule is never ask anyone to do something you won't do yourself. If I can't do this, then we won't do it at all. We'll find another way."

Jason looked up from holding the struggling man. "There is no other way." I'd never seen such rage in his eyes.

"Could you do it?" I asked. "Could you chop him up?"

Jason gave a slow nod. "I could bite his fucking fingers off one by one for what's in that box." He seemed to mean it, and it made me think I didn't know Jason at all.

"We can do this, Anita," Asher said, "and it will cost us nothing."

"It should cost, Asher. If we're going to do something this evil, it should bother whoever does it."

"It isn't evil," Asher said. "It is practical. It is even justice."

I held my hand out for the knife. "It's evil, and we all know it. Now, give me the knife. Either I can do this, or we do something else."

Damian just stood there, holding the knife. "Let me do this for you, Anita, please."

"Give me the damn knife."

He gave it to me because he couldn't do anything else. I knelt down by Thompson. "Where are they, Thompson?" I asked.

"No, no, Niley told me what they'd do to me if I helped you. He's fucking crazy."

"Wait," Zane said. He had found a small cleaver. "This will work better."

"Thanks." I took it, checked it for balance. I wasn't sure I could do it. wasn't even sure I wanted to be able to do it. In fact, I knew that I hoped I couldn't do it. But if we were really going to do this, I had to be the one. I did it, or we found another way. Charlotte Zeeman's finger was lying in a box. In less than two hours, they'd cut something else off. I'd killed the vampire, splattered Thompson with blood and brains, and he wasn't talking. He was a mean son of a bitch, but he was tough, too. Charlotte and Daniel didn't have time for him to be tough. We had to break him, and we had to break him fast. I gave myself all the reasons. They were good reasons, real reasons. And still, I didn't know if I could do it.

"We'll start with a finger, Thompson. Just like Linus did," I said.

He was screaming, "Don't, please, don't! Oh, God, don't!"

Asher was leaning almost his full weight on the flat of the man's palm, forcing his fingers to spread wide. "Tell me where they are, and it won't happen," I said.

"Niley said they'd cut me open and make me eat my own intestines. Says he did it once in Miami. I believe him."

"I believe him, too, Thompson. And you don't believe we'll do it, do you? You don't believe we're as crazy as Niley."

"No one is as crazy as Niley."

I raised the cleaver up. "You're wrong." I stayed frozen for one long moment I couldn't make myself start the stroke. I couldn't do it. Daniel, Charlotte.

"Has Niley raped Daniel yet?" I asked it in a voice that was so empty, it was like I wasn't there.

Thompson stopped struggling. He lay very still. He rolled his eyes upward. "Please don't."

I stared into his eyes when I said the next, "Did you rape Charlotte Zeeman?"

I saw the fear in his eyes. That flash that said he'd done it. It was enough. I could do it. God forgive me. I got the little finger and the tip of the next one, because he moved. But they got better at holding him down, and I got better at cutting. Thompson told us where they were keeping Daniel and Charlotte Zeeman. In less than fifteen minutes he would have told us the ingredients to the secret sauce or anything else. He'd have confessed to killing Hoffa, or dancing with the devil. Anything, anything to make it stop.

I threw up in the corner until there was nothing but bile, and my head felt like it was going to explode. And I knew that I'd finally done something that I wouldn't recover from. Somewhere in the first blow or the second, I'd broken something inside myself that would never heal. And I was content with it. If we got Daniel and Charlotte back, I was content with it. A hard, cold knot filled me. It was beyond hate. I would make them pay for what they'd done. I would kill them. I would kill them all.

I felt strangely light and empty, and I wondered if this was what it was like to be crazy. It didn't feel too bad. Later, when the shock wore off, I'd feel worse. Later, I'd wonder if there had been another way to get Thompson to talk. Later, I'd remember that I wanted to hurt him, wanted him to crawl and beg. That I wanted to take all the hurt that had happened to Charlotte and Daniel and carve it out of his flesh. Now we had to go rescue Daniel and Charlotte. Oh, one last thing. Thompson was screaming, high and piteously, like a wounded rabbit.

I shot him in the head. The screaming stopped.

43

I was driving the van down narrow gravel roads in the dark. I'd insisted on driving because I wanted something to do. I didn't want to just sit and stare out the window. But I was beginning to think I should have let someone else drive, because I didn't seem to be too real yet. I felt light and empty, shocky, but not guilty. Not yet. Thompson had earned his death. He'd raped Richard's mother. They'd tortured Richard's mother. They'd raped Daniel. They'd tortured Daniel. They all deserved to die.

Jamil and Nathaniel were in the back of the van with Roxanne and Ben. The lupa would not be left out of the fight, even though she'd had to be carried out to the van by her bodyguard. I didn't have time to fight with Roxanne, so she got to come.

Jason and Dr. Patrick got to ride up front with me. Zane and Cherry had been sent to the lupanar to get Richard and the rest. But we weren't waiting. I didn't trust Niley not to get creative. No, I didn't trust Linus and his master. How much control did Niley have over his pet psychopath? They'd already raped them. What else had happened to them by now? Niley had no rules. I knew that.

I was gripping the steering wheel so hard it hurt. The headlights cut a golden tunnel through the blackness. Trees crowded the road so close that they scraped at the van's roof with thick, clawing fingers. The trees seemed to squeeze down around us like a fist. The headlights glowed over the dirt road, but it wasn't enough light. It would never be enough light. There wasn't enough light in the world to chase away this darkness.

"I can't believe you did that," Patrick said. He was on the far side, pressed against the passenger-side door as if afraid to get too close to me.

Jason was in the middle. "Let it go, Patrick," he said.

"She chopped him up like an animal, then she shot him."

This was the third time he'd said pretty much the exact same thing.

"Shut up," Jason said.

"I will not. It was barbaric."

"I'm not having a good night, Patrick. Drop it," I said.

"The fuck you say," he said.

"Thompson was screaming, in pain," I said.

"And you killed him," Patrick said.

"Someone had to finish it," I said.

"What the hell are you talking about? Finish it!" His voice was rising, and I was beginning to debate how angry Roxanne would be if I shot him. After what I'd already done tonight, it didn't seem like such a big deal.

"How long have you been lukoi?" Jason asked.

The question gave us a moment of surprised silence, then, "Two years."

"And what's the rule about hunting?" Jason asked.

"Which one?"

"Don't be coy, Patrick," Jason said. "You know which one."

Patrick was silent long enough that the only sounds were the whir of the engine, the wheels on the road. The van rocked softly over the rutted road. Was it just my imagination or was there a sound underneath the engine's roar, a high, keening, scream? Naw, my imagination. My imagination was not going to be my friend for a while.

Patrick finally said, "Never begin a hunt unless you mean to kill."

"That's the one," Jason said.

"But this wasn't a hunt," Patrick said.

"Yes, it was," Jason said. "We just weren't hunting the deputy."

"What's that supposed to mean?" he asked.

I answered, "It means we're hunting the people in that house."

Patrick turned a pale face to me in the dark. "You can't mean that we are to kill all of them. Only one man cut off her finger. Only one man is guilty."

"They watched. They did nothing to prevent it. It's the same as doing it in the eyes of the law," I said.

"You are not the law," he said.

"Oh, yes, I am."

"No, you're not. Damn it, no, you are not!"

"Anyone who harms the pack without just cause is our enemy," I said.

"Don't quote pack law to me, human."

"How do we deal with our enemies?" I asked.

Jason answered, "Death."

"Most packs don't hold to the old laws anymore, and you both know it," Patrick said.

"Look, Patrick, I don't have time to explain it all, so here's the *Reader's Digest* version. Niley and crew raped and tortured Richard's mother and brother. We are going to kill them for that. All of them."

"What about Sheriff Wilkes and his men?"

"If Thompson helped rape Richard's mom, then he wasn't the only one. Anyone who touched either of them is dead. Do you understand that, Patrick? Dead."

"I can't do it," he said.

"Then stay in the car," I said, "but shut the fuck up or I'm going to shoot you."

"See," he said, "see, your conscience is bothering you."

I glanced at him huddled in the dark. "No, my conscience isn't bothering me.

Not yet. Maybe later. Maybe not. But now, tonight, I don't feel bad about what I did. I wanted Thompson to hurt. I wanted to punish him for what he did. And you know what, Patrick? It wasn't enough. It will never be enough, because I killed him too fucking quick.'' Tears were threatening at the back of my throat again. When the numbness and anger wore off, I was going to be in trouble. I had to hold onto the adrenaline, the rage. It would see me through the night. Tomorrow, well, we'd see.

"There had to be another way," Patrick said.

"I didn't hear you offering any suggestions at the time."

"What's bothering the good doctor," Jason said, "is that he didn't say anything. He didn't do anything to stop us."

I appreciated the "us."

"I didn't hold him down," Patrick said. "I didn't touch him."

"All you had to do was say, 'Stop, don't,' but you kept quiet. You let us chop him up. You let us kill him and didn't say a damn word," Jason said. "Your conscience wasn't working so hard while he was still alive."

Patrick didn't say anything for a long time. We bumped over the road, avoiding tree branches and dirt-filled holes. There was nothing but the darkness, the golden tunnel of headlights, and the engine-filled silence. I wasn't sure silence was my favorite thing right now, but it was better than listening to Patrick tell me what a monster I was. I agreed with him, which made it harder to hear.

Then something filled the silence that was even harder to hear. Patrick was crying. He huddled against the far door, as far from both of us as he could get, and cried softly. Finally, he said, "You're right. I did nothing, and that will haunt me for the rest of my days."

"Join the club," I said.

He peered at me through the darkness. "Then why did you do it?"

"Someone had to."

"I will never forget the sight of you chopping him up. This little girl . . . The look on your face when you killed him. God, you looked blank like you weren't even there. Why did you have to be the one to do it?"

"Would it have been better if one of the guys had done it?" I asked.

"Yes," he said.

"Please don't tell me this is some macho shit. That you're this upset because a girl did it?"

Patrick snuffled. "I guess it is. I mean, I guess it wouldn't seem so horrible if one of the others had done it. You're this pretty little thing. You shouldn't be chopping people's fingers off."

"Oh, please," I said.

"I will go to my grave seeing the look on your face at the last."

"Keep it up, and you'll go sooner than later," I mumbled.

"What did you say?" Patrick asked.

"Nothing," I said.

Jason made a small sound that might have been a laugh. If he only knew how unfunny the comment had been. I was having enough trouble with what I'd just done. I didn't need a sobbing Jiminy Cricket to emphasize the fact that I'd fallen into the abyss. The monster wasn't breathing down my neck; it was inside my head. Inside my head, fat and well-fed. What made me so sure the monster was home was the fact that I didn't feel guilty. I felt bad because I was supposed to feel bad and didn't. I had to have some personal line that could not be crossed, and I'd thought torture was it. And I'd been wrong.

Tears tightened my throat, but I'd be damned if I'd cry. It was done. I had to let it go—or at least push it back long enough to get the job done. The job was to rescue Daniel and Charlotte. If I didn't get them out, then it had all been for nothing. I'd added a new nightmare for nothing. But it was more than that. I couldn't face Richard if I let them die. I'd been angry with him, pissed, but now I wasn't. I'd have given a great deal for him to hold me right now. Of course, he'd have probably agreed with Patrick. Richard would be a very wise man if he didn't attempt to lecture me tonight.

But it wasn't just Richard. I'd met the entire Zeeman clan. They were so close to perfect that it made my teeth ache. The family might never recover from a loss like this. My family hadn't. I was counting on Daniel and Charlotte to recover from the torture. I was counting on them being strong enough to not let that alone be enough to destroy them. I hoped I was right. No. I prayed I was right.

Thompson had told us what room they were keeping them in. It was in the back, near the woods, as far from the road as possible. Not a surprise. There might have been information that Thompson had that could have been useful. Maybe I should have used less torture and more threat. Maybe that would have gotten us more detailed info faster. Maybe, maybe not. I was new at interrogation by torture, lacked the proper technique, I suppose. I would have said I'd get better with practice, except I wasn't doing it again. I might have the screaming meemies forever from just this one incident, but if I did it again, it was over. They'd have to wrap me up and put me away. I kept flashing on the feel of the cleaver biting into the floor. I remembered thinking that I didn't feel it go through the bone. I just felt it bite into the floor underneath. I saw the fingers go in a wash of blood, but not as much blood as you'd think, for some reason.

"Anita, Anita, the turnoff."

I blinked and slammed on the brakes, throwing everyone forward. I was the only one wearing a seat belt. I usually remember to have everyone buckle up. Careless of me.

Jason peeled himself off the dashboard, pushed back to the seat, and said, "Are you okay?"

I backed the van up slowly. "I'm fine."

"Liar," he said.

I eased the van back until I could see the white sign that said, "Greene Valley House." You didn't expect to find a house with a name at the end of a dirt road, but there you are. Just because the road isn't paved doesn't mean the people don't have style or maybe pretensions. Sometimes it's awfully hard to tell the difference.

This road was gravel. The gravel pinged against the underside of the van, even at less than twenty miles an hour. I slowed down further. Roxanne knew the house. She'd grown up with the Greenes' son. They'd been best friends until the hormones kicked in and he started trying to play boy to her girl. But she knew the house. There was a clearing about halfway down the road where we should park the van. The clearing was right on schedule. I pulled the van into the weeds. They whisked against the metal, whipping the tires. The black van was sort of invisible, parked in the trees. It was also sort of wedged. We wouldn't be moving it quickly. Of course, I wasn't planning on us having to make a run for it. My priority was to get Daniel and Charlotte out as unharmed as possible. I had no other priority. It made things simple. We secured the hostages, then we killed everybody. Simple.

Part of me hoped that Richard got here in time for the assault. Part of me didn't. One, I wasn't sure how he'd take the news about his family. Two, I wasn't sure how he'd take my game plan. And I didn't want to argue. I'd paid the price to get here. We'd play it the way I wanted it.

Someone touched my arm, and I jumped so badly I couldn't speak for a second. My heart filled my throat until I couldn't breathe. "Anita, it's Jason. You okay?"

The passenger-side door was open, and Patrick wasn't in sight. I heard movement coming up on my side of the van. It was Nathaniel. He tapped softly on the window. I lowered it.

"Everyone's out of the back," he said.

I nodded.

"Give us a few minutes," Jason said.

Nathaniel went back to the rear of the van without another word. He did follow orders well.

"Talk to me, Anita."

"There's nothing to talk about."

"You keep staring off into space for minutes at a time. You're not even here. We need you for this to work. Daniel and Mrs. Zeeman need you."

My head turned slowly of its own accord, and I glared at him. "I have done my best for them tonight. I have gone above and beyond my personal best for them tonight."

"Until they're safe, it's not over."

"I know that. Don't you think I know that? If I don't get them out alive, then what I did was for nothing."

"And what do you think you did?" he asked.

I shook my head. "You saw."

"I helped hold him down."

"I'm sorry about that."

Jason put a hand on each shoulder and shook me gently. "Damn it, Anita, get a grip. It isn't like you to wallow in the horror. You're a good soldier. You kill and keep going like you're supposed to."

I pushed him away from me. "I tortured a man, Jason. I reduced him to something that writhed on the floor, mewling with terror and pain. And I wanted to do it. I wanted him to hurt because of what they'd done to Charlotte and Daniel. I wanted to do it." I shook my head. "I'll do my bit tonight, but forgive me if it's a little harder to keep going than normal. Forgive me if I'm not superwoman, after all."

"Not superwoman?" he exclaimed, putting a hand on his chest in mock surprise. "You've lied to me all these years!"

It made me smile, and I didn't want to smile. "Stop it."

"Stop what? Cheering you up? Or is life supposed to stop because you did something horrible? I'll tell you the real horrible truth, Anita. No matter what you do or how bad you feel about it, life just goes on. Life doesn't give a fuck that you're sorry or upset or deranged or tormented. Life just goes on, and you gotta go on with it, or sit in the middle of the road and feel sorry for yourself. And I don't see you doing that.''

''I am not feeling sorry for myself.''

''You aren't all broken up about Thompson. You're broken up because of what you did to Thompson and how it makes you feel. You don't give a rat's ass about him. You're just weeping and gnashing your teeth about how much of a monster you are. Well, I get enough of that from Richard. I don't need it from you. So get your act together. We've got people we care about to save.''

I stared at him. ''You know what's really bothering me?''

''No, what?''

''I don't feel bad about cutting Thompson up. I think he deserved it.''

''He did,'' Jason said.

''No one deserves to be tortured, Jason. No one deserves what we did—what I did—to him. That's what the front of my brain keeps telling me. It keeps telling me I should feel sorry about it, horrified. This should be something that breaks me. But you know what?''

''What?'' Jason asked.

''It won't break me, because right now the only thing I regret is that I didn't have enough nerve to cut off his dick and keep it as a souvenir for Richard's mom. Killing him, even torturing him, wasn't enough. The Zeemans are like the fucking Waltons. To think that anyone could come in and take that away—spoil it forever—just makes me so angry—so angry that all I can do is kill them. Kill them all. There's no regret in me.'' I looked at him in the dark. ''There should be regret for something, Jason. I can kill and not blink. Now I can torture and not regret it. I've become one of the monsters, and if it will save Richard's family, I am happy to be one.''

''Feel any better?'' Jason said.

''Yeah, I do. I'm a monster, but it's for a good cause.''

''To save Richard's mom, I'd do a hell of a lot worse than cut a few fingers off,'' Jason said.

''Me, too,'' I said.

''Then let's do it,'' he said.

We got out of the van and went to do it.

44

Everyone had melted into the woods like stones thrown on the surface of some dark lake. Even Ben, who was carrying Roxanne, had vanished. I moved through the trees at a slower, more human pace. Nathaniel stayed with me like a well-trained dog. I almost wished he'd gone off with the others. His company was not comforting because though he was able-bodied and a wereleopard, I wasn't sure I should be taking him into a fight.

He crouched beside me, hand on my arm, pulling me down. I went to my knees beside him, gun ready. He pointed to our right, and I heard it: someone crashing through the underbrush. It wasn't one of us.

I put my mouth near his ear. "Get behind whoever it is. Drive them towards me."

He nodded and slipped into the trees. I got behind a large tree, using it as a shield. My plan was to shove the Browning into whoever it was and find out what was happening in the house.

Someone gasped, and now they were running full-out. I felt the movement in the trees without really seeing it. The shape-shifters were driving him towards me. Nathaniel had found the others and spread the word. If it was some innocent hiker . . . I couldn't think of an apology strong enough. Oh, well.

A figure crashed through the trees and right past me. I had to grab his arm and spin him around into the tree to get his attention. I shoved the gun barrel under his chin and only then realized who I had. It was Howard the psychic.

"Don't kill me," he gasped.

"Why not?" I asked.

"I can help you."

"Start talking," I said.

"Milo and Wilkes's deputies are up there, arguing about who gets to kill the man."

I pressed the gun barrel into his throat until he had to go on tiptoe. He was making a wild sound high in his throat. "Did you enjoy Charlotte Zeeman? Was she a good lay?"

He tried to talk but couldn't do it around the gun barrel. I thought about shoving the barrel through his throat until he gagged on his blood and died. I took a deep breath and eased down enough for him to speak instead. "Dear God, I didn't touch the woman. I didn't touch either of them. I'm a clairvoyant, for God's sake. I couldn't bear to touch someone during a rape or torture," Howard said.

I believed him. And I knew if later I found out he was lying, the world wasn't big enough to hide him. I knew with a cold certainty that if he were guilty, he would pay. "You said Daniel's at the house? Where's Charlotte?"

"Niley and Linus have taken her to use her blood to call up his demon. They're going to have the demon search the land for the lance. Niley plans on leaving tonight."

"You can't send a demon to find a holy relic," I said.

"Linus thinks the blasphemy of it will appeal to his master."

"Why are you running away, Howard?"

"There is no spear. I lied."

I eased up on the gun more and blinked at him. "What are you talking about?"

"You know how hard it is to make a living as a clairvoyant. So many horrible memories, and you usually end up working with the police for no money. I'd been using my powers to get myself in good with wealthy people who weren't so careful about the law. I'd promise them something, but it wouldn't be real. Then they'd be too embarrassed to go to the police about it. Or couldn't complain that they got cheated out of a stolen object. It worked. I only swindled crooks. It worked."

"Until Niley," I said.

"He's crazy. If he ever finds out I tricked him, he'll kill me and have Linus feed my soul to that thing."

"They're going to kill Charlotte to try and find something that isn't even here, you asshole."

"I know, I know, and I'm sorry. I am really, really sorry. I didn't know what he was capable of. Oh, God, let me go. Let me run away."

"You're going to get us into that house. You're going to help us rescue Daniel."

"There isn't time to rescue them both," Howard said. "They're going to kill the man and sacrifice the woman now. If I get you into the house, the woman will be dead before you can get to her."

Roxanne appeared on the other side of the tree, just there, like magic. Howard gasped. "I don't think so," she said. She opened a mouth full of fangs and snapped them near his face. Howard screamed.

She pressed clawed hands into the bark of the tree on either side of him and clawed long furrows in the bark. Howard fainted.

I left him with Roxanne and the vampires and Ben. When he came to, he'd get them into the house and they'd rescue Daniel. I'd take the rest and rescue Charlotte. There would be no choosing. No either/or. We would save them both. I had to believe it as I threw myself into the black woods. I unleashed that power inside me and sent it outward, casting like a net to catch . . . a faint, ruffling scent of evil. They'd know I was coming now, but it couldn't be helped. I ran like I'd run earlier in the day with Richard. I ran as if the ground told me where to go, and the trees opened up like welcoming hands. I ran in the dark and couldn't see and didn't need to. I felt Richard running, running towards us. I felt the hard edge of his panic and ran faster.

45

They'd chosen the top of a hill that had once been meadow, but some time today they'd bush-hogged all the grass and meadow flowers so that the hill was bare and broken under the moonlight.

In the movies there would be an altar and maybe a fire or two, at least a torch. But there was nothing but darkness and a silver wash of moonlight. The palest thing in the clearing was Charlotte Zeeman's skin. She was tied naked to stakes driven into the ground. I thought at first she was unconscious, but her hands flexed and strained against the ropes. I was both happy to see her still fighting and sorry that she hadn't passed out.

Linus Beck was wearing the proverbial black hooded robe. I guess if it saved me from seeing him naked, I could live with it.

Niley stood by Linus. He was dressed in the same suit I'd seen him in earlier. They'd drawn a circle on the ground with something dark and powdery. Charlotte was inside the circle. She was food for the demon, bait.

Wilkes stood not eight feet from me, to my right. He had a high-powered rifle and was searching the darkness.

Linus's voice rose in a singsong rhythmn that filled the night with echoes and movement as if the darkness itself shivered at the words.

Nathaniel and I lay on the ground at the line of trees, watching. Jason and Jamil were supposed to be on the other side of the clearing. A moment of concentration told me where they were. The marks with Richard were open and roaring. I'd never been so aware of the scent and sounds of a summer night. It was like my skin expanded outward, touching every tree and bush. I was liquid and barely contained within my skin.

I felt Richard and the others moving through the trees like a solid wind. The lukoi were coming. But they were miles away, and the spell was almost complete. I could feel it growing, swelling, like a dank, unseen fog. The evil was coming.

There were shots from the house, echoing up the hill. Wilkes turned towards them and I went to one knee and sighted down my arms. The first shot hit him in the middle of his back. The second shot took him a little higher up the back because be was falling to his knees. He stayed motionless on his knees for one of those seconds that lasted an eternity. I had time to put a third bullet in his back.

A bullet hit the tree next to my head, and I rolled back into the underbrush. Three more shots hit the bushes where I had been. Niley had a gun, a semiauto that might hold eighteen bullets if he'd modified the clip. Not good. Of course, it might hold only ten. Hard to tell in the dark from this distance.

I sidled up to a tree, leaned my arm against it, and sighted on his shape in the bright darkness. I pulled off one careful shot and he went down. I wasn't sure how badly he was hit, but I'd hit something. He fired back, and I hit the ground.

Nathaniel crawled to me on his belly. "What do we do?"

Niley yelled, "You cannot cross the circle, Anita. If you kill us, all you can do is watch Charlotte die."

I risked a peek. Niley had taken cover. I could shoot Linus, but I wasn't a hundred percent sure what that would do to Charlotte. I didn't know what the spell entailed. I just didn't know that much about sorcery.

"What do you want, Niley?"

"Throw your gun out."

"You throw yours out, too, or I shoot Linus."

"What happens to Charlotte if Linus dies in midspell?"

"I'll take my chances. Throw out the gun."

He stood and tossed the gun off the side of the hill. I couldn't hear it hit over Linus's chanting, but he'd done it. I moved out of the trees and tossed the Browning away. I still had the Firestar.

"The other gun, too," Niley said. "Remember that Linus searched you earlier today."

I tossed the Firestar away into the broken grass. It was all right. This wasn't about guns anymore.

I felt the spell close. Linus's last word reverberated on the night like a great brass bell that had been struck slightly off-key, but it echoed for all the flatness of the note. It echoed and grew until the skin on my body tried to crawl away and hide, creeping as if every insect in the world were under my skin. For a second, I couldn't breathe or move. Then Niley's voice came, "You are too late, Anita. Too late."

Charlotte was screaming through the gag on her mouth. Screaming, over and over again, as fast as she could draw breath.

I stared across the meadow and found that there was something else in the circle. I wasn't sure if it was the blackness of it that made it hard to see, or if it was like smoke, never exactly one shape. It seemed to be about man height, maybe eight feet, not much more. It was so thin that it looked like it was made of sticks. Its legs were longer than they should have been, bent wrong somehow. I realized that the longer I stared at it, the more solid it was growing. The neck was a long serpentine, bent back on its shoulders like a heron, and it had a beak for a mouth. If it had eyes, I couldn't see them. The face looked blind and only half-formed.

"You are too late," Niley said again.

"No. I'm not." I stood and walked out of the trees. Niley seemed terribly confident now that the demon was here.

"Only Linus can send it back to whence it came. If you harm him, then it will certainly devour the fair Charlotte."

I ignored him because I knew the plan was for the thing to eat Charlotte. Let them think I believed they intended to save her. Let them think she was still useful as a hostage. I wanted to get close enough to see the circle of entrapment they'd put up.

Charlotte had stopped screaming. I could hear her voice trapped behind the gag, but she was speaking now, not screaming. A strong woman, a very strong woman.

The demon paced the edge of the circle, flicking a long, thin, whiplike tail. It was becoming progressively more agitated, moving around the circle like a prisoner trying its cell.

"The circle is complete," Linus said. "You are mine to command."

The demon hissed at him, and the sound made the inside of my skull ache. It turned and gazed at me, though it had no eyes. I was on the edge of the circle now. I could see that Charlotte had closed her eyes, and I knew now what she was doing. She was praying.

I dropped to my knees beside the circle. I didn't feel anything from it. Which meant it wasn't meant for me. Whatever it was meant to keep in or out, I wasn't one of them. "She's pure, Linus. She's pure of heart and soul. She isn't a fit sacrifice for this thing."

"The pure are a rare and fine treat for my master."

"No, you can't feed her soul to it, Linus. Her soul is spoken for, and this thing cannot touch her."

The demon moved as far away from Charlotte as the circle would allow. It wasn't happy. "Give it its orders, Linus," Niley said.

"I offer you a sacrifice of flesh and blood and soul. Take this my offering and do my bidding."

The demon moved to stand over Charlotte. It snapped its beak next to her face, and she shrieked. The prayers stopped, and it laughed, a sound like grinding metal.

"It's a circle against evil, isn't it, Linus? Just evil."

"You're a necromancer," Niley said. "You are evil."

"Don't believe everything you hear or even read, Niley."

The demon raised fingers to the moonlight, fingers that ended in black knives. Charlotte opened her eyes and screamed. The Lord's Prayer would have been reasonable, but I blanked. All I could think of was Christmas. "And there were in the same country shepherds abiding in the field, keeping watch over the flock by night." I stepped over the circle. It was nothing to me. It was meant to keep out and in evil. I wasn't evil.

"And, lo, the angel of the Lord came upon them and the glory of the Lord shone round about them: and they were sore afraid."

The demon was chattering, snapping at me, razor claws slicing around me like fan blades, but it didn't touch me. "And the angel said unto them. Fear not; for behold, I bring you good tidings of great joy, which shall be to all people." I knelt and started untying Charlotte. When I pulled her gag away, she started to recite with me. "For unto you is born this day in the city of David a Savior, which is Christ the Lord."

I cradled Charlotte's naked body in my arms. She clung to me and cried, and I was crying, too. And I knew I had to get us out of that circle because I only remembered about three more verses.

"And this shall be a sign unto you; Ye shall find the babe wrapped in swaddling clothes, lying in a manger." Charlotte couldn't stand, and I had to half carry her. We stumbled near the edge of the circle, and the demon rushed us in a wave of clattering, snapping, horror. "And suddenly there was with the angel a multitude of the heavenly host praising God, and saying . . ." I stared down at the circle as I prayed, that carefully constructed circle . . . "glory to God in the highest, and on earth, peace, goodwill toward men." I erased the circle with my hand. I broke Linus's circle of protection.

The demon threw back its head and shrieked. The sound was like a rooster's crow or maybe a growl or maybe something else. It was as if even hearing it, I couldn't hold it in my mind.

It rushed out of the circle and fell on Linus. It was his turn to scream and scream as fast as he could draw breath. Blood flew in a wash, sprinkling us like rain.

And suddenly, there were flashlights and men yelling, "FBI. Don't move." FBI?

The flashlights found the demon. The light glistened on the beak, and blood shimmered on it as if it had bathed in it. If they hadn't tried to shoot it, I think it would have left them alone. But they fired into it, and I pushed Charlotte to the grass, hiding her body under mine.

The demon rushed into the feds, and they started dying. I yelled, "Bullets won't work! Pray. Pray, damn it, pray!"

I tried to lead by example and found finally that I could remember the Lord's Prayer. A man's voice echoed mine, then another. I heard someone else doing the 'Bless me, oh, Lord, for I have sinned' liturgy. Someone else was praying, and it wasn't Christian. Hindu I think, but every religion has demons. Every religion has prayers. All it takes is faith. Nothing like a real, live demon to give you some of that old-time religion.

The demon stood with a man's body raised to its mouth. The neck was cut and it was lapping the blood with a long, sticky tongue. But at least it wasn't killing anyone else.

Prayers rose up into the darkness, and I bet none of them had ever prayed so hard, in church or out. The demon stood on its crooked legs and walked back to me. Charlotte was muttering a new prayer. I think it was the Song of Solomon. Funny what you'll remember under stress.

It pointed a long finger at me and spoke in a voice that was deep and rusted as if it wasn't much used. "Free," it said.

"Yes," I said, "you're free."

The beak and the blind face seemed to waver. For just an instant I thought I saw a man's face, pure and almost shining, but I would never be sure. It said, "Thank you," and vanished.

Feds were everywhere. One of them gave Charlotte his coat that said F.B.I. on the back. I helped her sit up and slip the coat over her. It hit her at midthigh.

Sometimes, it was good to be small. One of the feds turned out to be Maiden. I just stared up at him in shock.

He smiled and knelt beside us. "Daniel is all right. He's going to make it."

Charlotte grabbed his coat sleeve. "What did they do to my boy?"

His smile vanished. "They were going to beat him to death. I'd called for backup, but . . . They're dead, Mrs. Zeeman. They won't ever hurt you again. I am so sorry that I wasn't there earlier today to help you, both of you."

She nodded. "You saved my boy's life, didn't you?"

Maiden looked at the ground, then nodded.

"Then don't apologize to me," she said.

"What is a federal agent doing posing as a small-town deputy?" I asked.

"When Niley came nosing around down here, they put me under with Wilkes. It worked."

"You called the state cops," I said.

He nodded. "Yeah."

Another agent came over, and Maiden excused himself.

I felt Richard arrive. Felt them slip through the trees. And I knew that some of them at least weren't in human form.

I called the agent over that had given Charlotte his coat. "There are some werewolves in the woods. They are friends. They were coming to help. Don't let anyone shoot them, okay?"

He stared down at me. "Werewolves?"

I looked at him. "I didn't know the FBI was going to show up. I needed the backup."

That made him laugh, and he started telling everyone to put their weapons up and not to shoot the werewolves. I don't think everyone was happy about it, but they did what they were told.

A woman in EMS gear knelt by us. She started looking Charlotte over, shining lights in her eyes and asking silly questions, like did she know the date and where she was.

Richard was suddenly there, still in human form, though he'd stripped down to jeans and his hiking boots. Charlotte flung herself from my arms to his, crying all over again. I stood up and left Charlotte to her son and the medical crew.

Richard grabbed my hand before I could wander off. He stared up at me, tears shining in the moonlight. "Thank you for my mother."

I squeezed his hand and left them to it. If I didn't leave them alone, I was going to cry again.

Another EMS came up to me. "Are you Anita Blake?"

"Yeah, why?"

"Franklin Niley wants to speak with you. He's dying. There's nothing we can do for him."

I went with him to talk to Niley. He was lying on his back. They'd set up an IV bag and tried to stop the bleeding, but he was cut up pretty bad. I stood so that he could look up at me without straining.

He licked his lips, and it took him two tries to speak. "How did you pass the circle?"

"It was meant to trap evil inside or keep it out. I'm not evil."

"You raise the dead," he said.

"I'm a necromancer. I was kind of doubting where that put me on the scale of good and evil, but apparently God's okay with it."

"You stepped into the circle not knowing if you would be safe?" He was frowning, clearly puzzled.

"I couldn't just sit there and watch Charlotte die."

"You would have sacrificed yourself for her?"

I thought about that for second or two. "I didn't think about it that clearly, but I couldn't let her die, not if I could save her."

He winced, closed his eyes, then looked at me. "No matter what the cost to you personally?"

"I guess so," I said.

He looked past me, eyes starting to lose their focus. "Extraordinary, extraordinary." His breath sighed outward, and he died. The EMS crew fell on him like vultures, but he was gone. They never got him breathing again.

Jason was suddenly beside me. "Anita, Nathaniel's dying."

"What are you talking about?"

"He caught two bullets in the chest when people were shooting at the demon. The feds were using silver shot because they knew what Linus was."

"Oh, God." I took Jason's hand. "Take me to him."

There were paramedics on either side of him. There was another IV, and they'd set up a lamp. Nathaniel's skin was pale and waxy in the light. Sweat covered him like dew. When I knelt beside him and tried to push my way past the paramedics, his pale eyes didn't see me.

I let the paramedics push me out of the way. I sat there in the weeds and listened to Nathaniel try to breathe through two holes in his chest. The bad guys hadn't shot him. He'd gotten caught in stray fire from the good guys. It was just a stupid accident. He was going to die because he'd been standing in the wrong place at the wrong time. No, I would not let an accident take him. I would not lose another person I knew to bad timing.

I looked up at Jason. "Is Marianne here?"

"I'll look." He went running into the chaos.

Nathaniel's back bowed upward. His breath rasped out. He lay back on the ground, horribly still. One of the paramedics shook his head and got up. He took some of the equipment and went to help someone else.

I crawled around to take his place at Nathaniel's side. I looked across at the other paramedic. It was a woman with a blond ponytail.

"Is there anything you can do?"

She looked at me. "Are you a friend?"

I nodded.

"Close?"

I nodded.

"I'm sorry," she said.

I shook my head. "No, I won't let him die." I wasn't evil. Everything that I'd done, and my faith was still pure. When I spoke the words, they were just as real to me as when I'd memorized them all those years ago for the Christmas pageant. The words still moved me. I never doubted God. I doubted me. But maybe

God was a more generous God than I allowed him to be. Jason was there with Marianne.

I grabbed her hand. "Help me call the munin."

She didn't argue, just knelt beside me. "Remember the feel of his body. Remember his smile. The smell of his hair and skin."

I nodded. "He smells like vanilla and fur." I knelt by him, touching his skin, but it was already growing cool to the touch. He was dying. I didn't feel sexy in the least. I felt sad and frightened. I bowed my head and prayed. I prayed to be opened to Raina. I prayed to open my eyes and look at Nathaniel and feel lust. It was a weird thing to be praying for, but it was worth a try. I felt that measure of calm that I sometimes got when I prayed. It doesn't mean you'll get what you asked for, but it does mean that someone is listening.

I opened my eyes slowly and stared down at Nathaniel. There were leaves in his long, unbound hair. I pulled them away. I held his hair in my hands and buried my face in it. It still smelled like vanilla. I rubbed my cheek against his, burying my face behind his ear into the silk of his hair. I laid a hand over the wounds with my face still buried in his hair. He made a small pain sound when I touched him. I don't know if it was the pain sound, the familiar smell of his body, or the prayer, but Raina spread through my body like flame. The munin rode me, and I opened to it, no fighting, no struggle. I embraced it, and her laughter rolled out of my lips. I rose up on my knees and stared down at Nathaniel.

I wasn't horrified anymore. Raina thought it would be a grand thing to fuck him as he died. I laid my lips against his, and his lips were cool, dry. I pressed my mouth over his and felt that fire pour into his mouth from mine.

My fingers found the wounds in his chest and stroked them, pushing my fingers into the wound. The paramedic tried to pull me off of him, and Jason and someone else pulled her away. I dug into the wound until Nathaniel's eyes opened and he moaned with pain. His eyes fluttered, pale, pale lilac in the artificial light. He looked up but didn't see me, didn't see anything.

I covered his face in soft kisses, and each touch burned. I went back to his mouth and breathed into him. When I drew back, his eyes focused. His breath eased out in something too low to be a whisper. "Anita."

I straddled his body and laid my hands on his bare chest. I covered the wounds with my hands, but I touched the inside of his chest with something other than my hands. I could feel the damage. I could roll his damaged heart in the heat that fell from my hands, that sank into his skin, that filled his flesh.

I was burning alive. I had to feed the heat into him. Had to share this energy. My hands left the wound on his chest and fumbled at my shirt. The dress shirt came off and vanished into the grass, but the tank top was trapped under the shoulder holster. Hands helped me slip the holster off my shoulders. It flopped heavy and awkward over my hips. I undid the belt and I think it was Marianne who helped me slip the belt out of the loops. I know it was Marianne who stopped me from undoing my pants. Raina snarled in my head.

Hands caressed up my bare back and I knew it was Richard. He knelt behind me, legs straddling Nathaniel's legs, but putting no weight on them. He cradled me back against his body. I was suddenly aware that we were the focus of the pack. They surrounded us like a wall of faces and bodies.

Richard's hands slipped off the spine sheath and the blade down my back. His hands found my bra strap and undid it. I started to protest, started to hold it, and he kissed my shoulders, sliding his lips down my back and sliding the bra away. He whispered, "Bare skin is best for this." That prickling rush of energy filled the watching lukoi, filled them and spread into me. The energy of the munin fed on that power, grew until I thought my skin would burst with it.

Richard guided my body to Nathaniel's. My bare breasts touched Nathaniel's chest, a brush of velvet skin against the torn flesh of his smooth chest. I shuddered against him, and that heat spilled from my bare skin. At first it was as if my naked flesh rode above his skin on a pool of sweat, then I felt the flesh give. My body fell against his with a sigh, and it was as if our bodies became plastic, liquid. Our bodies melded together into one flesh, one body, as if I were sinking into his chest. I felt our hearts touch, beating liquid against one another. I healed his heart, closed his flesh with mine.

Nathaniel's mouth found mine, and the power flowed between us like breath until it raised the skin from my body, and there was nothing but his arms around me, his mouth on me, my hands on his body, and distant like an anchor I felt Richard, and beyond him the rest of the pack. I felt them offer their energy, their power, and I took it. And beyond that, distant as a dream, I felt Jean-Claude. I felt his cool power join with ours and strengthen; life from death. I took it all and thrust it into Nathaniel until he tore his mouth from mine and cried out. I felt his body give under mine, and his pleasure rushed over my skin, and I threw it out into the waiting pack. I took their energy and gave them back pleasure.

The munin left me in that rush of startled voices. Raina had never been able to take power from others. That was my doing. So even the bitch of the west had never pleasured this many people at once.

I sat up, still straddling Nathaniel. He looked up at me with his lilac eyes and smiled. I ran my hands over his chest, and there was no wound, only a healing scar. He still looked pale and awful, but he'd live.

Richard offered me the dress shirt I'd dropped. I slipped it over my breasts and buttoned it. I didn't know what had happened to the rest of the clothes. Jason had my shoulder holster and knife. The important stuff.

When I tried to stand, I stumbled, and only Richard's arms kept me standing. He helped me through the crowd. They touched me as we moved through, running their hands along me. I didn't mind or didn't care. I put my arm around Richard's waist and accepted it for tonight. I'd worry about what it all meant tomorrow, or maybe even the next day.

Verne stepped out of the crowd. "Damn girl, you are good."

Roxanne was at his side. "I'm healed. How did you do that?"

I smiled. "Talk to Marianne." I kept walking.

The paramedics were rushing forward. I heard the woman say, "Holy shit! It's a miracle." And maybe it was.

Richard said, "I won't be looking for another lupa."

I hugged him. "No more auditions?"

"You are my lupa, Anita. Together we could be the most powerful mated pair I've ever seen."

"It's not just the two of us that make us powerful, Richard. It's Jean-Claude."

He kissed me on the forehead. "I felt him when you called the power. I felt him give his power to us."

We'd stopped walking. I turned to look at him in the moonlight. "We are a threesome, Richard, like it or not."

"A ménage à trois," he said.

I raised my eyebrows. "Not unless you've been doing more than just talking with Jean-Claude."

Richard laughed and hugged me. "He hasn't corrupted me quite that far."

"Glad to hear it." We walked down the hill, holding each other. Charlotte was lying at the bottom of the hill on a stretcher.

She reached her hands up to both of us. One of the hands was thickly bandaged. She smiled up at us. "Why didn't you tell me, Richard?"

"I thought it would make a difference. I thought you would stop loving me."

"Silly ass," she said.

"That's what I told him," I said.

Charlotte started to cry softly, pressing Richard's hand to her lips. I just smiled and held her hand. Life wasn't perfect, but standing there watching Richard and his mother, holding their hands, it was close.

46

Daniel's nose was badly broken. The perfect profile isn't quite as perfect. He says the women love it, makes him look tough. Daniel has never spoken to me about what happened. Neither has Charlotte, but on the first Sunday dinner after they both got out of the hospital, she broke down and cried. I was the one who went into the kitchen first. She let me hold her while she cried, saying how silly she felt, that everything was all right. Why should she be crying?

If I could do resurrection for real, I'd bring Niley and all the rest back and kill them more slowly.

Richard's family thinks I can do no wrong, and they are not being subtle about their plans. Marriage—we should get married. Under other circumstances, not a bad idea. But we aren't a couple. We're a trio. Hard to explain that to Richard's folks. Hard to explain that to Richard.

Howard Grant, the psychic, is in jail for fraud. He confessed to some things he'd done in the past. I told him if he didn't spend some time in jail, I'd kill him. His greed had started everything. He didn't touch Charlotte or Daniel. He was horrified at what Niley was and what was happening, but his lies set it all in motion. He couldn't get away scot free. I just gave him a choice of punishments.

The police think Deputy Thompson fled the state. They're still looking for him, and none of us are talking. I don't know what Verne's pack did with the body. Maybe it's hanging on their tree waiting for a Christmas that will never come. Maybe they ate him. I don't know, and I don't want to know.

The Vampire Council didn't send anyone to kill us. Apparently Colin overstepped his bounds. We were within our rights to kill him, and his people. He didn't survive his servant's death. There is no new Master of the City yet. Verne and his pack are in no hurry for Colin's replacement.

I wake from dreams that aren't my own. Thoughts, feelings, not my own. It is overwhelming enough to be in love, in that first heat of lust, but the marks are sucking me inside both of them. They're swallowing me up. Every act of sex makes it worse. So . . . no more sex. I have to get control of the marks first.

When I was sleeping with both of them, Richard catted around. Now that I've gone celibate, so has he. Jean-Claude, I think, knows I'm still looking for a good excuse to say, "Hah, see, you don't really love me." So he's behaving himself like some dark angel.

I took a month off and went back to Tennessee to learn from Marianne. Learning to control the munin is helping me to control the marks. Jean-Claude as my only teacher is just not a good idea. He has too much invested in me. I'm learning to put up barriers. Barriers so tall, so wide, so solid, that I'm safe from both of them. Safe behind my walls.

But sex brings all the barriers crashing down. It's like drowning. I think if I allowed it, and they allowed it, we could become like one organism with three parts.

Richard doesn't seem to see the danger. He's still naive, or perhaps I just don't understand him. I love him, but even thinking his thoughts, feeling his emotions, he's still a mystery to me.

Jean-Claude knows the danger. He says he can keep it from happening, but I don't trust him. I love him, sort of, but I don't trust him. I've felt his chortling joy as the power of the triumverate grows.

He told me once he loved me as much as he was able. Maybe he does, but he loves power more.

So, celibate again, damn it. How to be chaste with the two preternatural studs of all time at my beck and call? Be out of town.

I've taken every animating job out of town that I could for three months. I spend weekends with Marianne. I have a great deal of power inside me, not the marks, but me. I've avoided confronting that power as much as possible, but Jean-Claude has forced me to face it. I have to learn how to control the magic.

It sounds silly that someone who raises the dead for a living has been ignoring that she has magic inside her, but I have. I've always learned the minimum to get by. That's over.

Marianne tells me that I have the tools to survive in the triumverate. Until I feel confident in those tools, I'm avoiding the boys. Three months of not touching either of them. Of no one sharing my bed. Three months of not being lupa. I had to leave the pack to leave Richard. But I couldn't leave the wereleopards. They don't have anyone else but me. So I'm still Nimir-ra. Marianne is even teaching me how to forge the leopards into a healthy unit. She and Verne.

I've abandoned as much of the preternatural stuff as I can. I have to find out what's left of who I thought I was.

I faced a demon with my faith and prayer. Does that mean God has forgiven me my sins? I don't know. If He has forgiven me, He's more generous than I am.